REA

*Talking
Across the
World*

*University Press of New England*
*Hanover and London, 1987*

# *Talking Across the World*

## The Love Letters of Olaf Stapledon and Agnes Miller, 1913-1919

*Edited by Robert Crossley*

## UNIVERSITY PRESS OF NEW ENGLAND

| | |
|---|---|
| BRANDEIS UNIVERSITY | UNIVERSITY OF NEW HAMPSHIRE |
| BROWN UNIVERSITY | UNIVERSITY OF RHODE ISLAND |
| CLARK UNIVERSITY | TUFTS UNIVERSITY |
| UNIVERSITY OF CONNECTICUT | UNIVERSITY OF VERMONT |
| DARTMOUTH COLLEGE | |

LIBRARY OF CONGRESS CATALOGING-IN-PUBLICATION DATA

Stapledon, Olaf, 1886–1950.
  Talking across the world.

  Bibliography: p.
  Includes index.
  1. Stapledon, Olaf, 1886–1950—Correspondence.
2. Miller, Agnes Zena—Correspondence.　3. Authors,
English—20th century—Correspondence.　4. Love-letters.
I. Miller, Agnes Zena.　II. Crossley, Robert.
III. Title.
PR6037.T18Z487　1987　　823'.912　[B]　　87–8119
ISBN 0–87451–423–1

5　　4　　3　　2　　1

*This book is for*
*Mary Shenai*
*John Stapledon*
*Sarina Stapledon*

# ✑ Contents

## ᑫᓷ Illustrations

# ↜ Introduction

I

In the last months of 1930 British readers as various as the geneticist
J. B. S. Haldane, the Shakespearean editor John Dover Wilson, the astronomer Arthur Eddington, the scientific romancer and Outliner of
History H. G. Wells, and the novelist and children's author Naomi
Mitchison were making their way in astonishment and delight through
a chronicle of the next two billion years of human history. "You have
invented a new kind of book," wrote Dover Wilson to the author of *Last
and First Men*, "& the world of Einstein and Jeans is ready for it."[1] The
author was a forty-four-year-old tutor in the adult education movement,
a philosopher without a university appointment living in the seaside
town of West Kirby on the Wirral, a small peninsula between Liverpool
and the River Mersey on the east and the Dee estuary and North Wales
on the west. He had already published a specialist's book, *A Modern
Theory of Ethics*, in 1929 and, in 1914, a thin volume of awkward
poems called *Latter-Day Psalms*; but the name of W. Olaf Stapledon—
as he signed himself in 1930—was virtually unknown in intellectual
and literary circles. Readers of *Last and First Men* wanted to know who
he was, where his engrossing scientific ideas had come from, what
provoked the extraordinary inventiveness of his imagination. When
Stapledon wrote diffidently to Wells to apologize for what might seem
an appropriation of his ideas and methods, the great man wrote back: "It
is all balls to suggest that *First & Last Men* (which I found a very exciting book) owes anything to my writings. I wish it did."[2] Haldane, on the

1. John Dover Wilson to Olaf Stapledon, 6 November 1930. Letter in the Stapledon
Archive, Sydney Jones Library, University of Liverpool.
2. H. G. Wells to Olaf Stapledon, 30 October 1931. The letter is in the Stapledon
Archive at Liverpool and has been printed in its entirety as "Wells to Stapledon: A New
Letter," ed. Robert Crossley, *The Wellsian*, n.s. 7 (1984), 38–39.

other hand, was indignant that, as a biologist, he neither recognized the name of a person he took to be a colleague nor knew in what lab Stapledon had trained. In fact, Stapledon's degrees were in history and philosophy, and he had trained in no one's lab; but he had read *Nature* regularly, had long been thinking about both the evolution of humanity and the prospects for the future, and had spent many a night with a telescope on his rooftop studying the stars.

Over the next two decades the English reading public—and, to a smaller extent, American readers—had a chance to learn more about the distinctive mind and imagination of Olaf Stapledon. He produced a kind of sequel to his first work of fiction, a semiautobiographical growing-up novel with the misleading title *Last Men in London* (1932). He could occasionally be heard on the BBC speculating about the far future or analyzing the causes of unemployment in the present. He wrote more books in several genres: utopian argument (*Waking World; Saints and Revolutionaries*); social analysis (*New Hope for Britain; Youth and Tomorrow*); and philosophy for the layperson (*Philosophy and Living; Beyond the 'Isms*). But what most captivated readers in the 1930s and 1940s and what was rediscovered and reevaluated by new readers in the 1970s and 1980s was the startling succession of stylistically austere and intellectually vigorous scientific romances seeded by *Last and First Men*. In *Odd John* (1935) Stapledon imagined a group of precocious children rebelling not merely against adult authority but against the failures of the civilization of Homo sapiens. *Star Maker* (1937), for many readers his greatest achievement, is a modern *Divine Comedy* for agnostics, blending astronomy and theology in a dizzying spiritual quest for the links between human aspirations and cosmic design. The incongruously moving novel about a dog with a human brain, *Sirius* (1944), is both a striking exercise in psychology and an examination of the ethics of scientific and educational experimentation that the author considered his best work of fiction. He produced, among his other later works, a parallel history of two alternative futures in *Darkness and the Light* (1942); a visionary novel about the death of a World War II pilot, *Death into Life* (1946); an epistolary novella, *The Flames* (1947), about a hospitalized prophet who is the medium—or thinks he is—of intelligent solar beings; and *A Man Divided* (1950), formally and stylistically his most traditional novel and the last book published in his lifetime.

When Olaf Stapledon suffered a fatal heart attack in 1950 at the age of 64, his literary reputation was in decline. Sales of his final books had been weak, but his earlier ones had been discovered by such science fiction writers as Arthur C. Clarke and Theodore Sturgeon, on whom they had a powerful impact; in later years his fiction would affect the work of Brian Aldiss, Stanislaw Lem, and Doris Lessing. Some science fiction readers also became enthusiasts and kept Stapledon's name alive despite the fact that his writing was more difficult, more intricate in idea and design, less gifted in narrative than the ordinary science fiction novel.[3] But the true curator of Olaf Stapledon's spirit from 1950 to 1970, the years when his work was largely neglected, was Agnes Stapledon, his widow. Careful readers of his books could find many overt references to Agnes in his prefaces and some covert ones as well in the characters modeled on her: Pax in *Odd John*, Maggie in *A Man Divided*, the narrator's wife in *Star Maker*. And there was a famously mysterious dedication in *A Man Divided*: "To A in gratitude to her for being T." The Stapledons' private life, lived in the provincial suburbs of Liverpool rather than in the publicity of metropolitan London, was so private that no one outside the family knew that Olaf was thanking Agnes under the nickname Taffy, which he had used ever since 1919 to designate the woman he had fallen in love with.

Agnes outlived Olaf by thirty-three years. She was convinced that his literary stock would rise again someday; she edited the incomplete manuscript he was working on when he died and had it published under the title *The Opening of the Eyes* (1954); she preserved his study and his papers as they were in 1950; and she waited for the scholars to show up, as they began doing in the 1970s. But Agnes knew about some manuscripts that she didn't show to those who came inquiring to her house, papers that she didn't even show her relatives. In the summer of 1983, less than a year before Agnes Stapledon died in her sleep at a nursing home, two worn suitcases were removed with other boxes and cases from Simon's Field, the house in Wirral that the Stapledons built just before World War II. When a family house is sold there is no telling what long-neglected or forgotten items might be uncovered, especially when one of the occupants was a writer, especially when the other was a habitual saver. Most of the numerous manuscripts, letters, diaries, and notebooks found at Simon's Field were related directly to Olaf's literary, philosophical, and pedagogical work and were sent to the Sydney Jones Library at the University of Liverpool, where they now form the core collection of the Stapledon archive. But the two suitcases, plastered with old travelers' labels, were opened and examined by the Stapledon heirs and, since they seemed to contain nothing relevant to Olaf's literary career, remained in family hands. In 1984 the son and daughter-in-law of Olaf and Agnes Stapledon allowed me to open the suitcases. Inside, tied into neat bundles with coarse brown twine, were many hundreds of letters from Olaf Stapledon to Agnes Miller and from

3. For a full, judicious commentary on Stapledon's works and their influence, see Patrick A. McCarthy, *Olaf Stapledon* (Boston: Twayne, 1982). See also Leslie A. Fiedler, *Olaf Stapledon: A Man Divided* (New York: Oxford University Press, 1983); John Kinnaird, *Olaf Stapledon* (Mercer Island, Wash.: Starmont, 1986); Robert Crossley, "Olaf Stapledon and the Idea of Science Fiction," *Modern Fiction Studies*, 32 (Spring 1986), 21–42.

Agnes to Olaf, the great bulk of them written between 1913 and 1919. In Olaf's precise script in thick black ink and in Agnes's sprawling and more faded handwriting was the nearly complete record of a protracted romance conducted by correspondence while the two writers were, for most of the period, on opposite sides of the globe. The more than two million words they exchanged amount to something very like a vast epistolary novel, full of crisis and introspection and meticulous attention to their own microcosm and to the world at large, all culminating—like so many great novels—in a reunion, a wedding, and a revelation.

## II

The origin of the love affair between William Olaf Stapledon and his Australian cousin Agnes Zena Miller had the status of myth for Olaf. He felt it as the central psychological experience of his life, and it nourished his creative work in a way reminiscent of the youthful "spots of time" Wordsworth describes in the autobiographical poem on his artistic development, *The Prelude*. Again and again, in private and in public writings, Olaf returned to the moment in 1903 when he met the nine-year-old Agnes, visiting Liverpool with her parents, Frank and Margaret, who had emigrated to Sydney in 1893. His recollections of that encounter—a matter of a few details of color and costume, a gesture and a glance—recapitulate Dante's idealization of the youthful and inaccessible Beatrice, as described in the *Vita Nuova* and as depicted in the Pre-Raphaelite artists Olaf admired, notably in Rossetti's *Dante's Dream* and Henry Holiday's popular *Dante and Beatrice*, both at the Walker Art Gallery in Liverpool.[4] In 1908 when Agnes at fourteen was once again briefly in England, he wrote in his diary: "Five years ago in the Garsdale drawing room I sat and saw Agnes come into the room in a green silk frock. She warmed her hands at the fire, and I fell in love with her. I had thought of love before, but this was new, and love at first sight. She was nine and I was seventeen. I saw her for a week only. I wrote her letters, and she answered some, and in one sent me a piece of Lavender which I have now. Soon I got no more answers, I fear because my letters were stopped by Uncle Frank."[5] In 1909–10, when he

4. First exhibited in 1883, Holiday's painting was, like Rossetti's, a showpiece at the Walker Gallery, which, just before and after the turn of the century, attracted enormous crowds, among whom the Stapledons were frequent visitors. Prints of *Dante and Beatrice* were popular throughout the late Victorian era, and the painting was often used to illustrate school history texts. Earlier in his career Holiday had done a sketch of Dante and Beatrice meeting as children, but it is unlikely that Olaf had an opportunity to see it.

5. Entry for 30 March 1908. The Stapledon diaries are at the Sydney Jones Library, University of Liverpool. Although later in life he joked about his prolonged adolescence, Olaf's Dantesque fantasy, partly erotic and partly bookish, was not unique. An Irish commissioned officer recalls in his memoirs his similar experience on leave in 1917: "The high-light of the visit was clearly a certain eleven-year-old to whom I had lost my heart a year or two previously, and who sat in church each Sunday with her mother, brother and

Hotel Barbensi, (old palace)
Lungarno Guicciardini,
Florence.

{ December 31st 1909
{ January 1st 1910,

My dear Agnes,

Your picture of The Spit etc has just arrived. Thank you very much for it and for a letter of some time ago, which I was very glad to have. Please excuse pencil; our pens have run dry & there is no ink to be had tonight. If you can't read this you won't miss much. It is New Year's eve, & Mother has gone to bed, so I am writing letters, & I don't intend to stop because the ink has run out, so please, Signorina, forgive.

View from my room.

The first page of Olaf Stapledon's earliest surviving letter to Agnes Miller.

was teaching at Manchester Grammar School, Olaf started to write a ninety-four-line poem in couplets, beginning "I saw her first in green" and including the essential elements in the early stages of his attachment to Agnes from the time she was nine until she turned seventeen. In her eyes, as he says at the poem's conclusion, he saw

> The token that she and I
> In the far off by and by,
> Perhaps when the stars are dead,
> Shall surely meet and wed.

Olaf first showed the poem, titled "A History, 1903–11," to Agnes in 1914.[6] Although, as Agnes truthfully told him in a letter dated 22 November 1916, the verses are more interesting as history than as poetry, they show the effects of the Christmas holiday in 1909 Olaf spent in Dante's Florence, of his repeated readings of *The Divine Comedy* both in Italian and in translation, and especially of the image of Beatrice in the *Paradiso* and the transfiguration of the pilgrim-lover when he looks into her eyes. Not coincidentally perhaps, the earliest of all Olaf's letters saved by Agnes was a penciled note written to her on New Year's Eve 1909 from Florence, with several of the quaint line drawings with which he often illustrated his correspondence. From 1910 forward Olaf's courtship of Agnes was clearly also a symbolic pursuit of Beatrice.

Readers of Stapledon's innovative fictions of the 1930s and 1940s got tantalizing suggestions of the power that the Beatrice myth exercised over his imagination. The opening chapter of his cosmic romance of 1937, *Star Maker*, sets a vision of the galaxies alongside an appraisal of the narrator's marriage, "with its trivial romantic origin." The autobiographical narrator remembers meeting his wife when she was a child: "Our eyes encountered. She looked at me for a moment with quiet attention; even, I had romantically imagined, with obscure, deep-lying recognition. I, at any rate, recognized in that look (so I persuaded myself in my fever of adolescence) my destiny."[7] The most moving of all Olaf's versions of his Beatrice story came more than forty years after he first fell in love with Agnes. In the fourth "Interlude" of one of his last novels, *Death into Life*, the narrator addresses his middle-aged wife

---

younger sister and had the face of a Botticelli angel, with the same ethereal charm and the same slightly crumpled rhythmic grace. I had written poetry about her then, reassured by the thought that Beatrice had only been nine when Dante first fell in love with her; and my leave now was to be spent largely in her company." See Monk Gibbon, *Inglorious Soldier* (London: Hutchinson, 1968), p. 168.

6. The manuscript of the poem, evidently composed at different periods and with variants and revisions difficult to date, is in pencil and ink on five small sheets in the possession of John D. and Sarina Stapledon.

7. Olaf Stapledon, *Star Maker* (London: Methuen, 1937), p. 4.

and, comparing youth to age and past to future, he travels back in memory to the scene in 1903 in the drawing room at Garsdale in Liverpool:

Some fifteen thousand yesterdays ago there lies a day when you were a little girl with arms like sticks and a bright cascade of hair. In a green silk frock you came through a door, warmed your hands at the fire, and looked at me for a moment. And now, so real that moment seems, that it might be yesterday. . . . For in looking into your eyes I did (how I remember it!) have a strange, a startling experience, long since dismissed as fantasy, yet unforgettable. It was as though your eyes were for me windows, and as though curtains were drawn aside, revealing momentarily a wide, an unexpected and unexplored prospect, a view obscure with distance, but none the less an unmistakable prevision of our common destiny. I could not, of course, see it clearly; for it was fleeting, and I was a boy and simple. But I saw, or I seemed to see, what now I recognize as the very thing that has befallen us, the thing that has taken so long to grow, and is only now in these last years flowering. Today our hair is greying, our faces show the years. We can no longer do as once we did. But the flower has opened. And strangely it is the very flower that once I glimpsed even before the seed was sown. [8]

The evolution of the personal myth that Agnes and Olaf came to share can be charted in minute detail in the correspondence that is made public here for the first time. The collection begins not with the first magical encounter in 1903—the earliest letters seem to have been lost or destroyed long ago—but a decade later when the formal courtship-by-letter was initiated by Olaf. In early 1913, Frank Miller, the brother of Olaf's mother, Emmeline Miller Stapledon, had come to Liverpool with his family, as he did regularly every four or five years, to report to the home office in his capacity as manager of the Australian branch of Alfred Booth and Co., Shipping Merchants. While Frank Miller was discussing rabbit skins and kangaroo hides with Messrs. Booth, his eldest daughter was renewing friendships with various younger relations, including her twenty-six-year-old cousin Olaf. Agnes Miller did not look very much like a Pre-Raphaelite Beatrice. Shorter and less glamorous than her younger sisters, Rosamund and Ruth (known as "Peter"), she had a mass of unruly, wiry, light brown hair that she usually kept pinned up, a squarish chin and fleshy nose, and a full, attractive, open face dominated by large blue eyes set well apart against skin tanned in the Australian sun. Shy in conversation, Agnes was an attentive listener with the engaging habit of tilting her head to one side and leaning her face on a fist while she fixed the speaker with a steady and meditative gaze. For Olaf, "a mere bubble of ego" in those days," [9] that single-minded attention was flattering and hypnotic. Agnes was immune to fashion and dressed simply and inexpensively in a few well-

8. Olaf Stapledon, *Death into Life* (London: Methuen, 1946), pp. 103, 105.
9. *Death into Life*, p. 146.

worn dresses that she made herself and kept in constant repair with needle and thread; she disdained stays, powder and paint, and showy jewelry. In the Pacific waters off New South Wales she had become an accomplished swimmer and diver, and when in England she unselfconsciously donned her bathing costume to swim in the chilly River Dee with the male Stapledons, to her Aunt Emmeline's nervous consternation. She was not, she liked to point out to Olaf, an English lady but an Australian bush-girl.

When Frank and Margaret Miller and their other children departed for Australia in May 1913, Agnes remained in Europe. Her father had set aside £200 to give Agnes a year's study of music and languages on the Continent, in lieu of a university education. Agnes's coming independence from her family set the stage for Olaf's undertaking a serious effort to win her affection and her consent to marry him. While she was in England he took her dancing, accompanied her to the theaters and concert halls of Liverpool, joined her in long walks around Wirral, often reading Keats or Tennyson with her over a rural lunch. Olaf was solicitous and charming. He had earnest blue eyes to match Agnes's, a boyish smoothness of complexion, and a startling shock of windblown blond hair that (until it was trimmed back during the war) made his head seem slightly out of proportion to the rest of him. Agile, athletic, and full of energy, he had the lithe body of a cyclist, a runner, and a rower. At five feet, eight inches, he weighed 135 pounds, as he would for the rest of his life. Temperamentally, passion alternated with self-doubt in Olaf, and his eagerness to win Agnes was sometimes so urgent that she was distressed both by his intensity and by the despondency that could follow an evening spent together. But the fact that Agnes would be in Germany and France for most of the next eighteen months meant that she would get to see little of her fascinating and enigmatic cousin. Much of the wooing would have to be done in writing. The letter Olaf wrote on 30 March 1913 started a correspondence that continued almost unbroken until one week before they married on 16 July 1919. Inevitably, the first letter opens with Olaf recalling the impression made on him when he saw Agnes in her green dress standing before the fire in 1903.

Once the correspondence began, Agnes and Olaf saw each other perhaps a total of eleven or twelve weeks during 1913 and 1914: during a Swiss holiday in the summer of 1913, at Christmas in Liverpool in 1913, in Paris during May 1914, and again in Liverpool and Surrey during September and early October 1914. Olaf courted energetically in person and by mail, but Agnes repeatedly put him off. She completed her continental studies and returned to England in July 1914, and within weeks war suddenly engulfed Europe. As the hostilities threatened sea travel in the early autumn, Agnes hastened to book her return passage to Australia. On 12 October Olaf saw his twenty-year-old cousin onto the Blue Funnel liner *Aeneas*, docked in Liverpool, with their New Zealander cousin Dorothy Miller as her companion. He had already written her well over five hundred pages of love letters, and she had written about half that amount, but neither anticipated how many more pages lay ahead of them. Like others in that year, Agnes and Olaf did not expect the Great War to last very long; they never guessed that it would be almost five years before they would see each other again. A few days before Agnes's departure from England, Olaf, hoping for a reunion the next summer, wrote to her: "We will each go our way, and talk across the world a little."

As the months and years passed their conversation persisted, each contributing to it almost daily and submitting to the exigencies of a wartime postal schedule. The letters were often written in installments, each correspondent adding to her or his letter until the date of the next outgoing transoceanic mail. As a result, some of Agnes's letters in particular grew to thirty or forty pages in length.[10] While Agnes was in England, she and Olaf could communicate with one another through an efficient postal service within hours or, at most, overnight. When she was in Germany and France, each still could send a letter and get a response in just a few days. But even under relatively favorable conditions in the earlier years of the war, one of Olaf's letters would take five weeks to travel from Europe via Capetown to Colombo to Sydney; and Agnes's reply would either retrace that route or cross the Pacific to San Francisco and thence travel overland to New York before resuming an ocean voyage to England, and then, after the middle of 1915, it would be forwarded to Olaf at the front, where he was driving an ambulance. In the later stages of the war when mail service was less reliable, three or four months could pass between the writing of one letter and the receipt of its reply. Such constraints on spontaneity and immediacy might daunt would-be lovers in the age of the transcontinental telephone and jetliner, but Olaf and Agnes approached the daily ritual of composing with a fervor and resourcefulness that mark the last flowering of a letter-writing tradition now largely vanished.

Although written for the most part with an artless absence of premeditation, the letters of Agnes Miller and Olaf Stapledon—even in the current abridgment, which represents something less than one-tenth of the whole correspondence—have a natural shapeliness and coherence. With their minute attention to daily experience and subtle

10. In a letter omitted from the present selection Agnes described how she always kept her current letter to Olaf open on her desk "until the last post so that I can add, & then I add & add & always add to your letter" (18 January 1916).

gradations of feeling, their enactment of the psychological shifts and stresses of six years, the dramatic tension of political disagreements and external threats, their unusual degree of self-reflectiveness about the nature of letters as a genre, and even the intervention of a rival lover or two, they recall the texture of eighteenth-century novels. But Agnes and Olaf were living inside the story they were writing, and they could only rarely perceive the structure they were building. When they did perceive it, the immensity, the wonder, the precariousness of it all thrilled and scared them. Because of the distance in space and time that was the crucial factor in the great bulk of their correspondence, each was unable to gauge precisely the response of the other to any particular letter, and each had to struggle to keep alive the conviction that there was a real flesh-and-blood person, not a phantom or a figment, at the other end of the postal route. In one remarkable letter written from France on 4 July 1916, Olaf speculated about the discoveries an independent reader might make in their correspondence: "If all our letters were to be read through on end, alternately yours and mine, what a lot they would tell that we had not in mind to tell at the time of writing. They would tell of all sorts of changes and fluctuations and gradual evolvings that we knew nothing of at the time." [11] Almost no one except the original writers would have a motive powerful enough to sustain an engaged reading of *all* the thousands of pages of these love letters, but if the selection in *Talking Across the World* can serve as a synecdoche for the whole, then Olaf's fanciful speculation becomes a prophecy.

The romance of Agnes Miller and Olaf Stapledon is quixotic, improbable, charming, and often powerfully moving. Despite Olaf's fantasy of an external reader, it is evident that neither writer considered the correspondence as anything but an intimate and private exchange. They had, in fact, to overcome inhibitions at the thought of the censor, who was the unwanted third party to many of their war letters; and in November 1918, Agnes was chagrined that, after nearly six years of reading Olaf's letters, she had to make one of them public for the first time when the Australian customs officer demanded, as a condition for issuing her a passport, written proof of her fiancé's intention to marry her. Nevertheless, though the writers were shy and jealous of their privacy, both were acutely conscious of the letter as a literary form, and they liked to frame their confidences in large, public terms, embedding their personal situation in the universal world of story and alluding to other lovers real and fictional, tragic and farcical—outside the bounds

11. Even early on in their courtship, in a letter dated 11 March 1914, which is not included in this collection, Olaf imagined what it would be like if Agnes's letters were made public: "If I were to find them all printed and bound in a book, and I not having ever known you (as the Irish put it) I should say, 'Whoever wrote them, I love her.'"

of their stationery. This was a courtship conducted in full awareness of the history of lovers' trials, and so we can hear Olaf and Agnes likening themselves not only to Dante and Beatrice but to Pyramus and Thisbe, to Eros and Psyche, to Jane Austen's Mr. Darcy and Elizabeth Bennett, to Lorna Doone and John Ridd, to the Brownings and to Beatrice and Sidney Webb, to the suffering lovers in Elizabethan sonnets and *Othello* and *The Winter's Tale* and the modern lovers in Meredith's *Ordeal of Richard Feverel* and *Diana of the Crossways*, to the first cousins whose passion is the focus of Hardy's *Jude the Obscure* and Galsworthy's *Free-lands*, and to the allegorical lovers in the paintings of George Frederic Watts and the ludicrous and monotonous couple in a cartoon from *Punch*.

In their literary self-consciousness and their Edwardian gentility of style, in Olaf's habit of addressing Agnes with the archaic "thee" and in Agnes's fondness for exclamation points and for constructing theatrical "scenes" out of mundane events, the Stapledon-Miller letters are old-fashioned. Readers accustomed to sifting private letters for scandalous self-revelation or gossip about celebrities will come up empty-handed with this correspondence. Olaf and Agnes weren't well-connected enough to be able to serve up tasty anecdotes about poets or politicians. The most famous person Olaf knew was Julian Grenfell, with whom he had rowed at Oxford; but Olaf moved in different circles from his aristo-cratic, Etonian crewmate. Agnes lived on the same street in the Sydney suburb of Mosman as the governor of New South Wales, but she looked on the governor's family simply as neighbors, not as political figures. Although there is comedy and discomfort and even some suspense in the "subplot" of Olaf's Australian rival, a commercial traveler with the astonishing name Jack Armstrong, and still more in the last few months of the correspondence in a final and dramatic threat to the impending marriage, the definition of "scandal" would have to be stretched out of shape to encompass the events of these letters. The passions Olaf and Agnes express, though intense and often impatient, are chastely decorous. They are also quite real. When, after more than three and a half years' separation from Olaf, Agnes attended a working-class party of Sydney factory women who had all brought their "gentleman friends" for dancing and kissing games, she hurried home at the evening's end to pour out her grief to her absent, her almost ghostly lover across the world. Because of the physical and conventional constraints they had to accept in their courtship, Agnes's outcry is one of the most genuinely erotic moments in the correspondence:

You are in France—I am here & I can't have you. I have got to keep going without you. I must not depend on you to prop me up. I must be able to stand by myself. I may expect your letters & cherish them but I may not expect anything more. I must not expect you. —— And tonight, in spite of all my steeling, my soul is crying out for you, for your very self. If I could only see you with my eyes & touch you. If I could feel your arms round me holding me tight. If I could kiss your face, kiss your mouth & then bury my face against your coat & rest in your arms——ah if! even only once! (17 March 1918)

Whatever the changes in rhetorical fashion in the past seventy years, a reader from the later part of this century can have no trouble distinguishing this kind of feeling from mere eccentricity or posturing.

### III

The public event of the Great War shadows most of the years when Agnes and Olaf courted and lends their letters a social as well as a biographical interest, but before Olaf became directly involved in the war in mid-1915 his chief external preoccupation was the education of adult working people. In the late spring of 1913 he gave up his position as a clerk in the Alfred Holt shipping office in Liverpool to devote himself full-time to interests which he had fitted in during moments spared from checking bills of lading. Forgoing the business successes of his father, William Clibbett Stapledon, who had in the course of twenty years risen from service in his own father's shipping agency in Port Said to the board of five managers of the Holt Company's Blue Funnel line, Olaf was determined to make a living in social work and the adult education movement while trying to establish himself as a poet and essayist. In the autumn of 1913 he took up residence in the newly opened building of the Liverpool University Settlement, an institution that sought to get beyond almsgiving and implement practical remedies to the desperate poverty, overcrowding, and illiteracy in the city's huge slums.[12] Olaf had already been doing voluntary work at the Settlement for more than a year and had been looking after the welfare of poor children who attended one of the local Council schools. He would visit the dark, cramped dwellings of his "cases," explaining to their mothers how they could get medical attention for the children and free meals to combat malnutrition; when a child left school, he would give advice on the choice of an occupation.

As a resident of the Settlement, Olaf could spend weekends at his parents' large and comfortable house, Annery, on Caldy Hill near the suburban town of West Kirby, but during the week he lived at Nile Street, Liverpool, and began expanding his social work to include the founding of "study circles" for working men and women, informal discussions of

12. A short, well-documented account of the University Settlements in England, beginning with the opening of Toynbee Hall in London, can be found in Thomas Kelly, *A History of Adult Education in Great Britain*, 2nd ed. (Liverpool: Liverpool University Press, 1970), pp. 239–42.

English history open to anyone in the neighborhood.[13] Believing he was better at teaching than at visitations, Olaf put a great deal of energy into the study circles. He had already had one unsatisfying year teaching children at the Manchester Grammar School, but working with adults reawakened his commitment to education, though in ways that caused him to redefine his pedagogy. In 1913 he wrote a short article, called "The People, Self Educator," for the magazine published by alumni of his old boarding school. He outlined the conflict between two competing views of education and left no doubt about his own commitments:

The present age prides itself on its care for education. At no other time was there such a large proportion of educated people, nor so many various educational movements. Now the two great types of these movements illustrate my principle. On the one hand there is an educational system which is in some sense thrust down upon the people from above, an orthodox and somewhat tasteless system of board schools and technical colleges. On the other is a rudimentary attempt on the part of the workers of this country to organize their own education. With this lies the future.[14]

As he wrote, he was already putting his new principle into practice. In 1911 he had begun attending meetings of the Liverpool branch of the Workers' Educational Association, founded in 1903 and quickly grown to be the largest and most ambitious organization for adult education in Great Britain. By 1912 he was eagerly seeking tutorial work with the WEA. Typically, the association sent an organizer to a town to ask that people examine their own needs and, if they wished to study a particular topic, adopt a resolution at a town meeting that work on a course of their choice should begin. The WEA would supply the tutor.[15] Late in 1912, Olaf was dispatched across the river Mersey to the dockyards of Wallasey—coincidentally, the town where he had been born in 1886—to become its first WEA tutor for a course of twenty-four lectures on the history of industrialism.

For two years Olaf built up his repertoire of tutorial courses, which he

13. Olaf described the structure of these discussion groups in a brief article signed "W.O.S." in the *Liverpool University Settlement Report for Years 1911 and 1912* (p. 11), published in October 1913; a copy is on file at the Sydney Jones Library, University of Liverpool.

14. Olaf Stapledon, "The People, Self Educator," *The Old Abbotsholmian*, III (1913), pp. 206–7.

15. For an account, with examples, of how such courses came into being, see the work of the founder of the WEA, Albert Mansbridge, *An Adventure in Working-Class Education, Being the Story of the Workers' Educational Association, 1903–1915* (London: Longmans, Green, 1920). A retrospective survey of the experience of teaching in the WEA was made in a lecture by one of its earliest tutors, the historian R. H. Tawney, "The Workers' Educational Association and Adult Education," printed in his book *The Radical Tradition: Twelve Essays on Politics, Education and Literature*, ed. Rita Hinden (New York: Minerva Press, 1964), pp. 82–93.

carried to various towns near Liverpool: Preston, Southport, Birkenhead, Crewe, Workington, and Barrow. He wrote about the WEA and study circles for a number of local newspapers on Merseyside and in Cheshire, served on the Liverpool executive committee, and published an ambitious, if somewhat callow, series of five articles on "Poetry and the Worker" in *The Highway*, the official journal of the WEA.[16] At the same time he campaigned successfully for the establishment of a dental clinic in Liverpool, counseled juvenile offenders and helped them find employment after their release from prison, and spoke regularly at the David Lewis, a working-class club in Liverpool. When war was declared in August 1914, he was spending his second summer tutoring at the WEA summer school for working people at University College in Bangor, North Wales.

In aligning himself with what he described as "the effort of serious and zealous working men and women to fit themselves for their great task of re-making society," Olaf was not making a complete break with his past.[17] He had grown up in a reformist environment. His mother had corresponded with Ruskin and was committed to progressive ideas about education and social welfare; his father was a public-spirited philanthropist and a strong Liberal in a largely Tory part of the country. But Olaf's experience in the WEA moved him farther to the left than either of his parents. Under the influence of his WEA colleagues and, especially, in discussions with the dock workers, artisans, miners, and railway workers who were his students, he evolved a political philosophy that was more and more emphatically socialist and cosmopolitan. He had just reached a stage of frustrated uncertainty about English social policy and the ideology of nationalism at exactly the time when the declaration of war in August 1914 seemed to require an unquestioning allegiance to the nation as political entity and as cultural symbol. His letters reveal the emergence of the qualified pacifism that led him to choose what he regarded as a course of compromise, leaving his WEA work and applying, early in 1915, for service in the Society of Friends' Ambulance Unit.

Most of Olaf's struggle to decide how he would spend the war took place when Agnes was already offstage, making her way home to Australia. But she knew about his educational commitments and approved

16. Olaf's articles in *The Highway* began with a general survey of "Poetry and the Worker" in vol. VI (October 1913), 4–6; followed by pieces on Wordsworth in VI (December 1913), 51–53; on Tennyson in VI (February 1914), 87–89; on Browning in VI (April 1914), 125–27; and on Shakespeare in VII (January 1915), 56–58.

17. The quotation comes from one of a series of articles about WEA work Olaf wrote for local newspapers. This one, "The Tutorial Class," appeared without a by-line in the Warrington *Examiner*, 15 November 1913; it is identified as his on the basis of a letter to Agnes, enclosing a clipping of it, on 19 November 1913.

of them, though with a sense of continuing regret that she could not share more fully in the teaching he felt called to do. Agnes was a very dutiful daughter, and she felt grateful to her father for the money he provided for her year of music study in Europe; she also realized that that sort of education was no substitute for a university degree. Throughout the period of the correspondence—and indeed for the rest of her life—she mourned that lost opportunity, knowing that she would never be able to *do* the things Olaf, with his Balliol credentials, could do. She could share in his work, she kept reminding herself, better than if he had chosen a career in business, but her sharing would be as a supporter and sympathetic onlooker, not as a partner. Frank Miller's ideas about the education of women were unenlightened and typical of his gender, class, and age. His eldest child was trained in all the domestic arts, to give the tasks of baking, sewing, knitting, shopping, and child care their honorific title; and she received a musical education good enough to allow her to join her father and her sister Rosie in playing evening trios at home or to sing in a local recital but without being rigorous enough to equip her for a musical career. Ironically, Agnes's mother, Margaret Barnard Miller, had been disappointed in 1882 when her expectation of a scholarship to Newnham College, the new women's college at Cambridge University, had to be set aside because her parents "were not able to face the heavy expenses over and above the scholarship."[18] Agnes was not able to improve on her mother's bad luck. Instead, during the war she took some cooking classes at a local technical college, sang with the Sydney Madrigal Society, participated in a women's reading and discussion group known as "The Seekers," attended sewing circles to make clothes for Belgian refugees, found time to write still other letters to various Anzac soldiers at Gallipoli, and joined the Sydney branch of the WEA—not as a tutor, but as a student in order to study Greek civilization and modern history.

It is clear from Agnes's letters that Frank Miller was a powerful presence at Egremont, the Miller house in Sydney. Agnes was reluctant to voice her own opinions or make her own analyses of current political and social issues, and unlike the British Stapledons, the Australian Millers were a very conservative family. Although Margaret Miller was a Quaker, she was strongly prowar and proconscription, making her a renegade in the Sydney Friends' Meeting. Frank Miller was even more outspoken, and dinner conversations were sometimes monologues in which Agnes's father lacerated the "shirkers" in Australia and England who wouldn't take up arms against the Hun. It was not a receptive environment for the letters that began arriving from Olaf in early 1915,

18. From Margaret Miller's manuscript memoir, *Story of the Barnard Family and Their Friends*, written in 1949 and now in the possession of John D. and Sarina Stapledon.

announcing that he had chosen not to fight.[19] For Agnes, who no longer doubted that she was in love with him, the situation was excruciating—caught between a strong-willed father and an importunate fiancé and with almost no breathing space to think things out and express them for herself. She chose to be a noncombatant in the war of words in her household, but her effort to keep peace between herself and her father meant that her letters to Olaf became virtually her only outlet for candid talk and for a chance to test in dialogue ideas that were advanced as dogma at the kitchen table at Egremont.

### IV

Within four days of England's entrance into the European war, the Society of Friends in London convened an extraordinary "Meeting for Sufferings." The Quakers emerged from that Meeting with an open letter to the citizens of the British Empire, printed as an advertisement in many newspapers, calling for continued efforts to achieve a swift, negotiated end to the conflict and outlining the principles on which the Society would act if the war were to continue. Privately, a number of Friends thought the situation was already hopeless and were turning their attention to devising some form of emergency service, consistent with pacifist ideals, which would make it easier for young Quakers to resist the mounting patriotic calls to fight. By 21 August, forty-eight Friends were actively engaged in forming an ambulance unit that would operate outside military discipline but would provide an opportunity for exacting work to alleviate the suffering of injured soldiers and civilians and thereby would satisfy a sense of duty during a time of national crisis. At once, the idea of a Friends' Ambulance Corps provoked controversy within the Society. Older Friends remembered the work of the War Victims' Relief in the Franco-Prussian War of 1870, when Quaker volunteers strictly limited their ministrations to noncombatants; they feared that in a mechanized war ambulances would inevitably become entangled with the military effort and dilute the force of the Society's traditional peace testimony. "An ambulance corps at the rear," one member warned, "healing the fighters to fight again, is as much a part of the military equipment of to-day as the man with the bayonet doing his deadly work on the field of battle."[20]

Despite misgivings and a few resignations in various local Meetings of

19. For Frank Miller, Olaf's pacifism only strengthened the case against him as a suitable husband for his daughter. When Olaf first discussed his feelings for Agnes with her father, the meeting was uncomfortable. In the terse words of Olaf's diary for 3 May 1913, "He objects strongly to cousinship."

20. Letter of Charles E. Gregory, *The Friend* (London), 29 August 1914, p. 656. My account of the formation of the Ambulance Unit depends on the extensive coverage of the issue in *The Friend*, the weekly newspaper of the Society of Friends, from 7 August onward.

the Society, a training camp was established on 7 September, and sixty men began receiving comprehensive instruction in first aid, hygiene, stretcher drill, and cooking. In October, Sir George Newman, the physician who chaired the Friends' Ambulance Unit Committee, heard of an urgent appeal for medical resources along the French-Belgian frontier, where massive casualties were going untreated for lack of personnel and facilities. Full of energy and craving experience, the newly trained Friends constituted themselves as "The First Anglo-Belgian Ambulance Unit" and volunteered their services. By the end of the month a contingent of forty-three drivers and orderlies, three doctors, and eight ambulances crossed to Dunkirk and immediately confronted the spectacle of hundreds of wounded men laid out on piles of straw in railway sheds. "In the first room," one of the pioneer volunteers wrote in his diary, "there were some gruesome cases; most had been left from 1–3 days unattended. . . . The men were stoical and very patient under the pain. Their petition 'doucement! doucement!' was very pathetic."[21] In the next four weeks the Friends opened two hospitals, staffed several aid stations near the front, and had a headquarters and supply station operating at Malo, just outside Dunkirk. They thought of themselves as pacifist crusaders sallying forth, as one of their chroniclers said at the end of the war, "almost in knight-errant fashion, to look for work wherever [they] thought such might be found."[22] Although viewed with suspicion by the military authorities because of their refusal to take a military oath or to obey any order that involved the transport of munitions or soldiers to the front, the Friends' Ambulance Unit quickly established a reputation—more among the Belgians and later the French than the British—for extraordinary courage and efficiency. Unpaid and unarmed, performing work as often tedious, monotonous, and unappreciated as it was heroic, the Unit attracted Quakers and non-Quakers to an honorable and rigorous share in the national trauma. By the end of the war six hundred men were on active service in the Unit in various sectors of France and Belgium; a total of more than fourteen hundred served in the ambulance section at some time during the war.

As late as November 1914, as the first battle of Ypres raged in the vicinity where the FAU had established its stations, Olaf was still talking about applying for an army commission and enlisting after Christmas. If

21. From the Diary of J. W. Harvey now in the library of the Imperial War Museum, London.

22. *The Friends' Ambulance Unit 1914–1919: A Record*, ed. Meaburn Tatham and James E. Miles (London: Swarthmore Press, 1920), p. 8. This is the official history of the FAU compiled by men who served in the Unit, and I am indebted to it, as well as to *The Friend*, for many of the headnotes to the Stapledon-Miller letters. For a larger view of the prevalence of chivalric images and language in the Great War see chapter 18 of Mark Girouard, *The Return to Camelot: Chivalry and the English Gentleman* (New Haven: Yale University Press, 1981).

an episode from his novel of 1932, *Last Men in London,* is drawn from actual experience, he may, like his autobiographical persona Paul, have gone so far as to walk up to a recruiting office manned by a splendidly uniformed sergeant and only "scuttled away" from the inviting doorway at the last possible moment.[23] In a letter to Agnes dated 1 December 1914, Olaf described the agonizing doubts about enlistment, generated in conversations with colleagues and students in the WEA, that made him resist the patriotic "drumbeating," even though he as yet had no alternative plan in mind. *Last Men in London* re-creates his psychological crisis and the resolution of his dilemma in this way:

> A few days later Paul heard of a curious semi-religious ambulance organization, which, while professing pacifism, undertook voluntary succour of the wounded at the front. It was controlled and largely manned by a certain old-established and much-respected religious sect which adhered strictly to the commandment 'Thou shalt not kill,' and to its own unique tradition of good works and quietism. Some members of this sect preached a rigorous pacifism which very soon brought them into conflict with authority; but others, who tempered pacifism with a craving to take some part in the great public ordeal, created this anomalous organization, whose spirit was an amazing blend of the religious, the military, the pacific, the purely adventurous, and the cynical. This 'Ambulance Unit' lasted throughout the war. (pp. 195–96)

In fact, as Olaf explained to Agnes on 9 January 1915, he began to see a way out of his indecision about the war when he got letters from Agnes's cousins, Alfred and Beatrice Fryer of Rouen, explaining the work of a recently deployed Ambulance Corps operating in Flanders under the auspices of the British Red Cross and the Society of Friends. The committee that governed the Friends' Ambulance Unit had from the beginning intended to accept only candidates "who are Friends or closely connected with the Society."[24] Olaf was not a Quaker, and his only connections with the Society were the somewhat distant ones of the Barnard sisters Nina, Sallie, and Margaret—the last of whom was Agnes's mother. Nevertheless, he happened to apply to the Corps at a time in early 1915 when there was a shortage of volunteers, an urgent call for staff in both the ambulance section and the antityphoid hospitals that the Friends had established in Belgium, and a severe financial crisis in the Society as the costs of its relief work mounted rapidly.[25] The fact that Olaf could pay for his own training and that his father was willing to donate an ambulance to the Corps made him an attractive candidate. He spent the first seven months of 1915 pursuing what he regarded as

---

23. W. Olaf Stapledon, *Last Men in London* (London: Methuen, 1932), p. 60.
24. Minute Book of the Friends' Ambulance Unit Committee, meeting of 18 November 1914. The minute books are housed in the library at Friends' House, London.
25. Minute Book of the Friends' Ambulance Unit Committee, 10 February 1915.

the most satisfactory option available for a secular pacifist who was not absolutely opposed to the taking of life.[26] In July 1915, having completed driving lessons and a hospital course, and having recovered from an emergency appendectomy that delayed his spring departure from England, Olaf, in Red Cross uniform and brassards, arrived in Dunkirk with his custom-designed Lanchester car to begin three and a half years' service as a driver for the Friends' Ambulance Unit.

Olaf packed his letters to Agnes with information about the daily experience of the volunteers in the FAU: the hectic nighttime ambulance runs with lights out and wounded French infantrymen screaming in agony when they were jolted over narrow roads full of shell holes; the summer strolls through the Argonne forest, discussing philosophy or birdwatching or bathing in a stream with the sound of the guns in the background; the passionate debates about the passage of the conscription act in England and about the perceived militarizing of the FAU in its aftermath; the bitter winter nights in freezing barns when ambulance drivers sometimes cranked for an hour to get their cars started; the rowdy practical jokes, unQuakerly convoy talk, and fiercely aggressive rugby matches that sustained morale and saved pacifist idealism from priggishness or obsession; the horrors of the war's final months when the ambulances, following the advancing French army, moved for the first time through the devastation, hazards, and stinks of no-man's-land.[27] Ambulance work had seemed a glamorous wartime occupation in an age when automobiles were few and holders of a driver's certificate a fairly exotic breed. The reality, as Olaf came to realize, was considerably different from the anticipation. Many of his letters describe the boredom and frustration of day after day spent not engaged in a holy crusade but in cleaning mud off windshields, inoculating civilians against typhus, repairing punctured tires, and waiting for something to happen. By the time he reached Flanders in mid-1915, whatever romance there had been to the war and to the work of relief was sub-

26. In his only memoir of his World War I experience, aside from the mix of fiction and memory in *Last Men in London*, Olaf represented himself as resistant to military discipline but not an absolute conscientious objector: "I had no belief that killing, simply as such, must in all circumstances be wrong. It was war, modern war, that was wrong, and foolish, and likely to undermine civilisation. It was nationalism that was wrong; and militarism, and the glib surrender of one's moral responsibility to an authority that was not really fit to bear it." Olaf Stapledon, "Experiences in the Friends' Ambulance Unit," *We Did Not Fight: 1914–1918 Experiences of War Resisters*, ed. Julian Bell (London: Cobden-Sanderson, 1935), p. 361.

27. Olaf's colleague on the ambulance convoy, Julian Fox, recorded his own recollections of both the tedium and the gruesomeness of the war years in *The Man Who Would Have Been Blamed and Other Stories*, privately printed in Somerset in 1961 and available at the library of Friends' House, London. Fox's account of the final months of the Unit's work in no-man's-land supplements the sketchy information in Olaf's brief and hastily written diary notes and letters during that period.

stantially diminished. A tightened military bureaucracy restrained the FAU's "knights-errant" from searching out whatever projects attracted their attention; instead, the relief work was systematized, orders and permissions had to be obtained from military authorities, some sectors were closed to the Unit, and by the end of 1915, instead of operating as a fully autonomous body, the Unit was broken into several mobile sections, each of which was loosely but inextricably tied to a division of the French Army.[28]

The glory days of the FAU at Ypres and Poperinghe were already history when Olaf crossed the Channel, and there were seldom opportunities for Unit members to re-create the legendary heroism of the winter and spring of 1915. Much of the work was almost unbearably repetitious, dull, numbing—and, Olaf would tell Agnes, in some ways more difficult than being in the trenches. An American woman from Boston who was a volunteer driver for French ambulances made the same point, and without a male noncombatant's anxiety over appearing to be justifying himself too vigorously. Amy Owen Bradley told her correspondent that she thought her experience of the war had schooled her in a discipline that the young American men who began marching through France in 1917 and 1918 would not take to very easily:

There is so much that the boys can't imagine, possibly. Anyone can stand the fighting, but the sitting in the mud for days with *nothing* to do, and the dirt, and the routine, and the oppressive boredom is what tries and tests them. If they don't have ideals they are lost—there is no just getting along; they either live by their ideals, or lose them.[29]

For members of the FAU the concern was not merely sticking to their pacifist ideals through the tedium of ambulance maintenance and driving, but the worry that they would be perceived as what the French called *"embusqués"* and Frank Miller called "shirkers." Repeated requests from members of the Unit to undertake strenuous and visibly dangerous work near the front lines—stretcher-carrying, staffing field ambulances, working at casualty clearing stations at the lines—were turned down by military authorities who refused to accept men at the front not under their direct command. The failure to get that kind of

28. In a valediction after the demobilization of the Unit in 1919, Sir George Newman acknowledged the discouragement of many who had served in the final years of the war, and the great gulf between the splendid rhetoric with which the FAU had been inaugurated and the ambivalent pride in its accomplishments at the end: "While there has been adventure and chivalry and romance, and much of the movement and dust of battle and of the sounds and sights and echoes of war, there has also been another side to it all—grey, hard, apparently inequitable, deadening." "Farewell to the Ambulance Unit," *The Friend* (London), 21 March 1919, p. 164.

29. *Back of the Front in France: Letters From Amy Owen Bradley, Motor Driver of the American Fund for French Wounded* (Boston: W. A. Nutterfield, 1918), pp. 113–14.

assignment was Olaf's sharpest disappointment as an FAU volunteer. Even the Quakers in the Unit, whose religious principles could compensate for a lack of glory and romance in their work, were dismayed by the enforced menial work of endlessly polishing buttons and washing a chassis to pass ritual inspections, or worse, enforced idleness when there was clearly work that needed doing. In 1916 there was a sizable exodus of Quaker members from the FAU who felt that the relief work had become too compromised by the Unit's alliance with military authority and who chose prison as a more effective witness against the war.[30] For Olaf, who joined the FAU as a compromise to begin with, the entire period of his service was a struggle with doubts about whether he should remain and whether he was accomplishing anything significant at all. But despite perplexities about tactics, his pacifism grew in strength the more he saw of the smashed bodies and spirits of the men he carried in the double tier of bunks in his ambulance. As Herbert Read wrote in his war diary of the years 1915 through 1918, "Pacifism, before 1914, was an idealistic doctrine: it had not yet been tempered by universal war, and war had not yet reached the dimensions of universal horror. Pacifism, an expendable ideal in 1914, could become a rooted conviction before the end of the war—a conviction rooted in blood-soaked soil."[31]

Olaf's internal struggles and the divisions within the Unit were not the only, or even the most distressing, tension he felt about his war work. As he and Agnes continued to correspond throughout the war it became clear that Agnes—heavily influenced by her father's political passions—did not really approve of the idea of pacifism, though she always respected Olaf's work in the Unit. But Frank Miller was not the only source of Agnes's doubts. The propagandizing of women during the war in both England and Australia was intense; ubiquitous posters urged women to motivate their men to enlist in order to safeguard English civilization and English womanhood. One representative poster,

30. The Minute Book of the Friends' Ambulance Unit Committee for 3 May 1916 records the first five resignations from the Unit because of the Military Service Act and acknowledges growing dissent within the Unit over the committee's cooperation with the tribunals which heard cases for exemption from the act. On 17 May the committee, feeling that the FAU's political survival was at stake, forbade Unit members from publishing any dissent from committee policy. The disillusionment of Quaker members with the perceived militarization of the FAU is exemplified by the case of T. Corder Catchpool, one of the original forty-three members of the Unit who began working in France in October 1914. In May 1916 he resigned from the Unit, had his certificate of exemption from conscription revoked, was court-martialed, and spent the rest of the war imprisoned at hard labor. The evolution of his decision to leave the FAU is recorded in the letters he wrote to his sister, published under the title *On Two Fronts* (London: Headley Bros., 1918), especially pp. 93–109.

31. Herbert Read, *The Contrary Experience: Autobiographies* (London: Secker & Warburg, 1963), p. 62.

which can be seen at London's Imperial War Museum, shouts in large black and red letters:

SWEETHEARTS!

Has your "boy" enlisted?
If not, why not?
Are you selfishly dissuading him?
If so the shame of your Country
    rests upon YOU.
If you cannot persuade him to
    answer his Country's Call
    and protect you now
DISCHARGE HIM
as unfit!

On Australian walls, where strikingly inflammatory posters created, in the words of one cultural historian, "the most insistent and bitter campaign of persuasion Australia has ever seen," women saw representations of the slaughter of Belgian women and babies, warnings that their own treatment "would be worse," and appeals to "send a man to-day to fight for you."[32]

While Olaf came close to resigning from the Unit and going to prison after the passage of the Military Service Act mandating conscription in early 1916, Agnes (who, unlike English women, was able to vote) twice endorsed a conscription bill in Australian referenda in 1916 and 1917. Her position lost decisively both times, but it unsettled Olaf, particularly since he knew that the formidable figure of Frank Miller stood behind Agnes's arguments for conscription. While she tried to minimize the significance of their political disagreements, Olaf insisted that they were real and worrisome, and that the limitations of letters as an instrument of conversation, persuasion, and courtship became apparent as soon as a major ideological difference surfaced. The censorship regulations (which applied to Olaf's outgoing letters but not to the mail he received from Agnes) prevented a complete and mutual exchange on the subject of military service, and after a while Olaf and Agnes agreed simply to respect the other's position until they could meet and talk it over free from the oversight of the censor and Frank Miller. That the love affair survived and flourished despite such a fundamental difference may be the most remarkable feature of the entire correspondence. "Somehow I love you better for being in the enemy's camp," Olaf wrote hopefully on 12 January 1918. "What a plot for a melodramatic novel."

32. Peter Stanley, Introduction to *What Did You Do in the War Daddy? A Visual History of Propaganda Posters* (Melbourne: Oxford University Press, 1983), p. 8. This generous sampling of posters from the collection of the Australian War Memorial suggests the power of the visual imagery Agnes was exposed to in Sydney.

V

"Sometimes it is really hard to shake off the conviction that this war has been written by someone," Paul Fussell observes in his brilliant study of the mythologizing of the Great War in memoirs, poems, letters, and diaries.[33] The curious intersections between real life and literary imagination are at the center of Fussell's analysis of the processes by which the war experience was absorbed, transformed, and sometimes created in the act of writing about it. The letters of Olaf and Agnes exemplify to an often startling degree the extent to which two lives were constructed out of war letters, indeed, the degree to which their romantic affair took its life from writing. On New Year's Eve 1918, with the armistice in force and Olaf not knowing whether Agnes might already be voyaging to England when his letter arrived in Sydney, he wrote: "I don't know if you will ever get this or where you will get it if you do get it. Anyhow I must talk to you even if you never hear what I say." Agnes did just barely receive that letter before she sailed from Sydney, and her reply reinforced Olaf's perception that their correspondence had achieved something very like an independent life of its own: "You are a dear to go on writing just on the off chance, but of course you would, & of course I would too. Why, if you had been killed I think I must have gone on writing" (2 March 1919). Even after their reunion in England in the spring of 1919 the habit of writing was so strong, so much identified in their own minds with the genesis and sustenance of their love, that they continued exchanging letters and notes until almost the eve of their wedding.

Like Samuel Richardson's eighteenth-century epistolary heroine Clarissa Harlowe, Agnes and Olaf seemed always to have pen and paper at hand and were always ready to transcribe the day's or hour's events. The special value of this dual correspondence lies in the authenticity and power of writing that continually rises above minor infelicities of expression to present a convincing psychological portrait of the writers and a rich social history of an era. Each writer joins observation to reflection, personal experience to cultural generalization, self-exposure to the interrogation of ideas and values; together, they produce unintended marvels of coincidence, irony, counterpoint, and paradox in the structure of their correspondence that would be the envy of many novelists. The letters accommodate a variety of genres, from Olaf's fairy stories to Agnes's vignettes about "thrifting" at a cardboard factory, from Olaf's astrophysical meditations to Agnes's "wicked story" about an Australian adulterer, from Olaf's "lectures" on socialism and utopianism to Agnes's

33. Paul Fussell, *The Great War and Modern Memory* (New York: Oxford University Press, 1975), p. 241.

journalistic features on the Sydney general strike and the homesteading project for returning Australian war veterans. During the course of their courtship each of them carefully filed and occasionally reread the other's letters, so that even after the passage of several years they could make fascinating cross-references to, evocations of, or revisions to earlier experiences and letters. Between them, the correspondents generate a splendidly various text as each represents her or his world to the other and as each enacts the poignant effort to see and touch the other through words.

Aside from the pleasures and surprises of the intricate design of the whole sequence, readers will find many individual letters that have the literary sophistication, sociological detail, and immediacy of feeling that distinguish the best writing in the English epistolary tradition. At one end of the correspondence we can read Olaf's comic account of a near-riot in Liverpool when the Abbey Players come to perform Synge's *Playboy of the Western World* (25 November 1913); at the other end is Agnes's winning self-portrait in the office of the exasperated customs agent in Sydney who has interviewed one too many young women seeking a passport to marry her English fiancé (2 November 1918). The arrival of war in Europe as witnessed by Olaf from the remote and dim vantage of a workers' institute in North Wales is matched by the arrival of the great influenza epidemic of 1918–19 in Sydney as seen by Agnes through the gauze mask those who ventured into the city were obliged to wear. Letter by letter Olaf incorporates each of his acquaintances in the ambulance convoy into a gallery of types to amuse Agnes and himself: "the Prof," meteorologist and mathematician whose level of abstraction defeats nearly everyone else on the convoy; "the Artist," a cynical, worldly painter who does Agnes's portrait from a photograph and is given the menial job of painting golden croix de guerre on all the ambulances; Hodgkin, the antiintellectual young orderly who is "a model of a certain kind of loose-limbed luxurious beauty"; Pimm, the bulldog-faced fundamentalist aghast at the loose talk and freethinking of the agnostics on the convoy; "Amelia," a sleepy newcomer to the Unit who acquires his unfortunate nickname when he is praised for ameliorating the lot of his comrades; "the Doc," who gives Schumann concerts whenever the convoy can borrow a piano but whose exaggerated politeness makes him a perpetual mystery and irritation to Olaf. Agnes has her own portrait gallery of Australians, the most intriguing of whom, Jack Armstrong, is the subject of a story within the larger story of the romance of Olaf and Agnes. The continuing saga of Jack's effort to win her away from Olaf allows Agnes to be alternately coy, quizzical, satirical, and exasperated as she reflects on the foolishness of men in love. But Agnes's portraits of Jack are never without sympathy, whether she is describing him in the hot Australian night standing in his pajamas with his hair sticking out wildly from his soaked head, or copying out for Olaf a portion of a teasing letter Jack wrote about Mary Baker Eddy and Christian Science, or recounting the night he arrived at Egremont and, finding only Agnes and her brother Waldo at home, dispatched Waldo to a shop to buy tobacco for him and then squared off with Agnes across the table to cross-examine her about Olaf.

If these letters are full of vitality and invention, it is also true that their eloquence coexists with—and even depends on—an often touching inelegance of design and phrasing. The blemishes and clumsiness are as visible as the grace and energy in the Stapledon-Miller letters. Olaf had a weakness for Edwardian rhetorical swirls, which the present edition tames by abridgment but does not attempt to eliminate; Agnes's letters are less syntactically sure than Olaf's, and she uses commas and dashes liberally to create an impression of breathless enthusiasm about even the most humdrum of experiences. The letters that comprise *Talking Across the World*, it should be emphasized, are the product of two literary amateurs. Apart from a few columns on etiquette and grooming for young ladies written for a small weekly newspaper in Sydney, Agnes Miller Stapledon never published a single piece in her own name until she was eighty-nine.[34] Although Olaf had already begun publishing short discursive essays when he started courting Agnes in 1913, he was a virtually unknown author throughout the Great War. His 1914 volume of poetry, *Latter-Day Psalms*, went almost completely unnoticed. During the war he published a few odd pieces of journalism and allegorical fiction in out-of-the-way places,[35] and he struggled with poems that were mostly unsuccessful, though a few tries at vers libre eventually found their way, in revised form, into poetry magazines and anthologies after the war.[36] One long piece of writing, the much-bescribbled manuscript frequently mentioned to Agnes, occupied much of the spare time Olaf had while with the FAU. A philosophical manifesto, partly modeled on his earlier *Psalms* but partly in prose as well, it went through many drafts and at least two titles (*In a Glass Darkly* and *The Sleeping Beauty*)

34. In the nursing home where she spent her last year Agnes Stapledon wrote a brief personal essay, "A Blue Bird," about her struggle to liberate a frightened bird that had become trapped in her room and the Blakean questions the experience suggested. The piece was published in *The Lady*, 198 (25 August 1983), 338.

35. Notably, "The Road to the Aide Post" in the *F.A.U. Monthly Magazine*, no. 1 (January 1916), 11–14; "The Reflections of an Ambulance Orderly," *The Friend* (14 April 1916), p. 246; and "The Seed and the Flower," *Friends' Quarterly Examiner*, 50 (October 1916), 464–75. The first two of these were published anonymously but are identifiable because of attributions in Agnes's letters.

36. For a full listing of Stapledon's published poems other than *Latter-Day Psalms* see items B1, B2, C3-C6, C8-C13, and C15 in Harvey J. Satty and Curtis C. Smith, *Olaf Stapledon: A Bibliography* (Westport: Greenwood Press, 1984). Other verses and prose sketches from 1913 to 1919 survive only as parts of some of the letters to Agnes; most of them have been omitted from the present collection.

before he gave up on it sometime after the war. None of his published work from the war years has anything like the imaginative range, the maturity of thought, or the experimental ambitions that mark his later fiction. There are some fascinating foretastes of the substance and style of the great works from the thirties and forties in his letters to Agnes, but it may be that the letters themselves are Olaf's major creative work of the period from 1913 to 1919. Writing to Agnes was the one regular exercise in composition he practiced every week of the war, and the letters were a readily available forum for trying out ideas, voices, styles, and genres on a willing audience. The love letters served as an apprenticeship to his fiction, and they also stand as a literary accomplishment in their own right.

But to see these letters solely as Olaf's achievement or solely as a prediction of *his* career would be a mistake. Olaf always liked to claim that Agnes wrote more interesting letters than he did. His praises may have been compounded of a lover's flattery and the desire to escape his own grim circumstances, but Agnes's skill as an observer, her expressive range, and her manipulation of tone and voice all undeniably grew as the correspondence went on. Although politically and philosophically naïve, Agnes is often a surprising figure in her letters, her attitudes less predictable than Olaf's, her questions disarming, her feelings frankly articulated, her inherited conservatism always open to revision. Agnes would have resisted being called a feminist (she even asks Olaf in one letter if there is such a word), but many of the questions she raises and some of the stands she takes suggest a restless eagerness to stake a claim to her own identity, apart from either Olaf's or her father's expectations of her. If there are hints of the author of *Star Maker* and *Sirius* in Olaf's letters, in Agnes's we can find the origins of the woman who became, in her later years, a peace activist and vice-president of the British section of the Women's International League for Peace and Freedom.

By the end, a reader may no longer be so sure whose letters are more interesting, may in fact feel disinclined to try to judge at all between the aesthetic merits of Agnes and Olaf's writing. What is unique, finally, about this edition of war letters is the alternating current generated by each writer's dependence on an invisible but spiritually present reader who writes back and who ponders, comments, sympathizes, disagrees, complains, questions, encourages, teases, doubts, rejoices, and reinforces the other correspondent. Agnes is both author and auditor, and so too is Olaf. The rarity of having both sides of such an extensive correspondence enables a reader to observe the two parties talking to each other over great distances and gaps of time. While we may stand back and observe structures and ironies that could not have been apparent to them at the time, we also are drawn into the pleasure of exchange that brings both writers vividly to life. They liked corresponding; the act of writing was relatively easy for each of them. To compose a letter was a pastime and a solace, and the prospect of a mail delivery was an event always to be celebrated and commented on. What was difficult for Agnes and Olaf was the ever-lengthening wait between one writer's utterance and the other's response. That required a constant effort of memory and imagination. Both Olaf and Agnes often wished that they could dispense with letters and even language altogether and communicate immediately. In an early letter to Agnes at Berlin, omitted from this edition, Olaf complained: "Writing is such a slow way of conveying thought. Speaking is bad enough. I should like some method of wireless telepathy. If Marconi and Mrs. Eddy and Brahms were to get into partnership they might discover the thing. At present we are not so much better off than the deaf blind man who has nothing but hand-grasps to live on" (28 October 1913). Nevertheless, they made letters work for them with extraordinary patience and ingenuity. Reading the intimate record of the Stapledon-Miller romance is a lesson in the power of words to shape realities. The writers knew that their correspondence could at least allow their two disembodied voices to approximate a conversation that would link their minds until the world allowed them to join in body as well as spirit. In the last letter she wrote Olaf from Australia, dated 3 March 1919, Agnes anticipated the long-awaited moment when a boat would complete its twelve-thousand-mile journey across the world and deliver to Liverpool not another thirty-page installment of writing but an actual person. Then the words would at last become flesh: "I myself shall be the next letter."

## VI

The chief editorial problem in making this collection has been to fashion a coherent and relatively compact narrative out of a vast, meandering tract of manuscript. Very much that is interesting has had to be omitted, and inevitably what appears in *Talking Across the World* is more tidy and streamlined, less repetitive and banal than the full correspondence; but the governing principle in selecting and abridging the letters has been to preserve to the greatest degree possible the dramatic authenticity and continuity of the originals. While much of the "small talk" and family news (who is ill, who is visiting, who has gotten a new job) and the repeated routines and formulaic rhetoric inevitable in a correspondence of this duration has been excised, the selection is designed both to suggest a portrait of society at large and to convey some sense of the correspondents' ordinary lives, including the prolonged dreariness of the war. About 90 percent of the extant material remains unpublished, but the aim has been to include enough "exposition" and local detail to enable a reader to experience, with a minimum of editorial intrusion, the unfolding of the courtship, the family personalities and tensions, the major external events and pressures on the writers, the political issues and disagreements that were most central to their lives, and the inward scrutiny and outward extensions of self that are the essence of any interesting correspondence.

Many of the original letters are very long. Particularly during the war years, when transoceanic mail ships departed infrequently, Agnes and Olaf wrote incrementally, adding bits and pieces to their letters over a period of a week or more. Almost none of the letters printed in *Talking Across the World* are presented in their entirety, save Olaf's first letter to Agnes in 1913 and Agnes's letter to her parents six weeks after her marriage, which constitutes the epilogue to the correspondence. If the text of a letter starts with an opening salutation, the reader may assume that nothing has been cut from the beginning of the letter; if a letter begins TO OLAF or TO AGNES, then some portion of the first part of the letter has been dropped. Omissions within letters are indicated by ellipses. Unless a closing formula is printed, some material at the end of the letter has been excised. In general, for the sake of readability, ellipses have been kept to a minimum; the editorial preference for most of the letters reproduced here has been to excerpt sustained passages rather than to splice together selected sentences from various parts of a letter. Excerpts from lengthy letters composed over many days are dated by the day on which the first printed portion of a letter was written, when that can be determined.

Variety has been a crucial consideration in determining which sections of particular letters to print. In a typical letter Olaf and Agnes each might cover six or seven different topics (maybe even a dozen or more in a very long letter). But it has seemed prudent to avoid falling automatically into highlighting the most "obvious" topic from a letter: Olaf on the subject of his ambulance cases, for instance, or Agnes's frequent accounts of picnic trips into the Australian bush. The best instances of such frequently recurring motifs have been sought out, but choices have also been made with an ear for a rhythmic variation of subjects and styles that is faithful to the varying texture of the originals. Thus a reader will find war narrative playing off against nature walks, passionate discussion of conscription within the convoy and between Olaf and Agnes against homelier passages on music or food or games, the death of an ambulance driver in France against the death of a young Australian woman from tuberculosis, Agnes on her first overnight camping trip into the bush comically describing how she roughed it by sleeping on the sand against Olaf's simultaneous letter telling how he has just spent the night on the floor of a cold, filthy farmhouse in the convoy's only available billet, self-conscious reflections on the nature and limitations of letter writing against passages on stellar infinity. And so on. To some degree this texture is the calculated result of editorial selection, but it is worth emphasizing that the chronology of the letters is never violated. Although the process of selection may heighten certain alternations of subject or mood, all the juxtapositions and ironic parallels and contrasting perspectives are there in the uncut letters, part of the fabric of the original correspondence.

Some silent emendations have been made. Olaf Stapledon was a notoriously haphazard speller throughout his life; all obvious misspellings have been corrected, but his inconsistencies in the use of British and American spellings remain unaltered. Generally, punctuation has been altered very little, since Agnes's preference for ampersands and dashes is essential to the style of her letters. For clarity's sake some commas have been introduced where they do not appear in the originals. The full return address for a letter is printed the first time one of the correspondents uses it. Thereafter, an abbreviated reference to city or place is substituted. A shortage of writing paper during the war years forced Olaf to write some letters without paragraph indentations in order to save space, though in fact neither he nor Agnes was inclined to start a new paragraph very often except when beginning a new day's installment. Because long blocks of print are both hard on the eyes and disconcerting when there is a sudden shift in topic, this edition breaks some long excerpts into paragraphs. In general, however, the editing has been conservative, and has attempted to balance fidelity to the content and style of the originals with concern for readability.

Personal letters of this kind are full of allusions to people by first name or nickname only; because of censorship, place names in Olaf's war letters were usually indicated only by a capital letter or a generic reference to "a certain town" or "somewhere in Belgium." In addition, casual references to current events, titles of books or pamphlets, or public figures that came naturally to the correspondents in 1916 may be opaque to readers seventy years later. Every effort has been made to identify such allusions, but footnotes have been avoided in the texts of the letters. Brief identifications have been inserted in square brackets; for more substantial information, headnotes have been attached to many letters to supply historical or biographical contexts, to link the correspondence to the development of Olaf's literary career, or to fill in gaps created by the omission or condensation of letters. While the headnotes have been kept to a minimum, they are the ligaments that hold together the various parts of an abridged narrative and let it function as a whole. Unpublished sources of information for the headnotes include other letters of Olaf and Agnes to each other and to members of their families; Olaf's diaries; memoirs and notes by various members of the Miller and Stapledon families; and my own conversations with family members. Several libraries and librarians have also provided essential material and assistance: M. R. Perkin at the Sydney Jones Library of the University of Liverpool, home of the Stapledon archive; Joseph Keith and Julius Smit of the Library at Friends' House in London; the British Library; the Andover-Harvard Library of the Harvard Divinity School; and the Library of the Imperial War Museum. My own library at the University of Massachusetts-Boston provided an excellent collection of World War I memoirs and letters, and Hildegarde von Laue responded with patient resourcefulness to my frequent calls on the interlibrary loan services.

This collection could not have been made without the trust, friendship, hospitality, and warm support of the owners of these letters, Mary (Stapledon) Shenai and John D. Stapledon, the daughter and son of Agnes and Olaf Stapledon. They have taken me into their homes, given up many hours of their time to answering my questions, and kindly allowed me to remove the letters temporarily to the United States to be edited. Sarina (Tetto) Stapledon, in a variation on Agnes's experience, came from Sicily on a ship full of war brides to marry Olaf and Agnes's son at the end of World War II. She has taken a particular interest in this project and has tirelessly searched out and studied still more family letters and documents in response to my many requests for information. In dedicating this book to Mary, John, and Sarina I thank them for their generosity in permitting a family heirloom to be enjoyed and studied by a larger public. Agnes's sister "Peter," now Mrs. Ruth Fletcher, has shared childhood memories and photographs of Australia and helped make vivid to a North American the distinctive qualities of Australian landscape and locale.

The careful readings of the entire typescript offered by H. Bruce Franklin and Laurence Davies have been of great value in the final shaping of the book. The editorial staff at the University Press of New England has combined enthusiasm for the project with a scrupulous attention to detail and has made the last stages of my work unexpectedly joyful and efficient. Among many other persons who have given encouragement, advice, and technical skills to this project I thank particularly: Thomas Stapledon, Richard and Jean Stapledon, Susan Stapledon, Jason Shenai, Benjamin Shenai, Michael Fletcher, Harvey J. Satty, Curtis C. Smith, Beth Bagley, Richard Rogers, and Morgan Mead. For institutional support I am very grateful to the Commonwealth of Massachusetts and the University of Massachusetts for a Joseph Healey Grant in the summer of 1984, which allowed me to do much of the basic research in England, and to the College of Arts and Sciences at the University of Massachusetts-Boston for financial assistance with several aspects of the project. My wife, Monica McAlpine, and my son,

Andrew McAlpine Crossley, have both been amazingly patient and have taken time from their own projects to help me complete this one; I thank them for being exactly what Olaf later called his own family: my "homely, friendly, exasperating, laughter-making, undecorated though most prized community of spirit."

*Brighton, Massachusetts*                                                R.C.
*January, 1987*

An envelope for a letter written from France by Olaf Stapledon to Agnes Miller in September 1916 and bearing the military inspector's stamp and the seal of Section Sanitaire Anglaise 13 of the Friends' Ambulance Unit.

*Talking
Across the
World*

# ~~~ *1913*

[*The sequence of letters opens in the spring of 1913 with the first full
declaration of love by Olaf Stapledon. Olaf was twenty-six and Agnes
Miller, eighteen. They had already written to each other for ten years,
and on a regular monthly basis since 1911, but Olaf's letter of
30 March 1913 marked an entirely new phase in the correspondence.
By then he had finished his B.A. in modern history at Balliol, taught
at Manchester Grammar School for a year, worked nearly three years in
the Liverpool office of the Alfred Holt Company, spent four months
working for an uncle's shipping agency at Port Said, Egypt (where he
had lived as a young child), and undertaken social work in the slums,
under the auspices of the Liverpool University Settlement. Unhappy
pursuing a career like his father's at Holt, Olaf wanted to abandon the
shipping business to follow a vocation teaching adults through the
Workers' Educational Association. While he was considering that
change late in 1912, Agnes arrived from Australia with her parents,
Margaret and Frank Miller, for one of her father's periodic visits with
his employer, Alfred Booth and Co. It was decided that after a spring
holiday with the Stapledons at Festiniog in North Wales, her parents
would sail for Australia while Agnes remained for a year's study of
music and languages on the Continent. Olaf saw a great deal of Agnes
during the first months of 1913, and he fell in love. In February, at a
party in Hoylake on the Wirral peninsula not far from his parents'
house, Annery, he took Agnes aside and told her he had been fascinated
by her for ten years. According to his diary, she "was troubled, & said
she could not understand." In March she went to Reigate in Surrey to
visit her Aunt Nina, who would accompany her to the Continent. Olaf
moped and planned a new strategy of courtship. Three days before he
started wooing his cousin by letter, he wrote to his mother: "For the last*

*six or seven weeks I have had one face & one voice continually before
my eyes & in my ears & in every dream I have dreamed, and the whole
of every night is spent in dreaming, asleep or awake. This is literally
true." On 30 March, nearly ten years to the day from the time he first
noticed her in the drawing room of Garsdale, Aunt Louisa Kirkus's
house in Liverpool, he initiated an epistolary courtship by recalling his
earliest memory of Agnes in 1903 as well as a later visit she made to
England in 1908. "Elizabeth" was Olaf and Agnes's New Zealander
cousin Elizabeth Miller, who had been in England in 1906 and with
whom Olaf was briefly infatuated. "Dot" was Elizabeth's sister Dorothy, a student of nursing and physical therapy in Liverpool, who had
become Olaf's closest woman friend and confidante; they had no romantic interest in each other.*]

Annery,
Caldy,
West Kirby

My dear Agnes,                              30 March 1913

I had a very successful journey up to town and down to Liverpool
yesterday. I slept most of the time, and was pretty weary when I got in at
11:30. We have had a ripping day here today. Dot & I went a walk in
the morning, and Elsie & Doris came over in the afternoon. We all
wandered in the wood making a wonderful noise. Tomorrow Dot goes
to Garsdale as usual and will get your letter from Olga. I have to speak
for an hour in the evening, and defend myself in a debate afterwards. I
spend the week at the office and the Settlement.

Read the rest of this letter when you have a quiet time to spare. Be
very kind and read to the end. I think it is best to tell you everything so
that you may know where you are, and where I am. Therefore forgive
what will probably be a long letter.

You may not remember, but I remember a certain day some ten years
ago at Garsdale when we first met since you were a baby. You had a
green frock with white things on the shoulders. You came in and were
introduced, and warmed your hands at the fire. I, being I suppose a
romantic kid, was wonderfully impressed. It is rather quaint, and a little
comic, but from that moment I thought of little else but you for ages,
long after you had gone away. You became a kind of guiding star, and
the memory of you as a little girl grew so clear, that I can almost see you
so, opposite me now. I wrote letters to you, but after a while the replies
stopped, so I stopped writing, and began scheming how to get to Australia when I left school. Fortunately that did not come off, and I just
went on, and you were the star. Then I, being as I say, an impression-
able and foolish child still, decided I was tired of having a star so far

away, and decided I was in love with Elizabeth. She, however, very quickly cured me of that. (I tell you all this because I want to be honest. Forgive my prattle.) Then I decided I was a silly ass, and would be sensible, and not bother about these things. But somehow that spell which you have began working again, before you came again yourself. And I told myself I was a fool, and still the spell worked. Then you came again, and you seemed to me altogether wonderful, and I went quite mad, and must at times have seemed a strange and awful creature. Then again you went away, and I made up my mind that I would do all kinds of great things in order to be worthy to try someday to win you. So without knowing anything about it you have done me great kindnesses; and because you were the "star," I kept a lot straighter than otherwise would have been. So years went by, and I met lots of girls, and got mighty keen on some of them, especially in Egypt, but you were still the star; and though they were excellent friends, and I was fearfully fond of two or three, they none of them had that strange spell, save to a little tiny extent one, who had it because she was very like you in some superficial ways. Then Dot came, and I got to know her very well, better even than any of my college friends. So I told her all about it. And she told me to wait with an "open mind," and see how things were when you came, and she evidently thought more than she said, and I acted on what she *thought*, and made up my mind to break the spell at last. It was not easy to do so, but I argued the whole thing out in cold blood and decided I would have nothing to do with you because a mere memory, turned into an ideal, could not be you at all. But when I had decided that, there seemed nothing left particularly worth living for, and the star would not be torn down. Then you came, and I suddenly discovered what it is to be in love. It is a very different thing from mere worship, though love and worship may, I find, exist together. You remember I made you a pledge in an old letter,—the last I wrote to you. I have been at much pains to keep that pledge, but finally it seemed dishonest to pretend, and so I told you a little of this tale. I was very anxious lest I should worry you, so I only said a little. I thought there was no tiny chance of ever winning you, and somehow I hoped. But we were shy of each other, and that was miserable. Then we talked again, and you held out just a little hope for me, and for that I live.

Now I have put all this in a selfish way, talking about *my* hope & *my* chance. But, believe me, your happiness is more to me even than that chance; and if I did not feel sure, dead sure, that I can be all that you can ever want, indeed I would not even try to win your love. But in my heart I know it. I have nothing wonderful to offer you, but because I love you I am made strong enough to do anything and to bear anything. You shall see. If it is not so, both you & I will know it. But it is so. There shall be made a place for you, fit for you; and if ever, in time, I win you to love me as I love you, the place will be ready for you, and there will be an arm strong enough for you to lean on for ever. It seems too wonderful a thing ever to come true, and yet to me it seems like fate. It seems to me as if I had always known you, even in the back of beyond, before we were born here as cousins. If this seems foolish, forgive me. It is what I feel, rightly, or mistakenly. And it makes me feel almost as if to wait all my life in vain would not be more than a horrible delay, not a final failure. But all this is dreaming and perhaps only seeming. Here is the plain fact: that I love you; that I have thought of nothing but you since you came; that I would gladly serve you at any cost, of life or more; that I am going to show you that I am worthy, even if I never win you. But things are horribly against me. We are not likely to see much of each other at present as my work and yours are apart. But I shall contrive to see as much of you as I can, if you will let me. Yet I will try never to "be a nuisance," really I will. And if you think ever that I am going to be, *please* say, because it would not hurt my feelings a bit. Yet I guess I can tell without your saying. But if I am not ever to be seeking you out, even in foreign countries, you must say. Again, things are horribly against me because I must give up the office and carve out another career. I say I must, because one work I cannot do well, and the other I can, and am "called to." I fear I would give up even the "call" and everything else for you, even for the bare chance, but that I could not be worthy of you if I were to cave in and do what I am not meant to do. So I have deliberately to take the risk, and to renounce a pretty certain wealthy life for one that can never lead to much wealth. But you shall see that not long after I have made the change the "place" shall be ready for you, because I love you, and am stronger than before. But how is such a wonder as you are to be won by a mere ordinary piece of humanity! Wait and see if that piece of humanity does not shine a bit for you, and cannot be all that you can ever need; see if he cannot prove that he loves you more than everything in the world, prove by doing, not merely by talking; see if he cannot be also a good work-a-day friend on top of it all, and make you merry and talk to you (when his tongue is loosed) about all the things that interest you and him. Indeed, though I love you and worship you, I know I can do things for you that you cannot do for yourself. I do not pretend to think you are perfect, though you are so near it. I am glad you are human. I had worshipped an ideal, and now I am in love with a girl; the best of all girls, and infinitely dearer than the old ideal, yet strangely the same. Forgive my talking in this way for once; this letter is exceptional.

There is nothing more that need be said now. Do not worry at being made such a fuss of. Do not feel it is a "great responsibility," and that you will "feel such a pig" if it all comes to nothing. You are what you are, and you cannot help it. And if you fall in love with someone else instead, why, you need never worry about me, because through very love of you I should jog on all right, & not do a dramatic collapse. See? But if ever you find it in your heart to be won by a mere cousin, truly you shall never be sorry. Meanwhile let us at least be very good friends. Now that all this is said & done we know where we are, and we can talk naturally about things. If ever you tell Auntie Margaret give me the chance of talking to her. Show her this screed if you like. Do always anything that you like with regard to me. There is no need to answer this, save to say that you have got it. You see, I fear lest you might in answering say there is no hope at all, and if you were to say that I should only outwardly accept it, and inwardly go on hoping and acting as if there was a chance—while there is life there is hope.

Have I said too much? Forgive me, if so. Be very kind to this one letter. Write to me sometime about all you are doing, *if* you can spare time, & if you say anything about all this rigmarole do not fear that I mind hard sayings, or shall set too much store by fair ones.

This evening (Monday) I made a poor sort of speech ["The People Awake. What Will They Do?" at the David Lewis Club] which was followed by a good discussion. As I sat there thinking what on earth to reply, it occurred to me that I had made a poor show, & it was not worthy that any lover of Her Serene Highness of the Windy Hair should make poor speeches. And when it was my turn to reply I got up and talked as I have never talked before; and believe me, though I say it, it was good, & it woke them up. Do you see how the spell works?

Will you ever forgive me for this letter? I honestly think it was best to write it. If you think not, do forgive. I did it for both your sake & mine.

Dot said you were very old for your age, & very grown up. But behold you are none of these things, and I for my part, being disgracefully juvenile, am glad. Besides, like the windy hair, it suits you!

It is disgracefully late, well after 2 a.m. One must sit up sometimes.

May we meet soon. Good night, oh Star! At Festiniog I will really be very good, and not quite always staring at you and bothering you, especially as it will be the last you will see of your mother and you will want her, not me. Yet I am living for Festiniog just now, and I shall always be wanting to be with you. Indeed you shall be won, in spite of everything. Dare I say so? It is said.

Olaf

P.S. I am to have a great talk with "someone who knows" as to the chances of making a good living in the way I want. Because of you, not because of any hope you gave at all, but because of your being what you are, I feel that the work I have in mind might even be done through the office if necessary.

63 Deerings Rd
Reigate

4 4 13

My dear Olaf.

Its alright! I've read it right to the end. There's nothing to forgive. I'm glad you wrote it all out, it makes me feel all sort of funny inside but I suppose its alright. I'm a great believer in Providence so all I can do is to jog along just the same as usual & let Providence do the rest. It is strange, every word of it & I cant realise it at all, none of it. You see when I was made I think there was a certain part of me left out or else mine is a very poor specimen — that part called the heart — & sometimes I feel so mad & wild that I'm glad I haven't got a heart & feel as if I hope I never shall have one; so what is one to do with a being like me. Perhaps Providence thinks I'm too wild & young & fresh to work on yet so she is storing up all she has for me until I am older & quite different

The first sheet of Agnes Miller's letter to Olaf Stapledon, 4 April 1913.

63 Deerings Rd.
Reigate
My dear Olaf,                                            4 April 1913

It's alright! I've read it right to the end. There's nothing to forgive. I'm glad you wrote it all out, it makes me feel all sort of funny inside but I suppose it's alright. I'm a great believer in Providence so all I can do is to jog along just the same as usual & let Providence do the rest. It is strange, every word of it & I can't realise it at all, none of it. You see when I was made I think there was a certain part of me left out or else mine is a very poor specimen—that part called the heart—& sometimes I feel so mad & wild that I'm glad I haven't got a heart & feel as if I hope I never shall have one; so what is one to do with a being like me. Perhaps Providence thinks I'm too wild & young & fresh to work on yet so she is storing up all she has for me until I am older & quite different. So now you understand, don't you? I shall tell Mother all about it sometime & if you like you can talk to her afterwards. If you want to say anything about it at Festiniog do so, because while there's anything unsaid in that direction we can't get along in others, can we?

9 Valentia Road
Hoylake
My dear Agnes,                                           5 April 1913

Thank you for your letter. You are very good and I am very content. In fact just at present I am wonderfully pleased with life, though possibly I might be "pleaseder." By the way, you need not set up as an Undine and say you have no heart. You have a heart for the things for which you ought to have a heart, and none as yet for certain others. . . . As to fate and providence, I, with you, am inclined to leave much to it. Sometimes I think it needs a nudge. It is as imperturbable as a policeman at a railway crossing, I mean at the meeting of four streets in town. It directs the traffic admirably, but the traffic has to have horses or petrol or electricity to move it. But that is by the way. I mean it does not suit me, or rather it does not become me, merely to trust to providence in any serious affairs. . . . So there, oh heartless and mad maiden, whom that same Providence, of which we speak, has ordained that I should worship! It rests with me to worship in the grand style and not fatuously. Providence has no finger in that pie, unless you are Providence.

I am getting tied up in my own similes, so we will change the subject. . . . All week I have been very busy with Settlement work, mostly visiting in slums. I have also taken on the delivery of some small lectures, refused a treasurership and accepted a secretaryship! This last is a big and very interesting job, & I am rather bucked that they came & *begged* me to take it. (Of course there's no pay.) I have to try and organise "study circles" among working men and women all over Liverpool. I can't tell you all about it now, but I might sometime if you are not too bored. It means interviewing all kinds of people, & "talking them round," and writing reams of letters, and drawing up circulars, and advising people what to study, & getting sound leaders for each circle. In Bristol last year they organised these things, & got about 900 people to take an intelligent interest in various subjects & form circles. Liverpool ought to raise twice as many. But Liverpool is dense, not to say daft. It's a huge chance for me to get into the thick of these things, whether in the end I go on with business or not. I have been fearfully intent lately on settling up my affairs, and have come to a sound and irrevocable decision to move heaven and earth to get a job of the sort I want within three months, & if I fail to secure one, to settle down to business for good, & use ready made opportunities instead of making new ones. But business gives one so little leisure, & the other thing would give one time to think & study & possibly to write.

[*The first stage of Agnes's year in Europe was a visit with her cousins, the Fryers, who had left England to establish an engineering firm in Rouen that did extensive work in the building of the French railway system.*]

5 Rue Dufay
Rouen

TO OLAF                                          30 May 1913

. . . Last night I drank white wine & champagne & gambled! Doesn't it sound awful? I'm quite used to white wine but the champagne went to my arms & they felt as if they weren't mine & I've never gambled before. It wasn't a real gamble because I hadn't got any money. It was at Mme. Welby's. We went there to tennis & stayed to dinner & afterwards they got out the cards & dealt out for trente et un. I didn't even know how to play but they explained & we began. The first person who lost had to stump up one sou & then I realised that for the first time in my life I was playing for money! But I couldn't stand up & make a speech in the French language to the effect that I was not in the habit of so doing & that I hate cards at any price whatsoever & the more for money. So I just went on & didn't lose anything because I hadn't anything to lose & didn't win either, but next time I'll know what I'm about & won't play because it's a bad principle, isn't it? But it looks so awful when you are out to dinner to refuse to join in a game with everybody else. You might give me your views on the subject because I haven't any of my own, being only 19.

[*Olaf's effort to establish study circles for Liverpool workers landed him
a place on the executive committee of the Liverpool branch of the
WEA. His sudden epiphany under the stars gives a foretaste of the sort
of astronomical fantasies central to the great works of fiction he
produced in the 1930s.*]

Annery
TO AGNES                                                        6 June 1913

. . . Pauvre petite Australienne! I was delighted with your gambling experience because it was just what originally broke my principles. I am
now thoroughly unprincipled in this and all other respects. I suppose
there is something cheap and nasty about my mind, because I can never
rise to a negative principle. It always makes me rebellious to meet
people with principles of that sort. . . . Until someone shows me it is
wrong I shall stick to my unprincipled practice, which is really based on
the liberal principles of Shakespeare, Browning and the heroes of old,
who took life as they found it and swallowed it whole. Yet if you really
believe the nongambling principle is right, pray stick to it; for unstuck-
to principles are like weak links in a chain, whereby the whole chain is
weak. When I was at school, and very selfimportant, I made it a principle to stop people from smoking in a nonsmoking carriage. My hat I
did hate the job, and the smokers hated me! I gave up that as a principle, yet I generally persuade people not to smoke in nonsmoking
places, because it is a mean unfair trick. How killing! Think of a small
chubby kid solemnly announcing that though he did not mind smoke
himself, smoking being against the rules, he would tell the guard! Said
the mountain to the squirrel "Little prig!" You are tired of this discourse,
and so am I.

Last night after a committee meeting at which I was commanded to
write two articles and a letter to the papers within a week, I walked down
the new road towards the coast in the starlight. I was worrying about the
articles and other mundane things. Then I began thinking about Switzerland, and (with all due respect Miss) about you. While I was thus
occupied I looked up, and suddenly I had that rare and wonderful feeling of the great distance of the stars, and of their intent gaze upon the
earth. Everything happening on the earth grew not only insignificant,
by reason of that great space freckled with other stellar systems, but also,
in a strange way, of desperate importance, because of the intent gaze of
the stars. I wonder what these feelings mean, whether they are mere
tricks of the mind, or have some bearing on the true nature of things.
The stars are as a rule wonderfully soothing companions, clearing away
worry simply by implying insignificance; but when they begin staring at
one like that it is disconcerting. Do you know what I mean? As a rule

they seem magnificently to ignore this fourth rate planet of a fifth rate sun. Why should they stare at us, they who perhaps support as many beings as we have grains of sand? They put foolish self-important notions into our heads by doing so. It is not fair. Anyhow it was lovely to see them last night, and to watch the water, lying still, and asleep in the starlight. The night jars were beginning to give tongue, and away down in the fields an old corncrake was busily talking. He at least was intent on his own business whatever tricks the stars might play. . . .

Father is busy comparing routes to Interlaken. Boulogne seems to take the cake. I have a prodigious amount to do before leaving. I finish with the office tomorrow, after two and a half years in its service. I am sorry to leave everyone, but it will be good to be free. I have to plan syllabuses, write articles, and countless letters, interview a professor, attend a committee meeting, do some slumming, take a class, have a French lesson and go to the dentist, all before next Saturday.

[*Olaf and his parents, William and Emmeline, spent much of June in the Alps with Agnes and her aunt-chaperone, Nina Barnard. The letters resume after Olaf's return to England and Agnes's departure for Dresden.*]

Annery
TO AGNES                                                  8 July 1913
. . . I have come home to find my Study Circle affairs exactly where they were when I left, and two articles, which I wrote in great haste before leaving, have never been published, owing to some muddle. It is fearfully late for them now, so I am very disgusted, and everyone must think me a rotter for not having done what I said. However, I hope to get them into print in a few days. Meanwhile I must spend most of tomorrow "slumming," to make up arrears. May it not be as broiling as today. Slums are dusty and smelly, and I don't like slum flies. Having once got that up to date I shall get seriously hold of the Study Circle job. It is fearfully behind hand. We have to get unions and things to raise men for the circles soon, and we have not half enough leaders yet. I am in a bit of a panic. The rest of my time must be given to preparing for my two classes, when I have got the books together from goodness knows where, and seen my professor. Next month I have to spend a week at Bangor, in Wales, tutoring odds and ends of working men, and tripping over the Welsh Mountains with them. I look forward to that, and will tell you if anything amusing happens. It will be a new experience for me.

This morning I walked through the Birkenhead docks on my way here. The men were all just going to work, hundreds of them, swarming in at the shed gates, some big and burly, some crooked and lean, some young, some old, mostly smoking little clay pipes, and clumping along in big boots like Father's over mighty cobble stones. They are not a pretty sight. They came as a bit of a shock as a first sight of home after Switzerland. One feels mighty small dealing with such people, and I felt so today, stumping home from a glorious holiday, scheming "Workers' Education," while they had been scheming nothing but "bread and butter" since they were born. . . .

You said you were glad I came to Switzerland. I am glad you said it. You let me be with you a great deal. We did have a merry time together, as intended. I believe you would rather like to have me be a big brother, though you don't understand my wanting to be anything else. Well, let us be jolly good friends, better even than Switzerland made us. . . . Do you know you only just escaped having me in Dresden with you. If I could possibly have left things over at home I would have come (if it would have been acceptable to your highness & aunt) to learn German. I wanted to, desperately, but it was better not. By the way, I warn you that if the unlikely, but always possible, thing happens and we have a war with Germany, I am coming right over to fetch you like a good cousin. But heaven forfend anything so horrible. It is far less likely now-a-days than last year.

6 Burgerwiese 6III
Dresden

Dear Olaf,                                                    9 July 1913

I meant to write all this in German letters but I forgot so now I'll go on in English. I guess you're rather glad—but you won't be let off so easily next time, so beware! I tried to write down a few words this morning in German & I was horrified to find how quickly I had forgotten all about the blessed little curls and wriggles. I shall have to set to again solidly & do the alphabet. We had quite a decently good journey. My hat! we *were* glad we had taken your valuable advice & gone 2nd class. The third was so crowded & looked so dirty & stuffy—full of fat Germans all smoking like old chimneys & not a breath of fresh air anywhere. After about 3 hours I felt like a bit of wood—just anyhow—& I thought I was going to have a rotten time when suddenly I took a turn & pulled up & was able actually to read Browning. . . . There was a Deutscher und Frau in our carriage & we had a perfect fight with them over having the window open. Whenever we came in out of the corridor we went straight & opened the window & whenever they came in they went straight & shut it & this went on until Dresden. We never said a word & just then I began to think I didn't like the German nation much. They both had on cotton gloves & looked echte Deutschland all through. We didn't know of a hotel in Dresden so I exercised my German on our porter & somehow or other we got ourselves into quite a nice one called the Westminster—it was the name that attracted us & we slept like tops except that the top half of our beds preferred to spend most of the night on the floor—you know the sort—awful slippery feather beds like we had at Lucerne. Then next day we walked round like tourists & I stopped at every crossing & informed Auntie out of our "Guide to Dresden" where we were & where we were going to & where we had come from & at last we managed to secure quite nice rooms here in a nice street with lovely gardens opposite . . . Just now it's nearly half past ten at night & I'm sitting at my table by the open window writing to you by the light of my lamp & we've just come home from the theatre! We saw it advertised "Das Buch einer Frau" tonight & tomorrow night so we pulled ourselves together & went. Fraulein Ackermann our pension lady came with us & we've enjoyed it awfully, it was what they call a "Lustspiel" sort of light comedy. The acting was simply splendid & they spoke awfully distinctly, of course we couldn't understand much of the actual wording, but we managed to follow & Frl Ackermann erklarte eins in the intervals. We only paid 1 mark 50 & we could see & hear everything beautifully. Isn't it marvellously cheap?

Liverpool Reform Club
TO AGNES                                        14 July 1913
. . . I had lunch today with a man whom the slightest touch would shut up like a sensitive plant. I met him re study circles. He is a banker, small, thin and burdened with a dull prosy voice. He seems always to be trying to find the end of his sentences and never succeeding, so that he wanders on timidly from phrase to phrase, getting horribly bored with himself. He has that worried shy look that a certain sort of man always gets in business,—"there was a listening fear in her regard," as Keats says [in *Hyperion*]. He is a great social reformer in leisure moments, and a great "chapel" man. For some unknown reason he insisted on giving me a large lunch at the Bear's Paw, and intends to keep up the acquaintance. I respect him, because he is highly respectable, but I can't get excited over him, because, pharisaically, I pity him. I guess he may be one of those courageous people who know their limitations and ignore them by intention. We shall see. I am to have tea with quite another class of goods. He is tall, black, and bearded. He has a great flat forehead like the side of a house. He is in the post office, and though overworked he reads a lot. He once stuck up for me manfully in a debate when no one else did, so I like him. He is going to do wonders in the study circle line, as he has the power of making people like the subject and like him. . . .

*Next Day.* I had tea with the bearded man, and was surprised to find on closer inspection that he had no house-wall forehead, but a particularly low and curved one. It is strange how one can mix people up. At close quarters he looks exactly like a preRaphaelite artist, having remarkable large dreamy blue eyes under bushy black brows. I had a long talk with him largely about Rodin whom he much admires. Did you see "Le Penseur" outside the Panthéon at Paris? We discussed that, and compared it with "La Pensée," which is just a girl's head on a huge block of rock. It was a very pleasant tea that we had, though for study circles he has failed me absolutely, not through lack of zeal, but because of irregular business hours. After my history class, which consisted of one enthusiast, I came home across the river. The sun had set behind New Brighton, and the sky was burning. The lights along the Seacombe promenade were beautifully clear and cold against the strip of black land under the hot sky. The water was dark blue-grey, and very quiet. Evening skies are chastening things.

[*The Bangor "Summer School" at University College in North Wales, opened in 1913 on the model of a similar workers' summer institute at Oxford, gave Olaf his first experience as a residential tutor with the Workers' Educational Association and confirmed what was to become his lifelong work in adult education.*]

Bangor, N. Wales
My dear Agnes,                                         4 August 1913
   This will probably be a short letter as there is not much time for doing anything here. I am staying in lodgings with a man and his wife who are connected with the Liverpool University. In various houses about the town there are about fifty working men and women who are up here for a week or more, coming up one batch after another every Saturday. They go to lectures and are "tutored." I am a tutor and have four men and two girls to look after. One of my men is a miner of South Wales who in his youth was a "bad egg," getting through about £1 a week on drink. Then some Welsh chapel got hold of him and he was "converted," absolutely reformed in a twinkling. I don't understand how these things take place, but they do, especially in Wales. He told us all about it in a fine, simple speech in a big discussion we had on a certain big-clerical-gun's sermon. It was wonderful even to hear. He is a well dressed fellow, with a very clean-cut pale face all dotted over with little blue scars, the results of an explosion I suppose. He has ripping Pallas Athene grey eyes. I feel a bit of an imposter as he knows much more about his subject than I do. He speaks very clearly and precisely. In fact he is a very interesting man to have to deal with, and far the best of my

crowd. He is a lay preacher, and spends a lot of his time talking in public in his unassuming precise way, "converting" heaps of people I suppose. These things are wonderful. In fact there are so many strange and
wonderful things here that one gets a bit overwhelmed; and, through
lack of time to think about them, one will probably forget. It is useful to
be able to write a little down, even thus scrappily in a letter, as it fixes
things . . . .

But it is not only tutoring and discussing that we do. This afternoon I
went with 40 or so men and about five women over the Menai Straits to
Beaumaris to see the castle. We larked and joked and wandered about
under the charge, more or less, of a very boisterous young man who was
a working man and is now a WEA lecturer. He herded them about like
sheep, shouting at them with his awful Welsh accent. I have come to
the conclusion that though the working man can often make himself
learned, and fit himself to do a great deal of useful work, he cannot
nearly so easily get at the subtler and gentler side of education, and it is
only in such circumstances as these that one realises how important that
is. One gets mighty tired of a continual row and shout. Also when these
people get clever they are always in danger of becoming conceited. In
fact reverence for anything at all seems quite beyond the natures of
some of them. . . . Heaps and heaps of times I feel absolutely stumped
by the difficulty of making them feel that gentler and deeper side of
things. They have all suffered in their time, and have ingrained in them
the bitterness of a suffering man. One feels one has no right to preach to
a lot of people who have starved. I have never starved. I suppose the
thing to do is to get out of this lap of luxury one lives in and learn a little
of what suffering is, so as to have authority. But apart altogether from the
strength of mind needed, the thing is so impracticable. Yet one ought to
rough it a bit somehow, that is clear. Does this all seem very mad? I
daresay you understand what I mean, though I can't express it properly.
I am puzzled, stumped, not to say bowled out & dished, for the time.


Bangor
TO AGNES                                                         7 August 1913
. . . My views of these people here have rather changed since I wrote
last. You would love to meet some of them. . . . This afternoon I went
out with a *very* hard-up labourer to talk study circles. After we had done
our business we sat on a seat on the side of a steep hill overlooking the
bay and the town and all Anglesey. We talked about all sorts of things,
and finally he, knowing I was keen on poetry, brought out a Browning
from his pocket, and we turned over the pages and talked about various
poems, in the sun light and the sea breeze. He is a poor fellow who has

had a very rough time of it, and is nobly bringing up his children in the best schools he can find. He is tall, thin, wobbly at the knees. His head pokes forward, as if he was avoiding a blow. He has a low forehead and a little scrubby dark moustache. He is not a beauty, nor is he clever. In fact he is very slow, & can hardly express himself. But he simply loves reading and talking and thinking in his plodding way. He gives up every bit of his spare time to organising various educational movements. My country! I love that sort of man. Also he has a salutary effect on one; for he with his self-made education and crippled speech can get nearer to the truth of things than I can with all my expensive education and dreams. People are inclined to make fun of him, yet they all like him. It is sad that he is too poor to join in any of the excursions, and, worse luck, one can't offer to take him. . . .

You see, this really is a wonderful new thing to me—crowds of illiterate people all ravenous for knowledge, all on fire with a new idea of comradeship and with a new ideal, all ready to make a tin god of you or metaphorically to "spit in your face," as they would put it, according to your deeds, & the way you happen to strike them. Here also is a thing, affecting some five million people, trying to educate without bias a population that is split into ever so many rabid sects. Here also are men who have been driven from employment for their views, & persecuted by all kinds of secret means. It is a real live thing, is it not, however incomplete. And yet most people have never even heard of the W.E.A.

[*Her parents were back in Australia, Aunt Nina had left Dresden for Surrey at the end of July, and for the first time in her life Agnes was independent. She also was beginning to feel that a year of piano and voice lessons was not a real "education" of the sort that Olaf had had at Oxford or even that the WEA offered in its summer schools.*]

Dresden
My dear Olaf,                                    13 August 1913
Here am I all on my owny-own at a table with a yellow cloth, waiting for my Tasse Schokolade und Königskuchen & in the meantime saving time by writing to you. . . . I think I envy you your work horribly, though to me it is unintelligible, it's so tremendous, but it's so splendid. I wish I could do something really useful, something that would really help someone; my work doesn't seem to lead anywhere when it's done—& oh there's so much to do! so much. Fraulein Willenbucher tells me such lots of things about the different nations & about this old world & the way it is rushing along & breaking all its old bounds. I can never remember afterwards just what she has said but I know I get very excited

& so does she. Of course to her the German nation is the 'only.' I think quite a lot of things about Germany & England, but it never does any good because I forget straight off. That's just me all over. I want you to tell me lots more about everything & about England. I hear too much of Germany.

[*From Annery, at the top of Caldy Hill, Olaf had easy access to the paths along the estuary of the river Dee, which separates the Wirral peninsula from North Wales. The concluding fantasy of this letter anticipates the theme of his first work of fiction, published in 1930,* Last and First Men.]

Annery
TO AGNES                                                                17 August 1913
. . . After spending the evening talking . . . and listening to a thrilling Hungarian Rhapsody by Liszt, I went a lone walk in the night, down to the Golf Links, and by the edge of the cliffs. The tide was in, and patches of moonlight were running across the estuary, and the waves were falling upon each other's heels, and reaching out across the sand, sighing because the cliff was always too far to stretch. It was then that I did the thinking, about England and Germany, and about you, and things in general. You want to be told about England. Silly girl, what do I know about England?—just the outside fringe of one little movement out of all those activities that make a nation's life. Well, I know just this anyhow: The English above all races are gentle. They have their faults but they are never brutal. They have set the pace in all humane and kindly matters in Europe. They also have a very high ideal of unselfishness as individuals and as a state, though they don't live up to it. They have spent many centuries in evolving this high quality, and now will need sternly to exercise it in the settlement of their affairs. They have stood as defenders of the weak. They have made Europe fear to molest small struggling nations. Under Gladstone they defended Greece and Italy. The Italians can never repay their debt to us, & they know it. The English were the first to reform their own cruel ways with regard to slaves, & later, factories. They have stood up always for moderation against violence of whatever type. Their politics, though pretty foul, are far purer (or strive to be far purer) than any other nation's politics. They are tolerant of religious differences. They are, I believe, at heart deeply religious. Yet, after all these centuries of struggle for political freedom, they are ridden by professional politicians and by wealth; after building up a high ideal they are capable of land grabbing as in the Transvaal, of false trading as in the Chinese opium trade, of tyranny as in their ruina-

tion of Ireland, of miserable cowardice as in their anti-German panics, of mad jingoism as after Mafeking. And in spite of their gentleness they are now divided into those who have and those who have not, and the one often regards the other as inhuman, as something to be stamped out. In spite of their religious nature they are given over to hating one another & suspecting each other of treachery,—as the different social classes, & until lately even the different trades, hated one another. Then again very many of them are bigoted doctrinaires without any love of their fellows, & others are equally savage revilers of everything they cannot understand. But there truly is in England now a feeling, as it were, for a new religion, or rather not a new one, but a wider and more spiritual understanding of all sects and religions. I believe there never was such a deep and wide and sane "revival" as is now beginning especially in England. . . .

It's a strange world, isn't it? When I was down by the shore last night I kept wondering how long it would be before the earth dies like the moon into a barren crinkled piece of rock. At first it seems awful, horrible, to think of all civilization and all the work and heroism ending in that. Imagine those far off declining ages when a great race of supermen is vainly fighting against the cold, and knows what the end of it all must be. Imagine all the literatures and poetries and religions and social upheavals completed to the last chapter, and the last men and women, the flower of it all, dwindling in numbers, degenerating generation by generation and finally, a little species of frozen creatures round the equator, dying out. It's too horrible, or it would be if it were not for the one way out. I suppose it is quite inevitable (though almost infinitely distant) for the earth, & even the sun, must cool. But it really only serves to convince one that both individual and race *must* go on living some other way. One might be content to see all individuals utterly die save in handing down their works to the building of the race. But the race, when it dies, can hand on its work to nothing, it would seem. Therefore I will believe that the spirit of the race, as a being in itself, lives on. Also, even as the cells of the body have their own lives to live & die, & so make up the life of the whole creature, so may it be actually with us, the "cells" of the race. Again, I will believe that, as matter is indestructible, so is spirit, and therefore that the "soul" of a cell, & of a man, and of the race is eternal each in its own character. . . . Of all these things we know nothing, but it is sometimes a help to think about them. I wonder how it all strikes you. Perhaps you just say "God's in his heaven. All's right with the world." That is a very sound sentiment, if you don't lose sight of the fact that at any given moment, now, for instance, all is very far from being right with the world, and it is our business to put it right.

TO OLAF                                                22 August 1913
. . . I have never thought far enough ahead to come to the time when
the earth or world shall be no more. If I had, I shouldn't have been able
to come to any solution of the problem, but I shouldn't have been
afraid. I shouldn't have believed for one tiny second that everything &
everybody will crumble away into dust & be no more. At such a point I
should substitute "God's in His Heaven, all's right with the world." But I
like your solution & I am inclined to think it is as good a one as can be
found. If you find a better you will let me know, won't you? . . . This is
a most delightful way of seeking knowledge, but it's beastly hard luck on
you. I do hope you don't mind. Really it's very good for you to have to
write answers to all these questions, isn't it? The questions are so easy to
ask, but I couldn't possibly answer them for myself. Fraulein Ackermann & I are always getting tied up in knots over history & geography
& such material points & we make a rule to fish out the Atlas & the
history book almost every night & we learn quite a lot of mad things
that way.


                                                University Settlement,
                                                Nile Street,
                                                Liverpool
My dear Agnes,                                  10 September 1913
   Here am I once more in my own little bedroom-sitting-room, with
the roar of Liverpool pouring in at the open window, and a fat bundle
of "case papers" which will necessitate a lot of slumming during the
week. . . .
   How *can* one justify one's existence? The other day, at Westward Ho!
[on the Irish Sea in north Wirral] I bathed three times, and the last was
in the evening. Big green, white-crested breakers were coming in
grandly while I swam out against them. The sun was low, and golden.
Where the water was smooth, between the breakers, the sun had his
golden path, and along it I swam, towards America. Before each roller
broke, the green crest let the yellow sunlight through it, breaking often
into pale gold. Passing beyond all the breakers I swam out much further,
along the sun's path. There was nothing anywhere that was not beautiful and peaceful. There might have been no such thing as misery in
the world. It seemed so right and proper to be swimming there. It
seemed not only a pleasure, but a kind of religious duty. Well, and now
I am in quite another world, made, one would think, by other and hostile gods. The contrast is so stupendous. There was wide space, and
there are crowded streets. There was peace and there is turmoil. There

was beauty and there is—beauty still I suppose, if one can see it. But it's no use waxing eloquent. Eloquence is a cheap safety valve. . . .

[*Next day.*] This afternoon I went slumming. I had one revolting case which I hope I won't dream about, and certainly am not going to talk about now. But I also went to the house of a widow called Cusack. She was twice a widow, poor soul, and had two children by each husband. She ushered me into her crowded little room and sat me down and sat herself down by me and talked. Everything was going well. Her eldest daughter was learning to be a nurse. She herself was as brave and bright "as they make 'em." She had done 15 hours work the day before, but then it was her busy time. Her little boys were well, and she prattled about them. She had such a gentle, sad and yet bright, pale face. On a heap of odds & ends (she was cleaning her room) was a man's bowler hat, which is usual in widows' houses. There was just one unhappy thing in her room, and that was her poor little youngest girl (about 3) lying wrapped up on the sofa, looking very unhappy and ill. She had been taken suddenly ill the day before, having eaten something bad. The mother had given her things as usual, but was just beginning to get worried, as a neighbour's child had just died of some such complaint. So Mrs. Cusack was going to carry her little girl right off to the doctor, so as to be on the safe side. Meanwhile she looked over at her with such a calm yet concerned expression, as if she was too well used to calamity to get flurried. Personally I sat prattling there for ages in quite an aimless but interested way, which seemed to please the widow, for she gave me quite a genuine thank as I left. I hope I dream about her and not the other maundering unspeakable tipsy creature, poor unfortunate wretch. The only other incident was when a sturdy matron shouted after me as I left her "You're a proper young man to come running around, you are." She said it with such a hearty ring of liking that I turned round and laughed thanks at her, and was awfully bucked with myself for at least the length of the street. One does not see the fathers in the afternoon, which is a disadvantage. On the other hand one sees the numbers on the doors, instead of having to feel for them in the dark.

University Club,
Liverpool
TO AGNES                                            3 October 1913

. . . Your last letter is quaint, because when you have not known quite what to say, you have just stopped in the middle of a sentence and changed the subject entirely. The effect is rather that of a very broken telephone message with dashes for the buzz, but it is very charming. It gives a kind of post impressionist effect—colour without form. Of course this is all gross exaggeration, and for the most part the epistle flows on like the river down to Camelot. . . . Why do you invariably say, when you write, "This is a rotten letter, but next will be better," or words to that effect? The purpose of a letter is to give a picture of a person's life and thoughts; and that you pretty well succeed in doing! A letter is not a dissertation, nor an essay, nor a lecture (though mine are apt to be at times), but just a small portion of oneself snipped off and neatly packed into an envelope for postage. They also occasionally are aids to thought when one is writing them, but that is incidental.

[*Agnes's urge to describe the Australian landscape after getting a letter from her younger sister Rosie is partly homesickness, but it also reflects her concern that Olaf, who had never been outside Europe and North Africa, should have some definite images of her world.*]

Sentra Str. 3II
Friedenau
Berlin

TO OLAF             30 October 1913

. . . After dinner I was practising & it wouldn't go right & I was bored so I thought I'd have a rest & come back to it after & I closed my ducky piano & put on its coat to keep the chills out & I strolled round my room wondering what to do next when suddenly Frau Kramer bounced in & handed me three letters. She looked quite calm & uninterested but I was thrilled: Mother, Rosie & you. So I persuaded her gently to stop talking & go her way & then I got my rug & tucked myself up warm & comfy in my bed & read those three letters one after the other, first Australia, then England, then Australia again & then I had to wake up to Germany! Oh my hat! what a boon letters are, aren't they? & how ever would this old world jog along if it couldn't send its thoughts from one uttermost part to the other—or even across the North Sea. Rosie writes me such ripping letters. They make me all jump inside & just scream with delight. This time it was lots about a picnic they had had to Long Reef. I told you about Long Reef or Collaroy once, didn't I? It's where there is a great green grassy hill sloping down steep onto the beach & we toboggan & fall off & get bumped & love it & below on the beach it is yellow brown sand with frothy green & white breakers rolling up, & standing on the top of the slope you gaze far out into the blue Pacific—a great endless blue—to where sea & sky meet & when you turn to northward you see headland after headland jutting out into the sea all purply blue & getting paler in the distance till at last it looks like cloud & when you turn to southward you see more headlands but nearer & green &

with little houses & camps on them, & when you turn to westward you
see dry yellow brown grass slopes & gum trees & hills of gum trees & the
breeze is keen & comes from the sea all fresh & salty & it mixes with the
land breeze which smells dry & sweet of gum leaves & boronia & that is
Life—my life & my Homeland. Oh you must come & see it too, but
first you must have the spirit of the land—the bush spirit—the spirit of
sun & sea & sky, of salt sea weeds & warm sweet gum trees & boronia. I
can hardly believe I shall be there again with it all & soon, but I shall
yes I shall.

[*Edouard Risler, an Alsatian pianist and virtuoso performer of Chopin,
achieved wide recognition in recitals throughout Europe for regularly
playing the full cycle of Beethoven's thirty-two sonatas.*]

Berlin

TO OLAF                                                    16 Nov. 1913
. . . I had my lesson this afternoon, music I mean. Miss Davidson is
such a dear & I love it. I'm working at a Beethoven Sonata, just think of
the cheek of me asking for a Beethoven Sonata! She was going to give
me Grieg & I said couldn't I have Beethoven & she almost smiled but
she looked through her big Beethoven & found a sonata for me & it's a
beauty. It's so lovely to have such things for one's daily bread. Perhaps I
shall be able to play it for you at Xmas. "Play" it, we always say though
we know we only mean "have a dab at it." Isn't it glorious that you will
be at Annery for Christmas? I can't tell you how glad I am. I just want a
moor & a hill & heather & hills in the distance & a wood & everything
just like Caldy. Oh I am excited about Christmas. Do you know I have
only got not quite 5 weeks more here. No, Germany won't allow me to
be present at West Kirby on Saturday night 20th because I must most
particularly be present in the Beethoven Saal on Friday 19th. It's the last
concert of a series of eight which we have been going to every Friday
night for some time given by one great pianist called Edouard Risler. He
is just glorious & so quiet & matter of fact & dignified & modest. He
looks very steady & middleaged & quite ordinary & is not a freak at all,
no tricks or striking postures like such a lot of these mighty people. I like
Risler awfully. Every Friday he plays six Bach Preludes & Fugues beautifully & generally at least one Beethoven Sonata & then something
quite different. Once he played all the Kinderszenen by Schumann,
you know them, "Träumerei" & "Glückes genug" & lots of them, & we
pulled him to pieces afterwards like a pack of hounds. They were too
small for him somehow, quite out of his sphere & we all privately con-
cluded that we liked our own interpretation far better. Cheek. It's great
fun being a student.

[*The Repertory Theatre has long been Liverpool's most venturesome dramatic institution. Because of the very large Irish Catholic population in the city and the growing rebellion against English rule in Ireland, the Abbey Players were bound to draw a partisan and vocal audience.*]

University Settlement
Liverpool

TO AGNES                    27 November 1913

. . . On Monday the family went to the theatre, Repertory, to see the Irish Players do "Cathleen ni Houlihan" and also the "Playboy of the Western World." We had front-row-dresser seats. I sat between Dot and a beauteous Jewess called Jessica Wild whom I know through the W.E.A. I was divided between being natural to Dot and being, or trying to be, smart and clever to the brilliant Hebrew. The latter did not quite come off, but I gave her chocolates, which doubtless pleased her better than wit. Another W.E.A. tutor, also of Balliol, came from another part of the circle to talk to her several times, and to worship, I suspect. Anyhow she scintillated and he quietly admired. The first play is high tragedy. Do you know it? Cathleen is an old woman, who is really Ireland. She says wonderful things about her thousand lovers who have died for her, and about her four green fields that have been taken from her. . . . The language is wonderful, so full of imagery, and so Irish. Miss Wild was reduced to a momentary quietness and Dot had to hide her feelings. Don't tell her, but I know she was trying to be calm. There had been wild clapping from the Irish in the gallery when news of the French [liberators] came.

Next play, by Synge, was roaring comedy, and a skit on Irish peasant life and morals. . . . It is all excitement and jokes and strange Irish oaths and exclamations and weird situations. But the Irish in the gallery could not see Irish morals impugned in this way without hissing and booing and stamping, so that no one heard a word of the last act because of the babel. Not a sound could you hear but angry Irish protest. I don't know why they never got the police in. Liverpool is not used to rowdy theatres I suppose. At Oxford much worse riots were common, but the authorities were always ready with police. Uncle Willie, who was with us, said it was quite a new experience for him. The great joke was that the playboy appeared in a brilliant green and orange striped jersey; and green, you know, is the Nationalist colour, and Orange the Irish Protestant colour. So the colours of the two savage factions that have caused so much rioting in Liverpool were "sweetly blended in one blinding flash." Miss Wild was a model of patient but weary tolerance during the interruptions. Dot was genuinely disgusted not to hear the play finished. In fact it was quite an impatient Dot, and no wonder, as she does not often get a theatre, and to have this one spoilt was hard luck. Mother's head ached with row. Father, sitting behind with Uncle Willie, was simply chortling with delight, as the Irishmen amuse him. Uncle Willie was wonderful to look upon. He is a fine looking uncle at all times, but he sat there rapt. His eyes were lit up with amazement, disapproval, stern displeasure and a twinkle of delight. There is a lot of unnecessary drunkenness in the piece, hence his disapproval. Miss Wild, the re-fined, burst out in the middle "I *loathe* drunken men on the stage. I *never* think them funny."

[*Next Day.*] . . . Christmas day is in four weeks exactly. You will really be here before then. It is almost too good to believe. I know I shall forget that you want to see everyone, in the desire I have to see only you. Oh, you shall see them all plentifully. You will have Dot to prattle to all night. You will have Helène, and all your Aunts & Uncles and cousins and cousins' kids. You will be amongst English speaking people again. But always I will be there to fall back upon, and for as much more as I am allowed, and I shall be fearfully greedy of you, after all this long half year, since the station at Basel. You are not going home yet, poor girl, but we will make you at home with us in the meantime. And then after a little you will go home, and I will follow you there perhaps. But that last is in the dark of the future.

Berlin

My dear Olaf,                                                7 December 1913

I was wondering if there would be a letter from you this morning but there wasn't & I was rather glad because I owe you a letter & I feel such a pig when you write 2 to my 1. But please continue to make me feel so, I really don't mind a bit. This is not a letter, this is just a Sunday after-noon pause. . . . I have just fished out your last letter from my letter-drawer which is chock-full & points to the fact that I must have a turn-ing out before I come to England or my luggage will be overweight, but I hate destroying letters. Your last was a dear one. I wish I felt in a fit mood to write a decent one. . . .

It is running into months since I wrote to anyone at home except the family. You talk about my enormous correspondence but it has really dwindled down to one long letter & a stray p.c. per week & then Auntie Nina & Liverpool people & Auntie Sallie when I'm hard up & you. You're an extra but not a compulsory one. Frau Kramer said tonight, "Sie! Lütte! (that's what I'm always called, it is low German & means "Kleine") was tun sie heute abend?" "Ich schreibe." "Schreiben sie schon wieder an den Vetter?" "Jawohl!" "Na grüßen sie ihn mal von 'der Olch'." (Die Olch is also low German & means 'the old woman' which is the name by which Frau Kramer goes.) So you are to be "greeted" by "der Olch." She's very interested in my affairs & she has asked me so many questions that she thinks she knows all my private personal history, but she doesn't quite.

[*On 21 December Olaf met Agnes at Victoria Station, toured the London galleries and shops with her, and escorted her to Liverpool for Christmas. She remained in England, visiting at Annery, at Garsdale, and at White Lodge—Aunt Nina's house in Surrey—before setting out for France at the end of January.*]

# ✐✐✐ *1914*

[*In the first letter to Agnes after the holidays, when she was in Surrey preparing to depart for France, Olaf used a favorite metaphor for their courtship, viewing their lives together as a book, in which various phases constitute chapters.*]

Annery

My dear Agnes,                                                 27 January 1914

Here am I reduced once more merely to letters! It is Tuesday morning, and I have packed up all my books to go to the Settlement, so it is no use expecting me to do industrial history just now. . . .

But I want to talk to you about other things today. There is so much to say now, as soon as you are gone. You half reproached me once because I said some things could only be said in a letter. Then you said it was your fault. But it is this way really: When I am with you I have to remember always that you have not "read to the end of the book" yet. If I were to forget that, I should be "bustling you." But you can imagine that it is harder to say things to you so than if I were to think you felt as I feel. Now in a letter I need not so carefully remember that fact, so it seems to me. Therefore it is easier to talk. . . . Dear girl, how am I to do without you during all this time? Doubtless I must just work and count the days. And you also are to do without me, and that, I believe, is something now, though you will not be reduced to counting the days. I think that there is very much more hope for me now than there was, say, after Switzerland. Don't get in a flurry and say I must not hope too much. I shall not, because though I am sure in my own mind that you and I were meant for each other, to be man and wife some day, yet I know that it may never come off at all. You will not have to say a definite "yes" or "no" till I am in Australia, so do not ever worry that dear head on that score. That time is a long way off. Much will happen meanwhile. After Easter I will meet you in Paris, if and when I may.

[*Olaf's earliest WEA classes, in several towns on Merseyside, were in the history of industrialism. The question of the role of literature in adult education classes led Olaf to write a series of five articles on "Poetry and the Worker" that appeared in* The Highway, *the official journal of the WEA, between October* 1913 *and January* 1915.]

University Settlement,
Liverpool
TO AGNES                                           29 January 1914
. . . This evening I went to Preston and had a very interesting talk with people singly and in groups, in a fine room with plenty of huge armchairs. First came two girls, young things about nineteen, mere children in fact (!!). They talked about essay writing, and I probably helped them to see things a bit. Then came a man to discuss an essay. When he was cleared off two more came. Then began the fun. One is a tall bigboned fellow with a big thoughtful face and a sarcastic mouth. The other is small and mild. They started off by saying they did not like industrial history, but wanted literature. They wanted something that would help them to "see things," and get pleasure out of nature and out of thought. Industrial history merely made them feel pessimistic, as things always seemed to have gone from bad to worse. Meanwhile an ardent lover of industrial history had come in, and put up a very good defence, saying that it was necessary in order that we might improve society. I agreed, and gave a thumbnail sketch of human history as the story of the growth of ideas, ideals, and of high character in men. The big man grunted approval now and then. I said the social organism had often gone downhill, but that the difference between the ideals of a barbarian and an Englishman was an argument for optimism, whatever had happened in the last two centuries. Meanwhile two others had come in, and we were all sitting smoking, and letting our pipes go out. One of the original pair then talked about the blank minds of many of his fellow workers who could not delight in stars and clouds as he did, but who flocked to the football match. A newcomer said that if a man gets absorbed in those pleasures he becomes a dreamer and drops all active social life. "Good thing, too," said the big man. Well, we talked for an hour, and it was much more interesting than this bald account of it. I recited [Arthur O'Shaughnessy's] "We are the music makers" to them, and the big man said, "There's more in that than in all the history of trade unionism." I recited [Wordsworth's] "The world is too much with us," which was to the point. Finally we agreed to try to bring more

literature and general thought into our class meetings, and straightway
to found a study circle for literature. . . .

*Sunday.* . . . Write soon to me from France. You tell me to be patient
and brave, and to work hard. The first and the last are sometimes easier
than the middle command. I wonder if you understand. When you are
here the first is the hardest, and the second the easiest. Now, though, it
is different. Now will I give thee commands also! In France you will be
seeing and hearing all kinds of beauty. Never be content merely to say,
"I love it." Say also, "Now what exactly does it stand for? What is its
relation to other things I love?" Every beautiful thing is merely a window, more or less clear, through which one little part of the fair continuous heaven is seen. We have to fill in the unseen by our imagination,
and fill it in reasonably and as securely as may be. Also, when you come
across things ugly or terrible or even mean and sordid, remember that
they also are windows, though unclear, and that through them also part
of that continuous beauty is to be seen, if we only knew how. . . .
There is no more beautiful thing than a woman who is by nature and
culture conscious of the universe, to use a clumsy phrase; who in herself
is always listening to a voice which to some seems "the still small voice"
within, and to others seems the music of the spheres; who is calm and
wise by nature and culture; who is not "absorbed" in her listening to that
voice, but lives a full happy life, and in whose presence all people seem
to be at their best. This is very badly expressed and very parsonic; but,
true, I mean it.


Reigate
My dear Olaf,                                         30 January 1914
    I have just been reading your letter again. I expect you will be imag-
ining that I am annoyed, or in a towering rage at being 'bustled' so,
because you know you do imagine things, although you always think
you don't, but on the contrary I am quite calm & ordinary—only I am
sorry that I have made you wait so long for a letter. . . .
    Yes it was a good time at Annery. I loved it. But you be patient &
brave & work hard. I don't think you had better come Home when I go.
Why do you want it? I want to be just a little wild girl when I get Home.
Goodbye, your letter was alright. . . . Write again soon to me.
                                              Yours, Agnes
Is that selfish of me not to want you to come yet? No. I don't think so.


[*In Rouen Agnes once again lodged with her cousins Beatrice and Alfred Fryer.*]

Rouen

3 February 1914

. . . The town is full of people. It is very slummy where we live—not in
our own street—it is quite respectable & it is quiet because there is a
carpet of mud on it which deadens all sound & it has no pavé & no
tramway & it has the gate into the jardin des plantes, & nearly all big
houses, red brick & yellow stone patterns all over them & shutters
nearly always down, you know, don't you? But the people in the streets
are interesting. They are very dirty but they look happy, most of them—
the girls & the young men & the children & the older women too; but
there are such a lot of broken down looking men: the coalmen & the
dockers & the workmen & there are lots who don't seem to want to work
at all. Beatrice says the mills are always wanting workers but still there
are these crowds of ragged dirty men standing about in all directions &
blocking up the ways. Then there are the soldiers too in their red & blue
coats, lots of them, all over the place, in twos or threes or groups &
sometimes the proud possessor of a 'girl.' But are these rough working
men & dirty like your men? One doesn't see men like these in England
& it seems to be the prevailing class here, at least at our end of the town
where all the mills & works are. These men don't look as if they would
join a study circle. They don't look as if anyone does anything for them
at all, perhaps they don't want anyone to do anything for them & perhaps they don't mind being dirty & raggy. But I'm sorry for the women
who work in the mills. They look so pale & tired & they all wear dark
dresses & black shawls round their shoulders; lots of them are married
women & they meet their husbands coming out of their work & tramp
home together in the dusk, carrying their bread & packs & bundles.
. . . These slums are very dirty but Liverpool slums are more depressing. You've got a big work to do & your goal is a very clear one but it's a
long way off, isn't it? I want to help if I can, only I don't know how.

University Settlement,

7 February 1914

. . . Your account of Rouen is interesting. No, my people [in WEA
classes] are not of that kind. They are all respectable artisans, with nice
little houses full of nicknacks. They wear gold watches that belonged to
their fathers. They have bits of garden and grow tomatoes for a hobby.
But they are handworkers, and they speak strange tongues—accents of
all sorts. They are all, or nearly all, struggling to make ends meet. Some
are having a hard fight. They all call themselves working class people,
there is no snobbery about them. The people one deals with here at the
Settlement are more like the Rouen folk—dock labourers etc. Their
houses are miserable,—dirty, pokey and full of broken down rubbish.

They live in dread of the police and the rent collector. They are never settled, but flit from street to street. They are always married early, often married three times. They talk openly to a stranger of things we others keep very secret. We as a class are either foolish prudes, or sensible, or vile; but we don't shout things on the housetops. They are more acquainted with life, perhaps. They are overcrowded and have no privacy, and therefore no chance of thinking. But they will stick up for one another, and be generous to one another like none or few of us. They have no intellectual interests, and their understanding of social and political things is very limited. They are too hard pressed to care for anything but bread winning, and so it is only a few of them who will join in debates or study circles. I used to think it would be possible to get these people educated, but I am beginning to see how hopeless it is when they work all day and are dead tired at night, and when their surroundings are so sordid. It is all terrible, isn't it. Someday things will be improved, but very slowly. It is different with the class above them, the artisans—mill hands, silversmiths, joiners, printers etc. They are teachable even now, and many of them are keen to learn. Many of them think, and most could if they tried. But where is my goal? Really I don't know where it is, let alone how to get to it. I am not concerned in improving economic conditions, except in so far as everyone is concerned. But I leave that side to specialists. I want to educate a little. That is a clear end, but that is only part of the game. I have an idea that all this social upheaval and "new earth" has to result in a "new heaven" also. We have to work out a new culture, and a new philosophy, almost a new religion, certainly a new religious spirit, in fact an entirely new attitude to life. The old is all discredited and insufficient for the new world in which we live. The Victorian Age is done with. The last two centuries were a transition from the mediaeval. We have not really arrived at the modern yet. We are only feeling for it.

[*F. J. Marquis was warden of the Liverpool University Settlement, where Olaf had been living since its new building had opened in October 1913. The Settlement's residents formed a "care committee" to conduct inquiries designed to promote the education and health of children in some of Liverpool's poorest slums.*]

University Settlement,
TO AGNES                                    17 February 1914
. . . The poets and the preachers sing and preach of a green sunny world and Nature in the midst giving to all who need. Every fly and bird and beast is fighting Nature for a crumb. We only see those that survive. Every man is busy in the same war, with this difference, that a beast

cannot hold more plunder than it can use to keep itself alive, but men may hold much more than they can use. Therefore others suffer more. This morning I was two hours watching Marquis managing a court of appeal where parents come to appeal against a summons for keeping their kids away from school. We saw about fifteen cases. Some had lost control of their children and could not induce them to go to school. Some kept them at home to help in the house, some had diseased children whom they were neglecting. A good half of them were not far from drunk. One woman was at the weeping stage, and had a damaged eye from assault. One man, quite youngish, was present because of his daughter's child, a half caste nigger. But it's no use talking about these things. They mostly lied blindly and ridiculously. It was miserable. One or two were on the verge of mental deficiency. No I think that's enough. . . . This is the world that is green and overflowing. This is the great British civilization that stands for light and liberty. But what is the use of orating? It is no use trying to educate these unfortunates until,—until there are no more such. Society made them so. Society gave them hereditary taints of all sort, gave them drink and vice and misery, and then brow-beats them to make them send their wretched children to school. It was not God, but Society that made the Bottom Dog. Doubtless there's a bit of God's handiwork hidden in each one, but Society has smothered it, long before the poor creature came into the world, in some cases. And Society is all those lovable people who send their ships upon the sea, and drive their mills and build fine houses; and live in comfortable Settlements reading Goethe & Anatole France and dreaming dreams.

Annery

TO AGNES                                                    1 March 1914

. . . Today the sky is blue and hazy. Yesterday it was full of great clouds, piled up on one another. It struck me how splendid it would be suddenly to soar up between the clouds into one blue patch, leaving the clouds one by one behind and rising at last above them all, till the earth was a great sea of shining clouds below one, and turned at last into no more than a bright disc. One would rise into such thin air that the sky would at last be black like night and the sun and stars would shine together, and the white earth as well. I have a poetico-astronomical turn of mind! I am always wandering among the stars. I am always vainly speculating as to the life that may be on Mars and elsewhere, and in other systems. It is vain, but it is a pleasant holiday from this earth sometimes. If there is intelligence in other worlds how different must it be from ours, not merely greater or less, but utterly different and incomprehensible. Yet doubtless those souls also have their battles to fight, and their problems, and consequently their virtues and vices, and doubtless they love and hate as we do, at least it is to be hoped so. It is hard to conceive of intelligence without emotion. If they exist on Mars, those people must be faced with the problem of a rapidly cooling planet. Perhaps they have a long history of civilisation behind them, and having passed the zenith of it all are entirely busy fighting the cold. Or perhaps they have solved that problem successfully; or, having failed, are all turned spiritualists, and seeking some life less limited than the material. But what is the good of dreaming about them, except that it helps one to realise that man is not necessarily the only thinking creature.

[*Agnes arrived in Paris on 20 February and began taking lessons in French composition and singing.*]

chez Madame Jacques
13 Rue de Lyonnais
Paris

TO OLAF                                      8 March 1914

. . . I sat down at my table with a warm fresh wind blowing in onto me & mended stockings & other things that had got bust & I began to feel rather sad & sort of anyhow because it was mail day & my letters hadn't come & then the woman who lives en face about 20 ft. away from my window came to her window & began shaking her carpets & brushing things & she smiled at me across & I said "Bonjour Madame" & then she disappeared into the shade inside the window & I continued thinking how sad it was not to get my letters & then she came back to her window & brought a cage with four little gay canaries in it & perched it up on the window sill & the little birds began saying to each other how jolly it was to be out in the sunshine & how sort of safe & pleasant everything was in our little courtyard & I was glad & I liked to listen to them chattering away. Soon the woman came & took them back inside again & I was in a perfect *fever* to have my letters—when suddenly Madame Jacques arrived from the market, banged at my door, shouted "correspondance." I flew & she gave me two letters written in a well known hand & stamped with a kangaroo stamp & a little bunch of violets which she had brought for me. All my fever deserted me and I felt exuberant inside but just as calm as the dome of the Panthéon outside & I arranged my violets with great care & then sat down & read.

[*The paintings of George Frederic Watts enjoyed a vogue during the later Victorian era as exemplifications of a conscious, though nostalgic, striving for noble ideals. By 1914 Watts represented a quite old-*

*fashioned taste. Olaf and Agnes, who saw a Watts exhibit at the Tate
Gallery when they were in London before Christmas, frequently allude
to the paintings in this period of their correspondence.*]

University Settlement,
TO AGNES                                          12 March 1914

. . . When you go into Notre Dame you will see an avenue of very tall
columns (or piers, as they say), vaulting beautifully together overhead. I
think they will remind you of a beech tree avenue, and you will think,
perhaps, "I love the columns and the trees because of their straightness,
uprightness, and loftiness, and because they spring together." Perhaps
you will think of the steady and "aspiring" flame of a candle in a still
room. I might think of the slim column of smoke that rises straight and
"motionless" from a cigarette in a still room, quivering and breaking
outwards like the vaulting about a foot above the cigarette. Perhaps you
will think of the central figure in Watts's "Love Triumphant," erect, with
arms spread out and face turned up; or (another aspect of the vaulting)
of the brooding figure in "Death and Innocence." . . . When you see
the Venus de Milo you will perhaps worship her for her perfection, but
you may perhaps see, as I do, that she is haughtily sneering, as only
conscious perfection can sneer; and you will say "I have seen that sneer
round the nostrils of many fine ladies, it has a fascination, it is somehow
beautiful, but it just shows the difference between the Greek idea of
godhead, and ours. . . . Yet you will worship the Venus, and be very
sorry that her face is dirty. But you will not simply say, "I love her!" You
will think of what she meant to the men who conceived her,—a terrible, beautiful and often very cruel power. You will see that she is "classic," complete, looking down, not up, not "aspiring," since she is perfection, not compassionate either, just beautiful, to be passionately
loved and feared. You will notice also that her mouth is a little sen-
suous, and the mouth of one who despises curbs, for whom self restraint
has no meaning, since she is above the need of it. You will compare her
with that aspiring interior of the cathedral. The one represents divinity,
the other man, doubtless; but that Venus could not be the divinity of
that cathedral, nor would she for her part have her temples built so.
Then perhaps you will think that the cathedral was built by those who
were reaching up to a God who was reaching down, whereas we have
got so absorbed in that one idea of upward looking, aspiring (what with
our evolutionary theories and our feeling that the best is not the perfect,
but the most upward tending, worshipping or loving) that we must
needs have God himself, in a way, aspiring, working towards some
better existence. . . .

When you see terrible or harrowing or evil things, do not say "It is
overwhelming, I cannot fit it into my scheme of things; but I feel it must

be alright *in the end,* because I feel that God is good and it is wrong to doubt." Remember that *now* the evil is as real as the good, and that not only bodies but souls are crippled every day. Remember that millions of people do not feel that God is good. Remember that it is weakly optimistic cant merely to say evil exists to be defeated. What is cannot be undone. Or if it can, we cannot conceive how, and so we must not count on it. So many people fail to overcome evil, and are overcome. Think of all the pain and defeat and "badness" that has been mounting up through the centuries. Not a speck can be destroyed. Nor is it true that the spiritual quality of victory over misery counterbalances it all, for so often there has been no victory. You may look into your heart and say "I *know* beyond all doubt that all is for the best." I know also now. But do not let us shut our eyes on the facts. The world is not as we would make it if we were God. Let us not try to persuade ourselves it is, but absolutely accept the evil as a present reality and try to understand, in order to help. . . . I must stop this now, though I don't want to, and have heaps to say. I have been awfully dogmatic, but it is shorter to be dogmatic. I am not really so.

[*Psalms were much on Olaf's mind, apart from his disagreements with Agnes over the particular psalm he discusses here. He was writing the poems that formed his first published book, which appeared at the end of 1914 with the title* Latter-Day Psalms.]

University Settlement,
TO AGNES                                          24 March 1914
. . . My dear, I want to talk to you about something, and I don't know how to explain what I mean. Therefore, since it is difficult, don't think me an atheist and an ingrate if you don't see eye to eye with me and if you do not see the bogey that I see. You say "The Lord is my shepherd; I shall not want." It is good to think of you saying that lovely psalm. I say it also, being also in the green pastures. For you and me and many others it is absolutely true. But for many, perhaps very many, it is by no means true at all. They want always. Their souls are never restored. Goodness and mercy are only words to them. The house of the Lord, whether it be here or elsewhere, they utterly deny. It is not only that they are unshepherded and in physical distress. Strife and hunger has grown to seem to them the natural order, and he who withstands the law of strife is in their eyes a fool. They do not even say "my soul is athirst for God." The idea of God is utterly incongruous to their lives. That most beautiful psalm is a mockery to them, and they would say of it things that need not be repeated, calling it the thanksgiving of the capitalists. The only kind of psalm they care for is such as "Blessed be the

lord my God, who teacheth my hands to war and my fingers to fight"
(our old school psalm, by the way. Oh what a ringing time we had for it
too, and how we exulted!). Now my perplexity is this. I needs must accept the darkness of these people as true darkness in their eyes. How
then shall I complacently say "The Lord is my shepherd," when they
are utterly outside all gentle shepherding? My dear, you talk about Life
and Faith and Love for ever. For us yes, but for these others whose *souls*
are crippled from the beginning, owing to the unwiseness of their fathers and mothers and the whole elder generation? With a fearful vengeance the sins of the fathers are visited on the children. Therefore
when we sing that beautiful psalm let it be with an utter humility and
fear, knowing that for some unknowable reason we are favoured. But I
am talking like this not because I want to cast a shadow on your picture
of the world, but because I am coming more and more to hate the frame
of mind (which is not yours) that shuts its eyes to evil, and says "All will
be well, but this darkness has no place in *my* picture; blot it out with a
vague glory." These people are cowards. They are afraid to spoil their
peace of mind. They are secretly indignant that any nether wailing and
gnashing of teeth should jar them as they listen, with a kind of sensual
epicurean delight, to the harmony of the spheres.

[*Yvonne Jacques, daughter of Agnes' Parisian landlady, was an art student who acted as Agnes's guide through Paris and became her closest
friend there.*]

Paris
TO OLAF                                                          5 April 1914
. . . Monday night. 8.30. Do you see that blot? Well that blot has a
history & it marks a certain step in my character & disposition. I'll tell
you how it happened. Yvonne, as I said, was writing notes or copying
them for a manuscript & she is a chatterbox by nature & she couldn't
resist giving me all the tit-bits & I couldn't get on with my letter. Once
we both made a grab for the inkpot at the same time & we both stopped
being serious to laugh & she told me about a certain prim jeune homme
whom she used to sit opposite to at the Sorbonne & who was always too
"timide" to look at her until one day when they both dipped for the ink
together & made nasty splutters of ink all over their work—justement
comme ça—she said & we repeated the performance & the result is my
blot. . . . Then strange to say we both stopped work & I talked, talked &
I told her all about you! Would you believe it—no I wouldn't. I've
never talked about you to anyone except Mother & Dot. A few Aunts &
people have talked to me about you but I've always shut up like an
oyster & frozen like an iceberg, but here if you please—in a strange

land & in a strange language—I thawed of my own account. I loosened my curb for half an hour & talked. Isn't it a step? True, I was very annoyed about it this morning when I woke up. I can't bear to desert my own self—it hurts. But it was Yvonne who worked the miracle.

[*Olaf took a walk with his parents and Dot through the southern end of the Wirral peninsula to the Cheshire village of Burton. An ancient parish church prompted him to draw comparisons to the latest English cathedral, then under construction in Liverpool.*]

Annery
12 April 1914
TO AGNES                                    Easter Sunday
. . . Sitting in Shotwick church I got a-thinking of the many things that went to the making of it since its old Saxon foundation. In the beginning there was doubtless a pious village community that built some kind of a place with hearty pious labour. Then came the Norman rebuilding by some lord of the manor, directing his skilled villeins, and more skilled imported builders. Maybe he was pious, maybe he merely wanted to atone for sins. And they who did the work were either like slaves working for no reason but because they had to, or they were working for a wage and thinking of their wives and families. Yet in those days there must have been a genuine piety amongst them all, and a sincerity in their work. But later in the modern rebuilding methinks there will have been less devotion on the part of the builders, though perhaps no less honesty of purpose. Think that each stone that you see has been cut and placed by all manner of men from all manner of complex motives, and what a building it is! The glory of a building, doubtless, should be in the free eager work that has been put into it with pride of workmanship. Such are the old cathedrals, where, of course, a lot was left to the craftsman's individuality; so that the whole is like humanity, a beautiful creature resulting from countless little "free wills" that all sought the common beauty with their own means, and all cling together and yet have their own natures. But think of the new Liverpool cathedral. Rich men combined together to set aside some small portion of their riches that they might glory through the glory of Liverpool. A great plan, completely detailed, was chosen by competition, chosen by wealth and conventionality. And—well, you know—money got from slave trading and from screwing cotton workers is turned to the glory of God. Countless workmen are engaged at the market rate, set each to do his regulation work in regulation time according to the great plan. Each of them is thinking all the while of the fight that is life, of "making ends meet," of trade union action against employers, of next Saturday night's spree, of

Tuesday evening. Yesterday was Easter Monday and we all got wet. We all four took train to Hadlow Road, and walked thence to Burton for lunch. There are beautiful woods there, and the worn old gravestones of two quakers whom they would not admit into the cemetry. There is also a distant prospect of a wood on the top of a hill like my marginal scratch, only beautiful, with a great light behind it and green fields below it, so lovely. Burton is an ancient place full of wee little thatched cottages. One in particular is an an overhanging rock and is like a cottage in a fairy tale, like this only quite different, and beautiful.

BURTON

After a fat lunch we walked on to Shotwick through many fields. There is a fine old hall there where we ought to have had lunch, but didn't. The houses in those parts are all simple old picturesque brick houses, ornamented with brick patterns. There is also an old church where we sat a long while meditating and admiring the black oak panneling. Going home we all got soaked with rain. Father and I walked to Heswall along the coast at a great speed in sunshine and shower. In the evening Dot and I went to the Kerrs for a musical and jocular evening. There were friends with them and Mr Kerr was uproarious, and Mrs Kerr couldn't keep him in order, and Doris nearly had hysterics, and the noise was tremendous. Mrs Lawson, whom you met once at a Kerr tea in town, asked after you. An admirer of Elsie's was there with whom she had spent the day on the Dee. Then Dot and I walked home under the stars very slowly, talking about the heavens so quietly and "exaltedly" after all the merriment. Dot was not well in the middle of our walk after lunch, but recovered later. But we walked slow so

An illustrated page from Olaf's Easter 1914 letter.

the class war, of a maiden's buxom figure, of the Insurance Act or Home Rule for Ireland, of the next chance of shirking. Of the glory of God? Not they, save in rare cases. Mostly they will ignore such upper class ideas as "God." Some will be agnostics, or dogmatic atheists, most will be wrapt up in "the economic cause," when they are not wrapped up in football and "pictures." Very little of their souls will go through their fingers into those stones. There is no free eager individuality in that cathedral. Yet it's a fine sight to see it going up, with its tall cranes and scaffolding. And the people that are upon it are for the most part noble in their own way, at least as noble as the rich men whose whim compels the poor men to work on it. Yes it is all noble in its way, but what a higher nobility it might be! And the rich men are mostly sincere as far as they can see. But the cathedral is no true emblem of humanity, only a very true emblem of humanity in a very uncomfortable transition stage, as it is today.

[*On 5 May Olaf arrived in Paris to visit Agnes for a month, a journey Agnes's mother considered "unconventional." By day they visited Notre Dame, strolled in the Bois de Vincennes, boated on the Seine; in the evenings, usually discreetly accompanied by Alfred Fryer or Yvonne Jacques, they applauded the Russian ballet at the Paris Opéra, sang Brahms or Gilbert and Sullivan to the accompaniment of Agnes's piano, or read together from Daudet and Voltaire, from Keats's "Eve of St. Agnes" and Olaf's own psalms. They toured the countryside by car, and Olaf asked Agnes to marry him, but she told him to come to visit her in Australia and ask her again next year. Finally, after an idyllic day-long excursion to Fontainebleau, Olaf renewed his courtship more ardently: "I talked to her," he wrote in his diary, "told her how I love her, told her what she must feel, urged her desperately to feel it now, held her fast, & she was overpowered. Standing up I put both arms round her & kissed her again & again & urged, & at last she said 'yes,'—& was unhappy. So I gave her back her 'yes,' & it dawned on me that I might be harming her after all, & that she is not really in love with me." Olaf returned to England in uncertainty, but his trip had aroused great curiosity in Liverpool—a curiosity he rarely chose to gratify, though he gloated in his diary: "People must have thought we were eloping."*]

Annery
TO AGNES                                              4 June 1914
. . . My dear, for four weeks we have been together so much that I don't know where I am without you. Coming home in the train I kept thinking that I would write and tell you all that I have told you so often once

more, and sort things out a bit, so to speak. But writing seems such a slow & clumsy method after talking. Little girl, we had a very happy time together, didn't we? To me it was all just heaven, or nearly so. Sometimes we were so close together, metaphorically, that I made sure you were not only fond of me but that you loved me. And just because I got too excited about it I kind of frightened you away, but not very far away surely. . . . In the middle of last month I made up my mind that you should be won as it were by storm. And so I pressed for all I was worth. But I think I did it all the wrong way, though it didn't seem wrong to me at the time. And for about five seconds I thought you were won, and I went walking on the clouds. Then it dawned on me that I had made a little mistake and I came toppling down a horrid long way! . . .

What a shameless cousin you are! You have never really shown the slightest sign of being in love with me, but you just lead me on like the conventional sorceress and then at last you say "Oh but I don't love you, I can't somehow, so good bye, work hard and be good!" Now you will probably write me a letter sometime and if you say anything about these things it will probably be to the effect that I must just wait, and to make it sound more kindly you will say "be brave and patient." My dear, I'll do all that if necessary, but really is it necessary? Of course it is necessary to wait an age before we can get married, but not before we are engaged, or in some way or other agreed. . . . Look, it is like this. I have always been as it were holding out a hand to you. At last you have taken it firmly as a friend's hand, and whatever happens it is yours for good and all as a friend's, as a brother's. But now it is time to think it would be good to take the other hand too, or be wrapped round altogether by both arms gladly. It is the "gladly" that is the test. Oh I will treat you ever so gently now. I will not do as I did once and want to eat you up with love, so to speak (unless I think you want to be eaten!). I will not take what you cannot gladly give. But you *must* take what I am always eager to give. No, you shall not be eaten up, but covered up, with love. . . .

I am ready to do more psalms; want to get a good bit of that in before Festiniog. I will send you things as they get done, and you will give a word or two of criticism. When we meet let us sometime go over the whole lot together, if you are willing, and see if we cannot improve them together and bring them up to the standard of the passage you picked out as best. Will you? The "tone" that is right for them is the "tone" that you taught me long ago without intending. So obviously your help is necessary to make them worth publishing. Will you help me that way perhaps, or perhaps even work with me a little if you have time someday? Perhaps in the far future we may work together so a lot if you please. Sidney & Beatrice Webb labour to write statistical history books together. If you are ever my wife you shall do no such unskilled spade work, but you shall spare time from other things to help in the most delicate part of the work I want to do. (If, If, I am so tired of If!) Meanwhile help a fellow a bit now and then. You said once you would like to write things like the Daudet tales. Your letters are sometimes just like those. Some time, just for fun, select a really good subject, pick out just the essential parts of it, and write it all down in simple English (or French? better English because it's worth it), put the very best you know into it and condense it strictly. Then send it to me and I will let you off writing me a letter, and I will comment to the best of my ability. Perhaps you are too busy even for that just now, but it would be nice. It would be good to do that for all the most memorable experience of your foreign trip; but of course time is scarce. But do deliberately try once, because I have a very clear idea that if you try you can tell a little "tale" beautifully; I mean more than merely correctly and pleasantly, of course. That is just a matter of school composition. Letter-writing is good practice for recounting, but of course letters are slapdash and like a single coat of paint on a subject; and one doesn't bother about literary beauty in a letter! This letter for instance is all brackets, inverted commas, and sentences like trams—first the engine and then a string of trucks joggling afterwards. . . . You say the effect of last month will not "rub off." Let it rub on more. I am so desperately in love with you, little girl. Next time I write I will try to talk sense about things in general. This time it's just a love letter and rather muddlesome one.

Paris
Olaf!                                                              6 June 1914
I don't know what to say first, such a lot of things to talk about. I got your letter this morning, it was so funny to see your writing again, it made one realise that you were really gone. At first it didn't seem right somehow. When I said goodbye to you at the station I might have been saying "A toute à l'heure" mightn't I? But when I got to St. Lazare & climbed into the autobus with my bag & had to pay my *own fare*, I thought Paris was a very big city & I felt a very lone girl.

Annery
TO AGNES                                                        10 June 1914
. . . Miss [Nina] Barnard was here for Monday night and we took her a walk and kept her amused pretty well. I took her into town yesterday and she managed to make me garrulous about Paris all the time. . . . Miss Barnard went a walk with Mother and asked her, concerning you and me, if "it was coming off." Mother said she really didn't know. I talked to Mother once on the subject and emphasised the "uncertainty of my

prospects." The public at large has asked me all about Paris and been told exactly what they asked for and no more; except that I have been enthusiastic about the beauties of the city, and so on. But the public, as far as I am concerned, has no reason to talk, except the general one that I have been with you four weeks! . . .

My dear, I think it was a brilliant guess on my part ages ago when I took the first step of falling in love with you. It *was* a guess, you know, because I naturally didn't know at that age what really was necessary for two people to love one another. I knew nothing about the real being in love. So it was a brilliant guess, or rather it was fate. Yes it was fate, and it is fate. I am still ahead of you in the reading of the "book" you once talked of, but you have read further. And as for me, I have opened another volume.

[*In July Agnes came to England and joined the Stapledons for a Welsh holiday during which Olaf resumed the earnest courtship of his last days in Paris.*]

Llan Festiniog
North Wales
Agnes,                                                              25 July 1914

It is not twelve hours since I saw you, yet here am I needing to write to you. . . . Read carefully, and think. You have said you will marry me. That is a serious and definite fact. I cannot of course really think of it as a promise, because if it were a promise the public might be told at once. But for my private ear you have said practically "I love you, and someday I will be your wife, if all goes as I hope." I pressed a little for that "yes," and therefore you shall write and say (if you can) that you do not regret it at all. But the pressure was slight and you seemed not very unwilling! But I have been thinking that there can be no real "yes" until you feel as I feel, or rather somewhat as I feel. I have told you so often what I feel, and yet I feel as if the telling was all inadequate. The thing that matters is just this: I love you more than anyone else in the world, man or woman, old or young. I love you in such a way that I want to be with you not merely when we are happy and "on show," but in all moods and circumstances of life. You are glad to go walks with me, but are you glad to have me as the closest, most intimate companion? . . . Be won fully and finally. Be glad that I love you, and love me also with all your heart,—in whatever manner you like, but with all your heart. Look no more into the past of your life,—it was good but it was the opening chapter. Look into the future, which is to be with me. Get used to the big change that is to come, and be glad of it. My dear, how I do talk! But what else can I do just now? If a man has wooed a girl for a year

and a half and has lately had her in his arms and remembers still the
wonderful feel of her, so soft and yielding; and if she has said she will be
his wife and now is clean gone out of the land leaving nothing but that
thought of her,—why then, and if a fellow has been always afraid of
letting his feelings get the better of him and afraid of showing them too
much; then I say the poor bloke must be pardoned a little verbosity.

Bide-a-wee
Scarborough

Olaf,                                                             29 July 1914

Have you been waiting to receive a letter from me? Well I have been
waiting to write one. And I've had to wait till now, Wednesday morning,
before breaker. I got your letter on Monday morning just as we were
starting out for the day so I read it on the train going to Scarboro & then
finished it when I was waiting for Esther in the dentist's waiting room.
You didn't lose much time in writing to me & I was glad. . . .

Olaf, after I said goodbye to you & got to Scarborough & everything
was new & everyone was very friendly & kind but I was alone, I did
want you to be there & I thought all sorts of wild imaginations. I
thought I must be in love with you & I believe I was glad I had said 'yes,'
or I forgot all about that. Only now I don't feel like that any more, not
all frothy & smiling inside. Now why is it? I don't worry that I have said
'yes' because it *must* be right in the end, only I feel sort of dullish inside
this morning & I wish you were here, too.

[*As the German army advanced on Belgium and the various European
countries declared war, Agnes was at Aunt Nina's house in Reigate,
Surrey, and Olaf had just begun teaching in the WEA summer school
in North Wales, run by Evan Hughes.*]

Bangor, N. Wales

TO AGNES                                                    2 August 1914

. . . This evening eleven of us, half girls, were sitting talking in our dining room; and I as usual was in the background smoking and not saying
very much, but chipping in now and then. (More of the talk later.)
Then came the newspaper boys down the street, and Hughes got a paper
and read us the news—Germany & Russia definitely at war, all Europe
rising, German troops in Luxembourg, etc. Of course we talked about
the awful prospects, and it was a study to watch the different ways in
which people took it all. We all agreed in praying for peace, Hughes & I
for "peace at *any* price," even if it meant repudiating foolish treaties. I
don't believe there is as much in the affair as is made out, but certainly

things are very serious. Military preparations are going on about us and the coast is guarded, and people in police employ are being called back from their holidays. If the war spreads, and England fights, of course everything will be dislocated. There will be something like chaos. I don't believe England will fight, but she may. I still believe it will all be over in a fortnight, but it may be the beginning of unheard-of horrors, and goodness knows what may become of European civilisation. (Yet I still think it will all blow over and everything will be placid again.) But there is the question of one's little personal duties in this great world affair. Mine are clear, and most other people's in my state. So long as the war is outside of this island I stick to my work whatever dislocation there may be. If England is invaded I throw in my little mite with the rest and enlist. Having had a little training and being able to ride and being fairly sturdy one might not be useless; and like other people I suppose one would get used to the horror of being under fire (if one succeeded in not running away first time!). Mine would be a poor little mite, but "many mickles make a muckle." I have never really thought about these things before tonight, but I think this decision is right, though I am not *absolutely* convinced of the rightness of fighting (for civilians) even against an invader. A civilian might conceivably be more use, even in war, in some other way. Yet obviously that is the simple immediate attitude to take up as a starting point, to be qualified if necessary.

If the war spreads and lasts it may seriously affect your going home. My dear, for your sake I earnestly hope all will be well in that respect. But precious girls must not be sent upon the high seas unless everything is quite safe. Of course it will all be over before then, we hope, for all our sakes and the world's. And I personally feel pretty sure it will be over before then. Anyhow we won't worry till necessary. Oh, I want to be with you now to talk to you!

Now Agnes, cousin of mine, and very dear girl, we come to the point of this letter. I hope you follow the thread. Your letter has made me think again. And I am sure we must go on no more like this. All my best thought and attention has been centred for a long time on the winning of you. Under the circumstances it is bound to be so, & rightly it is so. But through one thing and another I have been lately afraid to press, or I have thought it wrong, and have just waited or seemed half hearted. So that you "feel dull inside," yet you are "sure it *must* be all right in the end." My dear, we have done with all that. I will press you now in season and out and make love to you with every bit of loving power that is in me. I am sick of half measures and half your heart. I will have it all now. You shall not feel indifferent and dull. The "life force" that I am spending simply in wondering and waiting has to be spent on other things—in work, and in growing into you, and in all kinds of *work* with you and for you,—and perhaps even in fighting (just an off chance). But anyhow from now until you are wholly glad you have said yes all my strength shall be used to make you love me really, and then a great uncertainty will be gone and all that energy will be set free. Now, girl, wake up! I love you. So that even all this world-crisis and possible confusion would seem nothing compared with my own personal love affair,—but that one tries to keep a clear view of things. . . . Agnes, I will wait no longer for your love. I have waited long enough, and now you can give it, if you *will*. To wait longer would be foolish, useless, dangerous. I have waited too long already, through some silly diffidence or other. You know you can never love anyone else now, and you know I cannot. You shall come back to Caldy simply ready to give yourself up body and soul to me, as I wait to give myself to you. You shall care for no other person in the world at all in the way you care for me, even as I you. You shall be always lonely without me, as I am hideously lonely without you. I tell you I am all on fire with you, and you lit that fire. . . . So come, not shyly, doubtfully, looking back like Lot's wife, but confidently. My dear, I claim you! I can't let there be any doubt any longer, in your mind or mine or the world's. I don't care what anyone says, I am right. The time for deciding is now. I think when we meet next I shall be very angry with you if you are not *sure*, and I shall scold you and give you up in disgust for the time being! Oh my dear, you know I cannot do that even if I try, so you are safe. I shall do to you what I did in Paris when I made you say yes. I'll give you no peace. . . .

You shall not answer this mad wise letter with sober doubts. When you left me you "thought you were in love with me." You *thought*? Then girls don't know themselves at all. You *want* to love? Why you silly girl, you solemn little sober doubting and altogether good for nothing girl, then if you want to love, be an ordinary human girl and love. Do you think it is done by writing and saying, "I feel it coming on, don't interrupt." It's done by saying "I *will* love." It was so I first loved you. Really it was. So from this time forth you are to be a new girl; see? Here we are on the verge of a great war perhaps, and all kinds of confusion, and yet I talk like this to you. Why? because whatever happens, if heaven and earth fall to pieces, we shall be stronger to bear it if we two love and have no further doubts.


Bangor
My dear,                                              3 August 1914
Here am I at it again! But how can I help writing to you every night now-a-days! You see I am taking you by storm. The long cautious advance across your frontiers is over. It took about eighteen months. Now I lay siege to your citadel. These letters are the deliberate cannonade

preparing the way for the final assault which will be a matter of hand to hand fighting. (Is it frivolous to use war as a simile?) Here in Bangor we are wonderfully out of the excitement. It is all like a fairy tale to us. But some of us are getting fearfully perplexed to know what to do. I heard from Dot today. She seems to be doing her little share by helping to prepare Red Cross organisation. I am going to write to the Settlement to see what I can do through them. But indeed it is all terrible and unrealisable. Everything here is so calm and beautiful in the lovely weather, and yet there is this unknown thing hanging over us. England will be very different when she has come through this. She will be both better & worse, but I firmly believe the balance will be great good. But many people may be ruined who at present are flourishing. And many great causes may be crippled. . . .

As for me, it is quite likely that WEA work will boom, as people may want a distraction from distress. Or it may fall right away. Anyhow we are going to do our very best to keep the torch alight through the winter. It is most urgently important that the movement should not lose ground. I am going to stir up my four towns with all my might, and try to make the winter a huge success as far as I am concerned. It does not sound very heroic to go on with one's ordinary peaceful work in this crisis. But it is clearly the right thing as long as there is a strong fleet to defend us. I won't get bitten by the fever for enlisting, just for the sake of the emotional satisfaction of it. Yet it does tempt one when one sees all these fellows marching about, & hears of the way people flock to enlist. But the whole thing seems to me exaggerated. There's more pressing work, though it is less heroic. Well, we'll see. But look, little girl. Suppose the very worst were to happen, the family resources be lost, the enemy in the country, and all things in confusion. Even so I claim you. God meant us two to love each other *whatever happens*, & to be a strength to one another. If there is fighting to be done I must *know* you love me, and feel your heart with me. I must know that we shall be married afterwards, if there is any afterwards. Because where there is really love questions of life and death, of future & no future, simply do not count against the fact of love. I am not selfish in saying this. It is better for both of us so. This is all badly put. We will talk about it when we meet.

[*Virginia Williams, the wife of the manager of Lloyd's of London, was a wealthy heiress who had befriended Nina Barnard when they were girls and had brought her home to be educated by her own governess. The financial independence of the Auntie Nina who chaperoned Agnes in 1913 and 1914 was the result of an annuity settled on her by Ginny Williams.*]

Reigate
Olaf you wild mad dear silly boy,                            6 August 1914

What am I to answer your letter with? How am I to answer a whirlwind by a still small voice? Impossible, even if I dared (which I don't)
and I can't answer by a whirlwind so I'm not going to answer at all &
you say the consequence will be that I shall be drowned with letters.
Tant mieux! say I, but I know it will take you a lot of time & I know you
have got lots of other things to do & I know all this energy ought to be
spent on other & more profitable things, that's just it, & there are so
many other things to think of just now, aren't there? But you'll have to
put up with that till I come back & then you say I've got to be a different
girl? Well, well, well, are you angry with me for talking like this? I'm
not really a stranger to you as you said in your letter you felt I was sometimes & I didn't mean to make you feel "desperately lonely" when I told
you "it was different & I felt dull & cold." You read my letter again. I *did*
want you all the time & now I want you too & when I think of the war
& try to be patient & brave, then I think of you too & I should like you
to make me more patient & more brave & perhaps I could do something
for you too. But you are so sure & decided—anyway about sticking to
your work. I have no definite work, so I just have to be ordinary & do
jobs & pay visits & take exercise & go to the dentist's & read the papers
& think & talk to Auntie Nina about it all. But oh what a selfish life it is
with everything to make life easy & quiet & insignificant & yet think of
the thousands & thousands who live in suspense & fear & dread & ruin.
Oh Olaf, Olaf.

Today I met the wife of the manager of Lloyd's Insurance place. They
have a big house & estate at Caterham & no lack of servants & she was
dressed like a duchess & has most charmingly wonderful society ways &
manners, but a sweet strong face & her eyes were full of tears today
when she came in & said, "Do you know dear, for us it means ruin."


Bangor
My dear Agnes,                                              6 August 1914

Things have become pretty bad since last I wrote, haven't they. I am
writing this in my room on Wednesday night, because it is no use trying
to go to sleep just yet, the evening has been too noisy and hilarious,
even in the midst of all this fearful business. We had a concert consisting of Welsh choir (lovely), glees, sweet Welsh folksongs about "Cuckoo
bach" etc., rag choruses with toy trumpets, etc. And all the while that
we eighty people were carrying on so gaily those two fleets were feeling
about for one another in the North Sea. I sneaked out once to get a late
paper, and the moon and Jupiter were shining together over the trees.
And the same quiet moon was looking at the North Sea. This afternoon

we had sports here, and I helped with the tea for those eighty people, quite a considerable labour, but I took care to get a good feed myself. They had cricket and sack races and three legged races and tug of war etc. and everyone made a great noise and was merry. But the war hangs over everything. People's minds are distracted from their work. Many have been called home to ship yards, offices, police etc. Tutors are far more worried than students mostly, because most working men don't seem to realise properly what it all means. I shall be glad to get away from this secluded corner into touch with things.

Bangor

TO AGNES                                                    9 August 1914

. . . Evan [Hughes] and his wife were telling me today a lot about their courting days. They were very amusing about it. I told them a good bit about mine, because we are so intimate now. It seems he "had a fearful business to get her up to the scratch," because she would say yes one day and no the next. But at last when she was staying close to Bangor three years ago he came along from Liverpool and stayed near her for a fortnight and "laid siege," and gave her no peace. "You should have heard the speeches I made to her. I tell you I gave her a bad time. I guess she didn't sleep those nights." (Mrs. H. interposed "Oh yes I did, blissfully.") "Well, I meant business, and at last I took her by storm, & went back to L'pool." "Yes," said Mrs. H, "and then I wrote & told him not to tell anyone about it because I wasn't quite sure yet. But he had already told everyone, so it was all up!" I laughed within me. Little girl, you shall be taken by storm. If I had the gift of gab like him I should have conquered you long ago. But I think I have only just wakened up and begun to *try* to win you. But how like their affair was to ours, on a small scale, except that he didn't care a rap for her when they knew each other at college. . . .

My dear, so many times I have come into my room & written letters to you after saying good night to everyone, that I often think how good it will be when this phase is over, and you & I together have to say good night to people, as this couple do to me, & go away together to rest. It's very odd to talk to a girl like this when one is not engaged to her, but I can so easily imagine you here now, saying perhaps, "Now let's go to sleep, it's awfully late." But we won't do late hours then. We will keep rational hours. You are wonderful, and all that, to me, but also you are "home" to me. And the thing I want most is that I may be "home" to you. Now when we meet again let us start that happy stage. Oh I will worship you as Beatrice was worshipped (as far as is possible for one who is not Dante!). . . .

I will be with you soon. Look you, it is the spirit of you I love

most because it is beautiful. I want to be in some real & close com-
munion with it; mystical and "spiritual," and also direct, intellectual,
if the two are separate. But also I love the dear body of you. And I wish
it was here in my arms again now, ever so close. When the body is near,
the spirit seems to draw nearer too. See? Good night at last, Agnes,
wife to be.

Bangor

Agnes,                                                    14 August 1914
   This is just a note to say I am going home today by boat. The trains
on this line are very disorganised; in fact there was a rumour that no
passenger trains would be running today. Anyhow in this weather sea
travel is preferable. . . . Last night we went out on to a certain view-
place & talked & smoked under the stars, our party & a few students.
We talked of the war in relation to social problems, and of the poor fellows rushing along in the trains over the bridge on the way to Belgium.
And someone had spread a rumour that I was going too, and half the
students had been asking me about it, and I had to disillusion them, and
merely say "Of course they may call out old members of the University
corps to serve at home, but I won't go fighting abroad if I can help it,
because that's not our business." And so I lost glory with them a little.
But all the while the stars were as quiet as ever, & if we seemed small in
the human turmoil of the war, the whole thing seemed infinitely
smaller under the stars.

[As *Olaf left the isolation of North Wales and returned to Liverpool the
reality of the war became inescapably visible to him. Meanwhile Agnes
and her relatives were growing anxious about her return to Australia
because the shipping lanes were becoming more dangerous for civilian
transport.*]

Annery

TO AGNES                                               16 August 1914
. . . This is to say that I intend to arrive at Reigate on Tuesday evening,
since Miss Barnard is so kind as to acquiesce in my inviting myself. . . .
So on Tuesday evening, and thence for all too short a while, we shall be
together. Just for a very little time we will be altogether happy with each
other, will we not? Say to yourself at this point "Yes, yes we will be
happy together, we two. Whatever else happens, we will be happy for
those days." Then there will be the time you are to spend at Garsdale,
and I shall have work to do; but we will see each other a good bit then
also. Then you will come back to Annery for a short time anyhow. And

about your sailing, well "Nestor" sailed the other day with 200 passengers. But we shall not let you go if there is any risk whatever. Think of me in England and you on the high seas chased by a German cruiser! No, that would be too horrible. We won't talk of such things. Yesterday I had a good little sea voyage from Bangor. When we reached the Mersey we saw all kinds of ships going in and out, several in government service with their funnels painted black, which made them quite unrecognisable. At the entrance of the river we were stopped by the guard boats, and told what signal lights to hoist as a pass word. Then we passed through the beam of a searchlight which sweeps the river right across. Caldy is quite peaceful, but Liverpool is a turmoil of holiday makers and war.

Reigate

Olaf,                                                                                                    16 August 1914

You asked me to write a line to Annery so here is one. It's going to be rather a *new* line. First thanks for your letter which came a few days ago. Perhaps there will be a note sometime saying when you are coming, if you still are going to manage to come. . . .

I began thinking of you & of all your wondrous threats of "taking me by storm." Oh yes—take me by storm, but *don't* make me excited, *don't* don't Olaf. Do you know for the last week or so I've been going through such a quaint lot of feelings. It's been horrible & I wasn't happy a bit, but last night after supper at 10.30 pm & after a long day spent with the Dornbusches at Windsor, Auntie & I sat & talked until nearly 12 & this morning I woke up feeling quite a different girl & I've been so happy all day—at home & then with Friends at Meeting & afterwards reading poetry to Auntie & I had some home letters this morning & we went out to tea & saw more Friends—then a lovely walk round home over the two commons in the sunset light. More than a week ago you know I talked to Auntie about you & she was a dear & she said to me that as far as Mother was concerned, she was pretty sure that Mother would say nothing to me one way or the other & would leave it absolutely to me— and many other things. Then that was like something taken off my mind & I began to sort of drift about in the idea that it was all fixed up. Then the war came, came & took hold of me & made me almost forget that there is a "very present help," "a hope & strength"—far stronger than the Kaiser & the Tzar all rolled into one. I can't believe that I doubted of this help. It makes me almost weep to think I could have. You always said I was strong to trust, & I thought I was too, but no, I only forgot a little & things seemed so black because I had little faith & things within were black because I believed that I had doubted, & then all the days I felt very tired & worried & I didn't love anyone much or you, but I couldn't help thinking about you & worrying & wondering how I could persuade myself or let you persuade me that I loved you really or well enough to promise soon to be your wife. . . . I have always talked to you about why I should not get engaged—about Mother, & about my being too young & about it being so far away in the future etc. etc. I have believed all these things & thought they were really preventing me, but now that's all done, but the one big & only thing remains which is that—yet I do not really love you. All those other reasons were only excuses. I thought they were mountains but they were only mole heaps. If really I were filled with the fire you are filled with I could be old enough & wise enough & I could so to speak conquer Mother & all the world, & I could wait a very age.

Don't say I am afraid to take the last leap, don't treat me as a child. I can't stand it. I want to feel like "Elizabeth" in one of Longfellow's tales: "I have received a call to love thee." I shall not say yes until I do; don't make me Olaf, but come quickly & make me to love you truly—as I want to, as you want me to. It is like a race against time. Come quickly. "Fly envious time till thou run out thy race."

Annery

TO AGNES                                          29 August 1914

. . . Since yesterday I have been thinking about our affairs and about the world in general. I want to tell you the result, though it is only a provisional result, depending on many great happenings. I don't want to seem dramatic or anything but quiet and sensible. You say you are not in love with me although you love me. I must needs accept that position, though also I must still believe that your love for me will prove to be a bigger and deeper thing than you think. Bless thee for it anyhow, in whatever degree it is! Well, for a long while I have been "pressing a suit" upon you, and always for one reason or another you would not wholeheartedly accept it. Meanwhile the little world in which we live has been greatly changed by the changes in the big world outside. The chance of my having to volunteer seemed at first very small but with the advance of the German troops it grows daily a more serious possibility. The war, one is beginning to see, is a more tremendous thing than has been upon the earth for many ages. For good or ill we have all to play some part or other in it, and our own affairs must sink before it. Therefore I fear I have no right any longer to press my suit upon you before you go home, and I will try not to do so.

[On the anniversary of the French defeat by Germany and the loss of Alsace-Lorraine in 1870, Olaf's thoughts turned, as they would repeat-

edly *in the next five months, to the problem of how to respond to the*
*call to arms.*]

Annery
1 September 1914
in bed chewing apples
Anniversary of Sedan

TO AGNES

. . . I told Mother I had been *thinking* of applying. She had just been
talking of the urgent need of checking the Germans. But my remark was
a horrid blow, & I felt like a murderer & a matricide. I proceeded to be
much enraged with me and her and the Kaiser. It was as if I had said I
was going to be shot tomorrow. So I have shut up for the present. But it's
rather disgusting to have to sit still and hear of the advance on Paris, and
to see all these fellows getting ready. Guess I *must* go sooner or later if
things don't vastly improve. But Mother would be all to pieces if I even
applied for a commission now. Might quietly apply without saying until
the actual offer came, which would probably not be for months. We'll
see. . . .

Between now and your going we will see as much of each other as
possible, and I will be whatever you want me to be, but I will certainly
be in love with you. The rest is God's affair. So also is the war. A great
and inscrutable God is he; a terrible and a loving. People will insist on
calling him the one or the other, whereas he is both. He, if he is at all,
has a mighty sense of humour. . . . He knocks the heads of the nations
together and laughs when they take vengeance not on him but on each
other, calling him their ally all the while. He fills the soldiers with madness, and makes young workmen to sacrifice wife and home and good
work in order that they may satisfy their own longing to be courageous.
He breaks off all threads of innumerable lives and innumerable noble
works, and bids men to kill, destroy, and cease from holiness. To some
he appears simply as a god of battles, to others as a good god harassed by
the Devil. Some say there is no god now, others say God is not loving
but terrible. Some see all around that he is terrible, and know by his
clear message in their hearts that he is gentle. The wise will accept God
as a war god and also as a loving god.

[*Olaf wrote Agnes two letters on 2 October, one to be sent to her imme-*
*diately at Garsdale, the other to be posted to South Africa to await her*
*arrival on board a Blue Funnel liner at Capetown on her journey*
*home. The first complains about her behavior toward him in the*
*present; the second imagines the degree to which in the future they each*
*will become disembodied to the other.*]

TO AGNES                                2 October 1914

. . . Now my dear I was very chilly and sour to you yesterday, simply because you "took me for granted." That sort of thing is horrid. I don't want to do it. I used always to *try* not to. But now I won't try not to, because I won't be treated that way even by the sweetest girl in the world. You say that when we have "muddles" you want to go home at once. I want you to go too under those circumstances. I get in a horrid bad temper, and wish you were at the other end of the world till you like me better. But let us not have any more muddles before you go. It would be such a pity if we did. I shall not try to take more than you want to give; but if you are indifferent to me, well, I shall be indifferent to you, and wish you far away, and I shall simply work and leave you alone. If you find you want that, you see how to get it.


Central Hotel, Workington

Agnes,                                  2 October 1914

You will get this at Cape Town, and I shall see you often between now and then. It is strange to be writing you a letter which you will not get for some weeks. I hope you will have had a merry voyage untroubled by German cruisers. We shall all be thankful when you have safely landed in Australia.

Now, it is no use my telling you news because you know all that I know at present . . . reading this letter a few weeks hence in the Southern hemisphere, looking back on all these days as far past and already prehistoric. How strangely far away England will seem by then! You will be settled down into the life of the ship, with new friends and new interests, and I shall be no more than a sort of phantom. Well, bless thee, and be happy, and do not forget. . . .

[*Next day.*] Go out to your home land and see if when you are settled there you do not hear a voice calling you back to England. When you have influenced your friends a little with the "good word" you bring from Europe, and when you have given more of yourself to your home (as is right) and when you have stored up in yourself more of that precious colonial ideal which is so much needed here at home, then truly you will begin to think of England again and then also you will begin to need me and to want to give yourself to me. It will surely be so. Meanwhile we will each go our way, and talk across the world a little.


[*Agnes stayed at Annery the night before boarding the* Aeneas *in Liverpool with her cousin Dot, who was returning to New Zealand. Olaf*

Annery
11 October 1914

Agnes, dearest of girls,

May the "Aeneas" carry thee safely and steadily all the way home, and may the voyage be a happy one and pass quickly! She is a good ship and a sea-worthy, and the Germans will not come nigh thee. But we shall be looking anxiously for her arrivals. Bless thee, maiden! I know we shall meet again soon, but I always realise your goings away so keenly. . . . Well, change is the order of this world, and I will be thankful for the long time I have spent with you, and look forward confidently to an even better era. You will not forget now, will you? . . . And if tonight you are heavy-hearted at leaving us all, remember when you are dropping off to sleep amid the sea noises that there is someone to whom you are dearer than all other souls. . . . And remember that if I loved you in Switzerland and Paris and elsewhere, it is all nothing beside the love I have for you now, and all my doing shall be worthy of you, and you for your part shall be always worthy of the best that I can give. . . .

At this very moment you are singing away upstairs, so happily. Get through life singing so. It is easy when all goes well, but let us two learn to do that also when things go ill, if ever they do. And we cannot expect to have things always so rosy as they have been.

Remember, you shall go through all the past two years in your mind again, and find out the real meaning of it all to you—Germany, France, England, music, and all that you have gained thereby in knowledge of the richness of life and in delicacy to appreciate the finer influences of it. And underlying all that you will find that there is a secret dear thing, I hope, which is our love for one another.

Good-bye for the present, my dear.

On board the "Aeneas"
[dispatched from Holyhead, Wales]
12 October 1914

Olaf,

The Captain just told us we might send letters by the pilot in 20 minutes time so we tore down from the boat deck & are perched on the sofa in our cabin scribbling. We are getting on alright. It all seems like a dream. Annery is most real—then Home & then the Aeneas. Thank you for your letter. I read it tonight & Dot read hers aloud to me. It was very dreadful saying goodbye. It wasn't the ordinary kind of goodbyes. I felt just like you said in Dot's letter. It will be alright tomorrow but today there was a sudden overwhelming feeling which made me choke.

Heaven, it is hard to go away & to be left behind. We felt two forlorn little specks without an anchor & we didn't want to do anything but now it is better & we have had dinner sitting one each side of the captain. He is a dear chap & will be very kind I'm sure. We are not struck on the passengers, but now that we feel better I feel sure they will look more hopeful. It is quite calm & I am a good sailor tonight. . . . Tonight I shall "think" before I go to sleep & ask that some day I may come back to you if it is best for both of us. Surely God knows what is right. His will be done. Good night—God bless you & make you not to be too sad.

Annery

Agnes, dearest of girls,                                    13 October 1914

Yesterday you sailed, and today I must needs write to catch you at Adelaide. When you read this, that good-bye of yesterday will seem a dim past event, but to me writing it is near and still horrible. . . . [This morning] I came home and behold there was a little letter from thee posted at sea. I read it, and behold I wept. If will had power I should have found myself winged and flying to thee, so very much I longed to be with thee again. Yes indeed, it was a different good-bye from all others that I have known, and very overwhelming. . . .

[15 October.] I cannot tell what you will be feeling when you get this; but I think you will not be caring less for me. But remember that a long absence blunts the edge of affections, and if as the months roll on you feel the past sinking into a blur, and feel very contented simply to be at home and have me as a distant admirer, do not think that therefore you are not meant to marry me and that you do not love me enough. To some extent you are sure to feel that. I shall also sometimes doubtless, and you will do so more. But keep alive for my sake the little flame that I have given thee, and if it declines let it never go utterly out. Keep it alive till I come again to make of it a bright fire of love. No, I will not let thee cool. I'll write to thee so often and so lovingly that thou will surely be eager for me even before the time when I can come. . . .

Do you know, when I am writing to you all kinds of foolish pretty little pet names and adjectives for you seem to come bubbling out of my heart and trickling down into the ink of my pen—names and phrases such as I would never dream of using to you in real life, because I feel always that your mind is not quite made up and so the little phrases never occur to me to say. But when I am writing to you that notion is only in the background; and so the phrases come flocking, and I have to drive them back with a smile at myself, because they would seem so odd in a letter, with no existence in real life. Yet sometimes a few of the

Agnes Miller, left, and her New Zealander cousin Dorothy Miller, right, aboard the *Aeneas* en route to Australia, October 1914.

company slip in, and I find myself saying "You know, dear, it is right" or "Darling girl, do not forget." And this time, if you please, I caught myself in the act of saying to you "dearie," as a Scotch lover to his lass, or as your own mother to yourself. But the word fits you when you are sweet and inclined to spoil me and are all smiles that make my heart jump for joy. Also, somehow in a letter I want to say "thou" and "thee" all the while, but in real life I should never remember to do so! . . .

Now I must stop! And if this letter is all love and somewhat in a minor key, remember it is only a day or two since we lost you two dear girls. But I myself am not in the minor key. Whatever happens you have put me in the major now until I die. For the world is clearly an affair of great hopes and fears and of long battles that are glorious which ever way they end. The world is like a great Beethoven sonata, not a Tschaikowski symphony. Yes indeed, in some funny old way there is much similarity between the world and Beethoven Op. 10, No. 1. And he, deeply puzzling, as in the picture you gave me, got as near to the true meaning of things as Shakespeare or Carlyle. And for a little understanding of him, not as a musical artist but as a musically speaking prophet, I thank thee and all those playings thou hast done at Annery. For music was a beautiful foreign language to me before you came.

S.S. Aeneas
just out of the Bay of Biscay

TO OLAF                            15 October 1914

. . . This is the afterlunch doze time & I am half asleep as I write. Most of the people are lying about under the boats on rugs & cushions but a few stray parsons and things are wandering up & down with their hands behind their backs. The sea is fizzling & swishing against the ship sides & the engines are making a great din in the background but it seems very quiet although all the air is full of noises, & when anyone speaks, that noise seems to be the biggest noise of all. Every day it gets warmer & warmer. I guess it will soon be quite hot & we shall be skipping round in white dresses & agitating for the swimming bath to be put up. Did you get my little note from Holyhead? . . .

Friday 16. . . . Last night we had an adventure. Dee & I were up under the bridge after dinner looking at stars & speculating as to how many planets there were & what their names were & whether they steered the ship by the stars etc. etc. when the Captain came up & we asked him to solve these problems, but he turned round & called to an old man who was leaning over the railing. "Mr. Reid, come inform these ladies"—so Mr. Reid came & he proved to be just as Scotch as the skipper himself. First we talked about stars & then we went round the other side to see the comet—Uncle's comet [observed by William Stapledon through the Annery telescope?]—& then Dot got very keen on comets & their doings & this Mr. Reid was just about to lie flat down on the deck & describe parabolas when the Captain invited them to come & do it in his room instead, so we all migrated & spent the whole evening—$1\frac{1}{2}$ hours—drawing hieroglyphics etc. on a bit of paper. Dot fired in endless questions & made sound remarks & was altogether sweet & interested & interesting. Mr. Reid is a scientist, an astronomer assisting at the Cape Observatory & as keen as mustard. The skipper & I sat quiet & excited & followed as well as we could, but Dot had the inside running alright. Her questions were absolute stunners & took away the poor little man's breath. He kept grasping the arms of his chair convulsively & looking keenly & timidly from one to the other of us as if to ask—now where is one to begin on such a huge problem? Then we would all laugh & again plunge into unknown depths. After Mr. Reid, the Captain had a go on navigation which is also a thrilling science & we got onto refraction & taking observations etc. etc. & then had some tales of his adventures in the China Seas & at last we left & sallied forth into the pitchy darkness of the boat deck for a last run before bed time.

Annery

My dear Agnes,                                                    21 October 1914

We have heard of your arrival at Las Palmas, and we hope to have letters in a few days. . . . Annery continues to miss your presence, in spite of the fact that Auntie Sara keeps us all alive with hideous forebodings about the war. She expects the Germans in Hoylake any minute, sees nothing but German success in all the news, and scolds our fleet for its inaction. She is of a mercurial disposition and cannot endure things to sit still. She is full of Nietzsche, whom she regards as a kind of diabolic supreme genius. It all lends interest to life! She and Mother never read anything but the papers, and all the most lurid passages in them. When Auntie Sophia was here also the house was simply a sanctuary of pessimists. . . .

University Settlement

Agnes,                                                          25 October 1914

I have just come back from Crewe where I was holding forth rather ineffectually on the growth of Prussia. It is really very unsatisfactory to lecture when you have to get up the subject as you go along, and do most of your reading in the train, too. Moreover this is not my subject, and I could have done much better at literature. Still, it is the subject of the hour, and one must just do as well as one can. All my classes are going pretty well; sometimes we have very exciting evenings, but sometimes things are a bit dead and I have to try and buck them up, which works all right when I am feeling full of buck, but otherwise not. . . . I see all kinds of people and get a lot out of it all, for myself, but what good it really does I don't always see. It's no use pretending that it is "university standard," because neither the lectures nor the students are really anywhere near that. I have to cover too much ground in the time. Sometimes people say things which make one see how utterly they fail to grasp the meaning of history, and one wants to weep. But others are too well read already to get much good out of a course that must needs be superficial and elementary. Well, well, it's all in the day's work; and if it's only pioneering perhaps it will lead to something real and substantial some day. . . .

*Workington*, 10.45 pm [28 October]. We have had a most exciting discussion again. There is a journalist called Moore who is very well read, very quick witted, and very cynical. He is at bottom a good fellow, but rabid as to his cynicism, which is a nuisance, as it is dangerous to let such stuff pass unchallenged, and if one does challenge it one has to enter into a long close argument which is almost sure to be a mere logical duel. He is engrossed in the great idea that all peoples have been eternally gulled, which is very largely true, but it won't stand being ridden to death. . . .

One fellow has left this class to join the colours today, a fine strong Cumberland fellow with a simple mind. But most of the class are much against the war, especially Moore, whose distrust of all governments necessitates that position. Heavens, I don't know whether we are more or less to blame than the German government. We have all been afraid of one another, and been in a hurry to get in the first whack. Talking to Eric [Patterson, another resident at the Settlement] has modified my views very much. Germany thinks about it *exactly* as we do only the other way about. Which, pray, is really right? Well it is all very perplexing, but the fact remains that we have to do our best to drive them out of France now, and more & more of us will be needed as time goes on. But there will come an age, far off, when people will talk about this time and say "That was just one of the cases when men could not realise their common interest. It was so between Athens and Sparta, & so between Florence and Venice, and between England and Holland, & then also it was so between all the states of Europe. The Athenian should have felt Greek, the Florentine Italian, and the Englishman European." And so it will be a hard thing if one has to drop all one's plans to learn to fight in a cause one is not confident about against people whom one cannot think of as enemies merely. But war is a hard thing for everyone. Think

of the millions of interlacing trails of private misery it lays! Think of all
the life ideals wrecked, first and last, and all for what?


                                                    S.S. Aeneas
TO OLAF                                 [undated; ca. 31 October 1914]
. . . We hope to get in [at Cape Town] about noon & are going to join
some party or other & do the sights. We had an awful farewell dinner at
our table tonight. Dee was well out of it. I felt like a fish out of water.
Champagne flowed at the command of a dashing coarse commercial
traveller at the end of the table, & one couldn't do anything but drink to
the health of the departing guests. I wish he were departing—Mr.
Geber—but he never troubles us; afterwards we had to grasp hands &
sing "for auld lang syne" & I'm sure I don't wish to see any of those
people again except the skipper who was on my right hand. He didn't
like it either, but he looked happier than I did because he's a man & can
talk rot to pretty women & be amused or pretend to be, but it makes me
sick. That's not our set at all. After all that pandemonium was ended the
skipper came in to see Dot & have a yarn & when he was gone I ran up
into the boat deck to blow the champagne away & borrow a book for
Dot & it was funny—I asked for one book & I came down with 12 in my
arms. The officers' and engineers' quarters were turned upside down to
find something interesting. Jimmy [Exley, a crewman] produced 10
thrillers from the depths & 2 other officers made up the dozen. Dot is a
favourite; she's so jolly & can always find interesting things to talk to
them about: I get on well with Jimmy in a steady old sort of way talking
about the tangible subjects such as engineering & slumming & sports &
friends & passengers and decorum & the care of my cousin Dot. But I
find it much harder talking to the others unless I'm being giddy & frivolous. Then it's easy enough. I didn't intend going on to another page.
It's such dry old stuff too. Don't think I've gone all off the lines. I haven't
really, it's only the effect of 3 weeks aboard ship with nothing to do but
talk & do nothing. I can't settle to reading. . . . I shall get your letter
tomorrow that you wrote ages ago, but I'd much rather be home & get
real proper letters written at a later date. Fancy four more wks! The sea is
good & she's a good ship & she's quite like home & we're quite comfy &
happy, but we *do* want to get home quick. . . . I don't know whether
you're a dream or Home is a dream, it's such a funny misty feeling. I
don't know where I am but it's alright. I'm going home & I know that
you are there at the other end—two landmarks.
    So good night & God Bless you Olaf.

                                                    with love from
                                                    Agnes

[*For several months after the declaration of war Olaf agonized over
whether to give up his position as a WEA tutor and enlist. His moods
alternated between the patriotic fervor of this letter and growing doubts
about the morality of the war.*]

Annery
TO AGNES                                                8 November 1914
. . . Things have changed since last week. They are calling for more
men. Conscription is not impossible, which will make an increase in
the commissions to be had. I devoutly hope they won't have conscription, because it will cause such fearful difficulties. But I do want my
commission. I am tired of letting other people fight while I dream. I
wish the training was not such a long job. That is the wearisome part,
especially as if there comes peace soon all the training is waste. But
there is greater waste than that in the world just now. Heaven what a
world! Belloc estimates the German losses up to date at $1\frac{3}{4}$ millions in-
clusive of prisoners. (Do you remember my prophecy that the war
would last a fortnight?) A man in my Preston class said the other day, "If
there is conscription I hope I have the courage to shoot myself rather
than go!" I admire that attitude, but I don't quite think it is sound. Killing is a low down vulgar trick not worthy of a civilized gentleman, but
our moral powers of suasion are not yet sufficiently developed to with-
stand the German armies, still less to make them retire; and as we don't
want the Germans here, we must needs fight. And we certainly can't sit
still and watch our friends die for us. So here is one more for His Majesty, and Kitchener, but more especially for England, which in spite of
her hypocrisy and snobbery and vulgarity is still England of Agincourt
and the Armada and Shakespeare and Browning and many millions of
passably noble souls. So here is one more for England, and also for Humanity. Alas! poor Humanity, like a mad thing tearing its own flesh.

[*William Stapledon subsidized his son's first book, a collection of poems
modeled on the rhythms of the Hebrew psalms. Published by a small
Liverpool firm,* Latter-Day Psalms *is now the rarest of Olaf's books,
much of the remaining stock having been incinerated during the German bombing of Liverpool in the* 1940s.]

Annery
TO AGNES                                               17 November 1914
. . . The Psalms are definitely going to be published, first edition of 500
copies at 2/6, second 500 paper-bound at 1/—I hope. I wish it could all
be done for 6d, but it would be too hard on Father's pocket. It's jolly

good of him to take the job on at all. In fact it's ripping. We have hit on a good title: "Latter Day Psalms." On the fly leaf will be this passage from Carlyle's "Latter Day Pamphlets."—"There must be a new world, if there is to be any world at all! That human things in our Europe can ever return to the old sorry routine, and proceed with any steadiness and continuance there; this small hope is not now a tenable one. These days of universal death must be days of universal new birth, if the ruin is not to be total and final! It is a Time to make the dullest man consider; and ask himself, Whence *he* came? Whither he is bound?—A veritable 'New Era,' to the foolish as well as to the wise." What do you think of that, I wonder. Father first suggested "Psalms of New Time." I thought it too ambitious, & "Latter Day Psalms" flashed on me. Then father jumped up to get a good extract & found the above on page 2. Critics will say the great Carlyle wrote "pamphlets" and the little Stapledon wrote "psalms," but never mind! . . . Now my dear, this book, which may or may not prove a success, should by rights be dedicated to A.Z.M. since she inspired it so, and helped directly not a little also. But how can I dedicate it when I am not sure if you would like it so? Well, there is a tacit dedication to you in most of the pieces, very clearly to be seen in some. And the whole thing strives to be full of the best of you. As to its attainment, I am alternately very disgusted and fairly satisfied. Someday something bigger and better shall openly bear your mark, if you will allow. . . .

With regard to my commission, things stand thus: I don't seriously *want* to go one little bit, & I tell everybody so, shamelessly. But since I obviously must, I want to go at once, and am in a positive fever to get at the job, & am full of the simple excitement & hope of experience & adventure. But the WEA stands in the way, & Mother would be very much overcome, I can see, if I were to go at Xmas instead of in March. So unless those difficulties can be overcome I shall stay till March. . . .

[*Workington.*] Last night I had tea chez one of my students with another as guest. They were chiefly engaged in trying to convince me that it was my moral duty not to get a commission at Christmas, and in arguing pessimistically about the war. There was a kid aged about four present, and I had to draw ships etc. for his majesty while arguing. I admitted the war was a catastrophe but wanted to make the best of it. They would not be comforted. I showed them my war & peace psalms, which impressed them, but only in so far as the sentiments agreed with theirs. One was the keeper of a boot shop. The other was a printer. . . . Another man told us some of the most ghastly and revolting war stories I have heard. They were his chum's experiences, & I have no doubt of their truth. I won't retail them. His chum had been right through the South African war, but he says the very worst of that was less than the everyday affairs in this. What you read in the papers is bad enough, but that is just nothing to the horrible (suppressed) reality. He was right through the retreat from Mons. He says it was simply a long fight for life on the part of individuals. There was no organisation left. Groups of men entirely on their own retreated from cover to cover as best they could, while some other miscellaneous group covered their retreat. He is a fusilier, but regiments were apparently entirely mixed up, and his nearest comrades were chiefly a Highlander and an Irishman. And he said, "Talk of running! An athlete wouldn't have caught me when it was time to retreat." But he only saw two British cowards all the while. Everyone else stuck to it to the last. He came home with a bullet through his shoulder, which is a let off. We people all agreed that we could not imagine ourselves not running away at the first shot, but of course there is no telling how one will behave in such conditions. But his stories of the trenches I will not repeat. Ever so many people are being sent home unwounded, but with shattered nerves. Officially "the army is tired out." Well, good heavens, can one sit still and wait till the spring under these circumstances! I hear rumours now that officers are wanted. If that proves true, goodbye WEA at once. Oh this miserable fool of a world! We are all part of it, and fools, and not worthy to look into the sky; for we all, the most peaceable, *want* to go and kill, or at least fight, which is the same thing. Education is a better thing than war, I suppose, and here one is, positively hoping to take on the worse job soon. And people try and persuade one not to, and one sets one's teeth against being persuaded, and could kick them for their look of disgust and disappointment in one. But heavens, someone has to do the job, however dirty it is. If only there was a real crusade-war instead of a miserable war of pot and kettle.

<br>

S.S. Aeneas<br>
Port Adelaide

TO OLAF                      [undated; ca. 29 November 1914]
. . . *Sunday morning* 8.30. We haven't had breakfast. We were all got up at 6.30 for medical inspection & the affair is only just over. We're lying 2 or 3 miles from the outer harbour of Adelaide & it's very warm. There is a purple haze rising from the hills & it all looks red brown & burnt up even at this distance. They have only had 9 inches of rain this year & the average is 20. Poor things & poor sheep & cattle inland. What must they be suffering! It's a sad country to be in just now, but it's my own home country nevertheless & My! but it was exciting yesterday at noon when we sighted the first land—that was Kangaroo Island, but it was near enough—every one of us Australians thrilled with pleasure & excitement. Then last night when we came to an anchor we could smell the land so warm & sweet under the bright starlight. I have never

known a heaven brighter with stars. It was a crescent moon but soon she disappeared to let the stars have a chance—then the Southern Cross shone out & Orion & lots of others which I don't recognise in this position. I used not to take very much interest in the stars before I left home. Now I have a new heaven to look at & it is good for me.

[*The book referred to in this letter is not* Latter-Day Psalms *but a more ambitious philosophical meditation on spiritual evolution on which Olaf worked throughout the winter of 1914–15. He mailed the "chaotic and incomplete" manuscript to Agnes on 6 April 1915.*]

Annery
TO AGNES                                                1 December 1914
. . . Now my dear, I want to talk soberly and somewhat humbly about a matter, and as briefly as possible, because I am heartily sick of it. I have been writing to you about the war in a rather feverish style, and talking about my going at Christmas. Well, I am not going at Christmas. That's fixed. I have my work to do, and I will see it through, and the better part of me knows very well that this is right. But the human part was carried away by all the drum-beating and by the longing to share in what so many good fellows are doing, and by shame at living at ease while others are in trenches, and by silent pressure of public opinion in all public places, and by knowledge that military life would be good for me, very, and indeed any kind of physical practical work after all this gasbag existence, and by a secret desire also to go right off and be a soldier for thee in the true romantic style. And so I persuaded myself I ought to go at once and I talked grandly about it, and then when it came to the point I found I really had no business to go at all yet, because, by all the stars, I must continue my four classes to the end, and I will complete the book I began, if I can do it decently. I have something to say and it must be completely said to the best of my power, and then we will see what is to be done. But drum-beating fills one with a wild desire to go off and be one of a great army, and live the grand foolish life of a soldier, & be universally (not quite) approved, and share in the deed of the age. . . .

As for the war, I grow more and more sceptical of Britain's self-righteousness. We want to win, of course, but how far it is really a war of principles it is very hard to say. Of course I may be prejudiced by the attitude of the more intelligent workers, that Britain is nearly as bad as Germany, but it seems to me that our foreign policy has really been as much to blame as theirs. . . . I don't know what you feel, but this war makes me feel more & more of a cosmopolitan. Patriotism is evil when it obscures cosmopolitanism. The papers do their best to stir up the baser sort of patriotism, which is a hostile, snobbish and egregiously foolish sort. They are succeeding very well. But England has helped to bring on the catastrophe, & so it is a point of honour with her to bear her share well, which she is doing. But as for me, I am humbled in my own eyes for turning from my past decision. I've been in a miserable state of doubt and vacillation, and I never thought I was so shaky. Really I very nearly went right off, & it would have been all wrong. . . . One more point: If by chance you have been at all worried by all my indecision and talking, Agnes, I am sorry. You are so far away, and it will be so long before you get this letter, and before I hear from you in reply. Say you forgive me for all this, and don't go worrying about me, except a little if you like. And don't go thinking I am absolutely unable to decide a thing & stick to it. It's not true, quite. And remember the temptation was to go, not to stay, to go now I mean rather than in the Spring. Here endeth the lesson. It has been a lesson, to me; and every time I hear a drumbeat I have got to remember.

[*Egremont, the Millers' home in the suburban district of Mosman in Sydney, was a typical high-ceilinged, one-story Australian house, wrapped around by a verandah, overlooking the Pacific. The name was taken from a line of Wordsworth: "Egremont sleeps by the sea." To reach the town proper, the Millers took a ferry across Sydney Harbour.*]

Egremont
Mosman, Sydney
Olaf,                                          9 December 1914
    I'm home.
    I have been home for nearly a week. We got in at 7 a.m. last Thursday & today is Wednesday, but I can't believe I'm home yet really. It feels like another port & I shall have to be moving on in a few days, but yet it is all so familiar that sometimes I forget I have been away at all. I only feel dazed & very stupid & rather uninteresting. I suppose it's only natural to be rather dazed at first when one suddenly falls plum-bang out of one world into another, specially when one fits so neatly into both worlds. . . . Everyone says I look younger than ever. Daddy expected me to be a woman & he finds I'm still a child. Isn't it heartbreaking? I don't know how to grow up. At least I don't know how to make them believe that I'm grown up. . . . I had two long letters from you this week, 21 & 25 of October—you *are* busy. And the beginnings of your book. I'm not going to talk about it this week because I haven't time & I haven't had time to read it properly. The whirl of life has begun.

Annery

TO AGNES                                                    16 December 1914

. . . We had a very good class [at Workington] though I had left my
notebook at home, & had to give it all extempore. We were doing
French social conditions. I told them all I knew about the general appearance of the South & of Normandy & Brittany (our motor tour). My
small French experience has been very useful. Then we got on to Conscription & then on to war in general, & outside my hotel, in the street,
a knot of us argued war. A strong antimilitarist tried all his arguments to
dissuade me from enlisting. He is a great dialectician, and he has
spoken at big meetings against war. He finally suggested it must be just
moral cowardice that was afraid to stand out against public opinion.
. . . Oh I am sick of all this mess we are all making. But there's collec-
tive responsibility & the burden must be shared, & the sacrifice. But
why should one kill & be killed? It's sordid, bestial, idiotic & soul-
destroying. The world might be noble surely in these days after so long
experience. But we bicker & fight and slander our enemies, and are altogether like monkeys. On the battlefield indeed there are noble things
that make one want to worship men, but it is all in such a silly cause.
Supposing Sydney & Melbourne were to heroically slaughter one another, or Liverpool and Manchester. Imagine a military clique in either
city (one rather worse than the other) and a gulled public full of Attic
provincialism, & you have an exact picture of Europe today. Yet how
can one shirk the burden that is fallen upon all? It's not moral cowardice, he can say what he likes; it's a sense of the oneness of humanity. It's
the obedient fulfilling of a divine purpose that is hidden out of sight.
But good heavens, I would sooner educate than fight, sooner get fond of
all kinds of men & women as I do in these classes, & feel that they are
fond of me, as I do, and sooner strive after a high unattainable ideal in
writing books, and sooner seek the hand of my cousin in her own land.
Oh, I'm sick of it all. Surely one must go, but it's not an inspiring thing
to do, it's just an obligation. And why do I say all this stuff to you? It
does no good, & I am sure I don't know what you think, if you do think.
Goodnight. I'm in a horrid rage with the world.

Egremont

Olaf,                                                       22 December 1914

    I got your letter this a.m. of the 8th November. I feel such a long way
away & I wish I could help you because you sounded so fearfully busy
about your classes & your book & so perplexed about enlisting. And
here am I doing nothing useful much but never having a minute to turn
round in & it seems so selfish of me & so unsympathetic not to have

time even to write a decent letter. I wonder if you have got your commission or whether you are waiting until the spring. I suspect the bombardment of the Yorkshire towns has made an incentive to the recruiting. It is so strange & terrible to think of the real horror of war having come right into our own country & among poor unoffending people who never dreamt of it.

Egremont
TO OLAF                                              29 December 1914
. . . Christmas has come & gone & now we're only waiting for New Year to be over & then we can fall to & get ready to go up to the mountains. It was a different sort of Christmas this year. I don't know why—it was a very happy one in our home—but it seemed quiet & I think we were all conscious of the cloud that must be hanging over so many poor homes. . . . We had 9 people to tea on Christmas day & then Dad took Rosie & me to hear the Messiah. . . .

We are going up the Mts. to Blackheath on Jan. 9th. We have got a cottage for 3 wks called "Cymbeline." I shall tell you all about the bush up there & the mountains.

Annery
TO AGNES                                             30 December 1914
. . . The other night I was reading the Indian poet Rabindranath Tagore. Do you know him? I have never really bothered about him before. He has translated his own poems into English prose. . . . The root idea is that the soul has to purify herself for her marriage with God, and has also to sing a perfect song before him—her perfect life. These things are very mystical and unreal in these days of war. Yet if you once get absorbed in them it is the war that seems unreal. The thing to do is to keep a balance in one's mind between realism and idealism, matter-of-fact and fantasy, and between the particular & the universal. It is easy to be entirely absorbed in this great affair, and feel that the world is war, and that war is all that matters now. It is also not very hard to look at it all from a lofty place and say it is a little meaningless squabble on a mean little planet, and even to the planet it is the event of—an age, but not of all time. But one has to keep a clear view of it all both from within and without if one wants ever to play one's part either outside it or inside it. I begin to think one will never be able to play one's part in the world, in one's small way, outside unless one has also played it inside this war. That is filling me with rather a scare as to the future. But enough of that. . . .

[*Midnight*] 1915. God bless thee, Agnes, and make thee to live happy and die happy. The whistles are shrieking their welcome to the New Year, and so are the bells—commercialism drowns religion in the contest, I fear! Was there ever such a new year, surely not upon this earth. Oh God bless thee, and all that are dear to thee. And God give us Peace, and help us all to bear our share and to forget ourselves. . . . Perhaps in 1916 we shall meet. Someone else may turn up for you meanwhile. You are absolutely a free girl. You have never committed yourself. But I for my part am dead sure, and always shall be unless facts undeniably prove me wrong. Now I must go to bed. My dear, it's odd, but every month that passes finds me more full of longing to be with you again. I ought to be getting used to your absence by now. All sane persons would! Girl, I want to feel you really in my arms once more, I want to feel that soft cheek again, and to have the real wonderful presence of you, and I want to be yours. And I want to strive after all sorts of great and marvelous things with you. But there is another thing to be done first. Goodnight. God be with thee. One little kiss for thee.

X Olaf

# 〜〜〜 *1915*

*[Beatrice and Alfred Fryer, Agnes' hosts when she stayed in Rouen in 1913 and 1914, told Olaf about the Ambulance Unit established by the Society of Friends and the work it was doing. From this point forward the Friends' Ambulance Unit became Olaf's goal for a kind of war service that would satisfy his desire to participate in the suffering without joining in the fighting.]*

Garsdale,
Liverpool
TO AGNES                                                    9 January 1915

. . . I am so glad you have grown to love the stars. I think the night sky is the greatest of all churches. One is not always in the mood to go to that particular church, for sometimes one is too busy with the earth to bother about the stars; but even at those times if one is forced to be under the stars a while, say walking home at night, one soon begins willy nilly to listen to them, and it is as if a door were opened in one's mind, and one were to walk out of oneself into heaven. There is only one time when the stars are not calming. That is when one is already in revolt against the earth and its laws. Then it is appalling to think of the inevitable machinery of the universe, grinding on for ever and ever, producing life and destroying it, careless altogether of its children, caring only about the will of the great Engineer, which will is by no means ours. That is a nightmare. Yet I think that even from that the best awakening is not to run away from it, so to speak, and drown oneself in this little world, but to stay out in the night and make oneself to feel that it is not just a great factory building, but indeed a church after all, wherein is a spirit or a God to be loved more than one's little self. Then it all goes right again. But it is hard to reach that point, and one easily slops back into egotism. . . .

[11 *January.*] Letters came from Beatrice and Alfred today, yes actually a quite long typed epistle from Alfred, about his Friends Corps. They have two centres, in the French midlands & on the Belgian front respectively. *If* I apply I shall only apply for the latter, but I have not carefully considered the matter yet. The great, very great advantage is that it would get one on to the continent at once; but then against that—well, one does not want to shirk the fighting. I'll tell you later.

> Cymbeline
> Hat Hill Rd., Blackheath
> 10 January 1915

Blue Mountains—just think of it Olaf—I wish you were here. I have wished for you so many times today. It has been our first picnic & I loved all the silver-stemmed blue gums with their tall graceful forms & the ferns & streams & the blue haze in the valley & the red sandstone cliffs away in the distance among the purple shadows & the big white dreamy clouds floating peacefully above the long flat hill tops. I loved it all with a great big rejoicing in the bottom of my heart & I longed for you to be here loving it with me.

[*Michael Graveson, from Wallasey near Liverpool, was a Quaker friend of Margaret Miller, Agnes' mother. Because Olaf was not a Quaker, his sponsors (as well as his father's offer to donate an ambulance) were important to his chances of being accepted for work in the Friends' Ambulance Unit. Robert Darbishire was Olaf's closest literary friend from his Oxford days.*]

> Garsdale

TO AGNES                                26 January 1915

. . . This morning I had two nice letters from two nice people. One was from Miss Graveson replying to a request that her father would be one of my sponsors for the Friends corps (in case they can find me a job). It was a sweet letter all overflowing kindliness to me and to the rest of humanity. She hopes I shall get a job, so that I may continue the social-work kind of existence. But I won't unless I can get an essential, strenuous & if possible perilous job; for it would be terrible to feel one was shirking hardship and danger. I shall not hear my fate for some time now. I have sent in a formal application, including Father's offer of a motor & expenses. But I want a more intimate & pedestrian job *if possible*, especially as Mother is worried about motor cars! My other sponsor will be Auntie Nina, so I have reason to be proud of my Quaker godfather & godmother! The second letter that I got was a long one from Robert passing judgment on my book. I opened it with a mixture of dread and deliberate nonchalance, fearing slaughter. But it began with "It is my quite private opinion in your ear that the psalms of David had best look to their laurels," which is a note of laudatory banter not common with Robert.

[*Ailsa Craig, whom Agnes said she had the best talks with of all her friends, left Australia at the end of 1916 to become an actress in London under the name Ailsa Graham.*]

Cymbeline
TO OLAF                                                          1 February 1915
. . . We've had 15 visitors altogether in the 3 weeks. We have all done the work of the house except Mother & it was light work—two meals out every day except twice we hardly ever got back before 8.30 pm sometimes it was 10.30—& there were glorious marches home along the roads in the starlight all singing or whistling & swinging along at a good pace. Rosie had her "gang" the first week—Jean & the 3 boys, Lionel, Cliff & Bill. Next week I had Ailsa, & the third week it was a mixture with family friends & all sorts of more grown up people. Ailsa was a dear. I feel that I have more sympathy with her than with any other of my friends—strange because she is the last made friend & the youngest. She is only 18, but she thinks & loves telling what she thinks to anyone who understands. We slept in a tent, Ailsa & I, in the bush by the house—one night somehow I told her about you and me. It was a knock & she was silent. Then she climbed out of her bed & up over onto my stretcher & I told her all about it & she kissed me very hard & we both somehow nearly wept, but we laughed at a lot that I told her. She said we must be a very funny couple. I assured her that we were very ordinary really & she said "Well anyway—I don't half like *that young man*. What right has he? I knew you long before *he* did."

[*Ruth Fry, Secretary of the Friends' War Victims' Relief Committee, had just returned to London from a visit to the Belgian front. The chairman of the Friends' Ambulance Unit Committee, who interviewed all applicants to the Unit, was the physician Sir George Newman.*]

Annery
TO AGNES                                                        10 February 1915
. . . On Monday I see Miss Fry of the Friends. I will tell you results. I am hopeful, from what I see in the "Friend," and I am getting very keen, and am always thinking about it all, which keeps one awake. Six

weeks yet, but there's a lot to learn in that time. So far they have carried over five thousand, no, very nearly ten thousand, wounded "into places of safety," and covered about 30,000 kilometres in all. That is the department I want, I think, but one must take what comes. . . .

We are in the dawn of a new age, a new truth; don't you feel it in the air, like the spring? Isn't it good to play a little part, however small, in such a spring? See—I am going to France to save life (I hope) and to do all kinds of odd jobs. But there is another thing too. I am going, I hope, to be some small practical use for once in a way. But also I am going to keep my eyes and ears open, and the whole soul of me open to behold the ways of men and women, and the terrible ways of God. . . . And afterwards, DV [*Deo volente*, "God willing"], I will put my little stone into the building of the new temple, and it shall be carved with care, for what it is worth. But first comes the spade work, and I want to begin. I say, do you think these letters are high flown idealism and dreamery? Do you think I am always talking about this subject? I *think* even more. You see, one must have a little idealist spice to season this appalling stew. It *is* a sort of gigantic stew. Whole tribes and peoples all in the pot wallowing in their own gravy, while the fragrance thereof ascends— whither? as Carlyle would say. A feast for the gods! Savage pagan deities, some would say. . . .

My dear, I do so want to *talk* to you. Writing is so slow. I want to talk as we have never talked before, real hard hammer-and-tongs talk about all things. But that is impossible while we live on two sides of a brick wall. The Pyramus and Thisbe chink is not enough. We have such a lot to teach each other. You can't learn through a chink, at least I can't. I want to make a breach. This is a double barrelled parable, for first the brick wall is the solid earth between us, second it is an intangible thing which must I suppose always be between us till I have found the way to convince you—make you love me in fact. Dot and I can talk on end and lose ourselves in the subject, because there is no intangible thing, no undecided question deep down behind. But with you and me, there is a fundamental query which prevents complete self forgetfulness, & must till it is answered. And yet you know when we do forget that question, or (better) assume it answered, we do find we have something sound to give one another. But now we must just wait, there's no time for lovemaking yet, and it would be out of place. But someday we have still to discover one another—after the war.

Egremont

TO OLAF                                               15 February 1915

. . . Harry Day of whom you have heard & who spent a few days with us up at Blackheath never spoke two words of his fiancée the whole

An Australian bush picnic at Blackheath in the Blue Mountains. Agnes is
seated in the center. Standing on the left is her sister Ruth ("Peter"); the boy
on the log is her brother Waldo. (Courtesy of Mrs. Ruth Fletcher)

time. He never mentions her to anyone—c'est bien pour l'homme dans
la rue—but I was grieved because we used to be very good friends. I
asked him one day why he didn't tell me ever about Daisy & he said
there was nothing to tell! & soon changed the subject. What rot! Harry's
two topics of conversation are architecture (his own of preference) &
courage—bravery rather—instinctive & premeditated. The last night
he was with us he showed me the plans of his own house which he is
building & he waxed very keen over them & all his modern conveniences & labour saving contrivances. It will be a perfectly sweet house
for he is artistic & knows what is what—but still never a word of the
future mistress of that house. Well, people are very different. Olaf, you

have spoilt me for these lads. They are all dears just as they always were & they are manly & they are bushmen & fine swimmers & they know how to manage a sailing craft & an oil launch & a picnic & they will get up at 5 o'clock & light a fire for you as Harry did when Ailsa went down early to Sydney—or they will get up & fossick round for their own breakfast to save your getting up—but there is something wanting. Oh Olaf am I a pig to be talking like that? Well you know I am not a deserter really—so I don't mind you. Harry was fearfully funny when he was up. I think he felt he was on the loose—he certainly looked so. He went round in the most awful old clothes & used to make himself look as much of a lory kin as possible just to amuse us. I didn't think he would deign to look awful because in town he is a model of convention & respectability—& all day he kept up a constant flow of twopenny songs interspersed with penny monologues. When we were in the house he was always popping through Mother's window & sitting on her bed talking to her. On the day he went down to town he appeared at 6.45 am. at our bedroom door & seeing Saidee & me fast asleep in our big bed he entered & stood & gazed at us until we woke up in a dazed fashion— then he raised his straw hat & beamed good morning at us & said he had come to say goodbye. Presently he went—& after waking all the other girls in his hail fellow friendly sort of way shouldered his suitcase & tramped away along the road in the fresh morning air to the station. From there he was whirled back to town & I haven't seen him since. Nice lad. Queer lad.

Garsdale

TO AGNES                                                   17 February 1915

. . . On Monday I managed to see Sir George Newman's secretary, himself being absent. The main thing that will stand in my way is that I am not a Friend—members of the society naturally get preference. But they are attracted by my offer of a car. At present I am quite in the dark, but I wrote a formal application to the big pot Sir G, and hope for a favourable reply, though they never can *promise* anything beforehand. I have to take St. John's Ambulance Certificate, which can be done in five weeks. I hope to start next week, and then it is just possible, though I fear very improbable, that I may be at Dunkirk in six weeks, i.e. end of March. They have a hospital at Dunkirk & a field hospital at Ypres. Of course one wants the latter, but only a few get there. At present they are dealing almost exclusively with typhoid, but in the Spring they expect to return to field Ambulance work. I have made up my mind to do all I can to get this job, & if I can't in the end, to get some other similar Red Cross job. There must be lots to do in that line, but I would sooner be with Friends, for I like them & also they are a corps with a reputation.

Moreover if one gets accepted for that off one goes straight to France. So wish me luck—Dunkirk & then Ypres.

                                                      Annery
TO AGNES                                              28 February 1915
. . . Learning to drive a motor is good sport, especially on narrow wind-ing by-roads with a ditch on each side—quite thrilling, especially for a novice. I am also learning all about the insides of the beast, and that is an arduous task in the extreme. My brain is full of "sparking plugs," "gudgeon pins," "carburetors," "exhaust valves," "clutches," & "throt-tles." Unfortunately it is also full of "scapula," "fibula," "complicated fractures," "spinal columns" and "femurs," and I begin to forget which are human and which mechanical. Add to that another category of "Metternich," "moujik," "zemstoo," "Kulturkampf," "Italia Irridenta," and "Magyarortzag," and you have a picture of the mental condition of your very humble servant. I have arranged to attend an ambulance class, after much fruitless search. I know the man who takes this, & he is one of heaven's born teachers, & he will arrange a special private exam for me as soon as I feel ready. Sir George Newman, replying to Mr. Graveson, says my not being a Friend shall not stand in the way, and he implies that he will probably have work for me. So I am content, for the time being. But there is a fearful lot to learn, & I still have my four classes, & this week an inspector is coming to two of them, and also I have a lecture at Birkenhead on "Poets' Gods" (if you please). Life is going to be very busy. I am fearfully keen and at the same time not alto-gether confident. Merely to hear the descriptions of these awful wounds and blowings to pieces turns me sick, I must confess. What it will be like to live with them I don't know, but I suppose one will get used to it, and one must just try to screw oneself up at first, and not make a fool of oneself. Anyhow, it will all be typhoid at first. Miss Graveson has been so kind to me in this affair, in lots of ways; and now she is going to get me access to the "worst" cases at the L'pool Dispensaries, to learn how to dress burns and wounds.

                                                      Garsdale
TO AGNES                                              9 March 1915
. . . I am fearfully busy with motor & ambulance & WEA,—simply up to my eyes, & my brain is a whirl. At driving I think I do very well—so they say, anyhow, & I should be quite proficient for *ordinary* work after a day or two more. I am not the slightest atom nervous, which gives one a good start. This evening I was at an ambulance class again—bandag-ing, & listening to a lecture on hemorrhage & how to stop it. A vast

time was spent on cut throats! There is a lot to learn, but I have a little
book for that & motors, & I take them everywhere. Now I am dying to
be finally accepted & have my uniform, & no longer be thought a mere
civilian shirker. Then there is inoculation for typhoid, & vaccination,
& then away. Put it at four weeks. I wonder. I saw a man today with a
cut nose that made a horrid mess, though it was nothing. It was revolting. What will war be like!

[The Friend, *the weekly London newspaper of the Society of Friends,
became one of Agnes's primary sources of information about Olaf's work
during his four years in the ambulance corps. "Peter" is the nickname of
the youngest Miller daughter, Ruth.*]

Egremont
12 March 1915

Thank you, Olaf, for your letters. They are a blessing. I wait for mail
days now like you do. It's such a trial when they don't come through,
isn't it? Never mind, it's better to wait for them & not have them come
than not to wait at all. I mean to write lots because it's quite a long time
since I wrote—the last was only a scribble in the train coming from
Ryde—& since then I have had a little short one from you in answer to
my first from home, and also a long good one just like I wanted telling
me all sorts of things—nice things. Your first letter made me think what
a queer girl I must have been when I got home & wrote you that 'dazed'
sort of letter. I didn't like myself a bit in those days . . . & now I feel
quite socially disposed & yet quite content just to be at home. Everybody is lovely but Olaf I have wanted you more than ever I did & I can't
have you yet—so I want your letters fearfully. Oh thank you for them.
Write often even if it's only a line. You will be enlisting in some thing or
other this month. I'd love to know about it. Will it be with the Friends? I
am glad of your "godfather" & "godmother." We were reading about the
Friends' work in the "Friend." It sounds very splendid. I should be glad
to think of you there if you can get the sort of job you want. I wish I
could know before 6 weeks what you are doing.

I love what Robert says about your book. I begin to like Robert, he
must be a good sort of chap. I hope with him that "you won't get killed."
If you did, it would cost me all my courage & strength &—faith to be
friends with the world & myself.

I should *be* friends. I feel I should because—why everyone has been
helping me ever since I was born. And all the little things of the last two
years have helped me & the big things more. You are the biggest thing.
Heaven! Have I ever written you or anyone a letter like this before! It is

only a confession on paper, for I have known it myself in all my veins for—well not very long. Oh God—& I want to cry.

I was going to write you about all sorts of things. I wanted to tell you about Jack. Shall I? That's serious. Jack Armstrong—he is in love with me—was—perhaps not now for I told him of "someone else."

I've fought against it & I've been ungrateful & childish & rude, positively rude & I hated being rude & senseless. A week ago it was arranged we should go down to have tea at the "Dew-drop" [Inn] with Jack & his twin sister Nell. We four "little Millers" went—it was a week day & they & Rosie came from town. I took the children from home. Jack's house is all rafters & timber & beams & things—no floor or walls or roof yet. It stands right in the beautiful bush about 100 ft above the water & the sun was setting red over the hills & glowing on the smooth water after a scorchy day. We all arrived & we had tea at a rickety little table in front of the house & we fetched cups & plates & things from the store-shed & we improvised seats on kerosene tins & pipes & planks, & Jack & Waldo made a fire & boiled the billy & the sandflies came in thousands & eat us bodily for half an hour & we were very unhappy, but after sundown they disappeared & left us to eat our tea. Jack was funny & we all laughed a lot. He had bought a tree in town that day & nothing would do but I must plant it, so he did the digging & I set it & wished it long life. Then we washed up by candlelight & packed our baskets & went & sat in a group on the rocks in the glow of the fire. Then it was time to go so we set off up the steep hill. I had Peter's hand. Jack talked to me all the way up the hill & Waldo got sick of us & went & joined Rosie & Nell. As we came up & over the hill we met the great yellow waning moon just risen from the silvery water against the dark crags of North Head on the other side. It seemed she had come to look for us. Then we went on the asphalt paths & tram roads & Jack talked to me all the way home—simply earnestly threw himself into it & unconsciously gripped my arm till I felt something would happen if he left go.

It was the real Jack—oh so humble & in his own eyes poor—but good & straight & burning—yes burning for me. I didn't know it burnt like that. I told him there was you, & he wasn't surprised, but he was silent a minute. Then he asked if you were someone whom he knew— & soon we were at our gate. He was very gentle & bade Peter goodnight kindly & then he shook hands with me & just said "We're friends—for always." It was so quiet & brave that I came inside & wanted to weep.

When I was putting Peter to bed she looked up at me & asked, "What was Jack talking all about?" I haven't seen him to speak to yet again. I'd like to talk to him sometime. On Monday night it was hot oh hot—95 degrees at 9 in the evening & we hadn't had a southerly for two days! I took Miss Graham home along the low path to her gate & then she

brought me back again to my gate & just as we came up into the light of
the lamp in the road opposite the Armstrongs' there was Jack in bare feet
& pyjamas leaning over his gate trying to get cool—& gazing down the
hill into darkness beyond the glare of the street lamp. He must have had
his head under the hose because his hair was standing up in a wild manner. I introduced Miss Graham & we stood a moment & talked. I was
glad Miss Graham was with me because I was so startled. I didn't expect
to see him there. When I came in I told Rosie I had seen a ghost!! & we
both laughed. Then we sat working & thinking & all the time I was
thinking of the glare of that lamp in the darkness lighting up that queer
white figure over the gate & gradually my thoughts shaped themselves
into that little poem of Kipling's—the Brushwood Boy.

> "Over the edge of the purple down
> Where the single lamplight gleams——"

And I looked up at Rosie & was going to ask her how it went on, when
her lips parted & out came the words clear & intense—

> "Over the edge of the purple down
> Where the single lamplight gleams
> Know ye the way to Merciful Town
> Which is hard by the City of Dreams?"

What a queer thing the human mind is. Rosie had got there by quite
another channel but we had both arrived on the tick.
    Well now that's all. I must go & do a little work before bed.
    Goodnight "best friend" Olaf

With love from Agnes

[*Sam Whittall, the secretary to the WEA class at Barrow, was a working man Olaf had first met at the Bangor summer schools in 1913 and
1914. A jovial atheist and socialist, he was Olaf's favorite WEA student, and the two of them enjoyed arguing after sessions, usually about
religion.*]

Garsdale

Agnes,                                                          14 March 1915
    I have only time for a scrap this week, I fear, as the mail is on
Wednesday, and Monday & Tuesday are fully booked with motoring,
WEA, ambulance class and hospital. . . .
    At Workington last week I stayed the night at a man's house. He was
of the sort that struggles to maintain respectability in vain, in memory of
past style. The general standard was therefore the most unwholesome
for the family. They put everything in the parlour and the rest ripped.

But they made me very comfortable, dear souls, and gave me such unheard of luxuries as a hot bottle & fire in my bedroom!! Never before have I been treated so! The kids were dear little souls, but just a bit "shop-soiled." The whole family was recovering from flu. These middle class people who have come down in the world are much harder to get on with than the real worker, who doesn't try to keep up an artificial standard of manners and language. At Barrow owing to the war the pubs close early, so my crowd had to adjourn to Whittall's house after the class, about half a dozen of us in his parlour, with beer bottles & pipes, and Watts pictures & Leightons looking down from the walls. We had the usual hard arguments and fun, and oh I'll be sorry when those evenings are over! We promise ourselves an extra fine discussion on the same lines on the last night, the subject to be the materialist conception of the universe. Won't there be a battle! . . .

*Tuesday night* 16.3.15. The mail goes tomorrow, & I have to go to the dispensary in the morning before catching my train to W'kington, so I am indulging in a pencil scrawl last thing tonight. This morning I went to the dispensary & helped to bind up cut heads, arms & legs, under the tuition of a Scotch doctor and a fairylike nurse. Then I went to the Royal Infirmary and with nothing to recommend me but brazen cheek & a plausible tale I was taken to see the out-patients and I palled up with the young doctor & he let me watch all he did. I saw sores dressed, fractured arms and collarbones (convalescent) re-bandaged, a girl whose leg was taken off long ago, & it won't heal, some horrid cuts, & a soldier who had had an operation on his toes. I am to go regularly to pick up tips. What I want most is to see fresh cases, especially hemorrhage. The place was chiefly notable for a mixture of scrupulous cleanliness, fresh air, cheerfulness, matter of factness & much silent suffering. In the afternoon I drove a motor about the less crowded parts of town. Then I came up & corrected essays, & wrote a tactful letter. In the evening I went to an ambulance class. A middle aged St. John man who had "been through" Antwerp was there, a gaunt & solemn person full of terrible tales & first-aid tips. He was very proud of a collection of German & Belgian buttons he had made. He made us shudder with his stories, & made us all very sober & quiet for a while. Our doctor is a jovial person just a tiny bit callous, but he also sobered under this man's influence. This has been a fairly busy day, hasn't it! The tactful letter was about my classes. The Committee which rules these matters says that as I cannot promise to be available next winter it must engage certain other persons definitely now to do my work. The matter can't be left open because the other persons (friends of mine) are dependent on the wage, & must definitely know their prospects one way or the other. So war or no war I have no work here next winter.

Egremont

TO OLAF                                                    22 March 1915

. . . I've got a rotten cold in my head & the rest of me feels anyhow. On such occasions I feel profoundly grateful that Providence has not made me a typist or a school teacher or a kindergartener or in fact anything in particular. Sometimes I long to be something in particular. I wonder if it would be good for me? If I had a "job" I should have to leave undone lots of things I do now or have time for. A certain (small) amount (alas) of music—a certain amount of reading—of writing—a good bit of sewing for myself & the family & the Red Cross—an afternoon's tennis almost every week—an occasional swim or picnic or visit to a friend & a small amount of housework & marketing. Would it be worthwhile to give up all those things to a great extent & *do* something? Again are the things I do worthwhile & do they sufficiently benefit myself or anyone else? Would they have strength enough of themselves to stand up in a body and say "Behold—we are Agnes' work." I wonder. At times things seem very trivial or futile—& one longs to have some one settled end in view—I mean means & end all in one. But I think it would grieve me to have to do what others wanted always & when they wanted. . . . I *should* like to earn some money just to see if I *could*. Did I tell you for your mere edification that my little jaunt over yonder cost £200 odd? Daddy had put aside £200 for the purpose—so I hit it very well—so did he—for neither of us had any idea how much it had cost until I got back here. But I'm glad I wasn't extravagant to the extent of more than that sum. It seems a lot—but it has meant a lot to me & it has covered a year & 7 months.

Annery

TO AGNES                                                   28 March 1915

. . . Down in the rose garden there is a patch of blue hyacinth, and by the tennis court there are daffodils sprinkled. The air is full of all manner of bird song, and a perky little stone chat is making sallies on to the path after flies. It is all simply lovely, and one cannot somehow realise that a few hundred miles away there is smoke and fire and stench and murder, and all uncharitableness. This tremendous contrast, which has become a commonplace by now, never really becomes a platitude. It is always new and awful. Personally I feel that any kind of half satisfactory "philosophy" that one had before the war now becomes utterly inadequate and looks precious and pretty and artificial, and most of the stuff one tried to write also. One has to readjust all one's ideas, and take care that they are founded on rock, not on sand. But one can't really do that until one gets there.

[*Among the Millers' neighbors in Mosman were the governor of New South Wales, Sir William Cullen, and his family. Class distinctions were more relaxed in Australia than in England, and the young bourgeois Millers were on easy terms with the titled Cullens.*]

Egremont
TO OLAF                                                            5 April 1915
. . . It has poured most of the Easter holidays—spoilt holidays for so many people & the town is full of country people who come from a long way back to see the Great Agricultural Show at Easter time. Rosie & I went on Thursday with Bill Cullen. We went in their car & heaven! we ran over a little boy in Mosman. He wasn't killed—he cried & we thanked God. We sat motionless in an agonised silence in the car, we three & Lady Cullen. It seemed centuries. Then Bill got out & the chauffeur got out & children crowded round & policemen—& it all seemed an awful nightmare & Monseigneur in "The Tale of Two Cities" flashed into my mind & I wondered why the crowd didn't want to tear us to pieces as they tried to do to him under the same circumstances. But Lady Cullen went into the Doctor's & we waited & we remembered that he had given a good robust sort of cry & then Beasley came out & said, "It's alright Miss. It's only superficial cuts." Then he fell to fix up the damaged car & after a while we all got in again & felt very tired & were whirled off to the show.

I couldn't bear to watch the horse-jumping. I am afraid of it always because at the last show I saw a merry little red coated jockey thrown & carried away on a stretcher. This time I thought everyone was going to fall & my knees nearly gave way. I was glad to leave that but it is always nice to watch the dear queer country people at the show, "out-backers" with wild moustaches & beards & freckles & broad brimmed hats & pipes—& young intelligent straight blue-eyed Englishmen from "the land" studying the catalogue & the wool & the cattle. I love the smell of the grain & to see the stalls of produce—it makes me feel so prosperous & so proud to be an Australian.

I brought away a wonderful splitting headache. Next morning it was alright & Bill came up to tell us that the little boy was almost himself again except for cuts, so that memory together with those jostling crowds, & sheep & cattle & horses & the smell of oats & barley & the pain of a burning head is all drifting away into space. Doubtless it will find a resting place in some far away pigeonhole where perhaps I shall find it some day all covered with the dust of years if it has not already vanished into thin air & become part of that thing in me which gathers impressions.

6 April 1915

. . . This morning I had my second dose of inoculation. It ought to have very little effect, so I will probably drive this afternoon. Last week I passed my ambulance exam, and tomorrow I expect a letter from Newman appointing a time for me to see him in London and get signed on and put under way. The motor matter is going to hold me up badly, I fear. Getting to France takes longer than one expected. . . . I am heartily sick of being at home in war time. Everyone must think one such a wretched shirker, & in retort I am becoming a crabby misanthrope. I would not go through another winter's "shirking" for all the WEA in the world. I believe it hurts more than bullets, though doubtless less than shell! The other day came a letter from Robert saying "Ideas must be fought with ideas. I will not fight German militarism with English militarism, but with ideas." I heartily agree. Don't you dream for one minute that an allied victory means the end of militarism. It means that we shall adopt much that is now called Prussianism. If we do smash Germany, heaven save us! There will then be such a seething bitter hatred in Europe as never was. Turn them out of Belgium certainly, but then what? I won't help to smash German homes. *I will not.* . . . If your father and I ever come to talking about the war I guess we shall argue most horribly, because we evidently disagree fundamentally, at least so it would appear from letters of his that I have heard read. If Germany is crushed Germans will be the freedom-desiring idealists of the future, and we the Prussians, for we shall be tempted to put our trust in arms. If the Germans were really the inhuman beings they are said to be force would be the only thing for them. But they are not, & there are many millions of pacifists among them, & Bernhardi says the German national vice is peaceableness. Against earthquakes, thunderstorms, steam rollers and Mohawks force may be the only weapon, but the Germans are not so. But why talk? Anyhow, so long as people are *willing* to fight there will be wars, and war should be as out of date and ridiculous now as duels and vendetta. If I get finally reduced to being a combatant I shall go down in my own estimation and up in everybody else's.

London & Northwest Rail
Dining Express
15 April 1915

The mail goes tomorrow morning, & I don't get home till late tonight. Just a line to say the world has considerably improved. I have joined the Friends' Ambulance Unit and my passports are being made out. I have now to secure a car, & that is going to be very difficult as all the best makers are busy on Government orders. I saw Sir G Newman this morning, a very pleasant old boy who dismissed me with a paternal handshake and "Very glad we're going to have you, my boy. We've got a fine bunch of boys out there. You'll like them." Then I rushed off to get a photo taken for passport purposes—all done in an hour, but such a ghastly grimace! Then I went to the office of the Unit & met some jolly specimens of the "fine bunch of boys" looking fearfully swank in their uniforms. I order mine tomorrow, cheers! So far I have only got the buttons, which are like this ⊕ in brass. There is an awful lot of stuff to get and all in a hurry, amongst other things a glorious woolly sleeping bag. But the car, heaven, the CAR. They give me full particulars tomorrow, of what I am to *try* to get. I also had to go & see Mansbridge, who runs the WEA. He wants me to do things in Australia when the war is over. He's a dear. He offered to train me up as his successor to run the whole WEA all over the world. He wants someone. But I assured him I was the wrong person, as my only ability is to do the actual teaching, I can't enthuse. He said, "Perhaps you're right, your genius is for teaching." So I put him on the tracks of Eric [Patterson], who ought to be duly grateful. But I did not say no to Australia.

London seemed to me brim full of soldiers and pretty maidens. Nearly every tenth person seemed to be talking French. Foreign soldiers in weird uniforms everywhere. Streets as crowded as ever, with all manner of motors. Ladies in spring fashions, my hat what hats!! . . . If it were not for the car I should go to Dunkirk next Tuesday. I fear one won't get much into the fighting, but there's no telling what luck may befall when once one gets across. Newman agreed that this is the quickest of all ways to the front. He refuses, he says, hundreds of applicants. One will be doing good work, that is the main thing; & the Red Cross is an honourable badge. I am happy at last, as happy as I shall ever be until I see you again. Oh girl, I am so longing for that. I know you are far too goodly in body & soul for mere me, but I love you, love you, love you, though the wobbles of the train won't let me write it.

If all the lads are as good fellows as those I saw today I shall not lack friends among the Friends. But there's one friend above all others—if she will still keep me for her best friend. Wait for me, pretty maid, it's worth while. Everybody is getting engaged or married before they go out. By the stars, if you were here I would forget the folly of it and take you by storm at last, & be engaged.

Annery
Agnes, 21 April 1915
I—I—I am the Brushwood Boy, *your* Brushwood Boy, and not Jack Armstrong, "nor another." Oh my girl, you have written me two such letters that I cannot find words to say the hope and fear and joy, and

sorrow also, that I have been feeling because of you. You say you want me more than ever, and so with one jump I also want you more than ever, so that sometimes all the war and the weary time that it may take and the doubt of it all sinks into nothing, and it is as if I were going to see you next week; and sometimes it is just the other way, and I am suddenly dismayed at the thought of all that is between us, to be put away before we can meet. . . .

*Later.* I have a lot to tell you, good news & bad. Cecil [Kirkus] was commanded to find me a car. He heard of a wonderful 38hp Minerva ambulance. After much telephoning to London and so on, we finally heard it was already sold. Then after more exciting days we secured a Lanchester 28 h.p. chassis, the ambulance body of which has to be built, which will take three whole weeks from the time they get the specifications from the War Office, & the War Office is slow. Meanwhile I have the chassis, with the original body (lent). It is a second hand car, but about as good as new. I am driving it every day, but the awful truth is that I am still utterly incapable of taking charge myself. . . . It is all so new & there is so much to remember—clutch, accelerator, foot-brake, gears, hand-brake, advance-spark, throttle, and air regulator, to say nothing of steering & tooting. Today, horror of horrors, I knocked a man over in Liverpool, & if it had not been for good luck should have killed him. He turned out to be stone deaf and also drunk, & I don't think the police will bother to take action as it was so obviously his fault. He was not really hurt at all, but he might have been, and an expert driver might have avoided him I suppose. Horrible. I shall dream of that. . . .

*Next Day* . . . When I knocked the man down yesterday, and was quite sure I had killed him (for he was well under the car) I had one huge thought which seemed to fill all my mind. Translated into words it was "Now show your 'first aid' knowledge is sound, even if you are a criminal bungler over the car." Now an emergency like that lays bare the roots of one to one's own eyes. . . . How very slight one's imagination is. We were so upset yesterday about what might have been one death, yet all the while thousands are being smashed to bits not far away, & we are quite used to the thought. When one sees the results I suppose one will realise. People ask one whether one is doing Red Cross work because of pacifist principles. I say that the first reason is that I decided to finish my lectures and then it seemed too late to start training to fight. Now I am beginning to add, "I think no less of other people for feeling it their duty to fight, & I respect them for doing their duty so bravely; but personally I grow more and more doubtful of the benefit & the morality of warfare, even in this war, and I feel Red Cross work to be my duty."

["*Little Mary*" *as a euphemism for the stomach was derived from James* Barrie's Little Mary, *the 1903 dramatic adaptation of his novel* The Little Minister.]

Annery

Agnes,                                                                29 April 1915

I have been and gone and done it this time! The doctor is nicely "undoing" it for me again. Since last I had the honour to write to you I got certain queer pains in Little Mary, but took little notice of them. Then I think I strained myself swinging the handle of the Lanchester. Anyhow on Saturday I went a fine drive with Cuth[bert Kirkus] up into the Welsh Hills, right into the cloud—so funny motoring in a cloud, you have to be careful. Well that went off nicely and I brought the car back to West Kirby at rather a fine speed, passing everything (which by the way I abjure for the future). On Sunday the pains were worse & I could not move with comfort. Dr King came, & after a day's consulting with a surgeon, behold on Monday they operated on poor little Mary for appendicitis! . . . This really is a horrid nuisance, because it will take six weeks to get strong again. At present I have an india rubber tube neatly inserted, as there was an abscess somewhere inside. But the doctor says 6 weeks ought to see me fit for France. . . . The Friends ambulance people will be a bit disgusted with me! They "urgently needed" that ambulance. I have been dreaming motors all night, it's horrid, & makes one sick of them. When I think that you will be thinking of me in France while I am here on my back in England, I am very sick.

[*The Anzac troops from Australia and New Zealand got their first experience of the Great War in the disastrous campaign on the Gallipoli peninsula in Turkey, begun in April and lasting until the Allied evacuation in January* 1916.]

Egremont

TO OLAF                                                          3 May 1915

. . . Today is a sad day & grey, for the first casualty lists are out—& our hearts ache for those who are lonely & they rejoice at the same time for the praises of our troops. They are true metal like the English aren't they? Thank God for that. Today I was talking to a girl whose fiancé is "on active Service." She is very calm & ordinary & very pale. She asked me to come & see her & bring my knitting. So I shall. I want to write a few lines to a whole lot of the boys in Egypt this week. I'm sure they want letters & I have been such a slacker. Haven't written for ages. Casualty lists are a new experience for us & we haven't got used to ourselves & each other yet under their dark shadow.

TO OLAF                                                            18 May 1915

. . . I can't believe the war will ever be over. It seems as if it has come to be with us always. I can't remember when it wasn't. Perhaps you will be in Australia this time next year! I hope that too. As Daddy says, "Hope is cheap & very comforting." So let us cherish it & make it grow. Olaf, you said in a letter that I seem to assume quietly that someday "we shall marry, but that *I* never seem keen on the prospect." Well "keen" is a funny word. You mean that I don't write lots & lots about my feelings— that I don't make a song of it really. That's because I'm a girl and you're not. I love your letters & all you say—but for me, I can't say things somehow. They don't go into words for me but I tell you—I think more about that prospect than about any other thing & with more joy— though at present it is a fearful joy, for I am afraid for you out over yonder. I am glad for you to be there, & I'm glad of the work, if you are glad, whatever the danger may be, but it makes me afraid.

[*Olaf continued to recuperate from his appendectomy. Walter Lyon,
with whom he had shared a flat in Oxford, took up social work and
became sub-warden at the Edinburgh University Settlement before the
war. He was killed at Ypres on 15 May, and a posthumous volume of
his poems,* Easter at Ypres, *was published in 1916. William Kermack,
another Edinburgh Scot, was, with Robert Darbishire, one of Olaf's
two closest friends from Balliol; he survived the crash of the troop-train
that killed and injured hundreds of soldiers near the English Lake District. The Australian Rhodes scholars Olaf knew at Balliol were among
the first group of Rhodes scholars at Oxford.*]

Annery

TO AGNES                                                           21 May 1915

. . . Really the loveliest thing here is the estuary after all, with all its various appearances—warm sand, ruffled water, and water smooth and rough in patches. And the boats, little fishers that come in every tide, bounding if there is a breeze, and gliding if there is not. No one would know there was a war, save for much bugling that goes on. One of my more particular college friends, Lyon, has lately been killed in France. I lived with him for two years, and respected him, though I never really got to know him well. He was an intellectual, very fond of German literature. He had published a poem (Hyperourania). He was very dreamy and most unmilitary in mind and body. He hated soldiering, but he always conscientiously did his drills & camps at Oxford, far better than I did. He is the third son of a widow, the third killed. The only other is an invalid. Kermack expects to be off at last, probably to the Dardanelles. A wire came from him implying that he was coming here yesterday, but he has not turned up. . . .

*Sunday.* Thurstastone Church bells are rising and falling on the wind so gently, as if they were talking, now loudly and gaily, now softly and seriously. The other day there was a fearful train smash near Carlisle, ever so many killed and hurt. You heard about it in Australia, I expect. Kermack's battalion was in that train, or part of the battalion was. . . . Did I ever tell you about Kermack? Yes, but never mind, here is a bit more. You know he was overburdened with extreme humility once. The first day I met him I thought in my conceited young mind, "What an awful mug!" Then chance threw us together, and his orthodox toryism and my general radical extravagance clashed every day. Then for some unknown reason he got awfully fond of me, quite ridiculously so, I thought. He sort of "fell in love" with me, and therefore I got exasperated and was beastly, and yet the conceit of me was flattered. My country, but we were ridiculous. He was always wanting me to go walks, or have tea with him, and I was always making excuses not to, and then being sorry. Then he got into fearful depression and felt he was a hopeless rotter and useless in the world, and really it was rather painful for everybody, but if I had been a bit kind to him and seriously tried to cheer him up he would never have got like that. . . . Have you lost any friends in the war yet? My deep sympathy, if you have. The Dardanelles affairs is no play. Advance Australia! I have friends there too, I expect, Rhodes Scholars. Now I must write to Edinburgh. I wish I could decently have gone to France last Christmas. It's miserable to be a shirker still, loathsome almost. Write to your still-idle cousin please. He really hopes to be in France when you get this, but of course there's no telling.


Egremont
TO OLAF                                                         1 June 1915
. . . I went up to post a letter & I had a little talk with the stars up on the hill & we decided between us that it was rather mean of me not to be engaged to you before you went away to France. It could not have been before I left England because I had not got there—but if you had gone away from Australia instead of from England it *could* have been. But as Mother says, it doesn't really matter so long as *you* and *I* know. This is what I am to say to you then—

> "I know not if I know what true love is,
> But this I know, that if I love not him
> Then can I love no other."

And that means that when it is time I am ready to be your wife. Are you glad? I'm glad. Sometimes it seems so near & very real & sometimes it seems far away & I can't believe it. But I know that whatever happens will be right. The means seem to be taken out of our hands but surely we can feel safe & glad to put our trust in that great Providence who knows so well what is to be—& that what is, is good.

Was it Providence who ordained that on the morning of June 3rd we should read in our papers "Killed in Action at the Dardanelles Lieutenant Logan, son of the Administrator of Samoa." His brother died of wounds only about 2 weeks ago. Poor Mothers. Think of that big grief. There is a quiet sort of grief in this home too, for he was a great friend of Rosie's & she is feeling it.

Annery

Best and dearest of girls,                                  23 June 1915

I have just arrived home after driving my imposing looking ambulance from Birmingham to West Kirby, and waiting for me were two letters from you and one from your mother. And now I am like a champagne bottle that can't keep itself corked up any longer, and I want to laugh and skip all to myself for joy at those three letters. . . . I hope to get a little work to do for the Liverpool & Birkenhead hospitals during this month, as I badly need practice at this motor driving game. I don't take to it naturally, and am always getting into small crises. Just now I backed into a door and smashed my tail-lamp, silly clumsy mug. Of course open country is all right, but traffic—I am still a fish out of water. The ambulance is of *the* very best, all grey, with great red crosses on white discs. I will draw you a picture of her later, or get a photo, and tell you all about her when I am better acquainted with her. I have to pass the Red Cross Society's driving test some time, and I am still such a fearful novice. I am a bit scared about it. Oh that one could do war service with one's intellect instead of one's clumsy body & five senses! Last week I went to see the surgeon, Mr. Crawford, who greeted me with "Hullo, here's the lad of nineteen!" He examined me, and was quite exceptionally pleased with the results of his work (and nature's). Yet he had the cheek to tell me to refrain from heavy work for a month, and to wear one of those beastly belts for a while. If doctors would tell patients the truth at once it would be better. He told me six weeks, & Father three months. I told the Friends six weeks & have been postponing matters ever since. . . . I am horribly scared now lest the Friends should not be able to take me and/or the ambulance after all. Their work has been so upset by the Dunkirk bombardment. And now comes news of another bombardment. It would be sickening to be stranded after all. . . .

You speak about casualty lists. There are so many now that I never
look at them, but one keeps hearing of "casualties" one knows. The
other day the Liverpool Scottish did a great charge, & suffered terribly.
Liverpool is in mourning. The Scottish are a crack territorial regiment,
& are used much for dangerous work. They are all sons of Liverpool
gentlemen. Don't you keep wondering what it is really all for? I cannot
rake up any enthusiasm at all for the issues at stake, but for the fighters
indeed I can. We think we are fighting for certain things, but we fight
simply because a myriad tiny causes all have worked that way—great
historical causes and multitudinous tiny personal causes.

                                                    Wentworth Falls
                                                    Blue Mountains
TO OLAF                                             3 July 1915
. . . I've been looking forward to writing to you. I haven't got anything
to say, but somehow I should feel lonely if I hadn't you to write to. Must
you write to me too? I had one letter from you last week & two the week
before, all since I have written to you, because there was no mail out
last week. I am so glad you are getting better. I've stopped being anxious
about that—your nurses both must have been dears. I'm so glad you
told the young one about us, you & me. It is a good thing & if it made
her happy too it is doubly blessed. Oh I wish we could have a good talk
instead of always exchanging thoughts in 3 months' time. . . . I wonder
if things will feel the same when the war is over. What a mystery the
future seems. Why do you talk about it not mattering to the world what
becomes of its citizens—whether you & I marry or whether we don't?
Why, it does matter a great deal, perhaps not individually but collec-
tively that every dust, every atom fulfills herself.

[*Olaf's account of the uprooted lettuces anticipates the episode of the
tragedy of the plant-men in* Star Maker *(1937).*]

                                                    Annery
TO AGNES                                            5 July 1915
. . . We spend much time in the garden now, watering, digging, tying
things up, and so on. Hoeing I find is a very peaceful occupation, and
digging of course is entirely soul-satisfying. Our garden is looking lovely
in spite of the dry weather. The heath is out, and the roses and all manner of flowers. The strawberries are doing well, and the lettuces. There
must be something very wrong with me, for when Father pulls up a fine
fat lettuce I do not think of the pleasure of eating it but of the disappointment the lettuce must feel at being pulled up in mid career after so

much zealous growing, pulled up even before it has begun to flower. I swear there is something of the cosmic tragedy in the pulling up of a lettuce! But I like them for breakfast all the same! And as for the cosmic tragedy, it is equally present at the death of Keats and at the killing of a gnat. We only think Keats' death more tragic because we can understand him better than the gnat, for we are decidedly narrow minded creatures. To us the difference between Keats and a gnat is infinite, but to the cosmic tragedian Keats is probably no more than a pleasantly buzzing gnat, and the gnat on the other hand is not so very much less in splendour than the great soul of Keats. I guess that is just rubbish, looked at from man's point of view, for Keats seems to reach so far upward into heaven that we think of him as among the stars (as we might of a mountain top at night). But from a higher viewpoint the difference between the mountain and the plane is nothing because of the difference between the mountain and the stars.

Alfred Holt & Co.<br>
Liverpool<br>
19 July 1915

Agnes,

    I am patiently waiting for a trunk call from London for my "sailing instructions," as Father calls them, so here goes for a line or two, just for fun. They never let me know anything, those Friends, and it is being very inconvenient, as I must certainly start first thing tomorrow. Meanwhile I am having much bother with tires—perverse obstinate things! I don't believe I shall ever get off at this rate, however I'll have a shot. Liverpool is buzzing outside the window, a distant typewriter is clicking somewhere in the office, and here am I in a little board-room surrounded by photos & original paintings of Blue Funnel liners. Every now and then Father comes in to ask if I have "got them" yet, and always I have to say no. Father is in his shirt sleeves (as always) rushing about with business letters, interviewing captains, etc. . . . This is a scrappy sort of letter, isn't it. I will try and drop a line just before I embark, if possible. When you get this I shall have grown quite used to my work, I hope, but the getting into it is very hard somehow, and really I should be so glad not to have a motor to look after.

[*H. G. Wells's* Mr. Britling Sees It Through (1916) *reflected the fascination noncombatants during the war had with articles of costume, such as arm bands, that displayed their service to the common cause. Wells's middle-aged titular hero imagined* "working at a telephone or in an office engaged upon any useful quasi-administrative work that called for intelligence rather than training. Still, of course, with a

Olaf Stapledon in the uniform of the Friends' Ambulance Unit, July 1915.

*'brassard.' A month ago he would have had doubts about the meaning
of 'brassard'; now it seemed to be the very key word for national
organisation."]*

White Lodge
Reigate

Agnes,                                                                24 July 1915
    We are all established chez your Auntie Nina, enjoying fair Surrey.
Today—no I must begin two days earlier. I spent two days in London
getting passports etc., & completing my kit. Also we all went to the theatre twice and the Academy once. In fact we enjoyed ourselves, & I was
busy also. Now I am complete in all respects, with my red cross brassard
(armlet) officially stamped, and my official shoulder cords & cap badge,
also my documents. On Monday I go to Folkestone with the car, &
cross next morning. . . . My postal address will be Friends Ambulance
Unit, Army Post Office S10, British Expeditionary Force. Nothing else
is needed. But you had better address letters to Annery & let them forward them, in case of alterations. But send an occasional word direct,
for fun. My dear I shall be longing for your letters, don't forget. . . .
    I hardly know anything about my new life, it's queer. I shall be glad to
be well at it & in it. Thresholds are restless places. Where are you now
at this moment, I wonder? It is so sad that for so long my loving you can
be of so little use to you, because of the war. But it is good to be loved is
it not, even so far away? Indeed it is good, I know it makes all the difference. Everything is different for me now, anyhow. It's so strange, when
one thinks about it, that one little being should be so deeply influenced
by the feelings of another little being at the other end of the world, &
the only means of communication just black scrawls on white paper!

Egremont
30 July 1915

My dear Olaf,                                                          Australia Day
    Daddy is "tuning up" his cello, so that means trios presently—he'll
be calling loudly for us to know if we're going to write all evening & we
immediately desert whatever we are doing as though it was of no account. We love doing trios, but we also love lots of things & we are
always doing something. I was firm tonight & refused an invitation to go
to the theatre. It was to see "Sunday" & I wanted to see it awfully, but I
didn't want to be with Jack. Jack's twin sister Nell asked me really, but
Jack told her to, I know, because I was there when he did. Nell's 'young
man' is going & I foresaw how 'square' the party would be. No—that
young man has got to be squashed somehow—it's quite impossible to

squash him: he does such fearfully kind things for me & then I feel sort of indebted. Last week when I went to the cooking school at the Technical Coll. I promised to have lunch with him between lectures—so I went & then he drove me back . . . & he went away & during the afternoon when he was driving round suburbs a thunderstorm came on & it *did* rain, & he remembered I had no coat or umbrella, so he went & *bought* me a brolly & took it down to College & left it for me. Now what *is* a chap to do under the circs? I felt a pig for not going to the theatre & yet I can't stand being made love to when I can't stand it—could you? He's taken to coming to fetch me from rehearsals now. I don't mind his coming—it doesn't make any difference to me, except that I *do* get tired of suppressing him sometimes & then it makes me annoyed, but I'm sure it elates him, at least he says so, & it's so harmless & he's so easily elated. What *is* a chap to do—(meaning me)?

[*The first of Olaf's letters to have to be inspected by the censor bears the marks of his inexperience at writing within regulations that forbade: the naming of geographical locations; mention of numbers, activities or physical condition of troops; enclosure of drawings, photos, maps, diaries, or writings intended for publication; criticism of military policy; and the use of languages other than English or Welsh (although French did get past some censors). At this point in the war the censoring was done by a member of the Unit—T. Bruce Ismay, appointed by the London Committee of the FAU—and so Olaf was wary of making critical remarks about his colleagues. The method of censorship was to cut out offending passages with scissors; since Olaf habitually wrote on both sides of paper, each indiscretion caused an innocent passage to be mutilated as well, until Agnes persuaded him to use more paper. Because correspondents were required to sign their full names, intimate letters had the paradoxically formal close, "Your lover, Olaf Stapledon."*]

Friends' Ambulance Unit
Army Post Office S 10
British Expeditionary Force
2 August 1915

Agnes,

Here I am at last within sound of the big guns. You know where I was to go. I may not mention the name. I had a considerable motor drive to get here, largely at night along bad and tortuous roads behind another (pilot) car. At 4 AM on my first

[CENSORED]

*Later.* My bad luck continued. The other day I bumped a heavy lorry and bent my front axle badly. Repairs will take some days. Meanwhile I am working in the garage here, which will be a very useful bit of experience. As a driver one has plenty of spare time; in the garage one works all day, so this letter must be very short. The censorship regulations are very strict here and I have not got the hang of them yet. There were a good many surprises for one on first arriving. We get a very poor idea of the state of things through the papers at home. Here everything is very flourishing and peaceful just now. There is sea bathing and a promenade thronged with people. The other evening we had a most wonderful sunset, one in a hundred. Some of us were on the sea front; it did us good. Later I hope to get interesting work further East, but at present I shall be knocking about within ten miles of this town—as soon as my car is right. She was in excellent condition before the bump. I was overtaking a big motor wagon & a lorry was meeting me. At the critical moment the motor turned towards me, & in avoiding it I hit the other. Everyone is very sympathetic at such bad luck. Accidents of that sort, & other sorts, are common here. The garages are always busy. One's French conversation gets practice. I find I am rather better than the average, & am even now rapidly improving. Later on a little Flemish will be needed.

[CENSORED]

One lives almost in luxury here. Out at the other stations things are much rougher I believe. There are many fellows here whom one hopes to make friends with, many of various social classes. It seems very long since I heard from you, the mails are so erratic. You know how much I want your letters, more now than ever before. Before one came the war seemed a small thing, because you seemed so much nearer than it. Now that one is up against it the war seems to overhang all things like a cliff ready to fall. It is so huge and incalculable. One is a very tiny speck that matters nothing to the war. Write to me as often and as extensively as you can find time for, so that the other and fairer world may keep its proper proportions for me. Other people here write to girls (naturally) but none, I think, to a girl so far away and so dear. Other people when they go home on leave see the girls they have written to, but I shall not see you when my turn comes for leave some day. But perhaps there will be peace next spring. Keep ready for peace, and for me.

Friends' Ambulance Unit
TO AGNES                                        13 August 1915
. . . I have no interesting news that I am allowed to give you, though there have been one or two small excitements now and then. If anything big were to happen we should not be allowed to put it in our letters, though it *might* appear in the papers! The other evening I went a

walk along the prom with a fellow who was originally an engineer, then began studying law & politics, and is very interested in social questions and all kinds of problems. We sat on a seat facing the sea and talked & watched the sunset. Over to the East we could hear the guns every now & then. Suddenly a sea-plane came whirring out of a patch of darkness & passed us, flying low & fast. Later that night, before going to bed, I sat in an open space to watch the stars a little while. They were very bright, with the Milky Way stretching right across the sky; and there were many meteors. In the distance trains were whistling. Occasionally a motor with one little dim light would pass. A surprising number of aeroplanes buzzed overhead, going off somewhere one by one, invisible, but very audible. . . .

I have really begun to make one or two friends here, including the above mentioned, who is rather out of the ordinary, and also a fellow I told you of before. But it is not only friends, but also acquaintances, that one wants. I have many of them, for everyone is very genial. A lot of us bathe in the sea before breakfast every morning and run barefoot on the sands afterwards. Bar jellyfish, it is very pleasant. I find it easy to look at all these things here with a kind of detachment because of you. Friends or no friends, bathes or no bathes, excitements or none, even dinner or no dinner (!), do not matter much, as long as one jogs along and is progressively efficient. What matters is in the future, & for the present what matters is in Australia.


Friends' Ambulance Unit
Agnes,                                    20 August 1915
Here am I lying on a sea shore "somewhere in France," between the plage and the sea. Round about there are children playing ball & making sandcastles, and there are gaudy French officers promenading. The sea & the sky are grey, and there is a constant roar of waves, drowned sometimes by the buzz of aeroplanes. It is afternoon. Today I have been busy evacuating a certain hospital. I had sometimes sitting cases, & sometimes lying—assis et couchés. My bus holds a lot, but I had her nearly full sometimes. Now I am off duty, & also playing truant from my car, on which I ought really to do one or two jobs, but they must wait till tomorrow; the call to write to you is too strong. . . .

Most of one's time off duty seems to be spent on the car, largely under the car. I am amazed at the complexity of the creature. After dealing exclusively with ideas and abstractions it is very interesting to be in touch with solid material mechanical facts. One gets to learn the nature of things, of steels and irons and brass and rubber etc., and the rigidity of the laws that govern the material world. You cannot force matter of one sort to do the work of matter of another sort. You can only put things in the right places and let nature do what she wills. It is all sufficiently obvious, but it is impressed upon one when one has torn the thread off a few bolts. It is all such very real and solid fact, beyond the limits of direct human will power; and sometimes one feels that the ultimate reality *is* really after all the obvious physical reality.

[*Olaf had moved from FAU headquarters at Dunkirk where he spent his first few weeks working in the garage to the coastal town of Nieuport and then to Coxyde, a convoy camp in Flanders from which regular ambulance runs were made to fetch casualties.*]

Friends' Ambulance Unit

Agnes,                                                    3 September 1915

I am at another place now, fifteen or twenty miles east of the last. We are under canvas here, about a dozen of us, a very merry dozen in spite of the soaking weather. . . . Driving here is far more thrilling than at Head Quarters. The roads are awful, bad pavé in the middle and quagmire at the sides, with a railway along one side. There is continuous heavy traffic and columns of troops. Beyond a certain part no lights are allowed at night, except an occasional flash from an electric torch. Last night I was out and it was pitch dark and somewhat a complicated manoeuvre to get past things. Every day (or night) there is a pass word to be given to all the sentries. Some of the little towns we go to regularly are simply ruins, and one has to beware of barricades across the roads. There is much of interest to see in daytime—troops and guns etc., and all manner of cars slithering about in the mud, also lines of trenches prepared "against adversity." There is a "soixante quinze" in a wood that we pass on the way to sundry places, and it makes an appalling savage row. . . .

[*September 5.*] Writing is not so easy here, but my dear, remember that however scrubby my letters are I am still always full of the thought of you, even at the strangest times and in the strangest places, such as lying on my back under the car tightening bolts! Heaven, but if I could be with you now in England or Australia, just for one whole day should we not manage to be happy? It would be better than the old days, & it will be in the future. You say that our meeting again is the rock on which you build. I am glad beyond words, and if we could have that one day together, though only the one, I think we should make one another stronger to get through all the waiting. But that cannot be. Never mind, someday for sure. Then no more mere letters, precious though they are, but at last Agnes & Olaf together forever.

. . . I seem to know you so well now, much better than when I left England. I have a little photo of you on my desk which speaks to me & your letters speak too. I don't imagine things & I shalln't get a shock when I meet you again, as you suggested I should. I love you more & more every letter not because I imagine things, but because I really find more & more to love as I know you better—& letters do speak. Yesterday just for fun I read a letter which I had from you before I came to England! It hardly sounded like you at all except in small patches & a certain ingrained way of saying things which is yours & which you have always had. But it is the *things* you say which change & it makes me feel how you yourself have changed since those days. I expect a letter of mine to you at that date would sound the same. Have you got such a thing or are you more spartan about destroying letters than I am? I wonder if you are; we never talked about that, did we? ever? Well, I'll own up. When I was packing up to go to England I had a huge burning of letters, mostly from girls at odd times & a few from older people I put by because I liked them. Also there were a whole lot of your letters written at odd times about 6 months apart! no, 2 months generally. Well I always looked forward to your letters even then, because they were nice & I was loath to part with them. So I tied them up altogether & left them locked up in my desk, & then when I got to England & had the awful state of affairs revealed to me—I remember thinking how funny of me not to have wanted to throw away those early letters. I might have known what was coming! Well, I went on keeping your letters still because they were nice, & I have gone on ever since. And now I need a new desk to keep them all in! Someday perhaps I shall have to give them up. Should one? Now why should one?

I'll tell you another relic just for fun. You know people tell me that a wise maiden should always endlessly withhold her favours if she intends that her lover shall endlessly seek them & prize [them] when won. Well I mean to be wise sometimes, but I've always been ridiculously frank where you are concerned, haven't I? I always used to tell you things I shouldn't have told. This letter is not very "wise" according to "people."

But this relic is nothing—only I refrained from telling you before because you would have said "There now, isn't it decreed by the Powers!" I must have been at the time about 9 or 10 years old, & I was waiting for a tram with Mother outside a little shop which no longer is, but I remember it quite well. I had hold of Mother's hand & I was swinging about & jumping round her just like Peter does now, & I remember saying distinctly on hearing that some friend of ours was "engaged," "Mum— what's 'engaged'?" Mother explained, & I continued. "I think 'engaged' is silly. When I get engaged—I mean, I'm not going to get engaged. I'm just going to get married straight off." "Oh," laughed Mother, "& have you decided whom you are going to marry?" "Yes—Olaf" (in a childish treble as they say in stories). That's true. It must be a pointing of Providence don't you think, for you had decided then, hadn't you? Another telepathic communication perhaps. I suppose I had better confess that I have decided to marry many other people since then before coming back to my original decision. But haven't you too?

Olaf,

Egremont

9 September 1915

I didn't get a letter from you this week, as I expected I shouldn't—or your photograph either, so that makes it all the more urgent for me to write to you because I *must* be with you somehow. A letter seems like a meeting. When you write you do the talking & I listen & when I write, it is your turn to listen, but they are both meetings & the week is so dull when I can look forward to neither one nor the other. . . . Yesterday instead of having lunch at the Technical College I rashly promised to go & meet Jack A. & have lunch with him. And I was annoyed after because I was so tired that I should have given my new hat not to have to go. However, I thought of the poor soul standing for hours on one leg & hours on the other . . . so I went & afterwards I was glad because we had a really interesting & suitable discussion—namely how *he* should justify his existence as a subject of HM our King at this time of need. I brought it on myself because I want him to go & do something useful. Everybody one meets says, "How is it that not one of the five Armstrong boys has gone to the war? Why doesn't Jack go? I think it is about up to him." Which remarks of course are neither here nor there, because it's no business of anyone else's. Well yesterday after talking about it in a general way Jack said, "Well I reckon it's about up to me to enlist." I said, "Do you Jack?" "Yes, what does Agnes Miller think?" So I answered, "If you think it is your duty to enlist—well I think it is too, & I should be glad if you did so." So he tilted his chair back & surveyed the table & me & things in general & soliloquized, "Yes, & without a tear she says it. Not even a sigh. That's the trouble!" Down came the chair with a bump & we both laughed. Then buried ourselves deeply in the important topic.

He says he *couldn't* kill & the whole idea of military discipline & training & the life is loathsome to him & he feels he could be more good in some other way. So we discussed ambulances & transport & finally decided that he is to go to London & work in one of the munitions factories because he has had some years training in an engineering school. . . . I hope you are not bored. I had to tell you all about it because I'm pleased with the result of my recruiting campaign.

Agnes, 10 September 1915

An altogether delectable letter came from you today. I had just come to the end of a spell of hard work. . . . I read it in shirt sleeves to the accompaniment of a pretty continuous distant bombardment. Both sides are very active now, so we have plenty of noise. There are big guns on both sides at it night and day. Our little village is never shelled; long may it remain so. I sat on that bench smiling over the quaint parts of your letter, and enjoying it very visibly, much to the interest of "mes camerades." At the end of it, heaven, the quaintness of the affairs of us two struck me all of a sudden, and I really felt as if I must either weep or laugh. One feels rebellious against the fate that keeps us apart now after so much inevitable being apart before. But it is no use rebelling, and anyhow it is all for the best (surely one feels it so) so long as we do indeed meet again soon. It will very soon be a year since I saw you, oh most cruel fate! It is strange and almost annoying, so to speak, to think what a very small proportion of our lives has been spent together so far, such a tiny number of months scattered over so many years. Months? Weeks rather. Sometimes all the rest seems a waste of time, but of course it is not really, any more than the growing time of a plant is wasted time.

[*Olaf often wrote Agnes playful fairy tales. The one in this letter is an apprentice piece for the opening and closing visionary passages, as well as for the play with time, interstellar travel, and the linking of individual lovers to universal community, in his 1937 novel,* Star Maker.]

Friends' Ambulance Unit

TO AGNES 16 September 1915

. . . The other night, a pitchy black night, I was one of the two who go up to the front. We call it the front, but it is very quiet as a rule—just a few shells, & they seldom come by night. But it was black as ink. My companion was a French doctor. When we had reached the point where lights must be put out and no horns blown, we proceeded very slowly along the central pavé, but every time anything had to be passed we had to get off the pavé into sand. All the while we kept saying "À droit" to the people & carts who would not get out of the way. Now and then my doctor got out and ran back to curse someone in loud ample French. The worst part is under some trees, and there we encountered much traffic going both ways. The side of the road here is full of great potholes into which a car falls with a fearsome bump. We had on board a load of six marines going up to the funeral of their officer, so we were fairly heavy. The doctor kept flashing my electric torch on files of troops, great lorries, & now and then a gun drawn by six horses; but one must not use the light much. Sometimes we would brush a man with our mudguard. Once we got jammed between two carts, but the crisis came when in order to avoid a lorry we fell into some unexpected chasm by the roadside. I thought we must have smashed all our springs, but fortunately, no. We got out "under our own steam" all right, but later we found that a certain amount of damage had been done in the nether regions. Soon we reached the deserted village and in the middle of a crowded street I clumsily managed to stop my engine! I did it several times that night, for some unknown reason. Well, we discharged our load, turned round, got a few wounded and sick and set off home again, accompanied by the crashing sound of the soixante-quinze battery. The return journey was similar to the other, and a cart with long planks sticking out behind tore our canvas work, making a rent some feet long. When we got home the engine was boiling with such slow running, boiling like a kitchen boiler. When I first came out I could no more have done this kind of thing than flown. Even now I am pretty clumsy. But it is nothing at all to what the Unit had long ago in a certain famous place [Ypres in late 1914] under a shower of shells, big & little. The old hands scorn this, though they confess they don't want more of the other. One gets night trips "to the front" about every three or four days, but it is not always black as pitch. The early morning trips are nicest, with all the world fresh and bright and cold. It is queer to see "Casino, restaurant," etc. still up on the walls of smashed buildings. Last night when I got in from a trip West I was hailed with abuse because six sevenths of the mail was for me. One of those six was from you, and worth seventy sevenths. So I made my "bed" and got in and read by the light of a candle and Jupiter. Other people came in soon & began to make cocoa. I begged a cup, and lay in bliss with your letter and an excellent cup of hot rich cocoa, trying to make out your pencil writing in the semidarkness. . . .

Are you in the mood for another fairy story? It's just foolery, but my heart is in it. Sort out the truth from the fiction if you will. The other night I decided to sleep outside under the stars, instead of under canvas. It was warm, and the stars were so bright. I took out my stretcher & sleeping bag, and a glorious leather rug belonging to my car. Having chosen a position (which happened to be in the middle of the path) I got straight into my bag all booted & belted, for I was on night duty that night. I then swept the heavens with my Zeiss glass (once your father's) and marvelled at the thousands of sparkles that make the Milky Way. Then two wicked people coming along the path fell over me, & in revenge each took an end of my stretcher and began pitching me about, causing language which need not be repeated. (The Friends' Ambulance Unit, especially this camp, is not exactly Quakerish in its language, I fear.) Well, when things had quieted down again I continued my observations. The Pleiades were in front of me, they of the "gentle peoples," the phrase [from "God" in *Latter-Day Psalms*] you praised. Jupiter also was present with his satellites, and stars without number. To one side was the pyramid form of a tent, and laughing voices came from it, and a gleam of candle light. There were dark trees also, and a sand dune. Along the road all kinds of vehicles kept passing, & each was stopped by the sentry with a sharp "Halt là," pronounced "altelà." It was Sunday night. It happened that there was no sound of firing at all that night, which made a Sunday feeling. After everyone had gone to sleep I still lay watching, trying to see the heavens deep, as they really are, not flat as they seem. At last I began to go to sleep. Why is it so thrilling to go to sleep under the stars? Suddenly far overhead a voice called me by name, with a musical singing sound. The voice of course was yours; what other matters to me? Immediately I soared out of bed, all booted & belted, and shot up into the cold air. There of course I found your very self, as real as I, dressed for walking (among the stars), with the woolly jacket and woolly cap. You stretched out two hands to me, and I took them & would have kissed the girl at once. But you leaned back laughing and said, "Don't be in such a hurry, you impatient thing." Wherefore we remained holding hands like children in a game, and looking into one another's eyes. It was verily you, & your eyes, such as I knew them, but with an added year. Then we soared, gathering speed every second. We left the dark world behind and leapt out of its shadow, the night, into bright scorching day. The planets also fell behind us, and the sun dwindled to a mere star. Still we soared. The constellations changed and many stars dropped behind us. All around above & below was starry sky, jet black with blazing stars, for of course we had left the air long ago. There was just you & me, smiling, playing this wonderful child's-game, each dimly seen by the other, each holding fast to the other's hands, and gazing intently into the eyes of the other, lest the spell should be broken. Tell me, is this a very silly story? After a while I bethought me that it was time for that belated kiss; but you still held back. So there was a scrimmage up there among the stars, ending with a victorious kiss on the cheek of the maiden, the soft cheek of the maiden. Thereupon all things suddenly changed. The sphere of sky remained indeed the black starry sky, yet somehow every star was seen to be a sun of tremendous magnitude. All the planets of all the stars were seen as worlds, and all living beings on all worlds were clearly seen. Far way there was the earth, with her dark continents and sleeping peoples. The battle lines were seen, and the fleets, and all the homes. We saw also into the hearts of all the soldiers and all those who were not soldiers. We felt with regard to each one "It is I." And the tired souls of all the horses were also open to us, so that we grieved for them; & the souls of all creatures great and small, down to the tiniest. And strange noble beings in other worlds were seen, and of each one we felt "It is I." We saw also worlds where life was hardly yet dawning, and worlds whence life had long since gone; worlds also where life would never be, rolling patiently along, lonely and humble. This is a fairy tale, my dear, but if you think hard enough it will all seem true, even though it feebly tries to tell the untellable. This vision was brought by a kiss, please note. It lifted us out of the mood for scrimmages. For a long while we stayed still, gazing together, conscious of all this. For ages and aeons we stayed so, watching the lives begin and die, watching the worlds do so also. Watching, but never looking from each other's eyes. But at last a feeling that this was not *all*, that there was another, deeper truth to unlock, made me take you in my arms (at last after all those aeons), and you lifted up your face, and it was as I have seen it before in the darkness once, solemn and happy. And you were kissed on the lips. We were a real flesh and blood couple up there in the skies, and we were dressed in the clothes of this world. Therefore the embrace was a very real and ordinary one, also gentle, and willing on both sides. But again came a change. Suddenly all time became now. That means nothing to us here, but in the fairy tale it meant that everything that ever happened or will happen was for ever present fact. The heavens also in their immensity were seen to be a very small thing, and an overwhelming sense came over us that a third person was present, one outside and beyond all creation, one of whom Life and Love are our nearest image. Then came the Truth. There the fairy tale breaks down hopelessly, and can only wind up by saying that the perception of that Truth woke me up, in my sleeping bag, alone.

Egremont

TO OLAF                                               18 September 1915

. . . This week I had your first letters from France. Two letters. I had waited 2 weeks & two days for them so I was very glad to get them. But I nearly *wept* with indignation or was it annoyance? when I saw that the first page was cut about by the censor in such a reckless manner that only half the page was left. It was all the part telling of your drive from where you landed to where you got to (won't that sentence mystify the Censor if he bothers to read [my] letters? which I hope he doesn't). It was very sad about the car getting banged. I nearly wept at that too. You do seem to have such rotten luck. But it will all come right in time. I am just so impatient again for news of you because that all seemed so new & strange & unreal. I wish there weren't any censors. It's more the idea of them than any real restraint which they impose, but the fact that one may not tell this & that harmless (apparently) episode is boresome.

You won't write on the backs of pages though, will you, because it would be tragic to lose both sides for the fault of one. . . .

Yesterday Mother read us some Psalms after breakfast. She always reads something nice on Sundays instead of "war notes." It is such a blessing. This family devours the war news so keenly & argues every move & finds it on the map, & I don't really feel a bit enthusiastic over it. I don't understand why. It's no good devouring out of a sense of duty. I wonder whether I'm just selfish or unenergetic. I think about all the men & boys away over the sea fighting, but I think of them as men & not as soldiers. I think of them as individuals, not as armies. I have no heart or mind for following the fighting on the map or knowing about it beyond that "we extended our front 12 miles" or "lost 50 yards of trenches"—& yet I feel that *we must* win.

Egremont

TO OLAF                                               24 September 1915
. . . We have just come up from Lady Cullen's—Rosie & Jean [Curlewis] & I. Every Friday she sends her car to the Hospital & gets a load of wounded soldiers. We see them glide swiftly down the hill past our house in the morning & toil slowly up late in the afternoon laden with flowers & good things. Today it was wet & they could not wander round the garden & pick the fruit as usual & boil their billy for afternoon tea— & they had to be indoors so Lady Cullen rang up & asked us if we would go down & play to them & talk to them which we were naturally very glad to do. Two of them, poor chaps, were blind boys a bit over 20—& their chums were so gentle with them & looked after them like a woman might but made no moan over them as some women might—only helped them & were very patient & considerate. I thought it was so very sad but they were so merry & kept chaffing themselves & each other about what they could see or what they didn't notice etc.—& in reality we were all a blank to them. Dear old Jean chattering away to them with her pretty goldy brown hair & bright young face. Lady Cullen calm & dignified & warmly interested in the men & all the time thinking of her own two boys over there. Rosie playing her violin to amuse them. Me playing the piano. Old Mrs White being dear & friendly. Ailsa & Amy on their horses prancing outside the windows & to think it was all darkness to these two poor boys. . . .

*Saturday morning.* . . . No mails at all last week, not even by America because they went down in the "Arabic." But there will be next week, I hope. How many hopes & fears & joys & sorrows went down also with those letters? After other disasters the "Arabic" seemed quite a small affair—but it meant just a worldfull of disaster to those concerned.

TO AGNES                                    25 September 1915

. . . Here I am writing to you as usual in this place. I came rolling along
after breaker "singing most joyfully" to myself & the world. Can you
imagine me sprawling over my steering wheel "singing" an endless
string of tags from musical comedy, Wagnerian opera, Beethoven sonatas, and sleepless nights. I never can remember more than a phrase of
each, so you can imagine the jumble, accompanied by the rush of the
car. Why is it so pleasant to "sing" in a train or a car? Once here, I
relieved the other fellow, oiled my twelve valve stems and cams, wiped
my paint work with a parrafin rag, polished my brasses, & retired into
the bus to have a quiet shave. It's a queer world. Yesterday we were all
grousing because of the stagnation of things round here, & talking of
trying to get sent to the Dardanelles; today, because there is a noise, and
rumours are in the air that we may get shifted to another part of the line,
we all feel "homesick" for our little village, in anticipation. Last Sunday
I went with an agnostic democrat to mass in the church of our village.
Did I tell you? The building was full of women and soldiers, about half
& half. People seemed on the whole sincere, one or two were moved,
one or two looked very bored. The sermon, in Flemish, seemed to
touch a few. The Gregorian chanting was beautiful. But, good heavens,
there was nothing really alive about it, as far as I could see. It was per-
functory, habitual. One would have expected either an empty church,
or an earnest congregation, so near to the front (for a church to be). But
perhaps really people *need* something habitual, matter of fact, and a bit
soporific.

I have found the only pretty girl in Flanders. At least if there is another I have not seen her, nor has any of my friends. She, the one I have
seen, is a flapper, and she has just sold me some mediocre cigarettes and
some bad tobacco. She is flaxen-haired, and has naughty blue eyes that
are mostly half-closed in a mischievous smile. She laughed at me for
wanting picture post cards of villages other than this, and I laughed at
her for being the only pretty girl in Flanders. She scowled at the two
Belgians who came in, but I being English (and of course a thing of
beauty) received her most languid mischievous smile in return for my
parting salutation. . . .

*Later,* next day, Sunday. . . . At noon yesterday, while I was writing
rubbish to you, one of our little motor section [Eric Taylor] was killed by
a high explosive shell, in one of the ruined villages, while he was putting a "couché" into his car. The wounded man was wounded again.
The French stretcher bearer who was helping our man marvelously escaped, though the shell fell only a few yards from them. The car was
half thrown across the road, & badly smashed. A French driver was also

killed & we went to his funeral today, a catholic funeral, musical and solemn. Our friend was a lad, almost, and very full of life. He always kept us merry. We continue to be merry, but that does not mean we are hard hearted, nor that we do not realise. Strange, isn't it, that one can go on placidly day after day with death never very far away from one's thoughts, and yet not be seized by the wonder of it; and then just because it is forced upon one like this, one goes wondering and puzzling—and getting no further. Heaven, what a fatuous remark. Most remarks seem fatuous now-a-days somehow.

Egremont

TO OLAF                                                   4 October 1915

. . . I read two letters from Gallipoli from boys I don't know written to their Mothers. It was all about the advance after the 2nd landing at Suvla Bay—the episode of the 'Lone Pine.' It was so real & dreadful & inhuman & life & death seemed so akin. So little they had to lose & yet that little was all they fought for. "The chap next to me was wounded too & we lay & waited for the stretcher bearers—he died. But they carried me away down to the ship & now I'm here." Now I'm here—& *he*? why he's there—why it's all the same only *he* died! Yes it's all the same to him perhaps, but what about his Mother or his wife? Why are we made so that our lives are so bound up with other lives that if they go before us we are broken too? . . . There are many who have lost their own friend already & many who will have to lose him yet. What if I were to lose you? or you me? What should I do? & what would you do? Must one in time forget & go love & marry someone else?

Egremont

TO OLAF                                                   8 October 1915

. . . Well, in "Egremont" there have been doings & talkings between Mother & Daddy & me & so forth & tonight Jack Armstrong has been over talking to Dad & Mother while I was out. It was about *me* of course & they didn't beat about the bush. Jack wanted to take me to the theatre & Mother told him why she thought it was best not. Mother was kind though, I guess because she understands & is sorry for Jack. Daddy doesn't altogether like Jack but he was as kind as he thought fit. . . .

I met Jack by chance last Wednesday up near the Tech. & had tea with him & a long talk about this everlasting nay. I have told him all about it & told him I have promised to marry you & he knows, but he can't get me out of his head & so he came over tonight to talk to Mother. I told him to. This morning I said to Mother that I thought it would all be nicer & better & easier if I were openly engaged to you & she said she thought so too—& it was so nice to hear that. Mother doesn't see any reason why it should not be known & Daddy seems to be gradually getting over the stumbling block of my extreme youth & incapability of knowing my feelings! As for me I have felt engaged for the last six months—more so every day! But if it were 'announced' I should feel more comfortable because it hasn't been quite easy lately, particularly about Jack. When you write back to me persuade me that I have not put the cart before the horse! I should have let you say all that—but you were waiting for me, were you not? Tell me it is alright, Dear, & then I shall tell people.

Friends' Ambulance Unit

TO AGNES                                          30 October 1915

. . . All but four of us have gone off to HQ to celebrate the anniversary of the Unit's work in France. I celebrate the anniversary of our last meeting by writing to you in peace and quiet at last. Of the four of us who are not at HQ one is away for the night on duty, the other two have just gone up to the front on the regular evening trip, and I am sitting at our American cloth dining table with your last letters, and (as a great treat) your photo. The fire is burning merrily, the clock ticks, the dogs are both asleep and the rats are scuttering and squeaking. We three had a cozy dinner all by ourselves—scrambled eggs and tinned peaches, followed by coffee and pipes round the fire. . . . Your last letter came via America. How I bless that mail, and the extra letters it brings. You tell me about Jack A's project of munition making. He will be well satisfied to be "doing something," and I wish him luck and contentment. I confess I cannot see how anyone who "*couldn't kill*" can make munitions. To be a pacifist and stay at home quietly needs great courage: to be a pacifist and do Red Cross work is satisfying: to be a pacifist and yet fight must be torture: to approve of war and stay at home quietly is unthinkable: to approve and fight is honest and unselfish: to approve and make munitions, while you are fit to fight cannot surely satisfy the soul. Personally I would not make munitions, I would fight. Whatever one thinks about the morality of war, many soldiers are saints. These old French territorials, for instance, "vieux papas" as they are called, are patiently sacrificing all they care for, and smiling all the while. They are not very courageous, from all accounts, but they are more courageous than one might expect old daddies to be, and they are patient beyond words, and gentle. But as to munition making—well it is good for women, invalids, *and* of course skilled mechanics, which I know Jack A is. Now, my dear, you say to yourself, "He's a bit jealous, so he says hard things." But faith he's not jealous a tiny bit, and he has a very friendly feeling for Jack A, from what he has been told of his character, but he can't quite approve of munitions for a young man who "couldn't kill." When a torpille goes off and lands well, it knocks in a trench, buries a few men, tears up a few more, and chucks others head over heels. One big shell has been known to kill fifty men. If one approves, better let the other fellows get a whack at one, it's only sporting. I know from experience that killing Germans does not seem half so evil when German shells are bursting anywhere near you. But killing Germans seems as bad as killing Allies when the soixante-quinze begins to reply. . . .

*Next day.* Last night nearly all our cars were out. I did one trip up to the front & back for four stretcher cases and two sitters. It was pitch dark & pouring, & every time the car jerked the poor fellows inside sang out. It gets on one's nerves. The traffic was pretty bad too, & the mud is soon going to arrive at the stage at which it cannot be got through at all. Please excuse bad English. I took six coffins and eight French stretchers up with me to deliver there, in the ruined town. The aid post of the Marins, where we went, is a cellar (of course). Last night it was full of people wounded and unwounded. Stretchers were everywhere, and French naval lieutenants were fussing round seeing to things. There were straw beds also where Red Cross people off duty were sleeping. On the little flight of steps leading into the place there were people carrying wounded in and out on stretchers or pic-a-back, and also people carrying in my six coffins (patent collapsibles). The attack had been quite a serious one for this district, where so little happens.


Egremont
TO OLAF                                               30 October 1915
. . . Tomorrow there is to be a long delayed English mail & I hope there will be a letter from you. I know there will because it is 17 days since the last. Then I shall be happier still. Letters really do mean a lot, don't they? I was puzzling the other day to know what would have happened to us if neither you nor I had written since I left England, now 1 year & 18 days ago. It is a mad supposition, because of course we couldn't *help* writing, but just suppose. Well I think we should both have felt differently now. The wonder of it really is that our letters have made so much difference, is it not? That instead of just remaining neutral so to speak we have wakened up & understood (I mean me) & grown closer & closer together even across 12000 miles of sea. . . .

Some weeks ago you said perhaps you might feel you ought to go back to your work even before the war is over & you asked whether in that case I would come to England to marry you (bar submarines!). I was talking to Mother about it, & she said she didn't think there was any need to consider that much—because she didn't like the idea of my going alone. The nicest would be if you could come out here to fetch me, but if that doesn't work & the war comes to an end, which we hope it may, then it would be almost time for the whole Miller family to set out once more on its 4 or 5 yearly visit to old England. So it will all come right one way or the other, some day. . . . I want you to come here though, because I want you to know & see & love all the things & places & people that I know here & love, & so there will be another thread in common. Up to now all the journeying has been on my side & I have got to know your world a little already so I want you to know *my* world too. Now I must stop for tonight because I want to write a line to one or two of the boys on Gallipoli. Poor chaps. I wonder what is going to be the end of all this turmoil & sacrifice of life at the Dardanelles. Goodnight.

Egremont

TO OLAF                                          6 November 1915

. . . I got a letter from you this morning & among other things it told how one of your men had got killed by a shell. You tell of it in so few words, just as if it were nothing—& to the world, indeed, it *is* nothing—only to one or two it is all the world. But it made me think "What if it had been Olaf who had been killed—& the other chap who wrote & told some other girl about it." It might so easily have been you—& then it would have meant so much to me that I dare not ask myself how much. I am not ready for you to be taken away. I never really thought it possible before until this letter came & it caught me all unaware. . . .

*Sunday night.* . . . I want to tell you a wicked story just to make you laugh. Jack told it me to show me there was still a spark of humour left in spite of circumstances & the war. There was a certain brilliantly illuminated picture-show (kinéma) in North Sydney—& this particular Saturday night it was packed to overflowing by all the youth & beauty of the neighbourhood. About the middle of the evening a man arrived in a most excited condition before the doors brandishing a loaded revolver in each hand & he threatened to shoot anyone who laid hand on him. So the Manager of the theatre came out to interview this gentleman & at last calmed him sufficiently to hear his grievance—which was that his wife was faithless to him & that she had stolen off with another man & gone into this picture theatre; wherefore he intended to wait there until he saw them come out & shoot the man, shoot his wife & then shoot himself. So the manager left him at it & came inside, had all the doors closed & the curtain lowered & addressed the audience in confidence, telling them the whole situation & adding that, to prevent the tragedy, he would have the gas lowered during the next picture so that those

guilty people might slip out by the side-door unnoticed. Which was
done accordingly & when the lights were again turned on there were left
in the hall—3 old maids and 2 little boys.

[*At this time plans were being made to form two convoys of the Unit
that would be attached to divisions of the French army, which would
pay convoy expenses. The new convoys would be known as Sections
Sanitaires Anglaises Treize et Quatorze; Olaf would end up in SSA 13.
However, his attempt to describe the change and the reasons behind it
was scissored out by the censor.*]

Friends' Ambulance Unit

TO AGNES                                     7 November 1915
. . . Don't let the censoring grieve you; one gets quite hardened after a
bit. Yours to me are never censored, nor *any* letters *to* me. It grieved me
once that everything I write to you must be read by someone else, but I
have long since got used to it, and spend my pity no longer on us but
upon the unfortunate who has to do the censoring. Of all thankless tasks
there is none more trying, surely! When we are done with wars we will
be done with censoring. Meanwhile I have discovered one thing, namely
that I may tell you more or less what I like about our doings and experiences at the front, but little or nothing about things here [Headquarters,
Dunkirk]. . . .

*Next day.* Last night I hoped to have a quiet evening writing to you, but
some fellows got up an adult school, and I thought I had better go and
keep it from being too religious! We had a quite interesting talk about
"The kingdom of heaven," in which I put up a vigorous defence of the
atheists, and tried to give them a character sketch of Sam Whittall, my
Barrow friend. Adult schools sometimes get fearfully insipid, goody-
goody, and solemn. People feel they *must* be serious and devout, and
often talk a lot of cant that means nothing (though the words they use
may have meant much to the first users of them). But when an adult
school is an unpretentious and sincere meeting for discussion, and
when humour is not taboo, then it is good. . . .

Today we have all spent on "service," anyhow. My bit consisted in
sawing and nailing to make panels for my car, the while my assistant
and myself made strange and hideous noises that were meant to be
song. We carried on till it was too dark to see the nail heads, and then I
talked in the garage door with an honest person who is always worrying
as to whether he should go home and enlist. I worry too sometimes (so
shaky are my convictions), but after each period of doubt I am more
convinced than before. We two finally agreed that our work at the front

is of a fair average arduousness and dangerousness, though so much less dangerous than the work of the small proportion of fighters who are in the trenches. My friend's father loathes the idea of his son's fighting, and my friend, being half a peace man himself, has acquiesced. I said we divide into two camps here: roughly it is the old cleavage between the Pharisees and the Publicans, only that the phariseeism is not a fact so much as a dangerous possibility. Meredith says, "The aim at an ideal life closely approaches, or easily inclines, to self-worship." That is a very pregnant saying, worthy to be noted.

[*When Olaf took his first leave from the FAU he could at last speak freely about his work, his companions, and his feelings.*]

India Buildings, Liverpool
Agnes dear,                                         18 November 1915
    Behold I am in Liverpool! And you are not. Alas, alas. Oh heavens it's sad to be as far from you as ever. There's a mail out this afternoon, so I am writing just a line to catch it. I am waiting at the office before going up to Garsdale to Mother who is up there with a cold. I arrived here early this morning in a swank sleeping compartment. I've been shopping & talking to people in the office, & to Father who looks very flourishing. No censor will read this letter, thank heaven. Oh very dear young woman (forgive ecstasies!) all the way over I have been haunted by visions of you, & all the way I could have wept because I cannot see you & be with you again here. Strange sudden thoughts of you have been flashing on me—tones of your voice, gentle tones & merry tones; and I have *seen* the very form of you, the adorable neck that is yours, and the smiling blue eyes. I swear I have felt my arms round you and my hand under a breast where the heart of you beats. The very, authentic heart of Agnes. Forgive rhapsodies, one cannot always be a Quaker.

Annery
TO AGNES                                             20 November 1915
. . . *At my desk in the Red Room,* a grey November day outside, a fire and a fag inside. Now for a little information. Our headquarters are as you know at Dunkirk. Our little camp is at Coxyde, a village 10 kilos from the front. The ruined towns at the front into which we used to go so often are Nieuport Bains and Nieuport Ville, the former of course on the coast. The railhead where we sleep in our respective cars once every nine nights, & where I used to write to you in my car, is Adinkerke, 8 kilos S.W. of Coxyde. The big hospital is Zuydcote, 10 kilos east of Dunkirk. This probably means little to you, but I may as well tell you

while I can, though there is a whole lot of interesting detail I had perhaps better not write even from here.

I have told you very little about my friends, because the censoring is done by a member of the Unit, and I didn't want to prattle about people to him. He is a decent sort I believe, & very shy and retiring. But now I am going to inflict upon you some little character sketches while there is a chance, and I shall refer to them perhaps by the letters put in front of their names here, in case you want to identify them.

A   *Richard Barrow*, the OC of the Coxyde camp, an original member of the unit, younger than I, from Kings' Cambridge. Tall, rather stooping, very fresh to look upon, quite *correct* in every respect, a terror for telling people what he thinks of them and hoping they will "get drowned in the well when they come in at night." Conservative & orthodox in his ideas, but ready to put up a sound defence of all his positions; a hater of bombast, revolution and melodrama. Very doubtful about not being a fighter, and modest about the FAU. A good speaker of French, and a reader of Zola and gentlemen of that ilk. He is suspected of being suddenly smitten by a certain very fair noble English lady who sometimes appears in these parts. He is a wonderful OC, for everyone does whatever he wants and yet there is no shadow of "disciplinarianism.". . . He is one of those I most respect.

B   *Sam Pim*, was our orderly at Coxyde, really a surgical person, but he wanted to get up there so came to do the washing up etc. Now he is off to Italy to the Italian Unit, & wants me to go too. He is a fine looking fellow, with firm thin lips and very "straight" blue eyes. He is always terribly respectable, and brushes his hair like a maiden. He is very strong, but has had appendicitis lately & has to be careful. Sam is a fearfully good person and very sincerely religious, and his religion is entirely founded on the Bible. He is in all respects a Quaker, save that he approves of the war and of fighting (like many others). He says very little, but what he does say carries weight. He has never been known to say a naughty word. He's a bit "too good to be true" at times, and inclined to be intolerant of weaker brethren,—not of the obviously weak & honest, but of the weak in high positions trying to seem strong. To the others, & to all, he is all generosity and heartiness.

C   *Lawrence Pimm*, no relation, drives his own car, not a Quaker, has a comic face with eyes half seer half faithful dog. Very pronounced ideas about "wine, women, & cards" etc. & tobacco, but very tolerant of people, & even gives tobacco to soldiers. Scout master, & very keen, got a shock when he heard the language of the FAU, having apparently been brought up in a glass case. He also bases all his religion on the Bible and is very earnest, but also has a splendid sense of humour, & a

Olaf's official service record with the Friends' Ambulance Unit. (Courtesy of Friends' House, London)

smile like a bull dog trying to laugh. Barrow "hoped he'd fall into the well," for Barrow likes all Pimm condemns, and yet they are both honest, conscientious, laborious.

D  [Arthur] *Pearson*, from the Victims, Irish, unintellectual, a hater of phariseeism, pi-ishness etc., a great talker and a very fine man with a car. There is nothing remarkable in him, but he is very sound & one of my best friends. We go walks & talk of nothing but motors, ships, mountains, & antiphariseeism, with just a word now & then about our own affairs.

E  [Henry] *Brown*, always called Father Brown or Daddy, from Chester, very rough diamond, big nobbly face, huge mop of fair hair, worse than mine ever was. Everyone wipes their hands on it and digs about in it, & gets knocked into next week in consequence of their offence. Very kindhearted fellow, with big blue eyes and deep voice. Always his clothes are in a state of decay and grime, worse than most peoples'. But he is a personality and a weight. Not practical, always takes twice as long as most people to do anything to his car. Seldom seen not smoking.

F  Another owner-driver, inclined to be boisterous but sometimes tries to be staid, wears his hat with a flop over to one side—it's the hat's fault, not his. Is consequently called the knut, in spite of his disreputable tunic. Has a very swank overcoat which gets saluted in the streets. Talks intelligently on all subjects that he knows nothing about. Friends with all manner of people who hate one another—a miserable opportunist. Drives his car with dash but no ability. Says he hopes to go to Australia. Initials—WOS. . . .

I have just read, though it was written months ago, a little book [Wilfrid Meynell's] "Aunt Sarah & the War." I will send it to you, for it is full of wisdom. If you have perhaps already seen it, pass it on. It has made me very nearly want to fight and share the full labour of these happy warriors, and be no longer embusqué. But I must not. For me it *is* wrong. I am torn more grievously ever between these two convictions, that war is wrong and that to die in war is noble. . . . Are we who will not fight really ungrateful renegades from England? We are haunted with that hideous thought, and sometimes, true, it makes one *want* to be hit by a shell, that the account may be fairly squared for ever. It's no small grief to think that England is calling one to fight, and thinking one a coward or a shirker. "Oh England, my England, maker of men." For those who stay at home there is persecution, and I escape that under cover of khaki. For those who go into the trenches there is death, and I escape that also, I whom you love, and therefore above all things you would have me to be a man. Can you really in your heart of hearts be proud of an Olaf snug behind the lines when your friends are dying in Gallipoli? "To thine own self be true," but I am often ashamed of the Red Cross on my arm. It's like "COWARD" written in blazing letters. In England I am ashamed before every soldier. I don't want to see you, dear, till I have sacrificed more seriously to the thirsty gods of war, not till I can look the most valiant in the face as equals. . . .

*Next Day.* . . . Tell me, do you *look* different from what I knew of you? You *are* different, as a grown woman from a child in some ways. But do you look different, or is it always the same dear fresh face? I say, are we "engaged," because if so I want to send you a ring. Let's be engaged in the ordinary sense, with the ordinary little gold convention. If only I could get hold of the size of your finger I would send a ring right out this mail. How can I evolve it, alas? But perhaps you don't want to be branded so brazenly till after the war. But then it is right and proper. Don't you want the credit of having a fiancé at the war? How *can* I get that small finger's size! Shall not sleep tonight for puzzling. Send me the size of it anyhow and suggestions,—what stones, pearl? pearl with little diamonds, or sapphires, or what? Or must it still be a tacit and unsealed engagement? No, sweet coz. But if only I had the size now.

*Next Day.* Wondrous fates! A letter has come from you suggesting, of your own free will, a public engagement. I wrote the previous paragraph last night: this morning brings your letter. So now we really are engaged. Agnes and Olaf engaged to be married! How perfectly glorious. And as to the ring, look you, I shall venture on one no later than tomorrow, guessing the size. If it won't fit, you must get it altered and debit me with the cost; that is quite often done, I think. I must needs guess also what you would like, but methinks I shall not go very far wide of the mark. But oh Agnes, in the eyes of the world betrothed to be my wife! Why ever did I leave you to do the official proposing? Wasn't it scandalous of me; but you see I had tried so often before, I thought I would give up assaults and sit down patiently to a siege.

Egremont

TO OLAF 21 November 1915

. . . I wish I could have a talk with you about *the* war & war in general. Daddy is so confident that we are on the right side & that our ideals are going to come out triumphant over all evil. It seems miserable to be doubting when he is so sure, but I feel glum at the whole thing. I know we *have* our ideals & I believe they are more noble than those of our enemies but the more we fight & get entangled the further we seem to get from those ideals & the more impossible does it seem of ever reaching our object in that way. We can't crush Germany any more than she can crush us, & when it's all said & done the settlement will be made by arbitration, won't it? Oh why fight? why fight? If we hadn't fought—the Germans would have been & swept through France & England & left a burning trail. There's something wrong somewhere—but where is it? Where did it begin that it should spread so like this into all the corners of the earth? I can't solve it. We can't begin to solve it until we stop fighting. What a work then. I pray that you may be spared to fight in *that* fight & I to help you.

Egremont

TO OLAF 24 November 1915

. . . The only real piece of news is that I met Jack this morning doing some business up near the College & he carried my bag for me & told me that he had enlisted! I just said, "Have you Jack? Yes I *am* glad" & pretended not to be very surprised or very interested but I couldn't get it out of my head all day. I know I'm responsible for it in the first place, & I know it's the right thing; he felt it too I'm sure, only he puts all sorts of things in the way. About 3 weeks ago he asked me if it would please *me* if he enlisted & I told him that it wasn't my affair at all, but it would please me to think that he was doing what he knew to be his duty. I said he wasn't to do anything for me but what he did must be for his King and his conscience. And he finally grasped that idea, & this is the result. It's a good thing, isn't it? I hope he won't get killed. Mrs. Armstrong would be inconsolable, poor old lady & as for me—well, *"men must work."*

I feel as hardhearted as an iceberg to be talking like this, but you understand, don't you? I shall probably hear the rest of it tonight because I am going over to town to French. Jack said he would come across with me. He hasn't told anyone at home yet. There will be great excitement. The girls will be pleased—& poor old Mrs. Armstrong won't know what to be. . . .

*11 pm same night.* . . . Jack is one of the most unconsciously peculiar people I know. He never will understand me & I never shall know what he's going to do next. Do you know, in spite of all that has happened, all the straightforward heart to heart talks, he asked me seriously if he might go to my parents & ask them for their daughter's hand in marriage! And he was apparently surprised & dejected when I said no & once more explained the situation definitely & for all. He is like a character in Dickens. I really can't account for him in any other capacity. He's quite sensible on an ordinary subject, but about me he really is *not* sensible. He talks inside out till he gets into a hopeless knot & then he says, "Oh I don't know" & we both laugh & then he begins again. But it's all serious and—oh I don't know either. . . . My temper is a little ruffled & my sympathy a little touched. Poor Jack. It is very late so I must say good-night & steal out onto the verandah with my goodnight first to the yellow moon & to my faraway lover, who is also my cousin. God bless him & keep him safely for Agnes.

Annery
TO AGNES                                        26 November 1915
. . . A good letter came from you yesterday to rejoice me. My dear you must not talk about "bettering the conditions of the lower classes." It is not done in the *best* circles! Call them simply the workers, a more honourable title. We know that "workers" should include people of our class too; but never mind, "lower" has a bad influence although it really means nothing. Also "bettering" or "improving" their conditions is to be rather avoided if possible, especially when talking to them. Who pray are we, to improve their conditions? Ours want improving also. At least in the *best* circles it is agreed that such phrases smack too much of his lordship condescending to his footman. . .

I am getting a simple ring made for you as a symbol. You are particular about jewelry, & share my distrust of it. But this is a symbol, & you will wear it, will you not? You may wear it or not, or take it off & lose it, or pawn it or sell it, without incurring my displeasure (!), but the symbol must be given as usual. It is to have a single whole pearl, the gold being worked into slender leaves. I have been laboriously designing it, with the help of another ring as model. The pearl is a little symbol of what you are to me, a symbol in its perfect roundness, its purity & its softness. It is also a symbol of what our love is to be, a perfect complete sphere, in which the two halves are indistinguishable. The leaves are the foliage of Mother Earth, upon which the pearl is like a flower. Inside the ring, following Father's example, I am venturing on an inscription, a wee one. There will be this little sign αω, which I invented last night. α is the Greek alpha & ω is omega. Both are small, not capitals, which are A and Ω, & are the divine symbol. But αω, the small letters, stand for Agnes & Olaf, & joined together they form a sort of little universe, a microcosm, essentially the same & yet different from the great God's Universe. Also I think we will have in the ring the good English word "Yea," which is the mighty everlasting yea of God to the world, and your blessed "yes" to me. These inscriptions will be very tiny, on the inside surface. I do hope you will like the ring. I am very fearful, since we have never talked on the subject.

London & North West Railway train

Censor next time!        [undated; ca. 28 November 1915]

Agnes,

Think of me jogging Franceward in a luxurious sleeping compartment! Hot water laid on, & all conveniences including early morning tea, & "get up as late as you like" except for catching the other train. I have just said good-bye to those two dear souls my parents. I *hate* goodbyes, especially this indefinite war sort. . . . What a world of partings, great & small! Mother has spent so much of her life parting from Father in the Egyptian days, & from me at all times. And she grieves so, even when she is showing very little. . . .

Well, here I am rolling back to the dreary old war. It's a fairly repulsive prospect, but for many it is so much worse. Your countrymen must be pretty sick that all their gallantry was wasted in Gallipoli.

Friends' Ambulance Unit

TO AGNES                    19 December 1915

. . . It is a clear bright Sunday-like day, cold and pretty. The slender feathery trees that are in these parts are somehow Sunday-like also. I am at our new place [Crombeke] alone in our dining room in a little country pub, about seven miles from the lines. We have two camps, this and another [Woesten] much nearer the front. I expect we shall take them in turns. Anyhow I am no longer in a state of anxiety to "get to the front." I don't care where I go, being thoroughly fed up with all things bellicose. Heavens, every time there is a bang one thinks just "bang goes saxpence," only it's hundreds of pounds. Early this morning while we were still in bed there was a ceaseless roar of bangs, indistinguishable from one another. And all day they have been at it pretty strenuously. There are rumours & talks and guesses on foot, but no one knows much, except that things are busy in our branch of the trade. . . . This morning they served out gas masks for us, & [we] nearly smothered trying them on, such stuffy things they are. This place is a little village much like the one I used to be at, but it is in the mud country not the sand country, so that the roads are worse. . . . We sleep in a wooden shed with an earth floor, quite comfy on the whole. But, my dear, I have a great access of ennui and general fed-up-ness and weariness of spirit. What must the fighters be feeling in comparison! Perhaps I ought not to say I am weary, but being in the habit of telling you just the truth—there is the truth. Barrow (the OC) knows very well I am writing to you. When he came in just now he grinned amiably. I have discovered that you are a talisman to unlock hearts. I have only to say a few words about a girl in Australia (tête à tête to people) and behold all sorts of confidences come flowing out.

Egremont

21 December 1915

 Why, oh why are you so far away, my Olaf? I can't fly over the distance tonight & all I can wish is that you were here, your very self. We are all tired and heavy with Peter's Christmas Party. It was this afternoon. . . . Waldo was Father Christmas with rosy cheeks & a long snowy beard, & it was pretty to see all the dear little girls & boys dancing round the Christmas tree with flags & banners. All the adoring Mothers sat in the shade of the big old pepper-tree, & the sunlight was dazzling with deep blue sky & great white clouds. Our garden is such a dear homely old thing. It's quite small, but it's all private & high above the road. It's not a spic and span garden, but there's a big lawn with nice strong grass & the old pepper-tree spreads its drooping arms on high over a good part of it, & the children have ropes & swings on the lower branches & there's a seat underneath it too where we have afternoon tea sometimes & sew & talk. *When* you come we'll sit there & talk sometimes—oh dear those times seem so misty sometimes, just like a dream, & I am afraid lest I shall wake up & find that all my love for you, & all your love of me has vanished into the air & I shall look after his place & he shall be away——; it is so *intangible*—all that I feel & all that I know of you is in my heart & in my mind, & what is that! a spirit. All that I can touch is the letters you have written me. I can lean my cheek on the same sheets where you rested your hand while you felt me, a spirit, in your heart, & your pen travelled lines & lines of little black scrawls, a journey from your heart to mine. Olaf! Olaf—what is this that we have between us & so near each of us which makes us go on writing lines & lines more of little black scrawls? It is something very wonderful & surely divine, because it seems to surround & pervade everything near & far, concerning me & even things not concerning me. I would you were here! . . . I say, I think I must have changed this year. Fancy me writing letters like this a year ago. What did I say when I wrote to you from Berlin? & what from Paris?

Friends' Ambulance Unit

TO AGNES                                            25 December 1915

*Christmas Day in the afternoon.* It is a warm damp afternoon, with soft greens and greys in the sky. Everywhere there are little water-colour pictures, so to speak—trees, flat fields and the sky. I have just been for a walk with a young fellow who was studying theology before the war, & hopes to continue it afterwards. This morning I spent chiefly in decanting petrol from drums to tins, a patient-ox-like sort of work. Now come cocoa & Xmas cakes, then talk, writing, reading, Xmas dinner, and soon afterwards bed. My bed has unfortunately collapsed, and subsequently has also been overturned by people who wanted me to get up; and this morning I arose from a mere mass of straw, rugs, and bits of wood, all strewn upon a decidedly damp earth floor. But what luxury to have a bed at all in these days!

It's weeks and weeks since I heard from you. There have been no mails from England for some days, but even before that it was weeks and weeks, i.e. over a fortnight. If you knew how I am longing for that letter. I lie awake at night and wonder when it will come and what it will say. There must have been a great scarcity of mails lately. The shed where we sleep is a big lofty place with beams running about in the roof at various angles. We have a stove alight at night, and it shines into the roof and dimly on to the beds, giving a sort of Peter Pan appearance. At seven o'clock in the morning Father Brown, who is our chef in the absence of the OC, turns us out of bed or makes himself objectionable in some other way. Between him and me there is an unceasing war of chaff occasionally materialising into blows and hilarious acts of war. We are a terrible childish crew. . . .

*Boxing Day, tea time.* We all sat down to our Christmas dinner last night round a table groaning under geese, trifle, fruit, crackers etc. etc. Suddenly in came a belated fellow with a huge mail bag from HQ. Two fellows doled out letters and parcels, calling out the names one by one. Lots came for me, but I was wanting one from you, so I watched every letter till almost the last, and then came a big one from you. My next door neighbour said, "There! Now you've got one from her you can be merry." Think of your Christmas letter coming exactly on Christmas day & at the great feast! Thank you for the little book enclosed. I will surely take to heart all that is in it and all that you say of it. I suppose it [poems of Elizabeth Barrett Browning] is the very finest expression of a woman's feeling that is in the language. I shall read it all now with a new understanding, because of you. You could not have sent anything that would delight me more.

Cymbeline
Blackheath

TO OLAF                                    31 December 1915
*Last day of 1915.* . . . This morning our verandah over at Chequers' has a clothes line from one end to the other, with limp still cold garments waiting for the breeze or the sunshine. Cymbeline's kitchen fire is crowded up with old passé wet boots—& outside is a mountain mist. The girls . . . have gone hatless & bemackintoshed into the village to buy in stores. Mother sat at the kitchen table & peeled potatoes & I read her suitable extracts from your 3 last letters which I am beginning to know well now. Now the girls are back with their bundles & the leg of mutton hissing away in the oven. Letter writing will be at a discount henceforth. It is sad that I can't write you anything decent nowadays. I think it is because there are too many people in the house & always too much doing. The fact is, up in the mountains one must be walking and picnicking in order to keep people cheery & interested, & our picnics generally last from about 10.30 am to 9 pm or thereabouts & there's no hope of writing; it is rather nice to have a wet day for a change, but people who haven't any Olaf to write to, & don't want to read begin to feel a bit dull. How do you ever write to me in all the upside downness & interruptedness of your surroundings? And you write such darling letters. Last year, when I came up here, after all the bustling & settling in was over, I began to be consumed with the longing to have you here too, & to share with you all the delights of being in my own native haunts again. I went on wanting you at every end & turn, & then sometimes I told you in a fearful way & then after I told it without fear, & now I want you to be here so that I need not write it any more.

I wondered if I should take another leap this year when I found myself here, but of course I didn't; I have been catching up to you so fast through the year & wanting you all the time so much that the time is over for leaps, is it not so? Only when we look back after some months do we see how we have leapt, while at the time itself we hardly realise a change.

~~~ *1916*

TO AGNES                                    4 January 1916
. . . Yesterday when I was lying on my bed I told myself a fairy story.
I was under the blankets, but I was dressed except for boots, and I had a
superior leather waistcoat on with sleeves. (These details are to give
local colour, as the journalists say.) I was lying flat with a nondescript
feeling of misery and a headache in my eyes. Everybody who had come
in to wash and brush up had gone away to dinner, and there was left the
lamp, eleven empty beds (or should we say bedlets) and me. Suddenly
there was a little knock at the door and I shouted "Come in." It was you
that came in, looking round curiously at the dimly lighted place. You
took a deck chair and set it beside my bedlet, and yourself upon the
chair. You put your hand on my "fevered brow," a cool loving hand,
capable of charming away all miserableness. You began talking then,
telling how you had felt the other day that I was ill, but could not come
before for certain reasons of magic; but as soon as possible you had
come. And then I caught hold of your arm and pulled you down to me
and kissed you, and kept hold, and said, "I'll never let you go again, so
you had better make up your mind to it at once." And you were glad to
be a prisoner, but you said, "Your friends will have such a shock when
they come back from dinner if they find us like this." And we laughed,
and I said, "They'll be very jealous, certainly." But you put my arms
away from round you and said, "No, dear, the time has not come yet,
but when it comes we will be parted never no more. Meanwhile get well
quickly, work hard, keep smiling, and love me always." And I said,
"Agnes, I love thee," and I jumped right out of bed and caught hold of
you with a fearsome grip and kissed your cheeks and lips and hair, and
your neck, which you hate having kissed even by your own father. And

you were dumbfounded, and you said, "You've got better *too* quickly, let me go." But I, "Agnes, I love thee," and you "And I thee." But you slipped away and ran to the door and were no more seen. . . .

*Sunday afternoon.* . . . With regard to war and peace I personally have no longer any doubt. Your father thinks the Germans would have "crossed France & England with fire & sword" if we had not fought. No, not England, nor France if France had not resisted. An unresisting nation may suffer much, but not fire & sword. Anyhow, can one not imagine a peaceful nation voluntarily martyred for the sake of the idea of peace? That would be a mighty and heroic example, were it possible. But all this is apart from the real question. It is no use to "suppose that England had not fought"—suppose Germany had not, while you are at it. The *fact* is that the nations are at war, while in each there is a minority strongly opposed to war. That minority is growing, through the centuries. The cause of the war (roughly) was the exaggerated governmental consciousness of Europe,—too much State. The actual state of affairs today is surely enough to prove that war is both useless (from any point of view) and also wrong, contrary to the trend of humanity's progress. And as to the ideals at stake, we are daily moving further and further from ours. You can not ever disprove the efficacy of force by means of force; for if you win it is by force. Nor can you discredit militarism by militarism, & it *is* militarism that we are under now. Nor can you reduce the State idea by making certain states defeat others. Nor can you disperse national hatreds by shellfire. It is not wicked in us to fight; it is just mistaken. All the heroism and self sacrifice is not in vain, but the glorious result of it will not be that at which it aimed.

[*The engagement of Olaf and Agnes was publicly acknowledged in the Australian branch of the family when Frank Miller set aside (without abandoning) his intense disapproval of his future son-in-law's pacifism long enough to offer a reluctant toast. It appears that he was the last member of the family to find out what was afoot, and Agnes was eager to make her father sound more enthusiastic than he probably was. "J.E.A." is Jack Armstrong.*]

Cymbeline
TO OLAF                                                                 8 January 1916
. . . At lunch time Daddy got up with his empty mug in his hand and said that until this morning he had not been aware that all the members of this party were acquainted with the fact that his eldest daughter was engaged to be married, but since such was the case he should like to

celebrate the occasion by asking for a little more tea! (Cheers) Later on they all drank *our* health, yours & mine, & I drank yours because I was thirsty & couldn't wait until they had finished. . . .

*Next day.* . . . Daddy is preparing to write to you! an official communication! Dad has been so sweet to me. I have always been shy about you with him before, but he's very pleased & I am sure he wants to pat himself on the back. I know he & Mother both adore their prospective son-in-law. What a delightful family we are, Egremont & Annery. . . .

*9 pm.* Dear, it is such a perfect evening, still & cool with a deep deep blue sky all spangled with starlights. Mrs. Whittell & I are at the table in the sitting room, she playing patience (I am trying to "play patience" too. I want you so much I could weep just for joy & grief) & I writing to you, in between us the lamp; the window is wide open & there are little chirps from the night creatures coming from outside, & a piano in the next house & no other noises except for the scraping of my pen. Mrs. Whittell & I have been talking—about *me* chiefly & you, & how good everything is, & how wonderful & interesting it is for people to love each other, & about two other young men who at one time it was thought would not have liked to hear that it is you I love & who loves me; one *was* Harry Day, & one *is* still alas! J.E.A.

[*The motley ambulances of Olaf's convoy had received hard use and were constantly under repair as the drivers awaited a new fleet of uniform Vulcans due to arrive in March to serve the convoy under its new name, SSA 13, an adjunct to the 16th French Infantry Division. In passing from the sponsorship of the British Red Cross to the Army of France, the men had to accept quasi-military discipline and a shared command between a Unit officer and a French lieutenant. While this internal reorganization was occurring, the new Military Service Act, mandating conscription and establishing tribunals to rule on claims for exemption, took effect in England on 27 January. Thereafter governmental regulations limited the autonomy of the Unit in choosing its own recruits. Because the FAU was founded on the premise that service must be voluntary and nonmilitary, these two developments undermined the Unit's already precarious moral position. In early 1916 there were 480 men in the FAU, but during the year many members left, some to become absolute conscientious objectors (risking a harsh prison sentence) and others to enlist in the army. Those who remained struggled to preserve a democratic basis in their daily routines, but the ambiguous status of the reconstituted FAU divided the Society of Friends at home and shattered the Unit's morale.*]

. . . The conscription bill is the main topic here now. We think it quite wrong in principle in spite of all its provision for conscientious objectors. Father is really quite grieved about it. To us here it is hard to realise it as a big fact, not merely a piece of news. The proper attitude to it seems to be one of acquiesence at present, I mean for the people at home. We don't want a row just now. But it is the thin end of the wedge against liberty. After the war it must go. By the way, did I tell you we are now all in the French army with French food & pay? We get 25 centimes a day! It goes in supplementing food. I was interested in your news about Jack A. He has done right, through you. I respect Jack A, but I should not have done so if he had munitionised. Some of my WEA people are munition working. I respect them for it, because they could not enlist & they are doing it at great cost to themselves, sacrificing their leisure & often their health. It is all wrong & mad, but they are doing what they think right. . . .

I am a bit jealous of all your soldier friends, for they can push and excel, but for me there is nothing but quiet stodgy plodding. But I have no business to grumble. Your soldier friends and my soldier friends of Balliol cause me much thought, also enthusiasm and sorrow. There is Lyon dead, & Julian Grenfell, & two Fletchers & ever so many others. There are still more like Kermack now in the thick of it. Yesterday as I was rolling through the village a young British staff officer walked across the road talking eagerly to a French officer. The Englishman was all bedecked with staff red. He carried his head forward & tipped up in a curious way, and I recognized a Balliol acquaintance who used to be most political and most unmilitary.


Cymbeline

Olaf,                                        16 January 1916

It is Sunday morning.

Dear my Olaf, I am sitting on an old wooden fruit box with my back against a great pine tree. All round under my tree there is deep shade with dry pine needles on the sand & I look across the little paddock, sunny sandy paddock with tall white gums & waving slender saplings to little weatherboard tin-roofed "Cymbeline" with its one chimney pot exhaling peaceful blue smoke against the dark pines in the next door paddock. Our paddock is always known to us as the "gangway" because last year when the boys were up here with us, Lionel & Bill & Cliff, also Jean & Rosie & I—"the gang"—we used to track across between the gums & pines, on our way to bed in Chequers Court, late at night by starlight & back to "Cymbeline" a'mornings for breakfast. Now "the gangway" only sees the three girls of the gang, & it wonders what has become of those three dear jolly boys who used to stride across a year ago. I wonder too what was the call that made them leave the gum trees! It is so peaceful here, except in my heart. My eyes keep filling with tears when I think of you, & of all the other boys & men away from us. . . . Perhaps, it is true, there is no solution to this problem for the present but to let it wear on & fret itself away & for each of us to help as best he can in his or her own way looking steadfastly to the future & never doubting but that wrong will perish, right will triumph. But in the future we must all *strive* & *strive* to secure that there shall be no wars. I hate to hear wise and farsighted people declare that there will be another & just as terrible war before the century is out. I think they must be men of matter; but *we* must be men of spirit & we must prove to them & all the world that they are wrong.

Friends' Ambulance Unit

Agnes,                                                   20 January 1916

Once more there are rumours afoot, and the order of the day is "Be prepared," as the boy scouts have it. It is a good westerly day, unfavorable to Bosch gas, anyhow. I am on duty, and next call is mine, so I have my car outside our estaminet and I am writing at our dining table, which a cheery Flemish matron is washing in slow stages. . . . I am rather afraid my car will prove too big for the work [at Woesten], the roads are so narrow, and shells have still further narrowed them. The work is different from our old aid post work at C[oxyde]; the roads are less crowded but more vile. Agnes mine, I am thoroughly bored with motors & things mechanical. Don't be disgusted with me. I fear I am not a born motorist like Alfred [Fryer]. Some people are geniuses at it. I just slog along and learn by bitter experience. The actual driving I like under almost all circs, but when things go wrong I am quite a mug at putting them right. Here endeth this grumble.

Our French lieutenant has a bull dog, Sammy. A real old ugly patient English prize dog. He is so good a bull dog that he looks deformed, with his jaws some inches in front of his nose, and his chops hanging down like curtains. He is so good a dog that his breathing is difficult & he snores horribly, & slobbers everywhere. Nature did not make him so; man did it, decreeing that he should be fit only for the bulldog grip, & fit for nothing else. But he is a dear old beast, utterly bored with life, but friendly in a gruff undemonstrative way. Dressed in motor goggles and a French military hat he is a picture. It is quaint to think how Life painfully evolved from the original protozoa to be a dog, an all-round prac-

ticable beast; and then man, just for fun, turned Life into a side channel & a blind alley, & made Sammy. Life has spread into many blind alleys, what with ancient flying dragons, & modern dodos and bisons. In fact all forms are blind alleys, in a sense, all save man, & he too for all we know. But no, he *must* lead on to higher & higher things. But the blind alleys (save Sammy) are not just mistakes, futile experiments. They are all beautiful in their own way, & necessary to the harmony of the whole
[CENSORED]
. . . But, look you, to think of being with you again someday is the only thing that makes this life tolerable. And to think that at this very moment you really exist and breathe, asleep doubtless at this hour! You really *are*, & I really *am*, and yet there is such a huge gulf in between. Oh love of mine, what thing is war that it should dare to keep us apart? A lot of politicians with swelled heads did a lot of evil scheming, and a lot of noble hearted but deluded people determined to hate one another and make a war. People thought in nations instead of thinking in Humanity. Result—blood swilling like yesterday's rain, and millions of individual lives destroyed or turned inside out, and everybody getting madder & madder. We have glorious sacrifices, thoroughly unselfish ideals being really lived up to, but mistaken ideals. We also have hoky poky, cant, phariseeism, hidden selfseeking. But by the time it's all over we will have also many new & holy things. We *must*, or it will all have been a devil's trick and a hideous hydrophobia, not a divine madness bringing forth wisdom. Humanity as a whole has upset its applecart. Granted that it has found gold at the bottom (rather to its surprise); it must not put the apples back all higgledy piggledy as before. What rot I talk. Goodbye. This is an extra letter. May it find some mail or other. And, dearest, when you read it, think that your so distant lover sat over it all an afternoon—nay much less, I forgot—but sat long in a horrid bad temper, but a rather healthily bad temper too. Think of him most illegally angry with the world for keeping him from you so long, most illegally angry, but most angry. Oh girl, girl—

Friends' Ambulance Unit
Dear,                                    22 January 1916
Somewhere in Belgium there is a wooden shed. At the moment a full moon is shining on it, low and yellow. There is a prim row of tall and graceful trees beside the shed, and an expanse of open field. Inside that building is a stove by which there sit two Englishmen. One is reading, and one writing. The former is a humourist and a sternly conscientious liver. The latter [Olaf] is attired in a sheepskin coat and a pair of very leaky dirty rubber boots (and a few other things besides!). The former, I

notice, is reading a pamphlet and frequently referring to a little bible. The latter has with him [Meredith's] "Diana of the Crossways." The former has never been known to say a naughty word. It is not so with the latter. The two of them have talked about religion, and have found themselves to be infinite spheres asunder and yet strangely in harmony. Each thinks the other mad, but somehow respects his comrade's madness. Neither of them are Quakers. They are the only two nonquakers present in this section. Both are strongly pacifist. . . .

Yesterday I had a long run with one patient, a bad case. He had fever, and also (quite incidentally) a bullet in his head. He did not look pretty, though he was well covered with bandages. Coming back I hurried, to keep an appointment with our dentist, and I got a puncture and was very wrath. Going I had to creep along, because of my man, and also because of the multitudinous troops upon the road, multitudes of bearded, helmeted Frenchmen tramping under heavy burden of kit up to the trenches. Things are changing rather here. The traffic is far more. We expected to be shelled in our village the other day, but it has not come off yet, in spite of aerial observations taken by an enemy plane. War, war always, futile, imbecile, miserable, and yet withal magnificent. Will it end this year? . . .

[*Next evening.*] We used to complain of having too little work here, but now we are always busy though there is no fighting to speak of. One begins to appreciate slack times when one realises that the winter is passing and the spring cometh wherein no man can slack—for in the spring I suppose they will fire off at one another all the shells they are busily making now, and there will be what a friend of mine vigorously described as a "bloody spring," like last spring, or worse. Good God why should we have another bloody spring! I am sure neither of the opposing armies wants it. It is as if certain foolish persons were to drive two great herds of cattle furiously one against the other. Why not have let them peacefully graze? And yet that simile is all wrong, for the instigators were part of the herds, & the herds were willing to be roused. In fact it must be admitted even by those whose faith is in democratic control that the war *is* really a great primitive folk war and not a curious accident and a "put up job." But it is none the less wrong because the peoples themselves half willed it. We should have outgrown folk wars, and "bloody springs." If we were not so parochial, and did not follow only our tribal gods there would be some hope. Yes, that is surely it! England's God and Germany's are parish idols in so far as they differ. All hail to Bahi the Persian prophet who embraces all the Gods and finds their common quality to be the one true God of all the worlds. . . .

Bedtime. We call the nights more enjoyable than the days. It's cosy and lazy in bed. Also at night one is not just a cog in the great war machine;

one is free of the whole universe, to wander at will. At night also there is less between Agnes and her lover,

Olaf.

[*Olaf's* embusqué *work in Crombeke was vaccinating the civilian population against typhoid caused by polluted drinking water.*]

Friends' Ambulance Unit
TO AGNES                                            26 January 1916
. . . The other day 20,000 shells were dropped into the ruined town [Nieuport] where I used to go so often before my leave. Our convoy there had a busy time. It must have been quite a considerable artillery attack. Here all is quiet. Long may it remain so. . . . One has seen and done a fair amount lately & one wants to grasp the meaning of it all. There will be plenty more seeing and doing soon. One gets over the stage in which one feels one is not doing one's bit unless a shell is whizzing alongside. But of course we are fearfully embusqué here, so long as peace continues. Yesterday evening a convoy of some fifty empty ammunition wagons passed through this village. They were hurrying at the fastest possible trot, horses sweating, wagons rattling, drivers smoking the pipe of peace. It made one realize what quantities, actually, of stuff are being fired off every day.

[*While he was at school Olaf had adopted* Mediocria firma *(Steadfast moderation) as his personal motto, inscribed on his bookplates.*]

Cymbeline
TO OLAF                                             27 January 1916
. . . What if the conscription bill goes through in England, will you not all be called on to serve your country in the appointed way? If you serve willingly in your own way why should you buck at being *forced* to serve in another way since it is all for the same cause? No one likes being forced to do anything, it goes especially against the English grain, but it's one thing to rebel against a cause, & it's another to rebel against being forced to submit to the cause. Tell me all these things, because I don't understand, & I do want to know what you are thinking & doing. . . .

[*Egremont.*] Saturday evening Feb. 5. Jack has just been over to talk to me. He came last night but the family was at home. He dispatched

Waldo up the hill to buy him some tobacco! & then came & sat next to me, whereat I picked up my knitting & retired to the other side of the table & faced about to meet the foe. It was the last shot. He asked straight, "Agnes, are you engaged to your cousin? Given him hand & promise?" & I answered straight too. "I have." He knew all the time, but I'm afraid he will never be satisfied. I am so much his friend that he can in no wise understand why he is not my friend. He says I have been his one friend for the last 3 or 4 years, more than any man or woman. And it *is* hard. . . . I wish things didn't happen like this. Jack wanted to kiss me very much, & he should not have let himself go like that. He kissed my hand a lot. Do you mind? I wish he wouldn't, but I couldn't stop him. He wished me everything good when I'm married & he said I am always to let him help me in any way I need, if ever. Soon he will go to the war & I shall be glad for him as well as for me. He is training hard in the Engineers Camp & is trying for his commission now; he looks so brown & fit with all the hard work. I hope everything will turn out right in the end for him as well as for you & me & everybody. When a man is straight & acts straight everything should be right. It will be in the end. Do you know, Jack doesn't really know *me* at all. He has put a girl up on a pedestal & made an angel of her, & he adores her & he thinks she is Agnes. I wish men wouldn't do so. . . .

*Sunday morning.* In your last letter you were talking about men getting married when they are on leave from the front. I'm glad you will not ask me to come & get married all in a hurry like that. It is not very right somehow, is it? I think that would feel like departing from the "Mediocria Firma." And that is a favourite motto of yours & mine, isn't it? I have it before me in your bookplate in front of your pocket R. L. S[tevenson].

It goes against the grain with me to snatch at joys precipitately so, just as it would have gone against the grain for me to have given you my "yea" before it was time. It is rather different I suppose if the girl lives in the same town where she will live afterwards & has her family & her own connections. But I don't like to hear of girls rushing from the other end of the earth to be married & part with their husbands again the next week. I know of two young doctors who are in France, & they both have cabled home for their fiancées to come over because they will have 2 weeks holiday in March & think it is a pointing of Providence that they should get married. I think they have mistaken the sign board. I think Providence is really pointing the other way & would have them be patient & wait until her own good time. No doubt it must be very nice for men when they come home on leave to come home to their own wife, but think of those poor stranded lonely girls. Of course there would be for them a kind of aching joy, but what blank bewilderment afterwards.

Men go to work, but the women must wait. I believe these girls go gladly, & are only too pleased to do anything to satisfy their men folk. I wonder if I should! I don't think so, because I think it is selfish of the men to ask them to go, & what isn't fair for one, isn't fair for the other. Say you agree because it would be horrid to think that I was being selfish myself. But if you were to give up the Unit & come home for good & couldn't wait—well that would be rather a different thing—only Daddy & Mother would not like it. They would let me go I think if there were no danger of submarines & other raiders. But I don't think I should like you to leave the Unit, unless to help in some other way. The whole thing is HELL & we've got to get out of it & it's all hands to the plough.


Friends' Ambulance Unit
6 February 1916

To Agnes greeting from her betrothed in the Low Country

At the risk of being censored I must tell you a little of the debatings and heart-searchings that I found going on at H.Q. The great subject is of course conscription. Yesterday we were told officially that all of us who are conscientious objectors to warfare can count on exemption if we apply through the F.A.U., and that those who do not apply must eventually go home and enlist or "be martyred," which phrase really means going home to live a private life under a government that apparently will not martyr conscientious objectors. Now the FAU seems divided on the subject. The large majority will take advantage of that exemption and continue to work as before, feeling that the FAU does stand for something both here and at home, and that the future of the idea of peace does to some degree rest with such compromising bodies as ours. But a minority are all eagerness to go home and "stand by their friends." The unwillingness of the Government to "martyr" genuinely conscientious objectors has taken the wind out of their sails, but some will probably go. Most of us will be very sorry to lose them and to see the Unit split, especially at this critical time. Personally I honestly should prefer to be at home quietly working than to be here, and I cannot feel that to go home is martyrdom! But if the Government fails to keep its promises to us, or the Unit becomes hopelessly military in principle, or if the war drags on so long that one feels confidently that one would be doing more useful work at home; then some of us will go. Meanwhile we want to help those who suffer through war, and we want to be in touch still longer with the greatest event of this age, in order that we may understand a little of the "psychology" of the age that is coming. Anyhow we don't want to be pigheaded and go looking for trouble, and we don't want to cause discord while it looks as if reason-

ableness would effect more for the peace idea than fanaticism can do, at
any rate in this stage. . . .

You say that sometimes the bond between us two seems so intangible
that you are almost afraid of waking up and finding it was all a dream.
Let the ring I sent be a tangible sign, until there is a better, and let the
new and happy publicity of it all be also a tangible sign. And chiefly
realise—I know you do—that whatever is felt in the heart is the only
reality in existence. . . . A feeling, whether of love or hate or aspira-
tion, *is* a reality within you. This is a dangerous line of thought and has
side tracks to the pit. But, like wine, it has its use in making glad the
heart of man (or maid). It is dangerous because it may lead to the love of
loving, not of a person. For another person is beyond that sense curtain,
and is as uncertain as all other outside facts. But my idea of you, and
yours of me, is so vivid and detailed and springs from such a multitudinous sense picture, that the idea cannot surely be so far from the
real spirit that is you. Indeed one is tempted to believe that two minds
can even pierce that sense curtain and apprehend one another directly,
so brilliant is the vision and so much more real than any of the sense
pictures. Anyhow, my girl, the war will not be forever, and every day
draws nearer to the end. . . . All the present will also fade into memory
and be a mere chapter in the past, not an endless question as to the
future.

Egremont

13 February 1916

This is Sunday evening at nearly half past ten. I mustn't stay up very
long but I want to have a little talk with you before I go to bed. We have
had Tristram Speedy & his nice newly-wedded wife over to spend the
afternoon & evening—they are in Sydney on their honeymoon. Now
they have gone back to town, & Rosie & I have washed up all the dishes
& tidied up things & now it is bedtime only I'm not going just yet, because I want to tell you that—Dear, the ring has come. I've got it safe
on my finger now & I am bending over it as I write. I love it more &
more every time I look at it. . . . This ring is a kind of revelation to me.
I did not think it would be so. I thought it would be light & thin & pretty
like all the flashy engagement rings other girls have—but behold it is
beautiful, and strong & firm & solidly wrought, & I am glad & afraid—
glad that you think me worthy of such a pearl & afraid lest I be unworthy. Noone has ever thought of me as you do—we are all half surprised. Yes, it fits beautifully but I must not grow any thinner. It is just a
slight shade bigger than I need, but it won't fall off because there are
some little ripples of flesh on my finger that stop it. It is quite safe but it
comes easily when I pull. I love the design you made, nice boy, & the

little furrows that go all round. They are very uncommon & so is the whole ring.

Friends' Ambulance Unit

TO AGNES                                    13 February 1916

. . . P[operinghe] is a quaint old town, with a big irregular square and churches and a "collège." It is always packed with traffic, mostly British, and today being Sunday, there was the additional splendour of the in-habitants in Sunday dress. Some few of the buildings are a bit battered, and many have shrapnel marks, like small pox, but otherwise it is much like a peace town. Our fellows at W[oesten] have had a busy time; some have practically not been out of their cars, or away from their cars rather, since 7 pm last night—nearly 24 hours. Unfortunately we must not send up help, & anyhow we could not just at present. This sounds very arduous, doesn't it, but we here are really having one long slack except for rare bursts, and anyhow the battle, *the* battle, will be alto-gether different. . . .

*Next Day.* If the war goes on for another year what will become of us? Somehow I have lately come to regard it as almost certain that it will end soon; but supposing it does not. My dear, how is one to live so long without you? In a year from now you will be nearly twenty-three and I nearly thirty-one. That is not late in life, for either of us, I know; and we are both very young for our ages. But all this time that we are not to-gether is the best age of our lives, and it seems so sad a waste. It may be longer even than a year—who can tell how long? When I think that there is a girl in the very flower of life waiting day after day, and I can give her only letters instead of myself, and can reach her only through her letters and not really be joined inextricably with her, and when I feel "She is altogether lovable and desirable, she is willing and she longs for me, and I love her," and when I feel how time flies and the war stays,— why Agnes, it takes all that faith of mine (so different from my evangelical friend's) to stop me from being childishly angry with the universe.

Egremont

TO OLAF                                    18 February 1916

. . . Tomorrow Monday Feb. 19th is going to be a great & blessed day in the present history of Sydney & suburbs. *The English & Expeditionary Mail* is going to be delivered. *The* mail. The one I have been growling over for weeks. It is 3 weeks since the last one, & everyone is starved & thirsty to the last gasp. . . . Each mail seems like a milestone on the road to Peace. Each mail seems the equivalent in Time of what Peace is in Eternity. Something vital to be attained, the end of one journey before setting out on another. If there were no milestones the road would seem endless. So thank God for milestones even though sometimes they are 3 miles apart instead of one. Goodnight now, it is late. Olaf, à demain! Courage!

*Monday afternoon.* I didn't go on with my letter this morning because your letter didn't come—*but it came this afternoon*, hurrah. It was not the right letter, but that didn't matter. It was very good to see your writing again & to know that all the time you are talking to me from away over there really & truly & not just in a dream, just the same whether I get your letters or whether I don't. I simply hate to have that vague indefinite feeling about you, & that is what comes sometimes when there is a long long gap between mails or when I have been too eager for you or too impatient. It's a kind of reaction—then if the mail comes soon it's alright & I get back to normal again, but if it doesn't I get more & more dull & you seem so far away. I have to say to myself sometimes, "It is all real. He is a real live boy, Olaf. His love for you goes on all the time & your love for him is a real thing too, not a myth. You are just as really lovers as any two lovers you may see talking together any day—only earth is between, & what is earth!" Long ago this feeling used to be a nightmare of doubt & uncertainty. Now it doesn't really matter because I know my love is strong enough to stand alone; it would always carry me through to you however long I had to wait—but all the same it is a rotten dull feeling.

Friends' Ambulance Unit

TO AGNES                                    21 February 1916

. . . Today we hear that all members of the Unit who conscientiously object to enlist in any service are to be given total exemption. It is wonderful that our supporters at home (chiefly Sir George Newman) have succeeded in getting so complete a concession. The result is that a very few people will have to go home to enlist, while the great majority, being conscientious objectors, are absolutely free indefinitely. I can't think how it was done! Some of us also signed a strong additional protest or declaration. I am exceeding glad to feel that I can go on here and yet be an out & out pacifist. At the moment there is a biggish bombardment going on, and shrapnel can be seen bursting over W[oesten]. It is queer to be in the midst of all this & all these "warring hosts" and yet feel absolutely free and not bound to any military allegiance. Heaven, I am sure now about it all, and glad I joined the FAU & not the army, as I might once have done.

TO AGNES                               29 February 1916

. . . Since I wrote last we have shifted. I am now cosily settled in my car for the night. We have all moved down into repos with our Division to a place [Rexpoede] some 15 kilos from the former spot, far from war. The guns can hardly be heard. We may be here days, weeks or months. We must be ready to go to the front in half an hour. We feed in a cheery dining room in a farmhouse and we sleep in our cars. It's just a glorious country holiday with just a little work now and then, & much repair work to cars. My car is in the farm lane with others. Some are in a field. There is heavy mud everywhere. My car makes a wonderfully cosy little two berth cabin—two berths on one side, a seat on the other and a little seat at the end. The upper berth is unoccupied so far, so I am palatially accommodated. Today I cleaned her up inside. The outer half of the floor (next the back of the car, where you get in) is left all muddy; the inner half is parafinned linoleum with a rug on it for bare feet! So I *am* snug. Just now I am attired in pyjamas with my sheepskin coat over them & I am sittin' opposite my stretcher-bunk, reeking of eau de cologne, & writing to you by candle light. The rain patters on my roof, but it is double canvas with an air space between. I would sooner sleep in my car (in any weather) than in most rooms. . . .

Imagine me, with three first aid haversacks over my shoulder and three rugs that kept tripping me up, & in my "strong right hand" a huge long bright curved old French cavalry sabre, chasing my friends among the apple trees because they laughed at my appearance thus accoutred. It was a fearful snicker snee too, four feet long, & sharp as a carving knife. I had the whole convoy & half the French army on the run before me. Glorious moment! Darling, I play the fool & behave like a schoolboy *because* I love you so & know you love me. The Frenchmen, our Frenchmen, called me "le Benjamin de la convoie" until they found out my age, which was a pretty bad shock to them. My reputation here depicts me as infantile, yet (strangely enough) prodigiously learned.


                                                    Egremont
TO OLAF                                  2 March 1916

. . . People are getting rather excited about Verdun. It is glorious, but I daren't believe it. I can't conceive of the war really coming to an end. At the French circle last night old M. Auchet, who fought all through the 1870 campaign, was nearly standing on his head with excitement. It was he who made the causerie with 'la carte d'Europe' as his foundation, & he boldly prophesied with the utmost of French confidence & enthusiasm that l'an 1916 verrait la fin de la guerre, et une Paix triomphante et glorieuse, pour les Alliés. He announced that the German attack had failed, that the French would not retire from Verdun & that this was the crowning of the beginning of the end & we hard unbending Australians who heard him began to be inflamed also for a minute & we clapped our hands & murmured assent of the old soldier's fire—but *we* don't catch fire like that. I think we are steeped in cold unbelieving caution & when the Consul added a few discreet & well-chosen remarks to M. Auchet's outburst it seemed to blow out all the flames & just leave a great silent hope glowing in our hearts.

Oh my darling. Oh how good—

Shall we give it till Christmas, or must it be next Spring? Let's say Christmas just for fun, & don't let's think of anything that might happen before then—& of all the things that will happen to somebody's lover & somebody's son & somebody's husband. Oh but I can't help thinking about them! But *you, my* Lover. You will take leave of your French Doctors & stretcherbearers & French Allies & your Camp & your car & you will journey to England with some of your F.A.U. friends & in London you will see each other off at the big stations & be sorry to say goodbye because even bad times have good points, & as you all journey on your own ways you will think it is a dream—& when you get to your own station you will know that it is real because of the home faces you will see all round you, bless them! If I could be one of those home faces I should be quite—oh I don't know, quite ordinary I think—& so be-wondered that I couldn't think at all or talk, but just watch—and watch—and be kissed, Mothers first & then Fathers & then Girls. When you come here it won't be on a station, but on Central Wharf. I shall come, we shall all come. I have often thought of myself gazing upwards from that dark wharf to find you & you looking down on all the upturned faces to find me—us I mean. There are ever so many girls on the wharf & ever so many men on the ship but only one will do, only the right one. Where is she? & where is he? Ah. There. And I'll "put up a hand" to you just like Lorna Doone did to John Ridd for a sign & you will put up a hand to me & then you'll have to wait years & years until they get the gangway fixed & you can come down. And afterwards we'll take you home to Mosman in triumph, & Peter will be very stand-offish & contradictory—& then we shall really begin to live, shalln't we?

Friends' Ambulance Unit

TO AGNES                                              24 March 1916

. . . Look you, cousin, it is no use your talking about this work as being part of the one great cause. "The one great cause" is really the getting humanity across this age of war with as little damage as possible. The other, the Allied cause, *is* a great cause, & to be left out is lonely. But the other is the higher. . . . What excuse have I to be here save that I must not fight for that cause? I ought to be ashamed to be here if I felt it right to help that cause. At the front I daresay we have more work than the men in the trenches, but less suffering and danger, far less. I have been in no real danger since—ages ago. I think we disagree about the war. I dare think that if I could talk to you you would agree with me. Remember that you hear one side. Think what the Germans are hearing. Don't trust newspapers much. I was a "doubting pacifist." Now I am sure as man can be about any great perplexity, any great problem in an age of transition from one great truth to another. . . . Agnes, if after all we disagree about the war,—I believe we partly do—and if secretly you would be prouder of me fighting although you are half a pacifist, why then we have found our first real difference perhaps. Well, it can't be helped, but I would gladly be your soldier if I honourably could. To be a soldier means hardship and danger during the war. To be a man of peace means a debt of honour, a huge debt, to be paid only by a lifelong devotion to one's fellow men after the war. If only one can rise to that devotion.

Egremont

TO OLAF                                                      26 March 1916

. . . I must tell you a nice thing that happened on Friday. I went to sew at the French Australian League of Help in the afternoon. It was the first time I had been there. I felt a bit shy when I went in. There were about 6 or 8 other girls sewing at the table, & I happened to know one girl so she introduced me to Mlle Soubéron who was in charge, & I fell to work. They were quite nice people & we talked of nothing in particular for a bit & then Mademoiselle S. came & sat at the table & brought a neat little basket from which she produced many letters. They were all French letters but she translated them into English as she read for the benefit of all. They were letters from French tommies who had received parcels of clothing from the league—letters from two "lonely soldiers" whom Mlle has adopted as her godsons & who write often to her. Letters of appeal from other tommies who had not received parcels, & who begged the favour of a warm shirt or a pair of socks from "the kind ladies in Australia" & the last a letter from that Soeur Julie who defended her convent & her 400 wounded soldiers so wonderfully last year. One letter was from a man in one of the African regiments, which are made up of "garçons difficiles" & this letter was *pathetic*. It was full of gratitude for the beautiful shirt he had received, but said that he had one great fear— namely that the letter which he had found in the pocket might not be for him "because it was so nice." Poor chaps! I had to hide my face under my hat & weep over all these letters that she read. They were more touching than I can tell. Tell me, are French tommies in real life so different from English tommies—are they different in their hearts? There were sentiments expressed in these letters which would hardly come from sensitive & refined women in our country, & they are only rough soldiers. Of course they express themselves most exquisitely & they express everything they feel—whereas we don't, or can't—but what I want to know is, are they an absolutely different people from us in their inmost feelings?

[*The new Vulcan ambulances had arrived, and Olaf's Lanchester was retired to the garage. Olaf now divided his time between driving and managing the convoy's supplies.*]

Friends' Ambulance Unit
4 April 1916

My dear, when you get this I believe you will be arriving at your birthday [25 May]. It seems almost impossible that a letter should take so long, but what with our out-of-the-way position and the censoring and the irregularity and slowness of the mails now-a-days I don't think this will reach you much before you are twenty-two. Last birthday found you in Australia, as this will. The one before found you in Paris and me with you. Do you remember that day? I triumphantly presented you with some flowers bought at the shop round the corner, and Yvonne smiled and looked mischievous. Funny old days! You can't think how hard I tried to keep my dignity at those little dinners in the Jacques' room where everyone talked French and I could only catch a bit here and there. I guess I should follow better now, though my French will always be pretty feeble. Those teas in the rooms of that young artist chap (I can't recall his name) were a fearful strain on one's linguistic powers too. Do you remember all four of us on the verandah, looking down into the street? Birthdays are mile stones; may our paths meet before the next stone after this. . . .

Yesterday was a perfect spring day, warm and bright. Many of our cars were out, but all were back in time for tea. We make our tea in our shed with a primus stove. Imagine a big wooden place with earth floor and half a dozen of us sitting about in deck chairs holding enamel cups and smoking pipes. Everyone was contented and talkative; and I think we made rather a picturesque little group, all in khaki shirts and bare arms, all in the shade, looking out into the sun. This morning was misty, and it was cold all day, but we have had our first taste of spring. There is a wonderful feeling, an indescribable unreasoning joy, in the spring; it is the thing that has been sung through the ages, and one of the most wonderful of all intangible and very real things. . . .

[*Another day.*] You don't seem to realise that in this place [Crombeke] one is about as safe as one is at Annery, at any rate until anything very big happens just here. Things happen all round about us in the bigger places, but here nothing. There is nothing here but an infernal noise. As I write the window is shaking continuously with the noise and rather distracting me. Bang! Great Scott there's a big'n! It's only at W[oesten] that things happen, and I seem to be permanently stuck in the mud here, because of the stores. So don't go imagining me in the midst of thrills and adventures, because it makes me feel rather sheepish to be pottering here. But then one has just to do what comes to hand and go where France tells one to go. (Confound that window!) We are really capable of doing ever so much more work than we have here now, and are spending most of our time still making the convoy more and more efficient and self-dependent. But we are not capable of doing a quarter of what might any minute occur if there were to be a big battle here. That is the way with all things military—semi-idleness and the possibility of sudden strains. The difficulty is that this life is apt to make one grouse without end, and feel rebellious. Before I went on leave we never bothered about grousing. Here we get very militarised and have lots of petty annoyances.—There I am, grousing again! (——that window!)

Pause, while I take a friend's watch to get a new glass from the village watchmaker's assortment. He has a little house tucked away behind the church. I walked into a small square room and found him, a fat fair Fleming, sitting at his worktable before the window. The table was covered with all manner of strange watches, and strange fascinating little instruments. He made me sit down while he looked for the right size of glass. The room was very bare, save for three china saints and a crucifix. In one corner sat his wife knitting and rocking the cradle. In another corner was an ancient man who might have been a Holbein creation. He read aloud from a Flemish paper, monotonously, and to me unintelligibly. Soon he departed and a French soldier of forty-four summers came in, also for a watch glass. Then we all set to work to discuss the great subject—"When will the war end?" Having thrashed it out with no result we listened to the Frenchman's account of himself. He said he did not care how long the war lasted. He was being fed by the government, and what more could he want? "But you are always behind the lines," said Madame. "*Rather*," said he, and we all laughed. Then he told us about the one time he had been shelled and how quickly he got on to his bike and rode away. (He was a Cycliste.) Then Madame went away and the baby squalled, whereupon the Frenchman got up and rocked the cradle with an experienced hand, talking the while. Then the fat watchmaker gave me a careful and formal lecture on the watch industry in general, rocking himself back and forwards on his chair like an inverted pendulum, and working the while. At last the job was finished and after adieus I retired, to tell you all about it. . . .

I am a very mediocre creature, not strong, but hither-thither-blown, perpetually deciding to be strong and perpetually failing, perpetually lifted up by an ideal and being dragged in the mud by "the flesh"; perpetually preaching & lazing, scheming & dreaming. Good night, dear. I can't write decently tonight. Bang, bang, rumble, roar, quiver, rattle, bang, grrrumpl, ratatatatatat, bang.

Egremont
TO OLAF                                                                    10 April 1916

. . . Re conscription: people out here say, "We *must* win the war, & that means we must have the men. If we haven't the men we shall lose the war & we shall be conscripted by the Germans. So let's choose the lesser of two evils & be conscripted by our own people." And by "winning the war" what do we mean? If "winning the war" means "smashing" Germany I don't believe we shall ever do that because we can not & will not fight her with her own weapons. I believe we should not be ourselves if we could smash her in that way. But we *could not* make peace now & leave our little noble Ally in the hands of the enemy & our small Balkan allies to share the same fate. You would not have it so, would you for the sake of Peace? What do the Belgians themselves say? Old Sir Richard Grenville was not just making a song when he cried

> "Sink me the ship, master gunner.
> Sink her or split her in twain.
> Let us fall into the hands of God,
> Not into the hands of Spain."

If we could get back all we have lost by any other means than by fighting for it, I would rejoice among the first that no more blood need be shed. Isn't that all we are fighting for? We have given up the idea surely of ramming Liberty down their unwilling throats—all we want is our own restored to us. In Peace time we shall do more than in war, there is so much noise going on that noone can hear. . . . I remember you were doubtful long ago about not fighting on the ground that you *would* fight for your own wife & your own family. Of course I know that to serve the individual exclusively is just as dangerous as to serve the state exclusively. I suppose we must call for our old friend "Mediocria Firma"— but it's often very hard to find her, isn't it?

TO AGNES                    12 April 1916

. . . Agnes mine, think of it! Think of my quietly writing letters to you when time goes flying past and we are never together. You say I am to think of you as part of me, that cannot be divided from me by absence or death. Indeed I think of you so. In some way that must be the fundamental truth, for we both feel it to be so; but *how* it can be so we cannot say. Therefore we live in a curious longing for what really all the time *is*! Agnes dear, it's strange to think how we two have got mixed up together; it's really a wonderful story, isn't it. "Lovers" is a word that can mean so many different things, from "The Winter's Tale" to Beatrice & Dante; from the "Brushwood Boy" to the Brownings; from "Peter Pan" to "Othello." I know you far better now than when I saw you last. Once I was afraid of you, as one is afraid of Artemis. Then I ceased to fear because I knew you better & you were to be won. Now I think I begin to fear again because I know you so much better still, & begin to realise Athena in you. She is the far greater goddess. Once I used to "lecture" you. Later I could not find an excuse for lecturing; now I think I dare not for shame, even if the excuse should ever come.

Friends' Ambulance Unit

Agnes,                   18 April 1916

Here am I at last at W[oesten]. I came up yesterday, and promptly went off on a sixty or seventy mile trip. Then at night I went up to the furthest aid post as a passenger in someone else's car so as to learn the lie of the land. There was a moon, so we saw quite a lot. The roads are very bad, worse than the aid post roads I knew up north, but practically without traffic. They are very muddy just now, and full of holes and twists. I believe we go up to about 400 yards from the first-line trenches, but that may be exaggerated. Anyhow the country up there is very much devastated. There is a line of tall trees (some intact, some broken off short) beyond which are the trenches. We had a long wait, listening to crackings & whizzings from rifles and watching rats crawling and scampering about in the moonlight, over heaps of all kinds of rubble etc. There are plenty of buildings, all very much knocked about, and all the fields are full of shell holes. It is a gruesome place, quite open, so that you can see the state of things all round about. There was absolute silence last night (except for rifles), and very little has happened for a week or two in this region. The worst of it is one never knows when it is going to begin again. We brought back a badly wounded man and had to take him very slowly indeed, & even so he shouted. We had set out at 10.30 pm and only finished the whole expedition at 3 a.m. Then came bed,—that spot of bliss. . . .

We are a dirty looking lot of beings in this weather, but we *can* look smart—for inspections. I am in charge, which is awkward, as everyone else knows all about things & I don't. But they are a good lot, & in the FAU the nearest you can get toward a republic the better control you have over people. At least that is what I find. Being in charge of a tiny affair like this is negligible in ordinary times, but in emergencies it is not. Yesterday when I was in HQ I saw lots of my old friends, and inspected the car of one who had been getting into hot places. The bonnet was pretty well riddled, but the engine practically escaped, and my friend was not touched. That was done at the old old place [Coxyde], not here. This letter seems rather full of semi-thrills. . . .

[*Another day.*] Last night I sat in bed repairing my sheepskin coat, which is always tearing. You would laugh if you were to see the home-made mending on it, and you would laugh still more to see me pushing the needle into it. Last night there was a fearful din from a battery close to us. Every gun made one fairly jump, even though one knew it was coming, and the whole place rattled, & you could hear the shell tearing along through the air. Shells make all sorts of noises according to their size & the direction in which they are going. Medium size ones approaching have a high screaming whistle, and going away the note is much lower, like a cart rattling. Side-ways on (so to speak) they make a noise like calico being torn. Big shells approaching are generally not audible (? they go faster than sound), but going over head they sound like the roar of a train. I have never heard that.

Cymbeline

Olaf,                                                    23 April 1916

Once more in the nice Cymbeline kitchen, but times have changed. Instead of a rollicking party of girls sitting round the table at supper time with combed & flowing hair, clad in gay Japanese kimonos, bare feet, bare arms, bare necks, now we have just Daddy & Mother & Rosie & Agnes reading, writing & knitting round the table in the lamplight, while the oven-fire crackles & flames & there's a horrid smell of milk that just boiled over a little while ago. Outside it's cold & starlight—not really cold, nothing like what you have, but we make more song about it & we sit with our brown jerseys & overcoats on & we go for a quick tramp along the road to warm our feet last thing before going to bed. It is a blessed thing to have warm feet & one doesn't realise it until one gets the blues with having constantly icy ones. I think I was really meant to be a black tropical girl, because I simply can't keep warm in cold places. When I come to you in England I shall have to invent some new contrivance for keeping warm, or better a new circulation.

But we are having a lovely little holiday & we are enjoying it ever so much, cold & all. I meant to begin writing to you when we first came up 3 days ago, but we have been out picnicking each day & in the evening when we get in we always have to turn to & light our fire & get a meal & wash up & then Daddy reads aloud or we are too tired & are ready for bed. When we walk home tired & happy in the dusk & watch the sun setting golden & glorious behind its banks of cloud, I always think how good it would be to have you here watching it too, & this evening dragging tired limbs up the long hill from the valley we turned to watch the twilight falling on far soft blue hills with the sky tinged with a faint blush of sunset & tender grey streaks of cloud above fading into open heaven & I longed to have you near to feel how quiet & still & peaceful it was. We passed two lovers arm in arm & I felt lonely.

This is Easter Monday. . . . Today we [walked] down a winding mountain road through Blackheath Glen into the Megalong Valley. All down the road there are tall sassafras trees overgrown with wild vines, & tall silver-stemmed gums & beautiful tree-ferns & thick undergrowth & on each side of the glen there are high copper-coloured sandstone cliffs with far away gums on top looking like twigs, some 5 or 6 hundred feet up. Then when the valley opens out, it is flat, or gently undulating, & some patches are cultivated & have little primitive homesteads built on them & one sees cattle & sometimes pigs & sometimes nice sheep dogs keeping watch under a timber wagon, & sometimes a burly drover or a farmer man and patches of brilliant green corn or yellow oats & nice barns full of hay & old quiet horses, & further on there are bush roads or tracks through stretches of ring barked country—not a tree with a green leaf on it, just forests for miles of grey dead timber all standing up waiting to be struck down by lightning or wind or woodman's axe. But down there also there are some of the most beautiful, superb gums I have ever seen. They are so splendidly athletic in their build—strong & tall & stalwart, the trunk & some of the arms twisted fantastically & knotted, & yet they are gracious & friendly, & some of the trunks are marked with dark reds & purples & pale yellow & green in flakes almost like tongues of flame. Sometimes these flame-tongues go in spiral bands up the trunk & then it looks like a twister column, & others are silvery white, or pale fawn or lemon yellow. We saw no red gums today, but I think these are more beautiful. . . . We passed the shady stream today where I read your letters which made us engaged in the eyes of people here. It seems a long time ago, doesn't it? It's only nearly four months. And now it seems the most natural & simple thing in the world to be 'engaged,' but then it seemed something new & unknown & strange & awful & exciting. Enid [Kirkus] & Frank [Noyce] can point to their wood at Ffestiniog & say that is where they became engaged—but you & I? Where can we point? To England & Wales & France & Switzerland

24th April 1916.

Agnes,

Last night a splendid budget came from you, & I read it in bed, and again after lunch I read it sitting in a field. You had been unwell, for which I was very sorry in spite of its affording me such a lovely letter! I am glad they spoil you when you are not well. You tell me of your being ill in Berlin, & how you grieved for your people. You think that was weak! Heavens, most of us don't worry much about other people when we are ＊ ill, I fear. You tell me also about Jack Armstrong. Good luck to him, he deserves it. He makes me want a commission.

Next Day. (There came an interruption.) Quite a lot has happened since I wrote the above. First came ▓▓▓▓▓▓ from HQ about a protest that is to be made against the ▓▓▓▓▓ behaviour of the tribunals and the equally ▓▓▓▓▓ way in which the FAU is being used as a kind of conscription for conscientious objectors. We insist that the Unit shall remain voluntary. We who joined long before there was any question of conscription do not want our Unit made into an underhand weapon against complete objectors. Some members are signing a strong protest against all this ▓▓▓▓ ▓▓▓▓▓▓▓▓▓▓▓▓▓▓▓▓▓▓ That is to ▓▓▓▓▓▓▓▓ ▓▓▓▓▓ We out here have had to decide on our attitude. It is a big thing to settle all in a hurry. They read us letters from Friends now in prison ＊ who feel that the FAU is cutting the ground from under them in their fight for free conscience. The letters were quiet, Quakerish

The letter of 24 April 1916, showing excisions made by the FAU censor.

& to a big pile of letters dating from somewhere early in the 20th century up till 1916 & say—There. Somewhere there. . . .

This is Anzac Day. April 25th. The first anniversary of the glorious & dreadful landing of the Australians & New Zealanders on the rugged cliffs of Gallipoli. That was Australia's first day in the great world & she is not going to let it be forgotten. In Sydney there are all sorts of commemoration services & parades & observances. It is not to be a holiday but a holy-day.

[*The heavily censored opening of this letter indicates how nervous the officials of the FAU had become about political criticism from their members at a time when the Unit's survival was far from certain. The issue worrying Olaf and others was whether English tribunals, which heard the cases of men seeking exemption from military service, might use the FAU as a "dumping ground" for problem cases, with the result that the Unit would have an influx of new members serving unwillingly; at the same time those serving in the Unit did not want to compromise the witness of the absolute conscientious objectors at home.*]

Friends' Ambulance Unit
TO AGNES                                              25 April 1916
. . . Quite a lot has happened since I wrote. . . . First came
[CENSORED]
from HQ about a protest that is to be made against the
[CENSORED]
behaviour of the tribunals and the equally
[CENSORED]
way in which the FAU is being used as a kind of conscription for conscientious objectors. We insist that the Unit shall remain voluntary. We who joined long before there was any question of conscription do not want our Unit made into an underhand weapon against complete objectors. Some members are signing a strong protest against all this
[CENSORED]
That is to
[CENSORED]
We out here have had to decide on our attitude. It is a big thing to settle all in a hurry. They read us letters from Friends now in prison who feel that the FAU is cutting the ground from under them in their fight for free conscience. The letters were quiet, Quakerish and very forcible. We have had to think very seriously, whether or not in this crisis we should go home to fight for freedom of conscience or whether we should continue here at our small but real work. I know you would be very grieved if I were to go. I know you look at the FAU as just one form

of the great war service, while I look at it in a quite other light. I know it would mean no end of horridness for many people if I were to go. I can't explain the ins & outs of it all to you, but realise that in England a considerable number of admirable people are suffering severe imprisonment rather than join the FAU. Realise that what you see in the papers (most papers) is an altogether distorted account of these things. Realise that we here are mostly very convinced and ardent antimilitarists and upholders of freedom. Try to realise, if you can in surroundings entirely out of sympathy with these ideas (Australia is so); realise that it is at least possible that these "martyred" people may after all be doing more good than we. If you feel all this you will understand that we are very sorely perplexed as to what to do. If I were to go back now you would be engaged to an ostracised person, & that could not be. In fact it would be altogether inextricable & horrible, and the mere giving you back your promise would be very far from squaring things. But I am not going back, not yet anyhow. The great majority of us are signing a strong protest against the various evils, but are saying that we will not resign simply because we don't feel it right to give up this work to support people who cannot conscientiously do this work. My dear, this is a fearfully muddled explanation, & I fear you will not understand it at all. It is muddled because there's the deuce of a noise going on from certain too near artillery, also there are things happening in the air. Bang! I am sitting outside. The earth seemed to shake with that bang & the air to split. It's getting rapidly impossible to write at all. . . .

From various directions comes the sound of rifles & sometimes of singing bullets. Occasionally the rat-at-at of the mitrailleuse is heard. Trench flares go up and brightly light the place. One passes by a spot where a shell scored a direct hit on the trench, the sides being blown out, & in course of repair. Rats crawl about & squeak. Talking is reduced to an undertone. Away to one side is the sound of some constructional work under way, & the clanking of heavy iron. Far away on the horizon are occasional brilliant pinprick flashes in the sky—shrapnel bursting somewhere down the line. . . .

*Another day*, and a lovely one. We are all lying on the grass having tea. I have got to the pipe stage. Our ordinary peacefulness has been somewhat disturbed the last two days. First they began dropping shells sufficiently close to be unpleasant. Then at night a farm was burnt and a lot of ammunition in it crackled away merrily all night. Then again they shelled and we spent the morning dodging behind trees while bits flew about, and in collecting bits between whiles. We were far enough away for there to be no serious damage done by fragments. One small piece fell on our wooden roof & did not come through. Then there was a lot of firing at planes overhead, which we found decidedly unpleasant, because things keep falling pretty profusely. A shell case came down six yards from me and buried itself three feet in the ground. All is quiet now, but we are still inclined to imagine that the wind in the trees is a shell coming, or a rattling cart is a shell coming, or a bee is a piece whizzing. It is a gorgeous day, and simply to be alive in it is a pleasure. We are all in scanty easy clothes—shirt sleeves turned up & collars off, & (most unmilitary) no hats. The sun is getting strong enough to brown us. The fruit trees are in blossom, the birds are singing their heads off. There are speedwell and all kinds of bright little flowers, and all one's limbs seem loosened from the winter and from heavy clothes, and the sun is in one's blood. The spring is a rejuvenescence of everything. Your lover, who should be feeling thirty, has incontinently fallen back into twenty again, and finds even that much dignity hard to maintain.

Annery
Agnes,                                                      6 May 1916
    Annery dining room is the same as ever. The fire burns merrily, and I sit in the rocking chair trying in vain to write as if I were sitting at the table. I have managed to get home before Father & Mother, who are due from Llandrindod this afternoon! I'll tell you all about my coming, for it was interesting. . . . The day before yesterday I had a joy ride in the front seat of someone's car from our place of "repos," Rexpoede, through smiling country, stopping twice to pick up malades to take to Dunkirque. The driver of the car was the fellow whose command I took in his absence up at the front. He is about 21, a farmer, a Friend, a young man of character; and when he and I are together we rag like children. That joy ride was the first step in my journey home, so I was gay. I played tricks on him all the way, switched off his current, pressed out his clutch, punched him in the ribs as he was turning corners, and finally had a free fight over the steering wheel, much to the amusement of the malades. Disgraceful conduct for two of the leading lights of a Friends' convoy, but what of that. The larks sang, the sun shone, and the world was green below & blue above. . . .
    Well, well, at Malo (HQ) I had a bath, the first for six weeks. (Please excuse these graphic details.) I got my papers and set off by train to Boulogne with other "permissionaires." We dined in Calais and slept in the FAU's hotel quarters at Boulogne, having reached that centre of British red tape at one in the morning. Next day we went through all the formalities and embarked upon multitudes of cheery British tommies, genteel officers, and pompous "brass hats" of all kinds. The boat was packed, & as we had to wear life belts she was packed still more! There were many Australians on board, & I devoured them with interest. They were a sturdy weather worn crowd, & their queer loose clothes

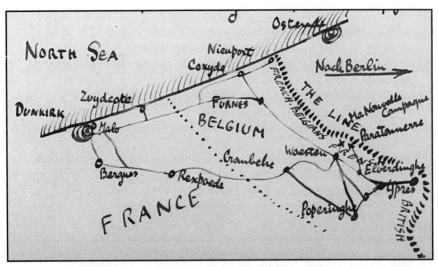

A small sketch-map of the convoy's locations during spring 1916, inked in a corner of the letter Olaf wrote to Agnes while he was on leave, 8 May 1916.

and big hats marked them off from the rest of us. They seemed mostly small men, which was odd. One of them only reached my shoulder, & I am rather less elevated than most of us. Their officers looked nice fellows and hard as nails, not nearly so genteel as the English in their immaculate attire but no less gentlemen. There were Canadians too, but they were less distinctive. Our voyage was fair, & interesting. At Folkestone we had a desperate battle to get into the fourth train, and finally that train also was packed tight. All the way up to town we were cheered, cheered on end, by the inhabitants of England. Houses and streets were full of women and children waving & shouting & wildly blowing kisses; and old men ploughing would stop as we passed and wave their hats. We of the FAU had need to think much, for behold us conscientious noncombatants, yet dressed much like British officers; feeling fully (surely) the love of England that others felt, yet anxious to prove that our work was not meant to bring victory to England. Think of us also definitely members of the French army, each bearing official papers headed "Armées Françaises en Campagne," yet bearing no French marks on our clothes. France, in her generosity, sends us all the way home (e.g. to Liverpool) free of charge, home & back. France calls us "soldats conducteurs," and feeds us always. Yet we are free volunteers, able to leave after three weeks' notice, and this while England & France are both lands of compulsion. We are free to leave, but having left our freedom would be short lived. But, girl, that journey over made one long to be a soldier and deserve those ecstatic cheers, and feel entirely at one with all those patient khaki hosts. It would be far the easier course, believe me. We are all discontented on our convoy and eager for more work. We want at least to bear all that others bear. It gets to be a burning desire. We do a fair average amount of work, & we are not entirely "embusqués," but sometimes one positively *wants* that great attack on our front which is always coming & never comes. Many of us have long ago decided that the most fortunate fate would be to get substantially wounded in a real action. Seriously we think so. We would gladly form a stretcher bearing unit to work in the trenches, but all such work is regimental. We would do anything, in fact, that would enable us to sacrifice without fighting.

Annery
Sweetheart,                                                          8 May 1916

Is that word nice or not? It's good English anyhow, and indeed thoroughly embedded in the language. I think it's nice, and genuine and simple. "Fiancée" is foreign, & might mean one pledged without love; but "sweetheart" is one gladly given. It is a country word too, and means a bonny lass in love and happy. And you are a bonny lass, besides being many higher things. "Betrothed" is more solemn, and "lady love" is either romantic or half comic. "Best girl" is a bit vulgar, but expresses much. "My young woman" is as honest as bread and butter. "My girl" is altogether complete and expressive. "Dearest cousin" might mean nothing, but from me to you it would mean everything. . . . Once you told me how you lie in bed on your verandah and watch things in the morning. If I could, and dared be so unconventional, I would invade that verandah very early, in the dawn, and you would be the Sleeping Beauty and I should wake you with a kiss, a most reverent, gentle kiss. But you would start up and blush and think of the conventionalities. Yet perhaps it would be as in Meredith's "Love in a Valley," and you would put your arms round my neck. Anyhow when we are married you will not mind if I wake you so. . . .

[*Next morning.*] You talk about Rupert Brooke. "Grantchester" delights me much. It makes me fairly chortle with joy. The sonnets are indeed fine, especially of course "The Soldier," and also "Safety," the truth of which I have begun to feel in Flanders, but only lately. Another sonnet I like much is the one beginning "Not with vain tears," about psychical research. It is very sound as a fundamental criticism of all spooks. If they *do* behave as the Society [for Psychical Research] says, all I can say is they are fools at the best and gibbering idiots at the worst. (I mean the spooks, not the Society, though that may be true too.) And yet, why of course, if I were dead and a spirit, I should be clamouring at the doors

of the physical to get back to you. The poem "Heaven" is—scrumptious,
the one about the fish. Compare Browning's "Caliban upon Setebos."

Egremont
TO OLAF                                                                9 May 1916
. . . At a meeting the other evening I had a long chat with a very much
alive & very nice grey haired lady called Mrs. Messiter. It was all about
Germany & the Germans. She was there in 1901 & met with great
kindness as did I also in 1913. It was good to talk of them & realise that
they are kindly human beings like ourselves. Oh dear, my dear, of
course I am one, heart & soul, with you in your ideals for the future of
Europe & for Humanity in general. Where you stand firm & I still
stumble is that I cannot make up my mind whether pacifists, idealists,
individuals ought not to sacrifice themselves & put their principles on
one side for the time being until we have won our way through this
chaos, & then when it is over & people can pause & think, take them
up again & try to educate people to them.

But no no, it was this in your letter that made my face burn—that
you should think perhaps I might be ashamed because you are not a
soldier. You feel that you are right in not fighting, & I know that you
feel so. When I read your letter I saw things all your way & forgot my
own, myself. You are living up to your lights & I trust your lights so
much that I cannot be "ashamed" of anything you do. Only I am perplexed about those lights. I do trust you absolutely & I want to think
exactly in your way—but I must find the way myself, because I've got a
mind of my own which won't be knocked down by my heart.

["Dag" was Agnes's nickname in Sydney. While Olaf was on leave Peg
o' My Heart was on stage in Liverpool. The furnace of the Mostyn steel
works lit up the bank of North Wales on the opposite side of the Dee
estuary from Annery. The harsh suppression of the Easter uprising in
Dublin was just a few days past.]

Annery
To the Lady Agnes Miller in Sydney,                                    9 May 1916
        from her betrothed.
    Dear, it is so long since I wrote to you! Seven hours, in fact! It is night
now, and I must sleep or they will wonder at my sluggishness. But just a
word first. . . . Tomorrow your lover is thirty. Heaven help me! I can't
feel that old. What is a fellow to do? I feel we are boy and girl lovers
still. Damn! It's a bother growing up! Oh Dag of my heart, we'll be boy
and girl as long as we live, even when we are greyhaired. In the new age
it will not be necessary to grow up. It will be an age of boys and girls.

You shall see! War, even the fringe of it, makes one feel that youthfulness is the highest virtue, and pessimism the deepest blackest crime. So, as I say, sweet Dag of my heart, let us gladly remain boy and girl. The heart of a boy and the mind of a man, that is someone's ideal, & a sound one. But thirty years are thirty years, and must be faced. May the next ten years for me be years of achieving, not mere attempting, anymore. . . .

*Next night,* in my room. Outside the moon is shining through mottled cloud and clear sky. The tide is up, and the Mostyn furnace is a big fiery star, reflected in the still water. The woods are black against the water, silhouetted against it in a black tracery of tree tops and branches. Our little winding pathway down to the gate is dim and mysterious, a path in fairy land. A pee-wit is crying, and sometimes a sleepy duck. A tiny breeze began to whisper in the trees, and soon tired of it. A train is heard as a peaceful murmur far away. There's not a sound of war! No guns, however far and faint! No whirring aeroplanes. Nothing but quiet water and English countryside. Somewhere in Flanders a French driver is at this moment taking his car along the aid post road, blessing the moon. There are guns, near or far, and perhaps they are unpleasantly near. There are wounded men waiting for him in a dugout, waiting perhaps since the morning. They are in pain, great or small; they are very tired. They are soaked in blood, maybe, in spite of their bandages. There is a difference between this world and that. But things are very far from right even here. . . .

Dear, this poor country is in a bad way, and grows worse. They have lost all common sense and prudence over Dublin. They are shooting far too many rebels, and some cases are grossly unfairly tried. This is not the way to settle the Irish business. And the whole rebellion was apparently a desperate attempt to forestall a military plot to crush the nationalists. Father is very indignant about it all. And the stories we hear of hopeless mismanagement by army authorities are very sad. It is simply the high commands that are weak. And alas for freedom! Habeas corpus & free speech are gone. Parliament is superseded by "the Government" too. I can't explain nor prove all this, but it is only too clearly true to us here. . . . At the front one is so cut off from home things that one does not realise how bad the present state (even) really is. It has been rather a shock to find out. But one has to cling to the hope of a general spiritual purification as the only way out of it all. It will come, surely, surely, but only if we all make it. Anyhow, in this war-stage pessimism is wicked. We cannot afford to grieve; or, having begun, where should we end? We must deny ourselves the luxury of mourning and of despair and of fear until a better world has been made. No black clothes now; no sad minor music, for it loosens the courage.

Friends' Ambulance Unit

Agnes,                                                                    21 May 1916

I am in my car in a green field among the buttercups. There are tall trees round us, under which our cars are supposed to be hidden from aerial observation. The grass is all mottled sun and shadow. Three red cows sit patiently munching, with eyes half closed and ears flicking. There is a blackbird singing, a wood pigeon cooing, and in the middle of the field is a little pool full of water-crowfoot, upon which a lot of little bright green frogs bask in the sun, or flop about, croaking most marvelously. This is war! I am lounging with my tunic off and my shirt sleeves turned up, displaying a pair of arms about the same colour as the khaki shirt. . . . We most of us sleep out of doors now, on groundsheets in a dewy field. The other night we lay in bed watching a great display of anti-aircraft shrapnel, bursting with bright instantaneous flashes far away in the dark. Also there were searchlights feeling about all over the sky, and Venus steadfastly shining through it all. It's lovely sleeping in a dewy field. You stretch your hand out into the grass and get it delightfully cold and wet. We have given up stretchers, and just lay our groundsheets and rugs on the bosom of Mother Earth. The dawns are beautiful,—when one can manage to wake up in time to see them. There are trees that whisper over our heads, and there are little owls that hoot, and frogs that eloquently croak and now and then a nightingale filling the night. Do you remember once long ago, while you were a gay school girl in Australia, I once wrote to you in praise of stargazing, and you answered that you had tried it and found it fascinating? I get plenty of stargazing now, in bed. In those early days it was marvelous that you ever had time to gaze at stars, so busy living you were.

Last evening six of us sat on a fence and stared at Venus and a distant air raid that was taking place ever so far away in the pale green sky behind some dark green trees. Several of us were also painfully revolving the problems that beset us in this Unit. When I got back from England I found that things had considerably developed. A

[CENSORED]

are leaving the Unit; none of whom I know well, but many whom I greatly respect. It has been made known to us that the time has come for us to make up our minds to tow the line, attain military smartness, refrain from expressing opinions on dangerous subjects, and obey the authorities, or else resign. Well all that is quite reasonable; one sees that a Unit under the military in the war zone must do all that. But it goes to make one feel that one might as well be in the army honestly working for victory. I have made up my mind not to leave except to go to other definite work. I want to find out about War Victims work in Armenia and Corsica, but not in this country, but that will take some time. At present we are really not doing enough here to justify our somewhat shady position. It is all "betwixt the shine & the shade," and smacks too much of evasion and the line of least resistance.

Egremont
TO OLAF                                        22 May 1916
. . . Jack has gone—at last. He embarked yesterday, & while we were having our lunch down on Balmoral we heard the ferry boats tootling "cock a doodle do" which is the sure salute to a troop ship steaming away down the harbour with her precious load of khaki. . . . He is determined to look you up if he gets a chance. Poor old Jack, it's very trying having goodbyes of that sort. He's very sentimental & works himself up to an awful pitch—& like you *I hate farewell scenes* of any description. I like to shake hands & say, "Goodbye Jack, good luck." He kissed me—& I felt nothing but fury. I am very sorry for him, but I don't love him a bit. I suppose if I had been another girl & been wiser I would have choked him off altogether long ago—I did try to at first—that was before I came to England, but by the time I got home again he had taken root so firmly that he could not be moved—& then I suppose I had a kind of feeling of responsibility because he said I had done & could do more for him than anyone else. So I kept on being kind at intervals with the result that it is really rather a relief that he has gone now. Perhaps all his new adventures will change him a bit & make him more amenable to Providence. I hope you will be able to meet him sometime so that you can see for yourself.

Egremont
Olaf,                                          27 May 1916
    What do you think is the latest? (This is quite unimportant news. I don't know why I have put it as a sort of leading article.) I have blossomed forth as a journalist! At least I haven't seen myself in print yet but I shall do soon. You will laugh or be disgusted when you hear what it is; I am too. Mrs. Curlewis is interested in a new weekly paper that is being started, for schoolgirls & young people. Jean is going to be a weekly contributor. I don't know what column she will take, but Mrs. Curlewis asked me if I would write the "dress letter" every week. Fancy coming to me for anything about dress! how amusing! I am noted only for doing without things or making my old ones do. She sent me a couple of sample letters & asked me to write a couple more in the same vein just to let her see what I could do. So I wrote a couple with much labour & groaning & sent them up to her & she rang me up yesterday & was quite

enthusiastic about them, said they could not have been better & she is sure the editor will be well pleased with them. I am to get 5/– a week & Mrs. Curlewis said that perhaps they would be able to increase the remunerations later & give me some more work. I hope they will give me another subject before long. The idea of writing about dress & things appalled me & even more than that the fact that it has to be done every week, whether I like it or not. But Mother said I ought not to refuse it, because it will be good for me to have some regular responsibility of the sort & will help me to concentrate & collect my ideas. But it's an awful nightmare to think that one must cudgel one's brains to produce 600 words about dressing every week! However I may get quite clever at pretending I know a lot about these things. . . .

*May 30th.* I liked your little scene chez mister the watchmaker. You know, you write little scenes like that very well. Those are the sort of little glimpses I should like to write for my journal. I can't expound things. I can present the picture & let people draw their own conclusions. Now tell me, there are conclusions to be drawn from many little scenes, are there not? That is mostly what Stevenson does in his books of travel.

Friends' Ambulance Unit

TO AGNES                                             4 June 1916

. . . I am looking out for some really decent lace, but I am not much of a judge. I saw some good stuff yesterday, but someone else had already bought it. It is interesting to see the making, with pins on a cushion. The women do a lot of farm work all day, with hoe or coulter or harrow; and in the evening they sit in the window and make lace. They are mostly quiet fair fat women, healthy and plain. The children are often very pretty, but a pretty girl is as rare as a hill. Their country is really quite pretty though, just now, what with the woods and countless little paths among the rye. Some of the rye is eight foot in height. We do a great deal of "coming through the rye," though we don't get the chance to "kiss a body." The rye smells so fresh and clean. It is a great relief after the awful stinks of this country. Then there are brilliant green flax fields, not yet in flower. And of course there are the hops, already nearly up to the top of their twenty foot poles. Beans, potatoes, & clover seem the other chief crops. The amount of weeding that has to be done is amazing. The cottage alongside of our present position holds eighteen refugees, old men, women & children. There is a garden plot in front of it, and one often sees a large proportion of the family squatting on the soil weeding and chatting in their inelegant tongue. By the way, one would expect that there would be no Belgians of military age left for civilian

life, but the place swarms with them—strong, stolid young men. They
are everywhere, carrying on their farming just as ever. You know, we
who are in the very country of these people don't think of them and
their nation at all as you do.

[CENSORED]

but for the

[CENSORED]

said. I would say more, but the censor would cut it out.

In your last letter [10 April] you stated as cogently as it can be stated
the official position with regard to the war. You put things well, and
your reasoning is always capable of making me doubt my own, for a
time at any rate. Your reasoning is thoroughly sound, but your premises
are all wrong, according to me, nay, according to the facts as far as we
can get at them. I should like to answer your letter point by point, but if
I did it would probably be all cut out. They appear to cut out everything
that does not accord with the official attitude, judging by my mutilated
letters home. (Our censor simply has to do as he is told, of course.) But
there is just this much that I daresay they will let me say: I am no theo-
retical "non-resister." In the individual sphere I will fight for a good
thing, because I know that in that sphere the principle that fighting is
*generally* foolish and wrong has been already firmly grasped & is in no
danger. But in the national sphere it has not been grasped. Second
point: it is not selfish soul saving & conscience appeasing that keeps us
from fighting. That would send us either to fight or to prison. We risk
our silly souls because we hold that this middle course is the most likely
to help open the public mind to the folly of the whole business of war.
Our souls are damned already on both counts. Thirdly: which is best for
Belgium—to see the enemy quietly retire after an arranged peace (which
might even be done today, if the opposite diplomatists really wanted) or
to have a bloody war fought step by step through their country? Good
God! Fourthly: Ten days in England would show you how we are slipping back politically, socially & I fear mentally, because of the war. We
*may* spiritually rise, but even that I begin to doubt. And I imagine we
did not go to war to purify our souls, but to do good. Lastly: Your premises come from the papers, & you forget the *very* strict censorship of
facts & ideas. You think if we had not fought there would be now German policemen etc. in England. Easy to fear it; very hard to see how it
could be. Germany was fighting an internal battle of freedom.

There, that is not to convert you, but defend myself. You ask if I am
*sure* my cause is right. No, not since conscription. But I know that if I
join the army it will be to escape from an uncomfortable position, to
shirk responsibility, and not to help the Allies. I won't join the army (yet
I am practically already in the English & the French armies. The differ-

ence is a shade only, but a vital shade), because the whole war (especially if we win) is the

[CENSORED]

by

[CENSORED]

and as I love England (more than many a soldier) I will not

[CENSORED]

even if to refuse means to be damned body & soul. Even if it were to mean shaming the girl I love, even if it were to mean slipping away from her altogether. It may be priggish and snobbish and unsociable and pigheaded and pharisaical and hypocritical and hyperidealistical not to fight. The kindly human thing just now may be to fight. But if I fight it will be through weakness & selfishness and a wretched desire for applause, and because I shall have shut my heart to the great Spirit that is trying to realise itself in every mind and every nation and in all liberties and human institutions. The Spirit is a live thing & a lovable. To obey it is not selfish salvation-seeking. I wonder how much of that will get through. It is scrappy stuff anyhow. . . .

Well, friend, I guess we have found a pretty deep difference between us, though I hope we are so close as to be able to kiss and be friends over the chasm!

Egremont

Olaf Mine,                                    11 June 1916

It is Sunday evening at 10 o'clock. Not the time to begin a letter! but I want to. I have been lounging on the drawing room sofa finishing the end of a thrilling & awful & blood-curdling story by Conrad—his latest book it is—called "Victory." The four characters of the book all get wiped out in the last few pages & only the onlooker is left to tell the tale. A truly disquieting & awe-inspiring book with a fitting & awful termination. I have put it all away into an inside pigeon-hole & feel it there settling down, but I can talk commonplaces with anyone & whistle snatches of tunes as if nothing were unusual. . . .

*Monday evening.* I had my two precious letters this afternoon. They were both written while you were at W. Dear, what a place! It filled me with fears for you. And when I had read through both those letters I folded them up against my cheek & kissed them very hard. Oh God— keep him safe. While I was reading them I wanted to utter a host of interjections to you about the things you said. Yes I know the conscription problem must be a very big one. I am naturally not in the swing of it like you are—but don't think, because I am so far away, that I do not sympathize with what you say about it. I want you to tell me about the things that are nearest in your mind. You see I haven't thought very much about anything in particular, & I have an open mind to take in what you say & try to understand how you feel, but I want to tell you this which I am quite sure of though I have never thought it out. If you were to decide to leave the Unit & go home as a conscientious objector & I were suddenly to find that my lover was an ostracised person—why of course, he would still be my lover. There would be no difference to me, dear heart. You would never be a stranger to me. You would always be the nearest, the most familiar friend, & if you were to talk of giving me back my promise why I would lock it straightaway up again in your heart & throw away the key. . . .

Look, I am quite sure that you are taking your share of the risks & labours—at W anyway. At first when I read your letters they did take my breath away a bit because they were the most exciting that I have had—perhaps you told me more than at other times—but I want to know it all. Anyway suddenly I thought—well, it's his share, & it's right, & other girls feel like I do when they get letters from their lovers who are doing their share—& why shouldn't I? & he? And I think now I feel more happy than unhappy—more proud than anxious, though there come times for both. I'll be very glad when you get your leave & go home. Men in the trenches are not always in the trenches. Men at W must not always be at W, & it won't go out of my head that men when they *are* in the trenches, are less of a landmark than men at W. That place is very open, isn't it? Tell me, why do they put you in charge of a place you have never been to before? Is it because you are old enough to know best? (That sentence was cut out of your letter, annoyingly.) I should like to have a peep into all these little things!

[*"The Reflections of an Ambulance Orderly," dated 29 March and published on 14 April 1916 in* The Friend, *was printed without Olaf's name, but Agnes's letter identifies it as his. The account of the mission of the FAU alternates comments on the stars and planets with dialogue describing a night evacuation of wounded; ideologically and stylistically the piece is clearly Olaf's.*]

Egremont
TO OLAF                                              15 June 1916
. . . Dear Ambulance Orderly, I like your "Reflections" very much. It was like a breath of fresh air in the old "Friend"—like a home sunshine. I think that is the right attitude for Pacifists: "while there is a chance for serving those who nobly suffer through humanity's error, we cannot stay at home." I hope you will be able to stick by it—conscientiously—because I can't help thinking that while there is so much to be done,

one ought to *"do" as well as agitate.* You feel that perhaps you ought to lend your support to those at home who are suffering slings & arrows for their peace principles, but is it not possible to lend to such your moral support while you lend to the sick & wounded your physical? It's not compromising because they are all one humanity & they are all trying to live up to their own lights. Anyway, the physical support is the more urgent, for the moment.

We read a few days ago a gruesome account in the paper of the first small charge made by the Australians in France soon after their arrival. They just calmly jumped over the German parapet & down into the trench & disposed of the various occupants & returned unscathed. And when I read it I sent up a thanksgiving from my heart that you were not taking part in such wicked barbarous massacres as those. I couldn't rejoice in the dash & courage of our men anymore than in the stupor of the surprised Germans. It was just wanton, useless slaughter, & I suppose that is only a sample of what the whole war means. I am proud that our men & all men have it in them to be dashing & courageous, but— oh that they should have to use these for killing their fellow men!

Friends' Ambulance Unit
TO AGNES                                16 June 1916
. . . Last night there was no end of a scrap. I was lying in bed in my car when it began. I was facing it and saw all the shrapnel flashes in the sky and the big shells far off landing with a dazzling blaze. The noise shook my bus on its springs, and made the flame of my lamp jump. After a while a near battery began and the shells from it roared away through the sky. Rifles & machine guns could sometimes be heard through the din. I lay awake ever so long but finally got to sleep, and next morning we learned of a British success. All today there has been steady firing from the various batteries, shells going & coming, roaring and singing all over the place—crash—roarrrrrr-bang—bang-whewww-crash, much tearing of calico & much humming-top song. Yet if one's ears had been stopped up one would never have known there was war in this continent, save for a few puffs of smoke. Tonight I am on duty, lying, dressed, in the inside of the bus, stretched on a seat, with my belt strapping me in from rolling on to the floor. It's mighty awkward writing! Please forgive the vile scribble.

I have just been reading another dear letter that came from you today, you blessed girl. I did not intend to write tonight, but now I must, even while strapped into "bed." Your letter was from Egremont. It spoke of lavender that you wore and was pressed against the desk as you wrote. I smelt the paper, and the scent was still there, & quite strong! . . . Much of your letter was about patriotism and wanting to win. I don't know, dear, but it all strikes me very differently. I won't talk about it, for reasons censorial and others. You must judge for yourself, be loyal to your view of the truth; and I will be loyal to mine. Believe me, anyhow, England is no less to me than to you. "England, my England, maker of men!" I am not a crank nor an extremist, nor a little Englander even, but I fear you have gone and got engaged to a fellow whose views are not presentable in polite society, and I am deeply sorry for you. . . . Can you really love with all your heart and soul one who does not even *intend* to live up to your ideal, but sticks to his own? If so you are a heroine, considering the relation of the two ideals.

[SSA 13 *was ordered north to Coxyde just as the major offensives at the Somme further south were beginning.*]

Friends' Ambulance Unit

TO AGNES                3 July 1916

. . . We are now back at the place where I was first introduced to the front. It is quite like a homecoming to be back here again. The other FAU convoy has made the place very luxurious, and it has an air of permanent habitation such as we are not at all used to. The shed is elegantly painted green, a sort of reseda green, by the way. We have luxurious washing accommodation (but of course no baths). We are a far more mobile convoy than the other, which is one to us. We also have the more reliable cars and by far the finer to look at. The little shed where I sleep is a sort of overflow place, quite cosy, but the floor is soft sand, so that all one's possessions are full of sand. Today we are being inspected by a lord, which is an unmitigated bore. I am also first call for the northern aid post. Now a days we keep two men and a car permanently there, and when they get a job and come down the next pair goes up. If there happen to be no runs one stays up there for 24 hours and then gets relieved. They have a little billet in a not-too-battered house up there, whence they get a good view of things. At the other aid post one sleeps in an excessively stuffy dug-out. We have a dug-out at our main station down here also, home made, with sandbags. It is popularly known as the funk hole. Personally I think it would be rather more dangerous to be inside than to be outside! . . .

[*Next day.*] We are hearing of ever so much steady progress by the allies everywhere just now. They are mighty happenings, filling the mind with diverse feelings. If they will bring about a speedy end of war, they are worth the sacrifice that gains them. But we are too ready to think that after the war all our troubles will be ended. It is *after* the war that the fate of a civilization will hang in the balance, and personally I cannot feel sure that civilization, nor individual life, is going to make a steady ascent towards better things. But it's all guess work. We don't really know where we are, nor what will come. "The gods are playing a great game with us for their amusement," says Sam Whittall [Olaf's former WEA student]. It's a glorious game & a glorious age, when all is said and done. And we have all got to ask ourselves continually and searchingly whether we are playing our proper part; and more particularly so when a wise and high-souled cousin keeps haunting one with those straightforward eyes of hers, that seem to ask always, "Are you sure, *quite* sure?" Again & again & for ever, Agnes mine, I am sure—not sure that this little modest job is the best & most that I can do, but sure that some vision or other of mankind as one great being has made it wrong for me to fight. For Jack Armstrong it is right, and for me, Olaf Stapledon, it is wrong. The state may compel, but that "vision" may more powerfully forbid.

[*"Gadget" became a widely used word in English during the Great War, perhaps from contact with the French dialect term* gagée *(tool). The title character of Olaf's* Odd John *(1935) was an inveterate "gadgetiser," improvising remarkable tools out of scrap material.*]

Friends' Ambulance Unit

Agnes,                                       4 July 1916

Last night two of us were up at the ruined town [Nieuport] where we used to go in days long past. It was a lovely evening, so before turning in we wandered all over the town. It is much more battered than before, having just reached that stage between habitability and a heap of rubbish that is most impressive in smashed towns. The church, once a mighty and solid building, is a chaotic mess—whole walls flung down and still intact, here a great mound of ruin overgrown with bright poppies, cornflower, & mustard, and often with patches of oats or barley flourishing on top, self sown. There is still one fine wall and windows standing; and a single pillar stands, with a very beautifully carved capital of acanthus leaves. All round the church is the grave yard, closely packed with beautifully decorated little graves of soldiers. Some are covered with growing flowers mixed with gaudy artificial ones. Some are tiled over roughly with fragments taken from ruined house-fronts, or broken slabs of marble, or a headless statue of a saint, or some unrecognisable piece of marble wreckage. All bear their little wooden crosses & inscriptions, mostly commemorating some Breton marine. Some say simply "Here lies X." One, equally carefully adorned, is the grave of a German. Some graves are fenced in with bits of iron bedsteads. Shell holes are everywhere, and here & there you can still come across a

man's jaw bone or ribs turned up by a shell and overlooked by the
"sexton."

The whole ruined town is a medley of yellow & blue & scarlet &
green of flowers & leaves. Tall clover grows in the great square, pushing
up between the pavé stones. The houses are all shattered, but some still
stand in an almost habitable condition, others are tangled wrecks of
beams & brick, gay wall paper hanging in shreds, bent iron work,
broken glass etc. In one room that has been laid bare we saw a little
white iron work cradle, "long since disused." Here and there on plaster
walls soldiers have drawn marvelous "works of art," faces, people, battle,
and subjects concerned with the Frenchman's one joke. Here and there
is a rough notice forbidding entrance, for military reasons; here & there
a patch of lettuces for some officers' mess. Everywhere there are cellars
& dug-outs, and everywhere soldiers. Here a scribbled notice "Very
good drinking water," here a shattered wall of pre-war advertisement
posters. Here suddenly the nose of a cannon pokes out of a window at
you. And from the one side of the town you look across fields & a river
to the trenches, the first line I mean, for of course there are trenches
everywhere. Last night all was quiet, save for an intermittent rifle fire
and an occasionally wild bark of a gun next door to our post.

All the countryside is enriched with loot from that town. Mirrors, bil-
liard tables, pianos, tiles, stoves, all have come from that town. Now in
these latter days there is no loot of any value, for countless searching
eyes have been over every square foot of rubble. But a shell may sometimes turn up some little valuable that is immediately snapped up by
someone near at hand. Last night after our walk we slept in our car,
rather than go down into a stuffy dug out. Each of us lay on a seat &
tried not to keep the other awake by turning & fidgeting & fighting mosquitoes & other vermin. Neither of us slept anything to speak of, because of the wretched insects. And at last in the morning we got a job,
much to our relief after that vile night.

*Some days later.* Having laboriously and ingeniously mended my foun-
tain pen I can at last write to you. I broke the pen in two ragged pieces in
an impromptu wrestling bout. It is now marvelously repaired with sticky
tape and bound with cotton. It is as good as new, save that it is short,
rather bulbous, and to fill it I have to put the nib end in my mouth and
*suck* up ink. Great judgment is needed to know when to stop sucking!
There is no news to tell you, save that our hitherto secluded position
seems to be becoming unpleasantly central; but I must not say why. Last
night from our sand dune we had a most glorious view, yesterday afternoon, I mean. We had all our glasses and telescopes out and saw all
manner of very distant easterly objects, and disputed about them with
the aid of a map. Some of us had been in the said places before the

war; the rest wondered whether perhaps we should ever be in them, before the end of the war. To the East also there was a most glorious pile of white cloud, beautifully moulded in great shoulders and buttresses and little delicate roughnesses. Such clouds always make me half drunk, sort of. And when the setting sun gilded them most of us forgot all the famous spires and towers and were amazed at the cloud's beauty. There was also a particularly mad tri-plane that kept reeling and twisting and flying upside down, flashing in the low sunlight.

The other night I was up in our ruined front town again and amongst other things I prowled round the ruined railway station. The floors of the various rooms were covered with old railway literature and unused tickets. I made a little collection of tickets for souvenirs for friends. I would send some to Waldo, but of course they are censorable, so he must wait. People at home always seem fearfully keen to get hold of any little souvenir, such as here one can't bother to pick up. Souvenirs are too heavy and bulky to take home. I never attempt to collect big things. That railway station must have been a fine hunting ground for souvenirs once upon a time. We slept in my bus in an old brewery yard that night, and got a job at 2.45 AM. After we had gone there was a little bombardment, and two shells fell in the brewery, one of them showered bricks and tiles on the spot where my car had been. I am glad the car was not there, for she would have had her canvas roof torn, & that would have meant much wearisome sewing for me, and I am not a great sempstress! This life does teach one to do odd jobs of all sorts, such as one would never have dreamt of doing before. Do you know what a "gadget" is? I don't know what it really is, but in the FAU it is any little contrivance such as a tool box cunningly made to hold all your tools in neat positions, or a strap screwed into woodwork to hold your shrapnel helmet when not in use, or a dodge for holding your brushes or oiler, or a home made ferule on a walking stick, or any home made or professional little convenience. Some people spend all their spare time making gadgets, or "gadgetising." I seldom do so, having other fish to fry, but sometimes I have a fit of it, and gadgetise solidly for a couple of days and then get fed up. My pet aversion is the making of gadgets officially commanded (suggested). I fear I generally avoid such work, unless it is something necessary and interesting. Your cousin is rather insubordinate and pigheaded and democratically inclined! My last gadget but one consisted of crude tailoring, as a result of which I now appear with khaki shorts & bare knees in Anzac fashion, that dress being now permitted at the front in this glorious weather. We cause quite a sensation with our bare knees, here where there are few British about.

Today I am on duty and must not go and bathe, alas. Tomorrow, Sunday, it is my turn to be orderly and that means a day of hard labour under the supervision of the cook, who is a great oar in his way, &

comes from John's, Oxford. Next day I spend in a place where to bathe would be most immodest as it would be in full view of—the enemy. So there is no bathing for me just now.

Here comes someone to borrow my glass to see if he can "see the shell leaving" a certain big gun. I don't think! Not except from just be-hind it anyhow. There is always something or other to look at here. Now dear, I am going to stop, because lots of people are coming up here and there is much talking. So here ends one more letter. If all our letters were to be read through on end, alternately yours and mine, what a lot they would tell that we had not in mind to tell at the time of writing. They would tell of all sorts of changes and fluctuations and gradual evolvings that we knew nothing of at the time. All the past has proved for the best for you and me. We will believe the present is also for the best, but truly I think we are both ready now. Further waiting seems not able to draw us more together. Well, we have got to wait, and take our chances, while all this great business gets itself settled. What I keep wondering is whether in the future years I shall be able to persuade you that it was right not to fight. Anyhow, we shall be able to look back on this time and laugh at it kindly. And the world, someday, will look back on this awful time and laugh at it, though grieving over it. For the world is apt to grow out of its wars and grieve over them, & laugh at its past dissensions. Good-bye, dear. This is a short letter, but I am busy just now. I'll write again soon. Perhaps there will be another letter from you soon. Oh, but I love my Anzac girl!

> Your own
> Olaf Stapledon

[*Aunt Emmeline, Olaf's mother, kept pressing Agnes to venture the sea journey and marry Olaf soon. She felt Agnes could be happy at Annery while Olaf was at the front and saw no reason why the two of them shouldn't live at her house even after the war ended.*]

Egremont
TO OLAF                                                    5 July 1916
. . . I have been wanting to write to you a lot, all the time, ever since late on Sunday night when we got the exciting news of the British & French advances. Surely this is the beginning of "the great battle"! Everyone is talking about it. We are all being very quiet but we are full of hopes inside & so optimistic about the end in view. *Isn't* it good news! I want to let off some of my exuberance on you, & make you excited too about 'the end.' When you discussed "our domestic affairs" in detail, that made me very excited—that was like the advance, & now the news from the front seems to say "gains consolidated."

After I had written to you last time I got another letter from you, the
last one before you left home, in which you told me Auntie's scheme for
Annery & us. Now in my last letter I'm afraid I turned the scheme down
in a very ungracious & seemingly ungrateful manner. That was because
I didn't quite get hold of the idea. I have been talking it over with
Mother, & we think that it would be very nice for us to be at Annery
with Auntie & Uncle for a time. She would not advise us to think of it as
a permanency—because it might not work satisfactorily. But we might
try it as an experiment. I should like to try—& like to make it work. It is
very kind of them & of course I can see that there are very many advan-
tages from our point of view. I was only afraid that I should get demor-
alised by living in someone else's house & having nothing to do—but
the scheme is, you say, that we shall really have some definite part of the
house that we can call our own—then I shall be able to bustle round &
do things, shalln't I?

[*Stationed briefly at an abandoned boarding house on a hill near the
coast, Olaf gets a bird's-eye view of the front and the thin strip of no-
man's-land between the opposing armies' trenches.*]

Friends' Ambulance Unit
TO AGNES                                            11 July 1916
. . . The sea is green, and on the horizon it is peacock blue. Between
house and sea is sand-dune and flat sea beach, and all is in bright afternoon sunlight. Have you got the scene? There is practically no sound
but the sea's even sighing. Today happens to be a very quiet day, unlike
the last two or three. We have had one job so far, and with any luck we
shall get no other till eight o'clock tomorrow morning. Twenty-four
hours' sea-side holiday with no formalities, no rush, no disputes! My
companion has been telling me how last time he was here they gave the
spot a dose of shrapnel, and a bullet pitted the wall just beside his
head. Today one might as well be in full peace, save for all the smashed
houses, and the number of bullets etc. one comes across in the sand.
Beyond all the ruins I can see with my glass a wind mill quietly turning,
and a certain tower beside it. If the wind did not shake my hand I could
see a man if he chose to appear there. That shows how narrow the actual fighting area really is, for it is all between us and that mill; and the
hypothetical man would be a bosche. And that thin strip that I can see
across is bordered on each side by wider strips of sporadic ruination, and
from our sand dune, back at our camp, you can see the two extreme
limits of these wider strips, and beyond those, on each side, war is
not visible, but only a kind of terrible report. And this great belt, so
very narrow on the map in comparison with its length, stretches away

away down many days' journey into the south. Now in all this there is
nothing of any conceivable military value, but I begin to fear it will be
censored. . . .

*Later, the same day.* There is a little spell of sunset time to spare before
we set off on another run. My companion slept all the afternoon. He is
a lad of nineteen, one of the large class who are sons of strict Quakers
and far from strict Quakers themselves. He has rather a bad reputation
to fight against, but he is not really at all a bad lad, though sadly uneducated. He has spent too much time frivoling. But he means very well,
can work both hard and efficiently *when* he wants to, and would never
do a mean thing. He and I get on very well together. I am feeling re-
morseful because I was a bit sick at having him as my twenty four hours
mate and not some more interesting person; but we have quite appreci-
ated one another, and there has been no lack of conversation. He is of a
fine build, rather inclined to dress like a knut—rather a shop-soiled
knut. He is a very clever slacker, but as I say he *can* work. He designed
our present sheds long ago. And he is a really fine motor bike rider. He
is reading now, and I have just finished communing with my friend
John Cotton (who is a tobacco). I am sitting at our open window watching a rather tame sunset. I do like sunsets, and I think that people who
consider sunset-worshipping fit only for superaesthetes and lanky poet-
asters are guilty of an affectation of austerity. Don't you? I am not afraid
to admit that a fine sunset fires me and purifies me. There is a wretched
little gun behind us blazing away and shaking all my brains out, so
please excuse any muddles.

Egremont
TO OLAF                                                  12 July 1916
. . . Tonight at the [French] Cercle I was talking to a girl about the latest
cercle engagement (quite romantic) & she said, "And you have an engagement ring on. Are you engaged, Miss Miller?"

I told her, "To a cousin in England."

"A distant cousin?"

"In one way—but otherwise a first cousin."

She seemed surprised & said people didn't often fall in love with
their first cousins, but I think it's the most natural thing in the world,
don't you?

Friends' Ambulance Unit
TO AGNES                                                 15 July 1916
. . . You say you would "like to be able to write little scenes," and you
suggest that the aim is to describe and then find a meaning. I suppose

so, but I guess the meaning should not be too patently found, or you fall into the conventional story with a moral. For instance, there's a fellow opposite me grinding coffee. He has the mill between his knees while he sits out in the sand on a chair. His whole body swings with the swing of his arm, and his pipe dangles loosely and swings too. He looks round occasionally at people amusing themselves, and then turns his bored eyes back to the inexorable mill, and grinds on with a cynical frown. I don't think he even knows he is frowning. He is half asleep with the hypnotic circling of his own right hand. His pipe went out long ago. Now and then I laugh at him, and he replies with a ludicrous grimace. I believe he knows I am telling you about him. Now must there be a meaning to such a little fact? Must one talk about the wearisomeness of monotony, or the glory of service, or the unconscious grace of the human body, or the amount of labour that is needed to keep man in his luxuries? All this should be rather suggested than said, should it not?

Just now we are full of the news of slow-moving victory. (Not "winged" victory indeed in this case!) People seem to think that this is a step toward peace. If so it is not in vain. But it might just as well be a step toward a twenty-years state of war. War may very well become a permanent institution if the scale on which it is waged were to be narrowed a bit, so that total production and total war expenditure in men and money should be equal.

Egremont

TO OLAF                                                                 31 July 1916

. . . We had a great grief this week; our friend Carl Brown has been killed in action. We don't know where or how. Rosie came across it quite by chance in an old casualty list that she found some days ago. "Corporal C. Bennett [Brown]—U.S.A. killed in action." He is only 18 now, enlisted at 16, was in the Gallipoli Landing, & went all through without a scratch until this—such a nice bright intelligent boy—the one bright spot in his family, I think. They are all a broken up sort of family, poor things, but they all looked towards Carl. I'm very sorry for them. He is the first of our near friends to go & the one we have done most for & towards whom we have felt the most responsibility. It made me afraid because it came so suddenly, so easily. And there are so many of them in it—precious boys all. Bill & Lionel & Cliff & Max &—I couldn't believe that it might have been you Olaf, but it would have come just as suddenly, just as easily.

[*SSA* 13 *spent the month of August* en repos *at Malo on the coast, just outside Dunkirk. During the rest period most of the convoy's work was devoted to ambulance repairs and cleaning.*]

Friends' Ambulance Unit
Dearest,                                              6 August 1916
    Your last letter to arrive was written on June 13, and the previous one was June 20. Your letters have great races with one another. . . . Don't go thinking, just because I sometimes write journalistically to you, that we are having as much as a tenth of our proper share of danger. We are scandalously safe, and there is no getting over the fact. And of course in repos in a football field we are safer still! The worst of it is that though we on the convoys do get a certain amount of real war, the vast majority of the FAU gets next to nothing of it. And worse still there are crowds of new fellows always coming out (popularly known as conscription-dodgers) and the authorities never seem to give them any serious work, and they spend their time bathing or being uselessly chivvied about. And the discredit of it all falls upon the whole FAU, us included. The FAU used to be considered rather a fine thing in the early days, but soon the world will say it is the lair of the conscription dodgers, and no more. We shall certainly get no credit from anyone after the war, militarist or pacifist. But we did not come for credit, so I suppose we must not complain. I fear the older FAU hands are not very fond of the swarms that come out at the eleventh hour or after the twelfth hour. There's a distinct cleavage in fact. Fortunately I managed to get out in decent time in spite of appendicitis. Yet one must not sweepingly blame the newcomers. Many, I know, were sticking to their guns in not coming out until they were forced. Many had good domestic reasons. But no pacifist principles could hold them back & then impel them to go at the eleventh hour. Many of them are very decent fellows too, but the general average is not very prepossessing. And of course they have not got their hearts in the work even as much as we have. I wonder whether all this will be censored! I shall never cease to regret that I could not have come out here earlier, when all the great times were.

Egremont
TO OLAF                                              7 August 1916
    . . . When I got the first of the four letters on Saturday morning somehow I wanted to weep because you think I am so far away from you in what you think to be right with regard to war & conscription & so forth. . . . In spite of whatever I may have said I don't believe there's a gulf between us at all. If you think there is, don't let it rest at that, talk to me, write to me—because if I am not with you I haven't got a firm

Agnes Miller at home at Egremont in Mosman, a suburb of Sydney.

footing anywhere. It's no good to say we'll agree to differ & each be loyal to our own point, because I haven't got a point; poor bewildered me! Come back & give me a hand, an arm. I'm so tired of being without you. As a family we are much nearer your point of view than other families here—though of course we never hear your point of view discussed in this country; and of this family I am the nearest to you, nearer than Mother in spite of her Quaker traditions. Don't say, dear, or think that, though the war has drawn us together, it might have done still more if you had been fighting—because I'm sure that is not so. If you had been fighting I should have approved because you were doing what you thought to be your duty . . . [but] I would not have thought seriously of Pacifism & its handful of ardent upholders—at least I might have marvelled at them but never thought of being one of them. It is only because of you that I have been wakened up at all, & I'm glad—although it is a new & difficult way & I have not yet learned to tread firmly. But I have the feeling in me that it is the nobler way & I wouldn't give it up for anything while I have strength & you to guide me. The only reason why your way makes me troubled, & sometimes a little bit ashamed is because your work does not take you into such dangers as the other boys'—you, & I for you, are not taking the risks of the fighters. But I know it's not your fault, you have told me, & I know you would take more, gladly, if it were possible. At present it is not possible, so I shall be thankful while I may. It's when I hear of a lad like Carl being killed in action—oh dear then I must be more ashamed than thankful. Thankful indeed that it is not you—but ashamed that it might not have been. So write to me as if I were one with you, dear, for I am really.

Egremont
TO OLAF                         9 August 1916
. . . I have been walking about town today looking in the shop windows & at people & feeling a bit cold, & thinking of you. I had a fit of jeweller's shops today—generally it's dresses or hats or lace or something—but today it was jewellers. Really jewelry, some jewelry, is a beautiful thing. I mean a thing of beauty. I love to look at it in the windows, not to possess because away from suitable surroundings things often don't look half as nice. If a ring is to look its best it must be on a beautiful soft white hand, at least all the rings I looked at yesterday should be—& who has a hand like that? Who could be bothered to have a hand like that? Best leave the ring where it is on its velvety flesh-tinted cushion. It looks beautiful there & dazzling: the opals & diamonds & emeralds & pearls & rubies. I didn't see any ring resembling mine in the least degree. There's one thing about my ring—it is so strong & genuine that it

doesn't look out of place on a sturdy brown hand like mine. I daresay it would look more beautiful on another kind of hand but still it is mine now—& it has grown to belong to my hand.

I was thinking of Ailsa [Craig] when I was looking at the rubies. She said, "If ever I have an engagement ring, I should like it to be one big burning ruby all by itself." *If ever*—just imagine "if," it makes one smile. But doesn't that show how different are Ailsa & I? She chooses one big burning ruby, & I choose what you had already chosen for me, one pure round pearl.

Friends' Ambulance Unit
TO AGNES                                        20 August 1916
. . . We had a surprise inspection the other day, and the Frenchman who did it (he came from [General] Joffre's staff) was very pleased and said he would see that after we had finished our next month at the front here we should get a move south to relieve a certain "very tired" convoy, which of course would take our place here. There is another plan in the air, which would take us, I believe, into the thick of things, but would split up the convoy. We hope they will not split us, because we have considerable esprit de corps, and think ourselves the smartest part of the FAU. The French let us wear the badge of their motor service—a conventional bursting bomb with A on it, but at present the British won't let us wear it in their area; but we hope to get that altered, as we are keen on our distinguishing mark. It is red and is worn on the collar. I have not got mine yet. I fear the rest of the FAU is not very popular with us just now,

[CENSORED]

. . . Yes, keep up your music always. We will not only delight ourselves with it, but help lots of other people, I hope. I keep seeing visions of our future home and you playing or singing, and people listening. *If if if,* we can manage to live that ideal quiet, busy life of home and outside doings, helping people to educate themselves, and modestly suggesting ideals to people, *if* we can do it really, and in no merely approximate style, think how glorious. We want to live on a very modest scale, don't we? I think no one has any right to live otherwise, especially now. We will not spend moneys on useless and soul-destroying things. We will reserve the main part of our funds for bringing up our children really well. (Think of being a father and a mother!) *If* we have any surplus wealth we will consider carefully whether we have any real right to it in this state of society, and if we have not, we will make better use of it. But all this is the ideal. The fact is sure to be only an approximation; let us make it as near an approximation as possible. It is a clear ideal, and an ideal for two people. I have no ideals apart from you. The world is in-

clined to say that marriage is a fraud and a fiasco. We will show that it
need not be. The world says people when they marry lose sight of everything else and become mere domestic animals. We won't. The world
says you must be on a great scale to be happy. Rubbish. The world says
you must take part in public affairs to do any good. We will try to do it in
another sphere.

Egremont
TO OLAF                                                        20 August 1916
. . . Last Saturday night Jean [Curlewis], Rosie's Jean, had a soldiers'
euchre-party. It was quite jolly, about 12 or 14 boys from the Convalescent Home, Middle Head, came with their poor stiff legs & broken fingers & gashed faces & there were about 9 or 10 nice girls in pretty frocks
to help entertain them. A nice sergeant major chap made a little speech
of thanks just before they went & he said it was very nice to sit in a
comfortable easy chair even if you played jolly badly & lost every game
(laughter) & to see the way the girls made merry & bustled about & did
all they could to make the boys happy again—was something that did
them all good (long prolonged applause). Then dear little deaf Mrs.
Curlewis said in her pretty way, "You've made us *vewy* happy by coming
here." Rosie & I were escorted home by two of our gallant defenders
whom we had never seen before—one was a blacksmith by trade, & the
other was, I think, a flirt. They were both aged 19 & enlisted two years
ago. Funny boys. The latter told us that the worst of it was when he
went away his girl got married to someone else—we agreed it was rotten
luck. The former, the blacksmith, told us that he never had no girl for
anyone else to pinch off him. We agreed his was the wisest plan. One
nice little English boy I was talking to said he had fought in France with
the Imperial Army, got wounded & had been discharged because he was
too young—only 17—so he came out to Australia to enlist with the
Australians. He must *like* it. We think we'll have a soldiers' party here
sometime.

Friends' Ambulance Unit
TO AGNES                                                      23 August 1916
. . . At night in my car. Yesterday some fellows came back from leave.
One of them, a very young and rather sentimental lad, but a thoroughly
good sort, got married. He and others were sitting in my car last night
when he told us. At first we did not believe it, but he insisted quietly
and he looked pensive and far away, and kept referring now and then to
"my wife." We knew he had been engaged for ever so long, and was very
much head over ears in it, but as he has very little money and is very

young we never thought he would really get married. He has been and gone and done it, however—married on Tuesday, back on Friday. I wonder how on earth it will all pan out. . . . They will have a hard fight, but at least they will meet every four months, and we have not even that. Two years soon since we were together, and very slight hope of meeting under another year. . . . Time flies! Thirty years to me and twenty-two years to you, and what a tiny speck of them have we spent together! First a fortnight, then a month, and then a number of scattered months and weeks. But even so it was only a spasmodic "being together," not a real living together, such as we want. It's positively ridiculous. Well, well, I must stop now and do something more edifying than writing to a phantom girl. Phantom! The odd thing is that your reality is so much more vivid than the reality of things that are here.

[*On 31 August SSA 13 set out from Unit headquarters in Dunkirk south toward Amiens. The next day the convoy of twenty-two Vulcan ambulances, mobile kitchen, workshop car, touring car, lorries, and a motorcycle reached the river Oise at Compiègne, where they remained until January. The Section was split into several working groups, some to carry wounded from outstations and some to evacuate ambulance trains. From this point on Olaf's letters bear the postmarks of SSA 13 and are no longer censored by a member of the FAU but by French military authorities.*]

> Section Sanitaire Anglaise No. 13
> Convois Automobiles
Agnes,                                        6 September 1916

At last! But it's only for an odd moment now, just to tell you the news. We are now some 300 kilometres down the line and I suppose about 15 kilos from it. We did the journey in two days, because a convoy is bound to move slowly. We did it quite successfully, though we shed one car ten minutes after starting! We came through glorious country and now are in glorious country. There is ever so much to tell you, but simply not a moment of time to do anything in. At the end of our famous journey we had a glorious fresh water bathe in one of the rivers of France. We then got orders to scatter over the country to various places. I (with an orderly) was sent to a little old town and found myself delightfully billeted in the grounds of a château. We arrived after dark, and the lord of the place, a count, came out with his family to greet us. He was a gay old bird, and they all prattled like the rain on an umbrella. He struck matches to see us by, & was satisfied that we were decent. He then struck more matches to show us his daughters and then asked us if we did not think them pretty, to which I replied "rather," or French to that effect; and they, being flappers, all shrieked and giggled. They examined the car curiously and cross-questioned us about everything. We soon got to be as good as friends of ten years' standing, and madame the countess began reluctantly to drop her laborious English and prattle French with the rest. We were astounded at our luck, and were looking forward to a very delightful week in a very delightful spot with very delightful people. We all stood gabbling in the dark for an age before my companion & I could get away to seek food in the town. At last we sallied forth with a French driver as guide. He told us there was very little work there, so we (after our journey) were pleased. Alas! While we were all making a scratch meal of bread & wine & ham, our motor cyclist found us, & delivered orders for an immediate departure to a far off spot. We debated the matter and finally decided not to go until the morning, as it was already nearly eleven o'clock. So all three of us went back to the château and went to sleep in my car. Next morning we made an early start without even being able to say good-bye to our kind hosts. It really was good to be with those people and talk with merry girls. We went away greatly sorrowing. They had been very keen on us because we were English. Our countrymen are few & very much sought-after all round this district.

Well, next day we reached our final destination, a nice little town on the edge of a perfectly lovely forest. Half the convoy is here, the rest being scattered at places quite a long way off. We plumped right into a lot of work, and have been really hard at it every day and night since. Crowded hospital trains keep coming in, generally at about 2 AM. We have not been undressed for many days, and if one gets three hours sleep at night one is very lucky. During the day all the time that is not spent in driving has to go toward *trying* to keep one's car in order. Very soon all the hospitals here will be full, & then we shall get a bit of rest, perhaps. We have made no end of a name for ourselves with the French authorities, and we and our cars are considered quite wonderful. In fact we are quite *the* sight of the town. . . . Another train is due at any time, the third in 24 hours; and of course it is not only trains that we have to manage. There is no doubt we have got as much to do as we could possibly keep up for any length of time, & it is very good for us! The wounded that we carry are of all sorts, but mostly pretty well begrimed with mud and blood, though here they are so far from the front. They have been wounded in victory. Everything to do with this place & this work has an air of victory, businesslike victory. It is all very terrible and very momentous. But I should like to have a hot bath and go to bed, with the certainty of no disturbance. Practically speaking we are all on duty always just at the present. . . .

[*Later.*] The other night we finished our work in a most excellent red dawn, the royal standard of God flung across the sky. When a train is in one loads up very quickly, drives off as fast as the wounded can bear to go, unloads at some hospital or other, near or far, rushes back through empty streets, swings into position before the station door, discharges empty stretchers, is loaded up again, jumps in and drives off once more; and so on without a moment lost, till the whole job is done. But as a matter of fact we generally manage to have a few cars waiting in the yard for their turn, because we are keen, & get the thing done pretty speedily. At last the médecin chef comes along paternally with a few kind remarks and tells us to go in & get some coffee & then drive away and sleep. At first the authorities were rather cold to us, but now they fairly fall over themselves with kindness and praises, and I rather think we have set an example and caused a smartening up all round.

SSA 13
Car No. 19
18 September 1916

TO AGNES

. . . It rains. There never was such rain. It roars. The forest gives tongue under it. The lane is a lake. I have put a tin basin out to catch water for washing in the morning, and I have dug out my rubber boots from the back of my front locker. The car slopes slightly, and a little river is oozing along the seat that is my bed, but I shall dodge it all right. I am not really going to write to you this evening, but I felt I must write just a wee bit because of your letter. It was a letter full of affairs. You put me to shame; you do so very much while I am drifting through a monotonous and rather idle existence. . . .

*Another day.* I have had a fearful epidemic of some sort of beastly little lice, caught, doubtless, from some passengers in my car. I could not make out what was the cause of all the beastly itch until at last I spotted the tiny little beggars and found I was overrun with them. Consequently I have been going in for drastic measures, and am now, I hope, free of the beasts; but a lot of clothes may finally have to be burnt, and I have been trying various methods of disinfecting the car. C'est la guerre. Did they thrive! They simply ate me up. Excuse these unpleasant details. Do you remember Mother and her "little friends," caught during visiting? But we don't worry much about mere fleas here, as long as they do not appear in large numbers. . . .

[*Later.*] Just at present my car is uninhabitable because it has just been disinfected after carrying dysentery, and if one goes inside one weeps and chokes. Disinfecting for that kind of disease is just a formality, I think, but it's a nuisance. The man was bad, poor fellow. I wonder whether he is still alive. The other day I had a mysterious journey with a corpse. (He was put on board dead.) He had been sent alive from one hospital to another and died soon after arriving. (One of us took him.) Well, of course he ought not to have been moved, & the receiving hospital would not have any responsibility; so they sent him back (per me) whence he came. Two orderlies came with me, but on arrival they practically gave me the slip & left me with a corpse that no one wanted. The people who had originally despatched him (alive) were terrified at having him sent back dead, & would not take him, quite disowned him in fact. The head man in particular was a miserable picture of guilty panic, talking very fast with tears in his eyes, & all in a half whisper. Of course in the end they had to take him, someone having uncovered his face & vouched for his identity. So at last we unloaded the white-blanketed stretcher, & I rushed off before any more could be said, & discussed the matter at our tea table. He was a lad of 20. . . .

*Yet another day*, and a beastly day too, for it has been spent chiefly with tyre-troubles. Just now I carried a curious case, a mad Bulgarian. He had deserted from his own people to the French out there, and the French had organised a voluntary corps of "navvies" to dig etc. in the war area. The corps was entirely for such as he, and is now hereabouts. This poor fellow had gone mad and was given to me on a stretcher with his hands and feet tied and a halter round his neck. He mostly lay still or tossed restlessly and murmured; but once he tried to get up. He seemed fearfully depressed and wretched, & lay on his face most of the time (with his hands tied behind his back.) He was a fine build of man and had a dark, ruddy complexion and a smart little black moustache. His face was covered with scratches, and altogether he was pretty disreputable. He had a strange childish expression of vacant misery, half-humourous but very pathetic. I guess he had not made a very favourable exchange by his desertion from our Balkan foe. I took him to a big army hospital along with an attendant and a smart interpreter of his own species. The hospital is pretty full, and the ward where he was sent was quite full, but he had to be taken in all the same. He was not very popular. They treated him decently enough, but with the sort of decency one would show to a sick bullock, or other beast. Poor Bulgar, I pity him. I wonder what kind of a life he lived before the war in his queer country. I wonder what thoughts he had while jogging along in my car, if madness left any power of thought in his brain. I wonder how often they tugged at his halter to keep him in hand. . . .

At present there is no chance of continuous writing, so I am going to try a lot of short things between "fables" & "psalms," just snapshots of all sorts of significant things. This will be a daring experiment & an innovation. I have thought of a lot of good subjects, such as little incidents

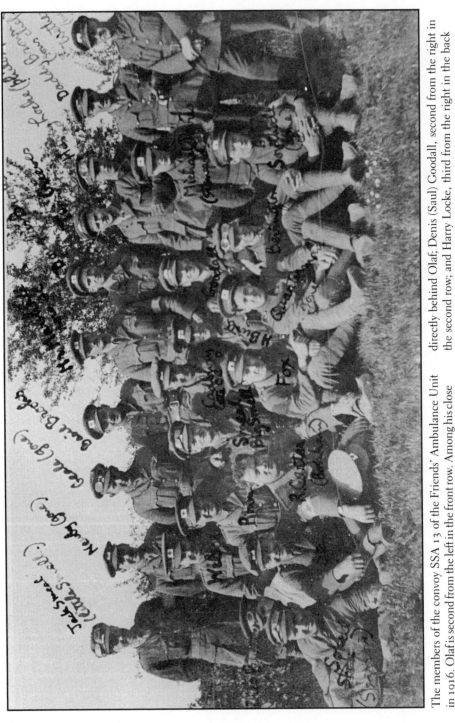

The members of the convoy SSA 13 of the Friends' Ambulance Unit in 1916. Olaf is second from the left in the front row. Among his close friends are Alan (Sparrow) Sokell, lying left of Olaf; Julian (Renard) directly behind Olaf; Denis (Saul) Goodall, second from the right in the second row; and Harry Locke, third from the right in the back row. The handwriting on the photograph is Olaf's.

out here that mean very much. If ever I manage to do any I will send
you some. I want to hit an almost impossible mark between prose and
verse, and to make things that are very simple, popular, & yet very full
of meanings.

                                                    Egremont
TO OLAF                                             23 September 1916
. . . I have had two letters from you to talk about . . . of July 25th &
August 6th—the first was from C(?) & the second from repos. The first
was a very exciting one—the sort I expect you call "journalistic." I like
the journalistic ones sometimes, e.g. when I am feeling optimistic, but
always I like to hear details of everything & conversations. You write so
well—you give us ten times as good an idea of your "life & times" as we
get from any of the other boys—naturally I suppose. It all depends
whom one is writing to, doesn't it? But some people will never go into
details even when writing to their own homes. . . .
    We're going to have another Referendum here for Conscription or no
Conscription. I'm going to vote for Conscription. Are you agreed with
me or no? I'm such a babe I oughtn't to have a vote. I can't weigh things
for myself, so I have to do what seems best according to other people
who know better. Here it is Conscription versus Slackers; & we don't
want to back the slackers, unconscientious slackers. The whole country
is being conscripted gradually by the Labour Unions, so National Conscription will take the upper hand over them & that will be a good
thing. Billy Hughes [the Australian Prime Minister] is being slated because he wouldn't decide it for us, & now it will cost somewhere between 50 and 100 thousand pounds. That does seem a sin, but I reckon
the people ought to decide it for themselves, it is too big a responsibility
for one man. If the Slackers win though it will be a worse sin. Poor Billy
Hughes then! You were very much against Conscription in England,
weren't you? But I wonder if you would be here. Surely it can't be the
same position.

[*According to the weekly newspaper* The Friend, *SSA 13 carried a
record number of ten thousand patients in September. Olaf's fear that
some of his letters were destroyed by the French censor is probably well-
founded; none survive between 18 September and 1 October—an un-
usually long hiatus for him.*]

                                                    SSA 13
TO AGNES                                            1 October 1916
. . . We are getting very busy. Our records show that we have done
more work in the last month than in the previous six months put to-

gether. We have done more than three times as much as any other FAU convoy in any one month. We are rather bucked. My only discontent is that as soon as one has cleaned one's car and got it really flashy, one gets hauled out again and four hours' work is gone in ten minutes. But it is good to be busy and to know you are necessary. Things here get increasingly busy. I have had an awful scare. Someone said the French censorship does not cut out censorable matter but destroys the letter. I fear lest some of mine to you have been destroyed. I shall be careful in future! I do hope they have all got through, because otherwise you will have been perplexed. We have a new OC, my friend the Anglo-Sicilian, [Charles] Marshall, the oldest man in the convoy. It is very decidedly a change for the better. I think everyone has bucked up, and certainly we have been run more sensibly already. I was suggested at one time, but I did not encourage the idea. . . .

The other day, as I was coming back from buying sugar biscuits to give a finish to our rather makeshift dinner for two (the two night men) I saw an astounding cloud. I was walking along a narrow street feeling virtuous at not having bought a bottle of wine, when I looked up and saw towering up the sky the very King of Clouds. I saw a splendid tower cloud once in Flanders, but this was more impressive. He stretched from the horizon almost to the zenith, and he was proportionately broad. The upper parts of him blazed gold in the evening sunlight, and the lower parts were all manner of grays. He was solid like a mass of masonry, and sharp-cut in all his moulding. Every detail was visible. One could see little grey crevasses in his golden regions, crevasses that were really huge gulfs. On a plane one could have climbed right up his goodness-knows-how-many thousands of feet, coasting in and out of all his creeks, or plunging suddenly into the body of him to corkscrew upwards and emerge into the sunlight again & again. He made one feel how very deep the sky is, and how smooth and flat the earth;—even her wildest Himalayas could not seem craggy beside his overhanging precipices. He was like half a planet, with the raw, cut surface turned toward the sun. I wish you had seen him with me.

Egremont
TO OLAF                                          4 October 1916
. . . Dad is beginning to think that I spend a terrible lot of time at my desk, & if he sees me there in the evenings he gets quite melancholy & talks about the pity of letting our evening music go, trios going to the dogs, no time for family life, and so on. However, we generally have a trio in spite of all my letters. . . . Daddy plays a beautiful Beethoven cello sonata. I have scrambled through it with him once or twice, but mine was a disgraceful performance. During the evenings, or else just at

bed time, Dad generally goes off into the drawing room & plays away to himself, sometimes in the dark, nearly always without the music. It always soothes him & keeps him happy. When he practises his Beethoven sonata all by himself I always feel terribly mean because I have not taken time to study & play it with him.

SSA 13

TO AGNES                                                    7 October 1916

. . . I have been reading your last three letters again. I read them all in one piece, and when I had done I was filled with a sort of warm glowing reverend joy because of you and because of your dear way of telling me all your doings and thinkings so frankly and fully and beautifully. To be quite intimate with a woman is a man's greatest possible joy I think, but to be intimate with *you*! There's no other prize in the world after that. Here is a rhyme for you "inspired" by one of your letters—

> Ailsa would have a ruby.
>    But Agnes has a pearl.
> Thus may you know
>    The heart of each girl.
>
> Ailsa is a glowing coal,
>    Or a goblet of red wine
> Through which deeply blazes
>    The light divine.
>
> Ailsa is a strong draft
>    To be quaffed by a king.
> But Agnes is the vital air
>    For a man's breathing.
>
> Life-long shall he know her,
>    Her whole of dread and dear,
> That are one soft splendour
>    Like the pearl's pure sphere.
>
> Who will give a ruby
>    To Ailsa? I confess
> I gave the pearl
>    And my soul to Agnes.

Apologies to Ailsa! . . .

Well, dear, I must stop, or I shall fall asleep over the paper. When we are married and there is no more need to write letters to you I am sure I shall still by habit take up pen & paper now & then and begin a letter to you before I remember that there is no need. After what you have said about war marriages I am burning to get married. And if you were in England you would probably be induced to substantiate your opinions by the personal act. I'd marry you this very leave, with ten days honey moon at Festiniog. But you are not in England, so you are safe. But darling I want that wedding day with all my soul. I am tired of barriers of earth and sea and barriers of convention. I want the whole of you. Wife! That's the magic word. It's better than sweetheart or betrothed or anything else. Goodnight Wife.

Egremont

TO OLAF 15 October 1916

. . . Well, Sydney is in a fermenting condition just now. I don't suppose your papers ever talk much about us, but in truth there is plenty to talk about. Things are working themselves up towards something or other for the great Referendum Day October 28 when Conscription or no Conscription will be decided. People seem to be very uncertain whether we shall get it or not. All the Trades Unions are dead against & very nearly all the Labour crowd. There are howls for Mr. Hughes because he has deserted them, & howls for everyone who follows Mr. Hughes. They, "the Antis," are raising wonderful arguments about the government wanting to get rid of the Unionists so as to import cheap coloured labour. They say Germany is beaten already, & there will be no need of more men. Australia has done enough, more than her share. The country will go to pieces if all the good men go.—There's not much in that because all the good men have gone long ago. Well now this is why I am voting for Conscription. We have sent out five divisions of fighting men & we undertook to keep them up to strength. We have kept them up in the past with the voluntary system, but now that system has broken down & we can't get enough reinforcements, & the men that we have sent are getting exhausted with the strain of the insufficient amount of sleep & relaxation—we hear that in our letters every week as well as in everyone's speeches. We *must* send help to them—we cannot desert them. It is said the more men you have the fewer are the casualties in proportion. That is a very great point. The more men you have the sooner will the whole miserable business be wound up. That is another great point for all parties. Another is that Germany, they say, is not beaten or subdued, if you like, by a long way yet & it may take many many months in the doing. But oh heaven forbid. Another reason is that Australia lives & dies with Britain—that if it had not been for the British fleet we should belong to the German Empire long ago. And while Britain is in need Australia cannot refuse her help, she cannot do too much.

Why should the generous brave men go & do their share while the selfish cowardly shirkers stay at home & do nothing for anyone but themselves? It doesn't seem fair. We all have shares in our country—

those who feel their obligation go & offer their lives in its service. Shall those who are too blind or too selfish to see their obligation be left off just because they don't see or won't see? The obligation is there whether they see it or not.

[*As the war continued, the ability of the Society of Friends to support all the FAU's expenses was severely strained. The generosity of William Stapledon, who as a manager for the Holt Shipping Co. continued to have a substantial income, enabled Olaf to purchase a badly needed fast car—the "Sunbeam"—for the Unit officer's use.*]

Annery
Agnes my own,                                    19 October 1916
    Here am I at my desk in the red room setting out to write to you as of old. It seems most natural and ordinary to be doing so, and yet so strange, if you can understand that paradox. There is ever so much to tell you, and I don't know where to begin, but the most tellable thing and the thing most present to me is that I find I am quite unable to enjoy the joys of being home on leave because you are not here. Each leave seems worse than the last. The first time I was so fearfully glad to get home that I could support your absence quite well. Next time your absence seemed more real to me than my own presence in England. And now, alas, it is worse than ever, and I am just a leaden loneliness, like an old coat that has lost its wearer and has been hanging behind the door till its own weight has pulled it out of the good human shape it knew so well. I am all dust and long straight creases. . . . Every time I come on leave I add a bundle of your letters to the big bundle in the bottom drawer of my desk. You would be surprised if you saw the bulk of all your letters. Every time I add fresh ones I dip into the old ones— little girl letters, mad young schoolgirl letters, formal letters that bore always a certain damp and chilly breath with them lest I should think you liked me more than just a wee bit, letters that alternately chilled and warmed, letters all warmth, letters of closest friend to closest friend, and the eager, weary, dearest letters that come now. They are the best. They are Agnes her very self with no chill caution. Oh most fortunate I, whom the gods have so blessed!
    Now for the news:—
    Accompanied by the fellow who is our cook I set out from Compiègne (our town) by train for Paris at 7.15 Monday morning. All the journey was through hilly woodland, mostly birch just turning brown, and all very lovely. . . . It took us 17 hours to get from Paris to Boulogne!!! Then came much red tape, a fine but crowded crossing, an encountre with a man [Herbert Sharpe] I knew at the 'varsity now an army chap-

lain, a delicate dinner at Euston talking old times with him and acting up to his supreme elegance, cleanliness & refinement as well as I could in my shabby state. (By Jove, he was immaculate!) Then a talk with an interesting FAU ambulance train man, and at last a luxurious sleeping car for Liverpool, and a glorious sleep followed by early morning tea, *hot water* and a nice breakfast. That was my first bed since last May. . . .

Well, being safely in Liverpool I went to the office & saw my important papa, looking busy & well, & Mother later also. I visited Auntie Louisa, who is getting much better but looks older. I had a tooth stopped, had tea with Auntie Sophia, & a chat. She is in some disgrace with her sisters because she chips marble instead of doing war work, poor Auntie! At last I went home to a good old Annery meal & the old piano player & a great spacious bed as wide as Siberia. . . .

*Next morning.* . . . Just a word about the new car. Marshall the new OC has no car & needs one very badly. The Unit was trying to get someone to bring a car out to drive for him, but I (accepting Father's repeated offer to me) offered to get a car & drive him about. He & I are the best of friends & he always tells me all his official worries & says, "Now what would *you* do, Stap? It's damned annoying, isn't it?" So I am giving up my ambulance and taking the proud post of OC's driver, & spare driver for all the cars. I shall get quite a lot of ambulance driving I expect, especially in busy times, but my main work will be taking old Marshall about to our various stations (the two extremes are 75 miles apart at present) and leading the convoy when the convoy moves to new work, & exploring new aid posts and front-work roads, when we get back to the front. I am seeing about the car now, & hope to drive her out, a strong reliable 4 cylindre 4 seater of some sort, about 25 horsepower. It will be a blessing to have a decent car to drive, but I can't pretend to feel enthusiastic. It's the best thing to do for all concerned.

[*In his utopian "book of dogmas," Waking World (1934), Olaf would later reflect painfully and in public on the contradiction between his socialist principles and the practical necessity of supplementing his income with dividends from his father's stocks in order to have time to write. His financial statement of 1916 is an accurate forecast of the kind of living he was able to make as a WEA tutor and a writer, and it adds some poignancy to a humorous marginal comment he had written on a letter to Agnes two years before (15 November 1915): "By Jove, why didn't I make my living by writing love letters!"*]

TO AGNES                                                         27 October 1916
. . . Financial statement concerning Olaf Stapledon M.A. Not a very
cheerful one:—Cash in the bank £ 235.16.0. Present income from interest on shares etc. about £ 80 per annum (not less). *Face* value of
shares etc. £ 2673. About £ 280 of this is safe in Bank deposits and Savings Bank. The rest is in such things as garden cities & suburbs and
reformed public houses! Father gave me all this at odd times, all thoroughly good things to support, especially the new pubs. Personally I am
surprised they all pay up so well. . . . Present expenditure just under
£ 30 per annum, probably considerably less in future. Prospects after the
war a practically certain, regular salary of £ 240 per annum from WEA.
No prospects of advancing beyond £ 400 in that line, and even that advance problematical. Possibility of considerably higher salary later on
from an inspectorship, but this is just an idea of mine, not very far-
fetched however. Vague possibility of additions from literary work, e.g.
Text Book of Literary History, for which there is I believe a real market,
also possible journalism. Well, if you can disentangle this rigmarole you
will see that the situation is not very encouraging. . . .
     The car is bought. It is a 12/16 horsepower Sunbeam in (I think) per-
fect condition. Father paid £550 for it, more than cost price. Of course
good cars are expensive. I only hope it will do good work to justify the
purchase. The man from whom we bought did not want to sell, but
there was no other car at all satisfactory. I feel the responsibility of having
let Father in for such a lot, but I do think it was the wisest thing to do and
perhaps the most economical after all. Certainly she is a splendid car for
the job, very smart, and smooth-running. We need smartness so as to
maintain our dignity against the French lieutenant who would *like* to
command us, and who must not be allowed to do so on any account. . . .

[*Another day.*] The Convoy's movements are uncertain. We may stay
long where we are, or we may get sent up to the Somme, where we
should have something very different from anything we have had so far.
Renard ([Julian] Fox) and I want to go to the Somme, and for selfish
reasons we both desire to become casualties, sufficiently severely hit to
get quit of the whole thing. Tell me, is it very wrong to long for that?
One feels ashamed of it, but it would solve many problems. We don't
want to die, nor to be crippled for life. But, good God, we want to have
done with it all & yet feel we have done our bit. And *I* want any mortal
thing that will hasten my meeting you, so long as I am not crippled for
that future life of ours. I would go through much to gain a speedy meeting with you. It's too far away you are. Other fellows see their girls on
leave,—Sparrow [Alan Sokell] for instance. But two whole years, and

more, will follow before I see you. Oh Agnes, it's all very well to bear it, but it gets so much harder to bear as time goes on.

Egremont
29 October 1916

Sunday evening.

It seems a very quiet & ordinary Sunday but the paper this morning contained a bomb concerning the great Referendum of yesterday, to the effect that the *no* Conscriptionists so far have a majority of 86,000 votes!! It is a bit of a stunner, isn't it? It is not complete yet because we haven't got the absent soldiers' votes. That may make a difference, but I believe they are by no means unanimous for yes, though one would expect them to be so. Nearly all the men in camp gave a solid vote for No! Well, I am tired with the whole affair. Poor Mr. Hughes will be tired, I guess. Daddy has it very much at heart. This morning when he read the results he said he felt like an Englishman, not an Australian at all & he was sick at Australia. I don't know how I feel about it, but I hope very much that the success the Antis have had may spur some of them on to enlist themselves. But probably the shirkers will still shirk, those who enlist will be the men who held back for domestic or financial reasons. Let's leave it for tonight—it's a wearying subject, & everyone feels a bit limp about it. If Dad knew I felt so limp about it he would be disgusted with me. Yet I am not an anti. I did want to send the men, our men, help & reinforcements. I am an anti-war, but not an anti-conscriptionist. Dad feels ashamed for Australia's honour. What would you feel?

Today I have written three letters, this is the fourth, but it's only the second love letter! At least it's not a love letter yet, but it may turn into one before it winds itself up. But I'm only trying to make you jealous. Are you not? not yet? The first letter was to Frank Day. Are you yet? The second letter was to Jack Armstrong—surely you are a wee bit jealous? The third letter & the first love letter was to—Ailsa.

The first love letter I have ever written to a girl! Well, she's gone now from my land, & she's on her way over to your land. They left yesterday by the "Medina." They should be in London early in December, so next time you arrive at Victoria Station & taxi up to Euston, will you look out for a dark eyed, red lipped (what word does describe her?). Her skin is clear & delicate & her teeth beautiful & even, & her lips fine & red, & her nose & chin rather piquante, yet so much more beautiful than piquante—taller than I am & rather smartly dressed. . . .

*Monday evening.* . . . We have decided that girls are of two sorts—outdoor & indoor. The indoor girls look dazzling at night & in town on a summer's day when they brush past you in the doorway of "the Stores," or sit by a window having tea. They take your breath away with their cool pleasant faces & their filmy transparent dresses. These girls are always daintily dressed & they never have a hair out of place & their skin is white & delicate. The outdoor girl looks best in the day time, on a tennis court down on the beach, playing in the sun without her hat. She invariably has a hot happy face & a red (sunburnt!) nose, but it doesn't show so much because the rest of her is brown or red. Her hair gets very much out of place, but it doesn't seem to matter much—her sleeves roll up & sometimes her shoes & stockings come off.

She may dress like a sportswoman or she may dress just like an ordinary nice girl—but try how she may she *cannot* look dainty. She is too much of an out-door girl in mind & body to look dainty. The outdoor girl puzzles over the indoor girl & cannot understand her. The indoor girl doesn't bother over the outdoor girl—at least that's the impression she gives—to an "outsider." We thank heaven we are of the latter, but when we go to chivoos & want to look decent we *do* envy the others their cool clear faces & their pretty clothes & their easy way.

[*Passing through Oxford, Olaf recalls the spring of 1908 when the Millers visited and watched the Balliol rowing team; among Olaf's crewmates on the "eights" team, the most famous of those who died in the war was Julian Grenfell. Walter de Stapeldon, fourteenth-century bishop of Exeter and a founder of Exeter College, is one of the oldest traceable ancestors in the Stapledon family tree.*]

Mitre Hotel, Oxford
TO AGNES                                    1 November 1916
. . . Just fancy being at Oxford! You once stayed at this hotel. Oh no, of course you were in rooms. Two dear little girls in fawn coloured silk frocks lying in a punt gliding up the Cherwell and one of them, all unconscious, was being piloted by her future "young man." Do you remember running along the bank watching eights? A good number of all those eager oarsmen are dead by now, and all the rest are very strenuously employed. This evening we arrived here after dark, so we saw nothing. The whole place is military. Balliol is a headquarters for cadet corps, and so are many other colleges. The streets are crowded with soldiers of all sorts and the characteristic Oxford girls, who are enjoying themselves no end these days!

Excuse this scribble. It is being written in bed, because it is most feasible so. If it were not to be written in bed it would not be written at all, so excuse, will you? It's so nice to talk to my girl a little last thing at night, with no more to do but turn out the light and tumble into sleep. . . . You fill this little room now. Who knows? Someday we may come to this very hotel together, and perhaps we shall have the room that has a picture of Bishop Stapledon of Exeter.

Royal Pavilion Hotel
Folkestone

Agnes best beloved,                                    3 November 1916

This is a huge and luxurious hotel full of officers and their women-folk. It is blowing great guns outside, and I am glad I am not crossing tonight. . . . Well, dear, here am I, your mere motor driver, on the brink of going back to that supreme boredom, the war. Fifteen months ago I stayed here with Father and Mother and wondered what it would be like on the other side. Guess I'm sadder & wiser now, and rather horribly sober and dry and disillusioned both about patriotism, militarism, and about consciences. I believe there is much self-deception on each side, much pharisaism and also failure to realise the situation, but on the whole I am clearly on the side of the conscience people, because they alone are guardians of the future, and all the fighting and smashing and hating only proves again and again that they are right.

But there is one thing I am not sober & disillusioned about, and that is you. I have grown to know you so much better in these fifteen months. You were the most real thing during all that time, more real than all the daily realities. And now at the end of this chapter of history here am I without any honours or distinctions or merit even, yet loving and loved by Agnes. And again & again I must needs swear to myself that this great good fortune shall result not only in personal joy but in good work for the world and in—children. Truly I think often of that future tangible expression of our loving. Do you? . . .

*Next Day*. Saturday 4th Nov. 1916. I am crossing this afternoon on a chilly grey windy day, worse luck. They are going to rob me of all my petrol, so I shall be nicely stranded at Boulogne with perhaps no means of getting petrol without my documents, and my documents 40 miles off. What a muddle.

France

Agnes,                                                4 November 1916

I am the other side now. I last wrote to you at three o'clock this afternoon. It is now half past ten, and I am staying here the night and driving to HQ tomorrow. I'll tell you about the crossing. My clean grey car was slung aboard and I sat in her for the voyage. The boat was very crowded, as usual. I asked the nearest people to come & sit in the car, and the one who came and sat by me was an Australian. He and his mate had a swig from a flask of rum, I having nobly refused that hospitality. We then began yarning. He had been through Gallipoli and Egypt and knew all the places over there that I knew, or many of them. He was really a Liverpool man, and told me lovingly of a little farewell dinner given by his sister at the Adelphi [Hotel]. We discussed Liverpool, he with a lowered gentle voice full of happy home memories. Then we got on to Australia. He came from Sydney. Says I, "I hope to go there after the war to marry a girl." Says he, "An Australian girl? I married an Australian girl. . . . It's two years since I saw my wife." Pause, after which he wriggled himself into a comfortable position and said, "It's heartbreaking, isn't it! And there seems no end to it." To which I grunted profound assent.

The moon showed dimly through light cloud. Our ship was without any lights. The deck was crowded with all kinds of soldiers, lying, standing, sitting, all wearing life belts, all very quiet, many trying to sleep. Some kept talking about the late channel raid, but mostly what talk there was seemed to be about home. A fellow standing near me was talking in a matter of fact voice. I overheard bits, such as, "She was just on the point of bursting into tears all the time, but she kept it back; she had to keep tight hold of herself." Meanwhile my companion, after discussing the war in terms that would be censorable and in a tone of voice still more censorable, settled down with his coat over his face and went to sleep. And now here am I in a hotel on my way to join the convoy. And all those men are likewise on their way to join their various units. I overheard one say, "Ay, before one went on leave one always had leave to look forward to, but now one has been, and there's nothing to look forward to. I suppose one will settle down to the old routine." When we were all pressing up to a door to go through formalities, the doorkeeper said, "Is there anyone here visiting wounded?" A grave voice said "Yes," and three poorly dressed civilian men struggled through the crowd toward the door. Leave is only given to relations to cross when the wounded man is not going to live.

Egremont
TO OLAF                                   7 November 1916
. . . I must tell you about last Sunday before it gets to be next Sunday, or I shall get muddled. Mr. Phillips is one of the voluntary workers at French's Forest Soldiers Settlement Farms. The Government has granted 200 acres out at French's Forest to be split up into 5-acre farms for poultry or fruitgrowing, & each farm has a 5-roomed weather-board cottage put up on it for the soldier or perhaps for his widow & family to live in. All the work is done by voluntary helpers—clearing the land,

"grubbing" as they call it, architecturing, carpentering, joinery & every-thing. French's Forest has been greatly boomed ever since Easter when they began work there. It is quite *the* thing for energetic little gangs to go out & spend their holiday working there & every Sunday morning great motor lorries go rumbling over there—through Mosman across Middle Harbour in the punt & away 7 miles out into the high bush land be-tween the coast & the harbour. Different suburbs have their own lorries, & different factories & government works, tramways, railways, & so forth. Each crowd works on its own farm & there is great rivalry—also great good fellowship & much horseplay & wry humor. They have 20 places finished already & some occupied & we had never been out.

O. J. P. [Mr. Phillips] was terribly keen for us to go with him, so we promised to go last Sunday to satisfy him. We took our lunch & our aprons & 9.30 AM found us up at the Spit Junction packed into the front seat of the lorry along with the rummiest looking crowd of voluntary workers you can think of. We were the only ladies & so we were much in evidence. "We" were a solicitor, a plumber, a government official, a retired squatter, a bricklayer (apparently), & a dozen or so other jocu-lar nondescripts of very mixed variety. Halfway down the Spit Hill we stopped to pick up two more enthusiastic old chaps with their tool bags & paraphernalia & as there was no room anywhere old Mr. Grey said he would stand on the front step—he's about 70—& all the rest of the crowd began accusing him of wanting to get near "the ladies." Much merriment ensued as we rumbled on down the hill. On the other side we had races with other lorries & finally got there about half past 10 AM. . . .

Just a bare piece of scrubland pitched on the side of a slope & all round it. Only a few trees about but plenty of bushes & wildflowers & tufts of grass, not green, sort of grey-brown-green. The bushes are surely a sort of eucalyptus with hairy leaves & stems—all had their early sum-mer deep terra-cottary red foliage mixed with the blue green—& as the sun got low in the afternoon we watched it flame through these ruddy leaf-buds & flowers. It is all high land there—we looked down on Mosman across gullies & beautiful hill slopes with the afternoon shad-ows on them. In the other direction, on the highest slope, there was a row of tall straight gums which gave me thrills of pleasure—they looked full of romance & wonder as if they might belong to the real French's Forest land. . . . Our first job was to go a message down to the store for the carpenters. Mr. Phillips is one of the carpenters. Then we got paint brushes & pots of paint & began our day's work painting the outside of the house. The master-painter in whose charge we were was a nice shy man called Mr. Lawson & he had a voice just like your father's. I en-joyed hearing it so much that I kept asking for information I didn't really need. I think he must have thought us a bit of a bore at first when he had to get down off the roof to fix up ladders & planks for us to stand on etc., but by the end of the day he was quite full of praises for his assistants & really we did work hard. We did the lower part of one side of the house, & the front verandah & all the back verandah & part of the scullery. Rosie made the fire at lunch time & got a big kerosene tin of water boiling & then the workers came in from their jobs on different parts of the ground & made their tea & went off again. It was a pretty high wind so we thought we would have our lunch inside—all our crowd.

You would have laughed if you could have seen your fiancée & her big sister having lunch with all their friends!! I suppose some stiff-necked young men would have been shocked but you would have laughed, I know—and thank heaven! The men brought in planks & made low seats on which we all squatted—irrespective of paint & cement & aprons & looks; we all dumped our lunch on the floor in front of us & the billys of tea in the middle where everyone could grab, & everybody talked and eat at the same time & we were all as happy as Larry, & Rosie & I forgot that we were really girls & not painters. Then they all smoked & I wished I had brought my pipe too! After lunch we fell to again & painted until about 4.30, then they told us to knock off & have some tea, & while that was in progress a man came along to break the news that the lorry had broken down. We struck tragic attitudes & laughed. "Oh," he said, "that's all very well, but you may have to walk home." We said we didn't care, but he went off to try & get us a seat on another lorry & came back with a long face. "No hope." So everybody assembled—grubbers, carpenters, bricklayers & all—& we set off en masse along the road. Everybody thought it was scandalous for ladies to have to walk home & we had several offers of a lift from the kindhearted people along the road. But we were really looking forward to the walk at sunset time. Mr. Phillips guided the party across country & we saved a couple of miles that way—it took us about an hour & a half & we were home soon after 7. It *was* a beautiful walk. We had the ocean on our left in the distance as blue as blue flowers, & the sunset on our right & the hills with purple shadows on them. We were pretty dead tired when we got in & it didn't wear off for several days, but the net result is that we caused quite a sensation! Mother has been accosted all the week by odd people who enlarged on the splendid way her daughters had worked out at French's Forest "& walked all the way home too!" The last person told her how Mr. Carter—one of the nice old chaps—made a speech about us at the meeting next night & the whole company gave us three cheers!! Isn't it amusing! Some men from the Government printing offices implored to be allowed to take our photos while we were at work on one of the walls & the lorry driver presented us each with a huge bunch of flannel flowers. We felt like little tin gods; it was quite dull to come back to Mosman & be nobody!

[*The winter of 1916–17 came early, and its severity became as large a part of the folklore of the Great War as the famously glorious summer of 1914 that preceded the war.*]

SSA 13

TO AGNES                                                 12 November 1916

. . . I am now taking up my new duties, & trying to live up to the proud position of OC's driver and driver of the best car on the convoy. Every one is fearfully enraptured with this car, especially old Marshall himself. I have only been back a day or two, but already we have done a good many trips, and today we ought to have gone far afield, but in view of the rumoured move they let me have the day to go right over the car in detail so as to be sure she is all right & to get the hang of her. Though she is an open tourer & quite small I have managed to arrange to inhabit her as if she was an ambulance, & I am in fact now "in bed" in her, diagonally lying across the stern section of her, half on the glorious padded seat & half on a suit case that Uncle Frank gave me ever so long ago (it's covered with labels of Swiss towns). She makes a cosy bed room, with the hood up, & the diagonal position enables one to lie almost full length. The only difficulty is undressing under the very low rakish hood. . . .

*Another day.* It is afternoon and I have struck work in disgust, and am sitting in the back seat of the Sunbeam in my woolly coat. Douglas Brooks, of whom I have told you that he and I are alternately friendly & rude, is curled up in the front seat snoozing. It's cold and bright. Frost last night, and I wished I had put on another rug. Busy day tomorrow again. There's no time to do anything that needs more than scattered quarter hours. That's what I hate. I have had such a dose of this car already that I am simply sick of everything to do with cars. And the professional pride of keeping a really smart car looking smart is not enough to counteract the boredom. I hope our expected move comes soon, and a bout of real busy work at the front. . . . Your friend Miss Cooper who says that poetry is one of the "real" things sounds nice. What we incline to forget sometimes is that poetry *is* life, or rather life *is* poetry; and the poetical expression in verse or prose or painting or sculpture or music is only a medium for the showing of the poetical reality of life, of all existence. Just now two old women passed carrying loads of sticks from the forest. The sun shone in their wrinkled faces as they peered into this car to look at the foreigner. My expression of that incident is not poetry, but the thing itself was poetry, the incongruity of them and me, the background of sun-lit tree trunks, and the distinct rumble of guns. They probably regarded their gathering of sticks as anything but poetic, and me on the other hand & my magic chariot as strange, wonderful, thaumaturgic. And I saw poetry in them & their stick-gathering, but in myself and this jumble of metal and grease I see nothing but an instrument capable of causing a lot of trouble and a person who is supremely fed up. That does not mean that poetry is a delusion, but that the real essential meaning of a thing is not necessarily to be seen at close quarters, just as a mountain is not visibly a mountain while you are climbing it. . . .

This letter is all Ego, sorry!

Mon dieu, qu'il fait froid! The ego in question is now embedded under all the rugs, coats etc. available, watching the moon rise between the trees. It's freezing merrily. My next door neighbour is complaining that the seat where he sleeps is covered with frost. My breath goes away in clouds. My dirty paws are chilly in spite of your mittens. One does not wash much in this weather! I am all dressed save for boots & tunic, expecting night work (but really because it's warmer in one's clothes). I pray that my radiator will not freeze & crack. It is well padded with rugs. November is so early for frost. I had better turn in before my arms freeze. Goodnight. This is a fearfully scrappy letter, and really there is very much to talk about. I have a cow in my box, as the Frenchman said when he meant a cough in his chest. Oh snug & blessed bed, even when it is the back seat of a tourer helped out with a suit case!

*Next Morning*. It really was cold! My boots were frozen stiff and my breath on my bedclothes froze as I lay in bed. And my washing water was almost unbreakable. The cushions are all sparkling like a Christmas card. This morning Sparrow & I went a brisk walk up and down the avenue, to get warm. The forest is perfectly beautiful, so bright and sparkling with fairy frost. The sky is cold and blue, and at dawn it was saffron & orange down the avenue.

SSA 13

TO AGNES                                              18 November 1916

. . . In your letter you tell of how you were going to vote, exercising your right of citizenship. I am sorry, but I earnestly hope that your side loses, most earnestly. I am no longer allowed to discuss such subjects, but though I sometimes doubt about the whole great matter, I am never at all in doubt as to that phase of it for which you are voting. No indeed, for whatever land. And against your vote I hope I would act firmly if need be. Odd, to think of our being so very deeply opposed on the one subject, and so very near on all others. Your voting, and bearing witness to your side makes me wish I could make some big sacrifice to bear witness to mine. But there, I must not talk about those things. Think for yourself, dear, and follow no one, me or another. If you were really sure, I am glad you voted. If you were not sure in your own mind, I am sorry. But don't pretend we are not far apart on the subject, because truly we are. But, dear, thinking and voting as you do, how can you do logically other than condemn me, utterly? You must. In your secret heart you do, even if you don't tell me nor even yourself. What a hideous coil we are all in! How can you, having voted so, do anything but disown me to your friends? . . .

Life becomes more and more monotonous here. Rumour has it that we shall move up to the front in a fortnight, but personally I doubt. Here there is nothing but much humdrum work, night or day or both. My work, my new work, is a bit of a change from the old. I drive the OC about to outstations and to official duties in the town. I am just his chauffeur, but unofficially his friend and confidant. The other day, for instance, we paused on a long trip at a certain much damaged town and had a good civilized lunch at a nice hotel—hors d'oeuvre, wine, coffee & all the correct things. Then whenever there is a train to evacuate I take the OC down and keep the car ready for official trips to hospitals with him and meanwhile I help a little to control the incomings and outgoings of the ambulances, jumping on each as it comes in and giving instructions and much chaff. And today I took the mechanic over to an outstation where a car has succumbed to the frost and we brought its radiator back here to repair, & tomorrow we take it back. That is nearly a day's job in itself. Then when we move from this place the Sunbeam will lead and shepherd the whole convoy. . . .

The Sunbeam has to be kept looking very smart so as to outshine the French officer's Hotchkiss, and I can assure you the latter car is not in the same street (metaphorically) either as to style or cleanliness as the Sunbeam. Funny life! But ye gods and little fishes I am aweary of all such hopeless lives as this. I want my dear girl with whom I so profoundly disagree in a matter that *may* someday be very much practical politics for me. Oh but I want my girl, and all else is just a long bad dream.

[*Many of Olaf's earlier letters contained drafts of poems for which he sought Agnes' reactions. In January 1914, when he first sent Agnes a copy of the poem chronicling the stages of his love for her, "A History 1903–1911," Olaf called it "almost my first effort at versifying" and dated the first part of it to his year teaching at Manchester Grammar*

Egremont
TO OLAF                                        22 November 1916
. . . Last night Rosie & Dad & I went to see a pretty little opera—half amateur, half professional done in Mosman by the Mosman Musical Society. . . . Being in an emotional & alert frame of mind with the singing, I couldn't help watching in the intervals a young man & a maid who were sitting several rows in front. She was just an ordinary looking sort of girl like me, with fair hair & blue eyes & a smile—& he was a great big strong dark chap—with a bronze complexion & shoulders as strong & square as a tower. . . . Just in front of me was an old school friend of mine with her husband. She looked dignified & matronly & absolutely placid—absolutely. It is wonderful how soon girls acquire that look of peaceful content after they are married. Lots of old school friends are getting married. There was one jolly young ruffian of a girl much younger than me who went & did it last week. . . . Dear, all these happy people make me long so much for our time to come. I am sure there is nothing else that counts beside that & we are the only two that fit together like these two do & all proper two's. Isn't it a blessing that we do fit so well! I feel that there is not one tiny spot of me that doesn't fit with you & vice versa. And yet you are "all a wonder"— strange boy that I know so well & yet so little & love so well all through.

The night before last I was wicked & sat up late when everyone had gone to bed & what do you think I was doing? Going through the treasures in my writing case & reading old poems that you have sent me now & then ever since I was a little girl. There were many you wrote long ago & only gave me this last time I was in England. I am going to show that little one—"A History of 1903–1911"—to Mrs. Irvine. You don't mind, do you? I went up to see her in the hospital & read her one of your letters & we talked quite a lot of you & she was such a dear. She was so surprised to hear our love—your love—dated from so far back, & so when she asked if you had written anything else except Latter-Day Psalms I told her of some of the little poems I treasure & I promised to show her this one. More for its history than its poetry, I told her. It is a quaint little rambling story, but it's very sweet & like a boy. When did you write it?

SSA 13
Agnes,                                          27 November 1916
Mud, rain, fog, frost, thaw, and more mud! One day running all over the country, next day a whole day's cleaning and tuning up. Next day

odd jobs and with luck a bit of time off. And so on. But it is so cold now that free time has mostly to be used in walking oneself hot. The pleasantest part of the day is always the night (!) tucked up nicely in rugs. My feet are becoming chilblains, and my fingers too, in spite of your mittens, which are absolutely invaluable. We are now settling down to a more or less quiet winter, with the pretty certain prospect of a busy spring. We shall none of us be sorry to have a quiet winter. And we hope to be up to full strength for the spring. The general feeling of weariness of it all is more pronounced in the convoy than it was last winter, partly because we are not as well billeted as we were, and also the food is being considerably "simplified." The margarine is generally pretty bad. Sugar is generally "run out." Jam is off; and so on. Yet of course we do very well compared with ordinary French troops. But we miss our own national diet.

It occurs to me I am already too late to wish you a merry Christmas. You will know I am wishing it when the time comes anyhow. I shall be imagining a real old Christmas party with games and stories and plum pudding and mince pies and crackers and paper hats and holly and mistletoe. You and I could enjoy a Christmas party together, such as the family used to have at the Scotts' or at Garsdale.

SSA 13

TO AGNES                                                8 December 1916

. . . This morning as I was running along a forest ridge to get warm I saw a hole low in a tree trunk, and the spirit moved me to peep in. Down at the bottom, below the level of the ground was a fine fat green woodpecker. Evidently I disturbed his winter sleep. He could not get out because I was in his doorway; so he had to squat at the bottom, cocking first one eye at me and then the other, as if he could not quite trust either. I was right above him, in the one position that was out of both his ordinary fields of vision. The poor old beastie kept up the alternate observation stunt like clock work all the while I was there, moving his green body restlessly the while, and looking daggers at me alternately from each eye. The splash of red on the crown of his head looked almost like an autumn leaf, but brighter. His beak was long and strong like a kingfisher's. The incident rejoiced me greatly, somehow. . . .

The other day my electric lighting dynamo went wrong. The mechanic was away, & I know little about electricity, so I was dished. Fortunately we found that our eccentric meteorologist [Lewis Richardson] was also an expert electrician. He and I had a morning on the job unscrewing, tinkering, cleaning and generally titivating, sometimes lying under the car in the mud, sometimes strangling ourselves among machinery inside. The professor was keen as a schoolboy; and when he had triumphantly set the thing right, and I thanked him with very genuine warmth he said, "Oh, but I enjoyed it. It has been a morning off for me, much nicer than washing plates!" Fancy having a fellow like that to do the scullery maid work! That is war all over. Of course it can't be helped. He is also a devotee of the international language called "Ido," a new sort of Esperanto. He is proselytising me, but I am not very enthusiastic.

Egremont
TO OLAF                                                    17 December 1916
. . . I had a letter from Auntie this mail concerning the Annery scheme & our future. Also another matter which she said, I was *on no account* to mention to you in case you should be annoyed that she had written. But I "mention" *everything* to you so it can't be helped & I leave it with you not to give me away & on no account to be annoyed with Auntie! My! One would think we were all the most touchy & susceptible parcel of folk imaginable. Auntie asked me if I had ever thought of coming over to be married in England instead of waiting for you to come to me. Have I ever thought of it! I thought of it in my last letter to you, didn't I? Well, I talked it over with Mother & she was comforting & reassuring. She thinks we ought not to go on being parted indefinitely, & I think she *would* be willing for me to go sometime next year, if nothing better turns up. She knows & I know that when it comes to the point it will be a plunge at any time. When one leaves one thinks of the leaving, not of the arrival at the other end. But dear, I think I must come to you before the year is out if you can't come to me. It doesn't seem fair not to, does it? I don't like causing a disturbance in this family, but I know they would bear up alright so long as the submarine danger was not too great, & after all *my* family is not the only one to be considered. And as for me I should be quite happy at Annery with Auntie & Uncle always & you on leave. It's just you & your leave that would make any place the best.

So all things considered, if by this time next year you are not here or preparing to come here—well, I shall be there or preparing to go there. Is that alright? You have been so good in not entreating me to come long ago. I'm sure lots of men would have done.

SSA 13
Agnes,                                                       23 December 1916
There is an old, old, very old woman who lives near us and goes out into the forest to gather sticks. Sometimes she goes by herself, sometimes a little girl goes with her. Many times a day the old woman passes the place where we keep our cars, and each time that she is coming back

with her load she is bent so low that her face is on a level with her hips and it is only with difficulty that she can raise her eyes to see before her. Her steps are very slow and unsteady, and her burden is always so unwieldy that the mere swinging of it nearly upsets her. She carries it in a curious way over one hip, so that her whole body is twisted like the face of a flat-fish. As she is passing one sees her ancient face, withered and very placid. Because of her very great stoop no one ever sees her face full, but only in profile. She never looks at anyone, but goes plodding on with her eyes to the ground. When she has passed one looks after her and sees her as a great moving bush of twigs and branches, with one mighty gnarled hand spread queerly over the waist of her bundle, holding it to her back. The girl also carries a bundle, but her going is in swift staggering stages, each followed by a long rest while the old woman comes up and passes her with never a pause. The girl is fresh to look at, fair-haired, blue-eyed. The labour is irksome to her. She looks round for things of interest, jerks her bundle into a more comfortable position, and at last drops it with a sigh, her whole body stretchng with the relief of the sudden freedom. But the old woman creeps on as steadily as the hand of a clock, and almost as imperceptibly. She wears a funny old dirty white sunbonnet, and on her feet wooden shoes that look loose. One expects them to clatter on her bony ankles. There is something weird about her. She is like a witch, but too serene. She is like some ancient woman in an ancient myth. There is something classic about her, something inevitable, and a divine calm. She has none of the childlike joy of the old woman in the picture "Words of Comfort." She is too wise to accept comfort. She has found out the world and she has no more dreams about it, nor about any other world. Yet she is not sad, still less bitter. She has seen the vanity of life; but she seems strangely content, as if all the while she held some great and solemn secret that was deeper than the vain world of pain-dreaders and joy-desirers, of little selfseekers and inflated idealists. I thought at first that she was like old, bent France, carrying load after load of sticks to the fire of war. But now I think she is the Wise Woman who takes whatever she chooses from the forest that is mankind to keep alight her magic hearth fire. And what purpose she has, and what good or evil potions she brews in her cauldron, no man knows, but only she. . . .

Last night as I was going to bed (first time), there was a great discussion. Picture: a dark but starry night, a line of cars in a forest glade, one car a tourer with hood up, and in it arranging his rugs and strapping himself in by the light of a little petrol lamp, Olaf; outside, prowling round the car, Big Smell [Routh Smeal], sometimes poking his head in, the better to talk, sometimes listening and watching the stars. The discussion was the usual that takes place between us. The gist of it was, on Smeal's part, "Nothing is any good really. There's no point about living.

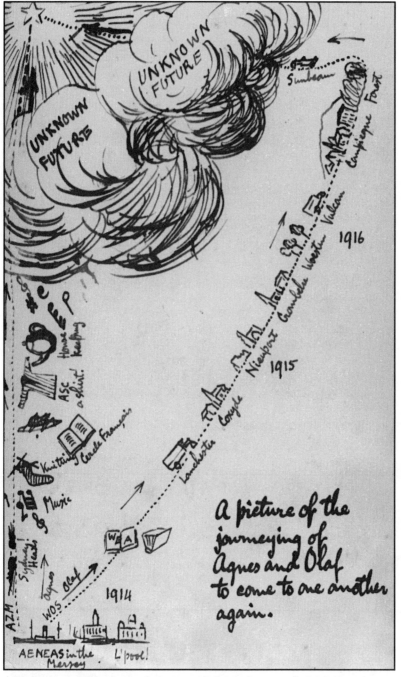

Olaf's cartoon of his imagined reunion with Agnes, drawn on the back of a convoy photograph and sent to Agnes late in 1916.

What is the object of it all? Goodness? Beauty? What are they for? What *are* they?" And on my part, "Why, Good Heavens, man alive, you seem to forget that you can't get right to the bottom by pure reason, simply because reason is only a guide, and must begin on some initial *feeling*. You can't *explain* the feeling. The world is very beautiful. Why? Good God, man, I don't know *why*; but it just *is*. What more do you want? If you care for a person you don't dissect the feeling & explain it all away and then say, 'What's the use of it?' You just love, & act accordingly. Well, it's the same in the universal as with the personal. The World is beautiful, & to be loved; and Evolution is supremely worthwhile. ("Evolution," in our talk, meant the universal striving to be good & beautiful.) You *feel* it to be. And *from* that feeling you start arguing, not against it." Etc. And this time, after much talk and much fumbling with rugs on my part, and prowling about on his, he said slowly in his deep voice, "I think I see what you mean." Then there was a long silence and stillness. Then he said, "Well, I'll be going to bed." Smeal is a seeker after reality. No fairy tales for him, no comfortable self deceptions. And what he thinks, he lives. He thinks cynically, so he talks & acts cynically. But he wants to grasp some more worthy truth, and when he finds it he will very surely act up to it. He has a big bulgy forehead, a snub nose, a straight mouth and bull dog jaw. I like him. He likes me sometimes, and sometimes scorns me.

Bed time now. Perhaps there will be a letter from you tomorrow, Christmas Eve, or on the day itself. It won't be Christmas without a letter from you. One more Christmas with the globe between us, but this will be the last, I do hope.

Cymbeline

TO OLAF                                                     30 December 1916

. . . The day before yesterday I got 2 letters from you which were a blessing—they were from Oxford & Folkestone & left me stranded on the desolate shores of England while you crossed to France with your car on a grey stormy afternoon. I am longing for the next letter, & to think of your having safely accomplished the rest of your journey. It's horrid to think of your having to go back to France, back to work, back to war—but I suppose it can't be helped. The whole thing makes me think more & more I *must* come over to you. I can't go on just being, being—doing here the same things time after time—because I ought to be over there where I can be with you when you are at home. I ought—I must—I will. I have often thought if my home had been in England all this time of course I should have turned & done something useful like all the girls. I should simply hate munitions making, & I would not like VAD much, but I should like to have gone to France with the War

Victims Relief People—the Friends. Do you think they would have young incapables like me? Even still I should like to do something like that when I come, but I know I should not want to leave Auntie & Uncle alone. However, I expect there is lots to do in all directions. . . .

Thank you ever so much, in advance, for the lace you are having sent for me. You *do* spoil me with things. But I shall simply love to have it. I *adore* nice lace. That is one of my few real extravagances! I shall use it for my trousseau & you shall know all about it later on. . . . Talking about Belgian lace—I had a most gorgeous present of some yesterday by the mail, & I don't feel quite happy about it, because he ought not to have sent it. He is Jack Armstrong. He says it is just a small token of his friendship in appreciation of mine—or words to that effect, & if it were only small I wouldn't mind so much. In fact I should be pleased, but it is a most beautiful silk lace scarf about 2 yards or more in length! What is a chap to do? I'll have to tell him never to do it never no more, but he won't obey orders,—& it would break his heart if I tried to refuse it,—because he says it's pure friendship, poor old John! I wish he had a girl of his own. What do you think about men sending presents to someone else's girl? Do you mind in this instance? I am afraid I can't alter the feeling that prompts him, but I think he ought to spend his money some other how, but then it's *his* money, & I am afraid it gives him most pleasure to spend it on me! Dear dear—what a shame! Why are things so? Why, the weest little wee thing that you send me would give me more pleasure than the whole world from anyone else. That's sad for Jack, but it's true, & you don't mind *that*, do you?

# 1917

TO AGNES                                                                    1 January 1917

. . . Today is the year's first day, and shall we not meet before the last of
it? If not, I think I shall burn to a cinder with just wanting you. And the
smoke thereof will blow round the world to you of its own willfulness
and—rubbish! Our tame professor [Lewis Richardson], the meteorologist, is going home on leave to his wife. Think of it! He wears a wedding
ring. The other day he lost it and raised a hue and cry through France
and lamented, "Won't I catch it when I go home!" Next day he found it
in his pocket. But heaven heaven! Heaven, I say, is just to go *home* to
one's *wife*. . . .

*Next Day.* . . . Remember, engrave it in your mind, that since we last
spoke together two long years ago we have each passed through many
new things and been changed. Remember that for all the deeper subjects letters are a very poor means of communication. We do not know
one another (intellectually) as well as we did before, not because we
have forgotten or grown apart, but because we cannot fully share all that
mass of experience that each has had since we last spoke together. This
is hard fact, and not to be abolished. It may be sad, but it is true. Yet I
don't think it is sad, for when next we meet I think we shall have all the
delights of discovery over again. But in the meanwhile, Agnes my girl,
let us in forming all our new opinions, faiths, loves, ideals, make a
mental reservation—"This is for the duration of the war. Afterwards it is
to be tested again, and either endorsed, changed, or put away." Not that
we must have the same opinions & ideals, but that before holding any
opinion or ideal irrevocably we must each truly enter the other's mind
to understand the other's faith. It cannot be done by letter, even apart
from censorship. . . . I say all this because someone, who has just
joined the convoy & is a true friend of mine already, was so dismayed at

the thought that you and I had gone through all this eventful revolutionary age with no means of spiritual touch but letters. We have made letters do well. But let us remember their limitations.

Rambling, imperfect, ungainly. But perhaps not wholly a failure. Love with understanding

Your friend
Olaf Stapledon

SSA 13

TO AGNES                               18 January 1917

. . . I have been sitting in front of the fire reading Walt Whitman, that astounding boisterous pleasure-loving prophet! I have hardly read him at all till now, & now it is time to do so. Do you know him at all? His stuff seems haphazard and undisciplined, but it is fine vigorous stuff whether one likes it or not. He seems rather obsessed by sex, even to a lover he seems to be so. But he is so refreshingly direct about it, brutally direct. Yet the tone is as pure as blue sky. And his obsession only consists in reading sex into rocks, atoms & stars. And sex *is* indeed the mighty thing he sings. And I am glad to be male since you are female. And in the photo of you painting the house your outstretched bare arm, which is beautiful in itself, is more beautiful to a man than to a woman and most beautiful to me of all men because I love you. Oh pretty arm, so firmly holding that old brush! The whole character of you is in that arm no less than in your face. And when I compare it with the similarly outstretched arm of Rosie on your right I see the difference of your souls. I want to kiss that little arm of yours for being so simple and brave and beautiful. I like you with bare arms. Beautiful things should not be hidden, not from a lover anyhow who loves the whole beauty of you from your hair to your little toes that paddle in the water on a summer day. According to Whitman the body is no less divine than the soul, and that is true. And in that photo of you I see much divinity, and I want to take it all in my arms and gently crush all its dear softness together against me. But all I have to give you in return for all that womanly beauty is a passably agile and light body of a man that people would say was rather a boy's, a chest that holds plenty of air, two willing but clumsy and unlovely hands and two legs like sticks, and like walking sticks—never tired. There's not much else, save a boy's face and a shoddy mop of hair and two eyes, one bigger and stronger than the other.

[*The working title of one of Olaf's lost manuscripts from this period was "Being and Doing." The apparent conflict between self-cultivation and*

service to others, between personal integrity and communal bonds was
to be a persistent theme of his later writings both as philosopher and as
novelist. Agnes had written in December of her own worry that she
spent so much time on household duties that no time remained for
spiritual growth.]


                                                                    SSA 13
TO AGNES                                                   22 January 1917
. . . Strange coincidences are always happening. The last is that your
letter all about being and doing and the duty of enjoyment, and the
choice between these two, comes just while I am reading a book in
which a girl raises that very question. The book is so very beautiful and
readable that I am going to send you a copy. I have been very good
about *not* sending you books lately, so you will forgive me this time,
won't you? It is a novel "The Freelands" by Galsworthy, that most noble
son of Devon. The hero and heroine are first cousins, so the book has
an added charm for us. The girl I think is just a bit like you in spirit, but
the boy (aged 22) is most unlike me. The girl is above all things honest
and a lover of beauty. The boy is a fighter. If you fall in love with him I
shall be jealous. The other people are wonderfully real and all have
something lovable in them. And through the book run great modern
perplexities, hoaxes, make-beliefs, and striving after beauty, and behind
all you will feel the mysterious presence of the very thing that all are
looking for in vain. And the whole human action takes place in glorious
English country. Find time to read it, dear, you will like it so very
much, because it is so sympathetic with all sorts of people, and because
it has a pretty love story in it. It was recommended to me by one of our
new-comers, [Thomas Tindle] Anderson, a most lovable person. He
came to us straight from Cambridge and the search for truths. He still
continues his search for truths by assiduous reading in all his spare moments, but being a very busy orderly and fearfully conscientious about
his work, he does not get much time for his reading. For a fortnight or
so he was taken into the mechanical department and astounded our old
mechanic with his profound ignorance and simplicity. He is a pale
roundfaced darkhaired lad with great big smiling dreamy black eyes,
and a certain firmness of feature and of expression. He is exceptionally
sensitive, has had nervous breakdowns, can't stand the sound of a file. I
don't know what he will think of shells, when the time comes.


                                                                 Cymbeline
Olaf My Dearest,                                          24 January 1917
     It's a cold damp morning & I am sitting in the warm kitchen with the
fire & the smell of vanilla cakes a'baking—beginning my letter to you. I

am feeling a bit forlorn. I want you very much, my Olaf. The postie just came along on his horse & I asked him about the next English mail & he said it wouldn't be in for a fortnight, but I don't believe that because it's a week already since the last came. That's enough to make anyone forlorn, isn't it? However I told him he was a heartless beggar & I didn't believe him, so he said perhaps he had made a mistake. He is a returned soldier & he has ceased to be interested in mails now. Come quickly the day when all the world will cease to take an interest in mails. . . .

Olaf, is it wrong of me to say it, but I often have a fear that someday we might have a little child like [Aunt Zena's] Joan. I always took it for granted long ago that cousins couldn't marry. I remember even when I was about 10—thinking what a pity it was that I would not be able to marry Olaf! & I think it must have been partly on that account that I took so long to get used to the idea of your being my lover. Once I had admitted this, frankly, to myself, it did not take me long to find out that I also was *your* lover—& then I told you in a letter or in several letters & that was the beginning of the good days, & the sad ones!——But there were snatches of them before. I remember sitting with you up by the cairn on the top of Moel Wynn, & I was troubled because of you & me, & you told me as we eat Susan [cake] & apples of your college friend who is the son of two cousins & I was quite reassured & happy then all the day, & when later we dropped down across the moor into that little cottage at Tan-y-grisiau I looked across the table to you & felt that it was good to be alive, & then we swung home across the low hills & were not a bit tired when we got to Bryn—only wet—& the family fussed over us.

Well just sometimes I am anxious again & I want you to talk to me & reassure me like a big brother, but anyway that is not a mountain any longer, it is only a pebble. Love itself is all that counts—& I *must* be your wife whatever happens. The great mountain is the war, but there is a way even over that—if God will.

## SSA 13

Agnes,                                                    30 January 1917

Frost, frost, frost! Day after day of it, bright, beautiful and bitter cold. Since I wrote last much has happened. We got a sudden order to trek, accompanied by a document "not to be opened until the hour of departure." Our journey was not a long one, but we took two days over it, and now we are in the town [Châlons-sur-Marne] you thought we had gone to when we moved six months ago. The War Victims people are here. The journey was made difficult by the frost. Every possible thing froze up. Hot water froze as soon as it reached the ground. One's fingers froze to everything. Last night a bottle of ink in a suitcase on which I slept all night was frozen up. Half a dozen cars were put out of action by frost on the way down, but we managed the necessary repairs on the road, and all arrived here. The first night I slept in a barn because the wind kept blowing out my lamp in my car. Otherwise I sleep in my car, but it is a bit chilly, and tonight I think I may move into the room, which is cold & stuffy. We are in a huge barracks and we hate it. There is not any heating apparatus, so it is practically as cold inside as out. The coldest night of all was spent on the way down. I believe the thermometer was not very far from zero Fahrenheit in the little upland village where we spent the night. It is about 14° now, here,—18 degrees of frost. This place is quite a big town, very far from the front, but at the base of the greatest of the French salients. If we are stuck here doing evacuation work forever, we shall be very depressed; but if this is merely a stage on the way to this new and important front, all is well. The other mobile FAU convoy is coming here too, and other English convoys are working with this army. We can be sure of having solid & important work here, but we are not at all sure how long it will be before we get to the front. . . .

Meanwhile oh for the end of the frost! The motor man is worse hit than anyone else in frost because the cars get so impossible to start, & things keep freezing and bursting; and of course lying underneath with few clothes on, a wind, 14° of frost, and fingers that can't catch hold of things, is worse even than sitting well wrapped up at the bottom of a trench. . . . This is not a letter, because everything is so higgledy piggledy and frozen up that one simply can't write yet. You know, don't you dear, that there's nothing I would rather do than write to you all the day, but it is not possible just now, so I am going to send off this as it stands and begin again very soon. Everyone is stamping about and shouting to keep warm. Your mittens have had such hard wear that they are already in holes, and I am wishing I had not lost half of the other pair.

[*Wells's widely read novel* Mr. Britling Sees It Through, *treading a careful line between patriotic sentiment and antinationalist propaganda, captured in eloquent melodrama the successive moods of amazement, loss, and determination in the civilian population's responses to the war. The letters of the young enlisted man, Hugh Britling, to his father near the novel's end capitalized on a vogue for the genre of "letters from the front." "The Seekers" was a women's reading club Agnes joined in Sydney.*]

TO OLAF                                           2 February 1917

. . . Mr. Whittell brought in a Sunday paper with big headlines about America having severed diplomatic relations with Germany. What do you think about America? I don't want her to go to war, but I want her to make a decent & fearless protest. All their little protests so far have been so petty & so selfish—only about the "rights of American citizens," & the property of American citizens & so forth. They have not protested for the rights of mankind as a whole, for justice & truth & honour. It's only for themselves. From the Allies' point of view I think we should do better if America remained neutral; but there was a little paragraph in Wells' book "Mr. Britling Sees It Through" which made me want America *not* to fight. It was where the young American explained that his country would betray her trust if she allowed herself to be drawn into war. He said America was the field for humanity to make a fresh start in, to turn over a new leaf, & it would be wrong for her to go back to the old lines. Do you think that? I have felt indignant with America not because she didn't fight, but because she held aloof & did nothing, just as I have felt indignant with people here who did nothing. I would not mind what they did—fight or ambulance or make munitions, so long as they did not just go on with their own lives as though nothing had happened. Fancy a man being content to do nothing when everyone else is sacrificing—some their limbs & lives. Two of our friends have got married & stayed at home.

Yesterday Lottie Armstrong was worked up because an old friend of hers had asked her to go a day's motor trip, & he is one of three brothers & all three are still at home just "living"—& says Lottie, "There's Mrs. South's boy being sent back to the firing line after only a week in hospital with fever, sent back because they haven't enough reinforcements. I think it's a shame! And I *will not* go out a motor trip with that man. I don't think it's right." She appealed to me. I think it is a shame too. That's why we want conscription—only for that. What do *you* think?

If a man hasn't the pluck, or perhaps the qualifications, for going into the army & taking his share of risks he might at least do clerical work or relief work of some kind. People won't enthuse over him, but at least he is of use. But to do nothing!! I wonder what you have been thinking about the Peace overtures of Germany. The papers mock them & twist them inside out. I can't believe they were honest. The Kaiser is such a hardened hypocrite, but it is horrible to think of the poor people starving in Germany, if that is true. Daddy who is reasonably optimistic & reasonably pessimistic pronounced the opinion that the end will come this year. He thinks the Germans are trying to bring things on & get peace somehow. Oh may he be correct! but I am afraid there will be a terrible

slaughter before it can come. Have you read "Mr. Britling" yet? I want
to read it again to myself. We are going to discuss it at one of the Seekers
meetings this year. Hugh's letters made me cry. Dad said after reading
one very harrowing one, "Well, it's quite understandable that the men
themselves wouldn't see beyond their own trenches. They wouldn't take
a broad view."—& I wanted to burst out indignantly, "No, & why
should they? poor men! Why should anyone see beyond all the filth of
it. They were not meant to, war is not the right way. It's all a hideous
madness."—but I couldn't have said anything without bursting into
tears, so I said naught.

SSA 13

TO AGNES                                          2 February 1917

. . . I wanted to talk about a book I have been reading about feminism
and marriage and love and the evolution of a nobler kind of society. The
point of it all is really very simple, namely that women, from being in a
servile state (economically and spiritually) under men, must become
free & independent economically and spiritually; and that marriage
must become a far freer, less legally-bound thing. But it's so hard to talk
properly about such things late at night and on a piece of paper that is
greasy so that the pen will not write properly. So I must stop.

Dear, you know how an electric wire conveys a current, and how if
the current is too strong for it the wire fuses—goes white hot and breaks.
Well, all this poor letter writing business is our electric wire, and it is too
thin a wire for the current of understanding and sympathy and love that
has to pass along it, that *must* pass along it. But so poor a wire it is, that
sometimes when there is most to say and most longing to be truly mentally, spiritually in touch with you, I don't want to write at all, simply
because I know I can't write down really what I feel & think, because it
is all unspeakable. That is when the wire fuses, when I just sit before a
blank page and wonder how we really stand toward one another after
these two and a half years,—wonder because my letters are really so
very unlike me. (It's not my fault.) And then I *long* to get right at you,
true real you, through your letters. And I long so much that we two
might freely give and take each the purest, best, most noble essence of
each. When we meet, girl, there will be such a lot to learn of one another. How shall we ever catch up? The best thing I have learnt in these
years of war is the sense of the supreme worth of sincerity in human
thoughts and feelings. I am always posing and pretending, but I am getting honester by degrees, and less flowery and rhetorical in mind, and
less interesting too, because alas when the poses are wiped away there's
not much left. . . .

*Next Day.* . . . Dear, when you talk of coming to England this year what can a fellow say? I want you so much. Yet I can't honestly feel that it would be right. It is one thing to be transplanted and quite another thing to be dug up and not properly planted again but just kept ready to plant at the end of the war. I do so desperately want you. But think! Eight days leave every six months with luck, probably only every eight months now. Unless one were to leave this job, but what then? No, I see nothing for it but the end of the war. If the war shows no signs of ending this year, then next year something *must* be done. But it seems to me that if you do come before the end of the war you will do best to stay with my folk rather than to wander into France. You could find plenty of useful work to do at home. If you cared you could do much at the women's university settlement at Liverpool. You would probably learn much about problems & people & life in general if you were to do that. And, dear, while we are on that subject—(the connection is more subtle than obvious)—in one of your letters you wonder if I mind your having presents from other people, from Jack Armstrong, for instance. Well why on earth should I? You are not my chattel! You are for ever a free soul. You remember how I used long ago to press you to *promise* to marry me. Well, that was most foolish of me, and you wisely knew it. Even now my claim over you is only a claim so long as, and because, you love me. . . . I am not your "lord." I will not be it. No man has the right to be "lord" over a woman. For man and woman are equals, of course. And in spite of all ceremonies and vows I shall always be just your lover and friend. My will is no law to you except while you will it so. You shall not "obey" me. Good heaven! The idea! You are not one of the women who were brought up to be pretty toys, dolls, "half angel half idiot." You are one of the newest and the most primaeval kind of women, of the new age that is dawning and the ancientest age that ever was, one of those who expect something more than protection, petting and slavery. You don't give up your will; you bring it to help us both. You don't live in a little artificial world, padded and scented; you live in the real great world, knowing it to be both beautiful and ghastly. We shall each learn from the other about life, about people, yes and about—God. Now where am I wandering? There's a noise now, and I must stop. All the above talk is just the result of reading [Edward] Carpenter's "Love's Coming-of-Age," a book which suggests that the world is only just learning what real full grown love is.

[*As SSA 13 moved farther south and west into the heart of France its members became isolated from their own countrymen. "Though in theory we were emancipated from mere patriotism," Olaf recalled twenty*

years later, "*many of us were in fact intensely conscious of our nation-
ality and anxious to uphold its honour in the eyes of the French. For
our journey south took us far from all traces of the British Army.
Henceforth we were to come across Italians, Senegalese, Algerians, An-
namites, American negroes, Russians, but no British.*"]

SSA 13

TO AGNES                                                    7 February 1917
. . . Now what has happened since I wrote last? We have made our
move and are now in a very satisfactory billet in a town [Ste. Mene-
hould] behind the lines. Our work is front work. The Sunbeam made a
trip round our aidposts today in rather wild hilly wooded country, all
considerably high above sea level. There was very little strafing going
on, though two or three shells did go singing over our heads and burst
behind us. Some of the villages are pretty well flattened out into mere
litter, and everywhere there are wonderful new "villages" of dugouts,
marvelously deep and elaborately engineered. It is rather fascinating to
wander round amongst them. Some of the roads are under observation
by the enemy, and on those reaches one does not loiter, for a car is a big
and obvious beast. And we were given the comforting news that a general's car was hit last week and the driver killed. So altogether we felt
quite like being "at the war" once more. This town that is our headquarters is well back from the lines, quite civilized and flourishing. You can
get a decent dinner in it, with the permission of the authorities, and a
snug afternoon tea most days of the week. Our billet is some funny old
stables by a little winding frozen river. The walls and roof & floors are
full of holes and the rats eat all our grub, but we have the place to ourselves, and we have put up our stoves and we raid the countryside for
fuel (wood). So we are warm! Think of it! And last night there were only
six degrees Fahrenheit of frost. And it has been so cold before, below
zero Fahrenheit often, that is more than 32 degrees of frost, and the
record is far lower than that. And we all have most awful colds and sore
feet. And one or two people have had slight frostbite in spite of being
well wrapped up. Oh it has been an experience, of its sort. And now we
are snug and the weather is improving. And the poor old Sunbeam had
to be towed to this place because the frost put her out of action at the last
minute.

Egremont

TO OLAF                                                    10 February 1917
. . . Last Friday I went to the French League to work, the first time
since I have come back [from Blackheath]. All the "casual workers" sit

at a long trestle table & sew on buttons & tabs or things. Sometimes I machine, but on Friday I sewed. It is always more interesting at the tables, because you can talk to other people or watch them & listen. The old ladies get up one end & the girls the other. I have some friends I have made among the old ladies, & often I sit & talk to Mrs. Jones. The girls are not really my sort, but they are nice girls. I sat with them this time until they all cleared out about 4 o'clock to go & have ice-cream sodas! They were such pretty, happy & prosperous kind of girls—all rather too well off to be "my sort"—but simply enough dressed in cotton frocks, two blues, & a pink & a mauve & a black & white (for a brother lately killed in France) & me in a green & white (my one & only, & last summer's at that!). The talk was all of the most open & honest gossip!— other girls & their nice complexions—clothes—"what my dressmaker is making for me"—picture shows—engagements & marriages—fiancés at the war. One of these girls since I saw her about 6 months ago has been down in Melbourne, got engaged & married, & her man has gone to the front & she is back home again playing the war-bride, & putting on funny little airs that we all felt & laughed at, & flourishing obviously her wedding-ring. She is still excited about her wedding & her trousseau but she looks a bit pensive sometimes, poor kid, when she's not putting on airs. Another girl, the one I like best, a solid pretty dark girl, with soft laughing brown eyes, & everything that money can buy, has been en- gaged for nearly two years ("but not announced all that time")—& now she is expecting her fiancé back from the war on a hospital ship in two or three weeks with a permanently useless right arm. It is 14 months since she has seen him. She wondered, aloud, if she would get a wire from him from the West. "Or a ring-up from Melbourne," someone suggested. She hadn't thought of that, & her eyes, half-shut, laughed again. "Fancy hearing his voice again on the telephone!"

[*In his old age Julian Fox, who had joined Olaf's convoy in December 1915 and shared his passion for jogging, recorded his memories of the FAU in privately printed stories under the general title* The Man Who Would Have Been Blamed *(Somerset, 1961). One of the most durable friendships Olaf made was with Harry Locke, whom he saw often for the rest of his life. Locke became head of the Education Section of the Rowntree Cocoa Works in York after the war, and with Patricia Hall he wrote a book on the relations between employers and employees,* Incen- tives and Contentment: A Study Made in a British Factory *(London, 1938).*]

Agnes,                                                          15 February 1917

The frost has gone (except at nights). The roads are muddy again after a month's dryness. The frozen rivers are breaking themselves free. It is glorious bright weather too, with a feeling of spring in the air. The country looks light hearted. You would never think there was a war, save for the prolonged and awful roar there was last night, and the rather too exciting aid post roads. Spring! Is it to be a bloodier than ever, or will peace come? I am bored with war, bored with cars and wounded men and officialism and flashy officers and shells (and bored when there are no shells also). The symbol of supremest boredom I think will always be a broken down blood soaked stretcher. . . .

*Later.* I have just been for an after dinner stroll with Renard [Julian Fox] up the steep little hill to the old little church and round the queer lanes that wander on the top of that citadel-like hill. We stood for a long time on the edge of the plateau looking at the distant flares and gun flash, and exchanging a word now and then. It is queer to see at your feet the lights of a flourishing village and beyond the lights of war. Renard is one of those quiet people who have the gift of making you struggle out of your own pettinesses and be serene. He has also the gift of being pleasant and interesting and even inspiring without ever opening his mouth save for a rare commonplace sentence or two. Just at present we are beset by rumours and we have been feeling rather as one feels before rowing a race. But as usual the rumours are proving "much exaggerated," and we are not sorry. Sparrow [Alan Sokell], whose car was hit the other day, proclaims, with a queer little twinkle and a Yorkshire accent, that he would sooner be a live coward than a dead hero. And Harry Locke, ex-metal worker, trade unionist, philosopher and revolutionary announced this morning that if anyone wanted a live bosch shell they could pick up plenty lying on a certain road, but he himself being a philosopher had left them lying, hoping that the night car would not blindly bump them. . . .

Now that the weather has changed one positively manages to wash once a day and we are all beginning to look quite clean. (My hat, we were a dirty crowd till lately! If you had seen me you would have run away a mile without stopping, for you would have seen the filthiest unshaven ragged object with black tide marks round his wrists and neck.) But now I am quite smart, when I put on my better tunic and clean my boots, quite smart enough to walk through this little town with you and take you to a patisserie for chocolate and cakes. We would sit down in the little inner room in a corner by ourselves so snug, so happy; and French officers would come in and sit at other little tables and look wonderingly at us. And American ambulance drivers would come in, and our own Englishmen. But we two in our little corner would sit watching and talking about it all with our heads near together for confidential conversation. And I would coax you to have more cakes and chocolate. And, being in a dark corner, you would let me steal your hand under the little table, just to enforce the conversation. But I must not go imagining these things, for it makes me so impatient and makes me sort of blaze inside with longing and indignation. It grows dangerous to think too much of such things. It makes me want to get away from all this and be just a free irresponsible individual with nothing in the world to do but seek you out and live with you. It makes me long to have you in England this year, war or no war. It makes me feel ready to give up everything just to be with you for half an hour again and die at the end of that brief spell of heaven. It makes me burn.

[*"Shooting the breakers" or "surfing," an activity utterly unlike what English people expected of a seaside outing, was the sort of thing that made Australia seem an unbuttoned frontier culture.*]

Egremont
TO OLAF                                            25 February 1917
. . . [Manly] is the gay place on the ocean side of North Head. It is fun to go there sometimes when you are feeling in a holiday mood & want to hear the band playing on the Corso & watch all the crowds of fashionable flappers & young knuts—"& the Lizzies & the Lils, & the 'arrys & the Bills." The whole place lives & moves on the Corso & the Esplanade. You will see it all some day with its bright lights & its noisy crowds & its cocoanut brown boys & girls, young men & maids—half of them in bathing costumes & kimonos, & best of all its sea beach, with a row of tall Norfolk Island Pines at the top of it & its white frothy surf below riding in to shore on the great green rollers. The beach is about a mile and a half long & has two great dressing sheds at each end, & a Life saving club & an attendant always on watch for sharks & changing currents. And you will see ever so many little black heads bobbing up & down among the breakers—& some daredevil ones out beyond the first row waiting to get "a shoot." Can you shoot the breakers? I can't much. I don't get enough practise, but you see the men & some girls get on the wave just before it breaks & ride right in to shore on its crest, their head & shoulders just sticking out from the bank of breaking foam. It's a fine sight. We went down on Saturday at the invitation of Gwen & Bea Arthur, who have been living down there in a boarding house for over a year. We arrived just about 5.30, undressed at the boarding house & paraded in bathers & bare feet & macks down two flights of carpeted stairs & across the esplanade—down the beach &

into the water. It was beautiful & frothy. We stayed in about 20 minutes & then stampeded up the beach again & across the street & up our carpeted stairs, only this time we dripped all over them. After tea we brought our rug out onto the beach & sat & knitted & talked & watched the cold green rollers & the grey ocean stretching right away to the sky. It got dark & when we turned away from the sea we saw a row of twinkling yellow lights light up among the pine trees—the beach lights. It looked so fairy-like & soft. We came in & got our hats & belongings & the girls came with us to the tram, stopping en route to listen first to the band, then to "mad Percy" holding forth & selling pea-nuts. It took nearly an hour to get home by tram & punt-ferry and tram again.

SSA 13

Very Dear One, 7 March 1917

Conscience bids me write duty letters long over-due but love bids me write to you. Love wins. After a long dearth I have been rewarded by a refreshing shower of your letters, the last of which came today. Lately I said that I do not reach really to the very soul of you in your letters. I am sorry I said that, for all your letters are full of the fragrance of you, and these last are so very dear. Of course there was something in what I said, for letters are only letters; but thank heaven for them all the same, and especially for the one that came this morning. It was written at Cymbeline while you were in charge of the family. It told of Peter and Jean and of Masefield Sonnets (which I cannot discuss because I have not a copy of them; only I remember that I thought them very beautiful, and true in a quite literal sense. They contain the gist of all the things I want to say and laboriously try to say.) You told also of Uncle Frank's illness and made me feel very sorry for him with a kind of impotent sympathy such as one feels for a shouting blessé while one jogs him about among the shell holes. ("Doucement! Doucement!" is the eternal cry, varied with Oh, là là, là là." Frenchmen never try not to express the pain they feel. I don't blame them.)

Egremont

TO OLAF 11 March 1917

. . . I do wish you and Daddy could talk & talk & find out each other's ideas & ideals. Daddy has had letters about the war from his three sisters, & at the end he looked quite down & said he was ashamed of his relatives, & he truly did wish he could have one letter from one of his own people which showed a more broadminded view & less of this unreasonable selfish narrowminded pacifism. I don't know if those were his words but that was the impression they left,—not a very nice one! I

Agnes' father, Frank Miller, Australian branch manager for Alfred Booth & Company's skins and furs trade.

know he is very fond of his nephew Olaf, but I always feel he includes you among "those miserable pacifists"—& it hurts. Mother thinks as he does, in spite of her Quaker ancestry.—You are really far more Quaker than she is in that particular line, but Mother is not so loud in her dispraises. I think she knows it hurts me, & I can't talk about it. I can't defend you with any convincing arguments. I haven't any but dim vague feelings & instincts & the biggest of these is that I love you & I trust you. But that is no good to Dad. Supposing you were to write to him & Mother at length, as you have sometimes written to me, & show him, dear, that although you may not think as he does, your ideals & aims & opinions are not miserable pacifism—pacifist perhaps but not miserable. I would love him to understand you better & think more of your way. Dad is so awfully level-headed. In our family he is the test. We get annoyed with him & his ways of saying things, & we argue & go off in a huff, but he is nearly always right. He seems to know at once if anything is genuine, & he lets us know when things are not. Mother is the impulsive—the enthusiastic—the sympathetic—the ideal, but Dad goes on all the time being the mediocria firma—the reasonable—the just—the good. Do you see? I can't bear that he should not be proud of you & of your ideals too. Perhaps it is my fault because I can't talk—but I can't.

Write then to him.

SSA 13

Agnes,                                                        13 March 1917

The world seems to be filled with two kinds of people, the doers and the seers. On this little convoy there are many of both kinds and one or two who hover restlessly upon the border line; but as the convoy is a convoy primarily with the object of doing it is very natural that the doers are in the ascendancy. Our commander is a doer, and so are (fortunately) the second and third in command. Of the rest the best drivers are mostly doers with very little of the seeing quality, but one, called [Edward] Wilson, is perhaps an almost perfect balance of seeing and doing. He is only a lad, and a quiet lad, but he is one of the very best drivers, one who is accurate, never flurried and always smiling. As to his seeing, this lad says little and yet I feel that he is busy looking at the world all the time with seeing, exploring, smiling eyes. I confess I am as much in love with this young man as you are with Ailsa. I am really quite ridiculously fond of him although he is not one of the people that I know well, like old Sparrow. "He likes me but I love him" (Browning). And the more I know of him the more proud I am of him and the more anxious that he should fulfill the whole promise that I see in him. It is very sad that his education has been cut short by the war, but perhaps he has learnt more out here than he would have done had he completed his Cambridge career. (He was "up" for one term only.) He is gifted with a godlike equanimity. Once when he suddenly fell to looking like dying he merely smiled at the Job's comforters and went and lay down for a few hours with a ghastly face and cheerful blue eyes. He is a tall thin fellow with dark hair, delicate features and a fresh colour. And his eyes are blue like yours and smiling. He is as mild and gentle as a girl, but perfectly firm and perhaps masterful, quite capable of holding his own against anyone, even big pots,—much to the surprise of the pots. His only failing seems to be a desire to seem older and soberer than he is, but he will grow out of that. I notice that he reads much and reads good books, and likes poetry. Now the greater danger of this young man as of many similar promising young fellows is of losing the vision that was born with him. Wordsworth's immortality ode seems to me false of Man, but terribly true of Englishmen. "Shades of the prisonhouse" are the smoke clouds of city life and of materialist civilization. Renard Fox, another fine driver and fine fellow, has lost much of that vision (if he ever had it). He is sternly practical, narrowly so. Wilson hangs in the balance.

[*Despite wide recognition of the Unit's efficiency and courage, neither the French nor British armies would permit the FAU to undertake work of greater danger closer to the front. Each time the proposal for stretcher-carrying at the trenches was advanced, the authorities turned it down because Unit members were not under military oath. At times SSA 13 firmly had to reject requests from the French army to use ambulances to transport men to the front; each such refusal imperiled the Unit's delicate relationship with the military command and therefore its very survival as a practical instrument for rescue and relief work.*]

SSA 13

TO AGNES                                                      24 March 1917

. . . We are beset by all sorts of rumours at present, and of course the official news is itself sufficiently interesting. On our front all is quiet as a rule, and we don't expect much will happen there; but one night there was a sudden and terrific spasm, an enemy coup de main accompanied by furious artillery work on each side. Our fellows up at the aid posts that night said it was very impressive as it started so suddenly, was so violent, and there was a general feeling that perhaps some great push was being attempted. However it was all over in a very short time. Then one night we had a report that the enemy was in full retreat from the next sector to us, and we were almost gulled into believing it and preparing to shift. Rumours, rumours, rumours! Meanwhile certain changes are really taking place, so we won't go to sleep. Our great disadvantage is always that the French military authority will not have its foreign motor sections take part in big offensives. That is after all only natural, as they feel they can rely best on their own men whom they hold under military discipline. Consequently we always get put in quiet places, although I daresay we are about the best of all their many foreign sections. By the way there has been talk of forming a FAU stretcher bearers corps to pick up British wounded between the lines. I gave my name in because—well obviously one simply had to volunteer for a thing like that. Such a job would finally justify the position of us moderate COs. However, the thing has fallen through. The authorities were not willing. It is a pity, for very many people would have joined, and it would have rehabilitated the FAU, and the heavy rate of casualties (about as high as in any job) would have been well worthwhile. I should hate the job in every way, but by all that's bright, it would be worth it! It would clear us of a great burden of responsibility, & it would quite definitely justify & glorify the moderate position. . . .

*Next day*, Sunday, and a lovely fine day too. . . . Here am I sitting down in our mess room which is really a stall in a stable. Others have just come in from [Quaker] Meeting. I did not go this time because last Sunday I was an "element of discord." I'll tell you. After we had all sat silent for half an hour and one or two people had made one or two conventional remarks, I broke up the meeting by asking a question. Very soon a rather heated discussion rose in which I kept asking critical questions and trying to get through all the soporific conventions. Nearly everyone in the room talked, and some I fear were rather disconcerted by the whole affair. There were people of such different views present, but most were rather of the conventional "meeting house" type, and one was an out and out Plymouth brother. And finally I got roused and defended my faith with considerable vigour, till the atmosphere was electric and we broke up and went across to the sleeping room and had a huge and merry rag with kit bags and top boots and other missiles. But after talking the thing over with Anderson, our sane and silent gentle saint (who helps to run the motor stores) I came to the conclusion that I would keep away today as a sign of penitence. Anderson is the most open minded of fellows and very well read. He is a paragon of all the Christian virtues, a very lovable creature with a ludicrous habit of talking in his sleep, of using all sorts of very strong bad language in a clear quiet voice in the dead of night, much to my delight who am very often awake to hear. "He's a —— ——, and I'll see him —— —— —— in —— first, the —— ——." Whereat I wriggle with delight in my sleeping bag and store up every word to tell him and everyone else in the morning. And poor Anderson would never say a mere naughty "dash" in real life! But seriously he is one of those whom I very much want to get to know well, but I am shy of being pushful. He is about twenty-two. He is very sensitive, nervy, almost lady-like, fearfully conscientious about his work, and about his leisure too, for he never wastes a moment but reads reads reads even in the general din that fellows are always making. He is a very great admirer of Meredith. I think I first introduced him to that great man. He and I often compare notes on books and things, but the conversations crop up haphazard. . . .

I do like this place. In front of the church there is a little walk at the edge of the steep hill. Sometimes I go up there in the evening and just walk up and down for half an hour or more. One looks down on the whole town with all its lights and huddled roofs. And sometimes the great light of a distant car appears far away and creeps nearer and nearer, winding along the road till it glides into the town. And one hears all the buzz of people in the streets, the clatter of feet and tongues and blown noses and the barking of dogs. And always there is some sound or other of war, or nearly always, and the flash and flare in the sky away toward the lines. And sometimes a plane will come creeping across the sky, just like a wandering star, and its dim whirring will be heard. And then perhaps the little old church will sound the time on little old clanking bells. And always the church itself stands over one and the huddled graves crowd round about right up to the edge of the cliff. Graves new and old they are, civil & military, gaudy and so simple as to be barely known as graves. (All this country is a graveyard. You keep coming on huge crowded cemeteries of wooden crosses, and scattered over the fields and by the roads you continually see the same little crosses and mounds.) But up by the church there are both the ancient & the modern dead and the whole presence of the living as well. It is a place that distills meditations as the marshes distill mists.


SSA 13

TO AGNES                                    29 March 1917
. . . I don't think this winter will ever end. Meanwhile what with the glorious revolution in Russia (if it's not too good to be true) and great movements of armies, and cryptic optimistic words by prominent people, one does almost begin to hope that the old war is on its last legs. Have you noticed how much less interest everyone takes in the war & how much more in peace during these latter days? At least that is the case here. Have you noticed also how in the early days the war seemed indeed to be a thing of nations? Germany violated Belgium. England (with majestic speed) turned herself into a fighting nation. France surprised us all with her national endurance & will. But now it seems as if the war were less the expression of national will than the expression of

sublime intangible fates and powers. The war sprang upon us; when will it leave us? We ask ourselves what it can all mean, and where is it that we are going, or being swept. To the ordinary man in any of the armies I am sure the war is now far more an act of incomprehensible fate, an "act of God" in fact, than it is an act of man. I think that is a healthy change in some ways, so long as it does not lead to fatalistic inactivity after the war. Because after the war there will be very much for human will to do and the only salvation will be through the increased exercise of human will.

I am talking like—like a bookworm! But what's a fellow to do? I want another nice long letter from you before we move. I have got into a "seam" of unreality and need one of your letters to pull me through it into a seam of reality. Everything seems vague, shadowy, unreal. The daily round seems the only real thing just now, and that becomes such a boring reality when there is no better reality to enlighten it.


                                                              Egremont
TO OLAF                                                  30 March 1917
. . . I must tell you about Thrifting. This week nearly over has been called Thrift Week. The League of Honour women have had a campaign to arouse people to the realisation of what thrift is, national & personal, & what it means to the nation at this time, & they are going to start war savings committees & certificates like they have in England. There have been lectures on the subject all this week. Rosie & I went to hear Mr. Meredith Atkinson on it last night. It was a good lecture, but an awfully small audience. Mr. M. A. must have put on about 3 stone in weight since I saw him last. He looks jolly well in it, but I like young men to be thin. He was very earnest about his subject & put things clearly & forcibly without ever ranting. After the lecture a funny old buster, white haired, sallow faced & firm featured, like one of the Fates, got up & began in a very Yorkshire way to deplore the shocking waste of food & foodstuffs in Australia. He said the women are not a bit thrifty & he knew that from experience because "two years ago he married an Australian young lady." (Sniggers from the audience & a great deal of screwing around to see if the said 'Australian young lady' were in the next seat!) "Well," he continued, "she's willin' enough to learn!" (Great amusement & interest on the part of the audience. Mr. Atkinson could no longer keep a straight face.)—"Now th'other day A went down to the markets & A bought fruit at 8d the case. But *she* didn't know how to make jam! Howsomoever A've showed 'er!" (Cheers.) But he calmed us down & spoke of the war that would come in our own country if we didn't make up our minds to thrift. He was such a queer old boy I shall remember his face just from the quick glance I gave.

But my part of the Campaign was in conjunction with the Y.W.C.A. They got workers to go round to as many of the different factories as possible & distribute literature & talk to the girls during the lunch hour. I went on Wednesday & Thursday to a cardboard box factory & a clothing factory. . . . The first day I didn't have to talk at all because I went with one of the secretaries & she had the gift of the gab, but yesterday there were three of us & we all had to put our shynesses in our pockets & talk to the girls individually & explain the papers. I can do that kind of thing alright when I know what I have to talk about. I'd like to go on with the work because it is good work & interesting & will help me perhaps to help you afterwards. Will it not? In the cardboard factory the YWCA want to form a club for the girls, & Miss Bignall asked me if I could take charge of that club, but I don't know about that. I don't know enough about how they are managed nor whether I could make things go. They were a much lower class of girl than those in the clothing factory—quite different in fact—although in this democratic country everyone is as good as everyone else! It was my first glimpse into a factory, & it made me sorry. . . . This is rather dull, isn't it? I always have to tell you exactly what I have been doing & thinking about. Thrift has been quite a big item this week.

Egremont

10 April 1917

Olaf, you would laugh if you could see me now, & you would have been surprised if you had come upon me at any moment of the day. Just now it is half past six in the evening & I have just missed the 6.25 boat to Mosman. I am sitting under the electric lamp on the wharf—it is quite dark all round except for the bright lights. The rain is pattering on the roof above & into the water on each side of the narrow jetty. Everyone has macs & brollies & everyone looks dejected—in fact as though they had all missed the last boat. I am wet, my feet mostly, but the rest of me a bit & my umbrella is a very limp companion—it has been hanging up on a tent pole all the day & the rain has been pouring down in it off the roof. It is Easter time you know & in Sydney Easter means "The Show." The Show Ground is a Soldiers Camp all the year but at Easter time it comes back into its own again. On Good Friday 98000 people were wandering round looking at the cows & sheep & pigs & grains & machinery & model homes & fat men & side shows & merry-gorounds. Yesterday, Easter Monday there were 112000 people wandering round & judging by our tent a good many of them must have come in to have their lunches & teas & odd meals. We are the Army Service, the Engineers & the 17th Battalion. *I* am the Army Service. We share a big tent of blue & white striped canvas that lets the rain in at all the seams & onto all the tables & everywhere where it isn't wanted. The floor of the tent is grass covered with sawdust about 4 inches deep & it's like walking through sand. The tables are rickety & very numerous & are all jammed up with chairs & people so that we, the waitresses, have to be always holding our breath in order to squeeze through somewhere. I only did two days of that stunt, Easter Monday & Tuesday. . . . The first day I was there from 9.30 am till 9.30 pm & when I set out for home on my long journey I was so tired in the back & achy all over that I felt more like screaming or talking to unknown people in the trams than just sitting & being quiet. We were dreadfully, gloriously busy that day. It was a record day at the Show. We took £125 in our tent alone. But we made up for it by the next two days which were unbearable, cold, stormy, rainy, a regular blizzard. The tent leaked, as I said, & we all got wet. There was a dear old Scotch body washing up for the "Engineers." The rain came through in bucketfulls over her head & down her back, but she held on to her job & never murmured. Only at last when some of the big guns of the depot came along & insisted on her getting a dryer spot she was heard to say in her broad uncouth tongue, "I reckon the boys are gettin' wetter na this for us.". . .

I had one lady on my table who was a character. She was an Englishwoman—middle aged, grey-haired, & strange to say I told her about you & how I was going to live in England. . . . She noticed my ring & asked, "& you have a fiancé too?" I nodded. "A soldier?" "Yes." "Where is he?" "In France." Her face softened & she said, "Oh you poor girl!" & then we talked some more. I didn't mind telling her about you even though she was a stranger, because she seemed so interested & kind.

[SSA 13 *had set up camp in* Villers Marmery, *a town just outside* Rheims. *On 17 April the French army launched a costly battle for the heights of Champagne, and Olaf worked day and night shuttling between a clearing station set up in a chateau in the village of Thuizy and a "boyau" or communication trench just behind the front-line trenches about three miles east of Rheims.*]

SSA 13

TO AGNES                                                                            11 April 1917

. . . I am at a deserted château that is an aid post. Our people on duty there have stood us coffee and now I am squatting down to write a line on a piece of paper on my knee. This place was once a great private house with marble pillars and a huge conservatory. Now the whole thing has gone to decay though it has not been strafed at all. There is a pretty big bombardment going on and the whole place is shaking and clattering with the shock of very many guns. But not a single shell has

Olaf standing in front of the Sunbeam at Ste. Menehould, reading a letter from Dot in early 1917.

come in here today. The enemy is inactive. We are living a funny sort of life at present, so ordinary in all outward appearance and yet it is one long excitement. In our village all is peaceful but——No, I had better not prattle, because of the censor. The most grievous part of it all is the weather, which is now miserably cold and often snowy. Just fancy snow & frost at this time of year! A lovely warm pair of brown mittens have come from you and I am wearing them now. Thank you so much, dear. They are doubly useful through being made with alternative covering for fingers & hole for fingers to come out of. . . .

Your father says the men in the trenches "cannot be expected to take the broad view" of war. And all the fellows that are near the front seem inclined to say that the people at home cannot be expected to take a broad view of war because they have had nothing to shake them out of their old conventional ideas. They go on thinking exactly as they would have done if there had been no war at all. Who shall judge between the two? . . .

You ask for photos. We are not allowed to send them, so whenever I get hold of any I send them by anyone who is going home on leave, & he sends them to Mother, & she sends some on to you. No one on the convoy has a camera except the French lieutenant. We are not allowed. A snap of me standing in front of my car reading a letter from Dot is now on the way to you probably.

SSA 13

Agnes, 20 April 1917

We have had the first dose. Twenty-four hours at the front & 24 hrs. working behind. Most of us worked 36 hrs. on end, or more. We had very good luck—only two fellows wounded & neither bad, and one car reduced to scrap iron. I drove sometimes the Sunbeam, sometimes an ambulance, & sometimes I filled up shell holes in the road, & sometimes I helped to drag dead horses off the road, but mostly I just helped to load ambulances.

11 pm, 21st April 1917. Sweetheart, I am sitting before a nice wood fire, writing by the light of it, in a big room in a château, waiting my turn to go up to our furthest point where I have already been all day. This place was very heavily shelled all day, but all is quiet now. I had one or two exciting moments up there, but here it seems to have been far hotter. The din has been awful. I'm fed up with offensives, though it must be confessed there is something hilarious about them, seen from our half ambushed position. The light of the fire has turned to darkness, so goodnight. Also the strafe has begun again. Oh Agnes mine, I long for thee.

*Another day.* Yesterday half a dozen of us had a pretty dance with three cars that got stuck in a badly shelled spot. One of them had to have repairs done to it before it could be moved. We were four hours at it, alternately working & seeking cover as the bombardment varied in seriousness. All the cars were badly peppered but we got them all away without serious harm to them & no damage to ourselves, though we had some quite narrow escapes. The convoy has been "cited," which means that we paint the croix de guerre on each car.

Egremont
TO OLAF                                                         25 April 1917
. . . This is Anzac Day, the day on which we commemorate for the 2nd time the landing—the brave gallant landing—but alas costly & almost fruitless—of our men on Gallipoli. It was a half holiday for all schools & for everyone else who could take one. I did. I went with Mrs. Day & Frank to watch the procession from a balcony & then on to the Show Ground for the big service. There were such lots & lots of soldiers— serious, neat men from the camps, new soldiers, & jolly weatherbeaten old soldiers with their colours & their crutches & their slings & bandages—they looked the jolliest because they had done their work, but there were lots of poor pale bent sick men who were not jolly—they made one sad & so did even some of the jolly ones. Frank wouldn't go in the procession. He couldn't have walked, it was too far. Poor boy is going to have this dreadful operation tomorrow. He must have felt a bit nervy about it, but he put on a terribly callous outside. The sciatic nerve in his leg is severed & they are going to try to join it. Mrs. Day, who is a trained nurse, knows what he is in for & she says it will be terrible pain. . . . Frank is about 24. He has been a wounded officer in London for some months & he has picked up a bit of "English officery" ways. He expects much more deference than he gets here, & he expects girls to smoke & drink cocktails. Not that all English girls do that, but you know that sort of thing *is* done by some people over there, & is not done by the same kind of people here. . . .
Harry came up on the balcony with us & watched the procession. I don't know how he could! Do you? I should feel ashamed to watch the men who had been to the war while I had stayed at home & built houses for myself & other people. Harry's friend who was married before the war has gone into camp & Harry who was married during the war has not gone. You may say, "Frank went to represent the family." Yes, but that does not acquit Harry. It is just as much Harry's duty to go & serve as it is Frank's. They are both men. It grieves me to see Harry still here. It grieves me for his own sake. I had almost told him so today as we watched all the men. . . . I wouldn't be so horrible as to give hints or be

sarcastic, but I'd like to ask him frankly about it. I'm sure it can't be want of money that stops Harry going, because his house is his own & he is a partner in his firm of architects, & anyway Daisy & little Max could go back & live with her Mother or board where Mr. & Mrs. Day board or do something or other. No, it can't be money that stops him, so if it isn't Harry it must be Daisy. I think the reason he doesn't go now is that he has left it so long he is ashamed just to arrive as the end comes, but I should be more ashamed not to arrive at all—wouldn't you? It quite worries me about Harry when I think of it. But one's object in going to the war should not be to satisfy one's neighbours—not even oneself except incidentally. It should be surely to fight for one's ideals & one's country's ideals if they are worth fighting for. In this war Dad says we are fighting for the Freedom of Nations—for Freedom—& he thinks the only way is through Fire & Blood to Light, & however black the fire & how red the blood the Light is worth the fighting.

When I think of it that way I think you ought to be fighting instead of saving life, except of course that your work has to be done by someone. It is as necessary to "winning the war" as making munitions, isn't it? Your ideal in general is the same as Dad's, isn't it—or nearly? & that being so, why are you different from other people? You don't approve of war, & I don't. You don't think war the only means & Dad does. But you are mixed up in the war for the sake of your ideal & you are helping other people to fight although you won't fight yourself. You said in your letter that however cruel & brutal the war, it is yet a divine phenomenon. If it is so, surely it must be right;—& it must be meant for all who are strong to go & take active part in it & win through & bring it to an end.

But is it a divine phenomenon? It has done lots & lots of good, but it has been so cruel & wicked & hard & savage. Oh, I can't really believe that God sanctions & intends war & cruelty, but if you think He does, well, I think you ought to fight, but I'm sure you don't somehow. I've got the wrong end of the stick. I wish we could talk. Even if I were convinced that war is not a divine phenomenon I think I should want to go & help as you are helping to relieve the suffering of those who do think it so, because they are doing what they think their duty & it is by so doing that they come to need our help. Even if one has "scruples" it doesn't seem right to stand altogether apart, though I can forgive people far more easily if they have scruples than if they haven't.

SSA 13

Agnes,                                                    29 April 1917

Let me see now, where were we when I last wrote? Anyhow we are in repos now in a quiet little village [Vavincourt], our first repos for eight months. Our last day at the front was rather eventful because they bombarded our village with some success and the main street was literally strewn with dead and wounded. Some of us English were pretty busy clearing up the mess. One shell accounted for about twenty men and a car, to say nothing of the top of a house. And most of those twenty were killed at once & the rest, I guess, were too badly smashed to last long. It was an ugly business. Shells were coming in while we cleared the street, & the only Frenchmen present were dead or dying. . . . Next day we left with our division for repos, and just after we had cleared out a shell fell in the yard where we kept most of our cars. It would have done much damage had we been there, and probably would have killed a good number of us. So our departure was lucky. For the first time in the convoy's history its members are heartily glad to be away from the front.

Our present spot is very peaceful and the spring weather has come. Yesterday in memory of ancient days with you I wore a celandine in my buttonhole. That is a little spring rite with me. There are lots of flowers of all sorts & lovely woods. Moreover we get milk, MILK! and eggs EGGS can be bought at twopence each. In fact we are living in great luxury. Helmets & respirators have been put aside, and caps have been dug out again at last. One undresses at night, UNDRESSES, and gets into a real bed (of straw), and one does not expect a shell to come through the wall during the night. There is no sound of war at all, but much singing of birds and bleating of sheep. And yesterday we heard the cuckoo and saw him lazily flap across a little glade. Oh Agnes, there is such a lovely lovers' walk down a little narrow valley the sides of which are steep and wooded and the bed of which is rich green grass. The little valley wanders on for some miles, changing its character now and then, but always small, intimate, and thrilling. . . .

Yesterday I walked down that valley with Sparrow and sat long with him watching birds and a woodman. There are cowslips and periwinkles, violets and wood anemones. We revel in all such things after months of winter, and after a surfeit of war. We are only to be here for a few days, and then we go with our re-formed division to a quiet bit of front further down the line than we have ever been before. Meanwhile we are really very busy trying to get the cars up to decent condition again. Soon we shall be hearing of great happenings in the region we have just quitted, and then we shall be both thankful and regretful of our absence. We should of course be there still had not our division suffered so much in opening the dance. Poor heroic infantrymen! Of course except during their actual attack we get it hotter than they do, but the attack must be incomparably more trying than any amount of town and road bombardment. But enough of all that. Last night some of us slept out in the orchard, and it was good to be once more à la belle étoile.

[*On 2 May SSA 13 moved to Ancemont, a few miles south of Verdun,
then a relatively quiet spot on the front. Near the end of May Olaf
went on leave. At this point almost a month's worth of letters are missing from both Agnes and Olaf, the longest such gap in the correspondence. Olaf guessed that something was wrong in his letter of 13 June.
It was not until 25 June that Agnes learned that many letters written
in May were lost when the ship* Mongolia *was sunk.*]

Egremont
TO OLAF                                                      25 May 1917
. . . I have been feeling rather sad in spite of my birthday & in spite of
two letters which came yesterday from you. But my word, I would have
been *much more* sadder if they hadn't come. You remember my telling
you about the girl at the F.A.L. (the League)—about the nice Kathleen
Hart who got engaged & married in that short time we were away at
Blackheath. Her husband went away a fortnight later to the war & Kathleen came back & worked on Fridays with us as before & talked about
her letters & what she would do when he came back & so on & so on.

Last Friday when I went—there were none of those bright girls & no
poor Kathleen. Her husband had died of meningitis in camp on Salis-
bury Plain before he had ever been to the front. I can't help thinking
about her. I overheard some relations of hers talking at the Red Cross. I
listened because she was in my mind all the time—but I was glad Kathleen didn't hear them. It would not have comforted her. If I were to lose
you people might talk like that of me. Curiously the circumstances are
much the same.

"Oh, of course it's frightfully sad—I'm most sorry for his Mother. It's
different for Kathleen. She's young, she'll get over it—she has all her
life before her, she's only 23! And you know it may be a pointing of
Providence. Why that girl could have been allowed to marry her first
cousin, I can't understand. It's not as though she hasn't had chances—
she's travelled a lot, she's met lots of people, & she must come back to
Sydney & marry her first cousin!"

—"But lots of cousins do marry & it's alright."

—"Ah yes, but it's a risk—& if he had lived I would have been afraid
for them."

And so on; till I was ready to weep for Kathleen. . . .

Sunday 27th. . . . When you wrote last (March 29) it was at the beginning of the big push & the Russian Revolution & America's entry & so
on. Things seemed to be going well then—at least on the move. We
were all a bit excited, but by the time your letter reached me it is all dull
& fizzled out again. Russia still doing no good & the offensive going
very slow—only some horrid bad news for us about the loss of the trans-

port "Transylvania" with ever so many men & the air raid at Dover with big loss of life again. It *does* all seem dreadful, doesn't it? We are all so fearfully tangled up in ourselves & each other that it seems almost impossible to believe that the final outcome can mean Freedom—Liberty—for anyone, victor or vanquished.

Annery
Agnes,                                                    25 May 1917, 11 p.m.
    My own, my darling. Your photo is looking at me with those quiet eyes that are yours, while I write to you in my room at home on the evening of my arrival here, and the evening of your birthday. I am trying to write in bed, because bed is a luxury not to be missed, and I have just finished munching a glorious apple that Father brought out of his cupboard. . . .

*Next Day*, and a lovely spring day, with me in cool mufti, writing at my desk. I have missed some of your letters and shall not have them till I get back to Verdun. I keep hoping that another one may come before then, because I simply must have something of you while I am home. I am sending you a copy of the "Soldier's Book of Love Poems," not a bad little anthology. It is not a book to read, but to look at now and then. It is interesting to note the different spirit in the earlier and in the later poems. . . .

[*With uncharacteristic sarcasm, Olaf describes his role during the Champagne offensive.*]

    It's fine to see a six horse limber going down a road at breakneck speed with the driver urging and lashing and the other men hanging on by the skin of their teeth, and shells crashing all round, nearer & nearer it seems, till at last one makes a direct hit, kills five horses and two men on the spot, while the other horse goes a bit down the road till it drops and the third man crawls out of the wreckage into the ditch. It's fine to see four or five cars all charging down the same bit of road until one of them has to jam on all brakes to avoid crashing into the limber the second after it is hit, and then has to creep gingerly round between the dead horses and the ditch while a shell bursts alongside it, breaks in its windows and pierces its body work with steel splinters. Once free, and away dashes the old Vulcan like a mad thing down the road with the poor devils inside crying out at the jolts, swinging, bumping, crashing across the railway line, past the sentry box where someone has propped the dead sentry up against his box for some reason unknown. Meanwhile the next car spots the wounded man in the ditch, draws up to take him on board, but the egregious idiot of a lieutenant who happens to be on board forbids the driver to stop under shellfire, so that (think of it!) the car goes on, leaving the man wriggling. Fortunately the third car has no egregious idiot on board, and draws up in spite of the crumps. The driver jumps out, & the orderly. They roll up the back curtain, put down the step, and with fearful gymnastic exertion they cram the man in on to the floor of the car. Then up step, down back, and away. Similarly it's rather fine, if you're driving your tourer & your OC down that road, at a speed far higher than the speed of the others, to be overtaken by your motorcyclist who shouts in passing that he has been hit, gets ahead of you, begins trailing one arm with blood dripping from it, slows down & wobbles, while behind him you come creeping home torn between anxiety not to run him down & anxiety to get out of it as quickly as possible. Oh it's all very fine & we deserve far more of it. But, ye gods what a damned silly thing is war! Fed up, FED UP! . . .

Father is well but very depressed about the war. He is as energetic as ever, as busy as ever, but perhaps a wee bit greyer as to the hair. He sees no end to the war and to the general mess up and waste of life and stuff. He thinks no good can come of further war, but he doesn't think people have enough sense or courage to make peace. The French soldier is beginning to scrawl up on the walls "À bas la guerre." A meeting of British soldiers, being asked to give a message to people at home, cried "We're fed up with the war," and again & again they persistently cried it. As for the bosches, when they are prisoners they are very glad to smile & be friendly and to exchange Prussian helmets for pieces of cake. Up at that furthest boyau of ours we had some Germans helping to load the cars, & they did it well; especially one smiling, kindly chap with whom the French stretcher bearers soon became very friendly. Of course there is really a lot of blind hatred & hostility, but less than of old. It's the miserable diplomatists that have not the courage to talk about peace, neither the Allies nor the Germans. The first day of our Champagne offensive they took a big crowd of German prisoners, mostly wounded of course, & all apparently rather in poor condition. Those that could walk came in parties and streams down to the dressing station along with those of the French wounded who could walk. Poor devils, they were in a horrible mess. One German I remember specially who was just about finished with the walk. But never mind the details. And as to revolting sights, the bombardment of our own village provided about as bad as you could have. And somehow it seems worse, more incongruous, in a comparatively civilized street.

But where am I wandering, from Annery & the pleasant things of home? The gorse has come out at last, making great islands of gold. The garden is mainly a food garden, rightly—potatoes, peas, beans, and fruit. The old lavish Annery fare is gone, and (between you and me) every meal is a secret and dramatic struggle not to exceed one's ration.

At the front one gets plenty of uninteresting food & more bread than one can eat. Here it's little and excellent food, & bread by the crumb. But good bread made of all sorts of things, not very hard stale French ration bread made of things unknown. . . .

Dear, you sometimes write about current political events, & sometimes I agree & sometimes not, but I can't talk about them freely from over there for fear of getting the FAU into trouble. And now I don't want to talk about them. But look you, your Australian public is a fearful fire eating public. Beware of its views. America under Wilson has, I think, done the right thing all through. Yet perhaps it is a pity they have come in after all. Who knows. Personally I think I will never fight for any nation, but would fight for Wilson's League, were it founded after the War. And yet I confess I am lost in perplexity about all these things and know only that the more people in the world are determined against fighting the less chance there is of wars. But, coming home & seeing everyone in fighting uniforms, reaping no end of honour & glory, one does envy them. They are each in his orthodox pigeon hole, & we are just straying heretics. They each have their sweethearts too, to go everywhere with them in pretty summer clothes and prettier radiant faces, so proud, so absolutely overflowing with kindly pride, as if they kept saying—"See! This is my very own lad home on leave. See his two gold wound stripes," or "see his ribbon," or "look, he's only twenty two and a captain." But my girl has no one to come home on leave to her and make her proud and radiant. . . .

*Next Day.* . . . Before I came on leave I used to go evening walks alternately with two people; one was Ned Wilson, the altogether lovable lad, and the other was Thomas Tindle Anderson of Kings Cambridge, commonly called Tindle or Tinners. With the former, Teddy, one walked with one's eyes open observing every bird, leaf and beetle and discussing its life history. Teddy takes such a jolly unselfconscious interest in everything that lives. . . . He and I sleep out on the top of the dug-out on fine nights and discuss the big owls that flap about and hoot. And in the morning he chucks a stone at me and (*perhaps*) we go and have an early bathe. Tindle is amazingly unlike Teddy in all respects. He goes walks simply to get exercise and talk. And so absorbed do we get in our talk that we generally get hopelessly lost in some forest and have to tear our way through thick undergrowth in the failing light and at last the darkness. We discuss the universe and one another's careers, but chiefly the universe and humanity as a part of it. Tindle is a saint. He is fearfully conscientious, but always with a genial smile. He is gentle, but in his work, which is to look after the motor stores, he is firm as a rock with people who try to get too much out of him. He is quite agnostic, and exceptionally broad-minded. I want to enlist him as a WEA tutor but the old thing is too doubtful of his knowledge. He has an idea of "keeping a corner shop" after the war, and helping people toward the light while he hands them packets of sugar.

Annery
My own girl,                                              2 June 1917
   Agnes, I have been trying to write a nice letter to your Daddy, but have not succeeded so far. I don't want to write about pacifism, because it's no use arguing, but I do want to write a nice letter with just a word or two about the war in it. I have tried two or three times unsuccessfully. It's so horrid to think of his having a son-in-law and nephew of whom he can't quite approve. I'll try again.

[*This letter contains four enclosures, each in a tiny envelope addressed to Agnes in various years: 1895, 1903, 1917, and 1999. The envelope for the last of these reads: "From a foolish fellow home on leave during the Great War* TO AGNES IN THE YEAR 1999. *Open it & read it for her, dear Agnes of 1917. She, poor soul, will not be able to. Poor soul? Glorious blessed soul or nothing." The text of the little letter follows.*]

Dearest,
   It will be all over when you get this. This war will be over, & you and I will be over. What we two shall be then, I don't know. But if we do live in some way or other, and can remember and feel, then we will be lovers still. Perhaps you smile at this letter, & perhaps I also must smile at it in 1999. But I in 1917, in the middle of all these wars and wonders, set down as a certain thing that for you & for me both then & now the main thing in all the world is that we love one another.
                                              For ever     Your Olaf

[*That drinkable water and electric lighting could be taken for granted at Annery but not at Egremont suggests the differences between middle-class comfort as Olaf and Agnes each knew it.*]

Egremont
TO OLAF                                              4 June 1917
. . . We had lunch near the [Manly] Reservoir which is just a pretty bit of artificial lake, with drinkable—at least boilable—water, a great asset in our benighted land, & after lunch Dad read some of Steven Leacock's "Further Foolishness" & Uncle produced chocs & peppermint creams & a naughty but delightful parody which I am going to copy out

for you here & now in case you haven't seen it, though I expect you have as you live in motor circles. I don't approve of parodies, specially of things I like, but there are some things you can't spoil even by parodying—that's rather a good test.

*Some Psalm*

The Ford is my car.
I shall not want another.
It maketh me to lie down in wet places
It soileth my soul.
It leadeth me into deep waters,
It leadeth me into the paths of ridicule for its name's sake
It prepareth a breakdown for me in the presence of mine enemies.
Yea! though I run through the valleys I am towed up the hill.
I fear great evil when it is with me.
Its rods and its engines discomfort me.
It anointeth my face with oil,
Its tank runneth over.
Surely to goodness if this thing follow me all the days of
    my life,
I shall dwell in the house of the insane forever.

After that we packed our baskets & followed the track right round the lake & further up the gully by the little stream that trickles into it. And the path was all overgrown with bushes & prickly bushes & wild flowers & they smelt beautiful. We all gathered bunches & wandered along chatting placidly until we came to the Pool Beyond the World. . . .

We're having electric light put in & the poor electrician chap has just had the bad luck to smash one of the drawing room globes & it will cost him about £4!! Rotten luck for him, I'm so sorry. It will be very grand to have the new light though. You luxurious people are quite used to it at home, but we have been striking our modest safety matches all these years & now we shall only have to pull the little knob & be dazzled by a flood of the softest diffusedest light from a shallow white globe hanging on a chain from the ceiling. Hurrah.

On the high seas
*Night.*                                                   4 June 1917
Agnes, if we are torpedoed I shall be very angry because I should have to get up in the middle of the night. Moreover this cabin is not particularly handy for a hasty exit. I came down from London with a Frenchman & girl who had just been torpedoed in a Jap boat. She was a vivacious little person, and told us all about it with sparkling smiles & grimaces of terror. She kept repeating that she was saved in nothing but her "chemise,"

and she turned back the throat of her borrowed or given blouse to display her own identical chemise. She said the English passengers were very cool, just smoking & laughing, but she was in terror, rather naturally. In the port that we have just left there is a lately-torpedoed hospital ship, a cheerful object lesson for us. . . .

I wrote to your father, but it was a poor feeble letter in spite of all my trying to do it nicely. I nearly didn't send it. . . . Ye gods! The ship is stopping for some reason; instead of the usual dash across perhaps we are going to creep. Now she's going ahead. I hear the telegraph bell each time, & the change in the note of the turbine's buzz. A Blue Funnel ran into & sank a submarine the other day.

SSA 13

Agnes, 13 June 1917

I believe I last heard from you on the 10th of May, and now it is past the 10th of June. Alas, Alas! When I got back after leave I was surprised to find no letters from you though there was one little one from Auntie Margaret. Father said he thought he had forwarded a lot of your letters to me just before I reached home. I don't know what can have happened to them. Anyhow I am hungering & thirsting for a letter. The fact that I have not had my Australian mail for so long is one of the stock "events" of the convoy. . . .

*Two days later,* and still no letter from you. The weather is simply roasting. While one works one drips all the time like a leaky tap, the sun is so strong. It's lovely bathing, anyhow. Today I shall miss my bathe because I have got a run. The other day I had a wonderful little evening trip to a certain place where one overlooks the enemy from the brow of a steep hill & sees for ever so many miles & long leagues behind his lines. We lay & waited there till dusk & then walked down into a ruined village right on the line where the troops live like rabbits in burrows, but where also they live like kings on all the fruit & vegetables that are coming up in the deserted gardens. But it was the view from that hill that I shall never forget. In that place no-man's land is not a desert but a glorious green place. But I must not talk too much about these things. When the war is over and we meet, then I will tell you about lots of wonderful places that I cannot write about.

I have begun to read "Mr. Britling," on your recommendation. It promises well. I begin the day at 5.30 or so, now. I sleep in my car with the hood down, under the open sky. It's lovely at 5.30, which is really 4.30 by sun time. I sit up and read or write till it is time to dress for 7 o'clock breakfast. We shall probably leave this place very soon. I don't expect it will be to go into an offensive yet a while, but that will doubtless come later. We are very indignant because the other two FAU con-voys, which were in successful bits of offensive, have had croix-de-guerre rewards, but we, just because our little affair was not so bright, have been given nothing, although of course under the circumstances our work was much more arduous than theirs. It's bad luck, especially as we were definitely "recommended." However, it can't be helped, & we ought not to bother about such things. Moderate pacifists tend to bother about such things just as tokens that they are not mere shirkers.

SSA 13

TO AGNES                                                    20 June 1917
. . . The convoy has moved. We are now further from the front than the convoy has ever been before, and further south along the line. It is lovely peaceful hilly country with rivers for bathing and woods and "hanging" gardens on the steep hillsides. We are in a little town [Vieil Dampierre], which is awkward for those who sleep in their cars, because everyone is always crowding round to look at the queer English. They have never had English here before, nor until this time any troops at all billeted with them. The girls of the place won't leave us alone, which is tedious, especially as they are not particularly good looking. They keep promenading up & down in couples by our cars, showing themselves off. They are not bad girls really, but personally I have no use for them. . . .

Yesterday Sparrow went off on a call and got a man who had just had his legs cut off at the thigh by a train, cut off almost at the hip. Seems unnecessary for that sort of thing to happen now, doesn't it. Renard went too & stayed in the car looking after the man while Sparrow drove "like hell" in the dark to reach a distant hospital before the man died. The man was a soldier (not of our division) and a cook, and kept giving orders about coffee & salads etc. whenever the pain knocked the intelli-gence out of him. Today, let's be frank, we have startled this peaceful place by a display of a very bloodstained car. (Bloodstained! the little word one uses for a hanky that has a spot on it!)

Cheers! Two long letters from you each in a big long envelope came on two succeeding days. . . . That Easter show must have been hard work. You do such a lot of things. I liked you to tell the unknown lady about us, though you must not say I am a soldier when I am not, but only a rather militarised civilian engaged in clearing up the mess. You say a lot again about war & me in one of these letters. I don't *know* whether the thing I am doing is right or wrong, but it seemed right when I began, and in spite of everything it seems right now though so very uninspiring. Don't be too hard on the fellows that don't do any-thing. They may be right in their own cases. As to me, I have deliber-

ately compromised because——But look here, I'm not allowed to talk
about such things. Heavens! I wish they'd bring off that FAU stretcher
bearers corps. That is the only real work for us. And this is only an approximation, and a restless business.

Egremont

TO OLAF                                                    25 June 1917

. . . I have had two more letters from you today by the next mail, & oh
such letters! the 21st & 29th April. How thankful indeed I am that you
are safe out of that dreadful battered village. You have really been "in
it," now, haven't you? & I am glad, but oh I am so very glad you are out
of it. . . . Who of your men were wounded? Any I know? That is, know
of? I am so glad you tell me things, dear. They stir me up & make me
stern & quiet & wild & anxious, but I would not be kept in a glass case
& have you tell me like most boys would, "The old Bosche made us sit
up the other day for a few hours but it's all over now etc."

I want to *see with you* & *feel with you* (as much as I can). I'm your
friend, your mate, your wife.

You may spare your Mother & perhaps even your Father, but don't
spare me because I want to be with you in every thing. I don't want to be
spared.

The news tonight hits *us* hard & in a very vulnerable spot, though I
suppose it is very small of us—me, I mean. The "Mongolia" mined in
the Indian Ocean—passengers saved but all the *mails* lost! We were
building our hopes on the "Mongolia"—she carried mails up till May
31st. This mail was April 29th, so there may not be another for weeks
& weeks. Were you at home in May? I do want to hear about home! I
want to hear all about everything you tell me, so I am bound to miss
something.

*Next day.* I had another letter from Jack this morning, written later than
either of yours—May 9th in fact—so I am hoping I may get another
still from you. Jack has been "in it" too—their dug-outs were raided &
gassed & a good many of them were knocked out. That's another mercy
for Nell's & Mrs. Armstrong's sake that Jack was alright—he was to cross
to England on May 10th for leave. I often wondered if by chance you &
Jack might cross together on leave. You have told me of encounters with
other Australians.

*Next day.* Glory! *Another* letter from Jack. That's three! Why does he!

Agnes,                                                26 June 1917

Hooraye! Five of our fellows have got the croix de guerre,—[Charles] Marshall the OC, [Henry] Brown the second in command, [Henry] Burtt the third, and Julian Fox (who incidentally is popularly considered the fourth), and [Harry] Locke who had his car destroyed and drove another till he was wounded. They are corps citations, not merely divisional. The wording of the document is very fine. (Things sound so fine in French.) I must copy it out for you when I get the chance. We are all immensely pleased and proud. We only expected a general citation of the convoy. This is better in some ways, though we should like the convoy to be cited as well. All those people richly deserved their crosses. The official account is that they were rewards for work on two days of the offensive, but really they are rewards for long tireless service in the convoy. On those two days they only did what everyone else was doing, but they set the example, and always have set the example. I, being only OC's driver and no candidate, had a wee bit to do with the settling who was to get the thing, only a wee bit. I am most pleased about Julian, who is rather sensitive about being thought a shirker from military service. It will take a weight off his mind. . . . I think it's up to me to get a croix de guerre, or to earn one anyhow. But when the time comes one forgets about such things and thinks only of the amazing facts of war. In fact in an offensive it seems almost sacrilege to think of little metal crosses and ribbons. Anyhow perhaps we shall not have another spell. No one *wants* the vile job, that's sure.

[*Eric Robertson (1887–1941), the most bohemian of Olaf's FAU acquaintances, was a Scottish painter whose personal behavior and erotic nudes occasioned controversy in Edinburgh. Perhaps expediently, he joined the Society of Friends in 1915 and was one of the growing number of men in the Ambulance Unit who, coming in reluctantly after the start of conscription, were more cynical than Olaf about the ideals of moderate pacifism. Robertson and his wife, Cecile, remained friends of Olaf and Agnes's long after the war. A retrospective of Robertson's paintings at the Edinburgh Art Centre in 1974 included several landscapes in oils and pastels of French locales from his period of service with SSA 13.*]

SSA 13

TO AGNES                                              1 July 1917

. . . A friend of mine who was engaged for a long time, a very long time, is engaged no more. You must guess who, because I don't want to put his name down in a letter that may be censored by people that know him. (Probably it won't be, but still it is not for me to risk it.) He long ago persuaded her to say yes and she never felt quite absolutely sure, though she was always very fond of him. Well, at last she feels she ought not to have said yes at all. . . . He has lost all faith in himself. He goes about being outwardly as cheerful as anything, but inwardly just bored to tears with himself. And all the while he is desperately anxious to be honest with himself & her. Don't think little of him. I am so sorry for them, but chiefly for him, because he feels it more, and feels his own weakness. Agnes! It sort of brought me up with a bump and a dread. Supposing you also were to find it was a mistake. Oh heaven, but you shall not, not even with all the muddles and perplexities that are round us. If you did I should——No, I'd make a mighty effort to bring you back again. But, do you know, dear, this business made me wonder how ever I should keep really in touch with you for so long without your—— No, I don't know quite what I mean. But it's so dim and make-believe and unreal, this business; and then there are all the puzzles and difficulties as well. What is an engagement? If you change your mind you are free. It's bound to be so. But oh never change your mind, never at all, dear. It would be so black a day. I can't imagine what it would be like. . . .

*Another day.* . . . Agnes, I want to say something. It ought to be said in words of fire, but since fiery words would only seem affected, I'll say it soberly. It's just this, dear—That fellow's broken engagement makes me realise better what you are to me, you patient faithful one. Your lover is always away from you, & doing less than the thing you would have him do, is far from you in place, in thought, in deed; and yet you love him. Oh never doubt! But I feel so—so full of shortcomings. Once I used to lecture you, and watch you grow. I did love you, but I was rather patronising. But now, Agnes, I can't lecture. There's no fear of my patronising. You are so far beyond the ideal I had of you, in many ways. . . .

*Next day.* . . . I went along to another fellow's car where certain people were having a little art club sort of affair. We have a professional artist on the convoy, a newcomer, Robertson, said to be a great portrait painter. We made him talk about Impressionism, PostImpressionism, Futurism, Cubism, and chiefly Vorticism. It was all more or less new to me. Some of us were very critical, but he had the courage of his convictions and at any rate made us see that these things are not just bunkum. He does not call himself a Vorticist, but he sympathises and sometimes paints Vorticist pictures. The idea seems to be to get from some natural scene all the most striking impressions in it and put them together in the most beautiful possible way. Perhaps there will be in the scene a windy sky, some dark tree trunks, a straight railway line, a sweeping hill. Well, you make a pattern out of these things. Perhaps the sky may come at the bottom of the picture, but that does not matter, because it is not a scene that you are making, it is a beautiful pattern. The result is, of course, a funny old muddle of pretty things, and personally I greatly prefer nature's way of painting pictures. But still there is something refreshingly rebellious and genuine—sincere—about the Vorticists. Our man thinks they will do a lot of good simply by breaking down old conventions that have cramped art for so long. You can be quite a passable realist painter without any real sense of beauty, but you can't be a Vorticist. Mind you, I think it's all a silly extravagance, but there is a root of good in it; and it is certainly a *spiritual* kind of thing. Robertson is very emphatic that a man cannot really be an artist without being deeply religious. And strangely, he goes back to ancient Egypt for his inspiration, rather than ancient Greece. He thinks all Greek art is very conventional, but the *earliest* Egyptian art is real live art. And by Jove, it's true. He goes also to Javanese and Polynesian things for inspiration. We had a great talk, not only about art but about the religious basis of art. In fact he is a fellow of ideas, and I must ruminate on them! His ideas apply to literature also of course, and are very largely the things one is always groping for, but one has to be sane about them and restrained and not go flying into extremes.

[*Agnes had enrolled for a course with Meredith Atkinson, head of the Sydney branch of the Workers' Educational Association.*]

Egremont

TO OLAF                                                               9 July 1917

. . . I am supposed to write an essay for Mr. Atkinson on the "Institutions of the City-State of Athens in Its Prime," & we haven't got a history of Greece, so I simply can't do it. I've wasted hours trying to find it in a big reference book but it's not there though I've found all the information I require on every other conceivable subject. That's the worst of dictionaries & maps & things when you are naturally given to wasting time. The class is tomorrow. I shall be getting pitched out if I don't write the essays, because I have signed my "death warrant" & pledged myself to fulfill the obligations of the class. Essay writing & anything like cut & dried work is an awful grind to me, but on the other hand I should like to get hold of a text book & find out all I want to know & also it's not nice to cave in to a mere essay. I must borrow a book. Q.E.D.

11 July 1917
. . . My Daddy is disappointed with me, and well he may be, for the driving of an ambulance for the French is not very creditable work for a member of a family that generally seems to get quickly into responsible positions. I'm sick about it, very. And of course it's my fault. There is very little scope for getting into responsible positions in the Unit and less on the convoy; but probably I could have done so if I hadn't always scorned it and always been so critical of the authorities. I'm feeling a pig. And just now I am more against the authorities than ever and it's silly of me, and only shows how right it is that I am not an authority myself! The truth is just that! But I'm sorry for Father, & you. There's absolutely no scope left for me now anyhow, so I must sit still and be good.

Egremont
18 July 1917
. . . I say, don't write to Dad any more about pacifism, it only makes him argumentative & annoying. I can't argue, unfortunately, never could—but it makes me all furious. It's not what you are doing that doesn't meet with Dad's approbation—he thinks the convoy work is a splendid thing, & he says he wouldn't think any more highly of you if you were doing stretcher-bearing or anything else—no, it's what you *think* that upsets him. He thinks pacifists are *very impractical* idealists. He reckons his ideals are exactly the same as yours but he thinks your ways of setting about attaining them are absurd & sentimental & impossible & illogical & all sorts of other similar adjectives. However he is pleased to make distinctions between pacifists & pacifists, & you & your Father (you will be glad to hear!) are "decent pacifists." Dad is very tiresome. He takes things so literally & doesn't make any allowances for people's character as expressed in their arguments. Mother & I are quite sure that if you could only talk together you would understand each other & each other's point of view ever so much better. But don't write to him any more about it. Write to Mother sometimes, she is not nearly so argumentative.

SSA 13
Agnes,                                                               18 July 1917
I am doing twenty four hours at the front, a very quiet front [at Maffrécourt]. Yesterday the two of us not on duty went a long walk into the region of trenches and listened to the "incongruous synchronology" of twanging bullets and a rather good band that played good music.

Why the enemy keep on pinking bullets into stones and mud I don't know. We had a great yarn with a lot of funny old types français that we know who, like the rest of our division speak a strange tongue of the Midi between themselves, but speak more or less intelligible French to us. You may be sure the conversation was largely concerned with "the one joke" of the French. That of course is usual. Dear old busters! Of course the young busters are just the same only more feverish about it. We saw the spot where a too non-chalant colonel was killed the other day, and we saw a lot of big stuff bursting on a place whose name you would probably know if I were to tell it. But the chief attraction was the music, which being plaintive and to us most rare made me want to bury my face in someone's maternal lap and weep, which would have been surprising to the vieux types with whom we were laughing. Doubtless they felt the same really. Well, we strayed back to our immensely solid dugout and read ourselves to sleep on novels or philosophy. But in the middle of the night we woke up to a rampagious crashing of guns. The bosches were trying a coup de main, and we began to prepare for work. . . .

We hear a lot about the grim reality of war. That's all true enough as far as it goes, but if you go deeper it's all intricate pretence and lies. The other day a very big person who happened to be visiting our village came in specially to see us privately and congratulated our decorated fellows and said (of course) we *all deserved* the croix, but he had only got a certain number to dispense; and he hoped to have another opportunity of giving us more later on. It was nice, because it was informal & he need not have come, so obviously he meant it all. But—ugh, what is a bit of red and green ribbon! Blood on French clothes is red on blue not red on green. The other night one of our fellows, lucky devil, got a bit of high explosive in his hand, such a tiny business, but by Jove he has got sick leave in England for it!! Now we are all praying for bits like that. But also the same bit in the eye would be less satisfactory! And poor old Harry Locke who got a bit through him in April is still languishing in a French hospital. And a ridiculous little doll of a man who always dragged a toy dog about with him even in hot places (an officer in the army) got his leg blown off it seems just after I saw him last and behaved like a brick. Human nature is odd! Eh bien, nous verrons, mais je suis ennuyé.

Egremont
TO OLAF                                                    31 July 1917
. . . It's a fortnight since my last letters & the next mail is in the unknown future. But I haven't quite given up hope yet in spite of all the postmen in the world. I have never missed a mail from you yet, never

since I came home—except of course when the whole mail was lost. I
know you always write at least a line. It just makes me a bit afraid you
might be ill or something, but I'll try & think the letters got delayed
somehow. The last was from England, June 2nd. I had one from Jack
from France dated June 14th, so there is quite a big gap—it *ought* to
come. Jack always signs himself "your devoted lover" & I can't stand it.
I'm sure the letter I told him not to in has been torpedoed. It's awful. It
used to be always "ever your devoted friend Jack." I think he must have
lost his head suddenly, quite unaccountably. About 4 months ago he
wrote me a letter in which he seemed to have forgotten you altogether,
he asked me to marry him. There was an enclosure for Dad & Mother
& one for his sister Nell. They never saw the light of day. The whole lot
disappeared in shreds into my waste paper basket, & now it seems like a
bad dream, but he signs himself your devoted lover! What *is* one to do!
Jack is so terribly thickskinned. I wrote plain English to him after that
letter, but I'm sure he won't swallow it. He's so weird. He writes to me
nearly every week & he keeps sending me things. I can't send them
back, it's too absurd. It's no good quarreling at this distance—besides it
takes two to make a quarrel. Nothing I write can hurt him—it simply
slides off. According to him the Queen can do no wrong.

He sent out his photo this mail. Mrs. Armstrong came over to see it.
She had hard work not to weep, he looks so thin & drawn & sad. I felt as
hard as nails. It didn't make me want to weep. Poor old Mrs. Armstrong. Jack is in hospital now—not wounded, a breakdown of some
kind. I'm sorry for him & I feel a beast, but what *is* one to do? Tell what
you think. . . .

August 1st. . . . The [WEA] lecture was interesting. Plato's commu-
nistic theories. Weird & awful! Do you know them? It's book V of the
Republic. What marvellous old chaps those Greeks were! These lectures are opening up an absolutely new world to me, quite a real &
thrilling world, & there's such lots more to discover. We have hardly
touched on art & architecture except in two lantern lectures which were
included in the course, & only on literature where it concerns politics.
One could spend a whole lifetime reading about all those things—it's so
interesting. I see the widening influence an arts course must have,—
wish I had had a university education now,—but I had my wanderyear.
One could enjoy a University course at any time. I'm awfully keen on
the W.E.A. I think education is much the best form of philanthropy. I
am so glad you are a W.E.A. I should like to be able to be a tutor myself. Why didn't I realise that before—then I might have planned my
studies accordingly. I have met one or two of the women tutors & they
are so keen & I think they do such good work. They are both different to
me, much cleverer & more alive. Do you remember Nedda Freeland

bemoaning the fact that she had been brought up only to watch other people playing their parts, to be a spectator, not a player? That's how *I* feel. Well, I must make the best of it until the war is over & then come you quickly & make me into one of the players. Take me from the outsiders.

SSA 13

. . . What you have said about the Thrift Club and your experiences at a factory are very interesting. I am fearfully proud of you when you do things like that. You would not, like so many people, go about it as if you were looking after inferior beings who were quite ignorant of their own affairs. That is the spirit that wrecks so much "social work." I am interested also in the WEA class. The subject and the method of treatment sound to me rather boring. Don't be disappointed in the WEA if that class is not really alive. Tutorial classes have two opposite dangers, one dead-aliveness, the other bright superficiality! What one wants is something both thorough and invigorating! After [the war] the WEA will find itself in a new position, and it may do well or ill thereby. One may feel that it really is in itself enough for all one's time and energy, or one may feel that it is only one little branch. . . . The thing I want to do, the concretest thing I want to do is to help people to like literature for its own sake or for the spirit behind it. I don't care whether it is to be in tutorial classes or otherwise; but as it is ordinary people and grown up people I want to get at, the WEA seems the best way. Of course, I don't want to stop at making people like literature, but that is the beginning.

Wilson (Teddy) and I have been two glorious runs (à pied, pas à voiture) over the grass hills. Once we took another fellow, but he was not much good. Teddy and I plod along together with some success, and come in after five or six miles feeling splendidly tired and well-lubricated and happy. Then we have a bath (in a *very* small tin basin), and then we lounge in the pride of our fatigue and talk to our respective guests. Really, there's a strange exaltation about lobbing on and on over the grass with a good spring in your toes. There's something primaeval in it; it takes you back to primitive man with a flint axe running down some swift animal just by perseverance and short cuts. Today there are sports, against a French battalion. If there were a mile I should run, but I am no good at sprints. Played soccer the other day and did excessively badly. Never mind, they are getting up a rugger team at last and I shall play, however badly.——War! Do you think it is rather shameful to be sporting while Rome burns? There is more work ahead of us somewhere. Meanwhile we sport with our friends the French. . . .

Robertson, the artist, is my chief problem at present. In many ways I dislike him intensely, and disapprove of his ideas and his conduct; but he is so different from anyone else here, that it is stimulating to get to know him. In fact, he has a lot to teach us, even if much of his talk is claptrap and fraud. He is rather a conventional rebel and artistic mono-maniac. I don't mind that, but I don't like the way he treats people he does not like. Nor do I like his rather sneering self-confidence. But we have toned that down a good bit for him already. He has a wife. I have seen her picture, and she is very striking, rather of the old Egyptian or Red Indian type, very hard-looking, hawk-like, with eyebrows like iron bars and a most delicately curved but cruel nose. In profile, her nose is nearer the perpendicular than her forehead, because her forehead seems to slope back so much. In all respects, she is an amazing contrast to my wife-to-be, and yet, strange to say behind all the difference, I seem to see something of the same noble and serene spirit in her picture as in yours; only that in her it seems fenced round with an iron spiked railing, and with you it seems a universal, wide thing like the sky. I expect old Robertson would not agree, which of course would be bad taste on his part.

Egremont
TO OLAF                                                                7 August 1917
. . . Sydney is all out on strike. It's only the beginning of it, but it looks like a jolly big thing. Sydney is quite an exciting place to live in—things happen in Sydney. Today, as far as we know, there will be no trams running, & a very few trains. It's the railwaymen's strike. The Government decided to introduce the card system so as they would be able to keep a check on the men's work hours. The railway and tramway shops have been a byword for the "Go Slow" system for years, & it comes too expensive on a hard pressed Government in war time. Everyone seems to be very keen to stand by the Government & fight it out—at least all the so-called decent people & the decent press. The unions fall down to it one after another like a pack of cards. It gives you an eyeopener to see how one thing hangs on another in a State. Trains stop—food stops—trains run again by nonunionists—miners refuse to supply "black" coal—no coal—no light—no heat—no ferries—no electricity
—no nothing—.
It hasn't come to that yet of course—it only began a day or two ago, but the tramway men were "called out" last night, so today it's a case of walk to the ferry or stay at home. I guess there will be a few trams run by loyal unionists, but they are not many in proportion. Unions are just as tyrannical as German militarists.
   It looks rather fishy—this strike all about a card system. An honest workman would not mind supervision. It's only the slacker whom it

hits. Perhaps I'll be driving a tram before the month is out! Russian women *do* things—It would be nice if *we* did things too.

Egremont
TO OLAF                                                            13 August 1917
. . . The Strike is still going from bad to worse—the silver lining of *that* cloud is well tucked out of sight. We have no butter since yesterday morning & can't get it for love or money. You will smile at that & think we are not so badly off if it's only since yesterday morning, nor are we indeed, but it is so annoying to have the butter waiting there by the ton up in the country & down on the wharfs because the regular wharfies are "out" & any person who touches any goods on any ship is declared "black" along with the goods & the ship & the firm that owns the ship. However the Government is going to take over the unloading of ships & there will be no lack of volunteers for the work. I have got very muddled as to who is "out" and who is still "in"—but they say the ferrymen masters & engineers will be the next to go out, & then we'll be nicely cooked. Isn't it a horrible state of affairs? It is turning into an absolute class-war. Many of the people we saw every day in town & nodded to as friends—the lift attendants in the depot buildings & so on—now look sour & only give a grunt instead of a cheery good-day. There's an atmosphere of antagonism everywhere. . . .

The surest remedy I see is the W.E.A. & I wish it could be very powerful & efficient & quick about it, the sooner the better. What I have been wondering lately is this—In the course of years, if these educational schemes go forward, the worker will rise up from his lowly place, he won't want to drive trams & clean engines & lade ships. He will want to do something better with his brains. Well then, who will do the rough work? Of course I have reductio'd it ad absurdum now, because I expect in reality this planet will be burnt out before we arrive at the stage when everyone is capable of doing something better than the merely rough physical, though necessary, labour. But theoretically, it makes one ask oneself if it is reasonable to suppose that all men were *meant* to have equal chances—whether it was intended in the scheme of things that some should be the masters & others the servants, that some should be exalted & others lowly, that some should work faithfully according to their capacity & earn all they need of material goods, & others should work just as faithfully in *their* capacity & yet should want on every hand for bare necessities. If it *was* intended so, it were mistaken kindness to educate the workers to do other than their own work, because their work is necessary to the whole world. It is the material foundation on which everyone else builds the towers—& (this is the point) surely every man was meant to do not only what is necessary but the highest he is capable of. Yes, that seems to me the keynote of service—of life if you like. Everyone is entitled to have the opportunity of developing himself to the full & even so there will be men enough to collect old bottles & empty garbage tins.

So long live the W.E.A. & all such associations. Is there any sense in what I have written? I think I have been going round in a circle. But these things are such problems—they get on one's mind—& one must out with them or suffocate. In old Plato's Republic he had three classes —the workers, the military, & the philosophers. He had a marvellous system of education, but it didn't include the workers—at least he trained them for their own work, but he didn't seem to think of training them for anything higher. The work was there & it had to be done by someone, & they knew how to do it, so he left it at that & gave all his attention to making soldiers & rulers. What do you think of old Plato?

SSA 13

TO AGNES                                          18 August 1917

. . . *Sunday evening,* after a feed of plums and apples officially gathered from an orchard near the lines, a deserted orchard. Ce soir j'ai le cafard. Mais je le supprimerai, or more correct words to that effect. Do you know, we have the most extraordinary convoy slang, a hideous mixture of French and English slangs. One never talks of "being on duty." It is always "j'assure la service ce soir." And never "lend a hand" but "Eh, vieux, un coup de main ici." But much of it is more slangy and more mixed than these phrases, such as "I've got a faim like douze éléphants.". . . Queer old convoy. One minute a fellow will be lying under his bus (otherwise known as voiture sanitaire, or just "voychure," or bagnole) emitting hideous imprecations of a harmless nature at some recalcitrant nut. Next minute he will be hunting rats with a tyre lever. Next he is found sitting inside his car nervously showing off his latest sketches to a friend, or solemnly discussing the origin and fate of civilization. One afternoon we all march to bathe, march in rather fine style for mere "Friends," so that the passing gros legumes look on with respect and the passing types join hilariously to our ribald French convoy-anthem made by one of us. Next afternoon we are scattered at our various jobs or sulking in our various cars. Well, I have suppressed the cafard up till now, have I not? But alas, ma très douce amie, it's only suppressed, not destroyed. Renard has come back from leave full of gloomy forebodings and despair about peace. And so I am in the dumps. . . .

A figure haunts me that is neither quite real nor quite a dream. It is just you of course. It is my friend of friends. These people here are all very well. Many are to be respected, many to be watched with interest, not a few to be deeply admired and loved. But they are all parts, facets; and you are the whole. There's Tindle; he's a dear generous conscientious lad looking for the truth; and he is the one I admire most of all. But he has his friends, and his circumstances on the convoy run slightly apart from mine. There's Wilson, also a dear. There's devoted old Harry who sometimes really does overpower one. But there's Agnes, that most fair dream. She is the whole, not a facet. Stopper! Lest we become maudlin, while Rome burns. But I do so want a letter, and more than that I want yourself. I want to be whatever you want of me (pourvu that I also approve!). And all this while if we don't drift apart a bit it's absolutely a miracle.

[*The torpedoing of mail ships led Agnes to initiate a system for keeping track of letters.*]

Egremont
TO OLAF                                                    22 August 1917
. . . I am going to begin numbering my letters to you & then you will know if you miss any & if so how many. Don't you think it a good idea in these troublous days? This letter is then no. 1, though really it would be more correct to call it the thousand & one-th! alas! The only trouble is that I shall forget to number some of them & then that will upset the applecart. It's very awkward, isn't it, for some letters to get lost & for one not to know which. In those letters you missed I *might* have said something very important. I might have changed my mind about you altogether, or I might have told you about my new hat, & there you never heard it & you go on just as though nothing had ever happened! I wonder whether I missed anything in your letters from April 29 to May 25. It all mattered to me at any rate, & I wonder what you missed of mine in all that long gap. . . .

I am sorry Uncle is grieved because you are not an officer of the Unit. I never thought of being grieved because it never struck me there *were* officers of the Unit, but would it be much better to be an officer? You are so funny—you never do the right thing that other people expect you to do. Why are you made to be so perverse, I wonder? I have got into the way of "swallowing you whole," so to speak, but perhaps I ought to blow you up sometimes, but it's not very fair for me to blow you up for that offence, because I am rather inclined to be like you myself. I really don't like disagreeing with people because I always have a suspicion that it is instinctive perversity on my part, & it's so rotten to be perverse just for the sake of being so. Sometimes one simply can't do the correct thing, because it's too absurd, but sometimes one could & one would rather not. Olaf, we shall have to be very severe with each other one day! . . .

The Strike is still getting worse & everything is very disorganised though the trams & trains are much better, however they seem to be only a very small part of the strike now. Miners, wharfies, firemen & seamen, carters, gas employees—all out. Dad's men in the store are out now, at least they have "ceased work" because the goods are "black"—so Waldo is doing a week in the store! He began this morning, Saturday, & he is to get paid union rates just like the other boys. . . . There are "Shore" boys cleaning engines & lumping coal & driving carts & wharf labouring. Phil Irvine is a "wharfie" at 14/. per day. Who wouldn't be at that price! And the volunteer coal miners get £1 per day, sometimes more. I volunteered at the Women's Bureau the other day, but I haven't been called up yet. There are thousands of volunteers. I put my name down as "waitress, shop assistant, packer, cook or miscellaneous." The family think I would be fine as a "miscellaneous." Don't you? I do hope the strike will be settled soon. It's such a miserable state of affairs. There have been one or two horrid incidents—a volunteer carter was attacked by many strikers & had to use his revolver in self defence & he shot one of the strikers & killed him. I wish it were settled. One war is enough at a time. What must it be like in Russia?

We have something unpleasant to look forward to during this week. The miners are route marching "on" Sydney, & heaven only knows what will happen if they come here. They are a rough lot. There will only be several hundreds of them, but there are other route marches in the wind entailing many thousands of miners from all over the country. The miners are the toughest of all the union crowds. I suppose they are in all countries. It's a good thing our premier is away—Mr. Holman. He's a weak reed. We've got a strong man in his place, G. W. Fuller. He seems to be a gentleman for one thing, & he talks straight. I wish you were here to understand and talk to me about strikes. . . . Dad thinks there ought to be martial law for government employees who strike just as there is for soldiers who desert. They are both betraying their trust. It is in fact "illegal" to strike; but what of that? The law could never be enforced. They have arrested several of the ringleaders, but that does not end the strike. Both sides are adamant, but who is in the right? I say—I want to know about socialism. What do you think about it? Is there much good in it? From what I know of it—and that is very little— I think we are not ready for socialism yet—what we want first is educa- tion, education, education. . . .

You know, Friday is my day for going to the factory in the lunch hour. I go through town to Redfern by train, rather a factoryfied neighbour- hood. The entrance to Hunter's is in a little narrow back-lane. . . . I go through a gate in a fence into a little narrow enclosure between another fence & the factory wall. There is an outside staircase leading up to the workroom & I generally stand in the sun at the bottom of the stairs & wait a few minutes until the 12.30 bell goes & the girls begin tumbling down the stairs putting on their hats & things as they come & they waste not a minute of their precious half hour. We smile at each other & say good morning & when the last one is gone I climb the stairs myself & go through the work room—full of machines & kid & scraps of leather trimmings & shoes in all stages—to the crowded narrow lunch room where all the girls are whose homes are too far away for them to go for lunch. I go from table to table & collect their savings & sign their cards & get them to sign my book—quite in the professional manner—& if there's time I sit down at the tables & have a few words with any who seem friendly. They are mostly very nice girls & they make it quite easy for me. We had to argue the strike a bit—they all blame the Government & constantly affirm it—that's their only argument. It hadn't really struck them that I should not be on their side—they were quite surprised & disappointed in me to find I still ride in the trams because "Oh Miss Miller—trams are black!" Well, last Friday I got there a bit early & had a ¼ hr. to wait, so I sat on a bench in the sun against the wall & under the staircase & read my book.

Presently a big shadow looms large in the gateway. I look up & there is a big friendly faced young man with an enormous brass trumpet affair. He dumps it on the ground & looks hard at me. I don't know what he is after, so I just look up at him & wonder. Presently he says, "What time's lunch hour?"

"Half past 12," says I.

"& wot's time now?"

I look at my watch: "25 past."

"I think I'll take a seat too," says he, plops down next to me & still looks curiously at me. "Lookin' for a job, Miss?"

"Not exactly."

"Out of work, then?"

"No, but I don't work here—come over from the other side."

At that point along comes another young man with a smaller trumpet, leans up against the door, tips his hat onto the back of his head, & grins approval. "Hullo Bill, what's all this?" (Jumped to the conclusion of course that "Bill" was "doing a mash"! Do you know what that means?)

"What a huge big instrument that is," says I, "what d'you call it?"

"That's a brass bass, Miss, a double bass, that is."

Arrives another young man with a cornet. "Halloa, nice sunny spot! See the lady's took a seat, so we may as well 'ave a seat too!" Plops down on the other side of me.

Arrive ever so many more men—the rest of the band in fact—all crowd in & round the door. The drummer holds forth & we all listen—he emphasizes his remarks with the drum stick. "See that roof up there? Victor Trumper put a ball up there once when 'e was playin' in the oval. Some hit, that! eh?" & more about the gods of cricket which I didn't understand.

Lunch bell.

We all move, I towards the staircase, they out to the lane to form their magic circle. Last thrust from an interested bandsman. "Are y'out on strike, Miss?"

We all laugh, & the girls come tumbling down the stairs all excitement at seeing the band & all the nice young men. They have no time for me today! I go up the stairs to the lunch room where they are all hurry to finish their lunch & get out to the band. We can hear the music faintly through many walls. At 1 o'clock when I come out the girls are having a fine time all clamouring round the gate & joking with the goodnatured fellows. I must put my penny in the box with the rest of them & I get a nod from my friend with the "big bass." I squeeze through the crowd at the gate & as I go away along the lane I hear the 1 o'clock bell & have a last glimpse of the band packing up & the little white-haired manager out on the landing trying to hurry his girls up & scolding them for being late—but not unkindly. A little scene full of life & good humour & well worth the price of one penny.

SSA 13

TO AGNES                                    25 August 1917

. . . Supposing we were never to meet again ever at all, in this life or another. It is too strange to conceive, like the world suddenly breaking in two. When you get this it will be about three years since we were together. What will you be doing then, I wonder; and where shall I be? Wars and revolutions and new social orders and new bright ideals are all very well, but I love a girl with all my soul, and she is far off by thousands of miles and three long divergent years. Social orders and ideals! What are they? The sun will shine no better for them. The west wind will be no more refreshing. . . . Is this a very silly letter? Ought I to be always stoical and calm? I don't think so, dear. But all expression seems so poor and cheap and false. Tell me that you still love me very much. Tell me that you don't love me less for my present work, nor for the three years' absence. Do you? Now I must go to bed. About a thousand bedtimes since we were both at Annery, and I used to lay in wait for you to catch and kiss you in the passage when you were going into your room, deshabillé and very sweet to see.

Your lover      Olaf Stapledon

[*Periodically the SSA 13 convoy rebelled against policies that smacked of militarism or infringed on their status as volunteers. The Unit's symbiotic relationship with the French army made it difficult for Unit officers to satisfy fully the men's wishes to dispense with a hierarchical command structure, but many felt that the current commander, twenty-three-year-old Leslie Maxwell, had gone too far in allowing a semimilitaristic bureaucracy to control their daily lives and decisions. The famous pamphlet on conscientious objectors, "I Appeal Unto Caesar," is now known to have been partially ghostwritten by Bertrand Russell.*]

SSA 13

Agnes,                                        2 September 1917

There's a beastly old row on among us here at present, and it has gone so far that I have said that unless certain changes are made I am going to leave the F.A.U. Sure, I don't want to go; it will make such a mess up, because I will not join the army. It will affect so many people besides oneself, and really when I think of you and of your father in this connection the whole thing is positively tragic. I won't go if it can possibly be helped. But it is no good to stick in a thing that seems to try and sit on both sides of a fence at once. . . .

*Another Day.* After lunch I went on to the top of the hill and lay in the long dry grass, sun-bathing. The sun is no mean deity. His heat rays and light rays and all his other wonderful nameless rays seem to soak right into one's bones. Life-giving rays they seem to be. One lies sweltering in it, with face and arms and knees scorching as if at a fire. And when one opens a cautious eye against his splendour he seems to rush blindingly in through the little eye-window into one's very brain. Through half-shut eyes one sees the grey grasses waving against a cloudless blue. Insects buzz; swallows twitter. Beside me stands a little wooden cross to a "colonel inconnu," killed in 1915. Beyond is the big new cemetery, growing daily with the graves of Frenchmen and Moroccans, and long-since-forgotten Germans. Beyond the cemetery lies the little church and our village of four farms. And there lie I luxuriating, chewing a piece of autumn grass. . . .

*Another day.* . . . I have also been reading "I Appeal Unto Caesar," Mrs. Hobhouse's careful account of the treatment of absolute conscientious objectors. She has three sons in the army (one was twice wounded) and one son is undergoing his second term of cruel imprisonment. One of the other three was in the Blue Funnel Office. I know him well. This book shows up some outrageous scandals. It makes one feel that England is not much better than Spain of the Inquisition. It shows the sort of thing to expect if one does leave the FAU. Ye great gods! Words fail. Of course in your part of the world nothing is ever heard of these shameful things. And of course I can't specify without breaking regulations. To my mind the point is not that the men are right or wrong in their views. The point is that no human being should be treated in that barbarous way, least of all a man who is obviously doing what he thinks right. Many have died of it. Many probably wish they could. Many have finally gone mad. Granted that their position of absolute resistance to the state is wrong—still surely this sort of action on the part of the state is wicked. But I am talking more freely than I ought even on this sort of subject. À bas la guerre, à bas, à bas.

Egremont

TO OLAF                                                    4 September 1917

. . . Yesterday was September 3—remember the date. It is a memorable one—. . . . I had about 1½ hours to spare & a headache, so I went & sat on a seat under a big clump of beautiful trees in the Domain & knitted & thought about everything—you mostly—& watched. The Domain is not a very proper place for a young woman to sit in all alone in the fading light—on Saturday & Sundays it is full of strikers & religionists & crowds—on weekdays of loafers—evenings of spooners & men—not full, rather solitary in fact, but nothing happened & it *was* beautiful. It is just a lovely park with great grassy hills & paths & big old trees. It runs out onto a little peninsula right in the harbour & you can watch all the ships. I have told you about that before. Jack took me there twice— once driving in his little trap & once à pied, & I was thinking then all the time not about poor John but about Olaf. But I didn't go right out to the point—at night by myself, of course. I stayed near the top & watched the last yellow light of the day among the quiet trees & the twinkling bright lights began to shine from the wharves & gleam in the water. . . .

I sat outside at the back of the boat coming home in the wind and thought about things & felt very small & very lonely somehow, & when I got home about a quarter to nine expecting to hear a trio going on, I found the family sitting in unusual chairs talking with Margaret & Miss Graham about something exciting. They stopped when I came in & looked mysterious. I had noticed a military cap & belt hanging up in the hall, but no soldier was in sight, & no Rosie——& suddenly Mummie threw the bomb——Rosie & Lionel [Irvine] are engaged!

Heaven! my little sister engaged! I simply could not realise it. Mother & I had discussed the situation only last week & I had told Mum she need not begin to get excited yet. Nothing would happen for a *long time*, & there those two young things took the law into their own young hands & sprang it on us like a whirlwind.

TO OLAF                                    16 September 1917

. . . Lionel has £200 or £300 saved or rather earned in the army. Beyond that he has another year of his engineering course to finish at the 'varsity before he can earn a bean. At present he has his pension & also some pay for doing press censorial work—a semi-military job—he is still in uniform although discharged. He is only 23, so perhaps it is just as well that there are financial obstacles to prevent their getting married for some time. I only hope these obstacles will not take on any more serious proportions for the poor old boy. He deserves to be happy. He has done his work. Do you know their engagement was just about as different from ours as it could possibly have been. We discussed ours for about $2\frac{1}{2}$ years & then became engaged. They discussed theirs for about $2\frac{1}{2}$ hours & became engaged there & then (& it was about 1 o'clock in the morning, be it said!) & they walked straight into Mrs. Irvine's bedroom without knocking—they saw her light—& proclaimed simply, "We're engaged"! They told me about it that Sunday night [9 September] when I first began this letter. I was dead tired, & it was after 10. They were boiling eggs hard for a picnic breakfast for the morrow. I sat on one table swinging my legs & they sat together opposite me on the other table swinging their *long* legs. They told me in answer to my question that until that famous night, a week ago, they had never said anything to each other which the world might not have heard! So evidently they had been going along their ways & had drawn nearer & nearer together without saying a word until suddenly they found they were both on the same path. How lovely that must have been, must it not? No wonder the dear kids are happy with their so newly found treasure. I disgraced myself that evening. I was so tired. We stopped talking & mused. Lionel took Rosie's hand & they looked so comfy & happy. I thought of you away there & me here on the kitchen table & the tears would *not* be kept back & I had to make a dive for my bedroom & have a good old cry in the dark.

SSA 13

TO AGNES                                     6 October 1917

. . . Well, what is to be talked about? I know—Jack Armstrong. In one of your letters you tell me that he still perseveres with you. I was sorry for him once, but the more indefatigable he is the less I pity him, the more I—am filled with primitive possessive desire to be with you. He ought to know better than to commit such importunity. No, I rather think that all (or most) is fair in love and war. I don't really blame him; but I want to dash his hopes forever by marrying you, soon. . . .

In your last letter you talk much of Sydney's strike troubles, and you set down clearly & naturally a great number of pros and cons in an unbiased way. The trouble surely is that class war is a fact, especially in Australia. There is indeed a barrier of misunderstanding between one side and the other. Education & economic reform is the solution; but you can't educate a people against their will, and no economic reform will work while there is still a great unevenness of social fortunes and great hatred of classes. Little by little the change will come, perhaps; but the class war is coming; and in England maybe there will be great tragedies before long. You see "we" *are* so much more fortunate than "they." You cannot get away from that fact. You say if all are educated none will want to do the poor jobs. Well, personally I find motor-driving a good enough job to satisfy my ambitions in some ways. But what you say is largely true. The answer would seem to be that society should (a) do away with as many menial jobs as possible, (b) make the unavoidable minimum of such jobs fit for a self-respecting educated citizen by paying them properly and allowing a large amount of leisure to the workers, (c) allocate all simple unskilled work in public services to be done by a sort of national service army of young men and women as part of their education. *Everyone* should be given at a certain age and for a limited time some such job, working hard but not excessively hard for a short time. Much could be done that way. But of course society as a whole is going to be pecuniarily poorer by these reforms for a while anyhow. Therefore at the root of everything is the vital need that everyone should be frugal, should do without harmful or useless luxuries. And always we have to keep in mind the ideal aim for education, that a man shall learn that however humble his work (e.g., stone breaking) he can find joy in it so long as (a) his work hours are short, (b) his position is respected, (c) his pay is enough to keep him from starvation, (d) his mind is educated to find joy.

Of course all this is very crude and needs a thousand explanations and qualifications, such as that a man's children must be given full educational chances by the state. All your remarks were plain sound sense; but I hold that mine are equally sound, and are the natural sequel to yours. No such society as the one I look for will come yet for many a long year; but some such is the ideal at which at present I aim. I am a socialist in most ways, but not a doctrinaire socialist. As to Plato's uneducated workers—no, we must do better than that. He based it all on Greek city states, and they were always in trouble. Besides, it was inhumane, snobbish, and Prussian, with all due respect to the most noble Plato. Men are not & never will be born equal; but they should each one of them (and each horse & dog also) have the reasonable chance of fulfilling the best that is born in them. Is it not so? I don't want to turn grass into rose trees; but I do want to prevent rich men from trampling on the rose seedling before it can fulfill itself. Nay—trampling on the poor grass itself so that it never becomes grass but is only a bare and beaten plot of earth.

[*The idea of inhabiting another mind—whether human or canine— became a recurrent motif in Olaf's later science fiction, especially* Last and First Men *(1930),* Star Maker *(1937),* Sirius *(1944), and* The Flames *(1947).*]

SSA 13

TO AGNES                                              12 October 1917

. . . Have you ever imagined what it would be like if one could really enter into the mind and being of another person? I should like to "be" Kerenski for a while, were it not that Russia would suffer thereby. Rather, I should like to steal into the minds of each of the men on this convoy, to see what it would really be like to be Tindle or Renard, seeing things as they see things, with their mental perspective, as it were. Renard's quaint narrowness would then be known to one as a steadfast practical faith; and Tindle's spirit would no longer seem too good to be true. I should like to be Ginger, the [convoy's pet] Aberdeen terrier, to feel the world as it is to him, and to relish all the thrilling smells that constitute his daily experience, and to explore the limits of his doggy mind. I should like to be this poor old autumnal fly warming his frozen feet on my lamp-glass, and occasionally moving in a senile way as if he were already half dead.

Egremont

TO OLAF                                              16 October 1917

. . . I have been reading a little book that your Father sent out to Mother, "I Appeal unto Caesar" about the conscientious objectors. Oh what those poor things are undergoing! It makes me miserable to think of, but one cannot help admiring them for their grit & devotion to their ideals. Oh what a wicked state of affairs! What lots of things need reforming. To read that pamphlet takes me back to the middle ages—it seems a different world to the England we know which is so sensible if material, & honest & efficient. I haven't ever known anything of penal laws, & it gives me horrible shocks to read of the awful treatment people have to undergo. And that men who are imprisoned because they denounce war should be treated as ordinary burglars & criminals seems almost unbelievable. It amounts to real religious persecution. There may be very few of them, but that is not the point. It is so wrong even to treat one man like that. I can't think how things can happen like that in England. The big question of the C.O. remains unsolved whether he is sent to prison or whether he is totally exempted by the law. I wish I could talk to you & I wish you could talk to me. I don't know what I think, nor do I know what you think. I suppose I find out a bit more every day, but so far it has not amounted to anything very definite.

Our last W.E.A. class turned into a discussion on conscription. I sat tight & said nothing. But it was quite thrilling. We were to write an essay on "Has the State the right to take a man's life?" I have not done it. I can't.

Egremont

TO OLAF                                                    17 October 1917

. . . I have been feeling rather sort of listless lately—about you. I don't know why it is—just, I think, because letters are so few & far between & so kind of unsatisfactory. I need so much to talk to you about everything. It isn't a positive kind of feeling in any way—it's just semi-negative—listless—perhaps as you feel when you "take things for granted." Don't know why I wrote all this—it seems so absurd. I was feeling rather frank all of a sudden. I don't think my letters have been very "keen" just lately, have they? Well, that is why. I believe it is a reaction after Rosie's engagement. When I saw them together I realised all in a sudden rush how much I wanted you. I knew what Mrs. Browning meant when she said that grief is greater than joy for grief is joy & grief. If I had been less selfish I should have had more joy in Rosie's happiness. Well, whether it was selfish or not I was passionately in love then, dear. . . .

Olaf, you said in your letter that it would be a miracle if we did not drift apart during this long absence. Well, if that does happen I think it does not mean that we come to love each other less. Love safely given & received like that surely could never turn into not-love. I think it means that we cannot understand each other as once we used, & for my part I think that part of it is inevitable in these times when such great new forces are at work all round us. It would be strange if we did not change at all, but it is not really strange that we cannot fully share the changes in each other. The best of letters could not do that & I think we must make up our minds to it. Do not you? I am not worried because I can't understand, nor am I worried at this fit of "taking it for granted" & I want you not to be worried either because I feel sure it will all come right in the end & if we could get away & look at ourselves from a distance we should probably see that this is all part of the unfolding scheme. More than two years ago—before I *knew really* that I loved

you—it used to worry me dreadfully to think that I could ever feel anything but exuberant towards you, but now it is different. One knows
oneself better. Life & Love are much more real things. One knows they
are solid & for all time, not to be blown away by any chance gust that
comes along.

[*As the war lengthened and as ambulance work waned in the colder
months, Olaf's longing to keep alive his teaching vocation led him to
set up miniature WEA classes in the convoy.*]

SSA 13

TO AGNES                                                    20 October 1917
. . . I am busy at present, what with the ordinary run of work plus various educational enterprises on the convoy, plus a sudden keen literary
fever, plus the building of a new shell-proof dugout (great fun) plus a
football match this afternoon, plus a car that has got some indetermi-
nable disease that gives me a lot of trouble. The educational enterprises
are Tindle's occasional essays (the last on "Past & Present"), & a small
industrial history class consisting of "Sparrow," the quaint old bird,
"Gertie," the second cook and formerly a printer, and one Evans, a
rather pharisaical but genial young journalist who was once second
cook but is now our orderly. That little class is great fun. We talk about
the Roman bath, the British village and the Saxon homestead, from
which you may gather that we have only just begun. I draw wildly inac-
curate maps & charts for them, and illustrate with sketches of ancient
British coins etc., and they comment, question, and are made to expound what they have read; also they write essays & we criticise them all
together.

SSA 13

TO AGNES                                                    27 October 1917
. . . Renard is outside reading over the stove, in the place that used to
be the living room of this quondam farm. This room was evidently a
fine room once. Look at the elegant frieze! But now, you notice, the
windows have very little glass in them, & not much of our celluloid
either, as we are short of it. The improvised curtains keep the light from
getting out through any chink to help bosche planes. We are really very
snug here. . . . [Denis Goodall] is reading a book of Harry [Locke]'s
called "The Making of Woman" (I think). Tindle is the great feminist
however. He says feminism was the thing that first made him think. By
Jove, you would like Tindle. He's a brick, and a main prop of the convoy. He has "doing" rather on the brain, and is inclined to take daily life

too seriously and super-conscientiously; but that is to err on the right side. There goes Henry Burtt through the room with an armful of gunk out of which he is probably going to make some wonderful contrivance or other. Henry spends all his time making things. He's a marvel. I should think he has only read about one book in his life. Henry and I when we are together invariably make fools of ourselves, and often come to friendly blows. We are one of the stock stunts of the show, though we are so different. Henry is a great lad for the girls. He has a hard matter of fact face with two dreamy black eyes looking out of it. He's a crock at present with a bad ankle. I am a worse one with a damaged thigh muscle. In fact for a few days I could barely crawl about at all. And I must play rugger again next week!

Egremont
TO OLAF                                     6 November 1917
. . . Last year when the Conscription campaign was in progress I went over on the boat with a young man & his wife—& re war & conscription he said to me, "I would not fight, not even if conscription comes. I would rather go to prison." I was interested because I wondered at him for getting married when all the other boys were off to the war. I thought more of him than before. But the other day I saw him again. "What are you doing now?" I asked. "Still with the Kodak company," he answered. We talked on affably, but I thought to myself—I should not be content to be the wife of a man who was "still with the Kodak company" when all the world was at war. You see, conscription did not come here, so there was no need for him to go to prison. But just put yourself in his place in a free country like Australia. You need not go to war & you need not go to prison, but I don't think you would be content if you lived here to go on with your daily work just as usual. I think you would have been drawn away to do Red Cross or relief work just as you have been doing. Would you not? If so I think you must be right in being there now. If you would not have gone, do you think it would have been more worthwhile to stick to your own work or to have joined the English C.O.s in their protest? Which?

SSA 13
Agnes,                                      6 November 1917
It is a foggy, muddy November Sunday, and in our great rugger match this afternoon we shall get well plastered. These matches are a great institution; they give us something to talk about for a fortnight before the event and a fortnight afterwards. We discuss rugger as seriously as if it

was the war. We estimate people's respective merits. We tragically whisper that so and so is "no use, you know." We exclaim, with eyes round with adoration, that so and so is glorious. We rearrange the whole program of our work so as to enable The Team to be all off duty on the Day. In fact it is just like school.

Now what is there interesting to talk about? I know. The other day was the French "Jour des Morts." Some of us dressed up and went to church to represent the convoy. It was a little old church, the church of our headquarters village. It was packed with pale blue soldiers, and in the background were about four women in deep black. The service began in the ordinary way, and seemed lamentably unreal, insincere. The priest muttered and rang bells and waved his hands & did genuflexions. The intoning was very bad. Then came a solemn solo on some sort of hautbois, rather an improvement. Then, after more scampered chants, the band in the gallery began playing some fine stately piece or other. We all sat and listened and were rather strung up by it. Then came the sermon, a rather oratorical affair, and yet somehow sincere. He spoke very clearly, slowly, and with much gesture. He pictured the supreme sacrifice of Christ, the similar sacrifice of any man who dies avec les armes à la main, en se battant pour la France, or words to that effect. He described sympathetically the mud & misery of the trenches; and then urged men, if they ever felt inclined to give up the struggle, to remember devastated France who needed their help. He pictured the souls of the glorious dead enjoying heaven. And his last words were a moving summary of all the sufferings of France since the war began. Well, one watched the pale blue congregation. Some seemed not to listen. Some were on the verge of breaking down. Perhaps they were those who had lately lost friends or had lately suffered in some other way. One sour looking man near me kept twirling his moustache and frowning, as if he disapproved of the whole business. Somehow that sermon, though in a way it was artificial in matter & form, stirred one terribly. For however artificial it was, there was the great tragic fact behind. One felt as if the little church were some ship in a great storm, sweeping toward a fierce coast. One felt that the blue mariners, instead of pulling at ropes and bailing the ship, were praying to imaginary gods of the tempest. I don't know. It was somehow terrible. One felt the awful fatal power of the world, and the littleness of men. Finally the band played Chopin's dead march as people slowly moved out with wreaths for their friends' graves. That nearly reduced some of us to tears, very much against our will. I can't explain. There was something more than the obvious tragedy of human death about it, though indeed that is more than enough in itself. Poor blue soldiers, with their short-cropped black hair, and their matter-of-fact French faces. They had such a strange shamefaced way of crossing themselves, rather as if they suspected it was a foolish superstition, but were determined to be on the safe side. They had seen hell all right, but they did not know at all what heaven is. . . .

*Next Day.* Alas, the rugger match was almost too fierce. I got temporarily laid out with a kick on the nut, was carted off to hospital for no reason but to fulfill red tape. The first thing I knew about it was when I found myself being washed in our billet! So at present I swank about in a huge & complicated bandage in a certain old château that is not a hospital. I hope to get out again tomorrow if the red tape can be disentangled. It was a fine game against a lot of heavy artillery men. Neither side scored in spite of a prolonged struggle. They played a bit foul, & laid out another of us for a moment or two. They say I fell on the ball and someone kicked my head instead of the ball. Anyhow I only have a cut scalp and a headache. And it's rather nice to sleep in a real bed again, & in *sheets*! The people in my ward are all slightly wounded, some even less than I. But alas most of them have got their hurt in war & mine was only in play. If only it had been a bit of shell & not a boot that had hit me I should be happy, & should get extra leave. Just my miserable luck!

Egremont

TO OLAF                                      13 November 1917

. . . Well, now for the horrible topic—I wish I were not 21 & hadn't got a vote! We are going to have another Referendum on the conscription question. It will probably be all over by the time you get this. December 15 is the date fixed,—& between now & then I have to make up my poor mind as to "yes" or "no." Last time I voted yes & repented afterwards. Ten to one I shall vote yes again & if not I shall probably not vote at all. I hate the whole thing. Some people are born with their minds already made up on everything. They are the happy-go-luckies. It is a torment to have such a terribly weak open mind as I have. I am annoyed with the authorities for making 21 the age qualification. People of my age don't know for themselves. They have to take the tip from their elders & betters. In the case of State or Federal elections it is an easy enough matter. You know one candidate is a gentleman & the other a bounder—one a Liberal & one a Labour & you stick to your own party & you don't worry about it, but in a big question of this kind it is different. Your pros & cons are not nearly so concrete. Well, I haven't thought about it properly yet. I shall probably have to tell you all my worries & thinkings later on.

TO OLAF                                         20 November 1917

. . . I wonder if perhaps you are at home now on leave—perhaps at this very minute waking up one morning at Annery. I have a habit of always thinking of you eight weeks ago, sort of. I don't realise that you are really there keeping pace with me at every fresh minute of the day. It is nice to think that. It makes you more real. I have read two books in the last three days. That is my record! I kept thinking how much you would have enjoyed them if we had been reading them aloud to each other. Of course you must have read them—"Pride & Prejudice" & "Northanger Abbey." You do like Jane Austen, don't you? I simply love her. Such really artistic delightful writing. Such books make me think of diamonds, small diamonds but perfect in workmanship. Absolutely genuine—clean cut, perfectly smooth & sparkling. Full of such delicious humour & such sound good sense, & although the ways & the language of that day are so very different from ours yet the characters are just such as we meet everywhere. I should like to have been friends with Jane & Elizabeth Bennett. . . . I should so like to be as bright & intelligent & sprightly as Elizabeth! No wonder Mr. Darcy "got it badly" when he did get it! I like to picture you in the characters of all the nice lovers—*my* Mr. Darcy!

I can see you at our first meeting thinking me "just tolerably good looking." I can see you later on watching me often rather curiously & I seem to detect a more severely critical look than any sign of approval. In self defence I avoid you or tease you & perhaps dislike your watching me & I think (as I do of so many English people) that you are cold & reserved—indifferent—unapproachable—& then suddenly one evening without any preparation you tell me that you love me & have been loving me for some time & I reject you rather vigorously & state my disapproval without any softening & you go away coldly without a word. . . . I can understand Elizabeth very well. I can understand her resentment at such a sudden & unexpected declaration. I can understand her disapproval amounting to positive dislike on that occasion. I think she would understand my despair & sorrow—almost shame at having won a love that I could never hope to return. If she had understood my feeling she would not have been surprised to find me weeping upstairs in the darkened drawing room. . . .

Then next I see the beginnings of changes in both of us—changes which make us feel how far away we both were before from the real thing & at last "my Mr. Darcy" comes to me—or rather I write to him from the other end of the world & say, "Dear Mr. Darcy—Once, a long time ago, you asked me to be your wife & I said no & I was very cross & horrible & now I am sorry. Everything is different now & I am different too & I understand & if you will only ask me once again I will not say no—indeed I will not."

And she did not.

Mr. & Mrs. Darcy were very happy after their stormy courtship, & Mr. & Mrs. Stapledon will surely be even more so to make up for all the long time they have had to wait. . . . Jane Austen really is a tonic as well as an artist.

[*The form of the book Olaf worked on throughout the war and for some time after kept changing. He gave Agnes periodic reports on it, sometimes describing it as veiled autobiography, sometimes as a medley of prose and verse; at one stage he thought of using an epistolary structure, modeled on his and Agnes's own letters. At first titled* In a Glass Darkly, *in later versions Olaf called it* Sleeping Beauty.]

SSA 13

TO AGNES                                                        2 December 1917

. . . The book I have been trying to write is now finished, all but a possible little epilogue. I have called it (for the moment at any rate) "In a Glass Darkly," for on the whole that seems the most appropriate title. It consists of some twenty five thousand words; very short for a book, rather long for anything else. . . . If finally I decide to publish it, I shall do so simply with the idea of giving some sketch, however crude, of the great thought-springs that are in men's minds today. Perhaps after all it will seem best to put it away and have no more to do with it, at any rate for some years.

[*Olaf's "closed up collar" was a recent modification of the FAU uniform required to prevent Unit members from being confused with British Army officers who had open collars; many FAU members regretted the loss of privilege and status when the collars were altered.*]

Annery

Agnes,                                                          8 December 1917

Home again! Cheers! And after such a quick journey. . . . Missed the connection for Liverpool, had an elegant light lunch at Euston, embarked for L'pool at 2.20. Now, on the strength of having in these latter days a closed up collar to my tunic, I travelled third. In the compartment were an RFC man, an RGA man, two infantry men one of whom was a New Zealander, and two young civilians of whom one was a discharged soldier. Very soon we got talking, first about the British and French fronts, then about the war in general. And I was surprised at the outspoken pacifism of everyone present. There was first a whisper then a trickle of remarks, then I said I was FAU and then everyone began to grow voluble about the war and the fact that if only some people weren't making a profit out of it, it would have been wound up long ago. The RFC man came from Preston. He was very bitter, in his broad Lancashire dialect. The discharged soldier talked a lot of palpably extravagant rubbish, but on the main points he agreed entirely with the rest. His extravagance was chiefly merely anti-monarchical. (Not that I am a monarchist; but I don't think the matter is worth bothering about.) The New Zealander was a lad who had not yet been to France, and all he cared for was looking at the scenery. But the rest! I assured them that the average French poilu was every bit as "bad" as they were, and they said, "No wonder." . . .

And so here am I home again, writing at my old desk in the red room to the girl I have written to so often from this place. . . . Annery is the same as ever, & Caldy is as lovely as ever. I have treadmilled the old pianola as usual. But somehow this time it does not satisfy me at all. I want handmade music again, and I want it made by your hands.


TO OLAF

Egremont
11 December 1917

. . . Last week I had such a frantically busy time. I had scarcely a minute to think of mails or anything else, but now that it is all over & the reaction has set in I begin to think it seems about an age since I heard from you or since I wrote to you. The three big events of last week went off very successfully on the whole. They were 1) the annual poor children's Xmas party at Killarney, 2) the Thrift Club party for factory girls at the Y.W.C.A., & 3) a lesser affair where the "talented Miller trio" played musical items between the acts of a children's play. We came through that fairly decently considering it was about the largest show Rosie & I ever played at, excepting in orchestra. There must have been between 400 & 500 people there in the Mosman Town Hall. . . .

Friday's stunt was the most thrilling. The [Thrift] party was such a splendid success, & we were all so pleased because it was the first one of its kind we have had in Sydney. It was the "Paying-out" party when all the moneys put in during the year were given out along with the interest they had acquired. Great excitement over a penny interest! There were collectors from about 15 factories & some girls from each,—there must have been well over 100 there. I began the party at home in the morning by baking about 4 dozen scones & a big sandwich cake. Then I set off to town with my bundles & a huge basket of flowers in addition. In the lunch hour I went out to the factory to see the girls & make sure they were coming down in the evening—set forth all the attractions—

games, flowers & supper etc. All afternoon we were fixing up the money, sorting it out & addressing the envelopes etc. Then we went down to the hall & another girl & I made about 3 gallons of coffee & cut up all the home-made cakes. Other girls decorated the hall with flowers & made ever so many little button-holes—one for each girl as she came into the room. The company began to arrive before 7 pm & all the collectors were installed behind long trestle tables for the "paying-out" part of it. Everything had to be signed for & checked properly—it was like being in a bank—& it was quite exciting recognising the different girls as they came in! So different some of them looked from when I had seen them at lunch time in their working clothes & print aprons. Now they appeared in silks & pale blue ostrich feathers & brilliants. . . . They all looked so spry & carefully got up & lots of them were as jolly & lively as sand boys. We had a flower competition—guessing their names—& that set the ball rolling. Then there were some terrible recitations which received thunderous applause & afterwards a little "causerie" about the Y.W.C.A. by the nice extension secretary, & afterwards supper & plenty of it & such lovely home-made cakes.

We "the committee" were quite proud of our party. My job was serving out coffee, but when it was over I went out & sat with my friends from Hunter's [factory]. They were so nice & so pleased with everything & they hoped we would have another party next year. Afterwards we sang God Save the King & the moment it was over, as if by instinct, the girls all rushed at the flower vases & stripped every one. The hall looked as if a plague of locusts had descended upon it all in the twinkling of an eye & left not a green leaf in the place. They do love flowers. Looking at those girls en masse I was wondering how they would compare with the factory girls of other countries. I think our girls would probably bear off the palm for general well-being & aliveness.

Annery
13 December 1917

TO AGNES                                        11.15 PM

. . . I am all adrift, all sixes and sevens and so bored, bored to tears with the war and my own stodgy self. This leave has been somehow unreal. It has largely consisted in going round talking platitudes to people about the war, and in slipping back comfortably into the artificial life that we all lead at home in our most excessive middle class luxury. Plates & dishes & knives & forks & furniture beyond the wildest need, & all so beautifully clean. Fires, hot baths, dainty food—& yet there are trenches in the world.

. . . I have told the bookseller to send you a wee book when he can get a
copy of it. It is William Morris's "News from Nowhere." You will like it,
I am sure. It is a sort of tale, and also a picture of a Happy England that
*might* be. Read it thinking of the things we want to help to bring to pass
when we are married. It is only a little book, and a very readable one.
Of course it is open to much criticism, but that matters not. It gives a
charming though rather limited picture. . . .

   Miss Graveson sent her love to you, sends it by me that is to say; and I
take the opportunity of sending it with an extra ration of mine—because, why just because you are such a dear. Miss G told us of Kenneth
Robinson an old school fellow of mine who is a CO. He stayed long to
help his father in business, and at last was called to a tribunal. His position was much like mine—ready to do anything but military service,
and very anxious to join the F. A. U. He trained for that, but the Tribunal
would not grant him exemption for it because, if you please, his father
& brothers were not COs. He was left at large for some time, but was
finally arrested and given eighteen months hard at Wormwood Scrubs.
You know what that means—solitary confinement with possibility of
going mad. He's a nice chap, so gay and unassuming and simple. Oh
England, for shame! And here am I sitting in mufti before a nice fire
with my feet on a thick fur rug and a meal preparing for me. Yet he and
I are of the same persuasion, mind you. The only difference is that he
was tied down by the need of helping his old father while I went off
before the conscription act came in. It is a queer justice that lets me do
the job I wanted and refuses it to him. . . .

*Sunday night*, the last night of leave. I go early tomorrow. This evening
Mother played some Rubinstein on the piano and part of it was a "melody" that you used to play. It brought back ancient days. Father and I
had such a wet walk this morning. Thurstastone was all one driving
blizzard.—But what's the use of writing you a sort of schoolboy diary?
The last night of leave is a poor night. It's bad enough for oneself but it's
worse for one's people; and their sorrow makes one grieve far more. It's
good to talk to you tonight, for I am not on the point of leaving you—
alas, partings need not worry us, for we have not yet our meeting. You
are always as near as ever, and as far.


                                                         Egremont
TO OLAF                                     18 December 1917
. . . Thursday Conscription Referendum. Everything is in a turmoil
about that. Public meetings pro & anti everywhere, eggs & other mis-

siles in constant use, papers full of it. Trams full of argumentative people. Posters everywhere. I am going to vote yes.

[*When Olaf returned, the convoy had left Maffrécourt and was "en repos" in Gizaucourt. Meaburn Tatham, who would take over command of the Unit from Leslie Maxwell on 1 January, was coauthor of the official history of the Friends' Ambulance Unit published by the Society of Friends in 1919.*]

SSA 13

TO AGNES                                        22 December 1917

. . . Our journey from Paris was uneventful, though it took twelve hours and ended with a four mile walk in the moonlight, tramping it with a Frenchman, discussing the war and the governments & the press. We reached the convoy in the middle of a meeting for the discussion of FAU reforms. The old & the new OCs of the FAU were both present. We put up a gallant stand for democracy, a very fine stand. The new OC is Tatham who was at Balliol with me. I knew him slightly. He was always a decent fellow, & may make a good OC. Next morning I had a walk & a talk with him. He is far more satisfactory to talk to than Maxwell. The latter in his farewell speech made very fine remarks about SSA 13, not concealing the fact that he thought us the star section of the Unit, and declaring that had he been an ordinary member he would have chosen to belong to SSA 13 rather than any other section. We are tempted to think it was not all butter—so conceited are we with ourselves as a convoy. He also thanked us for our criticism & help, which was rather handsome of him, considering what a lot of bother we gave him! While I was talking to Tatham about possible stretcher bearing corps he said, "Well, of course, I should think that as far as danger and arduousness are concerned you of SSA 13 have at least as much of both on an average as the ordinary soldier, because he spends so very long doing absolutely nothing far in the rear." I think that is a great exaggeration, but when we went into the matter carefully it seemed not so great an exaggeration as I thought.

Since I came back the Convoy has been getting thoroughly frozen up. Evidently it is going to be another hard winter. We do hate the prospect. It is impossible to keep warm except during hard exercise or in bed. . . .

*Next Day.* . . . The frost increases, and it becomes daily harder to persuade a bus to start. Two or three people have to take it in turns to grind away at the starting handle and apply hot cloths to the induction pipe

Agnes with her mother, Margaret Miller, and her sister "Peter" in the front garden at Egremont, December 1917.

for half an hour or more before she will fire at all. It is really pretty exhausting work starting a car in this weather. I keep three pairs of your mittens in service—one to wear inside my fur gloves for driving, one for writing, and one for knocking about outside; oh yes and one very old pair for dirty work on my car.

Cymbeline

TO OLAF 25 December 1917

. . . A happy Christmas to you, dear, in your far away village or barns or car, wherever you are.

If only you were here! or I there! It is unavailing to wish merely—but this is the fourth Christmas I have been here at Cymbeline without you, 1914, 15, 16, 17. It surely *must* be the last. Where is the use in talking, but I *must* talk. It seems that everything works up all through the year towards Christmas & one counts the waiting of all the past year at Christmas & the sum of it is very great. . . .

The result of the Referendum has left many a tear of desperation in its train. I forget the figures, but the main fact is that there is a very much larger majority for *no* than there was last year. I feel a terrible outsider because I cannot take it to heart like all my friends. Many of them are speechless with indignation & others are bearing their disappointment in silent agony. Well, you have got to take things as they are & not make a song because they are not as you would wish them to be. The sad part about it is that those gaps will be filled by men who are not the right ones to go—married men, & boys & families who have already done their bit—the willing ones. That is the wicked part about not having conscription. They may bring it in compulsorily yet—but then the fat will be in the fire! It is funny to me that Labour as a whole stands for no, & Liberal for yes. It is strange that even in such a universal question as that there should be such a distinct line drawn between Labour & Liberal. Is it the difference between educated & non-educated people? You would have voted against it, would you not? Your 'no' would have been the outcome of very different thinkings to the no of 99 per cent of the Victors in our Referendum, but the result is the same. There is the pity of it. The Quakers stuck to their no. Mother is one of their black sheep.

SSA 13
26 December 1917
Agnes,                                          Boxing Day

The moon is brilliant, and the earth is a snowy brilliance under the moon. Jupiter, who was last night beside the moon, is now left a little way behind. Venus has just sunk ruddy in the West, after being for a long while a dazzling white splendour in the sky. I have just come in from a walk with our Professor [Lewis Richardson], and he has led my staggering mind through mazes and mysteries of the truth about atoms and electrons and about that most elusive of God's creatures, the ether. And all the while we were creeping across a wide white valley and up a pine clad ridge, and everywhere the snow crystals sparkled under our feet, flashing and vanishing mysteriously like our own fleeting inklings of the truth about electrons. The snow was very dry and powdery under foot, and beneath that soft white blanket was the bumpy frozen mud. The pine trees stood in black ranks watching us from the hill crest, and the faintest of faint breezes whispered among them as we drew near. The old Prof (he is only about thirty-five, and active, but of a senior cast of mind) won't walk fast, and I was very cold in spite of my sheepskin coat; but after a while I grew so absorbed in his talk that I forgot even my frozen ears. (I had been wishing I had put on my woollen helmet.) We crossed the ridge through a narrow cleft and laid bare a whole new land, white as the last, and bleaker. And over the new skyline lay our old haunts and the lines. Sound of very distant gunfire muttered to us. Three trudging figures slowly drew near, three "poilus" carrying their kits and rifles. As they passed, one of them greeted us in our own tongue, for he had heard us talking. What a night it is. . . .

*Another day.* After heavy snow fall the world is now well blanketed save where tracks have been cleared. I have spent all the afternoon sliding on a pond. That sounds a pretty poor occupation during the great war, but it keeps one warm, & that is about the main object of life in this weather. There were about ten of us and we simply became schoolboys for the occasion. We made two wonderful long slides, and with practise we became quite expert at all sorts of fancy turns; and most of us took some awful tosses and one got a black eye, and I, in vaulting a fence at the bottom of one slide, landed in a lot of barbed wire, and we all got soaked with snow, and the French army watched and sometimes joined in. Then we came up for tea, and are now beginning to get cold again. One can't be grown up in this weather.

We are getting up a Shakespeare reading, and the play is to be "As You Like It." I find I am to take the part of—what do you think?— Rosalind! Alas, you should be with us to take that part. Anderson is to be Orlando. I shall think of you hard all the time, and so perhaps I shall be able to read it with a sort of rough imitation of your gentle voice and merry manner. I'll put all I know into it, thinking always of you. I shall try hard to *be* you for the evening. Our difficulty will be to keep warm while sitting still for so long. The other night we had to have a sort of political meeting for the detailed drawing up of our final suggestion for the reform of the Unit. It was a good meeting, but we nearly froze. It is not really cold yet, not as cold as it will be later, but even now one's boots are always frozen hard when one puts them on in the morning; and my ink bottle is always in need of being thawed out. Even in the barn where we have a fire, water freezes easily at the far end of the place. Last night I went to bed early, piled on all my clothes, and lay and read Bergson's "Evolution Créatrice" for two blissful hours. It is a great book, very difficult to follow sometimes, and often, I fancy, quite unsound; but it is fascinating reading, and in the main it is brilliant truth; or at any rate it is packed with sentences that are gems of bright truth embedded in a lot of questionable stuff. . . . This book is the last of a great series of three. I read the first before the war and made little of it. The second I have not read. This I am reading now because, having left my "In a Glass Darkly" at home, I want to read all round the subject for a while before making my final revision of the typewritten copy that is to be sent out to me later. I am making notes of little points to insert here and there in my effort. Guess that effort is to be the best I can do, however poor it may be in the absolute. But alas the thing is so slight, so small, in spite of all the hours & hours of work that have been put into it. There have been hours & hours of definite work at it, but ever so many more hours of half unconscious ruminating about it all during the times that I have been doing other things. Yet when it is all done the cold critics will say, and justly, "This work is a curious hotch potch of misunderstood Bergsonism warped by ill-digested ideas stolen from Meredith and Lowes Dickinson. The only original thoughts in it are original only in their crudeness.". . .

The other day someone in clearing out some straw came on a queer little beast hibernating. He was rather smaller than a rat and far more elegant, having a delicate brown back, a white underneath, with a black line dividing the two shades. He had a long and furry tail; in fact he was rather like a dormouse, only bigger and fatter & greyer. I saw him lying on his back in someone's hand with his four dainty feet in the air and his tummy rising & falling ever so gently with his slumberous breath. After a while he opened his mouth and yawned but did not wake up. Some sympathetic fellow put him by the fire, the warmth of which naturally came to him as a hint of spring, so that he finally woke up and ran away. The frost must soon have induced him to find another corner in the straw and turn in again for the rest of the winter. It was very strange to see the little beast in his winter trance, so peaceful he was, almost as still as death, but without death's stiffness. He let people wind his tail round their fingers and move his legs about and he went on heavily sleeping all the while. One kept thinking of Bergson's élan vital, the great universal Life, that lay in him patiently awaiting the spring & the opportunity of further creativeness.

It is the last day of the year. Best wishes for the New Year to my Agnes. May there be peace. May the world begin its new and happier age. May you & I meet and marry and begin our new & happier age also. With all my love

Your own     Olaf Stapledon

_ononon_ *1918*

SSA 13

Agnes,
3 January 1918

After a space of very many weeks two letters have come from you.
. . . In one you talked about our inevitable drifting apart in all this absence; and all that you said was wise and comforting, and rests on the
solid base rock of our now-long-standing love. It will all come right
when we meet. Meanwhile let us always be frank and say just what we
feel, so that we may know where we are, nicht war? Naturally I also
have ups and downs of feeling. Life would be unendurable if one were
always at the excruciating zenith of feeling. In the absence of summer
the little beasts hibernate, to save themselves for keener living when the
sun returns. With us also there must needs be much hibernating of the
keen spirit of "being in love." Be sure it will wake again in full vigour
when the time comes. I am not afraid of its not waking, afraid rather of
its waking so imperiously as to drown everything else. For even now its
hibernation is fitful. It is always waking up in the cold of your absence
and turning things upside down, and making me out of all patience
with fate, and out of all patience with everybody that is not you. But
when it is not quite so wide awake I am comparatively at peace with the
world, realising that it can't be such a bad world if it has Agnes in it
anywhere at all.

In one letter you talked about the FAU and my relations with it. I
only wish I had not worried you so much about my possible leaving.
When a thing gets into my head I can't keep it to myself; it always gets
trotted out to you, often prematurely. The question that was on the tap
is still not really solved, but it has gone so far toward solution that one
must obviously stay and see it through. We made a sufficient noise
about it, and are now busy working out details of our scheme for the
benefit of the officers of the Unit. It must sound very petty to you, but

roughly the question is whether the rank & file of the Unit are to feel & exercise individual responsibility for the actions of the Unit, or whether they are to be shepherded like sheep. In joining an institution like this one cannot really escape a big moral responsibility, and it is no use trying to shift it on to the shoulders of authority. It would be quite different in the army. There you do indeed surrender all responsibility. The very essence of the Unit is that you deliberately avoid that surrender—after which escape it is no use to try and fake up a more comfortable little surrender to your own self-constituted body of officials. As to the whole question of my being in the F.A.U. here is a summary of the matter: I joined largely because I was in a hurry to get out & do something, partly because I was nearing pacifism. (I was practically promised a commission before joining the FAU. There was not much question of pacifism at first.) My pacifism strengthened itself in the Unit, till now it is pretty firm. It is of course a compromising sort of idea in my case—simply "I'll do all that the state commands save whatever seems utterly wrong." If everyone were ready to do this work & no more there would be no war. That seems to me the reasonable and—what shall I say?—the gentlest course. And I do hold that reasonableness and gentleness are the qualities most needed today. Of courage and masterfulness the world has already shown itself to have a glorious sufficiency. Anyhow here I am in the middle course, the compromise, by no means contented with it, but aware that if I were to take either of the other two courses it would be less from a sense of duty than from the longing to be out of an uncomfortable position. . . .

Haste now. Love me. I cannot change from loving you, in spite of all hibernating.

Your own
Olaf Stapledon


Cymbeline
TO OLAF                                    6 January 1918

. . . Do you know, I don't often feel very happy. It seems so ungrateful of me, because I have so much that ought to make me happy, & so very much more of everything good (except perhaps contentment) than most people—think of my poor factory girls for instance! Yet I am not happy really—never joyous. To be happy one must forget oneself absolutely & be happy in the things that make one happy—forget oneself, yes, unless one has the luck to be oneself the source of one's own happiness. I shall be happy in that way when I get you again—but not till then. The only times I really forget myself now are in reading books, when I get wrapt up in other people. I can't look at a view & just enjoy it. I am too restless. I am distracted by other people & I am distracted more by myself.

Do you feel so too? Oh Olaf, what true peace it will be when you & I are together again! I sleep like a top & I eat—ever so much—& I am brown & sunburnt & I look very well & I *am* very well—but all this is only of my body. My spirit does not sleep—nor rest nor take food, nor pleasure. My spirit crieth out for thee.

[*At her family's cottage in the Blue Mountains Agnes reads Meredith's novel* The Ordeal of Richard Feverel *and recalls her earliest memories of Olaf when they met as children.*]

Cymbeline
TO OLAF                                            12 January 1918
. . . But to continue about you & Richard Feverel. I was reading the chapter where he first meets Lucy. No, not first meets—for he saw her when she was a child—but first looks at & loves. Oh such a pretty picture it makes, in a meadow by a river bank. She in a floppy sunhat eating dewberries—golden curls, rosy cheeks, silken eyelashes, smiles & blushes. He a handsome impetuous boy, untamed, innocent but *very* inflammable. He looks at her a long time & then he says, "You are *very* beautiful"—& somehow through all the differences of time, place & circumstance I could hear *you* saying that to *me*. I think our "first love" was just as pure & sweet as these two children's although we were not a passionate proud young Richard Feverel & a picture girl like Lucy Desborough. I know I'm not beautiful, but I know you *thought* I was just as sincerely as Richard did Lucy, & after all that is all that matters. He took her hand & held it. She said she must go & he looked in her face & asked, "Will you go & leave me?" & again "Will you go & leave me?" I could hear your voice, pleading, persistent, & I could see your face with that look in your eyes that makes my heart leap & choke my throat. Olaf! Olaf! I can read to the end of *Richard Feverel* but our story has to wait so long for its fulfillment.

SSA 13
TO AGNES                                          12 January 1918
. . . If you were here just now, sitting with me in this comparatively quiet corner of our billet, we would watch and listen together. Round the stove there is a ring of vigorous talkers all arguing rather flippantly about socialism. [Denis] Goodall, commonly called Saul, is the centre of it, and I fear he is doing no good to the cause with his flippancy and his knack of getting people's backs up. But really he is sincere and kindly and clear-headed. At dinner today Saul was forcibly carried out because he was supposed to have purloined the cheese of another table. But

look, beside me sits Richardson, the "Prof," setting out on an evening of mathematical calculations, with his ears blocked with patent sound deadeners. Over in yon corner is a little quiet bridge party, smoking and talking softly together. Over on that bed (lower story) sits David Long, formerly of Manchester University. He has settled down for a quiet read by the light of his hurricane lamp. That little fellow in the top bed, squatting on his kit bag and writing, is Tom Ellis, one of the workshop staff. He comes from Manchester too, and speaks with a Manchester accent. He is almost deformed, & was once paralyzed on one side, but he is full of life and has a heart of gold. Funny lad! He sings musical songs in a piercing voice, and can be very rowdy and unrefined; yet he is passionately fond of Dickens and Shakespeare, and yesterday at our reading of "Othello" he took the title part, and did it really well. It was a revelation, such strong yet restrained feeling he put into it. On that other upper bed is little [John] Rees, the head of our motor stores department, a quiet but firm young person, rather aloof from the general ruck, a good Christian in all senses. He was Desdemona, but did not put enough expression into the part. Did you hear that cynical tenor laugh? That was Robertson the Scotch artist. He is behind the centre block of beds. Of him one feels that underneath layers and layers of woolly muddled thought and egotism there must really be some secret splendour of Life. I guess he is the laziest and most selfish of us all, but somehow one feels more sorry for him than angry with him, because of the said sadly overlaid splendour of love for pure beauty. Poor lonely fellow. He never gets to know anyone, simply because he affects a strange attitude of superior bantering. There in front us sits [Francis] Wetherall, the head mechanic and engineer, grey-haired, spectacled, reading some heavy tome on rationalism. He is a close man. No one knows much about him, save that he has a strong unrefined sense of humour, an astounding command of bad language when he is wrath, and a faculty for singing funny Irish songs. He does far more work than anyone else. He is never happy unless working or reading some scientific book. He wears a wedding ring and is a confirmed old bachelor. He is self-educated with a vast disorganised or rather ill-proportioned store of information and ideas about evolution and natural science. Here beside me,—no, beside you, who sit between him & me—sits Teddy. You know him. He is rather laboriously writing a letter, and now & then turning in our direction to ask for light upon nice points of syntax. Teddy is gradually beginning to take more interest in the great world. He regularly borrows my "Nation" (most glorious of all journals) and my "Common Sense." Formerly his ideal seemed to be to keep clean and hale and full of the joy of pure life, and to be infinitely and unobtrusively kind to his neighbours. Now, he is more than that without having dropped any of that. Teddy's only fault is a lack of push, not of strength,

Dear Miss Miller
    The above is the wonderful
"Slapp" ! ! ! He is in the process of writing
to you. Why is it he takes hours and
hours over it? I pity you deeply!
It is hard enough to listen to his weighty
conversational styles, what he is like
when left alone to express himself without
interruption I shudder to think. It is
now almost midnight. He has sat in
the above position since six o'clock, refusing

A pencil sketch of Olaf writing letters by candlelight at an ambulance station. The drawing was done by the Scottish artist Eric Robertson in 1918 and was sent by Robertson in an undated letter to Agnes Miller.

for he is as firm as a rock. Perhaps the push will come later. Anyhow I lack push too, so I must not complain. Between you and the Prof sits Stap who has just had his hair cut very short and has suffered much chaff on the score of the visibility of a long scar that has been thereby laid bare on his head. "Daddy. what did you do in the great war?" "Look at my head, young man." But alas it was only an artillery man's boot! This same neighbour of yours is grimy, like the rest of us, and he is shy of sitting by you in such a grubby state. Otherwise he is much as you knew him, though (on dit) thinner. His right hand neighbour is the girl. I think I see her sitting with her elbows on the table looking round at people with a curious, interested smile, her face lit by the hurricane lamp. I think I see her brows drawn together in a puzzled expression as she wonders exactly why each of these people is here and not in the trenches. They look a pretty healthy, sturdy lot, don't they, and unashamed. Listen! There goes Harry Locke discussing Australian politics. I expect you would say he knows nothing about them. Perhaps, but I think he knows something about world politics, of which yours are a part. But goodnight now, dear Agnes. My pen is running dry, & it is bed time. . . .

*Next Day,* Sunday. Here am I, having got my car ready for duty, polished my buttons, shaved, peeled some potatoes of my own free will and out of the goodness of my heart, it being not my job at all. And now behold me squatting on my bed, a lower story bed of which the upper story is occupied by Goodall and the next door one by [Roger] Carter. He and I sleep "heads & tails," like sardines in a box, so as not to crowd one another out. This billet is a barn like the last, but we are far more crowded together. It is fitted up with beds, a very great luxury. Generally one sleeps on the floor—with a straw mattress if one has luck. These beds are made of crossed wire, and are very comfortable. The barn is rather smaller than the Annery drawing room, red room, and hall, and in the middle there is a big hole where the staircase comes up from a stable occupied by one honest but smelly horse. He gets mighty odoriferous in the night season. The barn accommodates us all for living, eating & sleeping, and as we are en repos, everyone is generally at home. At one end is a decent window covered with oiled canvas. At the other two little holes a foot square similarly covered. Consequently it is always pretty dark, and vast quantities of paraffin are burnt. Downstairs with Dobbin lives the motor bike, a mountain of hay, logs of wood that are forever being chopped up by shirt-sleeved English for our fire. Also down there at all sorts of odd times one may find two or three people each with a basin full of hot water begged from the cook's department. Each proud possessor of hot water plants himself down by the heels of Dobbin, strips, and has a hot bath. But hot water is very rare, and gen-

erally washing is no more than a lick to the visible portions and a promise to *part* of the invisible portions, in cold water outside. But in hard
frost even that gets omitted, & people wait for a change of wind and
wipe their faces every morning on a damp towel. My personal sorrow at
present is connected with boots. I have two pairs, one of trench boots &
one ordinary. The ordinary ones are old and dilapidated; the "trenchers"
suddenly began to fall to pieces, and as the divisional bootmaker says he
is too busy to mend them I had to send them to a town, where they will
be probably a month. Meanwhile I have one "holy" pair that are always
soaking wet. Consequently it is a very long time since one had dry feet
in the daytime. All these tragedies are nothing compared with the real
tragedies of the world today, but all the same they are amazing. . . .

*Another Day.* . . . I have been reading Nietzsche's "Also Sprach Zara-
thustra," but in translation. It is annoyingly pompous, and its ideal is
ludicrously egotistical; but it has brilliant truths in it here and there, and
of course it is interesting to read what the Germans so often profess as
their ideal, and to see how far they have really drifted from pure Nietzsche. It is a book to make one think, even if the thinking is often hostile to the author's idea. And it is wonderful to see how all these great
and so different books & men, like Nietzsche, Bergson, Mazzini, Meredith, Morris, Comte, Shelley, Swinburne, Browning, and even Carlyle—all seem to contribute some definite idea that is gradually proving
essential to the new faith. It is like a game of patience—fitting in the
cards in their right places. And in each case there seems to be so much
that will not stand the test, that is not the real true truth, and just one
brilliant idea that has been waited for by a puzzled world. . . .

As to Conscription, dear, you know what I think, & think with ever
surer confidence. You know what I think about the results of the Referendum. And you know how glad I am to think of your acting according
to your own conviction in the matter, however profoundly we differ.
Look! I feel very strongly about that subject, & in the future I may have
to act on that feeling; yet somehow I love you better for being in the
enemy's camp. Fair, noble, and misguided enemy. Certainly one or
other of us is misguided, and naturally I won't believe it is I! I'll snatch
you from that false allegiance someday, or be convinced and convicted
of profound error myself. What a plot for a melodramatic novel—He
and she in such bitterly opposed camps, & both by serious conviction,
not by mere chance.

SSA 13
TO AGNES                                    20 January 1918
. . . The most thrilling subject now is the slow but steady evolution of
the various nations & parties toward peace. One feels that there is now

quite a new air about it all. Personally I greatly admire the Bolsheviks in spite of their oppression of their enemies. The hope of the future is with them. It is they that seem to have the courage and the faith. . . . Peace is really coming at last. Then comes the beginning of real work at last. It will perhaps be an age of starvation and disorder and terror and misunderstanding and revolution, but it will be the age of the beginning of the new alignment of life, at least if we all try hard enough. . . .

Lately I have been thinking with little content about "In a Glass Darkly" and planning out considerable additions to it, & alterations. If I can get the additions adequately written the whole will be a far bigger thing than before, & actually a book. Was there ever a book that took so much re-writing? Indeed it has not been written, it has grown of its own accord & very spasmodically. I don't know if I am doing right or wrong in giving so much time & thought to this one effort. I don't know that I even care whether it is right or wrong. All I care is that the book when it is completed shall be sound. If in years to come the world (!) asks me, "What did you do in the great war?" and I have to say, "I wrote a book," I don't care for the world's condemnation, nor for anybody's; for if the book be the true & beautiful thing that I am trying to make it, it will justify me; & if after all it is nothing and I have to be ashamed of myself for a waster—well, there's an end of it, and one more man ashamed of himself won't harm the Idea, and the Idea is all that matters. And faith, I did not try to avoid the war so as to write a book. I did my best to get into the war while not betraying the Idea; and since the war would not have me on those terms more than as an ambulance driver—tant pis, and all the more obligation to serve directly the Idea by laborious thought & writing. . . .

The other evening we read "Twelfth Night" and I took Sir Toby Belch with much relish. We have some rather good readers amongst us, especially one [Frederick] Jeffrey who is called Amelia because (oh horrid pun!) when he first came to us he was sent as an orderly to an outstation where the drivers reported that he greatly "ameliorated" their lot! Amelia took Portia in "The Merchant of Venice," and did it with much spirit and delicacy. He is a nice lad, but generally asleep. At present we are having an epidemic of slight illness, due probably to some bad food or other, or possibly to the rather foul atmosphere of the stable over which we live. In the evenings, what with the stable, tobacco, acetylene lamps, the stove, and forty or more men, and the necessity for keeping the two wee windows shut because of the light, we get up a fearsome fug.

TO AGNES                                   27 January 1918

. . . On our run yesterday, in the midst of our breathless career, we met
a real live general walking with a friend. His gorgeous hat flashed in the
sun, and he was all splendid in blue & red & gold. "We" were Romney
Fox, Tindle and I. . . . Now Romney stopped & saluted, hatless as he
was; I merely broke into a walk & saluted, hatless as I was; Tindle, after
another hundred yards, and anxious not to be left too far behind, ran
past the general with his hand at the salute! The French don't much
mind about hatless salutes, and we *had* to do something. The meeting
of a general, all ornate with his golden oak leaves, is quite an event in
this our reposeful life, & to be caught with no hats, bare legs and very
ragged shirts, is as if *you* were to be caught in the city with your hair
down, though alas in your case the vision would be charming & in ours
it was merely disreputable. There is absolutely no other news at all to
tell you except that they read "Henry V" aloud while I was lying on the
bed of sickness [from dysentery]. I listened in great comfort and seclu-
sion while Renard as Henry stirred all our hearts with mighty speeches.
It was very interesting to compare it all with things of today. One dare
almost prophesy that there is less difference between men's minds in
Elizabeth's reign & men's minds today than there will be between men's
minds today & men's minds a hundred years hence. . . .

*Later.* Such a lovely day again, though colder. The young corn flashes
green, with a sort of surprising special significance quite unspeakable in
words. We walk among angels. Every sense message that we receive,
were we able to understand it or rather feel it fully, is a message from
heaven. Indeed the "special significance" of the green corn blades, the
shock of joy that it gives one, is the outward and visible sign of an inward and spiritual grace. The greenness of the corn is a messenger, an
angel in the exact sense. Some of these myriads of angels that greet us
every day we can recognise, but most of them we miss simply because
we are not ourselves spiritual enough to know them. The warm kiss of
the sun is easily felt to be divine, or a dive into cold water. The sight of a
gull stooping in its flight and alighting daintily on the water, that also
may be easily felt to be divine. And "my heart leaps up when I behold a
rainbow in the sky." But all the myriads of common sense-messages stir
me not. A fellow is chopping wood for the fire, causing me to hear a
series of bangs and crashes and human grunts. All this sounds merely
ugly to me, yet it is as divine as the lark's song; only I am not sufficiently
awake & alive to grasp its less obvious divinity. But I guess that the more
alive one is the more wide awake is one's sense of beauty, so that if one
were a perfectly alive free soul unhampered by the tyranny of pleasure

& pain one would recognise every message of every sense as a dazzling view of the world's soul. The artists are always talking about the "shock" of pure beauty that they get from some scene or some colour or form, and always priding themselves on seeing beauty where other people see none. And that "world of music" that you talked of is simply another instance of the same thing. Someone [the Pre-Raphaelite critic T. Watts-Dunton] said that the present need of the world is a "renaissance of wonder." True, we have forgotten the wonder of simplest things. For if your surrounding world is merely a texture of dead tints and noises and smells and tastes and touches, it matters not how intricately these things be woven, the result will be still dead, a world of commonplace complexity. But if the units are all dazzling angels, what a world it is!

[*Agnes describes a camping trip with her brother Waldo, her sister Rosie, Lionel Irvine, and various friends to the Cox River in the Blue Mountains during the Australian summer in January.*]

Egremont

TO OLAF                                                      30 January 1918

. . . We had four rucksacks with food and bathers in, & four bundles of coats, rugs & tentgear. That made a bundle each, & we looked a fine sight as we tramped through Blackheath about 8 o'clock on Tuesday morning. Odd hand packages were our billy, Waldo's camera & the vanity bag made of flowered cretonne. This last contained all the personal effects of the five lady 'rucks'—5 toothbrushes, 5 combs, some hairpins, some soap, a bit of rag & a bottle of Ellimans. Not a towel between us nor a looking glass! So we did not do too badly. We started off down the Megalong Rd. . . . and then we followed tracks & cut across gullies in order to get onto a ridge which we had decided would take us down to the river. *It was hot.* We melted. It was rolling cattle country & most of the timber was dead ringbarked. When we came to a tree with a shade we lay down flat with our heads on our packs & talked optimistically. . . . The last couple of miles was downhill—pretty steep going down to the river & I think I have never felt anything harder than the road. One's feet slip into the toes of one's shoes & get squashed flat. Do you know the feeling? It is all granite country down there. The earth is hard like baked clay & the surface of it is covered with tiny granite or quartz crystals. It gets very slippery—& hot & hard. The soil grows only bracken & gums & granite boulders, but oh it is beautiful country—so steep & rugged & so dry & parched & Australian! We got to the Cox about

2 o'clock & we dumped our bundles down & went in for a swim without wasting a minute. . . .

After the swim came lunch—now 3 o'clock & we had had breakfast at 6.30 & walked about 13 miles in between! Grilled sausages—grilled on sticks & eaten in our fingers. Four cups of tea, neat, without milk (we couldn't be bothered with a cow) & bread & jam. After *all* that we lay in the sand in the shade & looked up at the sky through the trees. I told you before about the casuarina trees? There was a double row of them along each side of the river. Great big massy trees like firs but not regular in shape. The river bed was very broad & only half of it had water in it—in the dry bed alas were forests of stinging nettle. But after a time one gets accustomed even to nettles.

We had our route planned out & accordingly we set off downstream again about 5 o'clock after a good rest. We walked along the banks under the trees—sometimes on sand—*that* was slow—sometimes on nettles—*that* was pretty quick. Now & again we came to reaches of nothing but granite boulders with the river frothing & tearing between them. Several times we had to cross & once it was great fun. We had to take off our shoes & paddle. In midstream Jean [Curlewis] dropped a shoe in, & the torrent seized it & carried it off like lightning. The owner of the shoe got the giggles & made for the bank & roared while Rosie & I rushed madly down the stream to try & rescue it. Rosie stepped in not wisely but too well & got wet nearly up to her waist—she retired & joined the gigglers on the bank while I rushed on alone over nettles & all & plunged in more wisely & intercepted the beast in full career down the next reach. Jean was overcome with laughter & gratitude & came forth to meet me as I approached & fell on my neck, tearing as she did so her jewels from her neck (one pink enamel brooch) & pressing them upon my reluctant head as I knelt at her feet. The others said I was much too fat to look romantic & the affair ended in compliments & laughter.

A little further down Lionel fixed on our camping ground & we fell to getting things ready before evening drew in. It was really a delightful spot. I shall often think of it. An almost flat space, partly sand, partly pine needles & a few low rocks with casuarinas overhead & the river tearing past at our front door so to speak. . . . Lionel & Waldo got the tent fly rigged up in a marvellous manner—quite an engineering feat under Lionel's directions. We had a wonderful soup sausage affair. I was cook & though we were all very uncomplimentary about it in preparation it turned out to be an absolute pièce de résistance. We made it in the billy & drank it in our enamel mugs & we made toast-fingers & dipped them in in a beautifully savage style. After that . . . we finished our final preparations while the real tea was boiling again. It was almost dark by this time & the boys lighted the big fire which was to burn all through the night. Such a fire it was—ever so many logs piled up—it made a glow all round & was so hot we had to sit quite a long way off. We finished our tea by the light of the fire & the moon which had just made its appearance over the hill. For an hour afterwards we all lay about in a drowsy way staring into the fire & noticing how beautiful our camping ground was with the little white tent in the centre among the dark trees, & that glorious rushing of the river so near us—& the moon keeping watch. . . . They made me sing lots of songs—Brahms, Schubert, old English "Barbara Allen," new little French songs & some of the "Just So's." Then another warm up by the fire & it was half past ten—bed time.

Don't let's talk about the night! It was fun in a way—when it was over—an experience if nothing else, but it is dreadfully uncomfortable sleeping on sand. We should have hollowed it out & made comfy places for ourselves but we didn't find that out until too late & then we didn't like to disturb the others. You see, we five girls all slept in the same bed, so to speak. All under the fly, 5 in a row with our heads sticking out of the top, & we had coats & rugs underneath us & two blankets spread over the lot. Alice [Graham] & I were on the two extremes. I think we got the worst of it because the blankets didn't stretch. It *was* fun though at first. We all got the laughs. When *one* turned over, we all had to turn. We were quite sure we were going to be eaten by dingos in the night & we made out a code of rules "In Case of Dingos." I was to be the first to be eaten, being on the outside, so the "Dingo Drill" was entrusted to me. I expect I slept quite a lot but it seemed to me that I only had about 3 hrs. real sleep. I saw the moon set & I watched Orion & the Pleiades & Sirius manoeuvering round over the tops of trees. I listened to the rushing water—I heard the boys throw fresh logs onto the fire. I heard the crackle they made & watched the sparks fly. I heard the kookooburras laughing away in the small hours, & at last the birds began to twitter & I turned then & faced East to watch for the dawn up over the hills. It was long in coming. At 5 to 5 I was thinking I couldn't lie a minute longer so I sat up & beheld through the back of our tent the three boys simply doubled up with laughter at sight of us—five tumbled young women & a heap of blankets. I laughed back at them & then the other four all woke up laughing & one by one we touzled creatures crept forth & shook our achy limbs & backs & made for the red ashes of the night's fire. It was still glowing & another log sent it sparkling up into the cool air of morning & the white sky. It is funny to wake up & find oneself dressed, isn't it? One feels so crumpled & screwed up & untidy. . . . We all voted for tea right away before our swim & fell at once to getting it ready. Billy tea & toasted buttered biscuits at a quarter to 6 in the morning down by the rushing Cox River under casuarina trees out of sight of man & all his works is quite a new & delightful experience for eight civilized mortals from the great town of Sydney, a town which probably has not heard of the Cox River & does not care where it is. . . .

Then we all came down & got into our bathers & had our morning dip. It was not lukewarm then by any means—it was cold & fresh. We glowed with it & hung ourselves out by the fire to dry, having no towels. After the swim about a quarter to 8 followed proper breakfast. Tea & gloriously hot herrings in tomato on toast, cooked by Jean. Cheese biccies & bread & jam. Such a feast! Then we broke camp & the camera fiends got busy (but without very much result) & we fastened up our packs & put the fire out & set off again down the river. . . . We saw a big snake lying sunbaking in the river bed, about 5 or 6 ft. long. We let it glide off unmolested because the boys were on ahead & we had no good stick. We saw a couple of very big iguanas too & chased them up a tree. Waldo saw a fox & many rare birds & lots of bunnies, otherwise nothing wild or alarming. Before leaving the river we had another good swim & a sunbake on the rocks for about an hour, then lunch & a rest, & then we said goodbye to the Cox & climbed our hill & thanks more to good luck than good management struck a track on the top of the hill which brought us right into Megalong & so home by the Valley Rd.

[*SSA 13 returned to Maffrécourt, where the Unit would remain until the end of the big German offensives in July.*]

SSA 13

TO AGNES                                        3 February 1918

. . . We have been on the move again, and are now settled down to the old old work. There is very little doing, but the moving is quite an affair, & I am on duty for two or three days also. This good old billet is a palace compared with our others, as it is a deserted farmhouse. But beds are scarce, and I have none, sleeping on the floor with a few rugs folded up to form a mattress, but I have got a good spot that is practically open air. The last convoy to be here left the place in utter filth, but they left behind some excellent board-shelves which I have commandeered for the public library; and so I have been busy reorganising all the books and cataloguing, seizing the opportunity just now when all the books are in. Quite an undertaking, especially scolding people who have lost or ill-treated books. Tomorrow I shall not be here, so it had to be done today. Tomorrow I wear my good old tin hat again for the first time for two months. . . .

Please thank your father for a letter that came today. I was very interested in all his political remarks. He thinks my side is as 1 to 100 compared with his. Wait & see. England is not Australia, and I guess my side is *very* much stronger than he thinks.

[*The Cadburys, a well-known Quaker family, owned the Cadbury Chocolate company; several family members were in the FAU, among them Laurence J. Cadbury, who was head of the Unit's motor division in 1917 and 1918. A* Student in Arms, *stories and sketches from the front originally printed anonymously in the* Spectator, *was issued as a book in 1916 shortly after the death of its author, Donald Hankey.*]

SSA 13

Agnes,                                                       4 February 1918
Yesterday I wrote you a scrap in a hurry; today I am beginning again, or rather tonight, and under awkward circumstances, for I am at an aid post with three garrulous Englishmen and two garrulous Frenchmen. The latter have gone but the former remain. One of them is making cocoa, which is now an almost unheard of luxury. He is the well-bred and well-built younger [George Romney] Fox, our best runner, and a charming lad although he is a bit too pleased with himself. Another is one [William] Meredith, formerly in Cadbury's works, a keen self-educating lad who suffers from two disadvantages, being neither of the well-to-do nor of the proper "working" class. He somehow always errs on the side of formality and over respectability; but he also is a good lad, a hard worker too. The third is the great and famous inhabitant of Liverpool, Alec Gunn, called the mitrailleuse on account of his endless rattle of talk. . . .

Goodnight. These silly little black twiddly scrawls that are our only lines of communication! Goodnight.

*Another day.* In your last letter you talk about "A Student in Arms." We have a copy in our library, so I shall be able to read it. People who have read it all seem to like it. I have spent the whole of today, an off-duty day, in putting little labels on all our library books and making rules and regulations for the said library! (Daddy, what did you do in the great war?) They are now all nicely sorted into classes, and I spend odd moments in strafing people who don't keep the rules, which is quite a pleasant task when you know that public opinion is on your side! Well, that's done anyhow. Tomorrow I must work on my car in preparation for next spell of duty. She's beautifully clean, the old bus, but there is a day's greasing and oiling to be done on her. All her paint fairly shines with oil and elbow grease. Her brass work gleams with a beautiful freshness; and the aluminium work of the engine is (to my prejudiced eye) white as snow. I spent much of yesterday lying underneath cleaning the front of the back axle and all the gadgets that are thereabouts. There is one awful blemish in her at present: someone has poked a hole in the inner canvas wall of the body, and I must devise some decent repair that will not necessitate taking down the whole sheet. . . . So there is plenty to do, and not much chance of getting time to complete the new library catalogue yet. And alas, my fur gloves *must* be mended, and my old leather waistcoat too; but as the latter has been discarded during this warm weather in favour of your knitted one, it will probably have to wait. Then there is a new job: I have undertaken to write a weekly report of intellectual activities on the convoy, to be sent to HQ!

You see what petty things I am doing in these days. They sound nothing in these days of world-cataclysms. . . .

*Next Day.* I will send this letter off tomorrow as a mid week letter, since the last was so short. We have borrowed a piano from an Officers' Mess for a few days. Poor thing, it is having a hard time. Tonight an informal singsong, partly good partly bad; tomorrow a lecture on Schumann with playing; next day we give a public concert to the division. I shall miss that, being on duty. But I am looking forward to tomorrow. We have put the instrument in the old farm kitchen. At the moment a crowd is sitting there in semi-darkness listening. I wonder what the rats think of it! We have a plague of rats here. They eat everything—cheese, clothes, even boots, and of course they run over people at night, which is disturbing. Under this place there is a cellar full of water, a most unhealthy place; all filth of ages is stagnating there. . . . But really goodnight now dear, I must go to bed, after a breath of fresh air and a stroll outside to make me go to sleep at once. How wide is *your* bed? Mine is just as wide as from the tip of my thumb to the tip of my elbow, but it's snug, except when you slip off onto the floor——Pause while the "Doc" played Schubert's Serenade, very nicely too, I thought. But it has made me feel sentimental. Oh goodnight.

Your lover
Olaf Stapledon

SSA 13

Agnes,                                                    16 February 1918

Frost again, almost as hard as ever. Too cold to work on one's car without grim determination and much pausing for swinging the arms, too cold to read or write in comfort, and often too cold in bed. Of course it's not really as bad as that. Probably if it were a real hardship one would not grouse about it; but as it is just bad enough to annoy, one makes a song. One spends all day putting one's hands into one's pockets or blowing one's fingers. I am busy at present. First, two fairly busy duty days, ending with a bus caked in frozen mud, then two days of work on the car badly behind time, then duty again. For real joy I recommend the washing of a frozen car with water that, instead of taking off the mud, covers it with a layer of glass almost instanter. And a wind like a thousand little safety-razor blades shot at you; and the old car valenced everywhere with icicles that grow visibly as you swill the water on. Altogether it was not a very successful washing, in spite of the liberal use of a screw driver to chip off the ice and mud. My last duty day was a busy one compared with what we sometimes have. In the night we had a gas alarm—all the sirens echoed down the valley in a most eerie fashion, and people began getting out of their blankets and investigating things and even putting on their masks. The four Englishmen, being a thoroughly sluggardly lot, lay abed hoping for the best. Needless to say the gas never came our way, & where it did go it hurt no one,—so our confidence was justified. When it was my turn to leave the place I started with two men in the car. We jogged along a hundred yards—Bang! not a gun, oh no far worse, a burst tyre, the first I have had for months. So out we got, Romney [George Fox] & I, and jacked up the hind leg of the old beast and changed the tyre; an ancient ragged relic it was. And the two "types" inside prattled and wanted to help; and other types passing begged for a lift and were sternly refused. Soon we were on the road again, but were presently held up by a big tourer that was frantically trying to turn around in a very narrow place. So we sat & watched, and evilly hoped that he would back too far and go over the edge for our amusement; but he didn't. When the road was clear we toiled up the screened hill, picked up two sick men on the top, two more further on, and kept on picking up patients until we were full. It was just like a bus, an omnibus! There was ever so much traffic on the road, & we were late, so it was exciting winding in & out, blowing a feeble horn, shouting "Eééé là bas!" and "À droit là!" and "Attention mon vieux," or when neçessary other things more powerful. . . . And then as luck would have it we came across an exceptional number of uncivilised American horses. (War horses all come from S. America.) They were being led in pairs. A large number of them took fright at us and flung about all over the place as we passed, so there was a glorious muddle. The air was a seething mass of horses' heels, as the journalists might say! Said Romney, "By Jove, I swear I've never had such a succession of thrills!"

[*Olaf describes an evening lecture on philosophy given by one of the younger members of the FAU to a mostly bored and impatient segment of the convoy, culminating in a lively religious debate.*]

After it, & after some discussion, old [Lawrence] Pimm, our literal believer in the Bible, got up and poured out a little real old Christian staunchness, damning the lecturer pretty fiercely by the way; and his voice was half-choked with almost vindictive emotion. It was tragic. Really I felt I could have howled as one does at a discord. The poor man affirmed & affirmed not merely his faith, to which he is welcome, but the intellectual validity of the defence of his faith, which is simply ridiculous. Also he gave himself away by saying, "I have at this moment a book which sweeps away the whole of so-called Biblical criticism, leaves it not a leg to stand on—I have not read the book yet, but I shall." Yells of applause. Oh horrible incongruity, jars, and nerve-wrackers. Poor old Pimm, I am so sorry for him, and I do so hate his old fossilized dogmas and his satisfaction that he is saved and we are damned. . . .

I am going to write to my-uncle-your-father soon; but I am going to spare him all great problems in my letter, never fear. The world is so rapidly coming nearer to my way of thinking in those great matters, that I am very content to leave it at that. But he wrote me such a nice letter that I must try to write a nice letter back.

Egremont

TO OLAF                        22 February 1918
. . . I have been reading [*News from Nowhere*] this afternoon while I was having a rest from labour. It is charming & I know I am going to enjoy it. I like Utopias. I like the way Wm. Morris writes. I have never read anything of his. His style is so simple & readable & easy (at least so far as I have gone) & yet it feels cultured & artistic writing. Don't you think so? Daddy remarked that "Wm. Morris was the chap who went wrong & turned socialist." Is that a fact? Did he really go wrong or is that only Dad? I like socialists of the right kind, like you. Tell me. Do you call yourself a socialist? If not why not? What do you call yourself? & just exactly what *is* a socialist? I want to know. I overheard two ladies at the French League the other day speaking in most vivid tones of our friend Mr. Atkinson [head of the Sydney WEA]—the sum total of their remarks being that "that man Meredith Atkinson is a rank socialist!" Well, if all socialists were neither more nor less rank than he the world would soon take on brighter hues. . . .

Feb. 27th. . . . I long for the next letters. There will be a gap, alas, very soon. Mails collected between Jan. 23 & 25 went down on their way from England to America. If you wrote anything particular near that date, do write it again please. The worst of it is everything is "particular."

SSA 13

TO AGNES                       25 February 1918
. . . My wonderful cousin beloved. I'm thinking it's sad you ever met me. If I had not been, you would have loved some Australian soldier

Olaf's own pencil rendering of his attempt to talk across the world to Agnes; it appears as a tiny marginal drawing in a letter of 3 October 1918.

man and you would have seen much of him before the war, & you might have had Rosie's luck during the war, and anyhow———all sorts of problems would not have been for you. But look, little cousin of mine, I have met you, for good or ill, & so there we are. And all the sorrow which was once just sweet-sorrow, & now becomes bitter because of the inexorable passing of years—it's the obverse only. The bright side is as bright as the sad side is dark. Words only, alas. Oh Agnes, Agnes, Agnes, I want you. In the old days, when I was always wanting to have you tight in my arms, it was like an unconscious premonition of the age when I should not be able to have you at all. The world is between us, and, dear, there's a whole other world between our minds now, after all this parted time. I have gone miles & miles from where I was when we were last together. I look back at myself as I was then and think, "What a child." And I am glad of that change, that mental journey; but I want to take you with me, I want that we should both learn from each other. But it cannot be done save by the living voice & the living daily deed.

[*The identity of "the Doc," the convoy pianist who figures largely in Olaf's 1918 letters, remains unknown. The nickname does not appear in any letters before February of that year, and he may have been one of a number of men transferred into SSA 13 at the end of January from another branch of Friends' relief services. Usually Olaf remembered to give Agnes at least one full account of anyone to whom he referred by nickname, but one of his letters, written between 3 February and 10 February, is missing, and it may have identified "the Doc."*]

SSA 13

TO AGNES                                        10 March 1918

. . . Yesterday while driving through a certain place I saw a French soldier with both arms round his horse's head and his lips a-kissing the old beast's face ecstatically all over. The horse seemed very pleased at these attentions. There was something strange about those kisses, they were so human, not condescending like the patting of a dog, but simply affection between equals. Poor old gees! They have a pretty hard time in war, and affection is not generally lavished on them, though they are generally decently treated. What have they done that they should be dragged into war? They fight for no cause. They are helpless slaves, driven hither and thither, kept standing in snowstorms, chafed with harness, whipped up steep hills with heavy wagons behind them till they drop dead. And then they are thrown into the ditch and left till someone has time to bury them. Or else a shell comes and smashes them and they are left to take a day or so in dying. But of course it is the same with the men, and they also are helpless slaves. . . .

*Another day.* . . . This afternoon's [rugby] match was played in broiling sun. We went there in two cars and found a band playing on the field and some hundreds of spectators. The opposing team was nominally one we had often met before and always beaten; but this time it was a picked lot chosen from twenty-five times as many people as we have to choose from. Moreover they were all got up smartly in uniform black rugger jerseys and white shorts, instead of being the usual rag tag crowd in bits of everything. They were a fine sturdy lot. I was playing full back after all, worse luck, and had lots to do and missed a whole lot of tackles and things—quite heartbreaking. But I brought one or two fellows down rather nicely all the same. They *beat* us by two goals to a try, much to the delight of the spectators; but we'll beat them next time with a more carefully organised team. Maybe I won't play, though, because I am so badly off my game. They stood us tea in a historic château afterwards, & then we drove home to wash & dine & feel pretty stiff. I have a bump like a walnut on my head and my jaw rather out of gear. . . .

    Last night we had a great treat, such as we have never had before. The captain of the divisional or regimental musicians came with his 'cello and another chap with a violin and they played to us all evening to the Doc's accompaniment on the borrowed piano. Several French officers came as audience, so it was just a bit formal. They played mostly what I thought was not awfully good music, and the violin was squeaky and the violinist far from infallible; but one or two 'cello solos were fine. He seemed to uninitiated me to play very beautifully, so delicately yet "largely," if you understand what I mean. Afterwards we made the Doc play us the Waldstein Sonata again. Perhaps I have got Beethoven badly on the brain, but anyhow that Sonata seemed to me worth ten times all the rest of the show. The rest one looked down at and judged and rather patronisingly liked. The Waldstein kept one painfully intent on every note. Every time one hears it there seems to be something new to get out of it, & all the while one feels one really gets a mere smattering of it. I swear it is the very music of the spheres. Someone has said that Beethoven is the greatest artist of the world. I can believe it. All the same he varies, even he. In my humble opinion the "Moonlight" Sonata is not nearly as fine as this great one.

Egremont

TO OLAF                                                    12 March 1918

. . . Can you pray? I can't pray consciously, even for you my darling. I try to some nights just before I get into bed. I stand & lean over the verandah rail & look out into the darkness over the water & up to the stars, but I am restless, restless. There is no peace in my soul. I look here & I look there & then I turn away from pretending & get into bed & think of a whirl of things & fall asleep.

I am sad. I should love to pray.

SSA 13

TO AGNES                                                   17 March 1918

. . . After all these years we ought to have got used to being in love with one another. All sensible people do; but somehow we seem to go on finding it as new as it was at first. Doubtless it is all this separation that does it. You tell me how you read "Richard Feverel" and read into the love scenes you & me. So always do I with all love scenes. I can't help it. You know I think that to an outsider our letters (mine anyhow, especially this sort) would seem very silly. Yours generally have such a lot of other things to save them and make them somehow things of beauty in themselves; but as for mine, I always feel them perilously verging toward the abyss that Punch has satirised: He—"Darling." She—"Yes Darling?" He—"Nothing Darling, only darling, Darling." That aggravating bogey haunts me. . . .

I have just come back from two days at a forest outstation with a lad

[Andrew] Hodgkin as my orderly. First we had to keep to the dug out, or at least we thought we might as well as odds & ends of metal kept buzzing too close to be comfy outside; but later we sat & basked in the sun, and next day we did a few little explorations in the neighbourhood, but of course we could not go far because we were on call, and also the available directions were few. Hodgkin is nineteen, and rather a model of a certain kind of loose-limbed luxurious beauty. He lives in his senses, quite honestly. He is a great nature-lover, & we had many discussions about beasts & birds. He found a dead mole & skinned it rather nicely, drying the skin in the sun.—Pen's dry, & bed time. Goodnight Agnes mine. More later.

*Next evening*, in a hurry, as I have been conscripted into going to a French concert to "cement the entente." Well, about my young orderly. I have never had much to do with him before save in a very superficial way; and it was strange that just this time I had been noticing his aforesaid languorous good looks and a strange spirituality in them. And also I had been noticing in him a curious likeness to Dot! Their features are not at all the same, yet there was something—I don't know what. Once he stood with his back to me so that I could see only his figure & his round helmet.—Do you remember a funny little round hat of Dot's? The effect was just the same! Well, the point of all this is that in the evening, as we were walking up & down outside talking about birds & beasts he suddenly disburdened himself of his "spiritual troubles," how he could not be interested in the things people ought to be interested in, like social problems, poor boy. How he had a beastly temper, & was apt to despise certain people, how he was a source of disappointment to his father because he could find no fixed purpose in life, and how he found no satisfaction in religion, but had a kind of religion of his own, the worship of life. We talked & questioned one another for a long time, and at the end he said he never did talk like that to anyone, but it seemed good to blow off steam, & he felt better.

*Next Day.* Our latest excitement, fortunately not censorable, is the garden. France allots ground for all her troops to cultivate, so that when we move on we shall inherit someone else's labour, & someone will inherit ours. We are arranging a dozen or so private plots and a larger common land for the unenterprising casual labourers. Teddy & I, with no knowledge at all, have booked a plot and shall doubtless water it with our tears before we have done. The crops are to be lettuce, haricots, petit pois, onions, carrots & radishes. I don't know what will fall to our lot. Today we had a meeting of plot holders, of plotters, a "conspiracy" in fact, to arrange about individual & communal rights. For the whole community there are only two spades, one and a half hoes and a rake, but we hope to eke it out with a few entrenching tools if we can purloin any. Personally I propose soon to sleep out in the garden. Teddy suggests that we sow grass only on our plot & have a tennis lawn (five square yards!).

Egremont

TO OLAF                                                                17 March 1918

. . . I have an adventure to tell you—quite an adventure. It happened last night. I went to a party in Redfern—a real "pay-yer-bob-&-bring-yer-gentleman-friend" party. It is as if *you* were invited to a party in, say, Minshull St., which is the only slumming neighbourhood I can re-member in L'pool—or Lodge Lane! This party was a "surprise party"—but I think the whole thing was more of a surprise to me than to the girl in whose honour it was given. Have you ever been to a factory girl's party & not been one of the superior race of hostesses but one of the girls themselves? At least one of the girls' young men? I should think very few people have. Well, I am one of them now—those few honoured people & I have rather the kind of feeling about it that the "Messenger from Mars" must have had when he got back again to his own planet. I'll tell you how it happened.

Mrs. Jackson, one of the nicest of the workers out at Hunter's boot factory where I go "a-thrifting," was getting up a surprise party in hon-our of her sister-in-law's 21st birthday. Mrs. Jackson must be about 36 or so & she has been a Mother to this girl since she was quite little. The girl herself works in another factory so I don't know her, but Mrs. Jack-son thought it would be nice to ask me to the party. One of the other girls put her up to it, the kind of forewoman, Miss Reavell. I felt it an honour to be asked, because you know how almost "hostile" girls of that class are to social workers—at least if not hostile, well, very stand-offish & suspicious. I must confess that I had a misgiving about going (inside me), but the friendly way in which they asked me showed not the least hesitation on their parts that I would be glad to come, so of course I just had to accept & look pleased. We each paid our shilling towards supper & the hire of the hall & I was asked to "bring a gentleman friend" with me! There is only one gentleman I *could* ask who would not have been horrified at the prospect, & he alas is far away wheresoever thou goest.

Would you have come with me to share the adventure? & not have been ashamed to be just 'one of them'—or to see me being treated as the other girls? I know you are a sport. I was kissed by a soldier, & I kissed him—but I didn't mind. It was all part of the game & I'm not ashamed. Annie Reavell met me at the tram because I didn't know the way to the hall. She beamed when I got out. I think she must have been wondering while she stood waiting if I would really come. Then we met some others—some girls from Hunter's whom I knew & some from

Miss Jackson's factory whom I didn't know & some "gentleman friends." The girls all looked so nice in their best frocks—two or three of them looked as well dressed as some of my smart friends, & as a whole they were much less powdered & "done up" than my friends. I don't know what they really thought of me—perhaps they didn't think—anyway I did as Rome did & they swallowed me!

There were about 22 girls & about 12 men. Two returned soldiers, 2 or 3 who looked *very* eligible & the rest the very young cigarette-smoking, lamppost-propping sort! Anyway they all had clean collars & they were fearfully jolly & lively & they enjoyed themselves wholeheart-edly. When we were all in the hall—a funny beflagged little place up a narrow passage & a back stair, with a fine old slippery floor & plenty of cobwebs round the walls—Mrs. Jackson went home to fetch Myrtle, & somebody's young man acting as M.C. got up & said, "Ladies & gentle-men, as Miss Jackson didn't know what she was in for & had been told she was coming to a Soldiers Welcome he thought it would be a good idea when she came in, for us to make a circle all round her & sing 'For she's a jolly good fellow' while one of the young ladies played the tune on the piano, & we'ld make it a real good surprise for her." So we took hands accordingly & waited pretty quietly until the warning was given that she was coming up the stairs. It was quite a thrilling moment. She stepped into the room or rather was pushed from behind by her excit-able sister-in-law & before she knew where she was she was surrounded by us all singing & proclaiming her a jolly good fellow. She hid her face in her hands till it was over & then she looked so pleased with life. The girls clamoured round & kissed her & then the boys all came along for their kiss—just like a wedding! She kissed them all & seemed quite at home. . . .

Then we fell to dancing & the "young lady" at the piano pounded away waltzes & rags & two steps all with the loud pedal down. It sounded *beautiful*! I was never at a party where there was so little ice to break! They started in right from the beginning & didn't waste a minute. As soon as the dance was over someone suggested the cushion game. I didn't know quite what it would be but I had an idea. We all sat round the room. Myrtle walked round in front of us with the cushion while the music played. I knew something must happen when the mu-sic stopped—I thought perhaps she would throw the cushion suddenly at someone—but then all games end in kissing! & where would the kiss come in? The music stopped. Myrtle stopped opposite the nearest man, dropped the cushion on the floor, knelt on it, he knelt down too & they kissed each other fair & square without a word. Then Myrtle took his seat & he took the cushion round & the game went on. It was all done so simply & naturally—it was nice to see! So different to the way it would have happened at one of our parties! The man would have looked as awkward as a goat & the girl would have blushed & made such a fuss & ended by 'not playing.'

I laughed at the others—but I was praying the cushion wouldn't come my way. While I was thus engaged the pause came & the cushion landed at my feet. It was a jolly looking soldier preparing to kneel down, but he couldn't, poor chap, because he had a stiff leg, so I jumped up double quick & kissed him & flew on with the cushion. I *was* amused at the idea of *me*! And it was so funny. I got right round the room once & when the music stopped I was between the soldier & another youth. I didn't know which to go to & while I was hesitating & the company was shouting advice the nice soldier came to the rescue saying, "Oh Lord love us, I *like* it!" So *that* was settled, & he proceeded with the cushion. What a blue fit 99% of my friends would have taken if they had been present at that little turn! I think I would have been struck off their visiting list! Tant pis. . . .

Two of the girls came along & saw me into my tram at 10.30, & once there among all the tram people I was back in my own world again. I came back to it with a bump. I thought hard about those girls all the way home. My head was full of my adventures. Such nice girls, good girls I'm sure. They are just like other nice girls except for education & atmosphere—yet that difference keeps us so far apart. We think of them as of another species, but they are really our sisters. I thought of their "gentleman friends" & how jolly they were, & I had a most irrepressible longing come surging up in my throat to have *my* "gentleman friend" here with me. Oh Olaf! One of the little Jackson girls said to me during the party, "Where's *your* young man?" I told her, "He's at the war"—& she looked very impressed. But oh! the war is so far away! Lately I have been steeling myself with hard facts. There is a war. You are in France —I am here & I can't have you. I have got to keep going without you. I must not depend on you to prop me up. I must be able to stand by myself. I may expect your letters & cherish them but I may not expect anything more. I must not expect you.—— And tonight, in spite of all my steeling, my soul is crying out for you, for your very self. If I could only see you with my eyes & touch you. If I could feel your arms round me holding me tight. If I could kiss your face, kiss your mouth & then bury my face against your coat & rest in your arms——ah if! even only once!

[*Work on the convoy became much more intense with the onset of the great German offensives that lasted from March to July. Although Agnes could follow newspaper accounts of the battles and try to guess at Olaf's relationship to publicly reported events, censorship required him to be vague about his movements and activities during this period.*

SSA 13

TO AGNES                                                24 March 1918

. . . It's hot, like summer. All morning I filled sand bags in seminudity, & this afternoon I continued in the same garb, save for a helmet that was added perforce and much against one's physical inclination. Now I am in the cool dugout, secretly hoping the enemy will continue to make it undesirable to work in the open till the cool of the evening. It's indeed a queer life. One day one is all too eager to get away from an uncomfortable spot, next day, after reading the dreadful British communiqué one has an urgent sting of shame at not being with one's fellow countrymen in their arduous doings. Both attitudes are foolish. The Spring is very early this year. Catkins are out everywhere, such cheery pussy-like things. Shall I tell you the real essential difference between winter & summer? During the former one hates washing; during the latter one simply loves it! Well, it is summer now, & yesterday afternoon after our work I retired to my car with a basin of water & had a fine bath. Chez nous one has baths of course absolutely in public, but the French seem to think it's odd, so I was modest enough to draw the curtain—also of course one is not supposed to go in for extensive ablutions while on duty; but it was so hot. . . .

This letter is not marching well, somehow. It's partly because I am sleepy after shovelling earth & drinking coffee with rhum in it, & partly because things are not quite tranquil, & people are loudly discussing the latest news. For dug-out repairs our foreman is the Prof, who arrays himself in russet overalls & a handkerchief under his tin hat to keep off the sun. The work is all voluntary, & quite unnecessary, so it does not progress very rapidly. The French laugh at us for doing it at all, as it is only for the protection of cars, not of men; still it's good for us & makes us sweat.

Egremont

TO OLAF                                                25 March 1918

. . . Evening—hot—still. There's a committee on in the dining room . . . all talking about the German offensive, trying to encourage each other & themselves. We are all thinking about it—terrible fighting. But we cannot know what will be the end of it all. Even here it feels like living on the slopes of a volcano. What must it be like over there in England, in France! They say this might be the beginning of the end, but what dreadful things might happen before the end. They say the

Germans *might* break through—they say Paris *might* be taken—& what
then? *what then?* But oh the dreadful cruelty, the waste & sacrifice of
life on both sides!

It is almost unbelievable.

It would make such a difference to us if we could get your letters a few
days after they are written instead of a few weeks & in some cases a few
months. Last week after waiting a whole month I had two letters from
you & they were so old that it didn't feel like getting new letters at all. It
felt as if I must have read them before. They had taken nearly 3 months
to come! They were written on Dec. 26th 1917 & Jan 3rd 1918 & I got
them somewhere about 20th March!

SSA 13

TO AGNES                                                    30 March 1918

. . . Since I last wrote all sorts of great & tragic events have been happening elsewhere in the war. You will have seen as much about them as
we have read here in the papers. I have nothing to say about it. It is too
big to discuss, even if one might. And as to our own local affairs of
course I must not talk. Heavens, I am sick of censorship restrictions! I
wish I could be with you and talk to you freely. It is hard that the one
thing we must needs think more about than anything else should be the
thing that one may not talk about, & that the things that are the most
absorbing events in our daily life should also be taboo. . . .

*Next Morning.* . . . It is a dark wet cold day, and la soupe is not yet for
an hour, & I have eaten all my chocolate. Have you ever drunk tilleul,
lime-tree tea? The types here drink it before going to bed. It is good
stuff, fragrant & soothing (advt!). We feed here with a sergeant, a corporal & six men, one of whom sits far from us & fires occasional words of
English at us, learnt at school. The sergeant is a fine black-bearded man
who ought to be Nebuchadnezzar the king. He has a royal way with
him. The corporal is a very human dear thing who wears a wedding ring
and (I guess from his talk) fears that his wife is not faithful to him. The
only other fellow who sits at our select little table is a small brisk towns-
man, who eats as if he were trying to catch a train or secure his food
before the harpies could foul it for him, as in the old myth. We are
strangers here, & rather shy & awkward, for these are not our own
people at all. But at the end of our two days we are beginning to settle
down and enter into things a bit—just when we are going. At another
place, where our own people are, we mess with a priest and a chemist
and have most fierce arguments and uproarious jokes; & beyond our
mess we more or less know everyone everywhere & are taken for
granted. Here they are only just beginning to realize that we are supe-

rior beings to the Yanks to whom apparently they have hitherto been
accustomed. . . . For us, who are a little bunch of English people
dumped in the middle of the French, it is strange to feel how little we
know of what our countrymen think of the war and how well we know
what the French think. Conversation is of course almost entirely about
war & peace and food and clothes and women, with now and then a
burst of pre-war agriculture or petit commerce.

SSA 13

Agnes,                                                    6 April 1918

Still no letter from you, but really I have no cause to complain as
things go nowadays. In the age of plentiful mails it was a disaster to miss
one week, but now of course a month or so is quite ordinary. Yesterday I
was talking with a French lad in the artillery, a very elegant lad, who has
a maraine de guerre that writes to him anything from four to eight pages
every other day. I told him that my last letter from you took nine weeks
to come, and he said I had great need of patience. I told him also that
mails are rare, and his eyebrows rose in elegant sympathy. As for him,
he is eagerly awaiting his leave, during which he is to have four days'
private holiday with "her" at some nice quiet little place. Of course the
whole affair is most irregular to English eyes, especially as, I suspect,
the lady in question is already married to someone else! But no one
seems to think the worse of that. They are a queer people the French!
He contents himself by saying that the marriage laws need altering. He
is only a boy, and particularly young and attractive, quite a budding
lady-killer I am sure. And he is so genuinely and openly keen. He can
talk of little else but his maraine. He is a staunch royalist, son of some
Angevin land owner. Our conversation was half English half French,
for he speaks English quite well and is proud of it. The maraine de
guerre idea is a curious one and seems to have in it much that is both
good & bad. It certainly gives the soldier man the keenest of all joys, the
joy of loving and being loved by a woman, and often it may lead to
marriage in the end. But on the other hand there are the funny muddles
like this lad's. Of course he has been horribly spoiled by the maraine,
used to get six parcels a week until the present change in such things.
And he has been horribly spoiled probably by many girls, so it seems
from his manner and his stories, especially one of a petite miss anglaise
who would not take a no—according to our young hero. . . .

Now at last another celandine season, and you & I much older than
we were when last we were together. In this state the clock and the cal-
endar are respectively the most comforting and the most distressing
things, for the former seems to tick off the weary seconds of war time,
working through to peace, but the latter seems to record the swelling age

of our separation, and taunts one with the expanse of days and months and years. And here we are, little specks in these present great military events, altogether negligible beside the great issues, and altogether unaware as to the future.

Egremont
TO OLAF                                                                8 April 1918
. . . I must have grown a little older & wiser, or perhaps it is only that I have lived a little longer & therefore love you still a little more & more. You have written of me—*political* me I mean!—as though I belong all to the enemy's camp, & wonder of wonders! I have not expired on the spot or grown sad with sorrowing or even shed a tear! Perhaps there is more truth in it than there used to be, perhaps in some points—such as conscription for instance—I am more sure myself of belonging to the "enemy"—but honour bright in my own personal views of "political me," I do not belong all to the one or all to the other. My reason, lighted by Daddy's constant forcible reasoning, urges me along one road—the enemy's road—& my instinct lighted by you & my love for you & for your ideals & mine draws me along the other way. *Perhaps* all those other reasons account for my not having despaired—but chiefly this one that I *know* now it doesn't really make a gulf between us. "You have grown too"—you say—"yet somehow I seem to love you better for being in the enemy's camp"—& I reply—"& I surely do love you better now that I know I can plant one foot in each camp & still keep close to you." So we'll only laugh now & we'll put the matter away in our inside pockets & we'll bring it out after the war & talk it all over.

SSA 13
Agnes,                                                                    15 April 1918
    This is undoubtedly the best billet that I have been in since coming out! It is a regular Peter Pan sort of little house. This place is a big camp of dug-outs, but our little wooden house is merely a light and fairy-like structure with a dainty gable roof made of pitched paper. Our accommodation consists of a bed-sitter and a bathroom-pantry! The former is about three metres by six, the latter about three metres by one. In the living room are two ample wooden beds and a stove and a wee table, also two seats. The walls are of grey paper that tries to persuade you it is grey and streaky marble. Our decorations consist of numerous coloured prints, a vase of cowslips and a jar of blackthorn bloom and young birch leaves. And it is all so snug and yet fresh, with one huge *glass* window that opens wide. Outside are the dugouts and lots of trees and budding things of all sorts. We have only just arrived, so we have not made any

A second-line trench in the Argonne, May 1918. From left, a French captain, Olaf Stapledon, a Moroccan lieutenant, the French lieutenant who engineered the trench, two other officers.

discoveries save that eggs can be bought at the co-op. I don't know why we have come in for all this luxury. The commandant of the place is reputed to have said, "We are going to treat them like officers because they are English." Certainly that is how we are being treated, and certainly we don't deserve it. . . .

Doc and I are looking forward to two days' peaceful reading and writing, far from the madding crowd, and disturbed only by the noise of allied guns. . . . The Doc is the most diffident apologetic polite person I have ever met. He is a dear, but so polite that it gets on my nerves a bit sometimes. He is generous. He would far sooner himself suffered much than his companion were to be slightly uncomfortable. Consequently one must always keep one's eye on him, lest he do some ludicrous thing. He is a dear, so quiet yet merry in his way, such a model of hard-working zeal, and so studious in his leisure. He is a budding professor of tongues. He is tall, rather slight, dark in hair & eyes, fair of complexion, and wears ever a kindly-innocent expression, chiefly in his wide eyes behind his studious glasses. He is our pianist, great player of the Waldstein, you know. I am lucky in having him for a mate here. Yet I never feel quite at ease with him because I always feel on my best behaviour, and I never get down to the real Doc through his politeness. We will try this time anyhow.

[*Agnes fantasizes about taking Olaf on an Australian picnic at a Pacific beach and wonders what a flesh-and-blood meeting will be like.*]

Egremont
TO OLAF                                                                21 April 1918
. . . There is only a strip of yellow sand between the lagoon & the sea & it looks like a gold bar on a field of blue, for you have to come to the beginning of the reef itself. Shall we have our lunch here among the sand hills—or shall we go out to the end first? It depends whether we feel hungry. Do you? "Yes, starving." So let's boil the billy for tea & spread our little feast here in the shade. I wonder what we shall talk about. I shall never be able to believe it is really you—*you*! Olaf of the letters. Olaf of the waiting—my Olaf—my lover! Will your eyes be always watching me? & when they have looked at all the beautiful hills & trees & the sea & the sky will they come back & rest on me? Oh I shall be happy, but I shall be afraid too of what those eyes will see in me. They will expect to find more than is there, & they may find, too, ugly things which they did not expect—but I shall not try & hide, & I shall not be really afraid because I know they will love me in spite of everything. I have been told I *stare* even at ordinary people I am interested in. What will be *your* fate? I promise not to "stare"—I shall just open my eyes very wide & take you all into my heart. Oh my dear, my darling! Just think of it! And after lunch we'll lie & laze in the sun—perhaps we'll read a book—I'll read & you can smoke your old pipe (do you smoke nowadays?) or perhaps we'll just talk or just lie & then we'll hide our belongings in the bushes & set off up the springy grass headland towards the sea.

SSA 13
Agnes,                                                                     22 April 1918
    Will this war go on forever? Shall I always be packing up my *two* haversacks for two days at an outstation? Shall I always be floundering in the French language, or cleaning my car, or washing my boots? Just now it is after dinner at an outstation. A French doctor is expounding a

new game of patience to a French priest and two English lads. At this
place we are positively priest-ridden. No less than three of them feed
with us, quite decent & really very interesting fellows, but just a bit
clerical. . . . What else is there to talk about in this poor age? Are you
more interested to know that SSA 13 has been cited? This I believe is
true, though I have not heard it officially yet. It is a good citation too,
and will give us a pretty bad swelled head. I will tell you details later.
The poor lazy artist man will have the labour of painting little croix de
guerre on every car. Won't he hate it!

[*Giuseppe Mazzini, the nineteenth-century Italian revolutionary, had
been one of Olaf's heroes since his teen-aged years when excerpts from
Mazzini's works were regularly read at his boarding school, Abbots-
holme.*]

SSA 13
TO AGNES                                                29 April 1918
. . . Another interesting person is a certain priest who is now a stretcher
bearer. He is a well-built man with clear-cut features and a little military
moustache, and kind eyes. His manner is very gentle, and just a bit
priestly-oily, but one has to put up with that. He cottoned on to me and
said, "You pronounce French with less accent than anyone I have heard
in your convoy—but with some accent, quand même. Will you come
and practice French reading with me? I should like to help." So off we
went and squatted on a bench at the mouth of his dugout and he
produced a book by Lamennais, whom I knew solely as the great pre-
cursor of Mazzini. I told him this, and a strange dark flash of dread
passed over his face, a kind of narrowing of his whole aspect. "Who is
this Mazzini?" said he. I told him, very briefly. He made no comment.
We then read passages from Lamennais for my pronunciation, & he
helped a lot, but soon we fell to discussing the subject matter. Lamennais, as you probably know, was a pre-Revolutionary philosopher and
religio. He was a pillar of the church who got into disgrace for his daring
teaching, but was subsequently reinstated. I gather that the Mazzinian
part of him was disapproved by the Church. Anyhow, what I read of his
is all most broad and sound. But this book that my friend had was of
philosophy vitiated by religious dogma. And so we did gentle battle together, the Priest & I, in the orchards and the ruins of France. And he
greatly surprised me by having read much modern philosophy (far more
than I) even to Bergson and William James. I propounded my own pet
views laboriously & most crudely in French (you've no idea how bad my
French still remains) and he listened eagerly, bowed forward, staring at

the grass. "Where did you get those ideas?" I shrugged my shoulders in the best French style. We continued arguing and arguing, and at last he said these strange words which must be put in French, censor or no censor: "Pour moi l'homme est foncierement mauvais. Et quand même je suis optimiste." Strange paradox! He explained that "pour lui" the solution was simply that God, the great power *apart* from the world, would save man against man's will, man's evil will. And he enlarged upon the vileness of men today, their jealousy of all who are a bit better off than themselves, their lustfulness, falsehood, and uncharitableness. Then I took the offensive and made him agree that "quand même il y a, depuis le début de la guerre, beaucoup plus de générosité, d'amour entre les hommes qui se trouvent dans les mêmes circonstances." And I insisted that Man in spite of all his vileness is the highest that we know of God, that the world is all trying to be alive, & that its point of success is just man, and that in some way God *needs* man no less than man needs God. And so on. That night, Sunday night, I went to our little Quaker meeting and *for once* I spoke, telling the priest's strange view and then my own. . . .

My dear, you ask am I a socialist? If a socialist is one who holds that the whole wealth of the community belongs absolutely to no individuals but to the community for the glory of the Human Spirit, I am a socialist. If socialism is a practical principle of politics I am far more socialist than individualist, *far*. But naturally the practices of socialism & of individualism are neither of them the single principle that is needed. We want a judicious mixture of each in its right place. But that Wm. Morris was a man who "went wrong" & became a socialist—! Heaven preserve us! He went wrong in that he ran socialism as a *practice* rather to death, perhaps. But he is one of the greatest inspirers of all that is best in England today, all the gentlest, most spiritual side of the Labour Movement, all the newborn love of real beauty as opposed to gaudy sham beauty. He went wrong in believing that human nature could be more quickly beautified than is alas the case. He was by nature an artist, a craftsman, and he turned to politics because he thought it his duty, just as Mazzini turned from literature to politics. And he did not make an immediate success of it.—But he is becoming one of the prophets of the new England (& World) that we all hope to see, or to enable our descendants to see. I don't say I am a socialist in the Australian sense of the word, for that I think is a narrow & materialistic sense. But in the true sense indeed I am, in that I believe that mankind must adopt a very great amount of practical socialism very soon or fall into a worse decay than has ever before been. I want to talk to you, dear. I wish you could talk to my father about these things. He is very moderate & cautious compared with me, but he is altogether on the right side in the matter,

—in the class war, for class war alas there is. Neither class is an end. Society is the end. But the rich class has made itself an end, & now the other must fight for itself because for the time that cause is the cause of Society. Of Society? Of Mankind, of God. But here we are again wallowing in wool, simply because letters have to be so condensed.

Egremont
TO OLAF                                                          12 May 1918
. . . I have just finished writing to Jack, a *very* nice letter to make up for all the mails I haven't written & all the letters & cards I have left unacknowledged. Poor old chap, he is wiser now. He has bucked up in health & spirits generally, owing to his stay in England on home service. I think his nerves were all to pieces before & that must account for everything. His last letter to me was just like his old self for fun & Jackobean style. I'll give you a sample. He tells how with much fuss & red tape he managed to get 8 horses to pull his ploughs (his job is "O.C. Spuds") & then realised that no amount of red tape could get enough food for them. "Finding feed almost impossible, I requisitioned through 'Ordinance' for a copy of 'Key to the Scriptures' by one Mary Baker etc. Eddy, but was disgusted & surprised when acquainted of the fact in writing that the *British Army* had never heard of it. Can you my Dear 'Fair Friend' ever expect us to win the war? However I procured a copy by transmitting some of my own hard earned 'dough' to Boston, & this priceless book securely nailed to the stable wall has deluded my horses not to *mind* what *matter* really is, & all goes well."

Old Mrs. Armstrong is a most ardent Christian Scientist & all this fun was of course directed at her. I read her the letter & she chuckled away till the tears ran down her face & she said, "Dear old Jack, he's always teasing me about Science. It's very naughty of him, I know, but he only does it for fun." Everything "dear old Jack" does is right!

[*Olaf celebrated his birthday on 10 May.*]

SSA 13
TO AGNES                                                          13 May 1918
. . . It is truly terrible to be thirty-two. I can't get over it. The only comfort is that on the whole I like myself better at 32 than at 22, which is at least a hopeful way of looking at things. But time flies so. One can't keep pace with it, can't live up to one's own great age. May next May see us two together at last. How calm and colourless it seems to say that, and what a lot it really means.

TO AGNES                                                                                 18 May 1918

. . . Today there is a trial going on, a court martial. Two men had a quarrel while drunk. One ripped the other open with a knife, with the inevitable consequence that his in'ards came out. It happened to be my job to carry the wounded man to hospital. I had to go very slowly to try and avoid dislodging too much of his machinery; and he could not be kept on his back by the orderly, because somehow on his side he was more comfortable, though it was so bad for him. I fear he had not long to live when I left him. Why do I tell you these things? Some people would rather die than write that sort of thing to a refined girl. But my dear, to know things like that cannot spoil any true refinement. And you are not a child. And it is good to know the truth; and such an item is only a tiny bit of the whole truth about war. I think you would rather not be told such things, but lo! I tell you all the same.

*Next Day.* . . . Here am I seated in the old Sunbeam in a cool breeze. They are busy painting the croix de guerre on her at present, and preparing little plates bearing the same cross for all the other cars. Some people think it is very wrong for a Friends' section to sport a cross of war. Maybe it is, but after all it must be quite obvious what kind of work an ambulance convoy got its medal for; and anyhow it would be a slight on the French if we did not put it up. A few days ago Thomas [Anderson] wrote an essay on "The Spiritual Significance of SSA 13." I suggested the subject. He said that we were "serving an apprenticeship to peace," for we were discovering that to serve without the stimulus of excitement and danger was spiritually harder (because of its drudgery) than more thrilling service; and after the war all service, he said, will be of that kind. But I think he did not allow enough drudgery to the soldier. In fact obviously he did not. I reckoned that we were learning chiefly to enter into the attitude of mind of all sorts of people and to sympathise with their ideals. Amongst ourselves there are such different sorts to begin with, and then we meet so many sorts of people. Moreover our queer position helps us to understand the various attitudes of soldier men, while yet we are sufficiently detached to make an unbiased judgment; and our other connections help us to sympathise deeply with imprisoned C.O. Yes, I think if we fail to learn to sympathise deeply with all sorts of people while yet keeping our minds "detached" we must be ashamed of ourselves, for the opportunities are quite exceptionally good. Another thing that we learn perhaps even more than the soldier is an almost inexpressible thing—the supremacy of the beauty of nature over the horror of war. It is easy to say that while you are comfortably aloof from the said horror, but nonetheless it is the true view, I hold. In the midst of the horror a man is apt to be overwhelmed by it. Those in our strange position can realise it without losing sight of the infinitely greater beauty of the world as a whole. Woe to us if we fail to realise the horror or the beauty. I believe that the great need after the war will be for these very two qualities—detached sympathy and a faith in beauty and goodness that is strong enough to afford to realise evil.

[*Antoinette Trebelli, daughter of the famed nineteenth-century French mezzo-soprano Zelia Trebelli, took the stage name of Antonia Dolores. She did not enjoy the operatic success of her mother, but her reputation as an "artistic" singer filled concert halls when she went on tour.*]

Egremont
TO OLAF                                              21 May 1918
. . . Last Saturday week it was the German Circle. At our last few summer meetings we have gone into the Botanical Gardens to read instead of in Fraulein Hasselman's room in town. But it was very disturbing in the gardens for we dare not be overheard talking in the hated German tongue & there were crowds of people all about, so we only attempted silly light comedies & we had altogether rather a skittish time with affected coughings & nudgings to warn each other of the approach of an enemy! It *was* silly. . . . When the meeting was over about 5.30 Ethel & Margaret & I invited ourselves to tea in Frl H's room. It was really like going back to our student days in Germany. Ethel [Liggins] & Frl H set the table & Margaret & I climbed down three flights of stairs & went out into the town to buy provisions. There are very few shops open on Saturday night, but we struck the right place—a veritable little Delikatessen-geschäft, but it was kept by a jolly little Italian man. Being Saturday night he was not supposed to sell tinned stuff & it was very amusing to see the way he kept the letter of the law & dodged the spirit. He was behind his counter all the time cutting cold meats & things. The customers crowded in asking for tins of oysters & tins of jam & things. He directed them where to find things on various shelves but he would have nothing further to do with them, nor would he take the money. He said they could bring it in on Monday! & all the time he was laughing away to himself as he cut his cold meats. We would have been annoyed at him, but he was such a merry little fellow. We were quite lawful customers ourselves. We bought only Schincken (ham) & Wurst (sausage)—a truly German repast. What helped very much to renew the feelings of our old German tea parties was that we were all in a state of excited anticipation about Dolores' concert. Have you ever heard her?

We persuaded Frl Hasselman to come with us when we had finished our jolly little German meal—Thee und "Cakes," Schincken, Wurst, Käse, Butterbrod und Banannas—& washed up in a very primitive style. We set forth all four of us in single file down the three flights of stairs through the dark still building. I led the way & lighted the procession with a half inch of candle that dripped all over my fingers. Out in the lighted streets we trotted along & I made poor old Ethel puff as I used [in Berlin] when I walked her from Fridenau to Wilmersdorf. All the world was *pouring up* the steps of the Town Hall, for although it was her fourth recital that week Mademoiselle Antonia Dolores is a name that rings irresistibly & draws people from far & wide. We were joined on the steps by Rosie & Marie Daniel & our little sextet bought its tickets & managed to squeeze through the crowd safely & establish itself in the back row & thereabouts. It was chock full & everyone was so excited. Fancy one woman's voice being able to produce flutters in so many thousand breasts! She came & bowed to right & left—a quaint little old fashioned figure. I thought she had stepped out of an old photograph. A frightfully conventionally corseted little figure in a tight cream high-necked, long-sleeved frock & with a wonderful train that had to be kicked round & made to behave before she proceeded to walk backwards or forwards.

She sang & I was disappointed. It was a very ordinary Ave Maria—the composer accompanied her. I really *was* disappointed but I would not admit it even to myself, & I was glad afterwards, for she so far outstepped my expectations that it would have been treason to condemn her for the singing of one Ave which did not suit her voice. Oh it was a revelation to hear her afterwards. I had the glorious feeling dancing inside me of "Art for Art's sake"—& somehow unaccountably of "Truth for Truth's sake." Have you heard that voice? I mean Dolores'? Such a wonderful voice—so many moods it has, now solemn & stately, as befits an old master, now elegant & smiling like an old gavotte, now plaintive & tragic as in the "Chanson russe" of today, now altogether irresistible & wicked in a teasing little English song with a French refrain, now peacefully content in—what song think you? Florian's song!

> C'est mon ami
> Rendez-le moi
> J'ai son amour
> Il a ma foi

& now most thrilling of all to me she sang from dear Handel's Samson

> Let the bright Seraphim in burning row
> Their loud uplifted angel-trumpets blow.

And her voice sounded for all the world like an angel-trumpet. Never has a trumpet of brass been so stirring to me. She must be at least a middle-aged woman, between forty & fifty, & as she stood there in front of the big company erect, her head thrown back, her arms by her side, she seemed to forget all about her train & her funny dress & her silly little fan. She was a beautiful, live, clean-limbed youth, one of the bright seraphim in burning row. If only I had had you there with me. How we should have thrilled together over that.

SSA 13

TO AGNES                                                      25 May 1918

. . . Last night, when it was about breakfast time on the 25th in your part of the world, I was sitting in my car writing, so I stopped to wish you many happy returns of the day, and I brought out my much-prized lock of your hair and tried to imagine that it was indeed you. God bless you oh Agnes of my heart, and may I be with you for your next birthday. Time flies. Keep young in body and mind. We shall have our spring time together yet.

Today I went for a lone walk in search of birds and beasts and flowers. I had small success, but it was a lovely walk, and the crowning excitement was in a certain wood that rang with bird song of all sorts; for here I heard often repeated two exceptionally full mellow notes, and I guessed the bird must be a golden oriole. I stalked it step by step through the jungle with my glass ready as if it were a gun. There were evidently other birds of the same kind, and they kept answering one another; but also there was a striking and often repeated melody of six notes, & the voice seemed to be the same as the others. So human and musical was this phrase that I thought at first it must be a man whistling. But the sound was too rich for any man's lips. It came again and again with slight variations. It rang through the wood drowning everything. And it was a phrase that might very well have come out of Beethoven's mind, so I thought. I stalked it very carefully, drew nearer & nearer step by step with long pauses, while the mosquitoes fairly guzzled on my arms and legs. At last I narrowed the search to one bush under a big tree. And now the sound was strong like some big flute thing. There was a sudden flutter, & away went the singer, & I only caught a glimpse of him through the leaves. Again I stalked and again three times, but with no luck. At last I was right through the wood in a little marsh, and here the mosquitoes attacked me in a cloud and I ignominiously retreated, & made my way home to dinner. But I must go to that wood again. It was the most highly developed bird music I have ever heard. It can't have been an oriole, and it was too loud and triumphant for any nightingale. Besides it was a big bird that I saw through the leaves. And its song was too full even for a blackbird. I can't express the glamour of it. The wood was like a haunted fairy wood. I am covered with mosquito bites, but what of that!

. . . Did I tell you before that I was to have this little holiday weekend at Newport? I am here, & not only here, but alas almost on my way home to civilization. We came on Saturday morning & this is Monday afternoon & tomorrow banks open & clubs open & schools open & work begins again for everybody. We're going to get our tea here & catch the last motor bus about 7.15 & we'll all be home tonight about 10 o'clock. We are four girls. Glad Armstrong is the cornerstone. I am her friend & the other two girls are her friends but I did not know them before. . . . The other two girls are Miss Maxwell & Miss Tange, but let us call them Sheila & Thelma respect*fully*, for short. Sheila Maxwell is Glad's latest "flame." Glad always has someone whom she is frightfully enthusiastic over. In fact her 'flames' are always so fierce that people live in expectation of an explosion & bust up. Nothing has happened so far on this occasion & I am also tempted to join in the fire worship of Sheila, for she is a most attractive & wonderful person. . . . She is a curious mixture, this young woman, of icy Scotch reserve & decorum, & most advanced & enlightened 'feminism.' Is there such a word? She belongs to the Feminist Club & is thoroughly interested in its movements & W.E.A. & in garden suburbs & improved housing etc. etc. In her profession she is a teacher of physical training & a masseuse etc. She was trained at the L'pool Gym, but I imagine a good many years before Dot. She has been the director of a big physical culture school in Vienna, I believe, & only left there because of the war. So although her father was a Tasmanian she has only been a real Australian for the last two or three years, & it is really wonderful the way she has found her niche. She is a beautiful girl to look at & she has a most fascinating way of talking & thinking. I can't think why she has not married long ago. Men are awfully slow to find the really splendid girls. But, my word, he would have to be an exceptional person who could understand & respond to— & love & win the love of such a one as Sheila Maxwell. One half is such a fine half that it is rare to find another half that would perfectly complete the whole. She is so strong & active it was like having a man in the party. You should have seen the way she went about getting firewood & breaking it & lighting fires & hanging the meat safe in a shady spot etc. etc. In some little sets of girls I am the one who does all those jobs, but in this set Sheila was so much more energetic & efficient that I retired into the ranks of onlookers. She has a bright clear complexion & she objects to powder! She wears thick walking shoes with flat heels. She doesn't wear stays—& neither do I—& she likes loose pinafore dresses without a waistbelt. She has original & artistic ideas about dress. I like that. She does exercises in very few clothes on cold winter mornings & altogether she seems brimming over with health & fitness &

cleanly wholesomeness. She makes you feel that it is your own fault if you get ill—you have been careless or not looked after yourself properly. . . .

I was feeling very young and inexperienced beside all these young women of the world. I think Thelma is only my age, but she seems older. She works in a bank & she has a flat with another girl & altogether she is more independent. Glad is about 16 months older than me, & no one knows how old Sheila is! But we think over 30. Girls who earn their own living have a great pull over girls like me who just potter round & do odd jobs,—& rightly so too. I have wild desires to be among them sometimes. Of course I really have the pull over them, because I have you, & none of them are engaged, but somehow you are too good a thing to brag about. I keep you *mostly* to myself, & wonder why I am engaged when there are girls like Sheila & Thelma to be had.

SSA 13
TO AGNES                                                          8 June 1918
. . . Last night, oh my own, I was made to read aloud to the artist [Eric Robertson] some of my literary effort. He sat in the corner with his hand over his eyes and "looked intense" (as he is always saying of other people) and I sat facing the darkling view and read for a good while. And sometimes we stopped & discussed, and sometimes he gave some valuable ideas and sometimes he just didn't understand and sometimes we simply agreed to differ. So slid the evening into the night. Then we went to bed and became confidential, and I told him much about you and me. And whereas the night before I had confidently declared that during the last year I had been happier than ever before, last night I found myself wallowing in the slimiest smotherest misery and despair and pessimism about the affairs of two lovers, Agnes & Olaf. He said, "If the war goes on you simply must get married before it stops. If she is twenty-four and you are thirty-two you must not wait any longer, for her sake specially." But what is to be done? First, it would be so wretched for you to come to England, leaving your own life behind in exchange for a husband for ten days every six months. That is what sticks in my throat most. And then anyhow women may not travel; and even if they might there is the risk. There seems only one solution, as we decided last night—that I should get just conveniently put out of action for all war purposes, go out to you & get married. But that does not happen. It *may*. But then one might get put out of action tout à fait, which would not serve the purpose. And yet sometimes one feels that even that would be better for both of us than this sort of life in death. . . . Time slips along from day to day and the months are like days and the years like months. The artist can't imagine how we can still love one another not

having seen one another for so long, but I assure him that waning love is not the problem. The problem is rather the reverse; it is—how to jog along contentedly with these sad circumstances, and how to attain the urgent urgent urgent practical necessity of getting married soon.

SSA 13
TO AGNES                                                            14 June 1918

. . . I am worrying horribly about our not being married. It's silly to worry, but then—how can one help. I have come into your life and muddled it, pacifist-cousin-antipodean-lover that I am. I have been trying to think how to straighten things out, but there seems nothing to do but to wait and wait. But I want to say something difficult to say. Our engagement goes on all this while simply because we go on all this while being in love, doesn't it? Supposing some day you were to feel "I don't love this shadowy cousin any more," the engagement would cease, and you would be free. I don't feel that I could ever cease to be in love with you. . . . But then, you have been in the past a bigger influence in my life than I in yours. If ever you should change (I cannot help praying that you never will) be altogether frank about it; that is all. I could not love you less for it, but you would be free. Don't say, as some girls would I suppose, that it is a kind of insult to talk of your changing. No human being really knows what they will be in the future. But, dear, don't think me cold and cheerless and unromantic. It is not being cold, but reasonable. I love you better now than ever because of time, & because after all in some ways I know you better now than ever. . . .

*Next Day.* This morning our mechanics got up at three o'clock to do some forging before the heat of the day. Three of them bed near my indoor bed. I heard them all getting up, & I turned over in blissful sleepiness. Presently from my window sill pillow I heard the old forge a-blowing—whirr, whirr, whirr; and after a while began a mighty blacksmith harmony upon the red iron. Sometimes one slept through it, sometimes one listened to it, sometimes it was wound into one's dreams. When I went out to wash they were still at it, taking great sweeping blows on the iron, one after the other, and as the hammers were of different sizes there was quite a chime, like the Harmonious Blacksmith, in fact. "They" are Bill Wetherall, the sergeant mechanic, once in the War Vic[tim]s, and once a marine engineer, Theo Burtt, a Unit-made mechanic, & various others of the same kind. Wetherall has his workshop car in wonderful & marvelous condition. All the tools are polished till they dazzle, and the whole car is one mass of gadgets of all sorts very perfectly made out of old shell cases etc. The department spend more time gadgetising for their car than in repairing other cars (owing to the efficiency of the drivers, who don't smash their cars!). Wetherall keeps his minions at it from eight in the morning till half past five in the afternoon, with intervals for meals. I would not be in the workshop for worlds. I like to arrange my own time, thank you, & not to find work when there really is no work to do.

And now please I want another letter from you. One is scarcely due yet, but I want one. Reading old letters is all very well, but I want a *new* one. I want to know the latest of you. How do I know what may have happened since the last? You may have become Queen of Australia for all I know. You may at this moment be performing your coronation ceremony on the summit of Mount Kosciusko, attended by young men & maidens black & white, and admired by the heads of all the tribes of the Kangaroos. If so—forget me not in that sublime moment. . . .

Years go slipping past so easily. I don't complain any more that time *drags* in your absence. I complain rather that the months pile themselves up so quickly into years. Time flies. I should like us to be twenty and twenty-eight at the end of the war! But it's no use crying over spilt milk nor spilt time. Look, I don't know what relation human love bears to the rest of existence; I only guess. But this I *know*, that I love you well; & that if that is not an event bound up with the foundations of the universe, so much the worse for the universe.——In the distance a funeral band is playing "Lead Kindly Light," slowly, faintly, in a drizzling rain. One more little wooden cross will appear by the little church. They are continually annexing new ground for the cemetery.

Good-bye oh Agnes, my darling. This is a letter in the blues.

[*Occasionally Olaf and Agnes wrote retrospectively, calling up memories from years long past in order to fill the emotional void created by their separation and painstakingly reinterpreting past experiences in the light of present feelings and fantasies. This letter can be compared to Agnes's note of 12 October 1914.*]

Egremont
Olaf,                                                        15 June 1918
Where shall I begin? What shall I say that is different from all the other many letters I have written to you!——Oh there is nothing new to say, but, Dear, I am wanting you so very much. I don't get used to doing without you. . . . When I stayed with you at Annery before I came home you spoilt me. You did things for me. You were always near when I wanted you. I never had to do my share of anything. I let you think for me. You loved me & you would have done anything for me. I knew you would & I counted on your love—without giving you anything in return. . . . It was all so nice (for me) that I thought it was the natural way

Portrait in pastels of Agnes Miller by Eric Robertson. (*Photograph courtesy of Harvey J. Satty*)

of things & I took it all for granted. When the "Aeneas" had steamed out of the Mersey & left Liverpool behind, Dot & I came down from the deck & went into our cabin—two woebegone young women among a strange ship's company, & Oh it was lonely! I felt forlorn as a little dog that can't find its master. I knew then all in a flash how it had been—I realised how much you loved me & I realised what that love had meant to me & it was too late to tell you—even if I had dared. I told something of it to Dot & she tried to comfort me & herself too—dear Dot. Then we curled ourselves up together on the settee & wrote little notes to people to send off by the pilot at Holyhead. I wrote you a little note & I forget altogether what I said. If it was not a love-letter it was because I was still afraid it might not be "the real me" who was writing it, because I felt I might change with some other person afterwards & then I should have hurt you dreadfully. When I wrote that little note I know I loved you more than I had ever done before. And now after all this long time & after all these changes & happenings, I come back again to that same desperately forlorn feeling I had an hour after I had lost you—(shall we say "found" you?). I need you all the time, but it is at these special times that I *know* how much I need you—& then oh my dear!——

Today I saw a girl with such a sweet beautiful face—she was in mourning & I know she must have a heavy sad heart, for her fiancé was killed in Palestine only a few months ago, & yet she was smiling & she was doing her bit as bravely as any soldier. She was helping at a garden fête. They had been engaged for four years & now he is killed. I could not help thinking of you & me.

SSA 13
TO AGNES                                              23 June 1918
. . . [Eric] Robertson's picture of you is done. He began it this morning, & now it is done. He has taken a subtle revenge on me for many evil deeds of mine, for this picture is sometimes so like you that I can't for the life of me keep my eyes off it. It is large, almost life size, taken from Cecil [Kirkus's] enlargement of your photo, but added to from my minute description and many other photos of you. I stood over him and kept correcting him discontentedly until all of a sudden it began to be you. It is not *quite* you now. It is not quite so gentle and gay, not quite so alive, but oh it is lovely, though less lovely than you. My dear, to look at it makes me catch my breath and want to cry or weep. There's some mysterious spirit about you, even about a picture of you, that bowls me over utterly in an instant. This picture, under a piece of glass stolen from a window that still had just one pane in it, is the centre of interest in the convoy now. Lots of people have already come in to my car to look at it and discuss the whole subject. . . .

*Later, same night,* before going to bed à la belle étoile. I am in my car alone. It is late but I must add a word. Harry [Locke] has been talking to me about you. I went round to his car with my new picture of you and asked him what he would do under these circumstances. He says I must be patient, must never ask you to take risks of travel even if you *could* be got a permit. . . . I said to Harry, "What can I *do?*" He said, "You can't do anything. You can only be patient & have faith." But that is not enough. It is a sin lamely to accept the situation. He said, "The only thing to *do* is to get your leg blown off, and you can't do that." Such a thing would hamper one fearfully, but it would not make one helpless. He said, "Oh Stap you're a lucky fellow." I know I am, but oh it's cruel good luck. And it is the two of us that suffer. That's the sting. Robertson said, laughing, while he drew you, "I can see by her mouth she must be able to see the priceless humour of being engaged to a thing like you." For heaven's sake see the humour, & then you will not someday see tragedy in it instead. . . .

*Next Day,* late at night. I cannot find my pen, but my heart is full of you, and so I must write [in pencil] a little. This evening as I was writing other things in my car Robertson & Goodall & Sparrow came in to— talk to me?—no, to look at your picture. Do you mind people falling in love with your picture? It is good for them. I do not know if this picture is really like your face, for I have not seen you for years; but I know it is like your spirit, for I have that in letters. . . . The Agnes of the letters has outgrown the Agnes that I first loved, & I have not enough out-grown myself. My mind has grown in scope & grasp, but I—alas! What can I do for you, oh my Star? I never can do anything for you. I am more unworthy than you think. But if ever a man loved I love you. . . . Love me. I burn for you. I long to hold you in my arms. And yet I am afraid. You are too lovely a thing for me.

Your awakened lover,
Olaf Stapledon

SSA 13

TO AGNES                                               30 June 1918

. . . We seem to be kept fairly busy just now, what with rather more work and rather fewer people to do it at the moment. But we still man-age a glorious bathe now and then, followed by a walk across country and a cherry-hunt. Cherries are scarce this year, but the other day three of us stripped a tree, and one of us fell out of said tree with a dramatic crashing of branches followed by a sickening thud, much to the amuse-ment of the other two. But it was a shame to break the tree. The swim had been a good one. We swam down stream over masses of tangled water-crowfoot that stroked one's body and sometimes lovingly tried to pull one under by the arms or feet, a queer and thrilling feeling. What else is there to tell of? One of my knees is the shape of a deformed vegetable marrow owing to mosquito bites. Our lettuces are coming on; our radishes nearly over. Alas what poor things to talk of during a world war.

The other day I sat on a hill with my field glass watching events. Shells suddenly began to sing over head and burst on the opposite hill where a few little blue figures were wandering. They scurried and crouched and ran, and one of them by bad luck chose the direction in which the next shells were to come. I watched him jump into a trench and bob along till he disappeared. Just then a shell burst ten yards ahead of where he had just been, and right on the trench. The smoke cleared, but I could see nothing. Evidently he got through all right or I should have been called to carry him off in a car. Meanwhile I myself was sitting in a perfect natural armchair of chalk and grass, surrounded by great scarlet clumps of poppy, blue borage, and yellow mustard; and below me the eternal orioles were singing unperturbed.

Egremont
TO OLAF                                                          2 July 1918
. . . I have had a long letter from Dot this afternoon, such a bonny letter, full of interest. I wrote her a long one & demanded a reply in kind. She is to be married on August 14. When you get this letter she will be already Mrs. Bert Wheeler & she will be so very happy, I'm sure. Dear Dee! Her chief anxiety about me is that I shall go building castles in the air about you & what you are like. I remember she wrote to you on the same subject before she left England. She seems to have a perfect horror of one's getting magnified impressions & being afterwards disappointed. It *must* be a blow, certainly. She says, "Even in one year one forgets heaps of things about a person, & then when one sees that person again one searches eagerly for the ideal things, & all the little irritating things one had forgotten come & rub themselves up against one & one begins to wonder where the old person is that one used to know & love. *Of course he is there all the time*, but it takes ages to get beyond one's dreams to reality & it is a very painful & very disturbing process." She adds in an outburst of honest Dorotheanism—"When I came home I went through a hateful time. It is just over now." I wonder if it is not possible for people to be parted without going through that reactionary process when they meet again? One could understand it in thoughtless people, but it is rather horrible that it should have disturbed so sanguine & thinking a mind as Dot's & specially when she was preparing herself beforehand for what might be. How will things go with us, dear? Dot & her man were parted only 1 year. You & I shall have been more

than four years apart. It will be horrible if we have to waste our first few weeks together in being disappointed. . . . So do—for the sake of our first few weeks—bring me down from my pedestal, however humble an one it may be. First you will see me with your eyes—think of me from now till then as other people see me. Don't think of what you have imagined—it is all wrong, truly it is. If I had the eyes & the nose & the mouth & the chin that *you* believe me to have, & the hair & the colour & the complexion & what else not! you wouldn't like me at all. . . . Next you will hear me speak, & probably I shall say just what every other ordinary girl would say—nothing to know me by that I am Agnes. If I only said ordinary things, it might be alright, but sometimes I shall say extraordinarily stupid mistaken things that you will be surprised at—& grieved too—if you don't get it firmly into your head first that I am only an everyday human girl, & then there will be "those irritating little ways" that Dot writes of so feelingly. And all these things are only on the outside & don't matter! & there are still all those other things to learn of that do matter! Somehow I am not so much afraid of those things although they are much more important. We are not so likely to go wrong over them.

SSA 13

Agnes, 6 July 1918

Just a line in case there is no chance of more this week. Our existence here is one of the queerest possible—midnight alarums & excursions, mid-day glorious bathes or very dusty running. It is quite theatrical, & the reality of war is nowhere. Were I to tell you about it all you would be vastly amused, but I can't. We are vastly amused during the day, but the shades of night put us into a vein of petty tragedy. . . . I am carrying about in my pocket (as being on the whole the safest place) the much bescribbled manuscript of the world's greatest and still unpublished flight of imagination, namely my book! If I keep it in my car the car will get blown to bits and burnt, like Harry's. If I leave it with our own embusqués they will get blown to bits. If I bury it the earth itself will be blasted. So I carry it, and shall be blown to bits *with* it. Quod erat faciendum. Poor old manuscript! It could not be read by anyone but me anyhow, in its so bescribbled-over condition. And if it could, it is so unfinished as to be useless till there is a real chance of working at it. Of course you understand, dear, that all this talk about blowing to bits is a "blague," because it is utter peace here; otherwise I should probably not be joking on that subject. But heaven help the infantry man in such battles as have been during this year. Words fail. But one's mind is full of the tragedy of the foot-soldier-man. The worst that happens to us is child's play for him.

[*At midnight on 14 July the "Kaiser Battle" began, the last major initiative before the German collapse. Although the ambulances of SSA 13 near Maffrécourt were kept very busy in the succeeding days, the heaviest casualties were to their east, at the Marne.*]

SSA 13

TO AGNES                                                          14 July 1918

. . . Now I am going to tell you my latest kit arrangements, because they are a wonder of organisation; moreover they have occupied my brain so much that I can't think of much else at present. Well, to begin with, under the front seat is a valise containing sundry winter clothes, my second tunic & breeches & a few odds & ends that are seldom wanted. Under the same seat is a small packing case full of books, sundries, spare grub, two little bags of socks & shirts & hankies, and my woolly waistcoat made by you (and worn at night even in summertime). Beside said packing case are boot cleaning things and my poor old decayed trench boots. Next, inside the "passenger accommodation" of the car there is a wee little cupboard or box containing maps, documents, writing materials, a box for spare chocolate (always empty), The Oxford Book of English Verse, cigarettes, spare matches, a little leather case full of photos, mostly of you, and nicely fitted into the side of the cupboard & easily accessible, the portrait of you, done by Robertson. . . . Among my car-rugs there are two boards folded together in a strap, and these are my bed. But also wrapped up in a groundsheet and strapped into the spare wheel is my sleeping bag—for times of peace that are for the present vanished. Next an old haversack containing eating apparatus, half a loaf, two ration biscuits, tobacco & cigarettes, sewing apparatus. Last my good haversacks containing my valuables & vital necessities— field glass, electric lamp, shaving things, & personal first aid packet, also passport, Keats his poems, & a wonderful pocket tool gadget. This haversack is the most precious item. It lives on the front seat, and serves as a pillow when I have to sleep there, and can be whipped away with me at a moment's notice if necessary. It and my helmet and business- gas-mask are constant companions. The other haversack lives in a corner inside. That is the lot, save for a wee tin basin, soap, brush, sponge & towel that are kept in a tool box. And in my tunic pockets, on one side a pocket book with some of your photos and letters & on the other a magnum opus. And in another pocket more of your photos and my lock of your hair. Altogether rather an extensive kit, but what matter since it all stows away efficiently? And anyhow that is absolutely the lot, not a speck of it is kept otherwhere than on the bus. . . .

*17th July 1918.* If you will look up the day before yesterday in the history of the war you will see why I tell you that we are not having one tenth as terrible a dose of war where I am now as we might have ex-pected. Anyhow this letter must stop. Things are not very conducive to letter writing, not that we are fearfully busy, by any means, but the mind wanders. Heaven have mercy on the souls of those who invented modern war!

[*When Olaf adapted the incident of the man in the ditch for the war section of his 1932 novel,* Last Men in London, *he described it as "the nadir of existence" for the semiautobiographical character of Paul, the ambulance driver.*]

SSA 13
Agnes,                                                          21 July 1918

We have settled down once more (for the present anyhow) to our usual peaceful existence. I can't tell you about the last week, or rather I don't know how much I might tell, and don't intend to take risks of being sacked or court martialed! Anyhow we had about one tenth of the unpleasantness we had expected, in fact we had a very easy let off. None of our fellows were hurt, and very few cars were hit, and there were few patients to carry, considering. On the other hand for a while it was quite sufficiently dramatic. Of course you will have seen in the papers all about the big battle of these days, and you will have guessed that we had only slight experience of it here. Yet, if you were to be sitting beside me now I should be able to tell you much that would be surprising and thrilling. But anyhow I am tired of it all. . . .

My dear, in the last scrap I did an awful thing for which I don't see how you will ever forgive me. I left a wounded man in a ditch under shell fire. Of course I thought he was dead. He was horribly smashed up. Of course I ought to have stopped and got out & examined him, but he seemed such a fragment of a man that I only slowed down to look at him and then went on. But subsequently he turned out not to be dead, & I myself finally took him to the rear. It is horrible to be guilty of such a gross piece of carelessness, for it was just carelessness and not blue funk, for I was not in a funk just then. I was too busy avoiding shell holes to be in a funk, and alas too busy to switch off my mind on to an unexpected subject. But never again, never never again. I shall now drive with the expectation of a wounded man at every ten yards, so as to be on the safe side. No one seems to blame me, but that is no criterion. People don't blame people on the culprit's own evidence, unless it is obviously an extremely bad case. But I shall remember that man now for many a long day. Poor chap, he must have died very soon after I got him away anyhow. Can you forgive me? I have been honest and told you anyhow. And I have learnt a lesson not easily to be forgotten. Can you forgive me? The worst point of course is that the place was getting badly strafed. I have no business to ask you to forgive me. Anyhow I am not likely to be guilty of that particular sin again; it has bitten in sufficiently. But I am always doing beastly things like that on the spur of the moment, things I would not dream of doing if I had time to think. Enough of that. I did not tell you before because the enormity of the offence had not dawned on me when I sent off the last letter. I was more impressed then at having had all my windows blown in and having crashed into a shell hole, though such events are merely external & unavoidable. It all happened in the same twinkling of an eye. My man must have been laid out by the previous shell. His bike was in the road, & I thought someone had chucked him into the ditch for dead.

Egremont

TO OLAF                                               22 July 1918

. . . Just these last few days there has been encompassing all our doing & thinking the news of the German check beyond the Marne & the subsequent glorious Franco-American advance towards Soissons & Château-Thierry—five good miles & in some places nine. Oh there *has* been rejoicing over it even far away here. What must it have been like in France & in England!

The accounts of the fighting & the havoc it has brought are awful, ghastly, & yet—one must rejoice! One must not stop to think what it has meant—we have got to such a state of things that we can not be too thankful nor too glad of the men who have wrought that havoc & brought us all 5 miles nearer to the end of this horrible nightmare. However much one would pray for Peace, one must pray instead for Victory since it seems that nothing but Victory will bring peace, & let us hope that our nation is doing the right thing in prolonging the war until a definite victory is reached, & let us hope they will justify their victory by making it the last war in history. Both sides are—or have been up to now—so nearly matched that it must take *ages* for one to completely vanquish the other. And when finally by reinforcements from a third great power the one *is* vanquished—what then? Is everything settled then? The end is hidden. When the news came, we thought it was going to be the final push. We could see the Allies taking village after village, town after town & the Germans returning helter skelter the way they had come—back across the Rhine into Germany. We heard the rejoicings over Victory, the ringing of the bells in London, Paris, New York, & then—& then best of all——the boys came home! We didn't really *think* it, but that is how one's wild imagination teased one on a wet Sunday afternoon with the rain pattering on the verandah roof.

Next day the papers calm down & one's face-the-facts, un-carry-away-able father comments quietly, "No—it's no good thinking of the great offensive yet. We shalln't be ready for it *this year*." Oh Olaf! It is three years & 9 months & about 10 days since I saw you. That's the way the world counts, but in my counting I have *never* seen you. It was all strange then because I didn't know. It is so different now. I am different. You are different to me. It is all real now & yet I have never seen you. If I should be warned beforehand that I must lose you I think I *could* resign myself to the future without you, if only I might see you first, & be with you & try to make up for all the time we have missed. But oh! to lose you in the dark & never to have seen you, never to have touched you—that would be too cruel! I would cry out against such a loss more bitterly than if you had already been my husband. A wife's grief would be more real, more warm for something known, remembered—but a fiancée's grief would have no comfort in remembering, for her life has never reached fulfillment. She is a cold mourner for something that she has never known & has lost. My heart leapt out to meet you when you said, "If only I might touch your hand for one little minute!"

SSA 13

TO AGNES                                                            28 July 1918

. . . Before leaving our last place we made good use of the piano, though it was getting very badly out of tune in spite of various amateur tuners. The Doc was made to play every evening. Imagine a little room full of beds & kit bags, and crammed with Englishmen & Frenchmen, & the old Doc playing away Schumann Novelettes, Brahms Rhapsodies, Mozart Sonata No. 12, Beethoven's Waldstein, Moonlight, Pathétique, & No. 20, MacDowell's Sea Pieces, & Wild Rose, Debussy's Arabesques etc. etc., while everybody sat (or lay) & smoked. Outside, the evening sky

[CENSORED]

darkened till at last it was necessary to shut the shutters to prevent light from showing outside; & then the three or four casual voyagers, who had stopped to listen at the window, were regretfully shut out. Imagine also on the evening of our departure the Doc playing in an empty room in which the piano was the only article save for three or four people sitting about on the stone floor. Imagine him still going on playing while the first cars go out from the yard for the journey. Good old piano! "Pas grand chose, mais, que voulez-vous, c'est un piano de guerre." The old thing is left behind. If ever we get back to that secteur, may we find it again. . . .

*[The following portion of the letter was later underlined in blue pencil by the Customs officer in Sydney. Agnes's letter of 2 November 1918 contains the explanation.]*

It will be September when you get this. It will be clear by then whether the war is going to drag on to the next summer or not. It is time we got married, whether or no. I can't get out to you. Will you come to England? I know very well that such a solution would be in many ways most unsatisfactory, and that the brunt of the trouble would fall on you, not on me. Passage money need not stand in the way, nor other finance. The danger of the voyage is serious, and cannot be overcome; but there you are. It just *is*. A permit could probably be got for you, so I am told, to come to England to do some sort of war work like VAD or WAAC. (Of course I would rather you held to the Red Cross.) You might get work near Liverpool, even near W. Kirby. Kitty [Stapledon, a cousin] for instance works at a Hospital at Heswall. We should get married during my leave (an extended leave perhaps). My dear girl, I know it would be a tremendous undertaking, and I know your people would be very reluctant, but what else is to be done? It has long seemed to me the only ultimate solution, but I have not said much about it because I kept hoping the war would end, and anyhow I kept feeling that I had no business to urge you to all that arduous change in your life while I went on as ever. But really it begins to seem the only thing for both of our sakes.

[As the French army advanced, SSA 13 followed, entering devastated areas that had been no-man's-land for so long that the landscape had become an unrelieved mixture of bleakness and gruesome horror. At Bligny, according to Olaf's FAU colleague Julian Fox, "the dead of four nations lay still unburied by the sides of the road." Olaf's own terse diary entry for 4 August reads: "Awful traffic. Dead men, stinks & ruin." Living conditions were primitive and offered little protection from bombardment. One of the drivers was killed by a shell in the village of Treslon, and in Poilly the flies, putrefaction, and disease were so bad that the Section had to abandon the station as uninhabitable. Trench fever and dysentery halved the convoy's strength, and "yperite"—mustard gas—was a constant threat.]

SSA 13
Darling, 9 August 1918

A line, no more. Thank you ever so much for a lovely parcel of food, all in good condition save the cocoa, & most of that I have secured. Butter excellent. Meat I keep for emergencies. It has all come *most* opportunely, just when it will be invaluable. . . .

This little letter is being written at odd times, a sentence at a time. We have been pretty busy, and very short of sleep, and generally quite

uncomfortable enough. Last night I spent in an old cellar being cold &
most painfully aware of the fagots I was sleeping on. . . .

We have a plague of flies and wasps. Of the former there must be
millions. Our only other plague is foul stinks. No, the worst plague of
all is the awful roads which are so fearfully bad for wounded men. One
creeps along, but one can't help shaking them up, especially at night.

SSA 13

Agnes,                                                11 August 1918

Today a lovely and long letter came from you, and three little photos,
for which many thanks. It is good to see your face after all the ugly
things one has seen lately. . . . Lately we have been so unsettled. I have
slept on various occasions in a stable, on a heap of rubbish, on a beautiful tiled floor and in a pig sty. No, I left the last before I went to sleep,
but others slept in it. Of course the pigs had left it ages before. You will
see by "The Friend" that we have had bad luck. Colin Priestman has
been killed, & David Long wounded. Really perhaps we have been
lucky in having no other casualties, for it has been fairly hot at times,
with the minor kind of "hotness" that falls to our lot. Most of the cars
have been hit, but none destroyed. I think we have so far fulfilled all our
obligations anyhow. It is a piggy, smelly, dusty, messy, nervy life, with
not the slightest excuse for feeling heroic but much disgustingness and
weariness. A fifty mile run on these roads reduces me to pulp, especially
at night. For the wretched wounded that one carries these roads are torture, alas. One creeps along and winds in and out, but one can't avoid
all the holes, especially at night. It is funny that of our own people,
some get all the narrow escapes and horrid half hours, others bring
peace wherever they go. I am of the latter sort. But the little difference
between our luck is of course nothing compared with the difference between the front line and motoring.

SSA 13

Beloved Cousin,                                       15 August 1918

I have been reading a book about the love affairs of two cousins,
"Jude the Obscure," by Hardy. It is a most black tragedy, a depressing
and miserable book; yet there is a grandeur and a truth about it that
makes it beautiful. From beginning to end all goes wrong with the two
cousins, not owing to their cousinship, but owing to a malicious fate.
They were beautifully made for one another. Cousinship seemed to add
a sympathy to their love unattainable by others. They had certain big
differences of opinion, yet their minds were very closely akin. They

were not a bit like you and me, save in their rare sympathy together and
in their intellectual difference. And this last was not permanent. We are
not likely, thank heaven, to suffer their evil fortune; but I hope we shall
be like them in love (unless they are made to change before the end of
the book. I am halfway through). Reading this book has made me think
much about you and me and our problems, so that I keep banging my
head against many obdurate brick walls. But chiefly I have been thanking heaven for the love of such a one as you, and longing to get to know
you again intimately as before, even far more intimately than before.
Mother urges me to urge you to find a way to England. I won't. I have
been thinking hard, & I think it would not be fair to you & yours,
though a great delight to me and mine. Oh Agnes dear, I am sorry for a
too zealous letter that I wrote urging you to come. I ought not to urge
you. And really though I want you very much I don't want you to be
torn up by the roots in that way for the pleasure of our meeting only
once in a while. It would not work. I am going on leave in three weeks.
I don't want to go half as much as I ought to. It sounds horrid to say
that, but what is a leave?—A rather awful journey of days, then suddenly a plunge into a new-old life and away again just as one is beginning to grow into it again. . . . I am sleepy, having been driving much
of last night and working much of today, and the rest of last night was
partly spent in wondering where the next shell would fall. I can't write
letters now. I can only read. We are kept too busy to think much. I have
not written any of my book for ages.

[*The dugouts were less secure than Olaf indicated to Agnes in this
letter. The day after he wrote, five members of the convoy were gassed as
they slept in their dugout, and three of them had to be evacuated to a
hospital.*]

SSA 13
Agnes,                                                    20 August 1918
    Once more only a note, as there is simply no time for more. One is
always either running, mending innumerable punctures, greasing,
sleeping or eating. . . . The chief topic of conversation is dugouts.
People are making little dugouts of their own, as there is not anything
like accommodation. It is amusing to see couples carrying logs about
and disputing as to how best to fix them, or in shoveling earth in huge
quantities on to places that are probably too weak to hold any more
weight. Parties also go in search of nice cellars, but seldom with any
luck.
    Let's have a cigarette and be at ease. There, that's better. I am sitting

on my bed, or on the floor space that serves me for a bed. On one side of me is the remains of a chest of drawers, in front of me a cooking range, and to the right a dilapidated grandfather clock. So I am quite civilized. The ceiling is intact. A barricade of bales of blankets is meant to keep off shell splinters from the window, & one trusts a shell won't pitch just here, because the walls are nothing much. I don't know why I talk in this journalese way when really we should be remarking rather on our comparative comfort & security, which is indeed remarkable. . . .

By the way, after my leave I intend to send you a series of letters embodying my book. One is not allowed to take MS home with one on leave, so I shall send it all home bit by bit. It is all nearly finished I think, but I can't send any till all is quite finished. What if the book were to take the form of letters to you? I am in love with that idea at present. The fact of writing to you helps to clarify one's writing. But now is not the time to begin.

SSA 13

TO AGNES                                                   23 August 1918
. . . I am having a war with my bed-neighbour, the fussy old Prof. He has barricaded himself with bales of rugs etc. to keep off shell splinters, bless his heart. Personally I don't mind the sort of splinters that won't pierce his barricade, but I do mind his stuffy barricade. Moreover we have a dug out of sorts, & if shells come anywhere near we all go down there & squat on the floor together. But last night was entirely undisturbed. It is as hot as Egypt now! One crawls about with one's face dripping. Yesterday I devoured much melon & much peaches (these luxuries having suddenly fallen upon us) and today I am *not* ill! If only one could bathe here. But we have a patent shower-bath of our own device, and it is in almost constant use, down here at our base. Elsewhere of course one does not undress.

Egremont

Olaf,                                                      27 August 1918
It is Sunday afternoon between 4 o'clock tea & proper tea. . . . This family always looks most awfully unpresentable on Sundays, at least until afternoon tea time. Waldo looks the worst of the lot, but Daddy runs him pretty close, though on different lines. Waldo wears the last old suit that he has grown out of & makes no pretence that it is not all patched & busty-out at knees & elbows. Waldo considers the lilies of the field in the way of clothes. He's not a "knut" except when he gets into his best suit & then he can't help looking an angel. Daddy, on the other hand,

does not lapse so much on Sunday in the way of quality but he lapses fearfully in the way of variety. I don't know why it is but on Sunday he seems to wear a bit of every suit he possesses—nondescript trousers, grey coat, navy blue waistcoat, any old tie, & to cap the lot he puts on an ancient of the ancient overcoats, & a battered old white helmet with four wonderful ventilation holes cut after his own heart. Thus attired he perches up on the top of the ladder in the garden & trims the trees, or does other odd jobs in the house or work-shed.

SSA 13

TO AGNES                                              6 September 1918
. . . Oh my dear, I do so long for you. You very likely don't know how much I want you, because one can't express it. But I won't say "come" because I cannot feel sure it would be for the best. Besides, supposing, just supposing, you were to come and I were to get killed while you were en route. It's not likely, but of course it is a possibility to reckon with. One's luck has been too good for one to expect it to last forever. If that were to happen, what a muddle and waste! And as for the other great difficulties—well, there they are. There's the dangerous journey, and the whole unsatisfactoriness. If you were to come I think we would have to get married soon—don't you? But alas it all seems such a phantom at present. The realities to me just now are such concrete questions as: shall I have a run tonight, having been out the last two nights? Is it going to be a very dark night or only a dark night? Is my gas-mask gas-tight? Has the road been chewed up since last night? Shall I wash a shirt tomorrow, or sleep all day? My dear, the other is the *real* reality, but this is the present reality. When I get home on leave I shall be in the real reality for a while, but when that will be is uncertain.

SSA 13

Agnes,                                               10 September 1918
   Rain, torrents of it. The top step of our dug-out is a pool, and a marsh is spreading slowly along the floor. Last night was pitchy dark, especially under trees. Lots of times I passed carts without knowing they were there until they were already abreast of me or half passed. And the road itself was only visible as the dimmest of glimmers if one kept blinking one's eyes hard to keep them fresh, & kept looking everywhere except at the road, so as to use the less-used parts of one's retinae. . . .
   The rain is crumbling this ruined village round our heads. In the last half hour three walls have come hurtling down in various parts of the place, each time with a noise that quite nicely imitated thunder. I hope

one does not fall on my car. My car is about the only one that has not
been touched by any enemy missiles this time, or at least not damaged
by any.

[*Caught between Emmeline Stapledon's repeated urgings to leave Australia and marry her son and Frank Miller's persistent arguments
against going to England, Agnes, not surprisingly, found it difficult to
keep track both of what she had said to Olaf on the subject and of her
own true feelings about it.*]

                                                      Egremont
TO OLAF                                    17 September 1918
. . . I forget what exactly I wrote in reply to your tentative proposal that
I should come to England next year. Anyway, last week I had a long
letter from your Mother on the subject, & since then it has been much
under discussion among us. I think Auntie really feels in her heart that
it is very weak of me to stay on & on here. She wants me to take the bull
by the horns & come. She thinks the passport difficulty might be overcome by pledging myself to undertake some specified kind of war work.
That, of course, remains to be seen—but supposing I am able to get a
passport she doesn't seem to think there should be anything in the risk to
stop my coming. I wonder if you & Uncle feel like that too. Personally I
feel that the risk is the only thing that has any weight with me at all, &
because of that risk I have felt it was right to wait here & be as patient &
as useful as I could. I wonder if it *is* weak of me? When I suggested this
to Daddy he was very surprised that I should think it weak *to wait*. He
said he would consider it weak & wanting in endurance to rush off now
after waiting until the 11th hour. . . . So I am to write back to Auntie—
a disappointing letter, I fear, from her point of view—that I will wait
here until your spring, & then come with luck safely, & without too
much risk to myself & anxiety to others. If—heaven forbid—things
should go badly again with the Allies & all our hopes of peace should be
dashed away into the unknown distance, I think in that case Mother &
Dad will reconcile themselves & let me take the risk whatever it is—
because they do realise that this separation can't go on forever. I think
they are right—do you not agree with them, that it is best to wait a little
longer & give time a chance to complete in our favour the job he has
taken in hand so successfully?

British Expeditionary Force
Dearest,                                   22 September 1918

I am on my way home at last, in a party of four, one of whom is Bonham [Roger Carter] and another the great Henry [Burtt]. We started with a ten mile walk, Henry & I, at night, in the moonlight, coming for a gratuitous air raid at the end of it. Now after two days travelling, we have just had an excellent English tea served by a rather dashing and charming YMCA girl all in bright blue silk—the girl, not the tea. Tonight we shall cross, with luck. Since leaving the Section we seem to have done nothing but eat omelettes & drink wine & coffee. . . . But the real crowning glory was last night in a glorious soft white bed, a perfectly scrumptious one, & a room with electric light & hot & cold water laid on. My hat! It seemed a wicked shame to waste it all by going to sleep in it.

[*As a partisan of the Russian revolution, Olaf saw the occupation of the Arctic port of Archangel and of Vladivostok on the Pacific by the armies of Britain, France, and the United States as a covert effort to destroy the new Soviet government, in spite of official claims that they were protecting Allied supply routes.*]

Annery
Agnes,                                     24 September 1918

Home again. . . . Now for a few facts of history, as little censorable as may be. Last July it was thought by the authorities that the big German attack was to break exactly on our sector as its chief point. There were therefore terrific preparations. We were told to be ready to be utterly wiped off the face of the earth at any minute, and indeed we all got the wind up pretty badly. But three days before the event it was found that the Bosche had changed his mind and much of the stuff was rushed elsewhere. We only came in for the fringe of that business after all. There was one unpleasant time, but nothing serious for us and very few casualties for the division. Then we moved to Aÿ, near Épernay, & waited there till wanted. Meanwhile very heavy fighting was going on round those parts. When our turn came the Bosches were retreating. We had a very mobile, busy, and filthy time, till the lines settled down, we being just to the left of Rheims. The motorists' main difficulty now was the badness of the roads and the length of the run back to Épernay, which took six hours there & back. This was our busy time. Then the enemy, having settled down, again began to shell behind the lines pretty continuously, and chivvied us about from cellar to cellar till we finally

A page of Olaf's self-caricatures showing him in a variety of characteristic convoy activities; included in his letter to Agnes of 24 September 1918.

had to move our base back to save the cars. Meanwhile a lot of our people got gassed more or less, mostly less, but enough to upset the service a lot. I had a very mild dose. Our casualties of all kinds that month were (curiously) just the same percentage of killed, wounded, gassed & sick as the percentages of the division. Things are quieter now, but we were still short handed when I left and still pretty well shelled. . . .

*Next Day.* If you suddenly hear that I have left the FAU and joined the army don't be surprised. It would not be from a sense of duty at all but from a gregarious instinct that makes one desperately want to do what others do, and from the purely selfish motive of wanting to better my prospects in the world. Out yonder one feels busy and part of a great happening and a very strong pacifist too; but here one feels different from everyone, and of course one knows that most people regard one (or would regard one) as a rotter. All one's friends are soldiers. Who am I to set myself up as having a conscience? It is obvious (I should have thought) to the meanest comprehension by now that war is wrong, that however bad the Germans are we shall not improve them by beating them, that a big allied victory would be a disaster for the world hardly less than a big German one, that in the present state of world civilization to kill is simply a damnable sin. A future age will take all this for granted, and greatly despise this age for its blindness. But—one can't stick out indefinitely against one's fellow sheep. I am feeling now more than ever before that I *want* to join the army and have done with it. Should probably get into trouble sooner or later for insubordination & seditious talk, but would try not. Would pray heaven not to send me to Archangel nor Vladivostok or any other of our immoral sideshows but to the good old honest Western Front. Should take the infantry, not artillery nor flying. Should make a very poor and indifferent soldier, & should always be wishing I hadn't. But the real difficulty is simply that I am beginning to feel that to be a member of the FAU while all one's friends & relatives are helping the war is not good enough, especially when one's own father is busy shipping troops from America all the time. The only difficulty on the other side is that Mother & Father would be much against my changing; but as things stand it must be very awkward for Father in his position to have a son in such a queer job as mine. . . .

*Next Day.* . . . I have conceived a horrid dread lest our time here so long ago be not enough to hold us together till the end of the war. All sorts of fears & bogies have been chasing through my mind today. *Come to me, and lay these spectres forever.* I am writing this late at night, and I am in the mood that I would sooner die now than go through another age without you. . . . We have waited four years; we can wait a bit longer if need be, can't we? But dear—I wonder if you really know how much you are to me. I have told you so often, & yet I never can tell you properly, until we meet. I don't see why I should love you so very much more than I love anyone else. I mean I don't understand the deepest part of my love for you. The surface part is clear, simply that you are a lovely girl, and a fellow is likely to love such a one. But below all that there is a something mighty. Perhaps it is just the accumulated power of habit, of having always loved you, or loved you for so long. Anyhow there is something strange that wells up inside when I think of you sometimes. . . .

Don't think that because my letters from home are more eager than my letters from France that therefore I care less & think less about you in France. It is rather that here one is articulate, there not. Such a lot of claptrap is talked about love that one is afraid of doing likewise, & yet there *is* that mysterious sense of something superhuman in loving. How do you love me? In what manner? I have a different mode of love for you on every day of the year. Dear, my not being a soldier has grieved you, in the deeps of you. And because of your grieving I have grieved with you. But there is another side too. Whether right or wrong, it has not been easy not to be a soldier, and the thing that made it so hard has always been—Agnes thinks otherwise. I wonder if you know what a difference that has made. Think how it would be if you had done something that *I* and all the world discountenanced. You would feel kind of—alone. But now I am beginning to get into the minor key unnecessarily. It is horribly late at night, a time when one's thoughts are apt to run in the minor. Cheers! I kiss thee in the spirit XXX. Good night. Keep young and full of life.

[*Agnes's first intimate experience of death in the final illness of a close family friend points up how insulated she was from the horrors Olaf faced almost daily in the latter stages of the war.*]

My Olaf,                                                                        Egremont
                                                                     29 September 1918

Where shall I begin & how shall I tell you of these last few days, the most full that I have known, I think, of anguish. Dear Maidie [Irvine] fought her last fight on Friday & passed away in the afternoon. I haven't told you much of her illness because there was mostly nothing fresh to tell, but it has been going on slowly, relentlessly for more than 6 months. Sometimes she used to seem better for several days. We would go & sit with her & talk of everything—books, & flowers, & picnics, & different events, people, dresses, & all kinds of news. She was bright then & jolly & happy & she always *talked* as though all this lying in bed was only a tiresome interval. She used to make plans with us for what she would do "afterwards" & we would all be cheered with her confidence & begin to hope—until the inevitable relapse came & then we were forced to remember the doctor's first words—"there is no hope.". . .

Mrs. Irvine took me in to see her when it was all over, the pain & the suffering as well as the little joys that had made life pleasant. She was laid on her own little white bed with her beautiful dark hair all let loose by her side. But now those tired eyes were closed & her white hands folded across her breast in the calmness that I think only Death can give. . . . I have been crying & I'm sobbing like a baby as I write—it may be very wrong of me & very weak, but I can't help it. It seems so sad for a lovely young girl like Maidie to die. We all went with her to her resting place—all the Irvines & Rosie & Daddy & I—& a good many other friends, both men & women. I had never been to a funeral before. Girls don't generally go, but it seemed best in this case, because she was a girl just like ourselves.

Annery

TO AGNES                                   5 October 1918

. . . This afternoon I helped Father with his bees. He has transparent pieces in the hives through which one sees thousands of bees busily working and going to and fro. Father loves his bees. If by chance one stings him he is far more grieved for the disemboweled bee than for himself, and if by chance he damages a bee, or finds some that have got drowned or that have died of cold outside at night, he is very grieved for each poor creature. They are indeed wonderful things, so very different from us, yet in some ways so strangely like us. They fascinate me. And it makes me unreasonably sad to see one hurt. It reminds one too much of the war and of the soldiers of the human hives. I do hate killing things, even rats. Things that live are so much more beautiful than anything that man's will can do. Of course things must often be killed, but the less killing the better. (Sermons in parvo.) . . .

[7 *October.*] Today, my last day at home, two great events have happened. The papers are full of Germany's acceptance of Wilson's terms and request for an armistice, and a glorious letter has come from you. As to the peace move, one prays that it will not be immediately rejected by the Allies, as a "peace offensive." Perhaps it may really be the beginning of the end! Perhaps it will all be over when you get this and I shall be on my way out to you. Perhaps, perhaps, but one cannot tell yet, and anyhow there will be long delays over demobilization. It is hard not to look at things from a merely personal point of view. The change in Germany is a world-event, and here am I immediately thinking of it in its bearing on you and me. Anyhow for both public and private reasons let

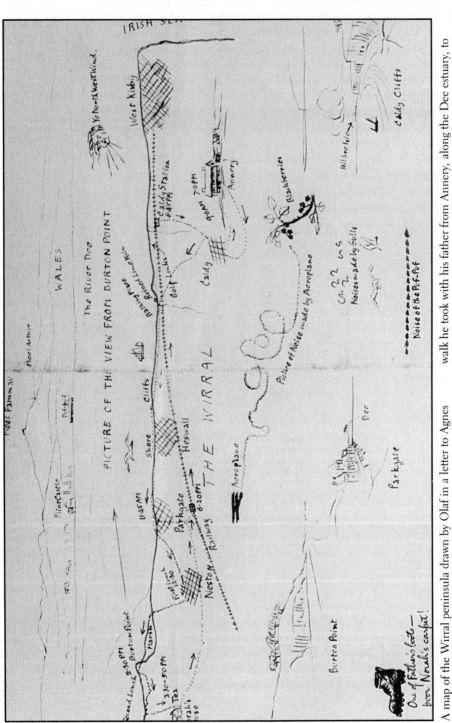

A map of the Wirral peninsula drawn by Olaf in a letter to Agnes dated 5 October 1918. The map is a comic illustration of a day-long walk he took with his father from Annery, along the Dee estuary, to his cousin Norah Stapledon's house.

us hope it results in peace. But I fear some of the Allies are likely to want to go on fighting. We shall see. In your letter you hope for a complete victory over Germany. Pacifism or no pacifism, I am sure that for the future peace of the world that is not what is wanted, but rather a draw. . . .

I must keep your letter to be answered from France properly, as I shall not have much of a chance on my last day here. A cupboard in my car is crowded with packets of your letters. Hitherto I have brought them home on leave with me to put away at home, but this time such a fuss had been made about taking written material home with one that I thought I would be circumspect and not break the regulations, for one FAU fellow has got into serious trouble on that score.

SSA 13

Agnes,                                                          13 October 1918

Great news, great rumours anyhow, & certainly great events. No chance of proper letter-writing, but just a note to say I am now with the Section again, after spending some days on the way, a very interesting journey. I am now once more in the old state of being always on the move. At the moment I am waiting in my car with several Frenchmen, & all are talking excitedly about the news and about our own immediate prospects. I want my lunch. Agnes, the end is coming! One can't believe it, can one? We shall meet soon, soon, soon—with luck.

*Another day & place.* This sort of business has at least the fascination of novelty, but it is hardish work even though there are no casualties. Our chief excitement is crossing pontoon bridges [over the river Aisne] as soon as they are put up. A big lorry has just broken through one. The roads—well, you can imagine what they would be like in an advance. Ruins are still smouldering as we pass through. Everything is at least delightfully different from what we are used to. Places that are still being shelled when we arrive become gloriously tranquil soon afterwards. Over all is the delightful sense that the fighting must surely soon stop.

This little note must go as it stands as I am going out.

Haste,
Olaf

Egremont

TO OLAF                                                        15 October 1918

. . . I wonder if you were all as excited as we were last Sunday, or was it only our inflammable press that upset us? On Sunday afternoon there were two special editions of the paper with most astounding headlines.

"Germany surrenders." "Cessation of hostilities." "Peace in sight" & so on. We couldn't really believe it—it seemed too big to be true, & in fact the morning papers of the next day were much calmer. What do you think about it? Could it have been the basis of a satisfactory peace, or was it only a 'try-on' on Germany's part? I don't believe in a compromise at this stage. I want it to be fixed up & finished off so that there won't ever be another war. Anyway the Allies are advancing while the governments are talking, so between the two of them may we not hope for Peace before so very long?

On the strength of this & in the face of the awful submarine disaster of the "Leinster," Dad went today to interview the Chief Collector of Customs with regard to my passport. He began by being very discouraging & said it was most unadvisable to travel as "at the present time" the submarine menace was more formidable than it had been at any period of the war. Dad explained that he didn't propose for me to go until about March next year, but he thought it best to make enquiries early in case I should lose time later by not having had my application in. Dad explained the situation to him & added that of course I would take up some kind of war work on arriving, if that would help the case at all. But Mr. Barclay said that that side of the question would not count for anything, as they were not letting women go on any pretext of work except in the case of Army nurses. But he said that the fact of our having been engaged for so long, & also the fact of your having *asked* me to come would be sufficient reason for securing a passport provided I could *prove* that I was speaking the truth & nothing but the truth. I therefore have the delightful task ahead of me of going over your ancient letters to find one which will convince the Collector of Customs that you did actually ask me to be your wife, & another to show that you also did ask me to come to England! The latter I have in so many words. "I can't come to Australia. Will you come to England?" It came by the last mail. The former is not so easy to find, as it was suffused over about a hundred letters, & never began in any one from the beginning. As a matter of fact, in the end it was I who "popped the question"—wasn't it?!! I can't tell the man that or he would think me an "impertinent hussy." I'll have a good old hunt & find something really convincing. I mean something that is suitable for publication. But isn't it beastly? However if it gets me my passport it will be worth its beastliness. He said that of course by next March the conditions may be so altered that it is almost useless to make arrangements already but he thought I might as well come along & show my proofs & then he would speak to the Minister about it. . . .

*Oct. 18.* When we were discussing my coming to England recently, it transpired that Dad is most awfully disappointed that you will not be able to come out & fetch me. He has sort of made up his mind to it at

last, but he hasn't got over the disappointment. It is partly on their account & partly on your & my account—chiefly ours I think. He feels
that it will be a great loss to us both for you never to have known me in
my own surroundings, for you never to have lived the Australian life
with us as we have the English with you. And then on their account
they would have the satisfaction of feeling that we started on a mutual
understanding & also it would soften my departure greatly to them to
have me go *with* you instead of alone. How far it really *matters* on our
account I can't say. What do you think? I feel I have *told* you a good
deal about myself & my doings & my country—& yet it is not the same
as seeing & breathing & knowing,—& certainly when I cross the water
some days on my way to town I am simply flooded with the beauty of it,
& it seems tragic that you should not know it too.

SSA 13

TO AGNES                                                    17 October 1918
. . . This world is a weary world. I don't like being shelled all morning,
but I would far rather be shelled all of a solid week than do one journey
down into the rear with badly wounded men over these awful roads at
night. It is impossible not to crash into holes in the dark, and each little
jolt causes cries to come from inside the bus, and a journey may take
three or four hours—hours of crashing and jolting and struggling up
steep slippery muddy banks on which you simply must not think about
the cries that come from inside, but only of the best way of rushing the
bus up—if she will go. And my nightmare is the thought of being stuck
in such a place with bad cases on board and having to wait perhaps
many hours until enough people come to push me out. Generally the
roads are overcrowded, but when you *want* people the roads are apt to
be deserted for hours. Ah, bon dieu! The other day I had a run which
(all told) lasted just twelve hours, including of course much waiting and
searching and one hasty meal of twenty minutes during a wait. Ten
hours is quite a usual time to be away on a run. Of course part of that is
with an empty car and matters not, but the rest is enough to drive one
cracked. Probably all this is censorable, but one can't always keep quiet.
The other day in a certain much shelled village I spent hours driving
round looking for certain blessés that were reputed to be there. At the
end of our exploration the colonel of a certain regiment came up and
said, "I know that all your section shows complete devotion to its work,
but I wish personally to thank in particular the 'messieurs' attached to
this car for the services they have done me." Whereat he shook hands
with us both and we (in the words of my companion) looked a bigger
fool than usual—because the only service we had done was narrowly to
escape running over the dear old duffer in turning a corner. However we

took the glory and bragged about it to our friends, who—unsympathetic brutes—merely said "toujours la politesse vers les Anglais." This enraged us, especially as it was true.

SSA 13

TO AGNES                                                    22 October 1918

. . . We have had another batch of citations. In fact about a quarter of the convoy sports the red and green ribbon now. The last three were earned, but some of the others have not been. In fact there have been scandals of a mild nature. Please note I shall never get one because my presence always has such a pacific influence that wherever I go the shelling stops! Teddy has one, and deserves it as much as anyone. But the thing is now so horribly cheap that the glamour is wearing off, save for the ever-undecorated old fossils like Sparrow and me. Of course Sparrow should have had one before several people that have got them, but he has never had the luck (?) to meet the necessary dramatic incident. He and I, on the sour-grapes principle, have decided we don't want one now. . . .

Last night as I was going to sleep in my car I thought of the last person who had lain where I was lying. He was a tall, thin, blue-eyed, spectacled, intellectual-looking man who had been badly wounded. When we had loaded the car he called for the priest (a friend of mine) and asked him to kiss him. The priest did so, gently, pitifully, and murmured a prayer over him. Then we got under way, and I was perplexed whether to go slow to save him pain, or fast to save his life. I tried both in turn, & finally made a compromise. But it was a long and bumpy journey. When we had almost finished it the other men inside rattled the window to call my attention. I stopped & opened the window. One said, "Je crois qu'il meurt." Pause. "Oui, je crois qu'il est mort." Pause. So I said (for there was nothing else to do), "Alors il n'y-a rien à faire. Il n'y a qu'à filer." So we proceeded, I now going at full speed since there was no chance of hurting him, & there might still be a chance of saving him. I nearly had a smash through scorching. We arrived & unloaded; and surely the man was quite dead, with his eyes still bright & blue and half open, and dust all over his spectacles.

Egremont

TO OLAF                                                    28 October 1918

. . . I haven't been to that man about my passport yet. It's a case of being there early in the morning before he gets busy. . . . I have picked out a letter to show we are engaged, but I'ld much rather not show it to him! I also have Auntie & Uncle's letters of that time saying how pleased they are—that might do. They were written just about three years ago from now, but I think we have been engaged much longer than that, don't you? That was only when it was made public. I feel now as if we had been engaged almost ever since that first night at Hoylake [on 24 February 1913] when you told me about it, but heaven knows I didn't feel so then! Thank goodness I came to my senses before you got fed up with me! You were a darling to wait so long & to be so horribly persistent. . . .

Auntie wrote this mail to Daddy, & rubbed in one point which counts a great deal with me & has done so for a long time. She said that if we were married & had had even only a few days together, supposing you were to be killed in the end—well nothing could rob me of those few days & perhaps even you might have left me the most precious leg-acy—your little child. Daddy, being a mere man & rather a matter of fact one, doesn't take much account of that point. Mother takes more of course—but you can understand that from their point of view it would have been very hard to spare me for three years for the sake of the 10 days I might have had with you once or twice a year. I do see their point but oh I do see *my* point too & if I were to lose you now in the end, oh Olaf why did I not risk it long ago & come to you? I can't help it, & it may be stupid but that thought is always hovering at the back of my mind even in the midst of all these exciting discussions & plans & preparations. . . .

Olaf, there's one thing I want you to tell me. I wish I had asked it long ago & then I should know——If you were to be killed directly or indi-rectly during the war, would you be content to have it so? We must all pass on one day & leave behind people & things that we love. (No one can *like* to do that & to feel that one's people are sad)—but apart from that would you give your life willingly for the cause for which England is fighting? You are so much against war as a means of securing an ideal that I have sort of got it into my head that you are not one with En-gland's ideal at all. And yet you must be to some extent or why are you in France? We can't talk of these things because of the Censor, you & I, & I'm all in the dark. I don't know this Olaf a bit. Do tell me, for it *might* make so much difference to me. If I felt you were content—no! proud, glad to sacrifice your life, me, everything to this ideal, I think I could be content too, & I would try to be glad. . . .

In August 1914 you & Dot & I were walking through Caldy village & you were reading the headings of the paper aloud as you walked. Dot & I were frisky & we weren't taking it in at all. I remember your saying, "You people don't seem to realise that this is the biggest thing in history." You were quite right. I didn't realise it one bit. I remember sobbing in an uncontrollable kind of way at Reigate when it first broke out in its huge black letters, but that was pure emotion—sensation. I didn't

understand what war meant until long after. I do understand it now,
from my point—from the point of the women who stay at home, &
though we here have not had the least physical discomfort to put up
with—yet war is stamped on our minds as the most cruel & wicked
thing that could possibly be—something we have had to bear perhaps
necessarily—perhaps it might have been avoided—but at all events
something which we must never *never* allow to happen again. In these
days of discussions as to an armistice & final peace terms, it seems
dreadful not to seize the first opportunity of peace & yet I'ld rather it
were fought on until the right terms are agreed on, than run the risk of a
repetition of this awful mess.

[*The wounded Abbé Saglio, Roman Catholic chaplain to the French
division for which SSA 13 worked, became the model for the French
priest in chapter 6 of the 1932 novel,* Last Men in London. *His even-
tual death, through medical neglect, touched Olaf almost more than
that of any other of his colleagues in the war.*]

SSA 13
TO AGNES                                                    29 October 1918
. . . Blood is getting on my nerves. I sympathise with Lady Macbeth in
her futile efforts to cleanse it. . . . Oh heavens, but I am sick of dealing
with shattered human beings. Always noise and blood and agonies, &
each single little tragedy is such a mere atom of the whole, & yet so very
great in itself. . . .

[31 *October.*] Today we are all very sad (underneath the usual hilarity)
because a French priest whom we know well and admire has had a bad
wound which has necessitated the amputation of a leg. He is now in a
very serious state and they only say that he *may* live. He is a fine man,
full of energy and kindliness. He was caught by a bullet while going out
to give absolution to a man who was dying. He lay some time till someone came upon him and began to dress his leg. Then another bullet got
him and broke his thighbone. I heard only two days before that he was
being quite careless in his energetic work and was sure to get hit soon.
He was a wonderfully tolerant man for a priest, and able to see & sympathise with points of view very different from his point of view.

["No. 42" *refers to Olaf's letter of 28 July 1918 in the numbering system devised by Agnes on 22 August 1917.*]

TO OLAF                                                  2 November 1918

. . . I have been in to interview—or rather to be interviewed by—the
Chief Collector of Customs about my passport. It was exciting. I've
been sort of effervescing ever since & I want to tell everybody I meet
about it. I have rather fallen in love with him because he was so nice to
me & so hopeful about my prospects. It was funny. I can't help laughing
inside when I think about it. There was he—the great man—just a wee
bit like your Father—sitting behind his lordly table, in a most lordly
office, full of ponderous spaciousness—& there was I an unpretentious
& rather diffident young person in a brown dress & a large straw hat
sitting opposite him on the edge of a lordly chair & between us open to
the gaze of heaven & all mankind one of your latest letters from France,
its two sheets pinned together by an official pin & looking as if they did
not know what to make of the whole affair. This is the first time anyone
but me has ever been allowed to read any of your letters since we were
engaged. So no wonder we felt shy—no. 42 & I.

Dad came with me, but I did the talking. He asked me a great many
questions as to dates & times & seasons etc. I had hard work to tell him
exactly when we were engaged! He said, "Which was 'the happy day'—
can you remember?" & he laughed right out when I told him there
wasn't one! I had taken the letter you wrote about our official engagement just to confirm what I said about the date of it, but he took my
word for that & I was glad, because the letter wasn't very sensible. He's
too young to see all these things! One of the first questions he asked me
was, "Now are you quite sure you want to go?" I had no difficulty in
answering that one. He turned to Dad & added, "You'd hardly believe
it Mr. Miller, but I've had hundreds of these young people in here after
passports. Half of them are the most hysterical excitable young women
I've ever come across. They take it into their head they will go to England & then directly they hear they can't get their passport, they absolutely raise Cain about it. They burst into tears, they go off into hysterics
till I'm at my wits' end to know what to do with them. I suppose we're all
alike when we hear we can't have a thing—we want it much more,
we'll move heaven & earth to get it. Now I'm not saying that your
daughter is one of that kind—she doesn't look it anyway." (I bowed. It's
good to know I don't *look* hysterical anyway.) "But this is what annoys
me," he continued, "I've taken a lot of trouble over some of them &
have managed at last to get a special permit. Never hear another thing of
them. Change their minds. Won't go after all." I hastened to assure him
that I was very reliable & would promise not to change my mind. When
he had all the information he needed he pressed a button & in walked a
shorthand girl. Between them & with a few corrective remarks from me
they drew up a petition to the Minister, beginning "I Agnes Zena Miller

etc. do swear that I am 24 years of age & am unmarried," & continuing with a brief outline of my life & transactions chiefly since 1914. Also a brief sketch of Mr. Wm. Olaf Stapledon his life & works.

When it was over I retired to the outer office to wait for it to be typed. The expressions & general behaviour of the clerks out there proclaimed that they had seen the likes of me before & knew quite well what I was up to. They were amused. Presently the girl came in & asked me to read the document & if it was correct to go back & sign it before Mr. Barclay. I went without Dad this time, & he was quite encouraging. Said he thought I had a very good chance of getting it on the facts I had stated. It would take two or three weeks to negotiate in Melbourne & when I got a reply I had better come straightaway over to him & we would see what ought to be done next. I said that if the war should end before Xmas I would like to go straightaway, but if it didn't end then Dad had his theories about it being less risky crossing in the warmer weather. To which this lordly personage replied, "Love knows no weather." Dear old soul! I quite agree, but I told him that I want so much to get there that I don't want to run the risk of not getting there at all. He came with me to the door & shook hands saying with a twinkle, "Now don't you go & pack up or anything like that, but I think—mind! I only think—it will be alright!" I could have hugged him.

He kept my letter. He said it would be quite safe, & they would all be too busy to read it! "Besides," he added, "they're all the same!" I don't know why he should have kept it. He underlined the important parts with blue pencil. I'll show it you one day as a relic. It *will* be a relic if it procures me my passport. I believe it's the letter you regretted having written afterwards! I didn't tell him that. They seem to lay great store on your having *asked* me to come.

SSA 13

Sweetheart,                                                 3 November 1918

I have just been cementing the Entente with champagne in a pub, a proper low pub, with the Artist, Saul, and Bonham, cementing also our affection for this place, which is a place of rest far from our recent haunts. Last night also we celebrated rest—with the same sparkling vintage, obtained never mind how in a city of the dead. This afternoon I went for a little lone walk beside a river, and coming on a place where we used to bathe months ago, and finding the pool smooth and tempting and romantic in the twilight, I was moved to strip and swim, though it is already November, and we have been lately keener on fires than bathes. I had a nice little lone swim and dressed in semi-darkness, and "feel better now," thank you, in spite of a cough which I brewed some days ago from rain or gas or both. We are all wondering if we shall see any more active war at all ever; things change so quickly now. . . .

There is now an air of unreality about the affairs of Agnes and Olaf. Get on with that trousseau, make all your arrangements, and come, come, come. Submarines are being recalled, praise heaven. And anyhow the war will soon end now surely. When at last we do meet there will be such a lot to discuss and arrange, and it will all be such fun, arranging the momentous policy of Agnes and Olaf. We will make a merry game of that same momentous and absorbing matter, won't we? I think your father and mother are generous and self-sacrificing in agreeing to your coming to be married in England. Don't change your mind! (Of course you won't.) I am going to turn over a new leaf from now onwards and live with more vigour and enthusiasm in all matters since I shall really soon see Agnes again. I have slopped along so lazily, because all has seemed a dream. "Agnes" began for me as a fearful and lovely and shadowy and very secret dream. "Agnes" became a dear friend, while the secret continued. "Agnes" became a sharer of that open secret, but still only a dear friend. "Agnes" became a multitude of letters that warmed from friendship to love. "Agnes" became the dearest single best friend, but she was a phantom, a spirit behind letters and cakes and warm woolly gifts. But Agnes will soon become once more a real girl of flesh and blood, as real as ever before, and more loving. And she and I will belong to one another. Soon. . . .

Tomorrow we must all work hard on our cars, for they are all wrecks, what with shell damage, collisions, and general decay. They are very different from what they were when we were here some months ago. But we have got them *all*. And of ourselves we lack now only some half dozen, most of whom will return in due season. Bonham, who was gassed over two months ago, got back today. There is only poor Colin left behind in a certain church-yard under a little wooden cross that bears a little British rosette and the curious inscription, "Mort pour sa patrie." Yes indeed, ours is a cushy job compared with others. I fear that thought must weigh upon one now to the end of one's days.

Good night. I live in the hope of having you soon.


Egremont

TO OLAF                                                         4 November 1918

. . . I spend all my time thinking about my passport & getting in a panic about my clothes & all the sewing that has to be got through before I can take advantage of it, & finally exulting over the war news. Turkey out of it on Friday—"fighting ceased." Austria out of it today! Fighting again has ceased! This is indeed a red-letter day. . . . Oh Olaf darling, if only we might know that hostilities had ceased on the western front! I think I should not know how to contain my joy at the thought of coming to you. Patience—patience. Now I need all the store of it I have saved up. I'm restless. I don't go to sleep for ages. I'm hungry all the day & then when I sit down to table I don't want to eat. I eat so slowly I get bored with myself. All I need else to do now is to wear tight shoes, sigh like a furnace, & write sonnets 'to your eyebrow'—those are the fashionable symptoms, but I'm sure Shakespeare would have included indigestion if he hadn't been too polite. . . .

Nov. 6th. The war news is so very exciting it seems waste of time to write or think of anything else. Will Germany accept the Allies' terms? Will she? If she does there won't be any more fighting! At least with words only. Not with guns.

It looks as if it might end any day, any hour. Oh what glorious news that will be.

Last night I went to a W.E.A. party. There were about 38 of us present, being students from about 5 different classes. It was held in a noisy little school hall not in the nice part of town & we were a gloriously mixed but very happy little company. Middle-aged & grey-haired ladies & young mothers from the Child Study Class. Young men of doubtful age from the Industrial History Class. Lots of girls & young women from the Biology & History classes, all in their best white frocks, & from our class 5 burly looking men & two shy girls of whom I was one, but I wasn't nearly as shy as the other girl. I went round & talked to people, & I do like those 5 burly looking men fellow students. One is a tram driver—one serves sausages in a ham & beef shop in town—one is a staunch trade unionist & the organizing sec. of the W.E.A.—one is just a 'businessman' of some kind—& the last I suspect to be a carrier, but I may be mistaken. *He* gave us a scene from Macbeth. I'm sure I caught a glimpse of his fine grey head sailing down Market St. on a carrier's cart. They are all nature's gentlemen. There were lots of recitations & some music. I was going to sing if there had been a gap, but I didn't offer because they had plenty of items & I was a bit diffident & my voice was tired with talking in such a noisy room. . . . I told Mr. Bland, our tutor, of my prospective departure & marriage & about you, & he was so nice & congratulated me so heartily. He & the "ordinary businessman" say they will come down & see me off & throw red, white & blue streamers on board in the old pre-war way.

[*Olaf's ambivalence about the croix de guerre was not unique. Siegfried Sassoon, like Olaf, suspected that the awarding of medals "became more and more fortuitous and debased as the War went on," and in his* Memoirs of an Infantry Officer *supposed that a psychological study of the Great War would need a whole chapter to explore "medal reflexes" and "decoration complexes." The place names in Olaf's citation had to be left blank when he sent a copy to Agnes; they have been restored from his original.*]

SSA 13

Agnes,                                          8 November 1918

Did I tell you the whole Convoy has been cited again, for work during Sept. & Oct.? This time it is a divisional citation, which entitles us to a silver star alongside the gold one on the croix de guerre on the cars. Many drivers have also been given the croix de guerre, including me. Most of them have divisional citations. Sparrow's name & mine were sent in (I am told) on the original list for divisional citation but were cut off because there were too many on the list. That is what comes of spelling one's name with a letter S instead of, say, a B or a D! So they sent our names in along with three others to the Service de Santé of the Corps d'Armée, so that our crosses are given not by a soldier but by a doctor. . . . The whole matter is a questionable institution, for it causes awful jealousies in our happy home. Decorations are bad in principle, but on the other hand they are useful assets to some people afterwards. For instance one FAU man who got a croix de guerre was delighted to receive, a bit later on, a letter raising his screw from his firm!! Moreover the general public, especially in England, where the croix de guerre seems a strange and distinguished decoration, thinks that if you have a croix de guerre you can't have joined the FAU merely to shirk! Here is the wording of our citation (Sokell, Goodall, Stapledon, Wetherall the most deserving of all because he is our head mechanic, and Livchitz the Russian driver of the French lieutenant's car):

> Depuis plus de trois ans sur le front. Ont assuré le transport des blessés en toutes circonstances, sous les plus violents bombardements, avec zèle, courage, dévouement infatigable, sans se soucier du danger qu'ils pouvaient courir, notament pendant les durs combats de la VESLE, de LA SUIPPE et de la HUNDINGSTELLUNG (Septembre et Octobre 1918)

Amen, so be it, I *don't* think.

It amuses me to be called careless of danger, me who have often had to refrain from speaking for fear of my voice going all of a dither! I am far more courageous than I used to be, thank you, but "careless," jamais de la vie! . . .

*Sunday afternoon.* The Kaiser has abdicated. The crown prince will do so very soon. The armistice should begin in a day or two, we all expect.

Having with great labour sewn on my resplendent ribbon with its little bronze star in the middle I have polished my buttons and boots and am ready to "swank" round the town. But as a matter of fact I have already been for two walks, and so after tea I shall refrain from swanking in order to write to you. . . .

News has just come that the whole of our Division has just been given a fine citation for its recent activities. They seem to be piling on the compliments, don't they. First came the stretcher bearers' corps and us with two flowery citations from the Division, then many individual dittos, and now the *whole* Division cited en masse by the Corps. France is great on la politesse, especially in victory. I have decided that my croix de guerre was given for two things: a) leaving a wounded man in a ditch last July, b) escaping from the gendarmes while trying to loot champagne a few days ago. By Jove it was a narrow squeak! Robin [Bird] and I had gone to a great cellar he knew in a great deserted town. The poilus had previously drunk most of it dry but we reckoned on getting some two dozen bottles for a convoy celebration. With great caution we explored and at last found a few bottles. Each of us burdened himelf with eight, and we began to retrace our steps through broken walls and littered courts. At the gate Robin looked cautiously out into the road and saw two gentlemen of the (military) law coming along. We hastily retired, deposited our bottles, and sauntered away as if merely sightseeing. The gendarmes came in and accosted us, telling us that even to enter here was forbidden. We were duly surprised, and I hazarded the remark, "C'est une maison bosche, n'est-ce pas?" Mais non!—said they. (I had been told it was.) Asked what we were doing, we said we were having a look round (which was neither more nor less than a black lie). We then beat a stately but hasty retreat, and saw them going into the room where we had put our bottles. In fact I heard one say, "Tiens! Les voilà!" But once in the road we hurried to the car and departed sans wine, sans glory, sans honour, and sans everything. . . .

*Next morning.* Vive l'armistice!

The telegram came through in English to this little French town, and one of us had to go to the post office and translate it. Personally I was taking a morning chauf-pieds along the canal when I met an elated artilleur who said, "C'est fini, la guerre."

—"Mais, c'est dans la communiqué?"

—"Oui."

—"Bon."

We are taking a holiday from car repairs etc. to celebrate it. Oh praise the lord for Peace!

Come to England soon, Agnes mine. I am all impatience. I can wait
not a moment longer than is absolutely necessary. Come, come, come.
 Agnes, come to Olaf,
  COME.

                                        Egremont
                                        11 November 1918
My Olaf,                                *Peace Day*
    It is 5 minutes before midnight, but I must write just a line because
this is such a great day. We had the news this evening at 7 o'clock that
the Germans have signed the Armistice. I can't believe it is really the
end of the war. The war seems like a whole life & I can't believe that
that life has come to its last day. What a tumult of thoughts must be
rising tonight from all over the world—mostly of thankfulness that it is
over & much rejoicing & alas! much sorrowing.
    Tomorrow we will begin a new chapter. . . .

17th Nov. . . . How I wish there might be a cable from you just to tell
me that you have come safely to the end of it. Everyone is cabling—
they say the Pacific Cable is chockablock. Soon I am going to get Daddy
to send a cable to you—or, best, to Uncle—to say that, dear, I have got
my passport!
    Life has been a ferment this week of rejoicing officially & unofficially
over a) the signing of the Armistice & the prospect of Peace, b) preparations for getting me ready to sail. Me! Just fancy. This is how it all
happened. I told you about my visit to the Collector of Customs to
apply for my passport. That was over 3 weeks ago, & we thought then
that it might be settled enough for me to sail in March. A week ago
comes Peace bounding on to us from the skies—surely from Heaven.
A false report of the signing of the Armistice came on the Friday before it & Sydney went off its head with excitement. Employees downed
tools & simply walked out of shops, factories, offices, tea-rooms &
the rest. Everyone waved flags or blew whistles or rang bells or banged
kerosene tins. It was a most awful din & all the while it was a false report. . . . When the real news came of course there were two more
public holidays—& once you had seen it, town was a very good place
to be out of. In the meantime I had heard nothing from the Customs
department, & of course I was beginning to fidget. Last Wednesday I
saw Mr. Barclay cutting his front lawn (he lives next to the Armstrongs
in our own street). I wanted to call to him awfully & ask if he had had
any word from Melbourne about me. Silly little ass. I was too shy & I
thought it might not do to track the Chief Collector home & talk shop! I
got past his fence before I came to my senses & walked home kicking

myself. I told Mother how stupid I was & she just said, "Oh what a
pity!" That was enough. I was off again with a firm foot & I called to
him over his front gate just as he was putting up his gardening tools. He
didn't remember my name or my affairs but he remembered my face.
I said "Miss Miller" & then he remembered the whole affair & was very
nice. He ended by promising to send a special wire to Melbourne to
hurry them up with the result that yesterday morning I received an
official document on H.M.S. containing my passport-form, your letter,
& a typed note advising me to arrange my passage & then fill in the
form & present it at the Customs department. I have had Sunday to let
off steam in & I am going to begin going the rounds with Dad tomorrow. I do want to have it all fixed and settled. I want to come in
December if there's a boat—it all depends on boats now. Isn't it thrilling
& wonderful?

[*After the war Lewis F. Richardson, "the Prof," had success as a meteorologist and statistician; he was elected a fellow of the Royal Society. In
1919 his book,* Mathematical Psychology of War, *was privately printed
in Oxford and dedicated to his comrades in SSA 13. Until his death in
1953 he divided his research between studies of weather and of the psychology of conflict.*]

SSA 13
TO AGNES                                                    18 November 1918
. . . I can't realise the great change that has taken place in our affairs,
nor the fact that you may be even now definitely determined to come
soon. I wish I were free *now*. I wish the armistice were a fixed peace &
my turn had already come to be demobilized. I wonder whether I shall
go home & wait a little for you, or go home and go out to you, or go
home and find you there. . . .
     Our billet is an icy loft, all windows that must be kept open to let in
the light. We have now one little stove in it, but that makes practically
no difference. I sit mostly in my bus, and go for a chauf-pied every now
& then. We are going to hire a joy room in the town [Aÿ], & some of us
are hiring private sitting rooms for our particular little families. But my
family is nobler, for it has secured a room and thrown it open to whoever wants a quiet place to read or write—and thereby (oh politic family) it has secured public fuel! And now before the room has even been
opened it announces that guests who wish to establish a *right* must sub-
scribe, & applicants keep tumbling in, too many in fact. The room
opens tomorrow. Of course one still sleeps either in the loft or in a car
(which is what I do). In engaging a room one finds that the first thing

naturally offered is a double-bedded bedroom. Oh France! But I expect England would be the same. They are surprised when you only want a sitter. . . .

*Later*, with a very shaky hand after helping someone to put on a tyre (and anyhow gloves are not conducive to calligraphy). Last night the Prof (Richardson) gave me for criticism a manuscript of his, a book on the psychology of war, a mass of abstruse mathematical symbols and equations. This morning I wrapped myself up and read it through, and subsequently he came himself to "be criticized." Of course the job was quite beyond me, I not being a mathematician, but we had a great discussion about free will and finally of course respectfully agreed to differ. My own book is causing me much tribulation. It must be absolutely *finished* by the time I am demobilized, but unfortunately the cold weather is unpropitious. It is so nearly finished in substance, but it needs a lot of work in revision and fair-copying. . . .

*Later*. Me voici, comfortably entrenched in the new reading room, a long narrow chamber with three windows, a fine fire, two tables, plenty of chairs, and an assortment of crude prints representing hunting and shooting scenes. Never since the Convoy began has one been so comfortable. It is quite a home. Beside me sits Bonham [Roger Carter] versifying, in front sits [Edward] Grace, our inimitable cook writing letters and his diary. By the fire is the Doc writing, and on the other side of the fire Pimm reading. (This all reads like the preliminary stage directions of a Bernard Shaw play. Do you know GBS? He is a tonic, nay more. He upsets all one's preconceived ideas about everything that matters.) On one of our walls is a highly respectable clock merrily ticking off the seconds that still separate Agnes and Olaf. . . . This room bids fair to make writing and reading quite tolerable. I hope we stay here for a long time yet. The other room, the "joy room," is much bigger than this, and is meant for making a noise in, for chatter and singing and general rowdiness. I expect that one will be very much used.

There! That is all of that subject. What next? Oh yes. This afternoon I was formally presented with my croix de guerre. The ceremony was simple. Brown, the second in command and acting chief, came along while I was going to tea, dug a packet out of his pocket and said, "Oh, glad I've met you: I can get rid of this." A piece of tissue paper enclosed the bauble, a bronze cross backed by two crossed swords, with a tiny head of La République Française in the centre, the whole hanging on the ribbon of which I sent you a snippet, and in the middle of the ribbon the modest bronze star. Gold starred crosses are given by the general in person, and palm leaves earn also a kiss from the general. Silver and bronze are given by the commanding officer of the unit at a formal parade, but of course we dispense with all that, being a family so to speak.

SSA 13

TO AGNES                                    22 November 1918

. . . We are trekking again, worse luck. We have left our nice little town, our cosy hired rooms and our feeling of secure establishment. Goodness knows how far we shall go now. Today's move has been very short, & indeed all the moves must be short, because of course the troops have to walk, & what is for them a long day is for us such a speck of a move that it seems hardly worthwhile loading up all our "gunk." My car was loaded with five tables, ten benches, the kitchen stove, and other household goods. . . .

*Another day*, still trekking. . . . Today's run was rather awful, all through ruined country, over awful roads and hills like steep gables. It is funny to find civilians in such places. One is used to them as deserted villages; but now in the midst of rubble and garbage one finds perhaps a little dirty pretty maiden with a kitten in her arms, or a lot of buxom dames drawing water. Such incidents enlivened the run, but with a heavy load and crowds of shell holes one got pretty fed up, especially moving "in convoy" and always either getting left behind or trying not to bump the bus in front.

SSA 13

TO AGNES                                    29 November 1918

. . . We are still trekking, the weather is soaking, everything is muddy, my car is nearly full to the roof with goods, the billet tonight is a very poor one, so I have spent an hour and a half in building myself a sleeping and living place inside my car by much thought and much physical labour among the benches and table tops. The net result is a compact heaven, though rather a grimy one. I have a lovely wide bed made on a table top, all ready to get into. Its only fault is that it is so near the ceiling that I fear there is not enough room to perform the delicate operation of wriggling into the blankets. I have a seat upon the kitchen stove, a writing table made out of a drawing board and an iron bar, two lamps (petrol or paraffin according to taste), a little talc window looking out upon the world, which is a horribly wet world, and a long narrow passage leading from my heaven to the said world, a passage hewn out among the benches, table tops, packing cases, and other gunk. . . .

War towns are of various classes. There is the fully inhabited place where we get all the joys of civilization but have to put up with a poor billet or hire rooms and trust to the official ravitaillement for fuel. Then there is the paradisal deserted but not destroyed town, where we have the pick of many houses with no more formality than chaulking up on a plank "Sparrow, Stap etc.," where there are arm chairs and tables and limitless fuel, where there are no rules to keep, nor proprieties, where the fair sex is absent, so that one can bathe in the main street. Then there is the more seriously strafed town where water-tight places are hard to find, where much of the first day has to be spent in searching for a room, clearing away rubble, putting ground sheets over the roof, and disputing over dry floor space for one's bed. Lastly there is the quite destroyed town where there is nothing to be had but cellars. Such is our armistice classification of towns. During the war each class might be unstrafed, occasionally strafed, frequently strafed, or (finally & most tersely)—hell.

[*The first of several delays in Agnes's journey to England came when she decided to discard her plan to sail from Australia to Vancouver after Christmas, proceed by train across North America, and then cross the Atlantic to Liverpool. Olaf's father urged the Millers instead to wait for one of the passenger ships from his own Blue Funnel Line to call at Sydney.*]

Egremont
TO OLAF                                    2 December 1918
. . . Dad has been reading one of the "Quite So Stories"—political skit on the "Just So." It was the one about conscientious objectors & it was horrid. I hated it. It resulted in a wild argument on my part & expostulation, & a long dissertation on Dad's part, & now I feel that in spite of 12000 miles that are between us you are the nearest of all my dearest to me. I haven't bothered about this question lately for some time, & this little revival recalls the feelings of many past occasions. Always I felt I had to turn to you for understanding & sympathy & underneath the thankfulness that you were you, & that you understood—there was always the weary war dejection, the anxiety, the unknown, endless uncertainty. Now it is so different. The war is over. I am coming to you. I shall see you soon, soon. . . .

The day before yesterday we had your reply to our first cable proposing that I should come home by the "Nestor" instead of the "Niagara." Dear old Blue Funnel. Yes, I think it will be much nicer to come that way & much more comfy for me, traveling by myself. I wasn't exactly looking forward to piloting myself & all my luggage across America. Dad went to the Agents to see about my passage & it's all fixed up. Isn't it glorious! I feel so sure & safe now that I am to come on a Blue Funnel. It is expected to sail about the end of January.

[*Horace Fleming, a bootmaker from Birkenhead, was one of the leaders
of the adult education movement in the Liverpool area. Fleming had
made Olaf's own boots—but made them too small, and whenever he
could in 1918 Olaf went without socks.*]

SSA 13

Agnes,                                          8 December 1918

This letter will probably miss you, but never mind. I will keep on
writing until I know definitely what you are doing, and then I will try to
catch you at various ports of call. Father says now that the "Nestor" is
leaving in January, so I do hope you will come by her, especially as she
is to come by the Canal. . . . Meanwhile I have had a letter from Horace Fleming, former warden of Beechcroft Settlement in Birkenhead,
asking me to see him as soon as possible about taking on work in residence there. (Such work is unpaid.) He says the place is "getting out of
touch with Labour," and is too middle class, and that he wants someone
to be resident there who can bring it back into the right way. During the
last year a L'pool professor has done the job, but not as a resident, &
apparently not with success. I have told Fleming that I cannot get away
for a couple of months anyhow, that I feel most unfitted for the job, as I
myself am now hopelessly out of touch with Labour & all local labour
organisations, that what I want is to teach, not to organise (which I generally muddle), but that I should very much like to work at Beechcroft
when I am free. I also said that I am quite decided to devote myself
entirely to adult education in one form or another, that the WEA by
itself does not seem to be sufficient, that I feel that the most urgent work
at present is this great intellectual (or spiritual) awakening, and that my
future wife is as keen as I am to take part.

[*A song popular among British soldiers began: "I don't want to go back
to the trenches again; Oh my! I don't want to die."*]

SSA 13

Agnes,                                          15 December 1918

It is Sunday, and I have just been out in the forest for the whole day
with the Artist. . . . The Artist is no use at seeing beasts & birds. He
always misses them. But of course a walk "à deux" is quite different from
a lone walk in that respect, for with a companion one is always talking
or making some noise, but by oneself one wanders silently at one's own
sweet will in strange & wild ways, and now one sits long at the foot of a
tree to watch squirrels, and now one stalks a bird, and now one hurries
from one district to another. I have a passion for that sort of thing. Yesterday, for instance, I did it, and now and then I came upon one or

other of the [convoy] artists squatting at the foot of a tree sketching, and sometimes they saw me & sometimes not, & when I got back I was greeted with a wonderful myth that I had been seen running hairy & naked & cloven-hoofed in the forest, a myth produced by Routh Smeal, one of the artists.

*Next Day.* . . . I say, when *did* we get engaged? I am blowed if I know. It was at no particular time, was it, but just at lots of times. It was a process, not an event. . . .

You ask if I would have been content to die in the cause for which England was fighting. I am still not allowed to talk politics, but be sure I should have been most discontented to die in that or any other cause at all. "I—*don't* want—to die; I—want—to go *home*," as the song says. But had one been knocked out one would have held that one was dying in the cause for which after all the FAU does stand in spite of its mixed composition, to uphold the attitude of being a pacifist who is eager to help those who suffer by war. I think it is a great pity that the FAU did not get the chance to uphold that position with more heroism. I believe that if half the personnel of the FAU had been killed "in battle" they would not have died in vain. Theoretically I should be "content" to die in that cause, very proud in fact, though for honesty's sake one has to admit that whenever there was any danger one's whole personality was gathered into one intense hope that one would not get killed or mauled. If one had had a lot of real danger that hope would have become a permanent obsession. As it was, it sank into the background as soon as the danger was over, and one began to pretend one was rather disappointed not to have had a finer opportunity of showing off one's calm and philosophic courage.

[*Because of postponements of her voyage, this letter was actually delivered to Agnes at home in Sydney. Some of Olaf's subsequent letters, however, were timed to be waiting for her at Ceylon, Bombay, and Port Said as she made her way toward England.*]

SSA 13

TO AGNES                                        22 December 1918

. . . I don't know where you will be when you get this letter. I am going to send it to Father to forward to one of the Nestor's ports of call. It does seem odd to think of your not getting this at home. Wherever you are, if you are homesick, dear, cheer up. The future is full of a great new life. And when you get this I, wherever I am, shall be waiting with eagerness such as I have never had before. . . . How I long for next spring, *the* spring of all springs. It is a late spring in both our lives. I suppose it is

not really the spring of our lives anymore, but it seems as if it must be.
Come quickly, happy April.

Egremont
TO OLAF                                              22 December 1918
. . . 20 days since I wrote to you! Who could have believed me capable
of such utter utter neglect? I for one could not. Could you? Oh such lots
& lots of things have happened. I think these have been the most exciting 20 days I can ever have spent. I don't know how I'll manage to remember everything to tell you but I do want to tell you everything—all
about it—because you are really included in all the parties & wedding
presents & excitements. . . . I must tell you that though I have not written for so long, according to the papers there has been no mail out since
my last letter. If there had been a mail I simply would have *made*
time—even if it had meant staying up until 2 in the morning instead of
only one. The boats have been fearfully disorganised owing to this horrible influenza epidemic. . . . In Sydney it has been wonderfully held
in check so far. It hasn't really broken out here at all, though there are
said to be over 2000 people cooped up in Quarantine Station, people
who have come from overseas & from infected ships. . . .
    I shalln't get an answer to these letters of mine—they don't need an
answer anyway—they are too—just spasmodic, but I ought to get letters
written almost up to Christmas, & I wonder if you will be able to write
to ports. No one seems to know yet what ports the "Nestor" will call at—
owing to influ!—nor when actually she will sail from Sydney. The latest
I have heard is February 4 (Daddy's birthday). . . .

*Boxing Day.* Now let me tell you of all the excitements there were at
home before we left [to spend the holiday season at Blackheath]. I don't
know which was the first, but I think my last day at the factory was altogether the most exciting. Several of the girls knew I was going to England to be married. I had told them some time ago, but I wasn't thinking that anything unusual would happen when I sat in the tram going to
Redfern on my last Friday. I was a minute or two late & as I hurried up
the lane one of the girls rushed up to me—a goodnatured, untidy,
homely looking girl—& seized my hand which she shook like a pump
handle saying, "Miss Miller, I 'ear yer goun' to be married. I wish yer
the best o' luck!" I felt pleased & I hurried on. When I came near the
factory I could *see* that something unusual was going to happen, for
there were rows of heads peeping from the windows, nudging each
other & whispering "Here she comes!"—heads that usually have lost no
time in disappearing from the workroom to make the most use of the
lunch half hour. I ran up the outside staircase and was met at the door

by Annie Reavell, the forewoman & a rather particular friend of mine. She looked very important & pleased as she told me to follow her. The machine room, usually deserted except by the few who sweep up the morning's debris, was now in a state of excitement—all the girls, about 50 or 60 of them, were assembled round the manager's table. There was a row of them about 4 deep all round the table—then a row perched on benches behind & the back row standing up on tables to get a better view. I was led like a lamb to the slaughter through the midst of this alarming crowd to the raised table where the little white-haired manager was standing. He asked me to take a seat—which I did, only too thankful to be not quite so conspicuous—while he proceeded to make me a speech & the girls all stared at me very hard & I wanted to cry. . . . It was altogether a very wonderful little scene & quite overwhelming. At the end he presented me on behalf of the girls with a most beautiful silver vase—a tall shapely vase & then I had to stand up & say a little word in reply to thank them all. . . . And you shall see & admire *soon* that vase that was given me on Dec. 6th in the workroom of John Hunter & Sons, Redfern. . . .

I have had a lovely travelling leather cushion given me by the ladies of our little Monday sewing meeting, & then I have had a lot of other lovely presents—in all of which you are included. Two beautiful hand-painted china cups, saucers & plates from Miss Turner—a lovely silver sugar basin & cream jug from the Graham family . . . and first of all, which I forgot to mention—I somehow don't like mentioning it very much—a cheque for 10 guineas from Jack A., written & delivered by his twin Nell. It seems he asked her to do it for him on the last night before he left for France. She walked down to the boat with him. It was like him—poor old John. I don't like thinking about it much.

SSA 13

Agnes,                                          31 December 1918

I don't know if you will ever get this or where you will get it if you do get it. Anyhow I must talk to you even if you never hear what I say. . . . Our great news is that owing to the working of the general demobilization about ten of our younger fellows are going to leave us to start next term at their various 'varsities. One went today, two go tomorrow, and so on. This looks like real business, and we are now all impatient to get away. Unfortunately I have no official claim whatever & must wait till the final disbanding of the convoy at the end of January or later. Meanwhile I am now stationed near the Belgian frontier doing ordinary work and trying to get the cars finally into condition before we give them up. . . .

The future is very far from clear, and I have a nightmare vision of finally dying without ever having seriously "done my bit" for the world. Anyone's bit is bound to be very tiny compared with all that the world does for him; but one does not expect to pay off the debt, rather to pay some little fraction of it. Oh I do want to talk to you and consult you about many things. Come quickly! It is no use talking to you any longer about the dull little affairs of SSA 13. All those are of the past, and it is the future that concerns us. . . .

Now I will stop this little letter and send it off in case it may just be in time to catch you at some port of call. I will write again soon, always little letters frequently, so as to have more chance of catching you with one or another. I hope your voyage will be a good one, and with nice people, and I hope it will be a quick one.

Good-bye dearie. I——but words are poor things.

With great love
W<sup>m</sup> Olaf Stapledon

# ✎ *1919*

Cymbeline

TO OLAF                                        3 January 1919

. . . Where are the words I want? I can never tell you how much I love
you. Someday perhaps you will know without my telling. I want you to
know but I shall never be able to tell in words. I want to tell by giving
you all that I have—& am—not much, but yet all—myself. You used
to persuade me that girls would never *want* to give themselves up—
would never be won in the end without a struggle. (That was in the days
when I was not ready.) You were wrong—the struggle comes only at the
beginning & afterwards one *longs* only to make the complete surrender.
I feel I want to perform impossible tasks for your love, as Psyche did at
cruel Venus' bidding.

SSA 13

TO AGNES                                        6 January 1919

. . . Well, girl, a dear letter came from you yesterday telling me about
your interview with a benevolent gent on the subject of a passport. I
laughed and could have danced for joy at that delightful incident, especially over the secret fact that the famous letter that you showed was the
one I subsequently said I wished I had never written. But in case of further difficulties—Agnes Miller, I do ask thee to be my wife. Agnes Miller, I ask thee to come straightaway to England to marry me. Agnes Miller, I implore thee to come. Agnes Miller, I love thee more than I love
any other soul. Now let him put his blue pencil marks against that if he
wants something definite. I, Olaf Stapledon, need thee Agnes Miller,
and beg thee to come to England at once. . . .

There is a sadness over us of SSA 13, for many of us have already left the Convoy. Teddy has gone, and leaves a void in my heart. It is queer without him. I wonder when I shall see him again, and I wonder how he will fare in the world. He will succeed of course, for he always succeeds; but maybe he runs a risk of over-respectability, having been brought up in a highly respectable and subtly pharisaical tradition, like so many young Friends. But by nature he is pure honesty, simplicity and generosity. And pharisaical is too ugly a word for the state of mind I mean. Teddy is a loss to everyone, and to me specially, for I was always a lover of Teddy. Saul [Denis Goodall] has gone too, to continue schoolmastering. He went in a hurry today, by special order obtained by his headmaster. . . . All this trickling away of members is very disconcerting. I hope we shall soon trek north and be disbanded.

Cymbeline

TO OLAF                                                  12 January 1919
. . . Do you know, I think I am so awfully lucky that I can share—at least a little—in your work. You might have been a banker or a cotton man or something that I should not have been half so glad to be interested in. Of course I should have been *interested*, whatever you had been, but W.E.A. is just the very thing I would have wanted to do myself if I had been a bachelor-girl & clever enough withal. I suppose all sensible wives get more or less drawn into their husbands' work—they mostly seem to take an intelligent interest in the details of it anyway—but still I don't think Mother can find as much real interest in skins & hides as I think I shall in the W.E.A. There is always a lot of small talk & personal details connected with every business & profession, but I think in your work there will be more for me than that, will there not?

SSA 13
Best Beloved,                                            13 January 1919
The news is that we shall probably leave for the coast in less than a week, and perhaps be home in three weeks from now!! It seems unbelievable. The end of convoy life! So many people that one has been closely packed with for so long will suddenly vanish. No more washing of cars, and greasing, no more wood gathering, no more rabble-ous convoy meals. For the loss of friends I shall be grieved, but for nothing else save the general outdoor life. . . .

I wish I was five years younger! I don't *feel* old, but I am falling to bits, and you will have a horrid shock when you find you are going to marry a broken down old man, who, though to the casual observer he appears to be about twenty, on closer inspection seems at least fifty-five.

So you know what to expect, wrinkles, scrubbiness, blear-eyes and general decay, a reluctance to lift great weights, etc. etc. etc.

SSA 13
TO AGNES                                                  18 January 1919
. . . I wonder if you will ever get this letter. Seeing that they do not yet know what route the Nestor is to take I should think Father will hardly know where to send it. Anyhow there is a chance that you may get it somewhere. Oh I wish I could be on that voyage with you. I feel a little jealous of your fellow passengers. Don't like any of them more than a tiny bit. Fellows on board ship are apt to make themselves nice while fellows at the far end of the voyage are merely impotently waiting and longing. I knew a girl that went a voyage (with her wedding cake) to marry a man in South Africa, but fell in love with another on the way & married him with the very same cake. I know of *two* other girls that did much the same thing, one of them on a Blue Funnel. Of course I know perfectly well you won't, but—I can't help thinking of those other girls and wishing I were with you. Oh yes, I am jealous for you. It's useless to pretend I am not.
     We are off in a hurry, so good-bye, dearie.
                                 Your lover      Olaf Stapledon


[*Schedules for passenger liners remained unpredictable in the months after the war; many were still in government employ, and those that had resumed service were subject to diversion for military use. The great influenza epidemic, just reaching Australia, threw timetables into further disarray, and Agnes's sailing date was repeatedly delayed.*]


                                                          Cymbeline
Dearest,                                                  20 January 1919
     This is only a little note & it doesn't count—but the "Niagara" sails tomorrow & I am sending this just in case there is no other letter of mine on board. The "Niagara" is the ship I was to have sailed by. My hat! What excitement if I had. You see how late she is, though she was down for Jan. 2. Everything is all upside down, first with influenza scares & disorganisation & then with the firemen's strike for higher wages & life insurance in case of influ. Any excuse for a strike! They certainly have a rotten job, but they are such a shifty lot. They change their grievance every second day. We have been absolutely cut off from New Zealand for months except for the American boats, & there have been good ships lying in the harbour for weeks doing nothing because

they can't get a crew. I hope the "Nestor"'s crew won't be affected. She has only just arrived in W.[estern] A.[ustralia] & they say there is some sickness on board, so I am afraid there may be further delays. . . .

Auntie said she thought it very important for us to have some time together before we are married. Do you think so? I don't know how I *shall* feel, but at present I don't want to wait any longer than necessary. I think if we wait just long enough for me to get my wedding dress & my "going away dress"—that would be just right.

[*The slow progress of the SSA 13 convoy to Unit headquarters at Dunkirk ended on 21 January. The drivers and mechanics then had to make the cars presentable and turn them over to the British Red Cross in Boulogne. Because his Sunbeam had been donated by his father, Olaf kept it; and after his certificate of discharge was issued on 25 January, he crossed the Channel and drove the battered car to a Liverpool garage. After taking the ferry over the Mersey from Liverpool to Birkenhead, he walked the last ten miles to his parents' house.*]

Annery
My darling,                                                     1 February 1919

This is to catch you at Bombay, where I hope you will see Enid [Kirkus] and Frank [Noyce] before they go. It is long since I wrote to you but not long since I thought of you, for I think of you in an undercurrent all the time, and there is less and less "under" about it as your approach draws near. I reached home on Sunday morning; it is now Friday afternoon. I don't think I have written since Fourmiés, the place where the convoy spent about three weeks. Thence we went to Dunkirk in two stages through Lille & Armentières, having said good-bye to our division at Fourmiés. We spent three fearfully busy days at Dunkirk getting the cars ready to give up, and arranging our own affairs. . . .

Father keeps telling me of new delays every day, the latest being that [the *Nestor*] must go to Brisbane. Alas, when will you arrive? End of April anyhow. Here is my programme, very rough.

| | |
|---|---|
| February ⎫ | reading, writing & something else of which I will tell |
| March   ⎬ | later. Also interviews. |
| April | AGNES |
| May | Wedding & Honeymoon |
| June | General settling down |
| July | Summer School at Bangor |
| August | Peace & Quiet, also swotting |
| September | Organising classes |
| October | Tutorial Classes begin |

TO OLAF                                    3 February 1919

. . . We were due to stay up [at Blackheath] another week & then come down to get me ready for "Nestor" on Feb. 22nd. . . . We were quite expecting to leave on Wednesday when Tuesday's paper came & scattered our plans to the wind with the announcement that the epidemic of pneumonic influenza had broken out in Sydney & that all the quarantine regulations & precautions were to come into force at once. All schools to be closed, theatres, pictures etc. Everyone requested to be inoculated as soon as possible—to wear a mask & to stand by the authorities in trying to fight the terrible scourge that had ravaged so many countries. There was no sense in our all coming down especially as the children's schools were not to open, & yet I had to pack & shop in case the sailing date remained fixed. Mother's idea was that if the epidemic were to spread & become very serious it would be best for me to get all my shopping done while it was possible, so as Dad & I had already been inoculated it was decided that only he & I should come down. So we came & soon joined the bemuzzled but otherwise indifferent crowd in town & I did very good execution in the way of a hat & several pair of shoes etc. etc. . . . Let's hope it has been taken in time & that there will not be the awful havoc there was in South Africa, America & New Zealand. Melbourne has got it pretty badly & it has spread to us with the returning soldiers & through the Melbourne authorities' scandalous behaviour in not declaring themselves an infected state. They had hundreds of cases & 30 or 40 deaths before they declared themselves. So far we only have about 50 cases in all, & with luck & care we may get free of the wretched thing. One of the first things Dad & I did when we got home was to go to Gilchrist, Watt & Sanderson's to learn my fate & the "Nestor"'s. Such a tale of disorganisation & upset as we heard! It seems the "Nestor," which is now quarantined in Melbourne, is first of all to pick up Queensland soldiers from many ships & take them up to Brisbane where she will probably be quarantined again! Then down to Sydney to be knocked into shape for passengers. In the meantime, after the ship is booked up fully the Imperial Government commandeers half the accommodation for Mesopotamian soldiers to be picked up by us at Bombay!! "I'm afraid you're likely to put in a couple of weeks there, Miss Miller," said Mr. Clarence looking at me with commiseration. "I don't anticipate your having a very comfortable trip." However I made sure that my name was not one of the 50 per cent to be crossed off & for the rest I'll take my chance. . . .

Feb. 5. . . . Rosie & I have been a great day shopping. We took lunch over & called in for Dad & took him down into the Botanical Gardens where we sat on a seat under a tree & breathed God's air *without our masks on* & ate our lunch. It is advisable to avoid eating in crowded restaurants nowadays with this epidemic in the air. The wearing of masks has been compulsory for the last few days & people in trams & streets & public places who have failed to comply have been arrested & fined 20/. or more. Quite a blow to be stopped by a bobby & fined. Oh they are dreadfully stuffy suffocating things, these masks. We had ours on the whole afternoon. It was quite a treat to go into a shop & try on a hat because you simply had to take it off to see yourself—you look hideous in any hat when your face is swathed in white butter muslin!

[*As Olaf's entrance into the FAU had been delayed by an appendectomy, so his return to civilian life was slowed by the need for another operation. The required bed-rest prevented him from following one tentative plan of sailing to Port Said to join Agnes for the rest of the journey to England.*]

Liverpool

Agnes, 14 February 1919

Now I will tell thee all about it. Some time last spring or previous winter, either from a kick at rugger or from the mere starting up of frozen cars during the winter, I got slightly ruptured. I guessed there was something slightly wrong, but it was not wrong enough to bother about, & it did not get worse. Later, we were far too busy for me to think about it at all, but after the armistice was signed I began to think perhaps I had better do something. . . . I came home, saw the surgeon who did my appendicitis, and was told to go to this nursing home in a week's time. Well, the operation, which was not a big affair, is over and I am patiently waiting to be allowed to get up, though they say I must spend at least a fortnight in bed, worse luck. This affair is nothing to do with my appendicitis affair, which has stood "the stress of war" remarkably well. I guess it is simply "tearing one's guts out" at starting cars with the engine stuck up with frozen oil. You can't imagine what a frantic affair it used to be, with a primus under the oil sump, hot asbestos on the carburetor, and ever grind, grind for an hour, sometimes. Of course, the kick at rugger may have helped, I don't know. Anyhow it is finished now, & there is but to get strong again. . . .

*Another day.* . . . The mail goes tomorrow, the last that will catch you at Bombay. Then Port Said, then England. Do you remember almost the first night of our first meeting (no you can't) when you said good night to me over the Garsdale bannisters, "Goodnight, Mr. O." And all your hair flopped down as you bent over and it brushed my face as you kissed me like a good little cousin? Do you remember (no) playing

spillikins in Grandma's drawing room? But I keep reminding you of all
these things so often.

[*Just before departing Sydney, Agnes received a last big batch of letters
from Olaf and suddenly knew that the epistolary stage of their courtship was coming to an end and that her definition of "home" was about
to change. The "pack of notes" was an envelope full of messages from
Olaf's colleagues, most of them a mixture of warm thanks for Agnes's
frequent gifts of homemade cakes to SSA 13 during the war and of
amused observations on Olaf's interminable letters to her.*]

Egremont
TO OLAF                                                    2 March 1919
. . . I don't know where I am. I have had the most beautiful mail—it
has showered in almost every day this week. Nov. 17 & 22nd, Dec. 8th,
14th, 22, 24, & 30th, including a pack of notes little & big from the
convoy. Oh it has been a happy week! Partly from these & partly from
excitements of one kind & another I have been in good spirits all the
day, & even managed to be philosophic when I heard that the "Nestor"
was put off from the 5th to 8th March. You will not share in my philosophy perhaps, but it wouldn't be nice to be depressed when the family is
so pleased about it. Your letters were all darlings, specially the last
one—because you talked about future prospects in the W.E.A. & elsewhere. By the way, this letter was forwarded by Uncle to the gent in
Adelaide with instructions to send it on to me if there should be time
before the "Nestor"'s sailing. It came with a little explanatory note in a
typed envelope. I thought it looked only some dull old thing & it turned
out to be the dearest thing the post could bring! The two previous letters
were also sent direct here by Uncle. I hope I may get some on the way
home. (Home?) You are a dear to go on writing just on the off chance,
but of course you would, & of course I would too. Why, if you had been
killed I think I must have gone on writing. I simply must write to you.
You know, during the last four weeks I only got one letter from you.
People kindly suggested that you must think I was already on my way &
had stopped writing on that account. But I refused to be consoled in that
way. I knew you couldn't stop writing.

Egremont
TO OLAF                                                    3 March 1919
. . . This is to be the end of the last letter from home. The mail goes
today via America & it will reach you about the end of April, I suppose.
Perhaps I may catch an earlier mail to you from Bombay if we are held

up there for a week or so as is supposed—& then dear, I myself shall be the next letter! Shall I come to London? to Liverpool? Will you come to meet me? Shall I spy you in the distance? What shall I be thinking? What will you? Look out for a girl just my height in a *very* dark brown coat & skirt & a funny little brown hat that perhaps you have seen in photographs. She will have features just like mine & hair that you know & her eyes will be watching & her heart beating—for you.

Goodbye till then. Come quick the day & speed the good ship "Nestor"

bringing to you
Agnes

[*Olaf's up-to-date information about sailing dates came from telegrams received by his father at the Blue Funnel office.*]

Annery
4 March 1919

Agnes dear,

So now the Nestor's sailing is postponed another week and she will not leave Sydney till the eighth. Alas! And yet I daresay your people will be very glad to have you for a week longer, and you will be glad to stay. But oh I am so tired of waiting. . . . There is a horrid & apparently unfounded rumour that the government will make all Australian passengers land at Bombay to make room for Indian troops!!! Father says it is unfounded and idiotic. . . .

*5 March.* There is snow on the ground, but the thrushes and robins are singing. Last March when they sang I was hopeless. This March I feel full of music like the thrushes. I can't sing as they do, but I am full of music all the same! I could pour out inky rhapsodies to you, but inky rhapsodies do not ring as true as bird-song rhapsodies, so I will be sober. I walked down to the shore just now, and saw the smooth water and listened to the little ripples licking the sand. There was not a gull or any bird present on the shore. I think they must have all gone to meet the Nestor. Oh for the wings of—an oyster-catcher or a dottrel! When you read this rubbish in Bombay and wish it was more interesting, comfort you with the sense that all the rubbish I ever write to you is merely a variation on the one delightful theme

which may be a very bad score, but it is a lovely tune. Or in another art:—

*Olaf loves Agnes,*
*and she loves him;*
*may these love each other*
*when their old eyes are dim.*

Your own rather foolish
Olaf


Annery
TO AGNES                                               10 March 1919
. . . Where are we going to be married? You ask me, and I ask you. It is
generally the bride's job to decide that, but of course things are different
in our queer circumstances. A few days ago came a letter from Auntie
Nina asking that and other questions, & wishing you could be married
from her house. Now the point is, what kind of wedding do you want? I
am personally an outlandish person with outlandish views, and I think
of ceremonies—the simpler the better, and the least ceremonious the
most sincere. The Church wedding service is rather a scandal, because
it makes both man and woman promise all sorts of things they can't be
sure of doing—does it not? (I have not read it for ages.) Anyhow we are
neither of us Anglicans. Of other services I confess I like best the rigorous simplicity of the Quaker plan. I believe I should like best, if it were
feasible, to go and marry you at Reigate Meeting House. . . .

You ask *when* shall we get married. I don't know how long a wedding
garment takes to make, but I should think it will be a longish job in
these straitened days. When it is ready should be high time to get married. The sooner the better I think. You may very well feel when the
time comes that you would like first to have time to get used to England
before getting used to being married. But that will really not take long.
. . . The main difficulty will be finding a house. It is most awfully hard
in England just now. People one knows have had fearful difficulties. I
think we should do best with a little house at Upton or some other place
this side of the water [the Wirral side of the river Mersey] and as much
in the country as possible without being out of touch with Liverpool.
There will be serious financial problems for us also unless my WEA
screw gets greatly raised. I have about £2000 worth of stock which
brings in a bit every year, but only a bit; also some three or four hundred
in the bank, and that is absolutely all. Father will give us generous help
I know, and he can well afford; for he always says he does not know what
to do with his money, and the way he chucks it to charities etc. is startling, e.g., the FAU got £50 a month from him for nearly four years, &
as to Ruskin College, the Liverpool Settlement etc. etc. etc., they must
account for many thousands all told. Then these hosts of poor relations

who are always getting sent to colleges or varsities, or trips to Timbuctoo for health. And he tells me all about them & what he is doing for them.

Annery
Agnes, best beloved,                                                        25 March 1919
    This will be, I suppose, the last letter that I shall write to you before seeing you again. I cannot realize it. . . . We reckon you are now at Colombo. I do hope the voyage is being pleasant. And I hope you will see Enid. I wonder whether you will make any friends on board. Probably.

[*The* Nestor *docked in Colombo in mid-March and Agnes disembarked for a railway tour of the mountains of Ceylon, under the chaperonage of a white-toupeed gentleman named Mr. Tarwell, who had three other young women from the ship in his charge—"a four-fold harem," Agnes wrote to her parents. On 29 March the ship entered Bombay harbor (the registered birthplace of Frank Miller, who had been born at sea in 1864), where it remained nine days, unloading bales of Australian wool and taking on 1,800 troops below decks and 56 officers to join the passengers on the upper deck. Enid Kirkus, recently married to Frank Noyce, was Olaf and Agnes's cousin from Garsdale, Liverpool.*]

Bombay
TO OLAF                                                                      3 April 1919
. . . I am in India—in Bombay—in Malabar—in Mrs. Wiles' flat—in Frank Noyce's bedroom—sitting in the bed in my nightie & my blue kim. I should have explained that Frank has decamped for the night, leaving me his room, & has gone to stay with the people down below.
    I have missed Enid, alas! & only by a week or 10 days. She could not stay longer on account of the heat. Isn't it bad luck? But never mind, Frank is here & he is being very nice to me & giving me a good time.
. . . I have been thinking & thinking about you. Sometimes on the ship I get frantically homesick—not for home (Australia I mean!) but for you. I get more & more at home on the ship & fond of it, but the voyage is too long, too long. This is the only voyage that has ever been too long. Even when I went home last time, the voyage was not too long! but now I wish it would end in a few days or a week. . . . I have lots of nice friends on board & the Captain & everybody is looking after me beautifully & the "Nestor" is the dearest ship on the sea & I have not been seasick & I have only fallen in love 10 times. We arrived in Bombay on Saturday March 29th & to my joy there came 5 letters for me from

you—also 1 from your Mother. The three earlier were from France—
the two latter from home—no, the last was from hospital. . . .

I had no word from Enid on arrival & thought they must have left
Bombay altogether. On Monday morning however I got on the track of
Frank's cotton affair & actually found him. He was ever so surprised. He
had been away & had only just arrived back the evening before. He had
been as far as Delhi to take Enid & the baby. Since I met him Bombay
has cheered up for me & I don't find it nearly so hot & dirty & unallur-
ing. I begin to find even that it has a distinct charm. . . . On Tuesday
he took me out to tea at the Taj Mahal Hotel—*the* place—& then a
little run round in the car before going back to catch the tender. We are
very much hampered by the "Nestor"'s lying about 2 miles out in the
harbour. At least it's ever so much nicer really because we get the cool
breeze without which we should be undone, but it is awkward because
we are so tied down to catching the tender. It is too precarious getting
small boats, because it's generally a bit choppy when the breeze is up, &
you get wet at best, & then there are sailing boats all full of jabbering
natives & it's not nice. The last boat goes back at 6 o'clock so that you
can't go to any evening function without staying ashore the night. You
can't stay ashore the night because there isn't a spare bed in Bombay.
Frank had arranged dinner & a theatre last night & he was very taken
aback when I mentioned that my last boat was at 6 o'clock. India just
begins to live about 5 o'clock & it is hard luck to be cut off from it altogether. However Mrs. Wiles kindly came to the rescue & invited me to
spend the day with her here & stay the night. . . .

Now I'm not going to write any more. I didn't mean to write so much
even. . . . I won't write to Annery or Garsdale because I'm so tired of
writing letters. You give them all my love in advance & tell them I'm
counting the days. How will the middle of May be for our wedding?
Between your birthday & mine. . . . Goodbye & this is really & truly
the last au revoir.

[*In mid-April the* Nestor *reached Port Said where Agnes visited Uncle
James Stapledon, who showed her around the house where Olaf had
lived as a young child in the 1880s. On 30 April the ship docked in
Liverpool. When she saw Olaf on the landing stage, he "looked just the
same—ridiculously juvenile," she wrote to her mother. "I thought I was
going to meet a man of 33—& there he was not a day more than 21!"
After a reunion lunch at the Blue Funnel offices, everyone returned to
Annery. But a few days later Agnes abruptly left to go to her Aunt
Nina at White Lodge in Reigate, Surrey, because she was tired and
Reigate felt more like home to her, and for another, more important*

*reason referred to only glancingly. The wedding date, once contemplated
for mid-May, became indefinite. "It has been," Agnes mysteriously
wrote to her mother on 7 May, "the strangest, weirdest, most incomprehensible week that I've ever put in in my life." The mystery
would not be explained to her parents until late August; meanwhile,
once more, she and Olaf were communicating by letter.]*

Annery

Darling girl,                                                11 May 1919

Twenty-four hours ago I began a letter to you, and here is another.
. . . Oh my darling, my darling friend, I have wakened into a new
range of living since you came. I wish I could wake you as you have
wakened me. I am all an aching desire that you should be happy,
strong, and blessed with loving as I am blessed. In the spring the crowding life of plants & birds seems to be the nature of all the universe. But,
dear, this lovely business of living is very short and for most creatures is
no less tragic than lovely. Today I saw a wretched little half fledged bird
crushed in the road. Down in West Kirby there is Mrs. Kerr, slowly,
painfully dying. Humanity's sorrows are fortunately beyond the reach of
one small mind, but sometimes we get terrible glimpses of it to blast all
our joy. Yes, this lovely spring and pure joy of life is a very rare & precious thing. And what is the end of all this rigmarole of mine? Why of
course—oh Agnes, love me, love me, not only for my sake, for I am
already blessed in loving you, but for your own sake that you may be
blessed too while yet it is spring time for you. . . . These few days away
from you seem more anxious and weary than all those years, somehow,
because now I love *you* and not a dream. I love a little girl whose hair is
soft and sunny, whose face is a little pale, but sometimes blushes, whose
eyes look generally away from me, but sometimes look right into the
heart of me. I love a little girl who has the sweetest Australian voice, and
certain dear manners of gaiety and gentleness. I love a girl who kept me
waiting very long so as to be sure, then was gallantly loyal to me for long
years, then lost herself on board ship and now is still all adrift and
troubled. Oh I love her all the more for that, for it shows her human, &
it has shown me her absolute honesty. I will not let her go. She is the
angel and I am Jacob. And what is it you are to love? A cousin of most
unremarkable appearance and undashing behaviour? A man who does
not seem particularly manlike? A muddler, and no man of action? A
philosopher who cannot express his philosophy? Silly girl, can you not
see behind all these things to the real me? . . . I am stubborn in love.
And if late events shook me for a while, I am solid again now, solid love
of Agnes & will to be loved by Agnes. "I am my universe," said I? Now I
say, "Agnes is my universe." She is no narrow universe. She is wide as

the constellations, deep as the First Cause. She is the radiant centre of all things, a sweet and wise comment on all things. . . .

[*Next day.*] Relations up here disapprove of the Reigate marriage, but that can't be helped. It is far best so. Father is keen & Mother acquiesces & the rest must put up with it. What am I to get married in? Do find out what Quaker bridegrooms wear. I am loath to buy a frock coat & never wear it again. I hate such garments. I have a "morning" coat, a tailed black thing, which I equally hate. In fact I hate all such respectable things, but one must do as will be expected of the Reigate Friends. What sort of a wedding dress are you having?

Annery

Agnes,                                                  12 May 1919
   You must forgive me for writing so many letters. When I am with you I feel I must have my arm round you lest you should desert me. These letters represent my arm. . . . Father and I have been sitting in the drawing room talking politics. He thinks the peace treaty very foolish, & even financially unworkable. He thinks Italy and France are doomed to revolution, but that it is just possible that England's changes may come without sudden violence. Great changes, good and bad, are surely coming. . . .
   As Father was talking just now I had a sense of the littleness of our present absorbing doubt and anxiety about the "state of your affections." Here is this tumultuous world all round us, and here are we two gifted to help things in our little way, yet still unsure about our own relationship. Why should we doubt any more after all these years? . . . Oh love me, dear, in a special way, our way, quietly but with all your heart, critically but tolerantly, never blindly, always with open eyes and a smile at my weaknesses and at your own. But above all things, dearest friend, don't be disheartened because I am only me and because you find no thrills. Thrills fade. The other love grows and grows. And when you begin to see through the image of me that you still respect and love (though you think you are not *in* love with me), love me more because you see me through and through. May I do so by you. In these days, my girl, I have felt like Ixion (was it he?) who rolled a great stone up a hill and ever it crashed to the bottom again and ever he began anew. When the stone is firmly on the top you will love me. I am like a man who spent years in building a solid stone house, and lived outside it till it was ready, and he went in and an earthquake shook it terribly. But it is solid stone and it will stand.

White Lodge
Reigate

TO OLAF                                                    12 May 1919

. . . I am glad you are coming back so soon. I do no good by myself. I can't think coherently—I just tie myself up into knots & feel as if I'll stifle—then I feel inexpressibly miserable & go out among people envying them—the grocer's daughter who serves in the shop & even poor dull or afflicted people I should feel sorry for—I envy them because they *know where they are*. Then suddenly this mood will drop off unaccountably & everything seems quite ordinary & I wonder what on earth I can have been in such a muddle about. That feeling is such a relief then that I would be happy if it weren't for the dread that the other will come back. My grip of things is so flimsy. I can't trust myself. I don't know what I'll be thinking about. . . .

Sometimes I'm quite jolly. I played the piano a lot last night & talked hard. Try not to worry too much about me & keep your faith that it is all right from the beginning.

Love,
Agnes

Annery

My darling,                                                14 May 1919

I did not intend to write again, but your letter has just come, and this will reach you before I do, and how can I leave you for a minute alone in that perplexity? It is all my fault for being so unprepossessing, but *you must get over that*. Except for that, which, hang it I can't help, we two are just cut out for one another, and you know it. Were we not very happy together sometimes last week? Say we were; believe we were. If you don't I'll break my heart and throw it away. You say I am to keep faith that it is all right. My dear girl, my faith that it is right for always never shook; I have only doubted about this present time, and I doubted only because of your doubt. But that is all past, and now I am quite sure in my own mind. When the postman came I was reading in the garden. I read your letter there and as I read it an unspeakable wave of longing seemed to lift me up and carry me to you. What do I mean? Just that you seemed very unhappy, and that I understand just what you are feeling, and that it must hurt you horribly, and that the only cure for it is for me to love you more and more. You say you cannot trust yourself. I trust you. I always knew it would be something like this when you came, but I knew you would win through it after a while. And now you are doing so. My dearest, to think of you unhappy all this time stabs me. When I come tomorrow give yourself up to me. Don't be thinking, "Do I love him or don't I?" Take it for granted. Lean on me. I am much stronger than you think I am, and than I thought I was. I am only weak when you don't love me. Make up your mind that we will be happy from now onwards, and we shall. If I thought you were still in love with someone else I might still fear. But you never seemed really to be in love with him in spite of those three weeks with nothing to do but watch him and admire him. It all convinces me that you are more mine than you think you are. Agnes dear, *you can never be happy without me.*

[*On Agnes' twenty-fifth birthday she joined Olaf and other relatives for a holiday in Festiniog, North Wales. This birthday message was not posted, but hand-delivered to Agnes's room.*]

Glasdo, Wales
Agnes,                                    25 May 1919

"Whatever can that lover of mine want to say to me now? He is always talking or writing letters." Thus thinks Agnes as she settles down to her breakfast in bed. "Many happy returns of the day," writes the lover, proud of this unimpeachable excuse for talking. . . . My darling, learn to make more and more use of me, spiritually and physically. Lean on me with all your weight whenever you are tired or depressed. I am a lover when you want a lover, & a friend when you want that. I understand a bit about you now, and about what you need. You need a little of the doctor & you must put up with him; but you need specially to be strengthened with love. Let me be *all* I can be. Love me more and more. And so you will get into the full sunshine.

Your own
Olaf

[*For Agnes, the time in Wales was an essential psychological stage in the courtship. She wrote to her mother that she fell in love again at Festiniog: "When I landed in England a month ago I lost the Olaf I knew—the one I had been writing letters to for $4\frac{1}{2}$ years. I thought the new Olaf would step right into his place, but no—after crossing the sea I found there was still a big river to cross before I got to the new Olaf." At Festiniog she and Olaf read Kipling's* Just So Stories, *including "How the Alphabet Was Made," in which the central character is Taffimai Metallumai, meaning "small-person-without-any-manners-who-ought-to-be-spanked"; she is forthright, stubborn, haphazardly educated, and devoted to her father. "Taffy" became the affectionate nickname Olaf used for Agnes for the rest of his life. When they returned to Annery, Olaf, in white flannels and Balliol blazer, took Agnes picnicking and boating along the Dee estuary, and, flying in the*

*face of Emmeline Stapledon's English proprieties, Agnes unpacked her*
*new scarlet and blue bathing costume in order to join Olaf for a swim,*
*just as she might have done in the Blue Mountains. She next visited*
*her Aunt Louisa at Garsdale.*]

Annery

Dearest in the World,                          11 June 1919, Midnight

I have just come back from a lovely midnight bathe, & I must tell you about it while it is all fresh, though I may see you before you get this. I went out after the family had gone to bed and when I reached the coast I found a high tide, a moon and little whispering wavelets, so I went down the cliff to the water. To my surprise there was a man lighting a fire by the old lime kiln. I shunned him guiltily and settled on the stones to undress. The water was smooth as oil, and beautifully warm. I swam round about with my (in)famous trudge, sometimes up the silver pathway to the moon, sometimes toward the still glowing northwest. A bit of current made me cautious, so that I did not go far from land. I longed for my Taffy, my darling Taffy. How thrilling it would be to swim with her in the moonlight, careless of the proprieties, careful only of the beauty and fitness of things. Someday we will do such things together and they will be our ritual of worship for the Spirit. Tonight after my swim I got out and stood naked and unashamed before the moon, and I stretched myself and felt well-pleased to be me, and to be still light of limb. Pride comes before a fall, and as I was stroking the wetness off me I stepped on a sharp something which made a hole and got full of sand. Having dressed I went to the man with the fire. He was lying wrapped up by his fire. After a greeting I said, "What is your job here?" "Fishing," said he, "I have nets to take in at one o'clock opposite Caldy station. The wife & family were here just now, but they've gone home, but I couldn't be bothered, since I have to be back at one o'clock. It's nice sleeping here. There's a bit of the savage in us still." I agreed, and we chatted about sleeping out, while we each smoked a Simon Artzt cigarette. He was a nice chap with a homely Lancashire or Cheshire accent. After a bit I left him and came home with the water still trickling from my hair, and making my shirt clammy. And I was gloriously cool and hungry, so hungry I could not walk straight. . . .

Now my dear, my darling, listen. Our telephone talk set me all agog, because you seemed so lost and gloomy and sort of frightened. You seemed to want me very much. That means you love me very much, which is good. But you seemed still distressed, Taffy dear. It is all quite natural as the physical reaction after so much being laid up, and it will of course go as you get fit again, and very soon you will be as happy as you were latterly at Festiniog, and so shall I. . . . My dear, I wish I could put both arms round you right now, right here, and hug you. I should like you as you were on the knoll with your hair down, only here by me now. Oh Taffy, we shall be far happier when we are married. I want my arms round you, and you laughing and blushing, and looking at me with that darling little merry smile of yours. I want to tease you a little as of old, & bite your little ears, and have you catching hold of a handful of my hair and—oh all as it has been before.

[*Olaf and his parents went back to Wales, and Agnes joined them briefly in the midst of wedding preparations. Once more, Olaf was jotting notes to slip under her door. "The Archangel" was Olaf's nickname for Agnes in her "English" and sometimes aloof moods, as "Taffy" represented her Australian "bush-girl" self.*]

Glasdo

TO AGNES                                                         24 June 1919

. . . Taffy, you have been a darling all this day—you always are so now. I wish I were with you now, & could have my arms round you now in bed, & could tell you by word of mouth all the above little matters of business instead of writing them. I wonder whether you are asleep yet, over yonder. Oh Taffy, I wish I were there! You are teaching me to be the kind of lover you like—in a thousand and one little ways. . . . And what I want is to be absolutely intimate, but never a nuisance, & always a help. And what I want of you is absolutely intimate friendship with Agnes & Taffy & the Archangel; & I want of you the spur, the curb, & sometimes the soft breast for a tired head to lie on. But most of all I want my darling Taffy of a thousand glorious looks & little moods & laughters. But don't forget the spur & the curb, they will be much needed. Little girl, you are a mighty power.

Late now, & I must sleep. Goodnight, little sleeping lassie, so near & still so far.

Glasdo

Agnes my own,                                                   5 July 1919

Now that I am actually sitting down to write to you I do not know what to say, so I shall just let my thoughts run on of themselves and "think on paper." This evening was too full of affairs and boot cleaning to be very memorable. Remember rather Saturday evening, as one of the happiest (in a deep mood of happiness). Remember that you asked me to come & sit with you on the sofa, and that you lay with your head on my chest (such a darling head it is, seen from above) and we talked so reasonably about things, and all our troubles cleared away like clouds before a new wind. And remember how you said you would gladly have gone to sleep just so, & you did not want to let me go. . . . We have learnt enough now to be sure that when one is not in love with the other it is not the end of all things, but a passing shade, to be utilized by both in other ways than just being in love. I feel much surer than ever that we can be the best companions in the world. And think what a big solid thing that is as a foundation for a life-partnership. Remember, dear, that in our home there is to be a little bedroom for me for when we want to be independent of one another, a bedroom-study perhaps, for the sake of space? This evening, sitting by the fire, you looked at me with such a gentle, warm, happy look that I keep seeing you so even now. Beautiful Taffy! You don't realize that you are sometimes very lovely to look at. Perhaps you will believe me if I say that sometimes also you freeze me like a Medusa head—but those times get rarer, and anyhow I am learning to see that other glorious face behind Medusa, and to wait. . . .

It is 12.45, & this is the end of my paper, so I am going to bed. And I only wish I could already go to bed with my darling & feel her going to sleep close to me. Come soon, oh 16th. On that night you won't be too much afraid, will you, little Taffy? You know by now that I can be gentle or eager as you want. It is not just for one act that I want to be with you at nights, but also for the long homely joy of being as cosy as we have often been on this sofa—and being so all night. The one act, little girl, must be, & you must be glad of it, & it will make you mine & make me yours more than any wedding service. Oh yes it will. Goodnight! Wherever you are when you read this, love me, find an even deeper love for me than you ever felt before. Your own queer but dear

Olaf

[*While Olaf called on all his mechanical training to try to put the Sunbeam in good enough condition for a honeymoon trip, Agnes returned to Aunt Nina in Reigate to await the wedding, now one week away. She sent Olaf his Quaker vow to memorize for the ceremony: "Friends, I take this my friend Agnes Zena Miller to be my wife, promising, through divine assistance, to be unto her a loving and faithful husband until it shall please the Lord by death to separate us."*]

Glasdo

Agnes, 9 July 1919

Are you in England or in Australia? I incline to think the latter, for today at Tecwyn I found myself scheming a letter to you just as in the old days of war—"I will tell her this and that. Perhaps I will make it into a fairy tale. And I will tell her how much I want her." Tecwyn was perfect. Would that you had been there. It was far lovelier than when you saw it. The lake was a brilliant blue that turned at the shallower parts to pale olive greens and warm browns where the red slates showed through. It was like a huge many-coloured transparent jewel. You would have loved it, and I should have—loved you. On the hills there were bright tussocks of heath that looked just like a giant's handful of amethysts thrown upon the hillside. Llan Tecwyn church, little homely place, made me ponder. I do wish you had seen it all, it was of rare beauty. I took it all as a wedding present from the gods of those parts. . . .

*Next Day.* . . . I am learning my part for Wednesday. It is nicely worded. If I forget it at the critical moment I shall say, "Friends—I want to marry Taffy. Amen.". . .

Perhaps this is the last letter I shall ever address to Miss Agnes Miller, that dear distracting spinster. . . . I am alternately awed and light-hearted at the thought of Wednesday & the future. Agnes, I will try to be man enough even for a wonderful girl like you. I will try. But some-times I feel like mortal Tithonus marrying the divine Dawn. I love you, anyhow.

Your Olaf

White Lodge
TO OLAF                                                      9 July 1919
. . . I'm having a busy joyful few days now getting ready for your com-ing on Saturday—then we'll have a busy joyful sociable few days here & then we'll have a glorious *unsociable* 3 weeks all to ourselves! It couldn't be lovelier, could it? & then we'll go back & *begin*. It will all be part of the fun, problems & all. Are you happy now? Don't let's be wor-ried by any old thing now. It's too good to be spoilt. Auntie & I have been listening to glorious music this afternoon—the Waldstein, & lots of Chopin & Schumann, & I sat sometimes just listening, sometimes knitting your "going away" socks, & always with a kind of background of you behind the music. One could not knit through the Waldstein—it seemed to take me away from everything but you. Dear me. I haven't time to be writing to you, but it's so nice. I sat down to write to Mother, & then I thought perhaps I'd send just a line to say good day on the morning you start on your journey. Speed Sunbeam, & keep to the left & don't get any punctures & don't dash along too much because I want you to be whole when you arrive here.

Now I really must stop. This is the last letter I shall write to my fi-ancé. I think it is the happiest I have ever written you. There is not much in it but we know now how to read between the lines, don't we?

I am waiting for you. I have something to give you. It is just

Agnes

## ~~~ *Epilogue*

[*Olaf and Agnes were married at the Friends' Meeting House in Rei-*
*gate, Surrey, on 16 July 1919. Olaf's best man was Denis "Saul"*
*Goodall, a colleague from SSA 13, and Madge McQueen, an Aus-*
*tralian friend who had been on the* Nestor, *took the role of bridesmaid.*
*The Sunbeam, which had seen Olaf through the last three years of the*
*war, carried the newly married couple through Windsor, Stratford, and*
*Oxford on their way to the Lake District, where they remained until 14*
*August. The long years of courtship constructed out of fantasies and*
*words on paper were over, and Olaf could exult in his diary during*
*their honeymoon: "My wife made love to me in a field (to the delight of*
*a dozen boys)." As a wedding gift, William and Emmeline Stapledon*
*had purchased a small house for Agnes and Olaf in West Kirby, but*
*because it could not be occupied until the following spring they had to*
*establish uneasy quarters at Annery, just as Emmeline had always*
*wanted. Frank and Margaret Miller did not come to England for the*
*wedding, because Agnes's sister Rosie was marrying Lionel Irvine in*
*Australia at about the same time. But Agnes had been sending her*
*parents running commentaries on events preceding and following her*
*own wedding day. Shortly after moving into Annery, she wrote to ex-*
*plain something she had concealed from her mother and father but*
*which would have to be faced when they came to England in 1920 to*
*visit her and her new husband. This letter supplies the details of an*
*episode on the* Nestor *that is hinted at in the letters Agnes and Olaf*
*wrote to each other in mid-May. Only here is there a complete explana-*
*tion for the evident tension between them in May and June and for the*
*unexpected delay until July of a marriage ceremony earlier anticipated*
*for late May.*]

370

The wedding portrait at Friends' Meeting House, Reigate, Surrey, 16 July 1919. Standing left to right, William Kirkus, Aunt Louisa Kirkus, cousin Alfred Fryer. Aunt Nina Barnard, William Stapledon, Emmeline Stapledon. Seated: bridesmaid Madge McQueen, Olaf, Agnes, best man Denis Goodall.

*Private*

My darling Daddy & Mother,

This is going to be just a little private letter to you & I'll write my regular one to Waldo this week so as to give you all the general news. I have just got your letters in answer to my first ones from England. I was almost dreading to get them because I knew you would be bound to be rather upset by my letters—& I hate to think that I should have added to your already strained minds & hearts just at the time when you were so bereft after Rosie's wedding & all the excitement of her departure to Narrabri. It all seems such very ancient history now & my world of to-day is so completely different to my world of May 1st that it seems useless to dig up the old, & yet I want to dig it up just once before I bury it quite out of sight & tell you of an incident that I want you to know about because it will give you the key to those early letters of mine & make things plain that were only half plain before.

I told you about my being so run down physically when I arrived—with the heat & the long trying voyage & so on. You attributed my mental depression *all* to that & I meant that you should do so because I didn't want to worry you any more than was necessary. I had a feeling deep down that everything was going to turn out alright & it has done so—as you see—but there *was* a reason for my kind of mental collapse & that was that I had half fallen in love with a man on the boat. I know you will find it as hard to believe of me as I did of myself, but so it was & there is no denying it. It wasn't just a shipboard flirtation. You know me well enough to believe that. If it had been, I should just have been thoroughly ashamed. It was something that went much deeper—& it was hard to root out, but it was not a thing to be ashamed of though it was a dreadful worry to me & to everyone at the time. When I look back now I see myself as I was when I left home—I realise how little I knew myself—how little I knew about human nature & with what blind self-confidence I was embarking on a big adventure. The whole thing sounds so unbelievable & so unlike me that the world seemed all upside down to me—I didn't know where I was nor what had become of the old me that I knew at home. It was Olaf who made me understand what had happened & gradually day by day managed to turn things right side up again. He said, & I see now, that it was the circumstance of our engagement that made it possible. You see, when we got engaged we were not together & never had been until I came. We had never been together at all & been wholeheartedly in love. When we got engaged I thought I was in love with Olaf—the whole man, mind & body & all—but really I only knew his mind. It was his letters I was in love with. But I was so sure that I was completely in love as other people are, so confident in my own wholeheartedness, that I did not dream I could run into danger. I was quite off my guard. So when I made friends with Captain Hutchinson (he was one of the officers who joined the ship at Bombay after six years' service in India) I found him a delightfully understanding & pleasing companion & we got on so well together that I didn't realise until the harm was done that it wasn't just disinterested friendship I was feeling, but the beginning of real love. You see, it all happened so quickly, between Bombay & Liverpool. It took me about a fortnight to discover where I was & then for the last week in the ship I was miserably impatient to be there with Olaf & get away from it all. I felt myself slipping further & further from him & yet I couldn't help myself.

I was so unhappy about it that I told Olaf all about it at once—the first day. It must have been an awful blow to him—my poor dear old chap—but he was wonderful. He might have given me up & thought I wasn't worth bothering over—but he seemed to think I was even more worth it than before, because it showed that I was a real human girl & not only the writer of a thousand letters. He was good to me & so patient & understanding & wise & helpful & loving & when I got to know him as he really is & could compare him with Balfour Hutchinson I knew that Olaf was far & away above the other & that if I could rise to him I should have a happiness as far above. At first it was only a mental conviction, but by degrees & slow degrees & often falling back & climbing up again my heart followed my mind & now both are as completely his as any wife's would be after being married six weeks *today*—to the dearest & best husband in the world. Auntie Emmeline & Uncle W. & Auntie Nina all know something about it. I told them because I couldn't bear to be pretending everything was right when it wasn't. Auntie Emmeline didn't understand—she was too grieved on Olaf's account to give me any real help although she was as kind as could be, but she talked about "duty" & "promise" & "principle"—& so on—& I knew that wasn't the main point. I was determined to break it all off unless I could love him as he loves me. So we waited—& not in vain.

That is all the old story. I did right to keep it back till now, didn't I? I didn't want to keep it from you altogether, because you would not have known your daughter & it had been a big thing to me while it was there. I don't know what you will think of me—whether you will blame me very much or whether you will make allowance as Olaf did—& help me to go on being friends with myself.

I thought I would tell you about it when you came & then it occurred to me that if you travel on the "Nestor" you might hear some rumour of the kind from one or other of the men who were there then & are still, & I would rather you heard the whole thing first from me. How I hate returning to it—even to tell you. But thank heaven it's all over & done with now, & I shouldn't be afraid to see Captain Hutchinson anywhere—though I don't want to except out of curiosity, & one good thing that it did which I shall always be glad of is that it brought Olaf & me much closer together right away & made us know each other.

Now I bury this world at the end of this letter & begin the regular one from the new world. I feel like a caterpillar looking at its old shrivelled skin, or rather like a bright butterfly looking at its old chrysalis!

Your loving Agnes.

[*By the following year Mr. and Mrs. Stapledon had laid full claim to their new world. Olaf was teaching history and literature in the WEA, but also moving in new directions. Soon he would begin working on a Ph.D. in philosophy at the University of Liverpool. Agnes became pregnant in the early autumn of 1919, and a daughter, Mary Sydney, was born in May 1920. Their son, John David, was born in 1923. The house at 7 Grosvenor Avenue, West Kirby was full, and Agnes was able to "bustle" as she'd always wanted. In the last year of the war Olaf had made a prediction to her: "In 1920 we'll look back at these sad days and laugh at the amount of letter-writing we had to do to one another, for in 1920 we shall never need to write letters to one another at all, God willing." Actually, the habit of corresponding was ingrained. Olaf and Agnes still occasionally wrote to one another, particularly when his tutoring work and later his literary celebrity took him away from home, or when Agnes in later years started going abroad for peace conferences. Even as late as the year before he died, in 1949 when Olaf made his only trip to the United States, he could still write home with boyish wonder about the sights of New York and about his efforts to get Agnes scarce postwar silk stockings as once he had searched out Flemish lace for her in the Great War. By sea and air he traveled to Lapland and Poland, Boston and Copenhagen; in fantasy he circumnavigated the globe and visited both the far future and innumerable other worlds. And in her fifties Agnes journeyed to Geneva and Stockholm, as once she had set out for Dresden and Berlin in the heady and confusing days of 1913. Always their travels begot letters, so used were they to talking across the world. As they lived and aged and grew closer together in the delicate symbiosis that Olaf took as his central metaphor for marriage, Agnes entered thoroughly and vitally into all his worlds, the real ones and the imaginary ones, and Olaf continued to celebrate Agnes in his fiction. But among all his journeys there was one Olaf never made. He died without having seen Agnes's caterpillar world. He never got to Australia.*]

# ✍ Index

Women's surnames before marriage are given in parentheses. Parenthetical names within quotation marks are nicknames.

*bers*); on fighting, 61–63, 106–107, 153–54, 158, 161, 184, 227, (*see also general entries on* Conscientious objectors; Conscription; Pacifism); financial worth, 181, 359; first meeting with Agnes, xiv, xvi–xviii, 4, 356–57; on French priests, 255, 297–98, 334; on God, 34–36, 37, 39, 52, 67, 69, 72, 126, 298; graveyard meditations, 158–59, 215, 247, 255, 307, 337; on the Great War, 51, 59–61, 63–67, 89, 121, 125–26, 164, 215–16, 325, 329, 333; hopes for stretcher-carrying work, 147, 213–14, 232; on human nature, 237, 298; on idealism, 5–6, 8, 18, 33–34, 66, 67, 72, 80, 110, 121, 130, 134–35, 138, 157, 168–69; ideas about women, 29, 193–94, 204–205; on the League of Nations, 227; learning to drive, 75–76, 78, 84–85, 88; learning new scientific theories, 264; literary activity during the war, xxxv–xxxvi, 173, 175, 258, 265–66, 274, 305, 312, 320, 343; love and destiny, xvi–xvii, 6, 9, 42, 46, 97–98; love in hibernation, 267–68; on love of cousins, 7, 200, 318; love's durability, 55, 228, 306, 359, 362–65; love's mysteries, 42, 307, 326; on marriage, 169, 204, 293; and material realities, 95–96; medical training, 75–76, 78–79, 82, 84; and "mediocria firma," 127–28, 138; on militarism, 82, 121, 137, 150, 184, 247; and music, 57, 104, 168, 236–37, 259, 281, 285–86, 303, 358; on Nature and war, 150, 223, 230, 300–301, 311; officer's driver for SSA 13, 179–80, 188, 190, 233; organizing convoy library, 279–81; and other worlds, 32–33, 102; physical appearance, xviii, 88, 133, 199, 352–53, 361; his "poetico-astronomical" mind, 32 (*see also general entry on* Stars); political differences with Agnes, 134–35, 153–54, 156–57, 161, 189–90, 198–99, 227, 273, 326; possible marriage during the war, 177–78, 205, 305, 317, 319, 321; and Quakers, xxvi-xxxi, 70, 74–75, 110, 126, 143–44, 214, 298, 359, 363, 368; receives the croix de guerre, 339, 343; on Russian revolution, 215, 251, 274, 323, 325; on separation, 53, 55, 84, 92, 99, 116, 125, 131, 170, 181–82, 198–99, 234, 246, 267, 284, 286, 293–94, 325, 372; on social work, 9, 12, 14, 20–21, 32, 239; and socialism, 180, 250, 298–99;

on soldiers, 62–63, 64, 106, 113, 123, 145–47, 185, 225–27, 255–56, 258–59, 292–93, 312, 325, 327; spiritual vision, 19, 101–102, 154, 158, 200, 212–13, 251, 269, 274, 275–76, 300–301, 326, 366 (*see also general entry on* Religion); surgery, 85–86, 88–89, 356; Swiss holiday with Agnes, 11–13, 27, 54; thoughts on the croix de guerre, 231, 233, 237, 300, 338–40; on tragedy, 24, 89–90, 247, 255, 273, 292, 310, 312, 318, 334, 362; utopianism, 180, 250–51, 261, 298–99; vaccinating against typhoid, 75, 127; visits Agnes in Paris, 39–42, 45, 54, 118, 136; visits a Flemish watchmaker, 137–38, 152; on vorticism, 234–35; on war ruins, 158–60, 162, 317–18, 321, 329, 344–45; warns Agnes about shipboard romances, 353; weekly reports on convoy activities, 281

PUBLISHED WORKS: *Beyond the 'Isms*, xii; *Darkness and the Light*, xii; *Death into Life*, xii, xvi–xvii; "Experiences in the Friends' Ambulance Unit," xxix n.26, 205–206; *The Flames*, xii, 251; *Last and First Men*, xi, xii, 18, 251; *Last Men in London*, xii, xxviii, xxix n.26, 314, 334; *Latter-Day Psalms*, xi, xxxv, 35, 39–40, 61–62, 64, 71, 101, 191; *A Man Divided*, xii–xiii; *A Modern Theory of Ethics*, xi; *New Hope for Britain*, xii; *Odd John*, xii–xiii, 158; *The Opening of the Eyes*, xiii; "The People Self-Educator," xxiii; *Philosophy and Living*, xii; "Poetry and the Worker," xxiv, 28; "Reflections of an Ambulance Orderly," xxxv n.35, 155; "The Road to the Aide Post," xxxv n.35; *Saints and Revolutionaries*, xii; "The Seed and the Flower," xxxv n.35; *Sirius*, xii, 251; *Star Maker*, xii–xiii, xvi, 89, 99, 251; "The Tutorial Class," xxiv; *Waking World*, xii, 180; *Youth and Tomorrow*, xii

UNPUBLISHED WORKS: "Ailsa would have a ruby," 177; *Being and Doing*, 199; diaries, xiv, xxvi n.19, xxix n.27, 3, 39, 317, 370; "A History 1903–1911," xvi, 190–91; *In a Glass Darkly*, xxxv–xxxvi, 258, 265–66, 274, 312, 313, 319, 320, 343; "The People Awake. What Will They Do?" 7; "Poets' Gods," 75; *Sleeping Beauty*, xxxv–xxxvi, 147, 258; untitled book (1914–15), 64–65
Stapledon, Zena (Miller), 201